Daniel Defoe, William Lee

Daniel Defoe, his Life, and recently discovered Writings

Vol. III

Daniel Defoe, William Lee

Daniel Defoe, his Life, and recently discovered Writings
Vol. III

ISBN/EAN: 9783337055509

Printed in Europe, USA, Canada, Australia, Japan

Cover: Foto ©Raphael Reischuk / pixelio.de

More available books at **www.hansebooks.com**

AND RECENTLY DISCOVERED WRITINGS:

EXTENDING FROM 1716 TO 1729.

By WILLIAM LEE.

ROBERT HARLEY, Earl of Oxford. Defoe's Patron and Friend.

IN THREE VOLUMES.

Vol. III.—The Second Volume of his Writings.

London :

JOHN CAMDEN HOTTEN, PICCADILLY. •

1869.

Serious Reflections

DURING THE

LIFE

And Surprising

ADVENTURES

OF

ROBINSON CRUSOE:

WITH HIS

VISION

OF THE

Angelick WORLD.

Written by Himself.

LONDON: Printed for W. TAYLOR, at the *Ship* and *Black-Swan* in *Pater-noster-Row.* 1720.

[TITLE PAGE TO THE 3RD VOL. OF THE 1st EDITION OF ROBINSON CRUSOE]

PREFACE

TO

THE THIRD VOLUME,

Being the Second Volume of Defoe's Uncollected Works.

HAVING in the preceding volume made such general pre-
fatory observations as then occurred to me, I have
little more to add than briefly to refer to a few of the Essays
herein, which appear to me of peculiar excellence ; and, to explain one or two things that might otherwise seem obscure.

I have already noticed the necessarily fugitive character of
Essays written under the pressure of the moment, and in the
midst of other herculean literary labours, as a reason why these
productions of Defoe's pen should not now be amenable to
severe verbal criticism.   I may add, that in the choice of his
subjects, he was not only bound to take up passing events,
often of little permanent interest ; but also to consult, with a
view of improvement, the taste and temper of the reading
public in that age.   Notwithstanding these limitations, I trust
that this Volume, as well as its predecessor, will be found to
contain so great variety, that few subjects of ordinary interest
are left untouched ; and that fine thoughts, happily expressed,
abound in almost every page.

The reader will find herein little of purely political or religious controversy ; but it may be needful to bear in mind
the great civil and social changes effected during the one hundred and fifty years that have elapsed between the composition
of these writings and the present time.   A sanguinary code of
criminal Laws has been repealed.   Education and intelligence
have extended the power and franchises of the people. Roman

b 2

Catholics, and even Infidels, have now the fullest Toleration; and the Press is freed from the absolute censorship and suppressive power of any Government. On these and kindred subjects the opinions of Defoe were undoubtedly far in advance of most of his contemporaries; but he rendered a loyal obedience to the laws of his country, in his teaching as well as by example. In some respects civilization may have carried us as far beyond Defoe as he was generally beyond the age in which he lived; but even on such topics, when occasionally touched upon, he may be profitably read, without our being supposed either to coincide or censure.

Among the Essays contained in this volume, which have deeply impressed the Editor, a few only can be specially mentioned, without extending the Preface beyond due bounds. Under date 2 June, 1722, I may notice an admirable constitutional and conservative Letter on Reasons for observing the 29th May, as being the day of the Restoration. In the same month is to be found an eloquent and impartial Character of the Duke of Marlborough deceased; and, in July, on occasion of the Duke's Funeral, some Reflections on the Instability of human Glory, not in my judgment to be surpassed for depth of solemn pathos. As a Contrast, showing versatility of great powers, may be mentioned the Satire in praise of Hypocrisy, containing an eloquent apostrophe to Fraud and Falsehood. In October following, he relates with sadness, the miserable career of a drunken, abandoned clergyman; and amidst some excellent reflections urges the advanced opinion that confirmed Sots should be treated as Lunatics.

In March, 1723, will be found a humorous story of Tea-Table Scandal, and a pretended description of the punishment inflicted in Siam on those who traduce the characters of their neighbours. With reference to the Jacobite Plot for which C. Layer, Esq., was executed, and Bishop Atterbury banished, I would direct attention to two admirable Essays, in the former of which, he graphically traces the physical and mental condition of a Traitor, from detection to Execution; and, in the latter, furnishes his readers with profitable reflections on the fall and banishment of the Bishop. His Essay on Public Faith, dated 10th August, deserves the consideration of all Rulers and Governments; and his Satire, in October, on

Public Spirit, in modern as compared with ancient times, is a very able performance.

It will be observed that on the 9th November, in the same year, Defoe notices the then new practice of concealing the writers of public Journals; and alludes in general terms to Bishops, Noblemen, and other eminent persons, as being then among such writers. On several subsequent occasions he sufficiently indicates some of them, with the exception of the Duke of Wharton. I am not aware that it has ever been publicly known that men of rank were then active contributors to the periodical papers; yet a List of them would include Bishops Atterbury, and B. Hoadley; Dr. E. Young; Sir R. Walpole; Lord Bolingbroke; the Duke of Ormond, and probably others.

The article for the 1st February, 1724, contains some severe strictures on the posthumous publication of the late Bishop Burnet's History of his own Times. In an ironical Essay against judicial Astrology, published the following week, will be found an amusing story how the Duke of Mantua sent the horoscope of a new born Mule to the most celebrated Astrologers in Italy, who supposing it to be that of a human being, answered accordingly. One of them, declaring it would become a Bishop, our Author adds, "he did not say he should write a History of his own Times." As the infirmities of age increased, I find in Defoe an increasing disposition towards grave subjects, and this pervades even his satires, often giving a peculiar fineness to the exercise of a faculty possessed by him in a pre-eminent degree. I think there will also be observed in this Volume a growing tendency to criticise the labours of distinguished contemporaries. This will be seen in his Essay of the 18th of April, 1724, on the Choice of a Subject, wherein he severely satirizes the inconsistent composition of the *London Journal*, and the impropriety of Bishop Hoadley being the responsible writer thereof. The Bishop's general signature, as a News-writer, was " Britannicus," and it will be found that Defoe returns to the charge on the 11th of July following, and several times subsequently.

Some apology may be thought necessary for my admitting the two Essays dated in August of the same year, relating to an unfaithful Wife, and the then defective state of the law as to any remedy. " To the Pure all things are pure," and as our author could not have fully stated the case in a less objectionable manner, I thought it best to insert the Articles, after suppressing a few words unsuited to modern ears. It is one of the many subjects on which the views of Defoe penetrated a century beyond that in which he lived. The same remarks are applicable to the Essay dated 10th of October, as from a Wife complaining of an unfaithful husband.

In the latter part of 1724 will be found characteristic accounts of the prison-breaking exploits of the celebrated John Sheppard, on which Defoe published at the time two separate pamphlets. Under dates 21st and 28th Nov. are two Letters written by Defoe under the disguise of a Niece of his heroine Moll Flanders. She expresses her admiration and love for Sheppard, whom she had desired to marry; and she deplores his untimely death. The short narrative of her own course of life as an expert Shop-lifter and Pickpocket is admirably conceived and sustained. She is quite incapable of appreciating any of the various motives that bring people together for pleasure, occupation, entertainment, or religious worship. These assemblies were only seen by her from a thief's point of view, as occasions for the transaction of her professional business. She is quite unconscious of any sinister reflection on Addison when complacently boasting,—" Cato was worth above 100 guineas to me, and yet I reckon the things taken, as we generally sell such things ; namely, at half value."

From the 12th of Dec. to the 2nd of January, 1725, are four communications commencing with one signed, " T. Experience," and cautiously revealing many circumstances of the ingratitude and injurious treatment Defoe had recently received from Mr. Mist. I have considered this matter in the Life of Defoe, and only specifically point to it here, that the reader may observe the deadly nature of the estrangement; and that it leaves Mr. Mist full of malice, and thirsting for revenge.

On the 29th of May, 1725, is a fine Essay on the great influence of Public Journals ; and this is followed by an eloquent and manly defence of Journal-Writers against the reproach of being mercenary. The Essay dated 31st of July, on Pope's Translation of Homer, must be admitted to contain a most happy and well sustained comparison. There was, at the time, much dissatisfaction, not unmixed with scandal, against the publisher, and Pope, his contractor. Bishop Hoadley, as Editor of the *London Journal*, became the exponent of the complaints; while Defoe, professing a reply to the Bishop, treats of the whole business on commercial and manufacturing principles. This Essay must have been very galling to all the parties against whom it was directed; and, if Pope even suspected that Defoe was the writer, his resentment in the Dunciad three years afterward, is amply accounted for. The King's long continued residence in Hanover during the year 1725, caused much distress and murmuring, especially among the middle classes of Westminster. The reader will observe the great judgment and delicacy with which Defoe handles the subject in his Essays on the 4th and 11th of *Sept.*, speaking plainly and truthfully, yet without any ground of offence to the government. The description he gives of the new district then erecting between Hanover Square and Hyde Park, is very graphic and interesting.

As a point in his personal condition, I think the solemn physical reflections on Death, dated the 25th of the same month, afford abundant evidence of having been written during one of the paroxysms of Stone, to which he was subject.

During the year 1710 Defoe had been attacked in the *Examiner* by Swift, and designated an "illiterate Fellow." He then defended himself, in the seventh volume of his *Review*, and retorted upon his assailant, showing himself fully a match for Swift in the use of sarcasm. It is remarkable that he should have returned to the subject in *Applebee's Journal*, after the lapse of fifteen years, as will be seen in the two Essays of the 30th of October and the following week. In the former of these he speaks, in the third person, more fully than before, of his own great attainments, as an "illiterate Fellow," but without directly pointing to Dean Swift. In the latter he illustrates "learning" by the character of a pedant. Both characters are admirably sketched, and in the hands of a competent artist would make a good pair of cabinet pictures. The article, dated the 18th of December, on Self Murder, in which Royal Gin is recommended as a specific, is a piece of Irony the most intensely solemn I have ever read. It seems to take the bony hand of him who is usually called "the King of

Terrors," and, with the aid of Gin, to grasp it as that of a most agreeable friend.

I notice as remarkable, that Defoe's last Essay in Applebee's Journal, reiterates the national importance of an English Fleet in the West Indies, during any War with the Bourbons. He had urged the same policy a quarter of a century earlier, on William III., when the expedition was determined upon, and Defoe was to have occupied a position of great responsibility connected therewith. It was then frustrated and abandoned in consequence of the King's unfortunate death.

It is also worthy of observation that Defoe's last Journalistic contribution,—so far as I have been able to discover,—the one with which the present volume closes,—advocates the great principles of Free Trade, which he had consistently held all his life.

Here then, at last, I lay down my pen. The materials collected and condensed in these volumes have been the Work of years. I lay no claim to literary excellence, nor deprecate fair criticism; but I trust it will be granted that I have brought to light much that was unknown as to the Life and Writings of Daniel Defoe, especially during the period extending from 1714 to his death in 1731.

WILLIAM LEE.

BAYSWATER, *Nov.* 1868.

CONTENTS

TO

THE THIRD VOLUME.

xiv CONTENTS.

NOTE TO THE READER.

To prevent the Reader having to turn back to the List of Defoe's Works, prefixed to the first Volume;—or, to search, in the same Volume, for the places containing descriptions of the Journals from which, respectively, the Contents of the Second and Third Volumes have been transcribed;—and also, to explain the Abbreviations, tabulated on the next page,—this preliminary Note has been thought desirable.

I. *Mercurius Politicus :* was a Monthly Historical Account of the most material Occurrences; commenced by Defoe in 1716, and continued many years. It was conservative in principle, and each number formed an octavo of about 64 pages.

II. *Mist's Journal :* was so called from the name of the proprietor and publisher. It was a Tory Paper, and its Title, in full, was " The Weekly Journal, and Saturday's Post." It had been some time in existence when Defoe undertook the control, in order to keep it within the bounds of moderation; but he was compelled, after a while, to abandon a charge so obnoxious to his own principles. Each number consisted of six pages, foolscap folio.

III. *The Whitehall Evening Post :* was Established by Defoe in 1718, on liberal conservative principles; and was continued many years after he ceased to write it. Each number consisted of a small quarto sheet.

IV. *The Daily Post :* was also Established by Defoe, and each number was contained in a small leaf, folio. Great part of the contents consisted of Advertisements. Party Politics were excluded.

V. *Applebee's Journal :* was,—from the name of the proprietor and publisher,—the common appellation of " The Original Weekly Journal, and Saturday's Post." It existed before Defoe's connexion, but he wrote all the *Letters Introductory,* or Leading Articles, for many years. It was of the same size and form as Mist's; but its principles were of the most liberal conservative character.

VI. *The Universal Spectator :* was commenced by Defoe, and his son-in-law Henry Baker. It was a weekly publication in large quarto. Defoe only wrote the first number, but the work was continued by Baker for some years.

VII. *Fog's Journal :* was the successor of Mist's; but less violent in its politics. I found in its pages only one communication, non-political, by Defoe.

NEWLY-DISCOVERED WRITINGS

OF

DANIEL DEFOE,

EXTENDING FROM 1716 TO 1729.

ABBREVIATIONS.

M. P. denotes Mercurius Politicus.
M. J. denotes Mist's Journal.
W. E. P. denotes Whitehall Evening Post.
D. P. denotes Daily Post.
A. J. denotes Applebee's Journal.
U. S. denotes Universal Spectator.
F. J. denotes Fog's Journal.

Against Self-Murder.

A. J., *May* 12, 1722.—Sir, Our Modern Authors, made
famous for the Pedantry of their Wit, having recommended, for Imitation, the Examples of the Romans for
a particular Virtue, call'd Self-Murther, it would be a seasonable Animadversion upon Their Conduct to put them in Mind
how far their Exhortations of that Sort have lately prevail'd
among us in *England.*

If *Cato* is recorded as a Hero, and a true Defender of
Liberty, because, when he could not beat *Cæsar* at *Utica*, he,
in a sullen Fit, would not try to beat him anywhere else, but
instead of killing Cæsar, killed himself; I say, if this made
Cato look great, and we are to esteem him a Hero, how partial are we to the Fame of those worthy Heroes of our Age,
who having gamed away their Fortunes in the late Bubbling
Age, and been gull'd of their Money by the *B——t's* and
A——e's, and *L——w's* of the Age,* have fled from the Face

---

* Sir John Blount, and Aislabie, both of the South Sea ; and John Law,
the Projector, are intended.—*Ed.*

of Poverty, by *the shortest Way*, to the Grave, and laid Violent
Hands on themselves, to shun the Infamy of a mean Figure in
the World?

If I am not misinformed, there have been abundance of
such Heroes in our time,—some say no less than 64 about
London only; and, with due Reverence to the Memory of
Master *Cato* of *Utica*, these Men deserve to be eterniz'd in
History, as much as he, that is to say, we should preserve their
Memory. Not among the Great, to whom we should make
Elegies and *Eulogies*,—erect Statues and Monuments of Marble
or Brass,—but among the miserable; who are Objects of our
most compassionate Thoughts, and on whose Fate we should
reflect with Tenderness and Sympathy.

The like Pity the Memory of *Cato* merits from us; but,
with Submission, not an Ounce of Praise, any more than to
say, that he died in the height of Cowardice made desperate,
which indeed is Envy and Rage; that feared and hated Cæsar,
but chose rather to Kill himself than try another Fall with
him; and to dye by his own Sword, rather than to dye fighting for his Country to the last Gasp. Pitiful low-spirited
Courage! that chose to dye a Freeman for Love of Liberty, but
afraid to fight for Liberty, that he might have lived a Freeman.

Much more valuable is the Virtue of the unhappy Monsieur
Le Blanc in *France*, on the Occasion of whose Death I take
the Liberty to write you this Letter: Monsieur Le Blanc was
a Gentleman born to good Fortune; his Father was one of the
late King of *France's* Harbingers, an Office of good Profits in
that Country. He had the Misfortune to Bubble his Estate all
away, in the late Mississippi Stock; and now finding, by the
new Liquidation, as they call it in *Paris*, that the little he
had left was reduced to about 23 *per cent.*, by which he was
sunk to so mean a Condition, as not to have Bread for his
Family, he threw himself into the *Seyne* to drown himself.
Some People, it seems, have unkindly prevented his Fate, and
restor'd him to that Misery which he chose Death to avoid,
having sav'd him from drowning; but another Gentleman, the
same Day, did the same, and tho' he was taken up too, yet
died; and a Lady, a famous Actress on the Theatre, did the
same, in the same River, a few Weeks ago, and for the same
Occasion too, having lost all she had acquir'd in many years

successful Labours.   I say, lost it all, by that cursed Bubble,
call'd *Mississippi* Stock, the *South-Sea* Stock of that Country.

Now if the Desperation of these People in *France* is so remarkable, what Work has our Bubbling made in this Nation?
What Blood have the Directors, and their Directors, to Account
for; of the poor Self-Murther'd Citizens, and Tradesmen, who
in Desperation at their Circumstances have been all *Cato's*, in
one Year's time, in this City?   How many have shot themselves through the Head?   How many have cut their own
Throats?   How many hang'd themselves, to shun the Shame
of their Disasters, and to be out of the hearing of the Cries of
their Families?   It would be incredible to Posterity; they
would question the possibility of it, if we should go into Particulars; and yet there is scarce a Man, that shall read this
Paper, but will be able to say he knows one or more who have
done thus.

I do not, by talking of their being Heroes, like *Cato*, triumph
in the least over their Disasters; I sincerely pity the unhappy
Persons, but it shows what kind of End our Wits have recommended to the Practice of Christians; and I fear the recommending Self-Destruction so much, has had no small Influence
upon the Minds of those whose Misfortunes have help'd the
Temptation, and all together, put Weapons in their Hands
against their own Lives.

Let both consider of it, and reflect upon their Conduct, as
they ought in Justice to do : FIRST, Those who have Bubbled
innocent People out of their Estates, and reduc'd them to
Misery, so as to make them choose Death rather than Life.
And SECONDLY, Those who have wickedly recommended to the
Miserable the shortening their Miseries, by laying violent
Hands upon themselves, which is, in short, launching them
out of temporal Misery into eternal.   As for the Colour of
Heroism, which is put upon it; it is one of the most con-
temptible and absurd Pieces of Vanity that ever was in the
World.   Erected in ancient times, when the Devil dictated
Morals, by Oracle, to the Roman World, as greatly serving a
Piece of Hell Policy, to the advancement of *Satan's* Monarchy
in that Age; but justly condemn'd and abhorr'd in all the
Ages of Christianity, and in all Nations of Christians, till the
Devil, willing to revive it, stirr'd up a set of Men to usher it

into the World again among us, just at a time when a Calamity was coming upon us that should suit the Crime, and make
it more in fashion than ever it was before,—a time when Men
were to be brought into a Condition more likely to hang and
drown themselves than ever before.

Sir, your Servant,

FELO DE SE.

On Protestant Neutrality.

A. J., May 19.—Sir, I remember some time ago, when the
News from all Parts told us, that the Plenipotentiaries were all
gone to Cambray to hold a Congress, and that the Assembly
would be open'd in a few Days, an impudent Fellow of a News-
Writer, whether Dutch or French I do not exactly remember,
put it into one of his Papers for a Piece of News, that a Company of Comedians were gone from Paris to Cambray to entertain the Plenipotentiaries till the Opening of the Assembly.

It was well he put in the last Part, *viz.*, That is was all to
entertain the Plenipotentiaries.   Some ill-natur'd critick, some
London Journal, or such like captious Wretch, might have suggested that he meant the Plenipotentiaries themselves; and so
have brought the poor foreign Wretch into the Briars, for a
Breach of the Laws of Nations, and affronting the Ministers
of Princes.

But the Man meant honestly, and indeed, as things look
now, if the Plenipotentiaries were to stay at Cambray till the
Assembly then intended were open'd, one might say, without
Offence, they would need something to divert them, or some
People would become a Comedy themselves; for if we may
believe the Accounts publish'd from abroad, many of the
Princes and Powers concern'd to meet there, are now drawn
up in different Figures, are engag'd in Interests quite contrary to what they were then, and are ready to go together by
the Ears, upon Points perfectly inconsistent with that Party
they took before.   In a Word, they are preparing for a new
War, instead of settling the old Peace; and we may probably
sit still in a little while, and see the Flame of War break out
in a great Part of Europe; and France, Spain, Lombardy,
Germany, and their Allies and Confederates respectively, cutting one another's Throats for Dominion as eagerly as ever.

I say *we may sit still* and see this, because, I hope, it will happen, if they do fight, that it will be such a War as England may thankfully say, we have nothing to do with it. The Conquest of the Milaneze, and whether one Popish Prince or another shall possess it; what is it to us? If it be true, that by Act of Parliament, England is not to be obliged to be at any Expense to defend the foreign Dominions of their own Princes; I hope, without an Act of Parliament, care may be taken that we may be entirely neuter in a War, that we have no particular Hand in, or concern about.

Solomon says, *He that meddles with Contention which does not belong to him, is like one that taketh a Dog by the Ears.* Prov. 26, 17. Be their Strife among themselves, 'tis all among my Lord *Thomond's Cocks*; they are all Papists, and all of a Side; and,—saving my Reverence to Crown'd Heads and Allies, —all Tyrants. Neither the cause of Religion or Liberty, I mean the general cause of Protestant Liberty, is concern'd in them; nay, nor is the Balance of Europe's power concern'd; the Barrier to England, or Holland, is not concern'd in it; and, in a Word, I do not know that anything belonging to Great Britain, or Great Britain's Friends, is concern'd in it.

Let them fight and knock one another's Heads off against Stone Walls, 'tis nothing to us; 'tis all their own, let them fight it out; I think we need not concern ourselves to part them. Indeed, when they have sufficiently maul'd and weaken'd one another, they would be an easier Prey to some honest, vigorous, Protestant Prince, that would take them, and turn them all out of Possession at once.

Italy is the Word now! *Italy* is the Bone of Strife, that these Men fight for. As it is, the Emperor has it, and we are not much the better for that; and if the Spaniards had it, I do not see we should be much the worse for that; and if neither of them had it, as I believe verily will be the case at last, I believe it would be much the same. But this is the Purchase they all run for at present, and this is the Prize of the Victors, and which they will value themselves so much upon the winning of; yet I cannot but say it is much better for Europe that none of them should have it, than that any of them should wholly engross it.

Still, let it go which way it will, I say, I think 'tis like to be the happiest War for England that ever happen'd in Europe; for we shall not need to care one Farthing who wins, or who loses; and consequently, need not spend one Farthing in the Quarrel. Our Business, in my Opinion, is to sing *Te Deum* on every Battle, let the Victory be whose it will, for all are Enemies to the Protestant Cause; and while,—like the Potsherds of the Earth, they dash themselves in Pieces against one another,—they leave the Popish Cause weak and exhausted, and unable to unite and fall upon the Protestants, which they would most certainly do, if they were prosperous and great.

Here is France, Spain, and the Emperor. They have been all persecuting cruel Enemies of God, and his Church in the World; they thought that they had rooted it up in King *James* the First's time, when the gallant King of *Sweden* redeem'd it, at the Price of a Bloody War, in which he lost his Life, but gave the Enemy a mortal Blow, which they never recover'd to this Day, or, as may be properly said, *never till this Day*. This persecuting Spirit is still in them, and among them, and now let them persecute one another: What are Protestants concern'd? Let them fight for Dominion as long as they please; as long as they do not fight for Religion, we have nothing to say to them.   Your Humble Servant,

PROTESTANT NEUTRALITY.

On Rumours of a Plot against the Government.*

A. J., May 26.—Sir, As the Secretary of State, in the King's Name, has declar'd there is, or has been, a Conspiracy, or Plot, or Design, call it what we will, to disturb the Peace of this Kingdom, I shall neither be so diffident, or so unmannerly, as to suggest the least doubt of the Truth of it; and though it is not yet thought fit to make farther Particulars publick, yet I shall not question but that, in a little time, we shall see the Reasons for all these Things, and be fully convinc'd that his Majesty has not been impos'd upon, nor has impos'd upon his People; and in this, I think, I am very loyal, as well as very just.

Yet I cannot but take Notice how oddly People would guide our Views to look for the Enemies they talk of; and

---

* This was the first mention of the Plot for which Bishop Atterbury was afterward banished.—*Ed.*

how they raise imaginary, and indeed most ridiculous Clouds, blowing from this or that Quarter, to support their Apprehensions, and amuse their Countrymen.

For my Part, I think that when People know that they have no certain Intelligence of such Things, they should either make probable Guesses, or let guessing wholly alone; for to what purpose do they turn our Eyes, now this way, now that way, to look for we know not what, and we know not who, or where? The Government, no doubt, have their Eyes everywhere, and when they see the Cloud, we shall see it too: But I cannot think our Coasting the World to make Guesses at Things, is of any use in the Case, unless it be to divert our Thoughts from the proper Place, and carry us to look abroad when we should look at home.

Besides, the Intimation of this Plot regards Things among us chiefly, if not only, as I see nothing mention'd in it relating to foreign Aid; on the contrary, 'tis intimated, that the Government has Assurances that it will not be supported from abroad.

To what purpose then do People run up the Straights to see what Ships the Spaniards are fitting out, and to enquire whether the King of Spain, who was so glad to close the last War, should be so forward to break the Peace, which was so advantageous to him, and should talk of shipping an Army at Barcelona to invade Great Britain?

But Barcelona, it seems is too near for these Men; and now they are carrying us to the frozen Zone, and insinuate, that great preparations are making in the White Sea, and we are, according to them, to expect a Fleet almost from the North Pole. To fill our Heads with these Things, they tell us, that " The Czar intends to repair to Arch-Angel, there to go on board his Fleet, which is design'd for some considerable Expedition, which is not yet made Publick."

This Piece of News is so wonderful new, and has such mighty probabilities in it, that you cannot do a better Piece of Service to the Government, or to your Country, than to talk a little Truth to them upon the subject. First the Czar is to go on board his Fleet there; but they do not tell us how he came to have a Fleet there, or whether he has any Ships there or no. In the next Place, whither can an Expedition be

directed from Arch-Angel? Unless it is supposed to go to
catch Bears at Greenland and Spitzbergen in the latitude of
86. As to an Expedition of the Czar's from Arch-Angel to
this Country, the Navigators know too much of those Seas to
think it rational.

Such Men would have us think the Chevalier is serv'd by
none but Fools, or Desperadoes, otherwise they cannot think
they would flatter themselves with any hopes for an Expedition
form'd at Arch-Angel. If the Czar has any Undertaking on
foot in that Part of the World, it can be for nothing but to
take possession of the North Cape, or to make a Voyage to
China, two Things as unworthy of the Czar as impracticable in
themselves.

Were these Men's Intelligence good, and such a wild Chase
was in the Head of the Czar; would our Government encamp
their Troops on Salisbury Downs, or Salisbury Plain, upon
Marlborough and Andover Downs, and all to the Westward?
Or would they not rather choose to march them Northward,
towards Newcastle, Berwick-upon-Tweed, or the Firth of
Edinburgh? .

Let us then set our Thoughts to rights in this Matter. The
Plot,—unless my Understanding is as dark as the Air was when
the Sun was in Eclipse,—does not lye that Way, any more than
it does from Constantinople. I will not say but the Czar may
have Ill-will enough to England, to try all possible ways to
embarrass us; but I shall never look for him that Way, because I do not take him for a Madman.

The Mischief then intended, if there is any such Thing in
Agitation, must, in my Opinion, be much nearer home; and
some say it is at home. How, and which way it is to be, or
was to be effected, is to me a very unfathomable Mystery;
and yet I cannot but say, I am as impatient as any of
my Neighbours to hear the Issue of it. At present, all
that is required of us is, to believe that there is such a
Thing; and this, as above, I will not so much as question a Word of, because of the Authority from whence we
have it.

But since other People are so forward to determine that
Point, give me leave to answer negatively, in spite of all their
Calculations.

Not from Spain, not from France, Assurances are given from thence to the contrary.

Not from Constantinople, the Turks and we are good Friends, and ever were so ; the half Moon never meddled, that I have heard of, with Matters at London.

Not from Arch-Angel and the North Kyn, unless the Czar is become Lunatick, and intends to transport himself where never Army was, nor will be again.

As then there is a Plot, it must be nearer Home ; and if at home, the Posture Things are in at Home is such, that if any of the Conspirators have a Cap full of Wit, they will be worse than Mad, if they stir. And, in the mean time, we must be half mad, if we are any longer frighted about it ; and, I must confess, I think those People deserve some Notice who put such wild Things as these in our Heads ; and if I were to judge of them, I should think it was part of the Plot.

Yours, &c.

A South-Sea Suicide.

A. J., May 26.—On Wednesday a Man walking under Lincoln's Inn Chapel, made an attempt to cut his Throat with a Penknife in view of the People, who therefore secured him, and carried him before Justice Hungerford, when, being ask'd the Reason for so rash an Action, he told his Worship he had been undone by engaging in the common Calamity, and having a very large family to provide for, was driven to Despair ; the Justice after some proper Admonition dismiss'd him.

Reasons for Keeping Restoration Day.

A. J., June 2.—Sir, On Tuesday last was celebrated the Anniversary of the happy Restoration. I cannot but wonder at the Contempt which some of our People put upon that Day, or, I should rather say, upon the Occasion of our celebrating it in the Manner we do ; and this makes me think it well worth while to take up one of your Papers upon that extraordinary Subject.

I shall not meddle here with the Nature of the Quarrel itself, which we have long had, about Keeping this Day ; that Part lyes, chiefly, just as the War did, *viz.* between Cavaliers and Round-Heads, Loyalists and Rebels, the followers of the

Royal Family in all its Distresses ; and the Generation of King-Killers, who went before them, and under whose prosperous Treason, the late King *Charles* the First lost his Life, his Son lost the Crown, and the whole Kingdom labour'd under that worst Sort of Tyranny, call'd Anarchy and Confusion.

But I choose to talk of these Things another Way, and I shall endeavour to prove that the most profess'd Low-Church Man in this Kingdom, those that talk highest of Constitution, Liberty, British Privileges, and the Supremacy of Vox Populi ; those I say, by the very Principles of a Whig, and by all the Doctrines of legal Right, in the Nation, those very Whigs, those very Low-Church Men, ought, on the Foot of their own avowed Principles, to commemorate this Day, and to be the most forward of any People in the Nation to have it observ'd with Ceremony and Zeal.

And first, I lay it down thus : It was not the King that was restor'd. I mean King *Charles* the Second. That is to say, not the King only, but it was the Monarchy. The King was indeed among the Regalia, but it was the Station of a King that was restor'd; the Name of King had been trampled under Foot as well as the Person, and the very Office of a King was restor'd, by the bringing back the Person of their King at that time, for which we commemorate this Day.

Now, let us ask those Men who dislike the Ceremony of the Day, the following Questions, which as I may say, are in their own Way :—

You value and honour the Memory of King *William*, and tell the World every Year what he had done for you in the Revolution. Pray where had been your King *William*,—where your Revolution,—all your fine Privileges gain'd, or rather re-gain'd at the Revolution,—if it had not been for the Restoration ?

You value the Accession of his present Majesty King *George* to the Crown, and cry up the Providence of it as another Revolution ; and the day before this of the Restoration, ye commemorated his Majesty's Birth-Day, and you did well; but what had become of the Hanover Succession if it had not been for the Restoration ?

You value English Liberties, and the Currency and Freedom of Parliament, by which the Constitution is made solid, the

Government itself supported, Law established, Property protected, and the People made happy, and you are right in all
this ; but where had all these been if it had not been for the
Restoration ?

How can those hot People that say so many fine Things of
the immortal Memory of King *William*,—and of the glorious
Succession of the Illustrious House of Hanover,—separate those
Things which Heaven has so remarkably joyn'd ?   Was the
Revolution a Blessing and not the Restoration, on the Foundation of which it stood ?   Is not the Reign of King *George*
a Blessing,—and is not the Restoration a Blessing also ?

These Men do not consider that the Restoration had in its
Womb the Felicity of all the Kings that have since Reign'd, or
shall reign, while Great Britain is a Kingdom.   In the Restoration, the Thing call'd Kingdom was restor'd ; the Government,
the Constitution, the very Throne was restor'd.   The Revolution
gave us but one King *William*, and the Act of Settlement has
as yet given us but one King *George ;* but the Restoration
gave us all, the King *William*, and all our Kings, and all that
can be of their Races.   This gave you the Throne they sit on,
the Crown they wear, the Sceptre they hold, the Sword they
wield.   Had the Monarchy not been restor'd, where had been
your Monarchs ?   King *Charles* must have died in Exile, as
King *James* did, King *William* have remain'd Prince of *Orange*,
and his present Majesty been what Providence should have
pleased to direct ; or have made a Restoration of the Monarchy
for himself, and by Dint of his own Sword.

But in the Restoration, all these Blessings were reserv'd.
The Restoration was big with all these Glories, and therefore
justly we call it the happy Restoration, the Blessed Restoration ;
and 'tis a truer Test of our Satisfaction in the present Government, and in the Succession of the House of Hanover, and of
his Majesty King *George*, that we Honour the Restoration,
and celebrate it with so much joy, than all your Clamour in
the Streets can be, than all your *Roebuck* Clubs, and such
other Artifices of noisy Loyalty.

The Restoration put an End to all the Blood and Rapine,
Terror, and Confusion of Civil War,—and, as we call'd it above,
—prosperous Rebellion.   The Restoration restor'd the Royal
Family to the Crown, and the Crown with the Royal Family

to the Kingdom; the Restoration restor'd the Parliament to
the full exercise of its Power, and the People to the free Election of their own Representatives; the Restoration restor'd
the Legislative Authority to its ancient and only legal Course;
the Restoration deposed the Sword, exalted the Sceptre, and
set the Civil Authority again to govern the Military; without
which we had been under the Government of a Standing Army
to this Day.

In a Word, the Restoration restor'd the Constitution, gave
the Laws their free course, Justice its full Exercise, the People
their ancient Privileges, and the Crown its just Authority.
How can we look on the Liberty we now enjoy, the Figure
we now make in the World, the Power of our Monarch, the
Wealth of our People, without Blessing the Memory of the
Restoration?

I have yet said nothing of the Church, and the restoring
to us the Religion of our Ancestors, and the pure Protestant
Worship of the ever glorious Church of England, all which
was restor'd to us by the Blessed Restoration; but I have
omitted it only because my whole Letter would be too short
to speak fully on so important a Subject, and that therefore I
leave to be handled by itself.

I think these Things, consider'd effectually,—for I have but
touch'd them lightly,—wou'd give abundant Reason to say, that
'tis wonderful how any People should be able to avow they are
for King *George*, and for the Revolution, for Liberty and the
Constitution; and not retain a due Sense of the Blessings of
that HAPPY RESTORATION.   Yours, &c.

The Plot in Favour of the Pretender.

A. J., June 9.—Sir,—Having, in my last but one, mentioned
to you the ridiculous Folly of those who send us Abroad to
look for the Plot, when it is plainly and publicly intimated to
be at Home; I desire, in one Paper more, to explain to you
what I honestly meant by it, and what honest Use we should
all make of it; for this Age is famous for Misconstruction.

As to the Folly of suggesting, as some ignorant People did,
a Fleet coming this way from Arch-Angel, I have spoken
plainly, and, I hope, sufficiently to that; I only add, that I am
since fully satisfy'd that many of the People that talk'd of that

Part, did not so much as know where Arch-Angel was, much less how far off, and how difficult and unlikely a Place it was for such a Business; so much greater is their Folly.

That suggestion then, appearing preposterous, and the Government,—if we may believe the printed News,—having received Assurances that neither Spain nor France will support the Plotters; I say, there can be no Reason for any Despondencies among us relating to the PLOT. And this is the End, and was the Reason of my exposing that simple Insinuation of an Invasion from beyond the North Cape. I think nothing can be of more Service to the whole Nation than to let them see, that tho' there are very good Reasons to believe that there is a Design on foot; and, that there is in those Reasons Cause sufficient to put the Government upon Preparations, and to be (for there can be nothing imagin'd from my Letter against that Part,) in a Readiness,—as we see is done,—yet there are no Reasons, that I can see, for the People to be under any publick Apprehensions, or to be uneasy and frighted. No Reason for running to the Bank for our Money, selling our Stocks under Price, sinking the Value of our Estates, and the like; as if there was some publick Calamity at Hand, and acting as People generally do, when they are under the Power of their Panicks.

There is a vast Difference between not believing there is any Danger, and believing there is more Danger than really exists; between being utterly secure, above the reach of an Alarm, and being frighted out of our ordinary Circle of Understanding. The Government is our Pattern in this Case; the King, we are told, has certain Information of a traytorous Design, &c. But does his Majesty act as if the Apprehensions were terrifying and amazing? Or does the Government shew, by their Preparations, that tho' they are vigilant to prevent every small beginning of Mischief, yet they are not at all diffident about the Event?

I take the Preparations of the Government to be a kind of open Defiance of all their Enemies; and to let those now concern'd see they are in a Condition here to give them such a Reception, as perhaps was not expected; and this was one Reason why I said, in my last, 'tis a Mystery to me, which I cannot fathom, how any Set of Men in this Nation, destitute of foreign Support, could propose to make any Attempt. Nor can I see that they have any rational view in it, except for their own inevitable Destruction.

And as this is evident, and ought to deter any Men in their right Senses from desperate Attempts; so it is a strong and forcible Argument with the whole Nation, to compose our Minds, to go on quietly with our Business, being fully satis-fy'd, that the Government is superior to all the Power of their Enemies, in the Nation.

I have heard it argued how great a Service it is, even to the Party itself, (who are suppos'd to be concern'd,) that the Government appears in a Condition so capable of crushing all that shall make, or offer to make, any Attempt against them; I say, a great Service in preventing their Folly, by shewing them their certain Destruction in the Thing. In the Time of the late Rebellion, many Gentlemen were taken up by the Government's Order, though without any Prosecution carry'd on against them; and they complain'd loudly of the Injury done them, to be imprison'd, when, as they alleg'd, there was no Proof against them sufficient to bring them to a Prosecu-tion. But I remember too, how thankful I have heard some of those Persons be since;—and some of very good Figure,— that they were prevented by that Kind severity from ruining themselves, as they had certainly done if they had run on as they intended.

The Sum of the Matter is this :—That as we see the Govern-ment in a Posture sufficiently able to suppress all Disturbance at home, and that we are assured there is no Ground of Apprehension from abroad; the People should sit still in Peace, and with the utmost Tranquillity, as to any Part they may have in the Matter. I speak this with respect to the trading indifferent Part of the People; who are, or ought to be, of no Party, nor meddling on one Hand or other, but whose Trade and Prosperity depends upon the Public Quiet. For what have Tradesmen and Husbandmen, Handicrafts and Manufac-tures, the peaceable labouring Poor; I say, what have they to do in these Cases? They suffer by the Alarms, Consternations, and Uneasinesses of the Generality, because all such Things are checks to our Merchants, injure Credit, stop the Employ-ment of the Poor, and perplex Trade; and they that study to make the People of England uneasy, do them the greatest

Injury imaginable. Peace alone propagates Trade, and Encourages the Traders; but as to themselves, they ought to have no Concern in these Things; their Business is Peace. To shew a full Satisfaction then in the Publick Safety, under the Protection of the Government, and of that Power which the Crown is Master of, is the best Thing that every Body can do; and they are the best Friends to the Nation, as well as to the Government, who promote it.   Your Servant,

TRANQUILLITY.

A Good Deed Embalmed.

D. P., June 9.—A poor Man, being come to Town from Tedbury in Gloucestershire,—in order to improve his Time in making Hay this Season,—was taken sick of the Small-Pox, and lay in the open Street, in Queen Street, on Sunday last. A great many Spectators gather'd about so compassionable an Object: but none offer'd to relieve him, except one Mrs. Shakleton, a poor Milk Woman, in Five-Foot Lane, near Old Fish Street, at whose House he is now charitably entertained.

Incessant Rain. Starving Haymakers.

A. J., June 9.—Among the rest, on Saturday, in the Evening, two of these poor Creatures stopt a Gentleman, by taking hold of the Reins of his Horse, as he was riding thro' a Lane near Hornsey, commonly called the Green Lanes, and demanded his Money. The poor Fellow, who laid hold of the Horse being not used to such Work, was so frighted, and in such Confusion with what he had done, that he turn'd pale, and trembled to such a Degree, that he could not hold the Bridle any longer,—and a Stick, which he had in his other Hand, which he had held up, as if offering to knock the Gentleman off his Horse, fell out of his Hand,—tho' the Gentleman offer'd no manner of Resistance, having no fire Arms, or so much as a Sword; but was going to give them his Money very quietly, when seeing the Disorder they were in, he told them Smiling, that he perceived they were but young Highwaymen, and had but newly taken up the Trade. He began to advise them very seriously to consider what the Danger of it was, and what End it would probably bring them to;—upon which, the poor Thief that had stopped him, burst

out into Tears, and falling down upon his Knees, told the
Gentleman their Miserable Condition, and that mere Hunger
had push'd them upon that dreadful Work. They begged the
Gentleman to Pardon and relieve them, protesting that they
had eaten nothing for two Days, and nothing but what they
had beg'd for ten Days, being not able to get any Work; the
Farmers not being able to begin Hay-Making. The Gentleman
gave each of them a Shilling; for which they were very
thankful.

Compassion on Famishing Thieves.

A. J., June 16.—Sir, You had a very good Story in your last,
of a couple of poor Hay-Makers, who, with Paleness and
Trembling, being young in the Trade, and driven to it by
Necessity, assaulted a Gentleman upon the Highway, and demanded his Money; I have enquired into all the Particulars
of the Story, and am assur'd it is very true.

This put me upon thinking of the natural Progression of
Crime in the nature of Man; and two very good Mora ls
occur'd to my Thoughts from your Story.

1. There are Extremities which the Nature of Man cannot
support, and which no Virtue, no Principle, will be a Protection
against.

2. That Men driven to such desperate Extremities deserve
our Compassion; both National and Personal Compassion,
according to *Solomon; Men do not despise a Thief who stealeth
to satisfy his Hunger.*

Family Distresses, and personal Distresses, such as Hunger
and Want, are even to human Nature insupportable; great
Spirits particularly cannot stoop to the Approaches of them,
they overcome at a Distance, and drive Men to Desperation,
the Effects of which we see terrible Examples of in Self-
Murthers, and in the Murthers of the poor miserable Objects,
for whom they are so anxious. I remember a poor Man that
murder'd his Wife and two little Children, purely because he
could not see them starve; and he then murder'd himself, mov'd
to the same, by the Fury and Rage that agitated his Mind to
the first bloody Action.

But I descend from those Excesses, which, I may be allow'd
to say, do not attend People, till after they are driven out of

themselves ; I name them for the sake of the Inference which
follows: If Men, by the force of these Distresses, are thus
brought to destroy themselves, and their dearest Relations, how
much more may they be driven to the trespassing on their
Friends, or on the Persons they deal with ?

How natural is it for us to pity poor Thieves who bring
themselves to the Gallows for Trifles, when we find that
Poverty and the Misery of their Families have driven them to
those Exigencies? Certainly, not Christianity only, but even
Humanity, extorts that Pity from us, if we consider what
we should do, if we were driven to those Exigencies ourselves ;
for, 'tis to be doubted, it might be said of us all, that if God
should give us Poverty, we should Steal ; that is to say,—for I
must suggest the Extremity,—that there would be some Difficulty to find an honest Man in the World, who would not
Steal before he would Starve. Let the Man who can say otherwise of himself, begin to cast Stones.

But now let me explain myself: By Stealing I do not mean
that he would go upon the Highway,—that he would go out and
break open Houses in the Night,—or any of that sort of Stealing ; but he would go and borrow, tho' he could not repay ;
promise to pay, though he could not perform ; make use of
another Man's Cash in Trade, which he was intrusted with ;
break in Debt many Thousand Pounds worse than nothing ;
and the like. And these People who do so, we know nothing of
the Necessities which drive them to it, but call them Thieves ;—
say they are worse than Highwaymen,—that they ought to be
hang'd,—and the like.

Let me then put in a Word for the Distressed, and for
honest Men made Knaves by insupportable Necessity.   How
readily did the good Gentleman pity the poor Hay-Makers !
And how do we hear him universally applauded ! At least, I do,
I assure you, wherever I have met with the Story.

Now how many Thousand such poor ruin'd Families do we
find every Day taking Sanctuary in Places appointed for the
Miserable ! And how much less Compassion do such Men meet
with, than the two Hay-Makers in the Green-Lanes ! Either it
was, that the two poor Hay-Makers met with a better Christian
than those unhappy Gentlemen do, who are forc'd to ask Favour
of Creditors, or else to be undone.   To be Bankrupt, and not

able to pay their Debts, is a worse Crime than robbing on the Highway; or else, which is infinitely more affronting to the Age; I say, the Men of these Times do not act by the Rules of Justice or Christianity.

The poor Men had eaten nothing in two Days, there was their Calamity; and it was occasion'd by the immediate Hand of Heaven, 'twas for want of fair Weather, (which they could not, it was not in their Power, to help), no Work was to be had, and without Work they could not subsist, and such dreadful Poverty put them upon that Breach of the Law, call'd Robbery.

What and wherein does this Case differ? A poor Tradesman is reduced to Misery, he has not Bread for his Family, his Trade falls off, his Debtors break, his Rent is high, he is brought down to Extremity, and having not wherewith to answer the Demands of his Creditors, he breaks; (that is to say, among the Merciless) he robs them; they fall upon him, they seize upon him, and he flies for Sanctuary to the King's Bench, to the Fleet, to the Mint; there he robs them again, as they call it: But why is it? 'Tis because, like the two Hay-Makers, he eats nothing perhaps in two Days,—aye two years;—for they will not give him fair weather to work for his Bread. He has nothing but Clouds and Storms from them, so that he cannot Work.

Let the Creditors consider the Desperation they drive their Debtor to,—that the want of Bread is not to be supported by human Nature; no, nor by Principle, nor by any Thing. And these poor Men,—no more than the two Hay-Makers, could not get Bread for themselves and Families,—but they were driven to the dreadful Exigence of Starving, before they fell into the Condition they are in; and how many, by the same Exigence, do the merciless Creditors drive to the Highway, or to the Street, to commit Things they abhor'd before.

And would these cruel People, call'd Creditors, do less themselves? Do we not often see those that refused Mercy come to want Mercy, those that have caused their Debtors to lye and perish in Gaol come to Gaol themselves, and perhaps to perish there too? So does righteous Heaven often times retaliate the cruelty of those who have had no mercy on their Fellow Creatures; and so they ought to expect. Indeed retaliating

SARAH, Duchess of Marlborough.

JOHN CHURCHILL, Duke of Marlborough.

(Defoe wrote several Poems in honour of his victories.)

Justice will always deal with them according to that happy Proverb of the King of Proverb Makers :—*That whoso stoppeth his Ears at the cry of the Poor, he also shall cry himself, and shall not be heard :* And, if I might, by way of Comment upon that Text, alter the expression, it should be thus; That *that Creditor who stopped his Ears at the Cry of the Poor Debtor, may come to cry himself as a Debtor, and not be heard ;* and, I may add, that I could name several inexorable Creditors, that have been Examples of it.   Yours, &c.

Character of the Great Duke of Marlborough.

A. J., June 23.—Sir, Among all the Heroes of the present Wearing-off Age, have you nothing to say, or no Room to add to the great Number of Elegies and Eulogies which appear upon the great Duke of Marlborough? It has been a stated Maxim among Men of Honour in all Nations, and by the Antiquity of it, and the Poetry, it should seem to have been so of past Ages,

> " Of the Dead
> Let none speak bad."

I have nothing bad to say of the great Person now in Hand. He was, when young, what some would not be, and, when old, what few could reach to be. His young Days we do not find promised for him what his Age produced, and in whom is it otherwise? The great Prince Eugene's History speaks not much of him till he appear'd in the Field. Men cannot shew the great Things that are in them, till they come to appear in the Circle of Action ; then they learn to Shine, and that Virtue which was conceal'd like an unpolish'd Diamond, under the roughness of its native Situation, has room to show itself, and recommend them to the World.

The Duke, exalted to the highest Pitch of Glory, has been loaden with accumulated Honours. England owes many good Things·to his Conduct; but, without lessening the Fame or Merit of the Duke, allow us to say too, that he has had good Masters. I hope there is no Injustice in that, nor any Offence.

It pleas'd Heaven, some Years before he died, to put a Stop to his Life of Action ; to render the Hero almost an Invalid, and to Eclipse, as to further Lustre, all those bright Articles in his Character, which gave him so much Splendour before, and we

C 2

might moralize very seriously upon that subject; but I leave
that to the Divines.

He had had the Misfortune to be, as it were, voted useless,
that is, laid aside, at several times, in two Reigns before; perhaps by the Power of Parties, perhaps otherwise, I don't meddle
with that; but now Heaven was pleased *to make him so,* for
Reasons higher than we can reach, and which we have nothing
to do with.

Under this last Disaster, for such it must be esteemed, the
Bounty of his Royal Master extended itself so far to him, as
to preserve to him his high Commands, the Posts in which all
his Wonders were perform'd; and tho' he might be render'd
incapable of acting, he was allow'd to be capable of possessing
the highest Post of Military Command; and this, under a
Monarch able for Command in Person, and so, not wanting
him in the Field, any more than in his Councils.

This extraordinary Favour of his Royal Master adds to his
Honour; but not this, nor all the Favours which Mankind
could bestow, could give him a Power of Action, (any more
than it could give him Life,) when Heaven put a Suspension
to the operation of his Genius.

He had once a Royal Mistress, generous in her Rewards, as
he could be extensive in his Merit; I cover that Part, with
saying he once knew how to serve her, and she knew how to
let him know he did not serve her in vain.

He amass'd Wealth in all these Services, to such a Degree,
as, I doubt not, satisfy'd his utmost Desires; For who can
tax his Memory with desiring anything which he ought not to
have? I will not suppose that he was not above desiring what
he could not want.

As he serv'd his Country in a Manner that gives us a loud
Summons to acknowledge him a great Man, as well as a great
Captain, so he serv'd a Country grateful to its Champion; and
as I will not detract from his Merit, so I will not say that his
Country has been very liberal in recording and rewarding his
Labours.

Let the Testimonies given at the Head of the Grants he
received,—the Honour of Acts of Parliament for aggrandizing
his Family,—for erecting him the finest Palace (not Royal) in
Britain,—for settling a vast Revenue upon him,—for entailing

his Honours upon the Issue of his Daughters,—with many other instances,glorious to his Family,and enriching to his Posterity;—I say, let these all bear Witness to the gratitude of his Country.

Let me add here, that the Treatment the Duke received from Great Britain, as his Country, and from the Monarchs of Great Britain, as his Sovereigns, will remain on record to Posterity, to let them see that whatever has been said by some, the highest Merit does not pass here, without a suitable Reward.

The Duke of Marlborough being dead, (16 June 1722,) it cannot be amiss to give our Readers the satisfaction of a Sketch of the great and various Figures he made in the World, and the Offices and Employments he enjoy'd under the British Government.   —   —   —   —   —

Against Publishing False Rumours of War.

A. J., June 30.—Sir, I cannot refrain sometimes putting a Whip in your Hands to lash yourselves, you News-Mongers, I mean ; and as long as the Smart will not affect you so much as it does our Half-Sheet Men, whose Labours you Journalists are supposed pretty much to copy after, so long I think you will not think it hard.

They have been all this Spring, and even part of the last Winter, preparing our Minds to expect the most bloody, desolating War to break out all over Europe, that the World has known for many Ages ; the Spaniards with all their Allies, France, Savoy, &c. were to begin a War with the Emperor in Italy ; how often have you all told us that War was inevitable ?

The next was the Turks ; they were preparing to attack the Venetians on the one Hand, and the King of Poland on the other, and their Fleet was fitting out ; so the Venetians were under great Apprehensions on that side, and even the Court of Vienna were very much alarm'd.

The next was, that the Czar of Muscovy had certainly determined to invade the Empire with a hundred thousand Men,—that was the least Number; and that his Fleet, which was composed of many more Ships of War than ever his Czarish Majesty had to fit out, lay ready at Revel and at Petersburgh to put to sea, and fall upon the King of Denmark.

Now give me leave to hint to you something of what better Intelligence informs us : Last Week I spoke with a gentleman,

upon whose Credit I can rely, and who, having resided at
Venice, came from thence about a Month since, and is just
now arriv'd here.   He assures me, that it is all News to
him, that the Turks had threaten'd the Venetians with a Rup-
ture, or that the Venetians were in any Apprehensions of it;
that they knew nothing of it at Venice, and that it was a surprize to him to hear of it when he came to England, for that
they had no Notion of such a Thing in any of the Parts of
Italy or France, through which he had travelled.

I ask'd him if he heard anything of the Preparations for
War in Italy; his Answer was, no, not a Word. The Emperor
indeed had changed his Governors pretty much; in particular,
the Viceroy of Sicily, the Duke de Montelcon,—and the Viceroy
of Naples, Prince Borghese, were removed; that the Duke de
Almanara was made Viceroy of the former, and Cardinal
Althan of the latter; and it might be that those Governors had
caused Troops to put themselves in a better Posture than
before,—and those *New Brooms* were sweeping clean; that is,
they were recommending themselves, by making a great
Bustle,—but nothing like a War. That as to a Spanish Fleet on
the Coast of Italy, with Troops landed at Porto Longone, and
the like; of demanding Firral of the Genoese for a Place of
Arms, there had been nothing heard of these Things where he
had been, and that he had been in the most significant Parts
of all Italy.

The like News I may have to tell you of, about the Affairs
of the North; one while you send the Czar of Muscovy on
a wild Goose Chace into the Calmuck Tartary, and another
time into Persia, to make War with the Great Mogul, and
open a Trade to the East Indies; but some People that come
from Petersburgh know nothing of the Matter, and we should,
I doubt not, find it so in his Enterprises which he was to go
upon in the Baltick, if we enquir'd farther.

Now if this be so, how merry a Story is it, to be told of us
Britons, that we, who pretend to keep all the World so much
at Peace; should, in our public Papers, edge, and whet, the
Expectations of our People, so much, as to make them expect
all the World to go together by the Ears, as if all Europe was
going to War with one another.

I need not exclaim against you News-Writers for imposing

these Things on the World, for it is your Trade to write, and yet 'tis none of your Business to answer for the Truth of what you write neither. But methinks it might yield us some Speculations when we see the easiness of Mankind to be thus put upon, to take every blind Story for Truth, and form Ideas upon those Things for stating the Affairs of Europe.

This seems to intimate how good a Posture Mankind are just now in to be deluded. No wonder the Bubbling Trade prevail'd so much upon us a little while ago. When Men believe anything, and everything, 'tis meet they should be cheated in everything; and this has been pretty much our Case, and may perhaps be so again. Let us guard against more Bubbles; and, I think, instead of believing everything, we should, for the future, believe nothing.   Your servant,

CREDULOUS.

Serious Reflections on Old Age.

A. J., July 7.—Sir, in your last Journal you told us a Story, how true we know not, of one *Mary Dennison,* of *Kirby Stephen,* in the County of *Westmoreland,* who was 131 years of Age. It is true long Life and length of Days is esteemed to be a great Blessing in the Scripture Dialect; but as we see Age treated in these Days, and as People carry their Age too, take it which way you will, I cannot but say, that if it be given from Heaven for a Blessing, we have brought it to such a pass, that much of the Blessing of it is lost to us, and that very many Ways.

The general Contempt put upon old Age by others, is now such, that it is hardly sufferable by human Nature. How can that Age be desirable that seems to expose the Person, not only to neglect and slight, but even to universal Derision ? Unhappy Creatures! the Soul is never old, but in its full Vigour and Exercise,—and this makes it the worse; also the Resentment of the injurious Treatment old Age receives, is the same in Age, or rather stronger; but the Powers being contracted by the Deficiency of the Organ, the Soul is reduced to an Incapacity of defending or revenging the Affronts.

If, as old Age cannot do itself Justice, so it were insensible of the Injustice it receives, there were some Equality in the Misery of it; but to have the same sense of Injury, and no

Power to do ourselves right, adds an exceeding Weight to the Burthen. Contempt is to a resenting Temper insupportable, and therefore while we are young and vigorous, we cast it off with Disdain, or effectually shew our Resentment, by avenging the Affront; but the old, decay'd, feeble Gyant, must be content to see himself the Scorn of the most despicable Wretch, and having the same Sense of the Grief, but no Strength of Body to act by,—and, to do himself right,—it gnaws upon his Soul.

This may be illustrated when the Children mock'd *Elisha*, *Go up thou Bald Head!* He turn'd about and curs'd them in the Name of the Lord. The meaning is plain,—he was an old Man, bald, and decay'd in Strength,—unable to turn back and chase them; and he prays to God to avenge him of those who he could not avenge himself of.

Would Heaven concern itself thus to give old Age the Assistance of his Power, and avenge the Injuries and Contempt they receive, the Man of a hundred would be truly venerable. But, as they seem not only scorn'd by Boys, the Contempt even of Dogs, and that Heaven itself is pleas'd to quit their Defence, at least in Appearance;—How can that Life be a Blessing, which seems to be, as it were, out of the Protection of its Maker, abandon'd to scorn, and derision of Children,—exposed to the Injuries and Insults of Youth,—divested of Power to help itself,—and as it were, left to the Alms-keeping of their own Posterity.

If it chance that the aged Person be poor, he sees himself left to perish, because he cannot Work; and at best, he is either a Petitioner for daily Charity, or demands it where he receives it with Reluctance, and ill Usage; namely, from the Parish.

If the Person have Substance, he sees himself surrounded with those that envy him the long keeping it from them,—and who gape for the Enjoyment of it at the Expence of his Life,—as if it was an Injury to them that he made use of it so long,—and that he ought not to keep them out of it; every Servant is a Thief to him, even his Children cheat and deceive him, presuming upon the Deficiency either of his Sight, or Hearing, or Memory,—and then, laugh at the unnatural Fraud.

All this, while his discerning Soul is as nicely sensible of the Neglect, of the Injustice, and of the Contempt he suffers under, as it was, or would have been, in the greatest Vigour of his

Youth; but his Complaints are not heard, his Reasons are run down with Noise, and he is told by the insolent Invaders, that he is an Old Man, and forgets.

His Remedy is found only in the Patience with which he torments his Mind; a Patience better describ'd by the word Anguish. Thus *Jacob*, when his importunate Sons so ill defended themselves for not bringing back one Brother, and yet pressing him to send the last,—*If I am bereaved*, says he, *I am bereaved*. So *David*, when under the Management of his haughty General *Joab*,—*These Sons of Zeruiah are too hard for me!* But he remember'd it, and made his son *Solomon*, who was strong and able, pay the Traytor home for it.

While thus Age is impotent, infirm, distemper'd, and unable to resent, and is continually loaded with Scorn and Contempt, insulted by those whose fathers, as *Job* says, *He would not have set with the Dogs of his Flock:* I say, where then is the Blessing, or the Benefit of Living, as *Mary Superannuated*, it seems has done, to the Age of one Hundred and Thirty one.

Your servant,
ANCIENT.

Capture of Pirates on the Coast of Guinea.

A. J., July 14.—Sir, I have suspended writing to you a long time on the Subject of taking the Pyrates upon the Coast of *Guinea*, and which I am now going to mention, because we were in some uncertainty about the Truth of it; and the Advices coming all but one way, and that one way being all but what we call Ship News, which, I remember, we did not use to give much heed to in former Times, all conspir'd to make us doubtful about it, yet since the World now universally seems to give Credit to it, I will for the present, and for the Argument Sake, beg the Question, and suppose it to be true.

First of all, I congratulate my Country, and particularly the Merchants, upon the News. This same *Roberts* being a bold, audacious, undaunted Rogue, as ever set his Foot on board a Ship in so wicked a Work; and has done more Mischief, and committed more Spoil, among the Merchants, than either · *Avery*, or any of that Godless Crew that we call Pyrates ever did. He has defied Mercy, out-stood Proclamations, declar'd Death or Victory to be the upshot of every Fight, and therefore carried his Black Flag, with a Death's Head in it, for his Ancient; and now he has his Reward, Death has been his Portion, tho' he deserved to have met his Death at the Gallows, rather than from a Cannon Bullet.

I have often thought, had those Enemies of all Nations (for such they were) been pursued, as they should have been, and as they might have been; had either more Ships been sent after them, or had those Ships which were sent against them, been better manag'd, and the Commanders done their Duty better, a shorter End might have been made with the Pyrates; I say, I have thought so. I do not charge any Body, but it has been a long time that these Sons of Hell have rang'd in those Seas, without ever having been met with in such a Manner before. How many honest Merchants have they impoverish'd! How many promising good Voyages have they ruin'd! What Insults have they been Guilty of! What Mischiefs have they not done! And yet, how long before the Hand of Justice could overtake them!

It has been spoken, with such Reflections as I care not to repeat, that whatever the Government has done in this Case, has been some how or other render'd abortive, and still the Rogues have rid Masters of the Sea; that is to say, have rang'd from Place to Place, and have not been met with; a Thing that when represented to Foreigners, they rashly conclude, that either the Government of *Great Britain* was very weak, or that the Pyrates of *America* were very strong, and stronger far, than we have Reason to believe they were; both of these Rumours produce no good Effect. To represent an Enemy as formidable, is to make him so; but let a few more of them be unkennel'd, as these have been, we should soon see the whole Nest of them roused, and they would dwindle away to nothing, and perhaps take Sanctuary in Madagascar.

But now to go back to these at *Guinea*. According to the Account we see now publish'd, almost all the Men of those three Ships are got on Shore, the Man of War having, as they say, taken only one Hundred and Seventy Prisoners.

Those three Pyrate Ships, by the Report of the same People who tell the News, were all Ships of Force, and must have two or three hundred Men in every Ship at least, perhaps more; so that if all the rest of them are gotten away, except one hundred and seventy, there cannot be less than five or six hundred of them on Shore. Now what can we say to all this? Such a number of Men, if they got on Shore with their Arms, (as it is very likely they might,) out of the Ships which were careening, they may still do an incredible Mischief on Shore; and particularly to the Settlements of the *African* Company, especially if they have also any small Boats. Nor can the Company's People raise Strength enough to attack them by Land.

What they will do for Provisions, is a Question by itself; that, indeed, they must range the Country for, and make as good Shift as they can. But I should, I confess, expect to hear of some desperate Attempt made by them on some of the Factories there; and I question whether any of the Forts on that Coast are strong enough to resist them. On the other Hand, if they have no Arms, but are only fled for their Lives, they will all perish, either for want of Bread, or by the Bows and Arrows of the Negroes; and we shall perhaps have an Account of their Exit, by some of them that may fall into our People's Hands there. As to those one hundred and seventy, who are now at Cape Coast Castle, some People ask what must be done with them; I confess it would be hard to hang them all there, because there may be some among them who were forc'd away into their Ships, who never went heartily with them, and so are not really Pyrates, and ought to be distinguish'd from the rest; otherwise, one would be apt to say they should e'en hang them all up where they are, and never put the Government to the Charge of bringing them hither, only for the sake of trying them. Taking them in Fight, is taking them in the Fact, and there needs no other Proof against them than the fire of the Guns they let fly at the Man of War. But that is none of my Business; wherever they are carried, they must be brought to Justice, there's no doubt of that, and we may hope the Coast of *Guinea* will now be pretty clear of them.

Yours, &c.

The Instability of Human Glory.

A. J., July 21.—Sir, I have employ'd myself of late pretty much in the Study of History, and have been reading the

Stories of the great Men of past Ages, *Alexander* the Great,
Julius Cæsar, the great *Augustus*, and many more, down, down,
down, to the still greater *Louis XIV.*, and even to the still
greatest *John Duke of Marlborough.*   In my way I met with
Tamerlane the *Scythian, Tomornbejus* the *Egyptian, Solyman*
the Magnificent, and others of the *Mahometan,* or *Ottoman*
Race ; and after all the great Things they have done, I find it
said of them all, one after another, AND THEN HE DIED, all
dead, dead ! *hic Jacet,* is the finishing Part of their History.
Some lye in the Bed of Honour, and some in Honour's
Truckle Bed ; some were bravely slain in Battle on the Field
of Honour, some in the Storm of a Counterscarp, and died in
the Ditch of Honour; some here, some there ;—the Bones of
the Bold and the Brave, the Cowardly and the Base, the Hero
and the Scoundrel, are heap'd up together ;—there they lie in
Oblivion, and under the Ruins of the Earth, undistinguish'd
from one another, nay, even from the common Earth.

> " Huddled in Dirt the blust'ring Engine lies,
>   That was so Great, and thought himself so Wise."

How many Hundreds of Thousands of the bravest Fellows
then in the World lye on Heaps in the Ground, whose Bones
are to this Day plow'd up by the Rusticks, or dug up by the
Labourer, and the Earth their more noble vital Parts are con-
verted to, has been perhaps apply'd to the meanest Uses !

How have we skreen'd the Ashes of Heroes to make our
Mortar, and mingl'd the Remains of a Roman General to
build a Hog-Stye !   Where are the Ashes of a *Cæsar,* and the
Remains of a *Pompey,* a *Scipio,* or a *Hannibal ?*   All are
vanish'd,—they and their very Monuments are moulder'd into
Earth,—their Dust is lost, and their Place knows them no more.
They live only in the immortal Writings of their Historians and
Poets, the renown'd Flatterers of the Age they liv'd in, and who
have made us think of the Persons, not as they really were,
but as they were pleas'd to represent them.

As the greatest Men, so even the longest liv'd,—the *Methu-
salems* of the Antediluvian World,—the Accounts of them all
end with the same ; *Methusalem* lived nine hundred sixty and
nine Years, and begat Sons and Daughters ; and what then ?
AND THEN HE DIED.

> " Death, like an overflowing Stream,
> Sweeps us away; our Life's a Dream."

We are now solemnizing the Obsequies of the Great *Marlborough*; all his Victories, all his Glories, his great projected Schemes of War, his uninterrupted Series of Conquests, which are call'd his, as if he alone had fought, and conquer'd by his Arm, what so many valiant Men obtain'd for him with their Blood. All is ended where ·other Men, and indeed where all Men ended: HE IS DEAD!

Not all his immense Wealth, the Spoils and Trophies of his Enemies, the Bounty of his grateful Mistress, and the Treasure amass'd in War and Peace; not all that mighty bulk of Gold,—which some suggest is such, and so great, as I care not to mention,—could either give him Life, or continue it one Moment, but HE IS DEAD; and, some say, the great Treasure he was possess'd of here had one strange particular Quality attending it,—which might have been very dissatisfying to him if he had consider'd much on it,—namely, that he could not carry much of it WITH HIM.

We have now nothing left us of this great Man that we can converse with, but his Monument and his History. He is now number'd among things pass'd. The Funeral, as well as the Battles, of the Duke of *Marlborough*, are like to adorn our Houses in Sculpture, as Things equally gay, and to be look'd on with pleasure. Such is the End of human Glory, and so little is the World able to do—for the greatest Men that come into it, and for the greatest Merit those Men can arrive to.

What then is the Work of Life? What the Business of great Men, that pass the Stage of the World in seeming Triumph, as these Men, we call Heroes, have done? Is it to grow great in the mouth of Fame, and take up many Pages in History? Alas! that is no more than making a Tale for the reading of Posterity, till it turns into Fable and Romance. Is it to furnish Subject to the Poets, and live in their immortal Rhimes, as they call them? That is, in short, no more than to be hereafter turn'd into Ballad and Song, and be sung by old Women to quiet Children; or, at the Corner of a Street, to gather Crowds in aid of the Pickpocket and the Whore. Or is their Business rather to add Virtue and Piety to their Glory,

which alone will pass with them into Eternity, and make them
truly Immortal? What is Glory without Virtue? A great
Man without Religion is no more than a great Beast without
a Soul. What is Honour without Merit? And what can be
call'd true Merit, but that which makes a Person be a good
Man, as well as a great Man?

If we believe a future State of Life, a Place for the Rewards
of good Men, and for the Punishment of the Haters of Virtue,
how full of Heroes and famous Men crowd in among the last !
How few Crown'd Heads wear the Crowns of immortal
Felicity !

Let no Man envy the great and glorious Men, as we call
them ! Could we see them now, how many of them would move
our Pity, rather than call for our Congratulations ! These few
Thoughts, Sir, I send to prepare your Readers' Minds when
they go to see the Magnificent Funeral of the late Duke of
Marlborough.   Your Humble Servant, &c.

D. P.—Paris, July 25.—Some Days ago the Dutchess of
Orleans made a Present to the Infant Queen, of a Wax Baby
three Foot High, with Diamond Ear-rings, a Necklace of Pearls
and Diamond Cross, with a Furniture of Plate for a Toilet, and
two India Chests, full of Linen, and several Suits of Cloaths for
the Baby, the whole for that Princess to play with.

Honesty not the Exclusive Property of any Political Party.

A. J., July 28.—Sir, I have been a strict Observer in many
particular Cases which come daily upon the Theatre of Action,
and I find that the Case of Whig and Tory, which has been of
late so remarkable a Distinction among our People, is strangely
alter'd ; and the wisest Man among the Gentlemen I converse
with, cannot give an Explanation of it, or lay down the Character either of one or of the other, so as I might know them
asunder. One time we find the Whigs a kind of honest
People, doing several good Things,—in Government they have
done much,—maintaining our Liberties, taking care that no corrupted Court encroach upon the People's Privileges, and the
like ; and while they did this, I very much inclin'd to be
a Whig.

On a sudden, I thought those they call Tories were turn'd

Patriots,—set up for Law and Constitution, pleading for Liberties and Privileges against the Whigs, complaining when they were invaded, exposing corrupt Ministers, and the like; and, like true Patriots, *I say*, standing up for the Laws and Constitution of the Country. And then I thought the Whigs, who my Eyes were upon before, were degenerated, and become scandalous for Avarice, Bubbling and Cheating the Nation, drawing in their Friends, and the like; and then, all on a sudden, I wish'd myself a Tory. Upon the whole, I find 'tis very hard to say which are the honest Men, or where they live.

When shall we see the Time when any one Party claiming the Title of Honest, shall shew it, by a steady pursuit of just Measures? Proving that they deserve the happy Title of Patriots, Men disinterested, and abhorring to carry on a private Interest at the Expence of their Country? I say, when shall we see such a Time? For my Part, I despair of it. But that which I now complain of, is still of as fatal a nature as the other; I find a Set of Men who call themselves of no Party, and indeed are of no Party, nor are fit to be of any Party; but,—watching for what we call Preferment or Advancement, publick Employment, and the like,— they reserve the Principles they have, if such Men may be said to have any Principles; I say, reserve them in Petto; *that is to say*, conceal them, till they know who their Patrons are, and what they would have them profess.

These Men act something like our Politick City Ladies, (Maiden Ladies I mean,) who do not discover which Way they incline, whether to the Church or to the Dissenters, till they see what he is to be that intends to Court them; and then kindly profess their Willingness to believe as he, who is to be their Husband, believes, let that be which way it will. These Ladies, it must be confess'd, shew more good Humour than ordinary; but no Body can charge them with having too much Religion.

Our Politicians, of whom I am now speaking, are willing to shew themselves so, and in such a manner, as that, whatever Party the Person is of, who advances them, they will be of the same. In this they may shew some Policy, but no Honesty; that is not to be expected. Now what is the Reason, that with every change of Times, the Dependents upon Courtiers and Ministers of State always forsake them when they fall, and are received by the succeeding Statesmen, and make their Court to

them, even in the quite contrary Extreme ? 'Tis only from the
certain Indifference they were in to Parties before they engag'd ;
for this Reason this Sort of Men ought never to be receiv'd
at all ; for he that thus lays wait for his Opportunity to get in,
is certain to use the same Falsehood when he is in.

Statesmen are always besieg'd with Flatterers, and so are
they always betray'd by them when they are drawn in to trust
them. Who have been worse used by these People, than those
who advanced them to the Dignity and Honour they attain'd
to ? Who were more implacable Enemies to a certain Noble
Lord in his Troubles, and push'd more heartily at his Destruction, than those Men who had been oblig'd to his Beneficence
and Bounty ?* *Et tu Brute !* is the Exclamation which great
Men have often an Occasion to make use of in complaining of
the Ingratitude of some whom they had, in the highest manner
oblig'd. On this account, I cannot but add to it, that these
undiscover'd, unfix'd Party-Men, are the most dangerous in a
State. As they choose no Party, but by the Profits which they
hope to make of them, so they abandon every Party, as those
Profits are abated, or dye off; if the Channel of their Gains
runs low, and the Tide, which at first they used, suffers an
ebb, they shew quickly on what account they serv'd.

Upon the whole, sir, I think it is worth while for you, who
write publick Papers, so to expose this fatal destructive
Temper of Men, as to let honest Gentlemen see and know who
to avoid, and be asham'd of; and to let the guilty People know
the World is aware of them, and that they cannot now deceive
Mankind, as they used to do. I may in a little Time let you
know the Faces of some of these Men, who walk about securely
doing Mischief, only by being conceal'd.   Yours, &c.

A. J.—This week died, in a Mad-House at Hoxton, Mr.
Russell, Brother-in-Law to Mr. Robert Knight, the late famous
South Sea Cashier.

On Falsehood : a Satire.

A. J., Aug. 4.—Sir, I have had some time ago an Inclination to have sent you a Poem upon Falsehood, and to give due

---

* He alludes here to the impeachment of his benefactor, the Earl of
Oxford.—*Ed.*

Praise to the Grace of Hypocrisy, the Modish Virtue of the Times: I mean not so much on Religion as in Politicks, though extensive in both, and my Poem should have begun thus:

> " Hail Men of Fashion ! Knaves of high Descent, ⎫ ·
> To every King, and every Government, ⎪
> Faithful alike, and with alike Intent ; ⎬
> Who for the Miseries of Mankind now live, ⎭
> Who smile to kill, and flatter to deceive."

But I do not find the Genius of the Times relish Poetry, so much as they did formerly, and so I think to digest my Thoughts with less Fire, and give you a Sketch of them in Prose. There was in ancient Times a Thing call'd Honesty in the World ; whether it was a Substance, or a Quality, even then, Authors are not agreed about it, and sometimes it was so loaded with Art and Disguises, that it was pretty hard to know it. However such a Thing there was, and it had that particular Character belonging to it, that it was full of Courage and Spirit; it would carry a Man through thick and thin, nothing could withstand its Bravery. Fire and Water, Hills or Dales, all was alike ; and it was the same, Humble in Prosperity, Stout in Adversity, the same in all Conditions, in all Seasons, Circumstances and Disasters, whence it became a Proverb in those Days, *Truth's as bold as a Lyon.*

Sed Tempora mutantur ! The Times are alter'd, and many a Turn and Return has happen'd among us,—and that of such a Nature, as has almost turn'd this old fashion'd Virtue out of House and Home ; at least, as the Sailors say, it has beaten it to its close Quarter, so that, *in short*, it does not walk the Streets so boldly as it used to do. I had almost said it dares not, indeed if it does, 'tis so often jostl'd and kick'd about, even in the open Street,—from Post to Pillar,—and meets with so much downright Knavery, or Falsehood, and Hypocrisy, that it is very rarely to be seen.

And since this obsolete Quality has been so long out of Use, or at least out of Fashion, why, to make a Virtue of Necessity, should we not as well take up and be satisfied with what is come up in the stead of it, and take it for the Equivalent? For, in a Word, if Falsehood and Hypocrisy answer our Ends, as well as Honesty answer'd theirs, is it not an Equivalent?

They say the Brutes have no Souls, and do not act by Principles of Reason; but I answer, that they have a something that answers all the Ends and Purposes of Reason, so far as they have Occasion for it, and so far it is a Reasoning to them. In like manner, if it should be said that the Men of this Generation have no Honesty, I might answer, that they have a (damn'd) something, that answers all the Ends and Purposes of Honesty, so far as they have Occasion for it.

If, to make this more eligible, and that our Felicity may not seem less than that of our Fathers, it should be said, that we have not so much Occasion for Honesty as our Fathers; or, which may come nearer to the Truth, that we do not understand the Use of Honesty so well as they did; I say, if it should be said so, I know not what Answer to make, but this: That, I believe, we understand how to make shift without it, better than they did.

If then our modern Knavery comes up in those Parts,—which we have most Occasion for it to serve,—to all the Purposes of Honesty; it may pass for Honesty to us, and in time we may live to see the Benefit of it more than we do yet.

Hail Glorious Fraud! Thou new-fashion'd Virtue! How art thou risen up to thy present Magnitude, in the Place of that weak and impotent Thing, call'd Honesty! And how much more useful art thou to us, than that was to our Ancestors! How many rising Families hast thou added to the ancient Gentry! How many flourishing Tradesmen hast thou plac'd among the Quality of the Day! And how dost thou daily heap Wealth upon all the Dealers in thy Craft! How evidently do Poverty and Honesty herd together! And where do they so generally end, as in the utmost of human Misery? While blessed Hypocrisy and gilded Knavery ride in the *Berline,* and are drawn about with a Coach and Six, from one End of the Town to the other, engrossing Wealth without Measure.

Happy Falschood! With what Pleasure dost thou roll in Prosperity, and how does thy Success confirm thee in the Hearts of Men! Who would speak Truth at the Expense of Fortune, and his own Interest; when, by the easy way of a little *leger de langer,* a Man may be as rich as *Crœsus,* as fortunate as *Lucius,* as happy as *Portius* and *Lucullus?*

Let Thread-bare Honesty keep House by herself, and let

them who love Poverty and Rags sit indolent and unactive at
her Door, waiting till those Ages of Weakness may return, that
shall value and restore her. But if we will be rich, happy,
fortunate, flatter'd, applauded, and cry'd up in the World, we
must be as the World are; and, as the World, be no honester
than our Neighbours, no better than other People,—embrace
the happy Favourite of the Times ; and what——— ? What we
dare not name, though so many dare be, and defend it.

Your Servant,
CAUTION.

Party Spirit may lead to Unnatural Conduct.

A. J., Aug. 11.—Sir, I have often seen the evil Consequence
of bringing our private Passions to concern themselves in our
public Affairs; and I have attempted, though Unsuccessful, to
expose the Inconveniences that proceed from it. I say unsuc-
cessfully, for we see it is impossible. When Men fall out in
their Politicks, they fall out in their Friendship, their Neighbourhood, their Societies, and everything,—as if the bein₂
Whig or Tory was Essential to the very Principles of Re
ligion ; and I should suggest, a Man could have no Conscience,
no Charity, no Religion, if he was not of my Party, or of
my Opinion in public Matters. This is as Unnatural, and as
contrary to Religion, as it is to suppose, that a Negro or
an Indian Servant could not be a Christian, and must not be
Baptiz'd.

Unhappy Temper ! Whither will it drive us? I have heard,
and desire they would not put me upon the Proof of it, That
a certain Man was refused to be admitted to the Sacrament in
a certain Congregation, because he had Poll'd wrong, or Voted
wrong, *as they call'd it,* in a certain Election ; and had, on some
other Occasions, show'd himself on the Tory side, *as they had
it again,* or, (as you may with as much Truth express it,) had
not been so flaming a Whig, so absolute an Incendiary as
he had formerly been. By this Rule, to be a Tory, is to be
Excommunicated from Christian Society, and even from
Heaven itself, as much as it is in the Power of Party to do
so. The Charity of this Usage is left open to our Remarks ;
indeed it is no more than what is done on many, if not on
every Side, and leaves us the greater Cause to Reproach our

Gentlemen, with the Breach of Temper in their Parties, to a most extravagant Excess.

Nothing has been more frequent, than for Fathers to disinherit their Children, Sons to Insult their Fathers, and Brothers to draw their Swords upon one another, from the unnatural Breach of Parties; and this, indeed, justifies my calling it Unnatural.

" You Ignorant Dog," (said a Worshipful Father the other Day to his eldest Son, the Heir of his Estate, and hope of his Family) " What! are you turn'd Tory? I had rather ten thousand Times you had been Circumcised, and turn'd Mahometan! Arn't you a Brute now, and would be glad to see your Father, and all your Family Hang'd? What! turn'd Tory? Go you Uncircumcised Renegade, go and turn Turk, and Act like yourself! But I'll circumcise your Fortunes I promise you. I'll take care, if the Devil must have you, he shall have you as Poor as you came into the World; as void of Money, as you are of Manners,—as Naked of an Estate, as you are of Honesty: Turn'd Tory! That is a Parricide, an unnatural Dog! Go, and see my Face no more, but sort with the Gang you belong to; and see what the Devil and you can make of your Bargain."

Was it not mighty agreeable to a Christian Father to use a Son thus? A Son especially,—seeing it was a Son that had never disoblig'd him in anything else; and had Acted perhaps strictly, according to Conscience and to Truth, and according to his own Judgment of Things, tho' not just according to his Father's Opinion,—or rather to his Father's Party,—which only Offence you see, Obliterated all his paternal Affection, all his Charity, all his Justice; and, in a Word, Enrag'd him to such a Degree, that his Passions carried him beyond Reason, beyond his Temper; stripp'd him of all that look'd like a Father, and Cloth'd him with the Rage of the Devil.

Thus we see it daily in other Cases, while all Fear of God, and Regard to Man is Obliterated, all just Usage of one another is dropp'd, and we fly into Rage on Things that not only are not suitable to deserve such Treatment, but Things that are in themselves Just, and so far from being Criminal, as that they are according to Conscience and Truth.

Where is Christian Liberty in this? And who are they,

who in other Things talk so loudly against Persecution, and
coercive Power? Is there any Persecution more Cruel than
that of the Tongue, and any Bitterness Greater than that of a
Party Temper?

What have our Passions and private Resentment to do with
our Public Interest? Every Man is, or ought to be, at Liberty
to Act, as his own Judgment and Opinion Guides; and if
Liberty is our due in anything, surely 'tis our due in this,
that we ought to be entirely Free in siding with those
People, or with that Party, which we think are most in the
Right.

But seeing we are so Impatient of Contradiction, I think
you should recommend it to the Legislature, to add this
blessed Establishment to our Constitution; namely, that
Fathers, and Masters, and Neighbours, and Preachers, &c.,
should be Empower'd to oblige all that may be Depending
upon them, to Vote as they, who they so Depend upon may
command. That the Parent should disinherit, the Preacher
Excommunicate, the Master of a College Expel, and the like,
upon the least Deviation from that Principle the Person was
Inducted to; and that, in a Word, all Inferiors should Act in
Parties, in Subordination to Superiors.

I shall in a few Days give you an Account of the Reason
and particular Occasion of this Doctrine, and to whom it may
be applied; for depend upon it, the Practice is become so
Fashionable, that it is great Pity it should not be Legal, have
the Sanction of a Law, and be made as Strong, as it is made
frequent by Practice.   Your Humble Servant,

                                              FURIOUS.

Uncertainty of History Written with Party Spirit.

A. J., Aug. 18.—Sir, I find all your Eyes at *London* are
turn'd upon the subject of the late Duke of *Marlborough's*
Funeral; and your Poets and Ballad-makers have been much
busy'd, in advancing his Fame, with Ribaldry, and Rhime.
Hard is the State of great Men in this World, whatever it may
be in the next; that their great Actions live but by so mean
and so vile a Help, as that of Pen and Ink Flattery. The
History of their Lives is at the Mercy of the Times that come
after them; and they are either, by Prejudices, run down to

Contempt and Forgetfulness, or by Parasites and Poets, run up to Monster and Romance.

If within seven or ten Years People can scarce prevail upon themselves to think regularly of Things past, or to entertain just Notions of Actions, or of the Persons that perform'd them; what must be the Case forty or fifty Years afterwards, when the Men, whose Memories could correct the Injustice of Historians, shall be gone off the Stage, and Men are at liberty to add or diminish, as they please, in the Story of Times past?

Actions of great Men, not unalterably recorded at the Time on which they were perform'd, and recorded by an Authority unquestion'd; are expos'd to the Mercy of Posterity, in a most scandalous and unhappy Manner. This is evident from the Histories of the few Ages since Queen *Elizabeth's* Reign, of which it may indeed be said, with some affliction, that we have not one faithful impartial History left; nor anything extant that looks back'd with sufficient Authority, and from which another Writer may justify his Ideas of Things then in Agitation. All the Writers of those Times are contradicted and reflected on, by one or other of those who followed them; and, except the Earl of *Clarendon*,—who wrote the Transactions of but a few Years,—there is not an Author but has been detected, exposed, or contradicted in the Accounts he had given of the Transactions of those Days.

With some of the Historians, King *James* the First was a *David*, a *Solomon*, a Prince inspired from Heaven, the best of Kings, and the wisest of Men, and his Fame is handed down to us as that of the greatest Man in Council of his Age; while at the same time, by others he passes for A - - - - - -, A - - - - - -, A - - - - - -, and A - - - - - -, and something else, not fit for me to name.

How his Son, King *Charles* was, and is still represented and misrepresented, is too well known; how he was reverenc'd, and even ador'd on one Side, but insulted and reproached with Crimes he never committed on the other Side; how he was persecuted, conquer'd, murder'd; all these Things are plac'd in different Lights, for Posterity to view and judge of them just as they think fit; all is left to the vulgar, and they left to judge of them by the false Lights of those Writers, who will not fail to represent them according to the Notions of the several Historians they are guided by.

Thus the Funeral Pomp of the Duke of *Marlborough*, his Actions, his Life, shall, without doubt, be handed down to Posterity, with a contradicting Variety, one Side representing Things one Way, and the other another Way; one Side shall represent him as he stood, in all our Opinions, in the first eight or nine years of his late Royal Mistress's Reign, when the Nation's good Opinion joyn'd with the Queen's, and when her Majesty thought nothing too great to say of him, or too much to do for him. Another Side shall represent him as they thought him acting from that time forward, in a manner, (to say nothing hard on that subject here,) differing from the Sentiments of the same bountiful Mistress he serv'd before,—and when we saw him remov'd, displac'd, and question'd, even in Parliament, as well as out,—nay censur'd, divested, and absented.

How shall Posterity receive these Things? How shall they form just Ideas of them, unless some impartial Historian should rise up whom no Man would contradict? And who should write with such unprejudic'd Faithfulness, as that all Party Scribblers, who now write under the Bribery of their own Passions, should give place to, and acquiesce with.

The Duke of *Marlborough* himself, were he now alive, and in the full Vigour of his Senses, could expect no other Fate. The Times are too much deviated from the happy Calm, that would give Room for such just and impartial Treatment of Men of Merit, or such plain and clear Relation of Fact, as would be necessary to give all Men an equal Esteem of those that were good, or Resentment against those that are bad. The Memory of the Duke of *Marlborough* shall be to Posterity just what Posterity can learn of it from the Writers of the Age, however partial and unjust; or from the yet more uncertain and more partial Voice of Oral Tradition. And he shall lye at the Mercy of the Pens, as all great men do now at the Mercy of the Tongues of the most ignorant, and most misguided Part of the People. They shall think of him either too high above his Merit, or too low beneath his Desert, just as he is rightly represented, or falsely misrepresented to them by the Voice of Common Fame.　　　　Your Servant,

　　　　　　　　　　　　　　　　　　　G. B.

Duty of Journalists to Discountenance Plots.

A. J., Aug. 25.—Sir, In these Times of Plot and Proclamation, I cannot but hint to you how much it is, not only your Interest, but your Duty, as a Writer of public Occurrences, to behave with a just Caution, as to the Parties, some of whom seem to be bringing themselves upon the Stage in a Criminal Manner, as also, to the Government; and I wish that, from your Example, the rest of the World's Instructors, (*I mean News-Writers*), would shew the like Prudence. I must acknowledge 'tis something difficult for a Writer to speak of Public Affairs, and not discover that he inclines, or leans, to one Side or other; but as Impartiality is your Duty, so it is not impossible to shew it, even on this occasion. What have you to do with Plots and Plotters? If they will involve themselves in Difficulties and Dangers, they must take their Fate; 'tis your Business to look on, Silent and Dumb. Plots against lawful Governments are Things no honest man can espouse, or be seen to encourage. If Governors do ill, God mend them; let not your Journal set up for State-Cobblers, whatever others do. If Subjects must, in particular Cabals, and in publick Prints, take upon them to heal the Breaches which Statesmen (however Impolitick) may make in matters of Government, there will be no End of the Confusion; nor is it often that any Attempts of that kind have any other End but the Destruction of the People that meddle with it. Leave those Things therefore, Mr. APP, to your politick-Sister, MIST, who sets up of late for a Patroness of the Parties, and gets frequently into the hands of the Law for her Labour; her politick Scribblers, grown bold by the Protection of the Petticoats, make it as natural, as it is necessary, to lay its Iron Hands upon them; and we hear, how it is with her on that Account. God send her a good Deliverance.

Let that be an Alarm Bell to us, and if we talk of Plots and Parties, let us do it with Decency. For my Part, when the Government says there is a Plot, I say there is Plot also. When Men are taken up and sent to Gaol, I am mighty apt to say it is for something; because I think the great Managers of Public Affairs never take up Men for Nothing. I am sure they ought not, and, I believe, they do not.

Let the Men who, being engaged in another Interest, are impatient of the present Tranquillity ; I say, let them disturb it, or endeavour to disturb it, as they think fit. If they finish their Course at the Gallows, they dye in their Calling ; and as this generally is the Upshot of such Things, they always leave their settling the Nation to the next Age ; so that there very seldom wants a Succession of Male-contents in every Government, either on one Side or on the other.

But, as I said above, what is this to us ? Duty to the Government we live under, dictates to us not to blow the Coals of Disorder and Tumult. While we enjoy our own Peace, we ought not to disturb the Peace of the Community ; and Charity to the discontented People, (be they of what Side they will,) should make us wish they would be quiet, that they may not bring themselves into Mischief,—let it be of what kind it will,—seeing resisting the Powers THAT BE, is always a species of Rebellion.

As then we are bound, both in Duty and Interest, not to disturb the Publick Tranquillity ourselves, we cannot excuse ourselves if we excite others to do it ; and on this very Account I am always soliciting you to meddle as little as possible in your Papers with the common Rumours of Plots and Rebellions, Insurrections, or the News of Insurrections, as well in Embrio as otherwise. 'Tis enough to us to relate the Facts when they happen, leaving the Speculations to the Speculators. If Men will Plot against the Government,—a Thing we freely disown,—we pity their rashness ; but all we can do for them, is to promise to publish their last Speech, &c., for them ; as for anything else, we must beg their Pardon, 'tis out of our Way. I speak now in the Language of a Newspaper, and, in the first Person plural of yourself and Assistants conjunctively, and you will find my Advice good in the Main, I am sure, let it be suited or not suited to some Palates.

All this respects your Duty to the Government, and to the Peace of our Country ; but let me tell you also, that Interest and Self-Preservation call upon us to use the same Prudence ; for why should a single Hand sacrifice himself for a Party ? Do Parties, at any time, concern themselves for Scribblers and Printers, when they suffer ; or, Volunteer in their Defence ? Have any of those who have done it, got any Thing but

Poverty and Punishment? For what then do Printers expose themselves, and what Thanks have they for their Labour? What is come of the Worshipful *Robert Frebairn*, Esq., Printer to, &c., &c., &c. Even our Friend *Mist* seems to live in *Tenebris*, and is fain to give it out that he is gone to Travel. Our *Dunkirk* Friend seems banish'd for Life, and many more are in Tribulation, *Felix quem faciunt* . . . . . .: Let us let all these Things alone, and tell our News so as to make our Friends merry, and not make ourselves sad.

Your Friend and Servant,
HENRY CAUTION, Junior.

The Plot Detected. Bishop Atterbury in the Tower.

A. J., Sept. 1.—Sir, Now I think the Caution I gave you in my last was critically done, it was timed to a Minute; for had we meddled now, in such a Juncture as this, how could we have talk'd to any purpose? Betwixt Safety and Honesty what could we have said? One Side or other would have been upon our Bones, say what we would.

Should we have exclaimed against Civil Power, laying its Hands on the Churchmen, and imprisoning the Fathers of the Faithful,—should we have pleaded Ecclesiastick Immunities, and that the Clergy ought to be esteem'd so sacred, as not to be judg'd but by the Laws of the Church;—how would Power immediately have fallen in, and said, with an Exclamation, must Clergymen be Traytors, and not be punish'd?

Should we have exclaim'd against the Wickedness of Churchmen's falling into Parties,—and Men, sacred by Office, dipping their Hands in Treason, after solemn Oaths taken for true Allegiance, and frequent Recognitions of the Power they live under, as lawful and rightful; and, that such deserv'd the utmost Rigour; how would the other Side fall on us, and say we were giving up the Church to be devour'd by Temporal Legislation.

Happy Neutrality! Mr. APP, let us stand where we are. What, say the Laws of the Land? And are the Bishops subject to those Laws? If they are, they knew it before; and if any of them break the Law, they must be judg'd by the Law. I hope if they are innocent, they will be acquitted by the Law too, and then all will be well again Mr. APP.

But, in the Meantime, still I cannot help saying I am against Plotting; there's something bad in the very Thing itself.

> " Plotting, by Nature, must be understood,
> To rise in Treason, and to end in Blood."

I must confess, I am always for letting Publick Things stand as they do, whether I like them or no. Attempts to alter them, whether on the right Side or on the wrong, are generally dangerous, as well to the Public, as to those that are concern'd in them. Governments are weighty Things, and like the Stone in the Gospel, whoever falls on them will be broken to Pieces, and whosoever they fall on, will be ground into Powder.

We may wish Things better than they are, and pray to Heaven for general Reformations,—and perhaps this may bring them about too, as effectually as by any other Method; for it engages HIM on that Side, who has Power to make Revolutions with a Word, as easily as we are able to think of them; but as for overturning the Establishments of the World by Plot and Insurrection, I have no Notion of it, at least of its being our Business.

Let these Things fall out as Fate and Right determine they should fall out. I am sorry for it when I hear Men involve themselves in Mischief; I pity them, but we can go no farther, Mr. App, if they are in, let us wish them well out again. God send them a good Deliverance; but, I say, we can go no farther, no, not an Inch.

This Thought puts me upon looking back into the History of Plotting in general in the World. I must confess, to me 'tis the most preposterous Thing in Nature for any private Men to plot against a Government; and, I have observ'd there is not one Plot in forty, take it thro' the whole World, that ever succeeded. They are always either detected or defeated, and then what Havock does it make amongst the poor Gentlemen, who are drawn in to embark; whereas the chief Agents, the first moving Causes, generally get away.

Plotting is a Thing necessarily committed to so many People at a Time, and in these, their Temptations are so many to betray it, that 'tis a thousand to one if it does not come out. There is the Fear of Danger on one Hand, and great Rewards on the other; good will, or ill will, all conspire to make Men false to one another, that 'tis next to impossible a Discovery should not be made.

What dreadful Hazards then do Men run that embark in such dark Things, and how seldom do they fail to be discover'd before their Designs are ripe for Execution ! Then if they go on to Execution, how unlikely to prevail against the standing Force of a Nation !

I remember in the late Rebellion and Usurpation, there was a great many Plots to rise, and real Risings, to restore the King; but all miscarried, and the King lost so many of his faithful Friends in those abortive Attempts, that it entirely ruin'd his Interest; and had not the Restoration of the King been at last brought about by those very Hands that had kept him out, he was so weaken'd by the Loss of his Friends in private Insurrections, that it was more than probable he had never been restored at all.

Plotting is a Thing, in my Opinion, next to Madness, and its Success next to impossible; and this—besides the Justice of Heaven protecting establish'd Governments,—makes it to me, I say, the most preposterous Thing in the World. Let those that are weary of Life, and in haste to be hang'd, go and Plot if they please; 'tis my Opinion none but Madmen or Desperadoes are ever drawn into it, and they commence Lunaticks when they commence Plotters.

I am, Sir, your Humble Servant,

ANTIPLOT.

A. J., Sept. 1.—Yesterday Sennight Dr. Francis Atterbury, Lord Bishop of Rochester, was examined before a Committee of the Council, at the Cockpit, Whitehall, and afterward sent Prisoner to the Tower. His Lordship was seiz'd at his House in the Cloysters of Westminster Abbey. Chandler, the Messenger, in his Search for Papers, &c., found a Parcel of Letters in his Room, which he took out, and shew'd the Bishop. His Lordship, when before the Lords of the Council, was treated with a respect suitable to his Character, and being told that his Offence amounted to High Treason, for which he must be committed close Prisoner to the Tower, he discover'd a very great Concern, and desir'd their Lordships would permit him to be carried there in his own Coach, which was adapted to the illness of the Gout, of which he is extremely lame. The same was readily complied with, and we are informed that Colonel Williamson, and Mr. Wace, the Lord Townshend's first Clerk, rode in the Coach with his Lordship to the Tower, where two Centinels are posted at the Door of his Apartment.

On Honest Decision in Political Principles.

A. J., Sept. 8.—Sir, I find your Letter-Writers take upon themselves lately to dictate Prudentials to you in your Writings ; and they do it upon a very poor, and corrupt Principle, namely that of Self-Preservation only. But if that private Spirit were to prevail Universally, who would at any Time act for the good of his Country in the present difficult Times ? Let us consider that, notwithstanding all the Prudentials which have been dictated to you in some of your past Papers, every Man is a Debtor to the Good and Safety of his Country, as far as consists with preserving, and keeping the Peace, and he who, when he sees a Party of Men pursuing the Destruction of the Community,—whether it be Men in Power, or Men out of Power,—and being a Public Writer, or Speaker to the People, yet holds his Tongue at such a Time, is like one who seeing a Flame break out in his Neighbour's House, forbears to alarm the People and cry Fire ; or seeing a Set of Rogues putting Fire privately to his Neighbour's House, or to his Neighbour's Barn, forbears to raise the Town upon the Incendiaries, and Endeavour to have them as well Expos'd as Punished.

How then, in this Difficulty, must we Act between Self-Preservation and Publick Duty ? It is a Difficulty which I must acknowledge, Mr. *Applebee ;* I can hardly tell how to advise you in, but I recommend it very much to your prudential Time-Serving Adviser in your last, to look on his Directions again.

For my Part, as the Scripture expos'd Neutrals in Religion, as Persons being neither Hot or Cold, a Sort of Lukewarm Christians, which God himself rejects ; so I think Trimming in Politicks, is what all good Men reject, and we ought always to Espouse one Party or another.

I have heard some of the warmest Writers of the present Times, and on the Side of the Government say, that an open

profest Non-Juring Jacobite is a fairer Enemy, and may be
an Honester Man, than a concealed Abjuration-taking, Oath-
swallowing, pretended Loyalist, who is a Jacobite in his Heart;
and I am really of the same Mind. If I were a Jacobite, as
we call a certain Set of Men among us, they should know it,
and I would profess myself so without fear; I might perhaps
take care not to lay myself open to the Lash of my Enemies,
that is to say, of those, who as a Jacobite, 1 must look upon
as my Enemies; but I would never be anything conceal'd, that
is to say, at the Price that such Things must needs be conceal'd
at, I mean Swearing against what I really espoused; but I
would own myself to be what I was, and suffer what I was by
Law to suffer.

But I hate this Trimming, that I must acknowledge; and
on this Account, I must tell you, who write Papers, that when
you think one Thing and write another, ye are not Trimmers
only, but Hypocrites.—I have read in a certain Journal, which
during the last Sitting of Parliament used to fill us with high
Encomiums of great People, and talk in the Clouds upon Characters,—when it was evident it was those very Persons he
Hated and would Expose. This is a particular way indeed
of ironical Satyr, but even this is better than saying nothing.*

I would fain have Men be all honest, profess themselves to
be what they really are, and speak out. I know you are an
honest Tory; but I won't take you for a Jacobite neither, yet
as you are what you are, there's room enough for you to speak
Truth in behalf of the Church, and in behalf of your Friends,
and yet not offend the Government, or any Body else that is
honest; no, or expose yourself to the Prosecution of great
Men,—then be not frighted at Shadows, and so terrified, as not
to stand to a good cause : If your Cause be not good, leave it;
if it is good, defend it, and then you Act like an honest Man.

I met a busy officious Fellow the other Day, who is worse
than a Jack in Office, for he is a Jack out of Office, and he
boasted how all the Writers of publick Papers were frighted
by his Management; " the *London Journal*," says he, " is turn'd
to talk of Trade, and he does it like an Ass mumbling of
Thistles : The *Freeholder* has been so often a Copy-holder,"

---

* This refers to the Duke of Wharton, and his Paper, *The True Briton.—Ed.*

says he, "that he begins to be a Peace-holder ; the very *Satur-day's Post* rumbles in the Clouds; and, instead of Treason, Mrs. Mist talks Philosophy, which she does too like herself, and just as an Italian talks High Dutch without Relish ; and as for my *Original* Friend," says he, " Mr. *Applebee*, he openly declares that whatever he thinks, he won't speak, and so we have them all under our Thumb."

I took him short with telling him a Story thus,—" No, Mr. ——," says I, " you are wrong upon Mr. *Applebee* too, for I heard him say t'other Day that you were a R——, so he is not Dumb,—he added," *said I*, " that you were worse than an Informer, for that you were of a Class with the Devil, first to Tempt and then to Accuse, for that you lately drew a poor Writer in to print an Offensive Thing, or Two, and then went yourself and accused him for it, tho' you had told him that Story yourself;" but all that's by the Way.

Upon the whole, I would not have you print Things that should give Offence to your Government, or be Indecent or Undutiful upon our Rulers; but for all that, you need not be Dumb neither, when you see an honest Man ill-used, you may say so ; if you see the Constitution insulted under Pretence of Vindicating it, you may expose the Knavery of Knaves I hope without a scratch'd Face, and may do your Country good Service, without bringing yourself into Danger ; or else your Country is in an ill Case, and honest Men are become Slaves more than I think they are. Adieu, MR. APPLEBEE.

Against Flogging in the Army.

A. J., Sept. 15.—Sir, I have often been desiring to write to you upon a Subject which would readily employ many Pens, and very many Papers, if it were thoroughly discours'd of; I shall, at present, only give you a Sketch of my Thoughts about it.

The Constitution of *England*, which we call happy, and which many Value themselves much upon, who understand very little what belongs to it, is in nothing, that I know of, more valuable than in that one clause, publicly declar'd by the People of *England*, in the Transaction call'd, *The Declaration of Right ;* which says, that cruel and arbitrary Punishments are illegal.

In consequence of this claim of Right, our Government, and

indeed our Laws, allow no Tortures, no breaking upon the Wheel, tearing the Flesh with burning Pincers, no ordinary, or extraordinary Question, in order to extort Confessions, and the like, as is the case in other Countries, nay, even in Protestant Countries too; and it is, I say, esteem'd an Honour to our Constitution that it is so.

In the next Place, another Beauty in our Constitution is, that Punishments are in some Measure suited to the Quality and Circumstances of the Person; Noblemen and even Gentlemen, if allied to noble Families, or are supposed to have any share of noble Blood running in their Veins, are not hang'd, tho' they are so sentenc'd by the Law, but, in regard to their Birth, are, by the customary Grace of the Crown, admitted to dye by the Axe, and on a Scaffold, prepar'd for that purpose.

Women, for the most atrocious Crimes, for which Men are hang'd and quarter'd, are, with respect to their Sex, and for common Decency and Modesty, not expos'd, as they would be, to be quarter'd, but strangled, and then burnt; nor are any burnt alive, as they are in other Countries, no not for any Crime whatsoever; and so in other Cases.

But that which I think seems not to agree with this happy Regulation, or, at least, not so well as I wish it might be said it did, is the severe Punishments oftentimes executed by Martial Law.

I have no View at particular Persons, nor am I any Member of the Army; but I have observ'd that the Employment of a Soldier is counted Honourable; they are all call'd Gentlemen, and indeed, to have serv'd the King or the Country in which we live, to have carry'd Arms under such a General, or born a Commission under our Prince; I think these do entitle a man to the Denomination of a Gentleman, as well as a Birthright. Families raised by the Sword, are in all Countries, and have been in all Ages, allowed to be Gentlemen. It was always enough to say, my Father trail'd a Pike under such a Prince in the Low Countries, or my Father fought for King *Charles I.* and lost his Life, or lost one of his Legs, or the like, in the Wars; I say, this was always Original enough to give any Man the Title of Gentleman.

It is the same Thing still; if a Man asks me what I have to shew why I call myself a Gentleman, and I say I have King

George's Commission in my Pocket, or my Father had a Commission in the Army under King *William*, and serv'd in such and such Campaigns, or my Father rode in the Guards, and the like; 'tis enough, no Man will scruple such a Claim to the Title of a Gentleman.

Now, if to be a Soldier is to be a Gentleman,—as I could say much more to make out,—what shall we say to the severe Punishments inflicted on Gentlemen, by Courts Martial, as above? And particularly such as tying a Gentleman to a Post, or to the Wheel of a Carriage, and there whipping him in an unmerciful Manner, as has sometimes been the Case in the Army? I remember a certain Officer of the Army was righteously made to give Satisfaction to a poor private Sentinel, who had been so used by him abroad, upon a Tryal in *Westminster Hall*, and was highly censur'd beside.

Whipping at the Cart's Tail has been allowed, and is allowed in our Law for Petty Larcenies, and small Thefts; such as Pick-Pockets, and little Thieves, stealing something under a certain Value. The House of Correction is also allotted to Vagrants, and *Bridewell* for Street Lewdness, and the like.

But to whip a Gentleman, a Man that has the Honour to wear the King's Cloth, and is entrusted with a Sword to fight for his Country, has in it something so shocking to Nature, that, (to me, I say,) for I impose my Opinion upon no Body else; but to me, I say, 'tis insupportable in the Thoughts of it, 'tis dishonourable to the Character of a Soldier; and, I doubt not, many a Gentleman that has been so used, would much rather have been Shot to Death.

It is therefore great Pity, in my Opinion, that General Officers in the Army be not prevail'd upon to consider that Part, and to find out some Manner to preserve Discipline, without such extraordinary Methods; such Things as sink the very Spirit of a Soldier, and some Times, nay many Times, has made them desperate, desert, and be hang'd, or be their own Executioners. An honourable Punishment a Soldier never declines; such was running the Gauntlet, as it was call'd, which, tho' it be a Lash, yet there is something Masculine in it; but to be Tortur'd, tied Hand and Foot to a Post; to be whipt like a Rascal, a Thief, or a Pick-pocket, it makes a Gentleman abhor the very cloth he wears, and refuse to show his Face any more; or, in Revenge, to go over to the Enemy, and be oftentimes a more dangerous Enemy than any of those he serves under. I could instance, in many Cases too, where such Severities have been fatal to the Officers themselves, when, in Time of Action, they have been remember'd by the revengeful Sufferer, but I leave that to another Occasion. I speak now with all possible Respect to the Officers, and only recommend it to their Thoughts to find whether it be not a Matter that deserves Amendment.

Your Humble Servant,
THE CORPORAL.

On Rumours of the Pretender Coming.

A. J., Sept. 22.—Sir, I believe you are none of those that correspond with the Chevalier de St. George, and I have some particular Reasons to hope you are not in the Plot. Whether you will imagine that I mean 'tis that you have too much Brains, or that it is for want of Brains, that must be left to yourself.

However, as when we write to you in London, *out of,* and from us, here in the Country, it is natural to ask you for News, or to send you News, so I will do both very concisely, thus: 1. We hear say the Pretender is lost, *there's News for you;* Pray send us Word whither he is gone, and that will be *News for us.*

'Tis a strange Thing the poor Gentleman we call the Chevalier can't take a Walk in the Fields about Rome, or ride out to take the Air, but all Rome must enquire whither he is gone; and 'tis as strange another Way, that when he is gone out, if every Body is not told where he is, we must be inform'd presently of it, and be bid to look out for him here. If he but takes a Gondola upon the *Tiber,* presently they tell us he is gone down to *Civita-Vecchia,* to embark for England; if he goes out to *Lucca* to eat Luque Olives, presently we are told he is gone there because 'tis a Republick, to learn Republican Principles, and how to manage in a limited Constitutional Monarchy. If he is gone to *Florence,* why then he is forming Alliances; the Duke of Tuscany's the most intriguing Court in Europe, and he is certainly gone thither to make a Plot.

If they can't find him in some of these Places, then to be
sure he is gone to France; and if in France, he cannot be long
ere we find him nearer home.   Nay some People will have it
that he is here already *Incognito;* that if he be here it must be
Incognito, that I make no Scruple to believe; but that he is in
England, I no more believe, than I do that he is in the Tower
with the Bishop of Rochester, or that it was for fear of his
opening the Gates of the Tower, and letting the Prisoners out,
that we are told in the Country, a stronger Guard was kept
upon them than formerly.

In short, if you know anything of his Perambulations, pray
let us hear from you; and that with speed, for we are mightily
alarm'd with his coming among us, when I am in hopes he
knows no more of it than the Man in the Moon.

I am next to propose a serious Question to you about that
Gentleman's coming into England.   I remember a very good
Saying of a Man of Quality, that was really a Friend to the
Chevalier, and to his Family, and believed that he was really the
Offspring of the Royal Family of Stuarts; when some of the
Party said to him, that the Chevalier was a coming,—and spoke
it with a mark of Satisfaction, as being what he was pleased
with, and thought his Lordship would be very well pleased to
hear it,—the Lord, on the other Hand, shook his Head, look'd
displeased, and said he was very sorry to hear it.   The Gentleman shew'd himself surpriz'd, and said, " Why, my Lord, what
Reason can you have for being sorry, I am sure you have a
Value for the Chevalier?"   " O," says the Lord, " and for
that Reason I would never have him come here, 'tis a Risk too
great for him; if ever he attempts it, he is sure to ruin himself, and all his Friends :"   Now my Question is this; can the
Jacobites, if their Eyes are open, desire he should make any
Attempt this way? and if I was to answer it myself, I would
say No.   If they have any Respect for him, they cannot.
desire it, for he is certainly undone if ever he attempts it.   If
they do not see it, they are Blind indeed; and I am perswaded,
by what I have observ'd of it myself, that this is his own
opinion, and that he will never be so out of himself as to
venture.

I would only add that I think those that sport themselves
so much with the Rumours of the Chevalier's coming, seem to

deserve the Censure of Mankind, nay, even of the Government itself; no Jacobite, in his Senses, can desire it; no Friend to the Government, in his Senses, can be afraid of it. To represent the Government as apprehensive of it, and alarmed at it, is to insult the Government, and make them look mean and little, as if they were capable of being afraid of the Chevalier ; and to make his Interest look Considerable enough to alarm the Government, neither of which, at present, do I take to be the Case. On the contrary, if I was a real Jacobite, and a Friend to the Chevalier, I should desire he might stay where he is, and run no more such Risks, as he has twice done, in which he has escap'd narrowly, and brought his Friends to Destruction, and I believe they will take it for good Advice to warn him against venturing a third Time, lest the Pitcher come Home Lame at last.

Your Humble Servant,
HUSHAI.

M. J., Sept. 22.—Moll King, a most Notorious Offender, famous for stealing Gold Watches from the Ladies' Sides in the Churches, for which she had been several times convicted, being lately return'd from Transportation, has been taken, and is committed to Newgate.

A Merry Story of John and Joan.

A. J., Sept. 29.—Sir, It is my Misfortune, I think, to be always furnishing you with dismal Stories; but as these are melancholy Times, what can be expected? The Tragedy following certainly deserves a Place in your Journal, and should be recorded to latest Posterity.

John and *Joan* were Man and Wife in the Parish where I live, and especially in an Alley leading to the Street, where a certain Church holds forth a Dial with a Hand to it to show what a Clock 'tis.

There was not in all our Alley an honester Couple, and as all our Neighbours can testify, a Couple better beloved than *John* and *Joan.*

John was by Trade a Cooper, but having great Losses by *South Sea* Stock, or some other Way, was become a Ticket Porter; and being a very honest, diligent Fellow, and well-beloved, had Business enough. *Joan* being bred a Knitter of Caps in *Worcestershire,* Knit Thread Stockings now, and got a good Penny to help out Houskeeping, and they lived mighty well together. They had now and then some little Bickerings together, *as who have not ?* *John* being pretty hot, and *Joan* pretty loud, they would sometimes make a little Noise in the Alley; but the Neighbours would always take it up, and make them Friends again.

It happen'd one Day, *a little while ago,* that *John* took a Vagary, having got a Cup in his Head, and he, instead of going to his Corner, as he should have done, got a Friend or two, and went abroad a Black-Berrying, and, to add to the Misfortune, being got merry, forgot to come home that Night. *Joan,* as she had Reason, took this very heinously, and the Consequence was, that when he did come, it occasion'd a dreadful Rebellion in the House; for, in short, the Peace was broke, *Joan* took Arms, and carrying her Grievance too far, declared open War against *John ;* nay, it went so far, and the Breach was so irreconcileable, that *Joan* would no more let *John* come to Bed, no, she would not Sleep with him; nor was it possible for Neighbours, as usual, to bring this Breach to an Accommodation, unless *John* would give an Account where he lay.that Night, and with whom, and bring good Witness to *Joan* that he had not lain with any Body else, &c.

John said this was dishonourable, that it was below the Dignity of a Husband, that he was Monarch within Doors, and accountable to none, that he would declare upon Oath, he had not done any harm, and the like; but that as to where he lay that Night, and with whom, that was an obstinate Humour, and a kind of Jealousy, which *Joan* had no Reason for, and he would not comply. The Truth on't was, *John* had been so Drunk, that he could not tell *Joan* where he had lain; and she had got some ugly Intelligence, that he had been where he should not have been, and this set up *Joan's* Back, so that she could not be pacify'd.

As it happens in such cases too often, that some wicked Body blows the Coals between Man and Wife, so one Day *John* and *Joan* being broken out in a terrible Fray upon the old Score, there comes in a She-Neighbour, an unhappy Jade, and she takes *Joan's* Part, with a devilish unlucky Tongue ; and after she had inflamed the Reckoning, as far as she could, and set them not a Scolding,—for that they were at before,—but a Fighting,—she comes into the Alley, cries *Murther!* in a most dismal frightful Tone,—tells the Neighbours *John* was a killing of *Joan,* and getting together two or three Women more of her own Sort, they got into the House, and there they all fell upon *John* together, and beat him most pitifully a good while.

But had this been all, *John* might have been the better for Correction; but it did not end here. *John,* a strong, sturdy Fellow, bore it a great while, they being all Women; but finding it was like to come Heavy, and scorning to cry *Murther* as they had done, rouses himself, and what with Kick and Cuff, master'd them all, and drove them fairly out of Doors.

The Woman that raised this Fray, being got out of his Hands, falls to Work with her Tongue, and sitting at the Door, " *O you Rogue,*" says she, " *what have you been a —— and a Drunkening, and now do you come Home here and beat your honest Wife; I'd have you made an Example to all Rogues, and a d—d to you ;*" and thus she went on a good while. At last she drop'd these devilish wild-fire Words, besides—*O what dire Effects have they produc'd since that, in this unhappy House !*—"*Ay,*" says she, " *if I was your Wife I'd pay you Home for it ;* you Doa *you, I'd give you your Heart full of it ; I'd go abroad too, and be hang'd to you, and stay out at Nights too, and a d—d to ye, if I thought fit ; an honest Woman can always be reveng'd of a Rogue, if she has a Mind to it,*" and the like.

John took no great Notice of what she said, but *Joan* heard it, and laid it up in her Heart. Now, Sir, what do you think has happen'd ? On Friday last, unhappy Day ! *John,* being a Porter, and plying at the corner of —— in —— *Street,* a Gentleman calls, " *Porter, Porter!*" *John* runs and gets the Job, which was to send him with a Letter as far as *Croydon* in *Surrey,* on extraordinary Business. *John* being a nimble Fellow, and the Gentleman offering him three Half Crowns for his Day's Work, and to bear his Charges besides, he undertook it. When *John* came thither, behold ! to his agreeable Surprize, it was the famous *Wallnut Fair* Day, and away goes *John* into the Fair to look about him. But alas ! alas ! how unhappy, how unfortunate ! He had not gone half over the

Field, but there he meets *Joan* at *Croydon Fair ;*—he met her, I say, full butt,—and a sad Meeting it was for poor *Joan,* and all along of that devilish Jade that had said what she would do if she were *John's* Wife.

The Second Part of this Tragedy, as what happen'd upon this unhappy Meeting, how *John* laid hold of her, how *Joan.* fought him fairly a good while, but lost the Day, and was forc'd to surrender Prisoner of War ; how cruelly *John* used her, and how he drove her home all the way before him, how she was revenged on him afterwards, all these must make a History by itself.

I am, Sir, Your Servant,

WALLNUTSHIRE.

Moral of the Story of John and Joan.

A. J., Oct. 6.—Sir, It is a sorry Fable that has no Moral. Whether your last Account of *John* and *Joan,* in the Journal of *September* 29, be a History or a Parable is not to my purpose to enquire ; but be it which it will, your Author has laid a Scene in *Low Life,* as it is call'd, and that very low indeed ; however give me leave to turn it my Way, and to my manner of Meaning, let his Design lye which way it will.

The Marry'd State seems to be like the Ocean ; no Calm so smooth, but has its Storms as rough. The Scene of Life is made up of Chequer Work ; the least Breeze of Wind rumples the smooth Surface of the Waters ; the Sea that is to-day delightful and pleasant, is to-Morrow frightful and threatening. The Winds that were still and hush Yesterday, when the Face of the Sea was like a Polish'd Looking Glass ; I say, the same Winds rising to-Day to a Storm, or rather to a Tempest ; the Waters will rise as if frighted at the Noise ; the Surface is all dreadful, Death and Horror ride upon every Wave, and the Disturbance seems to affect Nature herself.

I cannot but say, as I have with many serious Thoughts seen the Variety and sudden Change of the Face of the Sea ; so I have, with Wonder, seen the like Variety in the State of a Marry'd Life. To Day all Mirth and Smiles, embracing one another with the utmost Complacence and Delight ; to the Admiration of, and even a little surfeiting others with the troublesome Fondness of Behaviour ; and indeed the publick

Caresses of a Man and Wife are not always so agreeable to By-Standers, as the other may think them to be; but that by the Way. The next Day, nay perhaps the next Hour, we find the same Couple waspish, fretful, angry, sullen, or loud angry, and perhaps scolding, swearing, at last reflecting, reproaching, and the like; and after that, in private,—jarring and out of Humour, and scarce on speaking Terms with one another for some Time. There is the Calm and the Stormy Side of Life in every State.

> " Thus a seeming happy Pair,
> Who Hymen's Fetters wear,
> In publick fond, as Turtles are.
> The unwed, with Envy, their Caresses view;
> But, O! what would they do,
> If as they see their open Love, their private Feuds they knew?"

Now, Sir, to go back to my Allusion of the Seas and the Winds. It is true, that when the Winds blow high, when Storms and Tempests rise, and, when, by the Combustion they make in the Air, they disturb the Peace of the Waters; the Sea moves also, the Ocean is put into a Passion, the Waves rise and mount, till, in a Word, the whole Element of Air and Water, for they, *like Man and Wife*, are ONE, is disturb'd, and the Peace of the World is broken. But then take this with you, and remark it for the Moral that shall come after, That till the Husband, Air begins, the Wife, Water is calm and quiet; if he roars and swears, she will then indeed, and Reason good, rise and mount, and be in a Passion as well as he.

> " Thus when fierce Storms and furious Tempests rise,
> Provok'd, the Waters mount, and brave the Skies;
> But when the Winds abate, and Tempests cease,
> Quickly the Waves grow calm again,
> Spread a smooth Carpet on the Main;
> . . . . And show
> That whatsoe're by Force they're made to do,
> Their Inclinations are to Calms and Peace."

Upon the whole, Sir, let it be observ'd, that quiet Husbands make peaceable Wives; Exemplar Husbands make virtuous Wives. The Winds (the Husband) when they, like the Drummer, beat a Point of War, when they assault the Waters, (Wife) these cannot be blam'd for being put into Passions and Rage, even as violent, in Proportion, as the Force of the agressing Husband raises them to. 'Twas evident in your Story, *Joan* was not loud, till *John* was hot; *Joan* did not make Pots till *John* made Pans; *Joan* did not go to *Croydon Fair*, till *John* staid out a Nights.

Let therefore the haughty Agressor complain no more, till he proves that he does not begin the civil Broil; but if he raises a Storm in the Family, can he think, that when the Winds blow hard, the Waters will not be rough, that when the Storm rises aloft, the Waves will not rise below? No, no, only let him remember, that the Winds always break the Peace, the Winds always begin the Quarrel. I need go no further, the Moral speaks itself, I turn it back to *John* and *Joan;* if *John* would have *Joan* make a good Wife, let him remember she was a good Wife, till *John* began to be a bad Husband, and if he would have *Joan* to be *Joan* again, let him but mend *John*, and the Business is done.

Your Humble Servant,
JOHN-JOAN.

A. J., Oct. 6.—Since Saturday last, many poor miserable Objects have been seized in the Streets for offending against the Statute prohibiting the wear of Cloth Buttons and Holes; who had nothing to plead in bar of the Penalty but the old Proverb, *viz.*, " Needs must," &c. The Magistrates not having a discretionary Power given to mitigate the Rigour of the Act in such Cases, were obliged (tho' with great Reluctancy) to commit them to Prison.

The Ballad-maker's Plea.

A. J., Oct. 13.—Sir, I am very much discontented in my Spirit, and am afraid if you do not find me out some Remedy, I shall Plot and Rebel, and what not, *not against the* KING *tho',* *pray Mark that!* I am, Sir, by Trade a British Manufacturer, and I have often heard wise Men say, that all our Manufactures should be encouraged; for that it is by the Success of our Manufactures that our Nation is made happy, rich, powerful, and great, and our Trade carry'd on.

I need not run out here in a long Dissertation concerning the Excellence of our Manufactures; their Value abroad, and how they are of a Universal Usefulness in the World. The

Manufacture indeed that I am Master of, is generally for a
home Consumption, and yet I will appeal to you whether it is
not as useful in its kind, as any Manufacture of them all; in a
Word, I am a very useful Person in my Place, I am a *Ballad-
Maker*.

Now I find this ancient Art and Mystery of *Ballad-Making*
has suffer'd deeply in the Calamities of the Times, and is of
late very much, and more than ever discourag'd, and under a
sensible Decay at present. The Business is to have you be first
convinc'd of its Necessity and Usefulness, and then to be prevail'd upon to set your helping Hand to the Work of raising
its drooping Condition for the Publick Good.

The first Work I have upon me is to prove the Usefulness of
this noble Manufacture or Invention; for if that be secured, I
would hope it would be easy to find Friends to espouse it. To this
Purpose, I have many Things to propose; but previous to the
rest, and before I proceed upon the Merit of the Manufacture
itself, you are to understand, that there is another Thing belongs
to it, as most Manufactures have their Dependants, and this is the
great numerous Corporation of *Ballad-Singers;* this, tho' it be a
Lingua-facture, rather than a Manufacture, yet employs a very
great Number of Poor, who, *may it please your Honour*, are like
to be utterly undone, if this Manufacture be not supported, and
must of Necessity be maintain'd by the Parish; *that is to say*, in
the Gaols or the Houses of Correction. But I hasten to the merit
of the Case, and to give an Account of myself in the Capacity of
a Manufacturer, and of the Usefulness of my Manufacture.

And, first, Saving to myself the Liberty (due to me as an
Englishman,) of bringing any other or further Argument in
Defence of the Manufacture of *Ballad-Making*, and of that great
Lingua-facture of *Ballad-Singing*, as above, I must say, that I
am a Whig *Ballad-Maker*. And I crave leave to add, that the
Whigs have as much Reason to favour the Masters in these
Arts, as any Set of Party Men whatsoever; and I think I may say
a great deal more. *For Example :* Did not the famous Ballad
of *Lilly-burlero* sing King *James* out of his three Kingdoms?
And, speaking of remote Causes, did it not form the Revolution
of Blessed Memory? I hope that is a service the Whigs ought
never to forget.

Nor have the other Societies, or Parties of Men in this

Nation, been without their several and particular Advantages from this useful Society. Who can forget of what Universal Benefit that important Song (tho' since turn'd to an ill use,) was at the Restoration of King *Charles II.*, viz., *The K—— shall enjoy his own again.* I say nothing of the ill Use made of it since, but that it has generally turn'd to a dull Account to those that have been so foolish as to try it; in the Days of General *Monk*, it was the *Lilly-burlero* of that Time; and General *Monk's* Musick (they say) play'd that Tune every Morning after his coming to *London,* till the King. came himself, and then, you know, there was no more Occasion for it.

How many Operations have since been wrought by the Force of *Ballad-Singing,* I need not go far to recollect. The Riots in *Scotland* were usher'd in with a Song, call'd Awa, *Whigs,* Awa. The Mobs of Dr. *Sacheverell's* Time had *Down with the Round Heads,* an old Ballad reviv'd. The Hurries of the late Reign had the reviv'd Ballad of *Chevy Chace;* nay, even the Solicitations for the late *Callico Bill* were introduced with the Ballad of *a Callico Madam.*

But now, alas! We not only have no Ballad, but are in great Danger of losing that useful incentive (to Mischief) the Manufacture itself; and, I hear, the greatest Merchant in that kind of Goods has been taken up lately for something done *in his Way,* a little out of the Way, &c.

As to what he has done, and whether it be in his Way, or out of his Way, 'tis not much to our Purpose to enquire. But why must the Trade of *Ballad-Making* sink upon this Occasion? Why must we have no new Song to make our Hearts full glad on the approach of the new Parliament, or upon the Plot, or upon anything in which the Useful Faculty of *Ballad-Making* has been used to be exercised? This is really, in my Opinion, a National Grievance, and I hope it will be complain'd of in Publick, and I recommend it to you, Sir, to acquaint the World with it accordingly.

What! do you think I am so exhausted that I have not one Song in my Budget for King *George?* Do you think I cannot make one Stanza, for all the merry Times of Bite and Bubble that are past? Can I produce nothing worth while, do ye think, upon the Plot? And shall the jolly Fellows that may chance to Swing upon this Occasion, have never a *Passing*

Song for them, as well as they have a *Passing Bell* at St. *Sepulchre's?*

Never fear it, I can furnish you with something suitable to every Occasion, and you shall perhaps have a Test of my Performance very speedily.

Your Humble Servant,

JEFFREY SING-SONG.

The Folly of the Atterbury Plot.

A. J., *Oct.* 20.—Sir, I confess, as Times have gone, and as Things have been Managed of late in the Affair of the Public Funds, Stocks, Credit, and the like, we ought not to wonder, or be surpriz'd, whatever happens; and how strange soever Things may appear to us, it is not sufficient to say this is absurd, or that is unaccountable, this is irrational, or that is astonishing. Those Things which at another Time would have been the Amazement of the World, are now scarce the Wonder of half an Hour, the most unaccountable and impracticable Things are now become familiar to us, and never was that Rule in Philosophy more universally practis'd than at this Time, viz., That a wise Man wonders at nothing.

Who else would not be astonish'd and amaz'd to see Men of Estates, who might have liv'd Happy and Easy, who had Fortunes to lose, Families to risk, Honour and Dignity to expose; I say, who would not Wonder to see such Men as these dip their Hands in Conspiracies and Treason, and bring themselves into Misery and Distress for the Cause of Parties? To see *Cataline, Lentulus,* and *Cethegus,* in a Conspiracy against the liberties of *Rome,* who had lost their Fortunes by Gaming and Debauchery, or spent them in Luxury and Pride; to see these run desperate Hazards, and Attempt the Peace of the Commonwealth,—as the Consul said at that Time, it was what Nature guided to,—because they knew of no other way of escaping the Ruin their Vices had brought them to, or how to shun the Prosecutions of the Law for their just Debts; and thus we might say of several of the late Traytors concern'd in the Rebellion so lately suppress'd in these Kingdoms; but to see Men of Birth and Fortunes, Men of Character and Principles, fall into these Snares, that is astonishing indeed.

In the next Place, it would be a useful Speculation, and

serves to increase our Surprize, that in the present Circumstances of Government, and the Prospect that necessarily follows a Change, it should be possible that any Protestant, and Englishman, that has any Sense of Liberty, or any Sense of Religion upon his Mind, should be able to satisfy his Mind to enter into any Conspiracy against the present Government.

I would almost, (without Pardon from the Government for such a well-meaning Liberty,) grant, for the sake of the Argument, that all the Pretences of Mistakes in Management which these Men pretend to, were true, or, at least, in some Degree to which I am well assur'd of; yet suppose it, as above, who have you next ?   Have you any Body to set up but a Popish Pretender ?   Have you any Thing to offer to your Country but Popery, and its natural Consequence, Tyranny ?   And can you rather embrace these than submit to the present Administration, even supposing what you allege against it were true ?   Is not the Reign of King *George*, with all the Failings and false Steps you can load it with, much more eligible to Protestants than a Popish Tyranny ?   Was there any Thing to be offer'd in the Room of it, but Popery and a Papist ?   Other Arguments must be found, but as nothing except Popery can be proposed, or is pretended, how preposterous is it, for English Men and Protestants to engage in such Things as these !

It is objected by the Party, that we are not just in our way of Arguing, when we suggest Tyranny in the Case of Popery. But I must insist on the contrary, *for this Reason;* namely, that they cannot Name me an Example, where ever they were separated. Nor is there, that I know of, a Popish Prince in the World that is not a Tyrant, in the Sense that an Englishman would call Tyranny. Possibly the Tyranny may lye in the Manner of Government natural to that Country, not in the Person of the Monarch, for I do not reflect here upon Persons; but in our Sense, all Arbitrary Government is Tyranny. What then do we mean, who are Englishmen and Protestants, when we excite Tumults and Disorders, and practice against the establish'd Government of a Protestant Prince ?

But, to carry it farther, suppose these Mistakes, which they wickedly suggest against the Government are not so, and that they are not justly reproach'd with them; suppose everything is done by Law, and all Grievances left to the Decision of Parliament, and to their Pleasure for Redress. Suppose the present Government embark'd in the Protestant Interest, and Maintaining the Liberties of our Country; what then can a Protestant and English-Man have to Object? What complaint can he make, that is sufficient to justify his running into Plots and Rebellions?

But, as I said above, *we must now wonder at Nothing;* and since it is so, we have nothing to do but to take care that the Infatuations go as little a Length as possible, by convincing those that have Folly enough to embroil themselves, that they are Fools, that they will suffer as such, and that since nothing else will, Experience must bring them to a Sight of it.   Yours, &c.

Character of an Abandoned Clergyman.

A. J., Oct. 27.—Sir, In all my observations of human Affairs, and of the differing Circumstances of Men in the World, I think none can equal the Misery of a vicious, abandon'd Clergyman. Nothing seems to me to be more despisable in itself, nothing more contemptible to others. As the Preachings and Patterns, Words and Examples of the virtuous, pious and learned Clergy, are Reverend, like themselves; and are our Rules for Instruction, and for the Direction of our Conduct in the World; so, in the other, their Manners, their Examples, are our Aversion, our Abhorrence, and render them truly Odious to all that know them.

As the Degeneracy of the best Things are the worst in themselves, so by how much more valuable the Clergy are when they shine in their proper Lustre, by so much more hateful is the Object of which I am speaking, *viz.,* A Clergyman unworthy, wicked, degenerate, abandon'd; he is the reverse of the other, and moves just the opposite Passions and Affections in those that observe him.

In my late Travels, I saw an eminent Instance of this. A miserable strouling Thing, who call'd himself a Clergyman, was brought one Morning before a Friend of mine, a Justice of the Peace, and Chief Magistrate of a Corporation, for a Complication of Disorders in a Publick House, where he quarter'd. He had been quarrelsome, attacking a Person, whose Company he was in, with a red-hot Poker out of a Fire;

he had sworn several Oaths,—he had fallen foul upon the
Government by opprobrious Words,—and, to compleat all, and
which indeed might be the Occasion of all the rest,—he had been
drunk; for all which he was Charg'd in Custody of a Constable all Night, and brought in the Morning before the
Magistrate, who, upon a full hearing, and afterwards calling
him again before four other Justices, concluded, with their
full consent, to commit him to Prison.

What they did with him, or what he did after with himself,
is not to my present purpose; but the Picture of the Man
serves to confirm my Observation.

He appear'd in all the different Shapes of a Man detected
in what he ought to be asham'd of,—he was now high and
haughty,—immediately depress'd, and abjectly mean,—this
Minute again raging and loud,—the next in Tears and im-
ploring,—in another Moment he return'd and talk'd big, valued
nothing, and if they would send him to Prison, he must go,—
the next Moment all Humility and Intreaty, and the like. In
a Word, he huff'd, cry'd, scolded, beg'd, deny'd, confess'd,
would do anything, and would do nothing, all in the Circum-
ference of a quarter of an Hour.

Upon Enquiry into his farther Circumstances, it appear'd
that he had been the same Creature in several Places. That he
had rambled about; at one Place had run away from his wife;
in another had Pawn'd his Gown and Cassock; he had
preached here, and been drunk there; had been quarrelsome
and fighting with some, swearing and drinking with others,
and reading Prayers with others. He told the Justices he
was Curate of - - - -, a Town not above 12 Miles off; but
upon their offering to send thither for an Account of him,
confess'd he was not; and now, with all this wretched
Behaviour, it yet appear'd the Man was a Clergyman, and in
Orders; had had a liberal Education,—knew how to behave
better, and that he ought to have done it,—had some Learning,
and could Talk well enough.

This led me to think what a miserable Object this Creature
was; and what, above all the rest, he must think of himself!
If ever he troubled himself to think at all, how black a
Conscience within, and how odious to all without; for, as
I understood after, all his Poverty, and his other Crimes

were put to the Account of his particular Sin of Drunkenness.

I found the Magistrates inclin'd to Pity, and some would have dismiss'd him, as a crazy Fellow, not right in his Head; but, in short, Pride would not let him stoop so low to accept it; and when the Witnesses swore the Words against him, he cries out, as in a Rapture, " JESUS *forgive them, they know not what they do !*" as insinuating that they had sworn falsely; when soon after he confess'd the Words they swore to.

Yet, after all this, the Magistrates dealt tenderly with him,— admonish'd him, and having confin'd him some Time, he got his Liberty, without farther Punishment; tho' I hear he goes on in the same Course as before.

What a miserable Object now is an abandon'd Clergyman ! And how vile is the Degeneracy of the Sons of God, whose high Office in the Church renders them as Stars in the Firmament, while they continue to shine as they may, and ought to do ! I think indeed it would be the Wisdom of our Nation to take up all such; and to have a Law, that every immoral Clergyman,— I mean such as are found incurable, such as being often reprov'd, harden their necks; such as are incorrigibly wicked,— should be taken up, and kept in dark Houses, like Lunaticks, with good Discipline and frequent Exercise of it, till they give good Satisfaction of their being thoroughly reform'd. And that upon relapsing, their second Confinement should be for Life. I shall further shew the Reasonableness of this hereafter.

Your Humble Servant,

G. M.

A Curious Picture of Society.

A. J., Nov. 3.—Sir, I think we may say the talk of the Plot has taken us up Hours enough; and,—considering how dull and melancholy those Things have made us, it has been a great deal too much. Let us now take the Liberty to look about us a little, and see what the World is doing.

The Ladies are busy forming Assemblies,—I may almost say all over England,—where the extraordinary Virtues of Society are improv'd in a wonderful manner; such as Mirth, Musick, Gaiety in Apparel, and in Temper, and carry'd on to almost the utmost Extremes. Also Gaming, Love, and Intrigue; all which are become so extraordinary Advantageous to the Sex, that it begins to be a Proverb now in the Country, That when the Ladies are to go to the Assemblies, they are going to Market; or, as one maliciously said, *Carrying themselves to Market*.

When I come into Families within Doors, the good Hussies are universally at Work, cutting their Clothes a-pieces; that is to say, pulling all their Calico Gowns in pieces, and making them up into House Furniture, Window Curtains, Bed Curtains, Chairs, Couches, Skreens, &c., and that with such Precipitation,—because Christmas is at Hand, the Time limited by the Act for wearing Calicoes,—as if their being shap'd, and cut out, and destin'd to such Things as House Furniture, were not enough; but that the last Stitch must be set in them before Christmas, or all was to be Forfeited and lost.

All Hands are at work to unmake. the Ladies Gowns, Petticoats, &c., with much more Haste than ever they were made up. The poor Quilters are hurry'd Night and Day, and Quilt as if H——n and E——h would come together to make Bed Quilts, before the time should be laps'd,—as if making the Calico in the form of a Quilt for a Bed, was not a sufficient converting it into House Furniture, until the very last Stitch of the Quilting were put to the Work.

How does such a Trifle as this now embarrass all the Families in England, above the Degree of the meanest Shop-Keeper? The very Servants are busy, with Tears in their Eyes, demolishing the only Habit that made Gentlewomen of them, in spite of the severest Servitude, nay even in Spite of Age and Ugliness.

I hear some of the most sensible Girls are going into Mourning for the loss of their Calicoes, and a great Loss they have indeed; for all the Bounty of Mistresses, all the cheap Ornaments, that made it so hard to distinguish between Maid and Mistress, are laid down at once, to the great Mortification of the Maids.

And what are all the Plots and Intrigues of the great Men of the World to these more Weighty and significant Affairs, which at once engage the Ladies, and all their Dependencies, in such important Disputes? How much better had it been

for some of the Gentlemen now involved in the Labyrinths of
Politicks, that they had spent their Hours in the Trifles of
the Toilet, and been engag'd in Things thought otherwise
impertinent.

I mention this to hint, that, I must say, whatever Plots and
Conspiracies I ever met with in History, or in Memory, the
Plot we are now talking of seems to me to have been the most
unlikely, inconsistent, and improbable Attempt.

To attempt a settled Establishment, a Government fortify'd
not by Laws and Regulations only, but by strong Alliances,
ready Assistance, and several good Bodies of regular Troops
always at Hand ; and this with a Mob, a mere Rabble, and
conceal'd tumultuary Body of Party Men, to rise by Treason,
and Surprize a City of such Extent as this, where if they prevail'd in one Part, they would be attack'd from a hundred
Parts. Some may think it possible to have been put in Execution ; for my Part, I think 'tis all Witchcraft, and mere Madness and Precipitation, not only what they cannot Effect, but
what, whenever they had attempted it, must have ended in
their own Ruin and Destruction ; and that tho' they might at
first have put Things into Confusion, yet, I think, it must
at last have overwhelm'd all the Actors in a Torrent of
irresistible Revenge.

I do not say the Madness was such that no Men could be
found foolish enough for the Attempt ; for what Design is
there in the World so desperate, but some mad Men are found
that will engage in it ? But I cannot but say, I think those
who have so embark'd will not take it ill to be call'd mad, as
well as wicked, of which I shall say more hereafter.

I am Yours,
ANTHONY ANTIPLOT.

On Suspension of the Habeas Corpus Act.

A. J., Nov. 10.—Sir, I find our People mightily divided in
their Sentiments upon the present great Affairs ; I mean those
of suspending the Execution of the Habeas Corpus Act, and
encreasing the standing Forces ; that is, as some of our Neighbours call it, keeping up *a Standing Army*.

I find that those who were wont to be warmest against
lessening the Securities, on which our Liberties are founded,

are the easiest and most satisfy'd People, of all the rest, in these two great Points; and this inclines me to be easy too, whether my Reasons may be the same with theirs or no, that is to myself.

There are indeed some People that are easy with *every Thing*, and with *any Thing*, and who make no Inquiries into Things, are willing to let them go as they will go, without troubling themselves one way or other. I cannot applaud this supine Conduct, any more than I can imitate it; nor do I believe the Government expects, or desires we should, with a kind of National Indolence, acquiesce, without Inquiry, in every Thing. The Satisfactions of those Subjects are most durable, which are founded upon the most just and solid Information, the Consequence of reasonable Inquiries. Those who are satis-fy'd with any Thing, are also dissatisfy'd at any Thing; easily pleased, soon alarmed; to Day in perfect Tranquillity, to Morrow in the height of Faction and Discontent. 'Tis better by much that the Subjects should weigh the Publick Proceed-ings in just Balances, and consider impartially every step they see taken; then they would draw, as I say above, solid Con-clusions, and there would not be so many Mistakes about Things as there are.

It is true, the Habeas Corpus Act is, as we call it, taken off, or suspended; the Reasons for it are given in Publick,—the Parliament has thought those Reasons sufficient. So far we have nothing to say. One Point however is gain'd; namely, here is a visible Deference paid to the Value of this Act, it is acknowledg'd in Publick :—

1. That it is a very great Trust, or rather a Token of great Trust and Confidence in the Sovereign, when so valuable a Thing is committed into his Hands.

2. That the Liberties of the Subjects, as they were secur'd by that Act, is no small Matter; no Trifle, or Thing to be trifled with; it is what the Sovereign does not ask, but upon urgent Necessity of the State, and what the Subjects do not grant, but upon mature judging of those Necessities.

The Solemnity of doing this is a Witness to both these, and 'tis apparent also from the Manner when done; namely, that it is not an absolute Repeal, but a Suspension, or at least a Repeal limited to such a time; after which the Habeas Corpus

Act takes Place again, unless the like Necessity should call for continuing it farther.

I know some insinuate the Possibility, that in Ages to come, this suspending a Law of such moment, upon Trivial Occasions, should be drawn out into Practice, and be made Customary and frequent, upon frivolous Pretences, till at length it may be dropt for good and all : But as this is only a Suggestion, I leave it where I find it.

For my Part, I must acknowledge, that the Cautions used in the granting it,—the short Times limited for its Continuance,—and the prudent and wary Use that was made of the last Suspension ; all concur to satisfy my Thoughts in such an important Article, and which otherwise, I must own, I should have been among the uneasy Ones.

It was but a few Years ago, that the like Trust was placed by the Parliament in the Hands of the same Administration, and of the same Sovereign, and I do not find that any Room is left us to complain of the Uses that were made of it; that the Government coveted the continuance of it longer than was requisite, or extended the Power it contain'd, farther than the Necessity for which it was desir'd, call'd for, and evidently justify'd.

To speak as cursorily of it, as such a matter will allow : They merit to be trusted again, who have prudently used the Confidence already plac'd in them, and I willingly yield up the necessity of it also at this Time. But I may be allowed to say, I hope, that the frequency of these Exigencies will not prevail to make the Practice Familiar ; and, that nothing less than such a Necessity, as now justifies it, will be allowed to bring the Parliament to yield up such important articles as these are.

Should the People of Britain come to make Suspending the Habeas Corpus Act frequent, and upon Trivial Occasions, without absolute Necessity; it would be a sad Presage to me that in Time to come they might be brought to give it all up,—which every honest man would, I believe, be very sorry to see.

In the mean Time, I would not be misunderstood, I do not suggest, no not so much as in Thought, that the present Necessity is not such as fully justifies the Government in desiring, and the Parliament in giving in to, a Suspension of the Habeas

Corpus Act, at this Time; but granting, on the other Hand, that it ought to be done, not only now, but always, and as often, as such Cases as these are shall require.

Your Servant, &c.

Description of London during the Season.

A. J., Nov. 17.—Sir, I have often with the famous *Cowley* Pity'd you Gentlemen who live among the Clamours, the Noise, and Dirt of the Town.

> " The Hum, the Buz, the Murmurings
> Of that great Hive, the City."

But I think you are never so heartily to be Pitied as in Parliament Time, when the Town may be truly said to be full; when you have all the several Classes of the People about your Ears from all parts of the Nation, who have or pretend to have Business in Town, and who, put all together, make us say with great Truth, that the City of *London* is the most populous Place in the World; *for Example :*—

The Members of both Houses to sit in the Parliament.

The Clergy to sit in Convocation.

The Lawyers to attend the Term.

The Marine Gentlemen to attend the fitting out the Ships of War.

The Military Land Men to attend the filling up the Army.

Attenders and Dependers to seek Business at Court.

Innumerable Crowds wait upon these particular Classes, and pay their Attendance daily in the most public Places of Resort.

Projectors, Scheme-Drivers, and Case-Solicitors crowd the Parliament in all their Sessions, and fill the Members' Pockets with printed Papers of Cases, Calculations, Reasons FOR and AGAINST, on every Thing that comes in Debate before the Houses ; as if the Members were to borrow their Understandings from them, and then make returns in Laws, and Clauses to Laws, for the Public Good.

I care not to enter into an Enquiry after the several Sorts of People, or the Number of them who perhaps throng the Doors of the Convocation House ; because the Wisdom of our Superiors, generally has provided Ease to the Clergy from the

Impertinencies of those Attenders, by granting frequent Re-
cesses, so that the Doors are not so long open to the Interruption of these People.

Clients without Number throng about the Lawyers, and
fill Westminster Hall with Business of the worst Sort but one.

Well may we say the Town is in a hurry! Be the Business of all kinds what it will, how strangely does it Embarrass
the Heads of you at London; you look like Men not busy,
but rather Drunk, with Heads Intoxicated and Bewilder'd;
and how is this Amazement encreased when you hear of Plots,
and are a little Alarm'd with the News of Conspiracies, and
contrivances of the Jacobites in favour of the Chevalier.

Upon the first News, down go your Stocks! There's a Stab
upon yourselves, and by yourselves, because you apprehend
one from the Enemy. Away you run to the Bank for your
Money, as if the Enemy was at the Door. Why this is not
Drunk, but Mad. This is mere Lunacy, Desperation, and worst
of all Out-rage; 'tis, in short, the Extremity of Fear, and yet at
the same Time you say, you are not afraid. 'Tis serving the
Chevalier with the utmost of your Power, while you at the
same Time say, you are for King *George*. Is the running upon
the Bank, or running down other Banks, a token of Loyalty
to King *George?* No, no! but just the contrary; King
George seeks no Cowards, the service of Fear and Desperation
serves the Enemy, not the King.

In the Country, we live without suffering these Agonies, we
feel none of these Storms and Tempests; we mind nothing of
Plots and Plotters, but to hear of their being hang'd now and
then, as Fate and his Majesty's Affairs direct. When you send
us Word the great News is come to Town, and good Things
are done for the King, and the Nation's Interest; we make
Bonfires, and ring our Bells, and throw Squibs and Crackers,
and are very Merry; and when we hear Nothing, we are Easy
and Merry still, and hope we shall see another Bonfire one
Time or other; and thus we mind every one our own Business.
No Feuds, no Noise, no Clamour interrupts us. Nay, we have
not so much as a Ducking Stool set up at the Bridge, never
since the good Wives rose in Rebellion forty years ago and
demolished it, and have kept the Peace ever since.

And why can't you do the same at *London?* If you cannot

be satisfy'd with rural Peace, and the Pleasures of a Country Life,—yet methinks Men, even at *London*, might reason themselves into a political Peace; and, leaving the Parties to heave and thrust at one another, might separate themselves to a personal Tranquillity, that nothing should break thro'.

This would make you all as Loyal as we are in the Country, for King *George* need have no better Subjects in all his Dominions than are to be found among us; and chiefly among those of us that meddle least in the publick Affairs.

On the Madness of the Plot.

A. J., Nov. 24.—Sir, in the present circumstances of our public Affairs, there is so much Room for hourly Speculation, that I wonder our State Philosophers have given us no more of their Observations on them, than I yet meet with.

Certainly there cannot be so much Plot, so dangerous a Conspiracy, and so timely and imminent, tho', as some say, a yet imperfect Discovery, and nothing to be said of it.   I mention the Words *Imperfect Discovery*, because the King's Speech intimates that the Plot is still carrying on, which I suppose must be by Persons not yet fully discover'd; let us shoot a Fool's Bolt in this Matter.

First, I must confess, the whole Plot, so far as I am able without Doors to see into it, has been a most unaccountable Piece of Madness and Desperation, what even the wisest and most Polite among the Persons concern'd, must at last confess had (however much Contrivance in the Design,) no rational view of Success in the End, no Prospect but of Ruining all that should be concern'd in it, one Way or other, and of bringing the whole Nation into a Hurry and Confusion.

I remember in the late publick Entry of the *Preston* Gentlemen, from their Northern Expedition, the late Earl of *Derwentwater*, when he found they were past by the Exchange, ask'd where they were to go?   And when they answer'd him they were to go to the *Tower*, he return'd, "*I think they ought to carry us to* BEDLAM *rather than to the* TOWER."   I cannot but say, that if ever there was a Plot in *England* that savour'd of Bedlam, *this is it*, I mean, speaking my own Thoughts of it. A Plot without Foundation, except the Rage of a few exasperated People, and the Folly of those that are drawn in to join with them. A Plot form'd in the Desperation of a Set of naked, unsupported, but furious Tempers, against an establish'd, well-fortify'd Government; Arm'd with a well Disciplin'd Body of regular Troops, led by experienc'd Officers, and headed by invincible Generals; the Troops always ready, kept waking, and at a few Moments' Warning, able to form themselves for giving a warm Reception to Treason and Rebellion.

Are these to be attack'd by a Mob? Are these to be fought with, by a Set of Desperadoes, without Discipline, and without a form'd body of Troops? I know not what these Men might think practicable, but to me never any Thing was so preposterous. If there is any Sense in it, there must be more in it, than we have yet heard of; they must have such Armies *in nubibus* as I never heard of; and they must be brought to the Point of Action by such Measures as I believe nobody else ever heard of.

These are the Things which I say our State Philosophers methinks should enlarge upon, and should fill us with Argu·ments as their several Opinions guide them; some to shew the feasibleness of blowing up a Government with the blast of Breath, as well as that of Gunpowder.

Others should have given us their learned Dissertation upon Faction, and the invincible Power of Parties, and shewn us how a Rebellion may be managed without Weapons; and, that by the energy of Faction, Parties are wrought upon to Depose and pull down themselves, as effectually as others could be able to do it for them. Upon which Foot perhaps for the Future, Arms and Ammunition, Guns, Powder, and Ball, may entirely be laid aside and rendered useless in all Rebellions, Insurrections, or Treasonable Conspiracies in the World.

I have heard of a Book, said to be in the Press, and just now coming out into the World; what new Religion that may be which the Author of such a Book proposes, I know not; but I think there must be a new Religion suggested in the World, or else our modern People, who Act in these publick Matters, must renounce all Religion. For facing about against those Princes and Powers which we have sworn Fidelity to, will not do upon the Foot of any Religion, that we can give the name of Christian to, in the World.

We are now entering upon Evidence; visible Proofs of the

reality of the Plot in general, are now bringing forth, and one of the Persons has been brought to his Tryal and found Guilty. I would be glad to hear one of all those who shall ever be found Guilty, give some Account that he believ'd the Plot, supposing it had not been discovered, was ever Practicable in itself, or the Success of it Probable; then I would Philosophise upon it to you in another Stile, and talk of it in a Way by itself.

To me it has, I confess, been all a Piece of Madness, such that I must say, I believe all that have been concern'd in it, will at last Acknowledge, they should pass through *Bedlam* to the *Tower* when they are taken;—and be first punish'd for Lunaticks, then for Traytors. I leave the rest of this Observation to the after-wit of the Gentlemen to improve.

I am, &c.

The Sinfulness of Plots and Conspiracies.

A. J., Dec. 1.—Sir, When, in my last to you, I gave my Opinion of the Lunacy and Distraction of the Persons concern'd in the Plot now upon the Stage of Fame, I am to be understood to be speaking of what relates to themselves,—and their particular Parts in this hellish Design,—in which, as I said, they went on upon the most unpromising Undertakings, and in the most irrational, inconsistent Manner, that ever Men in their Senses undertook any Thing; this I say relates to themselves, and to the Plot as it respects themselves.

But now that I may go gradually thro' the other Parts, I desire I may not be understood to place all upon their Lunacy, for that would be to seem to reserve their Morals, whereas I must entirely give up that Part indeed; for as to the Morality of Plot and Conspiracy, that Part is beyond my Circle, and I see no Rules that can be call'd Christian by which it may or can be supported.

To plot and conspire against any Government, under whose Authority, and in whose Administration we live, and enjoy Protection, in common with the rest of its subjects, is Criminal and Abominable, be the Right to the Power that Government possesses what it will; for while we submit to accept its Protection, and claim the Privileges of a Subject, we certainly owe the Allegiance of a Subject, and cannot conspire against,

or contrive its hurt, without breaking all the Rules of moral
Right.

It is upon this Foundation the Church of *England* has always
inspired her Sons with Principles of Loyalty and Obedience
to the higher Powers; upon this Principle they have been
instructed passively to submit even to the Exorbitancy of
unjust Princes; much more then are they bound to preserve it under the peaceable, gentle Rule of just Princes,
governing by the Laws, and maintaining the Constitution of
their Country.

If our bare living under the Care and Influence of a
righteous Government, obliges us to pay Allegiance to that
Government as our Debt, both in the sight of God and Man,
as without Question it does; then Rebellion and Conspiracy
against the Government we live under, is an immoral Action in
the highest Degree; and to Plot and Conspire against such a
Government, is a Sin against God and Man, will be reveng'd
by the First, and ought to be Detected by the last. Nor does
our Opinion of the Rightfulness of the Possessor alter the Case
one Way or other, for the Debt of Allegiance is not founded
there, in the Right to Government, but in our accepting to
submit to live under the Authority of it; in which Case, if we
will not be faithful Subjects to the Government we live
under, we ought not to breathe in its Dominions, but be gone
off its Territories, and yet even then, there is a natural Right
of Subjection too; but of that by itself.

The meaning of what I now say is,—That the Present, and
indeed all Plots against the Government we live under, are
certainly immoral Actions; Wicked and Abominable, hateful
both to God and Man.

While then the Plot now in Hand is founded in Madness
and Lunacy on one Hand, and the Height of Wickedness and
Immorality on the other; it remains that we should justly
recommend it to the Abhorrence of all true Sons of the Church
of *England*, in their Doctrine, Discipline, and Worship. These
have always been the most faithful Subjects of their Princes,
and have recommended those Principles not by their Practice
only, but by Sufferings in the worst of Times.

Nor does it lessen the Honour and Character of these
Fathers of our Church, that one here, or one there, may have

deviated from the Practice of their Duty, or of what their sacred Mother's Institutions have instructed them in.

Let such, when their Guilt appears, stand or fall by their own Actions; it is an allow'd Judgment of Ages, that the Deficiency of Members is not justly a Reproach to the whole Body, much less is it a lessening of the Value of the Profession of Religion itself.

Let us go on then in a just Abhorrence of all Conspiracies against the Government we live thus peaceably under, and by a peaceable Example encourage it in others; this will be the best Testimony not to our Christianity only, but to our particular adhering to the Principles and Practice of the truest Sons of the Church of *England* in all Ages.

As I mention'd in my last, the Plot is now brought to Evidence; the Truth of its being, can be no longer Disputed; the Persons concern'd begin to appear Self-Condemn'd; one is convicted in form of Law, others Self-Condemn'd, by Flight and Escape. That there is a Plot remains no longer doubtful, and that all Plots against a peaceable Government, under whose Protection we live, are abominable, and to be abhorr'd, I have made clear.

I shall next Examine how we ought to behave in such a Time as this is, towards those who have fallen into the Snare of Treason, and who have Dipp'd their Hands in Conspiracies against their Country's Peace. How we ought to look on them as Enemies to their Country, and as Men who have,—to the best of their Power,—because it is apparent they would have—dipp'd their Hands in Blood, and brought us all into the utmost Confusion and Misery.

So far they are actual Murtherers.

What we shall say to them as willing to bring Popery upon us, and to overwhelm our Holy Religion in Superstition and Idolatry, is a Thing by itself.

So far they are profess'd Enemies to the Church of ENGLAND.

How we are to behave to such, one would think no Man should be at a Loss to know; but I shall enlarge upon that to a full Length very shortly.

In the mean time I am your Humble Servant,

ANTI-ITALICK.

Against Flattery of Princes and Great Men.

A. J., Dec. 8.—Sir, I have written several Times to you of the Plot, and of the Plotters, in which I hope my Politicks are as Orthodox as my Principles. I have done it without Compliments to any Body. Flattery is out of my Circle, it is a Manufacture peculiar to a Sort of People that I do not converse with, and indeed do not desire to converse with; just Governments desire and delight in the Services of faithful and useful Subjects, but they contemn Flatterers. A Flatterer, in Short, is a Plotter; he that Flatters Princes or Governments, evidently lays a Snare for them, endeavours to Deceive 'em, and so far he is, *ipso facto*, in a Plot against them, and accordingly, Flatterers ought to be treated as Enemies.

It was observ'd by a wise Historian, as well as Satyrist, in the Roman Times, that one great Token of the Degeneracy of the Romans, was the vast number of Parasites, that flock'd about the Imperial Court, and the Entertainments they found there.

It was owing to these that the most incarnate Monsters of Mankind were skrew'd up to such Stupidity in their Judgment of themselves; and were bloated and swell'd so with Pride and Insolence, that they who were scarce one Class in Wickedness below the Devil, fancied themselves to be Gods, and accepted of divine Honours, paid 'em by the Multitude. Temples built to them, and the like. Horrid, Impious, and Brutal! That while they brav'd Heaven with their intolerable, and inimitable Wickedness, they pleas'd themselves with the Adoration of the giddy flattering Rabbles, of whom it might be truly said, they knew not what they did.

Now to give all succeeding Ages a specimen of what they may expect from the flattering People; it would be worth while for all great Men,—who embrace the fulsome Delusions of Flatterers,—to observe, that the same Rabbles, and the same Courtiers, nay the same Prætorian Bands, who were the Flatterers of these Emperors, were often times, at last, their Murtherers.

How mean then must the Spirits of their Emperors have been in those Times, who pleased themselves with the Flatteries of their Courtiers, and valued themselves upon the empty Praises of Pedants and Poets, who soothed them in their Vices, and applauded them for those very Impieties for which the immortal Gods were sure to reward them with Plagues and Destruction.

But the World is now come up to a yet greater height of Folly, than in those Days; for Flatterers are not only accepted, but Rewarded; nay hir'd, and paid, with Stipends and Pensions, for employing their Tongues and Pens, in applauding the very vilest Actions of their Princes. Scribblers have been set on Work to support the Projects of Courts, and to call those Actions great, and immortalize them in their Writings, which have been in themselves most Infamous, and would have been to Posterity the most Detestable.

We need go no farther for Examples of this kind, than to the Court, and the Reign, of the late French King Lewis XIV. How many Orations were made in the Royal Academy of Sciences? How many Medals struck, and Inscriptions set up? How many Poems written and dedicated to the immortal Memory of the Great and Invincible Lewis XIV.? Applauding his Piety and Zeal for the Church of God, in extirpating the Protestant Religion, and cruelly Dragooning its Professors. His Virtue and Justice in Chastising his Enemies,—upon his unjust Invasion of the Dutch, and the barbarous Cruelties of *Swammerdam.* His Glory and his Fame, as a Conqueror, in ravaging the Palatinate, and the like Actions, the very vilest of a bad Reign; for which the whole World detested and abhorred the very name and mention of that Reign; and which in the end, Armed all Europe against him, till they made him Disgorge by Force, what he got by Violence, and beg for that Peace, which he had so often boasted, he gave the World before.

It is farther to be observ'd, that the Flatterers in those Days, viz., *The Paris Gazette,* (the *London Journal* of that Time,) principally Exalted, and spent most Pains to Applaud, the worst Actions of their mighty Monarch, recommending him most to the World, for those very Things for which he was most blameable. I shall, in its Place, give you some just Ideas of that particular Practice, so common to all Flatterers, and which renders all Flatterers so hateful, as I said at first, to all honest Men.   Your Servant,

                                        ANTISYCOPH.

Satire on the Pope Consoling the Chevalier.

A. J., Dec. 15.—Sir, We have now the Plot, so long talk'd of, come to the usual head of all Plots, (viz.) to be acknowledg'd at the Place of Judgment; so there is no more Room to enter into Disputes about the certainty and particulars of the Thing. As to the Nature of Plotting, I have declared myself upon that Head very freely already. Let us look abroad a little, Mr. App. They say the Chevalier is very Disconsolate, and much dejected at the bad News; namely, as I suppose it means, the disappointment of his Hopes, and the Disaster of his Agents.

As to his own Hopes, I cannot indeed enter into them, one way or other. One would be hard put to it to guess what it was he could be made to hope for, and upon what weak Grounds all his pretended Hopes could be rais'd; so that I can say very little to that, but that he might be much imposed upon, and Great Castles in the Air he might Build, and his People for him.

But the merriest Thing of all in my Opinion is, to hear the Holy Old Gentleman of *Rome* send him his Consolatory Epistle, encouraging him not to Despair, for that he would still be his Friend. What Consolation this can be to the Chevalier, I cannot indeed dive into, nor can I think that were the Chevalier personally that Idiot,—to say no worse,—that some would represent him to be, yet, I say, he cannot reap much Consolation from his Holiness' Letter, telling he would be his Friend,—I mean Consolation, with respect to his Cause. It may indeed comfort him with the view of continuing his little Pension, and that he should not want Bread; but can the Pope furnish him with a Regiment of Foot Soldiers, or a Troop of Horse? And if he could, can he give him Ships to bring them over, or pay them, any longer than they Quarter upon his own Ecclesiastic Dominions?

The Pope his Friend! An excellent Cordial! Pray how many Friends the more will that help him to in *England*, and how much will it recommend his Cause? That's one of the very Things, in short, that effectually Bars the Door against him in *England*, and that opens the Eyes of the abus'd Rabbles, when they have Huzza'd in his Favour.

The Pope his Friend! Why then,—What have we to do with him? For we have nothing to do with the Pope or with

Popery; we are Protestants. A loyal National Protestant Nation, Governed by a Protestant Prince;—and the Church of *England*,—as it is the Aversion of Papists, so is it the Bulwark against Popery;—it has been so for many Ages, and we hope will be so for many Ages to come. What then have we to do with the Pope, or any Body that depends upon him?

In my opinion they that sent the News over from Italy (viz.) that the Pope has written him such a Consolatory Letter, and that he had promised him to be his Friend still, were far from being Friends to the Chevalier, or his Party. For what was this but to Irritate, and Enrage the Spirits of all true Church of *England* Protestants against him, Arm them and their Posterity against him, as one who, being upheld by the Pope, must, in Gratitude, if he ever should come here, be an upholder of Popery, and support it with all his Power?

Nay, the Pope himself, with a Salvo to his Infallibility, must be exceedingly out in his Politicks in sending such a Letter to the Chevalier,—at least so as that it should come to be Publick; for he cou'd not but know, that such a Thing would certainly do him much more harm than good, if ever it came to be made publick in *England*. What Influence can such a Thing have in a Protestant Country, but to arm all the Protestants in the Nation against him?

On the other Hand, some imagine it has been a Trick put upon the Pope, and that his Holiness never wrote any such Letter; but that it was said so, merely to raise a general dislike against the Person and Party of the Chevalier; this indeed has something more of Reason in it, than the other, for it might with some shew of Reason be said by some, that ow'd him a Grudge, but it would never have been boasted of to the *English* People, on pretence of doing him any good.

But let us take it as we find it, 'tis none of our Business to inquire too far into the Truth of the Story; the Pope has, to comfort him, written him Word that he will be his Friend still. Very well! Why then the Pope is in the Plot, that's plain. And the first inference we draw from that, is this:—

1. Then every Protestant that is in this Plot is evidently in a Confederacy with the Pope against a Protestant King,—against a Protestant Church of England,—and, for the Subversion of the Prosperity of a Protestant Nation.

2. Is there no Course to be taken with this old Gentleman ? Is there nothing to be said to him, or to be done with him, to call him to an Account for plotting against King GEORGE ? Certainly, *Great Britain* may find out Ways and Means to shake the Foundations of the Vatican, and make the Old Mitred Idol tremble, but of this I shall say more hereafter.

Your Humble Servant.

D. P., Dec. 19.—On Sunday last died Sir Justus Beck, Bart. (the first Baronet of his present Majesty's Creation,) and also his Second Daughter, within half an Hour of each other. The said Gentleman always bore a fair character; but having had the Misfortune to lose a plentiful Estate through the late Calamity of the Times, it is believ'd the same was too much laid to Heart both by himself and numerous Family.

Of Humanity, even to Traitors.

A. J., Dec. 22.—Sir, Coming into a publick Coffee House last Week, in your Noisy, Populous, Murmuring Town; I heard one Man louder than all the rest, raving, exclaiming, and talking Treason by Mouthfulls, abusing and reflecting upon his Superiors. No Jacobite in the Parish could have done it worse, or in bitterer Language. When I came nearer to him,—for my Curiosity led me to desire to hear whåt it was this Fellow meant, and what he pretended to rail at his Masters for,—I found that all the Subject of his Discontent ran upon the late Instance of his Majesty's Clemency in re-prieving Counsellor *Layer*. I thought this must be some Man of a furious, merciless Disposition; and began to think of rattling him up, that he should pretend to prompt the publick Justice, and raise a Clamour against sparing a poor Man con-demn'd to die, or giving him a few Moments to prepare for an Eternal State. But he talked so loud, and his Mouth was so full of it, that there was not room to wedge in a Word between, or to get leave to be heard.

He cry'd, it ought not to be,—nay sometimes, that it could not be,—that it was Treason against the Nation, as well as against the King,—that the Plot was to burn, kill, and destroy City and People, and put the whole Kingdom into Confusion; that this was a principal Agent, and that he deserv'd no Mercy. He ran on to a great many ill natured ugly Things,

which I care not to repeat, especially in this publick Manner;
adding, how it might be an Encouragement to Treason and
to Plots against the. Government, and that if nobody was
punish'd, nobody would be afraid, *and the like.*

I did not like his Discourse by any Means. *First,* because
I thought it was against Nature, and above all, against the
Nature of a Christian, to obstruct the Mercy of any Government to the miserable. *Secondly,* That it was all out of the
Way, and none of his Business, and this made me extremely
desirous to know, what was the Meaning of it; when, upon
farther Enquiry, and drawing closer to him,—" *Let him alone,*"
says one that stood next, " *don't you know what is the matter
with him ?*" " No, indeed," says I, " but I think the Fellow's
mad, and ought to be punish'd." " Why, you don't consider,"
says he, " that, as I am told, this is one of those that took
Money of —— to pay so much a Day till the Man was Executed ; so, 'tis probable, he is in a Rage, that the Creature is
not hanged, that he might save his Money."

I was answer'd at once, and indeed struck dumb for a while,
reflecting a little seriously (whether this Fact was true or not ?)
on the Nature of Avarice, and on the Corruption of the Nature
of Man who is infected with it; how they will not stick to
affront and murmur at the Administration, interrupt the publick
Clemency, raise Clamours, and to their Power promote Dis-
contents in the Nation where they live, and which is still
worse, pursue the very Blood of those they point at, if their
private Gain be concern'd, or their Money in Danger. For
Example,—this Wretch would much rather a Man should be
put to Death than spar'd, so he might come off from his Wager,
and gain the Money he took ; nor had his Wager any concern
one Way or other that I heard of, with the Merit of the
Cause,—either with the Crime of the Man, or the Reason of the
Government's Mercy,—but mere Avarice, mere getting of
Money, which is certainly as corrupt a Principle as any in the
World, and has some Black Things in it, even too Black to name.

The Morality of the Thing itself then came into my
Thoughts, and upon what Foundation,—I mean Foundation of
moral Justice and of Charity,—any Man can enter into Wagers
upon the Life of another Man ; and thereby embark himself,
and all his Interest, if he have any, to get the Person destroy'd.

I would ask the serious Part of Mankind, and who are, I believe, the best Judges in such Cases as these, whether there is not a Degree of Bloodiness in this, and if it be not really a Species of Murther, let the Man's Case be what it will?

In my Opinion, I must own I think it is; but I would not set up for a Judge in a Matter so nice. Certainly, 'tis meddling in the nice Article of the Life and Death of a Man, farther than we have justly any Thing to do; and, as far as in us lies pushing this Way or that as our Avarice and Interest guide us; and if this unjustly pushing be at Death, let the Man be who or what he will, it is in itself hardly to be clear'd from a species of Murther. Let them think of it who are concern'd.

To say I want only to have Justice done, and a Criminal punished, is to say nothing; for as Clemency is an Act of Royalty, and it is in the Breast of the King to shew Mercy to a private Person, a Man, in his private Capacity, has no more right to anticipate the King's Justice, than he has to intercept his Clemency.

Leave the Judgment of Criminals to the Law, and shewing Mercy towards Offenders to the King, who in that particular is in God's stead, and is the only proper Judge, how, when, and where, to dispense his Mercy, and for how long.

But to interfere in such a Case, on so base a Principle, as that of Money, and a Wager; is a Thing, I think, cannot be too much expos'd, or too openly censur'd.

Besides, if I mistake not, such Wagers as these are included in the Act of Parliament against wagering upon Publick Affairs; if so, then 'tis unlawful another Way, and if it is not included, I must confess I think it should be included. It is not reckon'd a very honourable Thing, and in some Respects I think it is not very human, to censure or underwrite Insurances upon other Men's Lives. It is certain, such Insurances, were they made in *Italy*, would have more to say against them than perhaps they have here. But even here, the Person that insures another Man's Life, to reckon a Payment on his Death; ought to give a very good Account of himself, if the Man should come to any violent Death.

Tampering with the Lives of Men is a very nice Article, and ought to be very tenderly used, either one Way or another;

and to lay Wagers upon the Life or Death of a Man is in my Judgment an immoral Action; because it naturally engages us in Wishes, at least, if not Endeavours one Way or other. Our Interest lies to have the Person live or die; either of which is, in my Judgment, a kind of Murther. This I send to you only as an Observation on the Subject; let every one give their Opinion as they think reasonable.   Your Servant,

HUMANITY.

A Nice Case of Conscience.

A. J., Dec. 29.—Sir, when *Achan*, the first Sacrilegist, was detected and convicted of his Guilt, in stealing Things which God had consecrated and set apart in the Field; I say, when he was detected by the Lot falling so directly upon him, that his Guilt was, as it were, pointed out by the very Finger of Heaven: *Joshua* (without enquiring whether he was Guilty or not, for that was evident,) bids him *give Glory to God by confessing* the Particulars of his Crime.

It is a Question among Divines whether a Criminal can be a true Penitent, and may expect God's Mercy, if he does not, when he confesses his Offence, add to his Confession a full Discovery of all his Accomplices; so as that to the utmost of his Power they may be brought to Justice. I am not Casuist enough to decide this Cause, tho' in my Opinion, I incline to the Negative, namely, that he cannot.

But we are told on the other Hand, that it is a Baseness of Spirit, a Meanness and Lowness beneath a Man of Honour, beneath a Gentleman; that 'tis enough I am so unhappy to be detected myself, that I cannot without extreme Baseness endeavour to save my own Life at the Expense of my Friend's, and take another Man's Blood to deliver my own.

What I have to say of this amounts to thus much: We ought to distinguish Actions and Circumstances; there is a vast and manifest Difference in this Case, between being concern'd in an Action morally good, and with a good and justifiable Design, and in a lawful Manner, and being concern'd in an Action morally Evil, undertaken in an unjustifiable Method, prosecuted by wicked Means, and in an unlawful Manner: *For Example,* if any Man in open War was taken in an Attempt, by Ambuscade or Stratagem, to surprize and get into

G 2

the Gates or Works of a Garrison or Town,—this Man is by
no Means obliged to discover who were his Accomplices, either
in the Town or out of it. By oblig'd, I mean oblig'd in
Conscience, for that all Stratagems being lawful and allow'd
in War, he is not guilty of any immoral Action, he being a
declared Enemy, and serving faithfully the Prince whose Soldier
he was: But if, on the other Hand, one within the Town be
Confederate,—one who belongs to the Garrison,—who is in the
Pay of the Prince to whom the Town belongs, and perhaps
under Oath of Fidelity to him;—if he be detected in a Design
to betray and deliver up the Garrison, which is a Breach
of his Allegiance as a Subject, and Duty as a Soldier; if
he be taken in such an Attempt the Case alters: he is a
Traytor, a perjur'd Person, the Action is immoral, and he
ought not only to repent of the Crime, but as far as in him
lies, make amends to his Sovereign, by discovering all his
Accomplices.

If I have stated this Case right, then, not confessing and
discovering every criminal Confederate of a Treason against
a Government,—whether the Treason now brought upon the
Stage, or any other,—is certainly a further Crime, and a Bar
in the Sincerity of any Person's Penitence; so as, that according to the Christian Doctrine, such a Man cannot expect
God's Mercy, and cannot deserve our Charity, unless he makes
such a Discovery. If I am mistaken in my Notions, I desire
to be set right by those who can give a fairer State of the Case
than I have done.

But where then are our mistaken Notions of Honour, and
of a Gentleman? And how shall we bring these two nice
Extremes to be Reconcileable? 1. That it is our Duty as
Christians. But 2. That it is Base, and below us as Gentlemen. Hard is the Lot of every Gentleman at this Rate,
that he may come to be oblig'd to do some Things by the
express Laws of Christianity, which he is forbid by Laws of
Honour and a Gentleman. That he can one way expect no
Honour among Men, and the other no Mercy from his Maker.
That if he *does so and so*, he will be despis'd, and contemn'd
by all Mankind,—expelled the Society of Gentlemen, and left
to keep Company with Scoundrels and the Rabble; and if he
does not do it, he will be for ever contemn'd by God, and his

holy Angels, be expell'd Heaven, and the blessed Society of the Happy, and be left to keep Company with the Devil, and his Angels, &c.

And whence does all this come to pass? Is it really so, that Religion has any Thing in it disagreeable to humane Society,—that a Man is oblig'd by Religion to Things inconsistent with him as a Gentleman; or, that he cannot be a Christian, and a Man of Honour both together? No, No, far from it! Let no Man pretend to bring the Christian Religion under such a Scandal; you shall see the Reproach will fly back in their own Faces; *the Case is plain.* The Man ceas'd to be a Gentleman when he began to be a Conspirator,—when he enter'd into Treacherous Conspiracies against the Government, under which he liv'd safe, and received Protection from; he from that Moment stript himself of all the essential Qualifications of a Gentleman, and can never make any pretences to the character of a Man of Honour again, any more than he can to that of a true Penitent, till he has testify'd his Horror and Detestation of, as well the Fact (Treason) as the Persons (Traytors) who were concerned with him. To say a Man can be a Traytor, and a Gentleman, both together, is as inconsistent, as to say he can be a Christian and a Thief, or a Christian and a Murtherer both together.

There is a remarkable Case in the time of the late King *William*, and a General Officer of the name of *H——ton.* The King had, it seems, sent this Gentleman, *such he was then,* over to *Ireland* with some Message to the Governor *Tyrconnel;* and instead of coming over again to *England,* truly he goes over to the Enemy. It happen'd afterward, a few Days before the Battle of the *Boyne,* I think it was, this very Man,—for I cannot now call him Gentleman,—was taken Prisoner by a Party of the King's Horse, and brought to the King; his Majesty looking pleasantly at him, to see him so soon paid for his Treachery, bade them ask him some Questions about the *Irish* Army, and whether he thought they would give him Battle? He answer'd,—laying his Hand upon his Breast,—" *I believe they will, upon my Honour."* The King smiled, and replied, " Your Honour!" and with a little stop, added, repeating it, " Your Honour!" and turn'd from him with the Contempt he deserv'd; strongly intimating that he had already forfeited his Honour, and had no Title to the Privilege of being call'd a Gentleman, having prov'd false to his Trust.

Now upon this Principle, as Religion obliges him to confess his Accomplices, before he can have the Name of a Christian restor'd to him; so Honour and Justice require him to detect,—as far as in him lies,—and bring to Justice, all his Accomplices in Treason, before he can claim the Title of a Gentleman, or be accepted among Men of Honour. If it be the Vulgar Error of the Times, that our Gentlemen have such wrong Notions of Honour, as to despise him for this; he must Place all that to the Account of his Misfortune, in having taken such a wretched Step, as that of a Conspirator; and not pretend he is the less obliged to Act as he ought, because the common Opinion is wrong; but let him endeavour to rectify the common Opinion, by practising his Duty, and leave the Event to Time.

There is but one Objection against this,—and that is, that the Person being attach'd to another Interest, did not think the former Part of his Life Criminal, or that he was a Traytor, and that perhaps he had not sworn to the Government, and therefore was not under equal obligations, as those that had.

I shall clear up that Point in my next, and shall let the World see, that the Notion of not being oblig'd to Fidelity, because we have not taken the Oaths to the Government we live under, is no Argument at all; and, that those that have not taken the Oaths, are equally oblig'd to Loyalty and Obedience, and as much Traytors if they Conspire, as those that have,—except only the bare Addition of Perjury.

Your Humble Servant,
THE NEW CONVERT.

On Oaths of Allegiance, &c.

A. J., Jan. 5, 1723.—Sir, I have given you my Opinion so often and so clearly on Matters of Policy and Obedience to civil Powers, that I think I can't be so much as suspected of bad Principles in what I am going now to say. I am now to speak about civil Obligations or Bonds of Subjection, between the Sovereign and the Subject.

It has been much of Use in *Europe*,—and more in this
Nation, for a certain Time past,—to bind the People by Oaths,
Declarations, Associations, Abjurations. I think that Custom
began in an unhappy Time, and upon an unhappy Occasion; I
mean in the late Rebellion, when Covenants, Engagements, and
such like Hellish Inventions were made use of, to bind Men
in Conscience to Rebellion and Treason.

I cannot say, but I have many Times been sorry, to see
wise and just Governments pursue their Safety, by Measures
borrow'd from such evil Authors, and the Practices of Rebels
and Traytors. The Allegiance of faithful Subjects is well
secur'd by the common Engagements that bind honest Men;
the Allegiance of Knaves and Traitors we daily see is tyed by
no Bonds, secur'd by no Covenants, Oaths, Associations, or
Abjurations whatsoever.

The Present Reign has it to glory of, that they have added
no weight to this Load; King *George* has tyed himself with
the same Obligations to Allegiance which the Law had
directed before, so that what I am saying, does not relate to the
present Government, and I hope I shall give them no Offence.

But from the Revolution, downward to the Abjuration, the
several Laws for the security of the Government, and all the
Oaths and Associations that were before, center'd in the Oaths
of Allegiance and Abjuration; as for the Oaths relating to Offices,
how are they multiplied in the Time, and to what Purpose?

Since the making so many Oaths in the several Offices of
the Customs and Excise, have there been fewer Frauds, or
less Smuggling than before? And since the Oaths and Abjurations, have there been fewer Rebellions, and less Dissatisfaction than before? Or, has it been just the contrary, in
both? I leave the Question for any one to answer? What
then is to be done, says a Reader? Would you have the
Government to lay themselves open, throw down the Fences
the Law has set up, and encourage Rebellion and Treason, by
taking away the Perjury out of the Crime? No, no, by no
means! Now they are made, they must be continued; my
Argument does not so much as look that way. But I would
not have us, or the Government either, expect one jot more
Fidelity from the disaffected People for all these Oaths, than
they might have had (if the People were honest,) without them.

Oaths will bind honest Men, (Knaves and Men of no Principle value them not,) and honest Men are bound by Principles of Loyalty, without Oaths. Knaves having no Principle are bound by no Oaths; so that with Oaths, or without, the security of all Governments seems to me to stand upon the same Foot, (viz.) the Justice and Morality of Subjection to the Government we live under; the Christian Obligation on every honest Man to live peaceably and quietly, under those whom God has set over them. Where this binds us not, I cannot see that Oaths will have any Force, and therefore I must confess, I always thought those who have not taken the Oaths and Abjurations to the Government, are as much bound to their Obedience, in point of Justice and Morality, as if they had taken them; and consequently, merit as much Punishment as any when they rebel. And yet, by saying this I do not (at least I do not design to,) lessen the Weight of Guilt that lies on those, who are perjur'd by breaking the Abjurations they have taken; but give a due weight to the Obligations which are on others; who because they have not abjur'd, think themselves free.

I have observ'd, that some People lay a great stress on this Part, and they make great Exclamations on behalf of our present Government against those, who have dipp'd their Hands in Treason and Conspiracy, after they had sworn to the Government, abjur'd the Chevalier, and taken all the Oaths that the Law requires to ascertain their Submission; and without doubt, the Argument in the Case is very pungent.

But give me leave, Sir,—not at all lessening the just Reproach which is due to such Men, for joyning Perjury with their Rebellion; I say, not at all lessening their Crime, give me leave to argue upon the Distinction we frequently make, between such as Rebel, after having taken the Oaths and the Abjuration, and such as Rebel, not having taken them at all. Those they say are not so bad,—those Act what they profess, and we ought to expect no other of them,—and the like.

Now give me leave, I say, to tell you, I think quite otherwise; and that the Non-juring Rebel is, to Heaven,—within a very small degree,—and as to Man quite as much, a Person to be abhorred as the Abjuring Rebel, and deserves as little the Mercy of the Government he rebels against.

Every Government which affords me Protection, has a just
Claim to my Submission and Fidelity; so long as I do accept
the Protection, and think fit to live under its Dominion. It is
not material whether I have sworn Allegiance to the Government or no, nor does it alter the case; for accepting the
Protection of the Government is accepting it with all the Conditions of it, such as are for my Benefit, as well as the Benefit
of the Government. It gives me a just Claim to all the Privileges and Liberties of a Loyal and Faithful Subject. It
makes all the Favours of the Government their Debt to me,—
every Subject is forbidden to offend me, and punish'd if he
injure me. My Life, my Liberty, my Property, is the Government's care; and I claim to be preserv'd, as those Subjects
which are most faithful claim it.

Does not all this imply the strongest Obligation upon me
to Loyalty and Obedience? If I am a Traytor, I am (*first*)
unjust, (*secondly*) ungrateful, (*thirdly*) criminal, in being what
I appear'd not to be; in pretending to be Loyal, while I was
under all those Obligations, and being at the same Time a
Traytor. I am also a Cheat, a Deceiver, an unnatural Rebel,
unfaithful, and in the Nature of the Thing as much perjur'd,
as those that had sworn the contrary.

Every conceal'd, hypocritical Act of Submission which I
perform'd before I actually rebell'd and took Arms, was a
Protestation of Loyalty, in short, was an Oath of Allegiance; and
every Act of Rebellion I commit afterward, is downright Perjury.

What I did before to conceal myself was done to deceive,
and as it was only done to deceive, it was appealing to God
and Man for the Truth of it, when there was no Truth in it;
so that, in short, it was calling Witnesses, calling God and
Man to witness for the Truth of my Loyalty, when there
was no Loyalty in it. " Come, see my Zeal for the Lord," says
Jehu, when 'twas evident, all his Zeal was Avarice and Ambition.

But in short, Sir, the Nonjuror and Abjuror, *when they
rebel*, in my Opinion, are one as bad as the other; Rogues
alike, perjur'd and forsworn,—Traytors alike, and one deserves
no Man's Mercy more than the other,—that is to say, neither
of them, after so much abus'd Clemency, deserves any Mercy.

Your Humble Servant,
THE NEW CONVERT.

Description of a Street Outrage.

A. J., Jan. 12.—Sir, As I was coming through *Bishopsgate Street* one Night, I was surpriz'd with a Violence, which I thought could never have been practised, *at least unpunished,* in a well-governed City, as this is, or indeed in a well-governed Nation, such as we are allowed to be, even by Strangers.

The Street was quiet before, when, all on a sudden, I heard the Shrieks of Women just behind me, crying out for help most miserably; at which, turning about, two young Ladies, just stepp'd out of a Coach,—came running by me, frighted out of their Senses,—and two or three Fellows, with two Women, running after them, who had (especially the Women,) laid hold of the Ladies, tore their Cloaths, and threaten'd to strip them.

I stept in between them, and with my Cane gave one of the Fellows a good Knock on the Crown, that stagger'd him, and ask'd what was the Matter. This little Stop gave the Ladies time to get into a House or Shop a little farther, but they soon pursued them thither; and I had presently a Crowd about me, swaggering and huffing at me, that I began to look round me to see which Way I should make off; and, upon the whole, the Clamour was, d—— the ——, they had Printed Calicoes or Linen, and that was all one.

"Linen!" *said I,* "Why Gentlemen, that is not prohibited by Act of Parliament; as long as they are not Calicoes, Linens are allow'd to be wore, for they are our own Manufacture." "Are they not prohibited?" *says one of the Women,* an impudent Creature, "then we will prohibit them. *Our own Manufacture!* No, no, they are not our *Spitalfields* Manufacture, they are your d——d Scotch Manufacture, and your wild Irish Manufacture, let them wear them at home then, they shan't wear them here, so they shan't."

I would have argued calmly with them, which was to as much purpose, as a certain Author has it, as to *talk Gospel to a Kettle Drum;* for they began to crowd about me, and I was oblig'd to give them good Words,—tell them I did not know the Ladies, that they did not belong to me,—and that I only per-swaded them, that they might not bring themselves into Trouble; for, if any of them fell into the Government's Hands, they knew the Law, they would be infallibly transported. They made light of that,—said they knew where they were,—there was no Body dare meddle with them. " *Come, come*, Moll," says one of them, " *Let us go*, I have done their Business for them, I warrant them; they'll never wear them no more." And with this they troop'd away, and left me arguing and talking Law,—which as I said, *is talking Nothing*, to a Crowd of other Fellows,—for the first were all march'd off.

As to the Ladies, I know not who they were, but this I learn'd, that they were good sober Persons; that the Cloathes they had on, were one Gown of fine Holland, flower'd with the Lady's own Work, and the other fine printed Linen, within the Limitations of the Law, and particularly of the late Act of Parliament. But that notwithstanding this, the wicked Creatures had first torn them, by the Violence they used with the young Women when they first cried out; and after that, had thrown *Aqua Fortis* at them, to burn and spoil the Clothes, that I suppose, they would never be fit to wear again, if it reach'd them.

I do not say I saw the Clothes torn or burnt, or after they were so, but I heard that it was so; and I have seen several Ladies of my own Acquaintance since, who have been frightened, and threatened as they have gone along the Streets, for the bare wearing of printed or worked Gowns of Linen, and wrought by their own Hands too; which the Law expressly allows.

Now if this be the Case, that we are thus to be under the Government of the Mob; I desire to know, where is the Security to England by Laws and Acts of Parliament? And what must we do to obtain Justice, upon such a never satisfyed Sort of People as these are.

These People call themselves Weavers,—and perhaps they are so; and their Outcry is the same that it was, when they solicited the prohibiting the Calicoes, (viz.) the want of Work. The same busy people whisper about among them that the Printing of Linen will supply all the Places where printed Calicoes were wont to be worn; and that it will be the same thing. That they should be ruin'd as much by the Linen, as by the Calicoes, and the like.

Now I am not capable of entering into any Part of the Question here, or if I were, this is not a Time to do it. But seeing the Law—to gratify so great a Number of People,—did prohibit the printing or painting of Calicoes; I think it was enough, and they ought to be contented for a while. 'Tis Time enough when they can prove the Fact, and that their Woollen Manufacture is reduced by it; which 'tis evident is not the Case; for all the Woollen Manufacturers throughout the whole Kingdom have at this Time, and have received for a considerable Time past, so great a Demand for their Goods, that they really do not want Work any where, as I can make appear from several Parts of *England*.

But if these unsatisfy'd People will thus run their Heads against Stone Walls, and will, in Rebellion against the Government, commit such Violences as these; I think they should be told, that there is no want of Work in *Virginia*,—that they may, upon all Occasions have a Passage thither,—and may be provided for. And in the Meantime, our Magistrates would do well to consider of some Methods, for the more effectual apprehending such People, and bringing them to Justice. I shall add Something in my next, for the Benefit of Transportation; and how well some of our Weavers may do in planting Tobacco, as well as in other Manufactures.

Your Humble Servant,
CHESAPEAKE.

Against the Weavers' Outrages.

A. J., Jan. 19.—Sir, In my Last I gave you a short Account of the Insolence of our unsatisfy'd tumultuous Weavers, a Sort of People which the Publick about two or three years ago did so much to oblige, and show'd so much concern for, that if any thing in the Power of a whole Nation could have oblig'd them, one would have thought they had been bound to a stated universal Thankfulness, as long as the Trade of a Weaver or Manufacturer had been heard of in the nation; but there is, they say, Something in the Nature of our labouring Poor which makes them,

"*Always hate to be oblig'd too much.*"

Those People, not content to have two Acts made in their Favour, to the infinite Loss and Disappointment of the East India Company's Trade,—restraining and lessening their Com-

merce, I mean of the East India—to a prodigious Degree; and
by both which, the Woollen and Silk Manufactures were
evidently restor'd and Augmented; I say, not contented with
these, they are grown Clamorous and Tumultuous,—and the
People must still not wear any Thing but what the Weavers
please to have them wear; nay, not content to have the Use
and wearing of printed Calicoes so effectually prohibited,
that no Prohibition was ever known like it in England. Yet
now forsooth, they will not have printed Linen to be worn in
the Room of it, tho' those Linens be our own Manufactures,—
made by the natural born Subjects of his Majesty's proper
Dominions, and printed here in London, or within our own
Knowledge; so that we are positive they are the Workmanship
of our own Poor, every Way.

These are the Clothes they now clamour at, which is with
so little foundation of Reason, that they may as well plead not
only the poor Manufacturers must be provided for; but that
the Spitalfields Manufacturers must be provided for alone, and
all the rest Starve.

But that is not all neither, but the Manner of their complaining, which in short, is not by humble Remonstrance, and
Petition from their Masters and Employers, and in Concurrence
with them, as was the Case before, and by the very Method of
which, they carried their Cause; but leaving that soft, quiet
Way,—conformable to the Rules of Government,—which the
Laws direct, and which they are bound on severe Penalties to
observe; behold, they fly out to Fury, Rage, Violence,—threatening People in the Streets, to tear their Clothes off their Backs,—
and the like; and even to do as they Threaten. Now what
civilised Nation, what well ordered Government, can bear
these Things? and what must be done with these People, to
cool their Heat, and abate the Acrimony of their Temper, and
in the Meantime, what must be said to them?

I. As to what must be done to them, the Way is short and
plain, the Law is as clear in their Case, as in the Case of any
other Criminals in the three Kingdoms; they are to be seiz'd
upon in the Fact, that's the first Thing, then carried to the
Justice of the Peace, that's the second Thing. The Justice
knows his Duty, he must commit them to Newgate, or some
equivalent Place of Security, from whence they are to be

brought to speedy Justice, and being convicted, are to suffer as Felons; that is to say, be Hang'd,—only with this provisional Clemency, that they may be admitted to Transportation,—which is the last Favour they can obtain.

II. As to the Government bearing with them; it is really what one cannot recommend to any Government to bear with. It is what no Christian Government ever will, or can allow; to have Violence Exercised by the Passions and Rage of a mad Crew, upon innocent People as they pass quietly along the Streets. To have the Ladies harrassed and affronted, their Clothes abused and spoil'd; Women with Child, and unacquainted People, frighted, and laid Hands on, by a rude Mob in the Streets; and all this for Nothing but what the Law allows and directs them to do; Is this to be borne with? Is there no Justice to be obtained against this? Certainly there will be some Course to be taken with such flagrant Villains, to make them a Terror to themselves and others; and to that End, led me add a few Things.

The first Thing I would add, is to move the Magistracy, and the Citizens of London, to take some Measures with those People, that a sufficient Number of them,—such as are Guilty I mean, —may be detected and brought to Justice, and may accordingly be sent Abroad for Examples; and that those who remain, may be caution'd by it and grow wiser. Nor is it hard to do this, for as I am inform'd they are too many, and too easy to be taken. And then, that the other may be convinced, how unjust their violent Proceedings are, and how they ought not to act thus, that they may submit with more Quietness to the Laws; and in Case it should be true that they may still want Employment, time may come that other and better Methods may be used to procure them Satisfaction than this of Violence upon their Neighbours, and abusing People in the Streets. For they who have so often had Experience of the readiness of the Parliament, and of the Government to relieve them; cannot but think they will be ready again, when they find like Causes for it. Likewise then, honest Men will be ready to help and assist them, and to appear for them as they have formerly done; but this way Nobody can appear for them, or act any Thing, or say any Thing in their behalf.   Yours, &c.

On the Return to England of Transported Felons.

A. J., Jan. 26.—Sir, I have been often thinking to write a line or two to you about the desperate Temper of our wicked People, *I mean those they call convict Felons,* in returning from Transportation, as we see they do daily, at the peril of their Lives.

How they find Ways and Means at *Virginia,* and the Places they are carried to, to avoid the Servitude they are Sentenced to, and to get Passage back to *England,* is a Thing well worth Consideration; and I may speak of it by itself; but that is not the present Business.   No doubt Measures might be taken by the Government's direction to prevent it, and to make it impossible, so that the poor wretched Creatures should not have it in their Power to bring themselves to the Gallows as they do every Day; but of that, I say, hereafter, it is not our present Work.

But what Infatuation is it that possesses the People I am speaking of, that they should, at all hazards, nay, almost at a certainty of Death and Shame, push back *as they do* from their Transportation; to a Place where, they are, as it were, almost as sure to be taken, as they are sure to Dye when taken.

It cannot be the mere Dread and Terror of the Place and Labour they are doom'd to at *Virginia*; for tho' it be what may be call'd Labour, yet I affirm, it is the best and easiest of its Kind, that any Country in the World confines their Criminals to undergo.

It is not like the *Spaniards,* sending them to the Mines to Work a hundred Fathom deep in the Bowels of the Mountain *Potosi;* and dig up the Silver they are sure never to enjoy an ounce of. They do not Labour with Chains and Clogs upon them; as among the Marble Quarries in *Italy,* and in the *Appenine* Mountains of *Genoa.* They do not tug at the Oar, chain'd down to the Bench they sit on; as in the Gallies of *France* and *Spain.* They do not hunt *Sables,* as in *Siberia,* with the Extremity of Cold and Hunger, in the latitude of 72 Degrees North.

In a Word, their Labour is not harder, or their Usage worse, than many hired Servants in *England* on Yearly Wages; and 'tis evident, even before their Eyes, the Negro Servants, even in the same Plantations, and under the same Masters, are in worse Circumstances (infinitely worse) than they; as they are not only used worse, but are without Redemption, without Hope, without any End of their Misery, for them or their Posterity.

But here, their Time being out, which generally is no more than seven or fourteen Years, they are sure of being Free; and not only so, but have an opportunity of Planting for themselves, and that with such Encouragement, that nothing but a stated Aversion to an honest Life, or to a diligent Application to Business, can prevent their accepting it with the utmost Thankfulness. Nor are they without innumerable Instances on the Spot, which Way soever they turn, of good substantial Families, rais'd from the same Beginnings; namely, Offenders like themselves, made sensible of the Danger of Death which they had escap'd, and of the Benefit of an industrious Life, which was before them, have applied themselves to the planting of Land; and, by their own Labour and Application,—with the Assistance of the Country Bounty,—have, by little and little, rais'd themselves to good Circumstances; and, in the End, by a continual Addition, have prosper'd and grown Rich.

It is certain, that every Servant thus finishing the Time of his Servitude, has an Opportunity put into his Hand (as it may be call'd) to set up for himself; he may have Land assign'd him by the Country, and he may have Credit for Clothes, Tools, and Necessaries for his Support, till what he can prepare and plant may be brought to perfection, and then he pays by the Crop, and gains Credit till the next Crop; so that they cannot say they have no Stock to set up with, no Tools to work with, no Clothes, and the like.

This is a fair offer of Heaven to such Creatures to begin, not only a new Condition of Life, but even a new Life itself; and, which is very particular, here they are sure never to be upbraided with either the Crimes or Misfortunes of their former Life. To be reform'd, is so much real Credit to them; and is so valued by all about them in that Place, that it is equal, if not superior, even to not having been guilty at all.

Upon their being thus reform'd, and applying themselves with Honesty and Industry to a due Course of Business, they are as sure of rising in the World, as they are sure of Misery and Death in the contrary.

Who then, in their Wits, would decline wearing out with
Patience the Life of Servitude, which is in itself but short,
with so certain a Prospect of Safety and Success? Who would
choose to come back a thousand Leagues, to seek, in the Stead
of it, certain Death, Infamy, and the Gallows? And yet we see
every Day Examples of these Creatures, who suffer Death for
flying from their own Felicity; and, who choose to Dye with
Shame rather than to live happy and easy, at the small Expense of five, six, or seven Years Servitude.

Nor is it less wonderful to observe the Infatuation these
Creatures are under. They are not content to venture back and
to come over before their time, which is punishable with
Death; but they come into the very Places from whence they
went, and fall into the same Channel of Crime as that for
which they were sent away. If it was a Housebreaker, he becomes a Housebreaker; if a Pickpocket, a Pickpocket; and
that, in the very same Walks, and among the same Gang of
Rogues as before, as if they resolved to come to the same Jayl
they went out of. Whereas, would they but change the Place of
Action,—were the Felon transported from *England* to go back
to *Ireland*,—or the Felon transported from the City, to begin his
practice in the Country, and the Country Felon in the City,—
and the like; there might be some Room to escape. But
harden'd to a Degree, and secure of their certain State, they
come even to the very Spot they were at before; nay, some of
them have had the Impudence to come to the very Door of
the Prison, and some have been taken not far from it. This
is such an Infatuation, as indeed I can give no Account of;
and only take Notice of it as a Mark of Astonishment. I shall
say more of it hereafter.   Yours, &c.

Exposure of Astrological Pretensions.

A. J., Feb. 2.—Sir, I find our Astrologers and such cunning
Fellows, who tell us they peep farther into the Skies than other
People, are mighty willing to terrify the People here in *Eng-
land* with their melancholy Predictions of what is to be the
Consequence of the great triple Conjunction of the Planets,
which lately happen'd in the beginning of this Year. Such
People as those, I observe are always best pleas'd, when they
think they have something dismal to Foretell; something that

may fright and terrify the People, and make them uneasy.
Whether they find their Account in it by making the alarm'd,
disturbed People Inquisitive, and therefore forward to buy
their Books, that indeed I know not; but some how or other,
they do make their Advantage by it, or certainly they would
not go that way to Work.

In consequence of this humour of Frighting People, they
enter into a long Dissertation upon the unusual surprising
Conjunction of three Planets together at the same time; and
having cried Fire! Fire! so loud, that all the Nation has heard
them, 'tis natural for the People in return to cry, Where?
Where? and so they are set to Work, of Course.

I remember so long ago as the great Plague Year, the
People were just Alarm'd in this Manner, by the same sort of
Folks, and after the Plague was broke out, they made loud
Noise of its being Occasioned by the Conjunction of the said
Planets that Year; but it was very remarkable, not one of them
thought of its being a Plague that was to follow, till after it
was broke out.

So the succeeding Year, they spent their Verdicts much upon
the Appearance of a second blazing Star, which follow'd after
the Plague, for there was one the Year before; but not a Man
of them pretended to talk of its portending that the City of
London should be destroyed in three Days by Fire, till after it
was done. Then they could tell us how bright and fiery that
Star was, more than the other, which forewent the Plague,
which was Dull and Dismal,—how swift its Motion was,—how
low it hung over the City,—and went even so near the Houses,
that they thought they could perceive its Motion, and that it
certainly foretold the Fire, for it seem'd to regard *London*,
more than any other Place. But the Misfortune was, that all
these wise Sayings were vented after the Fire was out. Had they
told us this before,—had one of these cunning Men told the
Citizens positively their City would be burnt with Fire, and
himself, living near *Pudding Lane*, had openly declar'd it and
remov'd his Goods,—as Noah foretelling the Deluge, built the
Ark publickly,—then indeed we should have said he was a Rogue,
and was in the Plot to set it on Fire; or, that he was really a
cunning Man, dealt with the Devil, and knew it all beforehand.

But it was all in vain, 'twas not in Nature to disclose those

Things, nor could Art make any Discovery of what was not in Nature; and the same we say of these Conjunctions of Planets, which can by the Laws of Nature have nothing at all in them, or in their Meetings of that Kind to Influence us, for hurt or good. And, as a learned Author says very well, what has this Globe of Earth done to Saturn, Mars, or Jupiter, that they should Plot together at their Meeting, to hurt their Sister Planet? And what Advantage is it to them to do their Sister Planet any harm, if it was in their Power? Certain it is that the Planets in their Motions have no Power to meet, or not to meet, to cross, or not to cross one another, to do good, or hurt, much less to Influence the Actions of Men in another Planet.

We know, and are well assur'd that they are all dark opaque Bodies, and shine upon one another by a reciprocal Necessity, occasion'd by their position respecting the Sun; that they are prescrib'd by the stated Laws of their Motion, and can neither go in or out, to the right Hand, or the Left, but as those Laws direct. And 'tis by this Necessity of their Motion, that we can, by just Rules, discover the several Times, nay, the very Moment of their Conjunctions, Oppositions, direct or retrograde Movements, and the like. As they shine upon us, so we shine upon them, and the Sun in the centre of the whole System shines upon them all. As the Moon is a Moon to the Earth, so the Earth is a Moon to her. They are, in short, all of a Family, and you may depend upon it, have no ill will to one another; nor is this Earth one Way or other concern'd, or one Farthing the better or the worse for anything done by, or in, or from, the Influence of those Things call'd Planets, much less can their Meeting or Parting, their Distance Near or Remote from one another, any Way affect us who are Inhabitants of the Earth, to Dispose Nations to Peace or War, or expose them to Diseases or Distempers, Wet or Drought, Plenty or Famine. 'Tis all a mere Bubble, a mere Fable or Fiction of the Astrologers to get Money, by abusing and imposing upon the Ignorance of the People.   Yours, &c.

Against Fraudulent Lotteries.

A. J., Feb. 9.—Sir, Among all the Bubbles and Cheats which this Nation for many Years past has been oppress'd with, I think none have been more notorious, or carried on with more open, Barefaced, deliberate Knavery, than those Things call'd Lotteries; we suffer'd the Burthen of their Frauds for some Years, with little or no Complaint; till at Length they became a National Grievance, and the Government were oblig'd to suppress them by Act of Parliament.

As to the Lotteries established by Act of Parliament, they differ'd from those I speak of in this essential Point; Namely the Honesty. The Publick Lotteries pick'd no Pockets, made no Gain of the Adventurers, the Loan excepted; for which Interest and Security of Payment was given even to the Blanks, so that it was little more than drawing Lots, who should lend more or less to the Government, with some private Advantages to the Fortunate, and no Loss to any Body. But the Lotteries that I complain of were generally made up of such a Complication of Cheat, Thievery and Fraud, that no Sharping and Biting, at the worst Gaming Ordinary in the Town, were ever like it. And it was a Wonder to me, to see a Nation who had such wholesome Laws against Gaming, and so often reviv'd and repeated them, sit still so long, and suffer this worst Sort of Gaming, this Lottery Gaming to go on without Complaint, and their Pockets be Daily pick'd in so gross a Manner; without Applying for effectual Measures to prevent it,—but at last they complained effectually.

After the first Act of Parliament had pass'd for suppressing these notorious Practices, they lay asleep for awhile, and fear of the Penalty, made People shy of venturing for some Time ; but the Power of Avarice encreas'd to such a Degree, that in a little while they found Ways and Means to evade the Laws, and under the Colour of Sales of Goods, Sales of Numbers, and a great Variety of false Colours, the Lotteries were Reviv'd, and became as Publick as before, and the Cheats among them as Notorious; for in their Sales of Goods, of Plate, of Watches, of Jewels, the Lots were seldom equal to the Value, so that when a Prize was drawn, that was call'd 20l., it was very well if it was worth a Third, or at best a Half.

Two Essays the Lottery-makers had at this kind of Work, till both Times the Government were obliged to suppress them. It is true, the merciful Disposition of our Legislators made them content themselves, to prevent and put a Stop to the

Practice, without enquiring into the Guilt, or into the Persons Guilty, a Clemency which they had no Reason to expect; and whether a good Use has been made of that Clemency, let what is farther to be said, be our Guide to Determine.

Seeing the Door shut effectually to the continuing those Cheats at Home, away our Scheme drawers run Abroad, and one from this blessed Land of ours went over to *Germany*, where he proposed an Annual Lottery for thirty Years together. His Scheme was laid in *Germany*, and there his Lottery was to be drawn; but the Tickets were to be taken in among us, and it was the People of Great Britain whose Pockets were to be Pick'd of the Money. Nor was this all, but all the Towns of any Note Abroad, were in Time to be put upon to set up Lotteries, and all the hope was in Adventurers from *England*.

Some of those, especially those done by the Authority of the Respective Governments, were drawn, and much good *English* Money was lost among them; till at length, private Men carrying them on, the old Cheats were reviv'd, and the most infamous Proposals that ever any Men presum'd to impose upon Mankind were publish'd, presuming that *England*,—as if we were a Nation easy to be Bubbled,—would never Examine closely into the Matter. Such was that Notorious, Infamous Proposal, call'd the *Harburgh* Lottery, where,—as has been openly prov'd,—the Knaves of Projectors had Projected about 200,000*l.* into their own Pockets in Form of a Lottery; and under Pretence of a fair Chance to the Adventurers.

The Names of the Harpies,—those Robbers of their Country, who were the Authors, and Managers, and Sharers in this horrid Cheat,—I have nothing to do with here; Justice, I suppose, will bring them soon to Light, and sufficiently expose them, who,—in spite of large Professions to Honour, Principle, and Religion,—could be so far misguided by their Avarice, as to Attempt the worst of Robbery (viz.) publick Cheat, deceiving the Ignorant, and getting Money by the Plunder and Spoils of their injur'd Country.

How detestable an Undertaking this has been, how defeated, and how one of the most Guilty has already made himself a second Mr. *Knight*,—a *Scape-Goat*,—and is fled away to prevent a Discovery of the rest; and how some Knowledge of the whole Cheat and of the Persons, may yet be Understood, and his Flight be expos'd; these Things Time and the honest application of the Publick to do Justice, will we doubt not in a little while lay farther open.

But in the Meantime, not to meddle with particular Persons; the objection against the restless Endeavours of our People, to undermine, circumvent, trick with, and Cheat one another, deserves our Observation. Nor is there wanting Room for just Reflections on the strange Eagerness among our People, to throw their Money into the Hands of these Harpies and Thieves; and, as if they had desir'd to be cheated, running into their Lottery, with an Eagerness not to be described. This Humour of the People is indeed too great a Reason for the Forwardness of the Lottery-makers; for, when People are so fond of being Cheated, who can doubt of there being corrupt Agents, willing to cheat and deceive them, but of that by itself.

In the Meantime, all these Foreign Lotteries, whether they are all cheats or not, are Injurious to our People; and, we have generally every Year a justifiable Lottery of our own, establish'd by the Publick, and in itself Useful to the Publick Good, open for every Body to examine; and if there were Room to complain, was at least liable to be refus'd if we do not like it. Why should it not satisfy the adventurous Humour of the People, and why, as they are restrained from this Sort of Adventurings of private sham Lotteries at Home, should not those Foreign People be restrain'd from drawing them into worse Adventures Abroad? I hope to see this Grievance effectually suppress'd, and our Wives and Daughters, our Youths and Shop-keepers, may not have Room to game away their Fortunes and Credit, and be made a Prey to Knaves, in the Disguise of Foreign Establishments, City-Lotteries, and Town-Lotteries, Republick Lotteries, and I know not how many such Delusions.   Yours, &c.

Satire on Toleration by Ladies of Notoriously Wicked Men.

A. J., Feb. 9.—Mr. App., You are always talking Politicks in the Masculine, and directing your Speech from the Men and to the Men; as if we Women had no Interest in the World, no Share among you in Matters of State, or, in a Word, as if we knew nothing, heard nothing, never came to Court, and understand none of these Matters.

'Tis a Sign your Letter-Writers know nothing, indeed at least understand little of those important Cabinet Councils of the Tea Table; where the Ladies settle the most Weighty Affairs of the Nation, and without which, 'tis our Opinion, at least, nothing could be well directed.

How comes it to pass, that you never let the World know what we resolve in these great Things, and how our Votes pass? You tell the World of the Stock-Jobbers laying Wagers, whether Counsellor Layer shall be hang'd or no; but you never remark'd, how the greatest and most lucky Wagerer of them was directed in his Wagers,—at least in all his fortunate ones,—by Observing the Opinions and Votes at the Circle of Ladies twice a week, at M——s in Hatton Garden.

We foretold him, that Mr. Layer would be repriev'd a second Time, after the first, that is to say, we gave him our Opinion of it. He had the Honour to hear our learned Debates upon that Subject; and accordingly he squar'd his Exchange Alley Politics, and steer'd by our Compass, and he owns, he has been very lucky.

We had a long Debate about another Criminal the other Day, but we were not then so much upon this Point, whether he shall be hang'd or no, for that we leave to the Government, to whom it ought to be left; but whether we would have him hang'd or no. One Lady alleg'd his Vices,—" Hang him," says she, " let him go, he has been a great W—— master," and she run on against him, till she had put herself into a Passion, told us he had several B——ds, and I know not what of that kind, more than I can repeat. This began a great Silence about the whole Tea-Table; one whisper'd for more Sugar in her Tea, another for more Water, hers was too strong; one turn'd it off one Way, and another another; but I observ'd not one of the Company would second the Lady, or Vote the Gentleman to die for that Sin. At last, a particular Lady took her up, and said, " Hold, Madam, tho' 'tis a sad Thing indeed for a Gentleman to do so, yet 'tis hard to hang a Man for it." She enlarg'd upon this a good while, and at the End, when she came to talk of having B——, " Phoo!" says she, " I don't find we ever like a Man much the worse for that; if we have but the least Room to say he is reformed, and when he has a Wife he will leave it off. Besides,

Madam, I do not hear that this Gentleman has done much
that way, since he had a Wife; indeed, Madam," adds the
Lady, " I an't for hanging him for that; if the Government
thinks fit to put him to Death, let him go, I have nothing
to say to that; but if the Mercy of the Government offers
to spare him, I say let him live; as to w——g, he may be
better. And besides, for my Part, if I may speak my Mind,
I would never have a Man die for getting of B——s."

You cannot imagine, Mr. App., what Applause the Merciful Disposition of this Lady gain'd among us, and how soon
the whole Circle came to Rights again; the Ladies in a
Moment drank their Tea, and chattered as Merrily as ever.

Against Profane Swearing, Perjury, and Unnecessary Oaths.

A. J., Feb. 16.—Sir, I find our Reformers, or Societies for
Reformation, as they are called, very well employed in pursuing Scandalous People, and such as keep disorderly Houses,
and 'tis very well, I wish them Encouragement and Success;
but I wonder, among other Immoralities, they take no Cognizance of our common Swearing, as well in ordinary Discourse,
as in Courts of Justice, and form of Law.

Between those who do not, and those that cannot keep
their Oaths, 'tis a very unhappy Truth, tho' it sounds very
harsh to say of our Country, that I believe 'tis the Place of
the whole Christian World where needless Swearing, and downright Perjury is most in Practice; and I believe I might add,
where 'tis less liable to Punishment, and much of the Perjury
is certainly owing to the needless Swearing.

Mistake me not now, I do not say that we have no Laws
against that dangerous Crime, or that those Laws are not put
in Execution when the Crime comes before its proper Judges
in the ordinary Course of Legal Process; when an Information is brought to the proper Office, and the Judge thereby
inform'd that such, or such a Person has forsworn himself, a
Process is issued out against him, and he is of course Indicted
for Perjury, and Tryed, Convicted, and Sentenced; thus far
the Law is sufficient, tho' I will not say the Punishment is at
any Time equal to the Offence.

In some Countries Perjury is Capital, and if I may speak
my Judgment, should be so in all Countries; and had the

breaking Oaths been made Capital, the imposing Oaths would
have been more cautiously Practised in *England*. The making
Oaths familiar, is certainly a great Piece of Indiscretion in a
Government, and multiplying of Oaths in many Cases, is multiplying Perjuries, as well in making Oaths difficult to the
People, as in making the Breach of them appear of small consequence. The solemnity of an Oath is extremely abated by
the frequenting of Oaths, as it is in common prophane Swearing. Custom seems to legitimate the thing, it becomes habitual,
and is thereby practis'd by some, as if it were no Crime.
Nothing is more common with some People, and more particularly with those who are the greatest Swearers in the
Nation, than to say they think no harm in it; nothing is more
usual than to say,—" Such, or such a Man is a very honest
Man, and would be very agreeable Company if he would not
Swear so insufferably." Why says the other, " It is his Custom,
it passes for nothing with those that are used to him, and he
means no Ill, he thinks no Harm in it." Why might not we
as well say, when a Man used the worst, the most filthy, or
Treasonable Language that can be used, that he means no
Harm in it; and what shall we say to the Perjury of common
Swearers? I will write to you of that by itself.

If a Man speaks scandalous Words of the Government,
makes personal Reflections, or Reproaches the King, or his
Majesty's Government, he is immediately Prosecuted, and
Punish'd, sometimes Fin'd, othertimes Imprison'd, Scourg'd,
Pillory'd, as for Example, the Cobler of *Highgate*, the Brewer
of ———, and the like; and Justice requires it should be so,
for doubtless where Allegiance is due, good Manners also is
requir'd, and Slander and Reproach is a Breach of Allegiance.
Thou shalt not revile the Ruler of thy People, and why should
a Man be punish'd for taking King GEORGE's Name in vain,
and not punish'd for taking King GEORGE's Maker's Name in
Vain? Why, For affronting the King of *Great Britain*, and
not for affronting the King of Heaven? The former is reasonable, but certainly the latter is as reasonable; and I hope
I should not offend if I should say, there is more to be said
for the Latter, than for the Former.

I remember a scandalous Fellow, a Scribbler of the Town,
one $A^{(bel)}$ $Bo^{(ye)}r$, being Notorious for swearing by the Name

of God, and for calling upon God to Damn him, was by
another Writer call'd publickly a Blasphemer. The Profligate,
pretended to sue him for Scandal; upon which a critical
Question was put to an eminent Lawyer of this Nation, whether to prove a Man to be a common Swearer, was not in
Effect to prove him a Blasphemer, and whether to use the
Name of God on wicked and abominable Occasions, such as
the common lewd, and scandalous Discourse, which was the
Custom of that Wretch, was not Blaspheming the sacred Name
of God? And whether it would not be allow'd as such in a Court
of Justice? The Lawyer frankly gave it as his Opinion that
it would; and the Wretch, upon that Notice, let fall his pretended Prosecution.

But to return to my Argument; if common and cursory
Swearing be a species of Blasphemy, what is a common and
cursory taking of Oaths in a Cause of Civil Justice, and where
the Law has appointed them to be taken; I say, taking them
as common and .cursory Things, laying no stress upon them
and making no Scruple to break them? What is this less than
Treason to Heaven? It is a flagrant Violence offer'd both to
God and the Civil Government; 'tis a Breach of the Homage
every Man owes to Justice and to Truth; 'tis Injurious to
human Society, and the Person guilty ought to be expell'd
human Society, and die without Mercy.

But in considering the black Crime of Perjury, we must distinguish Persons, and Things; and here give me leave to tell you,
there are abundance of Kinds of Perjury, or rather this horrid
Crime appears with many Faces, and represents itself in many
Shapes. Some of them more Black, more Hellish and Frightful than others, but all of them capitally Criminal. I'll give
you a Climax of Perjuries, which I doubt History and Experience will tell you are, or have been, too much to be found
in this Nation.

1. Infant Perjury.
2. Ignorant Perjury.
3. Careless, Thoughtless Perjury.
4. Wilful, Malicious, Personal Perjury.   .
5. Custom-House Perjury.
6. Corporation Perjury.
7. Universal and Ecclesiastick Perjury.

8. Necessary, unavoidable Perjury, by which I mean, where men are oblig'd by the Laws, and their own Circumstances to take Oaths, which they cannot Keep.

9. National Perjury.

10. Abjuration Perjury.

11. Allegiance Perjury.

What a Black Scene of Crimes may be display'd upon these Heads, of which the People in this Nation have been, or are, Guilty, remains for farther Explanation.

Your Humble Servant.

Mercy, rather than strict Justice, the Glory of a Prince.

A. J., Feb. 23.—Sir, It has been a Question often Debated, and for many Years undetermined among Statesmen, Politicians, and Men of Letters, whether it is the Interest of a Prince that the Reins of his Administration be held with a Slack, or with a Stiff Hand, or if you will have me put it into my more intelligible Words, whether Nations should be governed by Lenity and Clemency, or Strictness and Severity.

You must understand as you go, that it is supposed that both are kept within the Rules, Laws, and Limitations of the Country to be govern'd; but even in the Execution of those Laws, is it better that a strict and severe Execution of the Laws, and of common Justice should be the Prince's Practice, or that his Justice should be mingled with Clemency and Mercy?

There are some, and those not a few; nor are they despicable for their Character and Judgment, who have been of Opinion, that the Strict and Stiff Rein is the best, and that a remiss or soft Administration is dangerous to the Public Peace; and consequently to the Felicity and Safety, whether of King or People. They say in Justification of it, that the Lenity and Clemency of the Prince, Serves only to harden Offenders, encourage Factions, and promote Tumults, and Insurrections in a Government, and at last begets Revolts, and even Revolutions themselves. That when the Subjects see the Prince does not strike, they always think he dares not; as if Reason demanded, that if he durst, he ought,—and if he could, he would. That to *hang well, and pay well,* was the State

mottoe under the Administration of *O. Cromwell*, the most
fortunate, as well as the most daring Usurper that the World
ever saw. That executing Justice, and adhering strictly to the
Laws ought not to be call'd Severity, and to say such a Prince
administered severe Justice, is to talk Nonsense; that if
Princes break the Laws, the People never forgive, or fail to
take hold of it, if the weakness of the Prince gives them Occasion. Why then should the Prince lay himself so low, as
by his Clemency to let his Subject insult him? These Men
add that History and Experience are full of Examples in favour of their Opinion, where Acts of Grace, general Pardons,
and particular Remissions to Traytors have serv'd but to harden
them in their Rebellion, and arm'd them against their Sovereign, on presumption of his Clemency; and several Princes
have been overwhelm'd and destroy'd, by the very Wretches
they had formerly Pardon'd, and let go; as King *James II.*
for Example : That Gratitude is not Obligatory at all in the
System of Politicks, and to think to oblige the People by Acts
of Kindness, is to think like a weak Politician.

These, I say, are some Men's Notions on this nice Subject.
I do not tell you they are right, nor indeed can I say, I think
so, as human Affairs now go; for the Natural Inclination of
Men in Power to Tyrannise over the People that are under
the Government, is such, that they need no Prompting in
such Cases.

But on the other Hand, Clemency, Mercy, and a generous
Disposition to pity and spare the miserable Objects of Justice,
is so Heavenly a Temper, is so truly Great, so Godlike, and so
recommends the Characters of Princes to the Praise of good
Men, and to the Affection of the wisest of their People, that
it is great Pity there should be any Reasons of State, why
all the Princes in the World should not Practice it; and
nothing but the most ungrateful Abuse of such Clemency in
the People, who stand in need of it, can be a true Reason for
any Abatement of it.

Wise and just Princes are generally Merciful Princes; indeed I believe I might say they are always so; for there is
abundance of Clemency and Mercy, consistent with Justice.
It is indeed sometimes injurious to the Prince's safety to be
too Merciful; I will not give the many Cases which are com-

monly produc'd, as Examples of this Criminal Clemency.   In some Reigns past, the Whigs say King *William* was too Merciful, and that he spar'd those who had they been hang'd, as they deserved, had never perplex'd his Affairs as they did ; I say nothing to that, but this, that others charge King *James* with the like, and that if he had taken off some principal Heads, which he had Reason to know were too much his Enemies ; the Revolution had never happen'd. Whether either of these have Truth in them or not, is not now any of our Business ; but I must add this, that whoever he is, that having once received Mercy at the Hand of his Prince, when he was within the reach of his Justice ; ought certainly to expect no Mercy or Pity if he Offends again.

This abus'd Grace of the Sovereign is oftentimes the Occasion of future Severities to others that have not been equally Guilty.   Princes are but Men ; they have Passions and Affections, as we have, and 'tis provoking to those Passions, to see the Clemency they have extended to their worst Subjects abus'd, and the Crime Pardon'd, renew'd by the very Person pardoned ; and if such Things harden the Monarch's Heart to the entreaties of others, it is not to be Wondered at.

But notwithstanding all this, 'tis certainly the Glory of a Prince to be Merciful, and to Treat his People with Lenity and generous Pity, as far as the due Execution of Justice will allow ; for there are Crimes which it would be Criminal to Pardon, such as wilful Homicides, Parricides, Assassinations, reiterated notorious Blasphemy, and the like, these I am not now upon ; but I speak of the general Tenor of an Administration.   'Tis certainly more to the Interest and Safety of the Sovereign to hold the Reins with a gentle Hand, than with a strait and stiff Hand ; it Rivets the Person of the Prince, in the Account of his People, it engages them to his Government and to his Measures ; and, in short, strengthens his Hands upon all Occasions against Faction and Sedition ; and many other Blessings both to King and People attend it so, that indeed my Vote and Blessing must go for a Merciful rather than a cruel and inexorable Government.   I shall descend to particulars hereafter.

The Force of Conscience Irresistible.

A. J., Mar. 2.—Sir, There is doubtless a Fate or Enchantment upon the Words as well as upon the Actions of Men; and they are no more Free Agents, in what they speak, than in what they do. What secret Springs they are which Act this Part within us, and how mov'd; what Powers Influence the Tongue to speak either what the Thought never conceiv'd, or even something Contrary to our own Conceptions; nay, somewhat premeditately resolv'd against in the Mind, is very hard to describe. But that the Fact is so, common Experience confirms, and there are Examples of this kind to be found, even in Matters of the highest Moment; nay, more in Matters of the Highest, than in those of meaner Concern.

For Example, in cases of Treason, Murther, and the like Crimes, how often have we seen, that when the Guilty Persons have apply'd themselves, with their utmost Skill, to conceal their Guilt, and to make their Escape from Justice; they have by a mere *Lapsus Lingua*, by a Faltering Tongue, or a wrong Step, or a tremor in their Joints, or by some unconcealable Part of their Conduct, been their own Betrayers, discover'd the Crime, and detected themselves; I am at present on that Part which respects the faltering Tongue.

A great and remarkable Story we have to this purpose, in a Person, who some years ago was Executed at Tyburn for Murther; which Murther he had committed about Eighteen Years before, and had made his Escape beyond the Seas, where he liv'd all that Time, and till I suppose those whom he expected would prosecute him were Dead, when he return'd Incognito, and continued in *London* undiscover'd some Time.

It happen'd that going along the Streets one Evening, near the Place where he had done the Fact, upon an accidental Quarrel in the Street, two Gentlemen drew their Swords, and one being Wounded, Murther was suddenly Cried, and the Person who had done the Mischief ran by this Man. The People following, he began to run among the rest; but the Mob gathering about him as if he had been the Murtherer, he cry'd out as he thought, "*I am not the Man*," but by a powerful Mistake,—secretly overruling his Tongue,—said, "*I am the*

Man." It was in vain for him after this to say, *I am not the Man* : But however, going to repeat the Words, he committed the same Mistake a second Time ; " *I tell you,*" says he, " *I am the Man.*" " Well," says one of the Crowd that laid hold of him, " we believe you, that you are the Man, and we take your own Confession for it ;" says he again, " *I tell you, I am not the Man, he is run into that Alley.*"

The poor Gentleman believed he had said, *I am not the Man* from the first ; and when they charg'd him with saying, He was the Man, he flatly denied it ; but it was too late then, it was to no purpose to attempt to convince the Crowd, against his own plain Confession, or to stifle a Truth which had so strangely discovered itself. In short, the People hurried him away to a Justice of the Peace, and the Justice committed him. When it came to be examined, the wounded Person acquitted him ; but by his being thus made Publick he was known, and charg'd with the Murther he had really committed, which he presently confess'd, and was executed as he had De-serv'd eighteen Years before.

Many Examples of this kind are to be found in History, which I have not room to mention in the Compass of a Letter ; but to bring down the Observation nearer to our present Time, we may make it Familiar by the following Story, which I heard some Years ago. The Tale is told thus :—

Young D—al was a Model of native Eloquence, and of Hereditary Gravity, known in the Nation where he dwelt for a Genius, particularly enclin'd to Speech Making, and by the like Family Propensity, more especially addicted to it at such Times, when most might be said with the least Signification. This Gentleman being a Member of a Society which he often frequented, it happen'd that the Danger of the Protestant Religion in this Nation, which was a popular Subject at that Time, was occasionally the Subject Matter of Discourse in the Society, to which he belong'd, as above. It seems some of the Society had made some Oblique Reflection upon the Conduct of some of D—l's Ancestors in these Matters, when the young Orator, fir'd with Zeal for the Honour of his Progenitors, stands up and addresses himself with much Formality to the Chairman, or what else he might be call'd, who presided in the Society, and harangued to this purpose.

" Mr. Ch——an,

" It is well known that my Father was one of the LAST Men that left the Fortune and Influence of King James, and how he acted under King William, I need not recite ; my Father has on all Occasions Testified his Zeal against POPERY, and I doubt not but he would be the FIRST Man in this Nation that would be for bringing in the Chevalier."

N.B.—He would have said the LAST Man, when he said the FIRST.

He would have proceeded in his Speech to other Matters, which he had in Petto to say, and having Minutes also in his Hand to help his Memory: But he was surpriz'd to find all the Society fell into a violent Fit of Laughter, himself remaining perfectly ignorant of the Slip he had made ; his surprise was also encreased, when a certain Person, who sat near him, returned upon him by way of Answer, *And so Mr. Ch——n,* says he, *we may suppose we have the Secret History* OF THE FAMILY *laid before us ;* all this while the young Orator stood as one amazed, and notwithstanding knew nothing of the Matter, till he was told his Error, and even then it was some Time before he could be persuaded to believe he had made any Mistake, and standing up to rectify it, *I wonder, Mr. Ch——an, says he, what the Gentleman means, I am certain that I said* THAT HE WOULD BE THE FIRST Man. Here he stopt, the Society Laugh'd again, and he went on, *I say, the* LAST MAN *that would be for the Chevalier.* Thus according to the Custom I am speaking of, to mend the Mistake he left it worse than he found it.

It was an irreparable Misfortune to the poor Gentleman, and worse than all the rest, that this Mistake fell upon a Word so liable to be noticed by the Society ; and that, very unhappily for him, most of the People then present were of the Opinion, that the Truth which he would have suppress'd if he had spoken what he meant, was fully express'd in what he had spoken by a Mistake, so that if he had spoken Right, he had spoken wrong ; as on the other Hand, when he had spoke wrong, he happen'd to speak Right.

From the sequel of these two Accidents it may be observ'd, that when People act in Disguise they are often discovered by a Fate upon their own Actions, and upon their own Words, which it is impossible for them to shun, they are made Evidences against themselves, and they bring themselves to the Bar of common Opinion, when nobody else could do it.

There is no Occasion to record the rest of this unlucky Story; it is only added, that the Gentleman made what decent haste he could out of the Company, that he might not Discover the Confusion he was in, and I hear he remained ever after a perfect Convert to the Doctrine of Infatuations.

This Story, Sir, may serve for a very good Introduction to what I have hereafter to say upon the like Subject.

Unprincipled Journalists Rebuked.

A. J., Mar. 9.—Sir, I have observed among you Journalists and other News-Writers, whether Quotidian or Tertian, or otherwise, that the main Credit of every Writer depends much on the Credit of the Party he writes for; and consequently the Effect your Writings have upon the Age, is influenced by Numbers. That if the Party, which the Paper espouses, is numerous, the Paper rises, because the Numbers of the Party read it; so that, in short, your Merit is not the Question, but the Strength of your Party. I am told that one of the Leaders of the Scribbling Troop, who flourishes at this Time, is said to keep' five Presses at Work; that he writes for itinerate Papers, besides almost every Week two or three Pamphlets. So that the Public is indeed rabbled by him, and he may rather be said to rain upon them with his Lucubrations every Day; I had almost call'd it by a coarser Name. Now what is the Reason of this continual Emission? Is it because of the real need there is of the Light he gives? No, far the contrary; but his Party is known, he has Readers, and therefore he writes.*

When a Man's Party fails, he fails. What is the Reason why your old Visitant the *Flying Post* is so sunk and so decay'd of late, who boasted so loud in former Days? Is it not that his Supporters decrease, his Party separates; Bubbles have exposed them. So many of that Sort of Whigs have made themselves Odious, that their own Friends fell on them in their *South-Sea* Villainies, and laid them naked to the whole Nation; and when that weak Brother would have spoken in

---

* There can be no doubt Defoe here rallies himself; perhaps to avert suspicion.—*Ed.*

Abatement, it abated him too.   Again, this *Harburgh* Buhble,
a Cheat in its Proportion, worse than the worst Part of the
South-Sea.   How has it fallen among the same Sort of Men?
And as their Chief is expell'd out of one Society, the greatest
of the Nation, so their Defender grows as despicable among
Writers.

But let me return to those who now fancy themselves popular.   Three Things I lay to the Charge of them all, and a
fourth they may take among them, and let it fall where it
will fall :—

  1. Speaking falsely.
  2. Speaking foully.
  3. Speaking maliciously.

Of these three, I think it might be easy to Convict any of
them before a Jury of Impartial Readers.   The Fourth is of
Speaking Ignorantly ; that they detect themselves in every Day.

  1. As to speaking falsely, they are not only guilty of the
Fact, but, which is worse, when they are convinced of the
Falsehood they Refuse to make just Reparation by acknow-
ledging the Mistake.   No, they say 'tis dishonourable, and it
injures their Paper ; and this has sometimes brought them to
the Bastinado, Gentlemen having been oblig'd to Cane them
into it, and bring them to do Justice *au Coup de Batton*.   A
Worthy good Friend of mine, the other Day had a Paragraph
publish'd upon him by Name, very Injurious to him, and indeed in a matter of Consequence too, and the matter of Fact
entirely False, and not only false, but Groundless, and without any Apparent Foundation.   Upon this, he went to the
Author, and ask'd him if he had any authority for it, he
own'd he had not, common Discourse excepted, and of that,
he could say no more than that he had heard so, but he had
forgotten where, and of whom ; my Friend assur'd him, in the
first Place it was False, and gave such Testimonies of it that
he owned he was convinced it was so, and that he was imposed upon.   My Friend then urged him to put in a Word or
two in his next Paper, only to give Notice that it was otherwise ; but here he shrugged up his Shoulders, desir'd to be
excus'd, and at last flatly denied it, alleging it would be
a Disreputation to his Paper.   As if it were not more Scandalous to publish an injurious Falsehood upon an innocent Man,

and insist upon it, after being convinced of its being so, than to make a soft Publication, that they were misinform'd. How many innocent men have suffered thus, is not easy to reckon up.

2. Speaking foul and unmannerly *Billingsgate* Language. This want of Decency cost Old *Tutchin*, that wrote the *Observator*, such a Thrashing, as in Effect threshed the Grain out of the Chaff; I mean, thresh'd his Soul out of his Body. And many an unwary Author has been oblig'd to stand Kick and Cuff on that Score; and I cannot say but more have deserved it.

As to their speaking Maliciously, that may take up a Time to speak of by itself. I call it Malicious when Men fall personally upon any Man's Character, insulting and reproaching him, and perhaps taking Advantages of any of his Mistakes, to expose, and perhaps ruin him. This is a Hellish Practice, and merits to be punishable by a Law.

I am not going to Compliment your Paper, Mr. App, as being free from all these, tho', if I could have charged you, I should certainly have made the Complaint Publick by your Means. But I take this Occasion to hint to your Fellow-Writers how unsufferable these Things are; and I would perswade them, if it were possible, to avoid such Scandalous Practices, that it might be no Sin to call a News-Writer a Christian; and that Gentlemen might not think they ought to treat a Journalist, or Writer, like a Scoundrel, upon all Occasions. The Advice is just, the Request reasonable; that I am perswaded there are not above three or four of all you Authors but will acknowledge. I may give you Hints of their Names in a proper Time.

I could end with observing, and wish it were more observ'd, how easy 'tis for every Writer, even with the utmost keenness of Satyr, if he finds Occasion for it, to lash any Crime, expose any ill Practice, and tell any Story, without Railing and ill language. Decency is a kind of universal Law, 'tis due to every Body; and he that forsakes it, has not much Title to a Share in human Society. *Billingsgate* is not the Language of Gentlemen, or of Christians, but of Barking Fishwives, Carmen and Porters, Wenches and Oyster-Women. Shall the Writings and Labours of you, Gentlemen Authors, descend to these?

It cannot be without infinite Scandal to the Performance, and in Time the World will be weary of the Reading Part; for tho' Salt and Gall is agreeable to some, and a little too much to us all, yet honest and modest People grow Sick of it in Time, and generally speaking loath it at last, and leave it off, the consequence of which is, that like the *Flying Post*, nobody reads them, and they die and are forgotten by the World.

I am Yours, &c.

Scandalous News-Writers further Corrected.

A. J., Mar. 16.—Sir, When I mention'd to you in my last the Scandalous Method of News Writing Authors,—who daily obtrude upon the World scurrilous Reproaches, and malicious personal Reflections,—I did it, not to warn you, for your Practice is known, and publickly commended, for avoiding these Things; but 'tis to let the wise Writers of the Day see their own Pictures if they think fit. I thought to have said something to the Unchristian Part of it, tho' I do not see that those Things are of any great Weight as the World goes now, either with Writers or Readers; but, that the Method is Infamous and Scandalous is Matter of Fact, and may be argued upon.

How to correct it, is hard to Propose, unless I should recommend to the Injured, to give personal Correction to the Authors; but how often have some, nay, most of them been kick'd, cuff'd, can'd, &c., and what Amendment? But besides, this would put the Executive Power of Justice into the Hands of every particular Person; which is contrary to the Rules of Government directed from Heaven, as well as against the Laws of the Country in which we live.

To sue these Wretches for Damages in a due Course of Law, is a Method,—as our Proceedings at Law are now carried on,—too Prolix, too chargeable, and too troublesome to make it worth while for Persons to do themselves Justice that way; so that upon the whole the best Way is to deal Civilly, but importunately with those Men, to perswade them to blush at the Practice, and leave it off.

I am not for arming publick Justice against them by any Means; I think the cutting off the Right Hands of *John Stubs* of *Lincolns Inn*, Esq., the Author; and *William Page*, the

Printer, of a Libel, in Queen *Elizabeth's* Time, was an Execution very terrible, considering that there was neither Treason nor Felony in the Paper they Printed. But this may add to the Argument which I am upon, that ruinous Prosecutions may be avoided, for should personal Reproaches be punishable by the Laws, and be Prosecuted by the Government, as in Queen *Elizabeth's* Time, when such offences were punish'd by losing their Ears; I say, should it be so, How long some of our present Journal Writers would wear their Ears is Matter of Speculation !

From this Part I come to the Subject of speaking Truth; and here I would argue, not the Justice, the Necessity, the Reasonableness of our Newspapers giving out no false Accounts of Things, no false Reports upon Persons and Nations, but the Advantage which it would be to themselves. And here, by the Way, I do not insist that the Writers I speak of should be accountable for the Truth of their foreign Intelligence; for as it comes over in other publick Papers, or in private Correspondence, it is enough that every body knows they can write Nothing of an unquestionable certainty, and that such Things are to be taken with Allowances, for differing Accounts, that may come afterward. Nor is this a Deceit to any one's Injury, they only tell us what they hear, and we know it before they speak it, so that it is taken, as they intended it, and there is no Fraud.

But in their Home Intelligence the Thing differs exceedingly. Here they MUST speak Truth, because they MAY. Here I would caution them not to Kill People before they are Sick, or bury them before they are Dead; not break a Tradesman before he Fails; and make poor Shop-Keepers become Bankrupt by reporting them so. How many have been thus Ruin'd in this one City of *London*, by malicious wounding their Reputation in Print, and bringing their Creditors upon them without Cause, God only knows.

Such Things as these should make a Writer tremble; whereas on the other Hand, we have People now at Work, who if they can but pick up something to make a Paragraph, they value not who is injured, or in what Manner.

How many virtuous Ladies have these Men reproached? How many Husbands and Wives have they Parted? How many Men have been made Jealous of virtuous Wives, and

Women Jealous of virtuous Husbands, and the like? Nay, what Quarrels, Duels, and Blood have they been the Occasion of?

Your Paper, without flattering, Mr. APP., stands the clearest of any I meet with in the Town as to those Things; and you have not been asham'd to rectify the few Slips which you have made. May you continue the same Caution, and let me tell you, if once your Paper comes to be Remarkable for speaking Truth, and shunning with Care, all False, Scandalous Reports, it will be justly look'd upon, and read with Respect by the best Men, and valued as the best Intelligence in the Town.

But our Writers will answer, as one of their Honest Paragraph-makers did once, in my hearing;—" Why, if we will write nothing but Truth, we must bring you no News, we are bound to bring you such as we find." But those who value the Reputation of their Writing, and of the Paper they publish, will go upon a different Foundation; and this makes me say, that the only way to establish a Paper, is always to write Truth. By a constant adhering to Truth of Fact, and correcting any Mistake that may inadvertently happen; an Author cannot fail to Establish the Character of his Writings. It is true, that the bitterness of Writing is what now recommends, but this is the Degeneracy of the Age, not their Virtue; and obliging the worst Part of the Taste of the World, will never recommend us to the Reading of the wiser Part of the World. Satyr is indeed what the World loves, and the Gall and the Salt, gratify the Splenatick Part, and those Papers that Rail most often times sell best; but this is a Province no wise Man will enter upon, nor any honest Man care to perform after that Manner. Let the World be gratified in their Gall at the Expense of themselves, not making a Cats-foot of the Publick Writer, to make the Reader laugh, and the Writer cry. You are wise in the Choice you have made of a moderate Way of Writing, by which you at the same Time please your Friends, and keep your Paper, and its Publishers, Writers, &c., from the daily Torture that others feel, and from the Scandal of being a Defamer, and a Slanderer,—Characters no honest Man can be easy with. I shall not flatter your Paper, or any one else; but there is an Art to reprove the Times, and yet not to Arm the Powers you are subject to, against you or your

Paper, in Justice to themselves, and in Justice to other Complainers. ADIEU.

A Nuptial Tragedy.

A. J.—Geneva, March 5.—We have the following tragical Relation from Casal. A certain young Couple in the Neighbourhood of that Place being come to Church to be married, it happened that a Fancy took the Bride to answer *No,* instead of *Yes,* to the usual Question propos'd by the Priest. Which unexpected Disappointment so enraged the Bridegroom that he stabbed her immediately to the Heart. Whereupon one of the Bride's Relations pistol'd the Bridegroom ; after which the Friends on both Sides, to the Number of fourteen, miserably murdered each other on the Spot.

A Dish of Tea-Table Scandal.

A. J., Mar. 23.—Sir, I was the other Day, at a TEA-TABLE Conversation, among some Ladies of Quality, and I happen'd to come there, when the Characters of some Ladies of the Neighbourhood were just upon the Scrutiny ; and really, I must acknowledge, the Ladies who were the Judges, shew'd a most laudable Zeal against the Levity and immodest Behaviour of those other Ladies, who had the Misfortune to be tried in that dreadful Court, call'd *The Tea Table Inquisition ;* but I must also acknowledge, that their Proceedings, however just, were very severe.

Imprimis. There was Lady *Lucia* ——, condemned, *Nem. Con.,* for letting a Gentleman kiss her in a Parlour next the Street, the Window being open ; and it was Witnessed with this Aggravation, namely, That she look'd behind her afterwards towards the Window ; (it seems her Back was to it before :) This they said was a Clinching Circumstance, and put it out of all Question, and even beyond Contradiction, that the Amour was Criminal.

There was a Lady of my Acquaintance by, and I whisper'd her to know if I might have leave to speak a Word in behalf of the absent Lady ; they granted it presently, and I was call'd the Counsel for the Defendant. I owned the Title, the Person being absent. I said, I humbly objected, That the Circumstance of looking behind her after she had been kiss'd, was

wrong interpreted ; and that it did not argue that the Amour
was Criminal, but the Contrary ; for that if it had, she would
ha' looked behind her before she was kissed, not afterward.
This held them a little in Debate, but I was Over-ruled.

Item. She took Coach at her Mother's Door with one single
Gentleman, and drove away ; staid out some Hours, and came
home with the same Gentleman and two more.

In answer to this, another Lady interposed, and said she
must be heard as an Evidence for Mrs. *Lucia,* for that she
was an Eye-witness to both the Passages ; that the Gentleman she went out with was her own Sister's Husband ; that
she went to Dine with her Sister that Day ; and that the two
Gentlemen that came home with her, one was her own Father,
and the other a Gentleman that made Love to her. This
being very positively asserted, and the Lady that asserted it
being of a good Reputation, she was, tho' not without much
Difficulty, acquitted of that Article.

Item. That at Church she was observed to look off her
Prayer Book, tho' she held it up as if she had been looking all
the while upon it ; and that when she turn'd her Eyes off, it
was toward a Pew where two young Gentlemen sat, and
for that Reason, they said, it was very probable she was in
Love.

Mrs. *Lucia* was condemned upon the first and last Indictment without any Mercy ; she was only acquitted of the
second, and that was not without Difficulty, as above.

Mrs. *Annabella* ——, was Try'd and Cast, For that, she
being a young Lady and new Married, pretended every two or
three Months to have Miscarried, and made great Publication
of it among her Neighbours ; when indeed she had never been
with Child, by which Means she caused herself and her Husband
too, to be most egregiously Laugh'd at.

Miss *Abigal* ——, was censured, For that, being but
a young unmarried Lady, she had for some Months past,
walk'd along the Street,—notwithstanding she was well in
Health, and had learned to Dance,—thrusting out her Body
leaning herself back, as if she was with Child.

Memorandum,

She was not absolutely condemned, but it was resolved
nem. con. That it was well if it did not prove a true

Jest, and upon that Resolution, it was order'd that she be well watched.

There were several other Ladies of good Reputation, who were try'd before this Court of Ladies, and cast too, yet still I observ'd, that none of the accus'd Persons were present, or had Fee'd any Counsel to Plead for them; but when I objected the Hardship of it, began to talk a little of its being Unjust, &c., I was taken up short, and told I should not trouble myself about that, it was not the ordinary way of proceeding in that Court;—that they acted by a higher Authority,—that they were not tyed down to those Formalities, their Methods of Justice being peculiar to themselves. I had no more to say, indeed, but came away after a decent taking Leave of the Ladies, with only telling them, I hop'd I should never have the Misfortune to be indicted in their Court; for that I thought it would be much easier to be acquitted at the *Old Bailey,* tho' the Crime might be greater. The Ladies a little resented what I had said, but excus'd me for that Time, by telling me they had Ways to punish all those who should venture to object to any of their Proceedings.

But when I was come away, it put me in Mind of a Letter publish'd in one of your Papers against personal Scandal, in which, tho' I think your Author may be right in some Things, he is certainly wrong, in omitting the Notorious Injustice of our Tea Table Court,—as I call it;—where, in common Discourse, the Reputation of the most virtuous and innocent Persons in the World, is sacrificed, and torn in pieces by the Judgment of Slandering Tongues to a degree unsufferable, and which requires some immediate Remedy.

This put me in Mind of an admirable Way, which they say is practised in the Kingdom of *Siam,* with any Person, who has publickly, in Discourse, defamed, or slandered another. The guilty Person, whether Man or Woman; for there is no Difference made in this Case, is stript Naked from the Waist upward, and in that Posture is carried or led thro' the street where the injured Persons live, and Proclamation made, to whom, and in what manner, the Offence was committed. Upon which all the Friends of the Injur'd Persons, and all their Neighbours, come out, and strew upon the Offender the Seed of a kind of poisonous Herb, call'd in their Language, *Chequo-*

tineschi.   This Seed is moist, and of a Clammy substance, and
would be sure to stick close to the Flesh of the Offender.   At
the Door of the injured Party they stop, where the Person
injured is called out, and is obliged, or, if he decline it, some
other in his or her Name, to sprinkle warm Oil upon the
Offender with a Bunch of that same Herb.   Then the
Offender is set in the Sun, at or near that same House,
being tied to a Post, only, with the Hands at full Liberty.
The Effect is that he will be tormented with the most intolerable Itching that could be imagined, (a true Emblem of
the Itch of Scandal, which was the Occasion of the Crime):
but if the Person offer to Scratch him or herself, or rub,
then the Place so rubbed or scratched, will immediately
Blister, and will also blister the Fingers or Hands it is
rubb'd with.   And then the Offender is to stand, till the
Person agrieved come in Person, which is not to be either
under two Hours or three Hours, as the Sentence may direct,
and release the Bonds which tie the Person, and throw on
the naked Part of the Body a healing Water, which will
Allay the Itching, and heal the Blister in a few Days.   And
this the Injured Person is not to do neither, unless the
Offender beg to have it done, and then they are obliged
to do it, in Token that they are fully satisfied with the
amends for the Offence, and fully reconciled to the Offender.

O ! if such Justice could be obtained in these Parts of the
World, Mr. APPLEBEE, how effectually would it cure that Itch
of Scandal, that so universally overruns the Nation !

Your Servant,
TEA-TABLE.

Portraiture of the Miseries of a Traitor.

A. J., Mar. 30.—Sir, You know that for some Time past, I
have avoided leading you into the Bogs and Briers of Publick
and Party Differences; and I believe you have found the
Sweetness of the Retreat you have made from the hazardous
Part of Journalizing.   You shall never be harrass'd if you
follow this safe Method ; I say, you shall never be harrass'd
for Printing false Lists of the Plotters, and Naming the
Innocent to the Crimes of the Guilty.   Plotting and Plotters
are black and terrible Things, and the last are in a fair Way

to be made a Terror to themselves, as well as to others; be it
to them as Fate and their own Folly have determined them.
We may Pity them, and Pray for them as Fellow-Creatures,
with the Permission of Heaven, led into Temptation by the
Instigation of the grand Evil Counsellor and Enemy of
Mankind; and in that Reflection we may, and ought to be
Thankful, that we are not abandoned of the divine Protection,
so as to fall into the like Misery, no, nor into the like Wickedness.   But as Persons guilty of such Crimes, as for which
Publick Justice appears armed to Punish them, (there we leave
them,) we can go no farther with our Pity than as above.

But waving all these Things, and leaving every Tub to stand
upon its own Bottom; I could not but take Notice to you (in
this Manner,) of the State of Human Life, under the Strange
Extremities which sometimes Men unhappily are brought
into; and among the rest, give me leave to represent to a
serious Reader, the several Circumstances of a Man's Life,
who is situated as we see some Men now are, and have been.
Suppose a Person first taken up, put in Prison, and perhaps in
Irons, and close Guarded for fear of Escape : I have no regard
in this to the Prisoners at present in the *Tower ;* I would add
no weight to the Afflicted; I do not meddle with Mr. *Layer,*
or any body else, let those Gentlemen make such Use of it as
they please.

But suppose, I say, a Person committed as above, for some
Capital Crime, left to his own Anxieties, and restrain'd perhaps
from the Comfort of his Friends, from the Use of Pen, Ink,
and Paper; and, which is worse than all this, conscious to himself, (for there lies the Sting of it all,) that he is guilty of that
for which he stands accus'd.   What Horror must fill his Mind !
What Ideas of Things to come must he form in his Soul ! Here
he has Time, you will say, to Repent.   But Heaven does not
always give Men like Notions of their Crimes; and the usual
pretence to being in the Right (especially if it be a Party
Treason,) oftentimes Cheats Men out of their Penitence.   But
whether they Repent or Repent not, the Appearances of Death
must be very Frequent to them ; and it is hard to describe the
several Shapes the Spectre shews itself in to them, all suitable
to the Circumstances they are in.

In this Case, I believe the most Comfortless, and in the End, the most Injurious, are the Thoughts of coming off; and either not being sentenc'd, or not being Executed, after they are Sentenced. For these foolish Supports serve but to sink them deeper, when they vanish again out of their Hopes.

It is true, there is a Fortitude of Mind able to support a Man under these Things, and to give him a stated settled composure of Mind, not to be conquer'd even by a View of Death itself; but then this must be founded upon the Innocence of the Person, or the goodness of the Cause he suffers in, all which I barr'd against in my first proposition. I am supposing the Crime to be really a Crime, such as Treason, Conspiracy against the Life, or Government of the Sovereign we live under; which, as I formerly wrote to you, can not be Innocent. Against this, no Fortitude founded on a Principle of Virtue can be pretended,—but all must be Agony,—and Horror,—or Rage and Desperation.

After living under the Misery of a painful Confinement for some Time, I am to suppose the Criminal at length brought to Tryal; and, after what Defence he or his Counsel have been able to make, the Jury withdraw to consider a Verdict. O! that a Painter could be found, who in lively Colours could describe, on his Cloth, the inside of the Man's Soul, in those two or three Hours; while the Jury are contending with one another, whether the Man shall be a Man, or a Corpse; an Embodyed Soul, or a dislodged Soul, and a macerated, quartered Carcase; whether he shall be delivered, or deliver'd up; in short, whether he shall Live or Die!

But it is not in the power of Art. It is not to be done. No Colours are lively enough, any more than they are to paint real Light, or the full brightness of the Sun. No, not only not Colours, but not Words. Language is deficient; nothing can Express it. No Ideas of it can be received by any one, but him who has been in the same Condition.

Well! after this Miserable Interval, comes the unhappy Moment, and he hears himself pronounced Guilty! Having received Sentence, goes back to his Dungeon, where he beats the Air with Sighs, and reproaches himself with the Misery he has brought himself to; and has now nothing to think of, but the Ignominy of Death, and the Terror of the State that is to follow.

But not to enter into that Part,—and make your Paper invade the Office of the Divine's,—I look another Way. Suppose the Time of Execution being at Hand, perhaps the next Morning; in the Eve of that very Day comes down a merciful Reprieve! How are they often obliged to open a Vein, and put the Blood into Motion, to prevent the sudden Transport prevailing over the Heart, and the Joy being too strong a Cordial for the weakened Spirits to bear, without Swooning.

Now here are two violent Extremes. But what's the Man's Case, who in the course of two or three Months, may five or six times be left under Express Orders for Execution; and yet, at the last Gasp with the utmost Application, and after often despairing of Success, still obtains a Reprieve; and this from but a little Time, to a little Time. The inside of such a Man I would be glad to see, or to hear it impartially described; I scarce think the Man himself could satisfy my Curiosity in this Point.   I am, Sir, &c.

Satire on Censorious Old Maids.

A. J., April 6.—Sir, I sent you a Letter a few Days ago concerning a New Court of Judicature Erected among the Fair Sex, which I must call The *Tea-Table Court*; as some of our little Courts on Extraordinary Occasions are call'd Pye-Powder Courts. I acquainted you with some of the Proceedings of these Ladies, against their own Sex especially; and how like (exactly like,) the *Spanish* Inquisition their Proceedings are, allowing for the Want of Power only.

I shall as opportunity offers, acquaint you with some of the Proceedings of these Ladies Inquisitors against our Sex, for they assume the right of Judicature in their Way over both Sexes, and of all Degrees. Nay, I doubt not, but they pass their Sentences and Censures even upon their Governors, as Things come in their Way; for they know no Government or Governor, when they are in their Chamber of Justice, (as the *French* call it,) and when the Actions of the Greatest in the Nation come to their Bar, i.e. the *Tea-Table*. But this Part they are prudently pleased to Act more in Private, than other Things; because they are not willing to be disturbed in their Business.

But I happened the other Day to get Intelligence of another

class of these Lady-Inquisitors, which I must Confess, alarmed
me much, because I was told they were of another Species of
Women, and particularly such, as were more Cruel and Merciless than the other, being a Furious and Voracious kind of
Females ; nay, even a kind of Amazonian Cannibals, that not
only Subdued, but Devoured those that had the Misfortune to
fall into their Hands.   I say, I was much alarmed at the
Account I had of this new Sort of Inquisitors, for I thought
that in a free Nation, as this is, we should never have such unlimited Power, such Cruelty unmixed with Mercy, such unre-
lenting hard Heartedness suffered to be Practised.

But so it is, Mr. APP., and this new Set of Cannibals exercise their Cruelty in such an Outrageous Manner, that whoever are so unhappy as to fall into their Hands, are sure to be
Devour'd ; nothing can live under their Cruelty.

To hold you no longer in Suspense, and to convince you
that I do them no Wrong, I shall tell you that this *Tea-Table
Court*,—if it be fit to call it a Court,—consists of a Bench of
OLD-MAIDS.   These, having made themselves Judges, and
clothed themselves with a Self-made Authority, are so Cruel,
and so Voracious, that no Mercy is expected from them ; it
is not in their Nature, they are a Sort of People who have no
Compassion.

Philosophers say, there are Natural Reasons to be given
for every Thing that Nature does ; and so, in this Case, they tell
us, that the Reason why Old Maids are without Compassion
to their Fellow-Creatures, is evident in the very Nature of the
Thing : (viz.) that no Body having had Compassion upon them,
and the Age having been so Cruel to them, as to shew them
no Mercy, but to leave them to the dreadful Condition in which
they become the Contempt of Mankind, *Lex Talionis*.   They
are justly entitled to make returns in kind, and to have no
Mercy upon Man, Woman, or Child that comes into their
Power.

It was my unhappiness to be at a House one Day when a
Committee of this terrible Body of Justiciaries were Sitting.
It seems the Business of the Day was over, so that I had not
the Opportunity to hear any of their judicial Proceedings ; but
they were diverting themselves after the Fatigue of Business
was over, and drinking a Dish of Tea, to exhilarate their old

Eyes, and abate and establish the Chagrin of their Tempers. And here, seeing them in their kindest Dispositions, I had the opportunity to Learn, that their very Diversions savour'd of those Sour, and acrimonious Liquids which flowed in their Veins, instead of Blood; that Venom and something Noxious was mingled among their animal Spirits; and I am perswaded, and therefore Caution all the young Ladies of my Acquaintance with it; that if an OLD-MAID should bite any body, it would certainly be as Mortal, as the Bite of a Mad-Dog; and Physicians will tell you, that the Rage of the Spirits in both, proceed from the same Cause, of which I might give you a Physical, or anatomical System, but I have not Room for it here.

It happened, while the Ladies were in Publick, and the Doors open to admit Company, a little pretty Miss, a Neighbour's Child of about 4 Year old, had come into the House to play with a Lodger's Child that was in the House, for the Mistress of the House was (you must note,) an OLD-MAID. I say it happen'd, that this little Miss came into the Room, and being a most admirably pretty Child, that every body admired,—the Lady-Maids took its Features and Appearance to task thus: "L——d," says Mrs. *Bridges*, aged two and fifty, "I wonder what they see in this little Brat to make them so fond of it; methinks 'tis a very Indifferent Creature, she'll be as far from a Beauty, as *Moll Cut-Purse* was from Handsome." "Nay," says Miss *Nelly*, the youngest, being one and forty and a quarter; "you wrong *Moll Cut-Purse*, I assure you I have seen her Picture, an Original of Sir *Peter Lely's*, and I can Vouch she was a very comely Jade." "Ay," says her Elder Sister *Nancy*, *Ætat. suæ* 57, "So have I, and I think she was a very Handsome Woman. But this Thing will have nothing to boast of; she will be large Featured, her Forehead is too broad, and she will have so little a Nose." "Ay," says Miss *Judith*, (about 61,) "but she has something in her worse than that, I can see it in her Countenance, she will be a bold Hussy." "A bold Hussy," says Mrs. *Abigal*, (aged 64), "you soften it too much, if she been't an Impudent W——e, I have no Skill in Physiognomy." "Why aye," says Mrs. Margaret, (past 50,) "her under Lip hangs out, and that bodes ill indeed upon her Virtue." "Virtue," says Mrs. *Nab* again, "I tell you she will be a W——e, or it must be because no Body will ask her the Question. I see it by the make of her upper Teeth."

Having thus talk'd upon the poor Innocent Lamb,—and Damn'd it to Wickedness,—even before it could speak plain; One of them Spit at it, another Frighted it, a third Pinch'd it, till they set it a Crying, and then inhumanly turned it out of the Room, and bid it go away, a little squalling Bastard. "I warrant," said old Miss *Abigal*, "it came of a W——ing Breed."

Now if this was the Justice of the OLD-MAIDS, Mr. APP., to the poor little Babby that could give them no Offence; what must the young grown Ladies expect to suffer who fall into their Hands? But that belongs to a Story itself.

Yours, &c.

Old Maids. The Other Side of the Picture.

A. J., April 13.—Sir, I have read your last Journal, wherein you have publish'd a Letter scandalously reflecting upon the Elder unmarried Ladies, who your Author universally Reproaches, without Exception. Now this is so unjust a Method, that I expect Satisfaction from you, as you would be esteem'd a Person (PRINTER) of Honour; and, that I may make my Demand appear perfectly, and unexceptionably ·Just, I explain myself thus :—

In giving an Account of a Court of Female Justice, as you call it, or an *Inquisition*, (which, by the way, is undeniably malicious, because it alludes to the highest Injustice and Cruelty), *I say*, in giving this Account, your Author calls the Ladies that he brings in as Judges, OLD MAIDS.

This your Letter-Writer makes a Term of Derision, and like a Man of more Injustice, than the Judges he pretends to censure; takes all the unmarried Ladies of above 30 or 40 Years to be Old MAIDS, within the Compass of his Satyr, as if they were all equally Guilty.

Now, I humbly conceive that there are two Sorts of Ladies who ought to be excepted out of his Buffoonery, and are not the proper Objects of the general Satyr bestow'd upon the other, and these are,—

I. Those who, either by Religious Vows, or by other private Engagement; by Choice, not Necessity; remain Single and Unwed. These are neither touch'd with the Scandal of having never been asked, or tainted with the Sourness and Morose-ness of Humour with which you reproach the OLD MAIDS you mention.

II. Such as for Defect of Fortune, *say it be the late South-Sea Calamity*, or such like Disaster of their Families, are sunk below the Views they had, and the Figure they were bred to; and,—scorning to Dishonour their Education, and the Blood of their Ancestors, will not,—for the mere Satisfaction of being married,—be fettered to Scoundrels, and degenerate into the rate of Mechanicks; but choose to live Single. The Age being at present such good Judges of Virtue, Beauty, Sense, and Manners, as not to take the best of them, without that Alloy of Money, of which they are thus barbarously Plundered, just in their Prime, and perhaps just in the very Article of Matri-mony; and, as it were, in the very Arms of a Lover.

III. A Third Sort are such Ladies who being perhaps a little over Nice, and having good Fortunes, (come of good Families,) good Faces, and good Breeding, have rejected many such as others have call'd good Offers; being difficult and hard to be pleas'd, had rather live as they are, than Marry where they cannot Love; that is, in a Word, had rather be completely Happy in the dear Enjoyment of themselves, than completely Miserable in the Bondage and Chains of unsuitable Matrimony, which without doubt, is the worst Condition in the World.

Now, Sir, let me add here with plainness, that I am one of those they call OLD MAIDS; and under one of these three De-nominations. I shall not for the present humour your Curiosity so far, as to tell you of which. Tho', that you may not tax me with being so rude, because I am an OLD MAID, I shall acquaint you with it at last.

But before I come that length, commend me to your Letter-Writer, and tell him what the Degeneracy of his Sex makes a sad Truth; namely, that the just Character of the Men is such, and the Age is so generally, I had almost said universally, Debauch'd, Wild, and Rakish, or Haughty, and unsufferably Insolent; that—I believe I speak it with an unanswerable Authority,—there are more Ladies of Fortunes, Beauty, and

Breeding, who have had Admirers Plenty, and never wanted
Opportunity to match equal to their Rank, who yet remain
unmarry'd, and venture the Reproach of *being Old Maids;* I
say, more at this Time than ever were known in the Memory
of the oldest Person alive.   The Reason is to be found in the
Degeneracy of the Times; and, in a Word, your Sex is come
to such a Height in all the most disagreeable Articles, that an
honest, virtuous Woman must, and ought to have an Aversion
for Marrying, it being indeed a terrible Venture.

I wish your Letter-Writer, (if he is acquainted with any
Thing of the Town,) would concern himself to tell the World
how many Gentlemen,—some of Quality, and that not of the
lowest Rank in the World at this time,—live separate from
their Wives; nay, how many of them there are, whose Virtuous
Ladies are forced to separate, because they dare not suffer their
Husbands to touch them.   And let him add, if he can, when,
or at what Time, or in what Age of the World, there were so
many of the kind as there are now.

I remember in my Travels, not many Years, coming to
a certain large City, but not *London,* or *Westminster;* and
happening to be in Company where there were some Ladies,
not of the best Characters; one of them, who was not ashamed
to own her Profession, declar'd her Resolution to leave the
Place.   Not, as she said, that there was not People enough in
the Town to give her Employment, and Profit too in her Way;
but to use her own Words, *She scarce knew a Man in the
whole City, that an honest ——— could venture with.*   This was,
if true, a wretched Character of the Virtue of the Generation
we live in.   •   •

Now, Sir, if this be the Case in any Proportion of that wild
Woman's Expression; can it be any Reproach to live unmarried?   You should first remove the Scandal, and wash
clean the Characters of your Sex.   Prove that there are Men of
Virtue and Honour enough, in Proportion to the Ladies, who
merit the Character, and that they may find such if they
please.   If that could be proved, you might then reproach us
with being OLD MAIDS; but till you do this, I must tell you,
that the just Reproach of your Sex's Debauchery, will rather
make the single Life of the Ladies a Mark of reserved Virtue,
than a Brand of Infamy.   And now I have set you a Task,

an *Herculean Labor*, cleansing the *Augean Stable* is a fool to it; you had better be the Town Scavenger, or in plain English, a Tom - - - - - man, to rake in all the Filth of the City, than. meddle with it. And therefore take friendly Advice, and leave the Subject; let it drop, it will but fall in with a Proverb, The more you stir, the worse you'll stink. The Ladies are infinitely and laudably to be justified; for better be without a Man, than with a Rake. And where to choose, who knows?

Your Humble Servant,

CELIBACY.

Reflections on the Death of the Bishop of London, and Banishment of Bishop Atterbury.

A. J., April 20.—Sir, If in the Middle of the Devotions of the Holy Week, I laid a few Moments aside, which I might otherwise employ, in writing to you some Trifles, or gratifying the Levity of the Day, and diverting your Readers; but have now written something more Grave and Uncommon; the most Serious, and consequently the best Part of them, will (I doubt not) excuse me, and perhaps be pleased with it.

We have two eminent Instances this very Week, (as I may say,) of the uncertainty and changeable Disposition of human Affairs, even among our dignified Clergy, I mean the Fall of the late Bishop of *London*, and of the yet Bishop of *Rochester;* and these put me upon making the following Reflections.

Death has levelled the former with the Dust! The Civil Power is, for Aught we see, levelling the other in a differing Manner; as to the *How*, or *How Low*, that we do not, neither is it our Business to enter into it. But be it as Fate and the National Justice shall determine, the Thing is the same, as to the Moral of it. Death or Banishment! What are they? To the Essence of Life, and the Scene of it, which we are all appearing in, they are the same Thing; namely, a removing the Person from the Stage of Life, or from the Place where he acted his Part before. And, as to a Mind unfortified with Virtue, they are in their Proportion equally Grievous; yet on the other Hand, could we steer a steady Course thro' the World, sit loose and easy in every Part of Life, and give no more Weight to the World than it deserves from us, neither of these would be near so grievous as they really are in our View.

Pray Note, I am speaking now of Banishment, abstracted from Crime; for it will for ever be True as the Poet says in another case : That—

"Guilt is all the Pain of Punishment."

But to abstract this,—What is Imprisonment? What is Banishment, to men of Virtue? And, indeed, what is Death? The Soul elevated by the Power of heavenly Vision is able to raise itself above them all. But then, I say, it must be supported by Virtue and Innocence, as to the two first; and of Religion in the last. And therefore I do not bring the Case of the Bishop in Bonds, or other Gentlemen in the same, or like predicament, into this Case farther than as to the Fact; namely, that there are such Persons, and under such Circumstances.

But speaking of the Condition of Mankind, no Station is void of its Trouble, or free from the Changes that are common to Life, but such as, founded upon the solid Basis of Virtue, make the Soul uncapable of being impressed by them when they happen; this is the Station which, I say, is either liable to no Changes, or they are no Changes to that Soul, for they make no Impression on him, no Alteration in him.

To BE, or NOT to BE, is all the specifick difference between Life and Death; and to him who, sitting loose to Life, is thereby prepared for Death, of what Value is the Difference? The Change is not of more Importance, than it is to a Family to remove its Lodging or Dwelling; nor indeed so much in some Cases.

To be appointed to Live in this, or that Part of the World, or not to live, in this or that Part of the World, is still the same, and can be of no Concern to a Wise and good Man, since he is sure he shall remove from thence again at last; and that his great Journey (to Heaven,) shall not be one Step the longer or the shorter, for the alteration of his Situation here. But then, take this still with you as you go, that this is always provided the Mind is entirely clear of Guilt, that no Crime is the Occasion; for to suffer as an Evil-doer is justly Grievous, and indeed there can be little else in Banishment than the Crime, which is the Cause of it. *Adam's* expulsion from Paradise had no bitterness in it, but that of being expelled for his Crime;

as to the Beauty of the Place, indeed something might be said, but all the Ante-Diluvian World was a Paradise in its Degree, and when the Garden of *Eden* was forsaken of its first Gardener, (with Pardon for the Expression,) all *Adam's* Pruning and Cultivation would make it nothing compared to what it was before.

I have heard of some who have said, that the bare being confined from any Place, would make all the World nothing, and of no Value to the Mind, excepting or in Comparison of, that one Place; and if we were forbid, or restrained from going to, but any one Country in the World, all our Happiness would be Centered in that one Place, and we should never enjoy a Moment's quiet in any other; or be easy till we could get leave to come at that one Place.

This is, in the first Place, a most preposterous Suggestion; and, in the next Place, I cannot allow it to be True. What some vicious Tempers may dictate to them I know not, but there is no Manner of Philosophy in it at all, nor indeed of common Sense.

I am loath to say too much on this Subject; yet I would make no Man's Troubles heavier than the Justice in whose Hands they are; for particular Persons are nothing to us. But I am supposing a Man to have a Mind free from all Manner of publick Offences, and either Banished by his private Satisfaction of Life, or by any other means from his Native Country, or the Country he was as it were Naturalized to, which is much the same. I see no more in it than as the Merchants of the World, who for Bread confine themselves to live in the torrid Zone, in the Lybian Deserts, among Pagans and Negroes; or in the Frigid Zone, as in *Hudson's Bay*, *Davis's Straits*, &c., where they converse with Bears and Wolves, Foxes and Tygers all their Lives, and when they Die are to Freeze into a lump of Ice, till they are Thawed by the general Conflagration.

Yours, &c.

On Government by Parties.

A. J., May 11.—Sir, There was a Book publish'd in *London* some Years ago by a well-known Author, the Learned (to say nothing else of him,) Mr. *Toland*. Learning, without all doubt he had, but for anything else, 'tis enough to say he is in his Grave, *de Mortuis nil nisi bonum;* I say there was a Book publish'd by him, with this subtle Title, *The Art of Governing by Parties.*

If all Mr. *Toland* advances there be true, Parties are in the main no Disadvantage to the Nation, or to the Government; only provided that the Government find themselves strong enough to govern these Parties as well as to govern by them. Governing by Parties, is call'd by the Politicians, playing the Parties one against another; by which means the Party who are Out, are always a Curb, and a Bridle to those which are In, and the Parties which are In, are always a Terror and a Stirrer up to Vigilance in those which are Out. In a Word, they are mighty useful to keep one another awake, and make one another Uneasy; and in their uneasiness, very often the easiness and safety of the whole Body may consist. All this, I say, is upon Mr. *Toland's Hypothesis,* and according to his Notions of Parties.

If I was to be asked, whether it is best for us to be divided into Parties, or no? I must answer that, *Negatively,* certainly it were best to have a Nation of one Heart, and of one Mind, as well in Political Principles, as in Religious, if that were possible. There is a great difference between there being a Set of Politick Statesmen in the World, or in a Court, who can make their Advantages of the Divisions of the Subjects, and setting one against another, form their own private Interest from the Contention and Strife of others, and the Halcyon calm Enjoyments of a Dominion entirely united; where the King and the People have not only one Interest, but one Heart; where the King has the Hearts of all his Subjects, and the Subjects equally enjoy the Favour and Affection of their Prince.

But as the World never was of one Mind since there was but one Man in it, and never will be so again, so long as there are two; and since Divisions must come, the Politick Statesmen will make their Advantage of it, and make their Market of both. When the subtle Angler fishes for Gudgeons, he takes a long Pole, and rummages and disturbs the Gravel at the bottom of the River, makes an Uproar in the Water, and raises the Stones and Sand; and then the Fish come blindly together, and are caught with the more Ease.

Thus I have seen a Press Gang, when they have wanted Seamen, set a couple of Fellows to Fight in the Street, thereby drawing a Crowd together; and while one takes Part with JACK, and t'other takes part with GILL, the Press Gang come upon them all, and sweep away from both Parties the People they want.

It is true, it were to be wish'd there were no such Things as Parties among us, *as above*, and that we were Religious without Separation, and Loyal without Faction; but as Offences must come, and Divisions must happen among Mankind, as above, 'tis the wisdom of our Ministers of State to work the Safety of the Government out of the Mistakes of the People, and out of those very Feuds by which, *if left to an ungoverned* ARISTOCRACY they would destroy all Civil Government in the World. Thus the wise Mariners have so improved Navigation, that those dangerous Shoals and Sands, and those frightful Rocks, which in former Times made the Northern Seas be the Terror of all the Navigators of the World, are now artfully made assistant to Preserve, instead of Destroying those that sail among them; affording them, by the help of Buoys, and Sea-Marks, safe Harbours, good Roads, Skreening them from the Fury of Storms, and contrary Winds, by breaking off the Sea, and sheltering the Ships under their Lee; so that when our Ships get in among the Sands, or under such or such Rocky Headlands, they are now Safe, even in those Places where they would, without that Skill or Caution, have been most assuredly wrecked.

Of this, the blessed Apostle St. *Paul* set us a Wise and Politick Example, when he was in danger of being Murthered by the Mob in the famous Tumult at *Jerusalem*, when the enraged *Jews* threw Dust into the Air, in taking off their Madness; and cry'd, " Away with such a Fellow from the Earth, it is not fit that he should be suffered to live." The blessed inspired Man, present to himself, and with a turn of Wit, and Superiority of Genius, peculiar to himself, knowing there were Factions and Parties among them, and that they Hated one another, as much as they Spighted, and were Piqued against him,—immediately turned his speech to the Point in which they disagreed, played the *Pharisees* against the *Sadducees*, talked to them of their future State, and the Resurrection from the Dead, which the *Sadducees* deny'd, and setting the two Factions together by the Ears, made his own Safety the Effect of their Quarrel.

This is certainly a shining Example of the Art of managing Parties, and I could give you Modern Instances of the like in our own Times, of which I shall be more particular in my next.

Discordant Parties sometimes the Safety of States.

A. J., May 18.—Sir, I must own the Doctrine of Party Making is a nice Thing to handle, in this Age especially, when we are upon Arguments that seem to recommend it as useful and even Needful in a Government; but as I write from just Principles, and aim sincerely at the common good of my Country, I cannot believe I shall be wilfully misconstrued by any Body, that have the like honest Ends in view. To illustrate what I Mean, by saying that *the Safety of a Nation or Government may sometimes be formed from the discordant Factions of the People.* I think the best Way is by History and Example, to lay before us what has been, and thereby shew what may be done again by wise and just Governments, and gallant Princes, for the publick Good.

In the late Civil Wars of *France*, begun and carried on between the Factions of the *Guises*, and the King of *France* then Reigning, namely, *Henry* III., the King found himself Oppress'd by the growing Power of the Princes, as they were then call'd; and that he was really in danger of coming under a kind of Tutelage to the Duke of *Guise*, and the Cardinal *de Lorrain*.

During the Power of this rising Faction, there was a strong Party in the Kingdom, call'd the *Hugonots*, or *Protestants*. These had, in the former King's Reign, supported by the Admiral *Coligni*, and the Prince of *Conde*, maintained no less than four Civil Wars against the Government; and had behaved with so much Gallantry, that they brought the Court, as often, to give them Peace upon such Terms as left them with their Swords in their Hands, always in a Condition to maintain that Peace, or defend themselves by Arms if it was broken. Till the Court Party finding they were not able to reduce them by Force, attack'd them by Treachery; and under

the Mask of Friendship, and a Wedding, surprised all the
Heads of the Protestants, and had them, whom they durst not
meet in the Field, murther'd in cold Blood, in a most villainous
and execrable Manner.   This was what we call the Massacre
at *Paris*, in which above Thirty Thousand Protestants fell by
the Sword of Treason and cold Blood Assassination, and among
them, all their Heroes; their best, and bravest, and most ex-
perienced Leaders and Commanders.

Yet all this did not so quell the Protestants, but that the
rest, flying to their Arms for Safety (or else indeed they had
been all Murther'd thro' the whole Kingdom,) they boldly
stood upon their Defence; fought with, and many times defeated, and routed the Catholick Party, and supported, or
rather raised from the Dead, their dying Cause, till at last they
brought the King of *Navarre*, afterwards the famous *Henry*
IV. to own their Cause, and appear at their Head.

The Duke of *Guise* on the other Hand made himself Head
of the Catholick Party under the King, and almost, whether
the King would, or would not; and as he was a Prince of great
Fire in his Temper, as well as Conduct and Bravery in the
Field, so he made himself popular, and especially among the
Parisians, by his zeal, as they call'd it, for the Catholick
Religion.

But this Popularity grew so great, and the Duke raised
himself so much upon it, and carried it so high, that he became
not only uneasy to the King, but seemed to awe and govern
Affairs in a manner unsufferable; representing the King himself
as favouring the *Hugonots*, and as betraying the Church, and
the like.

In all this, he appeared to be supported, not only by the
Princes of the House of *Lorrain*, who were his Relations, but
by the *Spanish* Power; which was then not only great, but
justly formidable to the *French* Court.   The Alliances and
private Entrigues that the Duke carried on with *Spain*, were
such, and the Duke himself swelled so much with the Hopes
he built on them, that he carried it every Day more Haughtily
and Insolently, even to the King; often coming to Court,
attended by such numerous Crowds of his Followers, that it
seem'd as if he came with a Guard to support him in some extraordinary Attempt; seldom appearing in Publick, without

Crowds of Rabble in the Streets, Hollooing and Shouting him
along, calling him the Defender of the Catholick Church, the
Champion of their Holy Religion, the Scourge of the *Hugonots*,
and crying out to him to drive the *Hugonots* from the Court.

As this Party had in the preceding Reign, Massacred the
Protestants; so in a Word, they now so treated their King,
that his Majesty,—God's just Judgments so far concurring and
permitting,—resolved to deliver himself from the Danger he
found himself in, by the same Method; and, in short, caused
the Duke of Guise to be Assassinated, by 12 of the Guards, just
at his entering into the Council Chamber, and the Cardinal of
Lorrain to be Murthered in his Lodgings in the Palace at the
same Time.

After this, the Party, exasperated to the last Degree against
the King, supported, as is said, by the Tumultuous Parisians,
broke out in open Rebellion against the King, expelled him
the City, with the utmost Indignity; and, in short, Headed by
the Duke *Du Main*, Brother to the Duke of *Guise*, and supported by the *Spaniards*, rais'd a Bloody furious War against
the King.

In this Distress, the King, who lost not his Courage, for
being thus powerfully Assaulted, gather'd his Strength about
him, and prepared to give them the due Reward of their
Treason and Rebellion.

But that he might serve himself of the Division which had
so long raged in his Kingdom between the *Catholicks* and the
Hugonots; he secretly managed the *Hugonots* in such a
Manner, that those did by no means joyn with them, (at that
Time) yet the Protestants immediately took Arms all over that
Kingdom in Defence of the King, against the Faction of
Guises, which now began to be called the League, or the Holy
League.

Thus the King, who would have been otherwise overpowered
by the *Guisan* Party, played the *Hugonots* against them, and
thereby preserved himself and his Government from being devoured in the first Rage of that League; and by the Assistance of the same *Hugonots*, afterwards reduced them very low,
till they were driven by the same Desperation and delivered
themselves. The City of *Paris* being besieged, reduced to the
most dreadful Extremity of Famine, and at the Point of being

taken, a Priest was sent out, who Assassinated the King, by which Murther the Siege was for the present raised, and the War transferred to other Hands, as in the History of those Times may appear.

I think this an eminent Instance, where the Factions of the People, were the Preservation (*Treason and Assassination excepted,*) of the King, and of his Government. The next Part of the same History will afford another Example as eminent as this, of which hereafter.

Another Historical Example of the Same.

A. J., May 25.—Sir, In my last to you, I gave a Specimen of the Benefit of Parties to a Government, in the true History of the Faction of the *Guises* on the one Hand, and of the *Hugonots* on the other, in the Kingdom of France; by the Management of which, alternately, the Government, and the Person of the King himself, was preserved.

First by the Strength of the *Guises*, and the Vigour of the Princes of the House of *Lorrain*, the Party of the *Hugonots*,—who were two or three times at the Point of Oppressing the King's Troops,—were reduced, their Armies routed, the Prince of Conde Killed; and the whole Body brought low enough to accept of such a Peace as his Majesty pleased to Grant.

After this, when the *Guises*, making haughty Pretences of their Services, began to impose upon their Sovereign, and in their Turn to oppress him, and after the Killing the Duke of *Guise*, and the Cardinal of *Lorrain*, to call in the Spaniards, and form a League against the King, in which, the greatest Part of the Nobility of *France* took Arms against their Sovereign; his Majesty, by the same Policy, Faced about to the *Hugonots*, Plays the King of *Navarre* against the Duke *Du Main*, and so got the better of the *Guises*.

As to what followed in that History, viz., that the Leaguers were pleased to deliver themselves by Treason and Assassination; Murthering the King by the Sanctified Dagger of a *Jacobine* Friar, that does not at all concern this Part of the Story, or the Application. It is certain that till that horrid Assassination, a Villainy which no Prince can be guarded too strongly against, I say, till that, the Animosity of the Parties was the Safety of the Government. It was the Wisdom of the

Administration so to Manage them, as that they were alternately in direct opposition to one another; and Consequently,
one Side might always be had to expose and ruin the other.
By this Management the Crown kept them both low, as occasion required, and supported itself by Knocking the Heads of
the Factions one against another, till at last the Priests, seeing
themselves going to wreck and the *Hugonots* joyn'd with the
King, took another Course, and for the Safety of their Church,
murthered the King; in a Word, they stabb'd *him for God's
sake*, and supported Religion by the Royal Blood, Killing the
King, their Sovereign, in the Name of the Lord, and Sancti-
fying the Villainy, by specious Pretences of Safety to the
Catholick Faith.

" In Nomine Domini incipit omne Malum."

Give me leave now to bring you to an Example in History
nearer Home, more recent in Memory, and more familiar to
our Knowledge; and this was in the late Miserable Times of
our unhappy and unnatural Rebellion.

After the War between King and Parliament was at an
End; after the fatal Stroke was given, and the Royal Crown,
not only thrown off from the Head of King *Charles* I., but his
Head, in a Villainous and Execrable Manner, severed from his
Body.   It was, I say, after this, *twelve* years before the happy
Restoration of his Son King *Charles* II.

During that Time, the Rebels divided in Factions and
Parties among themselves, such as Presbyterians, Independents, Levellers, Politicians, Royalists, and the like.   Was
this their Security, or their Curse?   Was it the Injury, or the
Happiness of the Loyal Party?   Who from that Incident will
deny, but that the Division of Enemies is the Protection of
just Right?

The Cavaliers, or Loyal Party, taking just Measures, notwithstanding they were everywhere overpowered in the Field;
yet by taking these two Parties by a just Handle, and playing
the Presbyterians, who were Disgusted, against the Independents, who were then in the Saddle, knocked the Heads of
one against the other; and by this very Thing brought about
the Restoration.

It was plain General *Monk* was a Presbyterian, and most,

if not all his Army were so ; such as were not, and were very
violent the other Way, he wisely garbled his Army of them,
and left them behind him ; and not letting them know anything
of his Design, tickled them with the Honour of Governing in
his Absence in *Scotland*.   At the Head of the Presbyterians
he brought in the King ; and, which many of them might be
truly said to do, not in Affection to, or Zeal for the Person
of the King, or of Kingly Government, but in true Hatred
of the Independents, and in Revenge for their Tossing them
(the Presbyterians) out of the Administration.

Who now will say, that a Division of Parties may not be
so Managed as to be not only good, but even needful in a
Nation ?

Extracts from an Essay continuing the same Subject.

A. J., June 1.—. . . . . . . The Learned say a Sermon is
no Sermon, without an Application ; and that all the rest is but
beating the Bush without catching the Bird.   There are some
Men in the World,—upon what Principle we will not now
enquire,—that can abjure the *Chevalier*, and yet act for his
Interest ; swear to King *George*, and yet act against him, and
against his Government. . . . . There is a third Sort,
who have a Secret reserv'd Attachment to the *Chevalier*, and
his Interest, and so Careful are they to conceal and reserve
this attachment, that they submit Conscience, Honour, Religion, and the Faith of honest Men, all to their Politicks ;
take all the Oaths and Abjurations that the Government can
form for its Security, publickly joyn in Praying to God, (*Mocking God, I should call it, as well as mocking the World*,) for the
King's Life, and at the same Time, Plot and Conspire to
Murther and Destroy him.   These are a Sort of People for
whom our *English* Speech wants a Name ; and as for the Principle upon which they Act, we want Words to express the
Horror that honest Men conceive at it.   Here is Defiance
given to Heaven, and to all the avenging Methods of Providence to do the worst against them.   Here is the just and
righteous Judge of all the Earth, called upon, and appealed to
on a Pretence that is, in its Original, False and Fraudulent, a
Thing affirmed for Truth, and God called upon to Witness it,
who knows, and who, the Appellant knows, sees it to be a False-

hood, and that the very Appeal is in itself a horrid Fraud, made only to deceive, and intended to cover Treason and Blood. But to leave the horrid Circumstance, a worse than which, I think, never happened upon Earth since *Judas* betraying Christ with a Kiss, and the execrable *Jews*, crucifying the Lord of Life, I say, leaving this, I come now to a fourth Sort. . . . .

. . . .

Queen *Elizabeth*, as Story tells, was twice happily preserved by the Disagreement of those who had agreed her Destruction; the Villains not agreeing to the Time when, and Place where, they should post themselves for the shooting at her. I have something farther still to offer upon this Head, but have not Room for it here.   I am, &c.

A Satirical Answer to the Essays on Parties.

A. J., June 8.—Sir, It is allowed by Philosophers, especially by the Moderns, upon an Enquiry after the *Summum bonum*, that there are two Sorts of GOOD, namely, *Good* for *something*, and *Good* for NOTHING. The Person, Mr. APP., who has written you several long Discourses upon the nature, and the rise and progress of Parties, had done mighty well, if he had left off there; but since he has come to talk pretty much upon the GOOD of Parties, and the good Uses they are applied to by our cunning Statesmen, intimating that it is mighty well that we are divided, and split into so many Pieces and Parties as we are, of which I must confess, I think just the contrary, Pray, Mr. APP., do me, and some other of your Readers, the Favour of asking that Gentleman which of the GOODS may these Party Divisions be assigned to, among us,—Are they good for something, or good for Nothing?

As to their being good for something, a great deal of Pains has been taken to make out a kind of Advantage, which, by the Artifice of Statesmen, is sometimes found to be made out of those Things; and you, giving us several Instances out of History to confirm them. But what do all these Instances amount to, any farther than to shew that the Parties were first the ruin of the Country, and of the Country's Peace and Happiness when they began; only that at last, Wise Heads made Shift to prevent the Nation's Ruin by the politick Management of the People.

In particular, as in the Case of *Henry* III. of *France*, after
the Fury of the Parties had raised five several Civil Wars
between the *Royalists*, and the *Hugonots*,—been the Death of
Eleven Princes and Dukes, and 100,000 Men in several Battles,
Sieges, and Skirmishes,—occasioned the Murther of 30,000 Protestants on one Side, and cutting in Pieces the Duke of *Guise*,
and the Cardinal of *Lorrain*, on the other Hand, all in cold
Blood ; the Killing of the Prince of *Conde* in hot Blood, namely,
in Battle ; and, last of all, the assassination, and horrid Murther
of the King himself in Religious cold Blood by a Fryer ; I
say, after all this, the good from these Parties, was, that the
King before he was Murthered, supported himself about three
Quarters of a Year, whereas all the Mischiefs above, were first
of all occasion'd by the Factions and Divisions in the State,
and among the People.

In like manner, in the Reign of King Charles II., the
divided Interest of the Parties ; namely, the *Presbyterians* and
Independents, was Politickly made use of by the Trusty Friends
of the King to bring to pass the Restoration. But take it
with you as you go, and pray do not forget it, that this
good was not produced out of that Evil, till first the dreadful Effects of the Factions and Divisions were felt throughout
the three Kingdoms ; namely, not till a seven Years' bloody
Rebellion, and twelve Years continued Usurpation, in which
the Factions, thro' God's Judgments, getting the better,
300,000 Men's Lives were lost, almost all the Loyal Gentlemen in *England*, and their Families were ruined and undone,
the King himself taken Prisoner, bought and sold, insulted,
hurried about from one Gaol to another, and at last most in-
famously Murthered. I say, after all this, besides the Blood
shed in *Ireland*, and in *Scotland*; after all this, the Parties,
having run themselves out of Breath, and falling out with one
another, the King took the Advantage, and made them be
Instrumental to his Restoration.   ·

Now, where is the good, pray, out of Parties, at the Foot of
this Account ? Is it any more than a small Benefit out of an
infinite, horrible Confusion. I say, a small Benefit, because,
in the first Case, the Benefit was indeed but trifling, and in the
last, the Restoration would certainly have followed, and been
carried, over the Bellies of both the Parties, for the whole

Nation was sick of the rest; Rump upon Rump had surfeited the People, and the whole Kingdom groaned for a free Parliament.

In a Word, all the good I can deduce from these Things, amounts to little more than that of a prudent Skipper, who sunk his Ship, to drown the Rats; or of a good old Woman, who burnt her Bed, to kill the Bugs. If your Author can make any more of it, Pray let us hear of it; for my Part, I think Parties, and Divisions among us, are all from Hell, and only are permitted by Heaven to be the Torment of just Princes, the Terror of the most upright Ministry, and the Plague of a whole Nation.

Exeunt Omnes.

PETER.

On some of the Evils of Political Parties.

A. J., June 15.—Sir, I have spent some Time in writing to you in answer to the important Question, Whether Parties were any ways Beneficial, or to be made Beneficial to a Government? Give me leave to enter a little now into another needful Enquiry. What is the main Evil of Parties? And why are they so bitterly exclaimed against?

I shall scarce venture to answer this fully, and determine what is the main Evil; but I may venture to let you into some of the particular Evils that we daily feel, and have for many Years felt from them; I say, some of them, for their Name is Legion, and they are many.

1. One of the first, is the Breach of all good Nature, and good Manners between us, and the constant Revilings, Slanders, Reproaches, which they daily throw at one another in Conversation, and at all Mankind that do not please them, to the ruin of all good Neighbourhood, Charity and Decency.

2. Libelling and Defaming one another in Print, Raising and publishing Scandal, and which is worse, Slander, upon innocent Persons; without regard to the Morality of such Treatment, and directly against the Tenour of the Ninth Commandment; in a Word, against all the Laws of Civility among Men, as well as of Religion towards God.

I must confess, Mr. App., this Way of Party Libelling, and of Publishing private Personal Scandal, is by the devilish Rage of Parties, (for there it began,) grown up to that Height, that no Nations in the World (I believe) practice it like us, and no Government like ours, both bear with it, and are injured by it so much.

I do not in this confine myself to the present Government, all the Ages of Government in this Nation have complained of it; printed Scandal poisoned the Minds of Men with the Venom of Malice against the Person of the Royal Martyr, and enflamed their Minds to a degree of Rage that reach'd up to Heaven; made them furious, and implacable, and prepared them for the bloody Execution which followed.

Who can stand before the fury of Party Scandal? What Authority can resist the Force of Party Slander in Print?

Life and Reputation are parallel cases. He that regards not his own Credit, has every Man's Character at his Mercy. If, as the Wise Man says, *A good Name is better than Life*, by the same Rule, *Slander* is a worse Sin than *Murther*, and as in all well-governed Nations Penalties are proportioned to the Nature of the Offence; so I think, indeed, the Slanderer's punishment should exceed that of a Murtherer's; but then, as Printed and Party Slander are of a degree so much greater, so much more flagrant, they merit a greater Punishment suitable to that degree.

The nature of this Party Slander seems to be such, and to be carried so far, that it does more than kill the Person, of this, or that Man or Woman it points at; it Murthers all his Favourers and Defenders; all that speak but in his Excuse, or but venture to Dissent from the publick Raillery. Nay, it goes farther, it blackens Families, brands Societies, Nations, nay, Princes, Kings, Queens, and Governments of all Sorts.

This was the Case, as I have said, of King *Charles* I., and how much short of this, did Party Clamour strike in a late Reign? When the most virtuous and most religious Queen that ever this Nation knew,—her own and eldest Sister only excepted,—a Princess full of Goodness, and Beneficence,—full of Tenderness, Charity, and Humility;—was attack'd by the most vulgar, most infamous Scribblers, in the vilest Manner imaginable, even to Ballads and Songs.

Inimitable Party Slander, at the same Time, followed many of her Majesty's most faithful Servants, and those that were the most Inoffensive, had ordinarily the greatest Share of it.

The present Age is far from being free from the like Inconvenience, at least, as far as the Engines of Slander dare appear to act; but the Wisdom of the present Administration has carried a stricter Hand. And yet how has King *George* been treated upon by them, how bold have the Spreaders of Faction been ! And how much farther they would have gone, if Justice had not exerted its legal Power to restrain them !

Again, what Length do Religious Slanders go among us; and how are we every Day, as it were, pulling one another's Throats out *for God's sake !* As if to slander and reproach one another, were a Part of Religion; and, that Want of all Charity denominated a Christian, and Want of Good Manners a Gentleman.

These are some of the inimitable Virtues of Party-Making, and of the inexpressible Advantages of Parties themselves. You may perhaps meet with some more of them in my next.

On Personal Slander.   Against "The True Briton."

A. J., June 22.—Sir, Give me leave to dwell upon this Weighty Subject of Personal Scandal, it really concerns us all. 'Tis no Compliment to your Paper, but a Debt of Justice, which the Nature of the Thing pays you; there is not another of your Brother Journals where the Complaint of this Crime,— which all the World thus complains of—can be made, for they are all Guilty of it themselves.

Party Scandal has run a dreadful Length among us, and as I find it now working its Way out into the World again, with the utmost Artifice and Cunning; I think it is an incumbent Charge on us all to warn against it, and to give some Marks by which you may know it.

When a Slanderer is coming out with his pointed Spears, with his pointed Arrows,—for his Breath is an Arrow, and flies by Night,—and a Weapon that wounds in the Dark; when he makes his first Essay, you find him covered with Panegyricks; the Men he designs to wound are seemingly forced by himself against the very Weapons he fights with.

If he aims at the Person of the Sovereign, he first runs out against all those that would detract from his just Character; panegyricks him with the Title of Deliverer, Ransomer of his Country from the Plots of preceding Reigns, extolling his Personal Merit, his Readiness to the Interests of his People, his constant Care of Religion and Liberty.

If he points out any impending Dangers, and the bad Consequences of such and such Councils, he never fails to close it with telling how secure we are, that these Things can never affect us, while such a Prince holds the Reins of Government; but fails not to groan deeply under the Apprehensions of what may happen when the King may rise up in *Egypt*, who knows not JOSEPH.

When the Defamer is prepared to exclaim against AVARICE and AMBITION,—when big with Slander,—drawing his Lines, and breaking Ground in the Dark, to make Approaches upon a great Person, a Minister of State, or other, whom he resolves to blast with his Breath; when he has pointed out the " Miseries of the Nation, where the Minds of their Statesmen are infected with AVARICE and AMBITION, and the melancholy Prospect there is, when we see Men of the greatest Abilities becoming *Tools* to a *Court*, where they ought to *Preside*, making no other Use of the Advantages Heaven has given them to support others in the Ruin of the State;" *I say*, when he has flourished thus in Raillery, for it cannot be called Satyr, the Slanderer fails not to add,—

" Our Age affords no living Instance of this Nature, such is the Care, Justice, and Reputation of our Governors, and the Independency of both Houses of Parliament."

When the subtle Insinuator has been exercising his Talent to form a Design of attacking the whole Legislature,—when he would slyly impeach the Honour and Justice of the Proceedings in the House of Commons, he first harangues upon the dreadful Consequences to our Liberties;—" If ever an Evil Minister should, by Pensions and Places, be able to corrupt the Minds of the Members, and intimidate them with the Loss of their Employments;" he never fails to smooth this over with the hypocritical Daub as follows :—

" This Manner of enslaving us cannot be in our Time, there being so glorious a Spirit in both Houses for the Support of our present happy Establishment."

Can any Thing now have the Spirit of Slander more than
the first, and the Colour of a Satyr more than the last?

Slander has two Instruments, by which its Poison is openly
or secretly always vented, and the very Essence of its Venom
insensibly conveyed by a Kind of *Effluvia* imperceptible to
common Eyes, and, which thus penetrate, as the Slanderers
imagine, into the Vitals of the Person they would kill :—

> 1. *Defamation.*
>
> 2. *Insinuation.*

I think the Slanderers of this Age have pretty well done
with the first, because they are tired with the Whip of Correction, and a Coward being a constant Adjunct in a Slanderer,
they dare not suffer for the Cause they assert; Shame covers
them with Fear, and they have ceased for a While to rail, and
now they go to Work the other Way. A famous Knighted
Pen began this Method, till he sickened of the Cause, and
then turned about, and was contented to be paid, and hold his
Tongue. This was in the late Reign.

INSINUATION is now the last Refuge of Slander. The *True
Briton*, when he comes to dip in this Dirty Work, is no more
a BOLD BRITON, but a sly *Insinuator ;* like a broken Tradesman
in the *Mint*, who flatters himself with a Negative Honour, that
he is not a Prisoner, he is a Shelterer. He applauds his self-
opinionated Wit; namely, That he is not a foul-mouth'd
Slanderer, he is a Shelterer. He shelters himself under the
Protection of *Inuendo ;* and, as he thinks like the *Tarantula,*
bites laughing.

But is not this Slander? And is there not equal Rage
and Venom in the Design ? Are not these some of the Chil-
dren of Envy ? Who only grin and snarl under the Chariot-
Wheel of *Virtue ?* Where's the Courage that should attend
Truth ? If the Fact is True, the Charge may be True ; why
all these Subterfuges and Retreats behind the Skreen of *Double
Entendre ?* Why is Panegyrick hung out for a Sign, when
Satyr only is to be sold in the Shop? Why fawning Words
from the Teeth outward, and the Gall and Poison under the
Tongue inward? Truth is as bold as a Lion ! Old *Andrew
Marvel*, the King of Satyrs, has this bold Couplet in one of
his Satyrs, and which indeed should be in the Title of all
Satyr :—

" *Truth's* as bold as a *Lion*, I can't be afraid,
For I'll prove *every Tittle* of what I have said."
Vid. BRASS HORSE AND STONE HORSE.

He that writes Truth, writes Satyr. He that cannot say he
speaks or writes Truth is a Slanderer. Slander is no Satyr.
If it be Truth, speak out Man ! Fear not. If it be not Truth,
no honest Man will speak at all. I shall carry this a little
Farther hereafter.

On Cypher-Writing.

M. J., June 22.—Sir, I being one of your constant Readers,
observe, that many of my Fellow-Students apply to you, on
any emergent Occasion, for Advice, Information, &c., as to a
general Intelligencer. And, though I have been your constant
Reader some Years, yet have never taken that Liberty before,
but, being willing, once in my Life, to do you that Honour,
I thought I never should have a more proper Occasion than
now ; for, being of an inquisitive Disposition, I have been
puzzled in my Thoughts for some Time. In short, Sir, the
Occasion of giving you this Trouble is this :—

Being in Company lately with some of my Acquaintance,
we were talking of several Subjects now in Fashion, and, among
others, of the modern mysterious Way (to use the Words of a
late Author) of decyphering Words wrote in mysterious Characters. And one of our Company did assure us, that there
are Persons now in *England* who can decypher a Letter wrote
in any Characters, and some who can find out the true Letters,
and put the Words, though the Language be unknown to
them. So that when they have done that, they know not the
Meaning of them without an Interpreter. Now I, who have
no opinion of the Art of Conjuration, could not conceive which
Way this could be done by any other Art ; and, as he could
not inform me where such Persons were to be found, so, for
the Reason aforesaid, he left me under Uneasiness of Thought
which Way to know the Truth of this Matter ; for I thought
that to find this performed, would be more curious than all
the Arts of *Hocus Pocus* that ever I saw, besides the Usefulness of it. For, as it may be very useful to many Persons, as
well in a private as in a publick Capacity, to have Ways of
writing their Secret, though innocent Affairs, to one another,

in Characters known to few, if any, besides themselves; so it would be of great Satisfaction to the Publick, to find that no Persons can carry on any Correspondence, by Letters, against the Interest of their Country, so private, but that some People can discover it. Also it would be a Means to deter any one from it, when he finds that his Meaning can be discovered by some, in whatever Characters he writeth. At length I considered with myself, who should I apply to, but to one, who, (if I mistake not your own Words,) hath dipp'd into all Arts and Sciences, and, I suppose, all Mysteries, and one who hath seen a great deal of the *Hocus Pocus* Art.

Then, prithee *Mist*, put on your Conjuring Cap, and try at the few following Lines; and if you find them beyond your skill, be so candid and ingenuous as freely to acknowledge your Incapacity in this Art, and desire some other more mysterious Sons of Art, to do it for you. Let me have the true Meaning of them in plain *English*, in some of your Journals shortly, or else let it be known, that there is one Person, at least, in the World, who cannot believe that there is any certainty in this Art. And, to help you something forward on your Way, I assure you, that these are all *English* Words, and not Words without any Signification, but the Sense of them coherent; though, perhaps, not in the most polite Style, according to the Modern and best Way of writing *English*, because such Words are made use of as may make the greater Difficulty in the Discovery. And take this also along with you, that if, upon Trial, you do not find them to be of an innocent Meaning, you may assure yourself, that your Art fails you, and you must turn over your Books once more; for neither you, nor any Man living, can put any ill Construction on them, if they give the true Meaning of them, which will be known by the Key, which shall be faithfully transmitted to you, as soon as you have decypher'd them, or acknowledg'd your Incapacity in this Art.

Please to insert this, with the following Cypher, in your next Journal, and you'll oblige many of your Readers.

I am, Your humble Servant, &c.

pmos kwafroz rmyzo kgy3o7x 829vmqyd4 ca39zxowz nft reysrod6ywz xmoz& hwasi m67eyw yfxc vm&ag cuzx&gz usa

xmocz&dloz 49bopaz& hoe&qax ysv6 rejc67pondxmz 24z6
vmoM kwerygo ie63pa4d qwec xmo9w qod46p zyhforvz
xepnwtz xm&ag zelownais 273 8w6j xmoag basi y7x6 maz
k&ekdo wouzef paxm o5k&waosr& hexm zmop vmux qgej
resxwngM ruyzoz 398q&wosx oq8&ruz kg6r&o3.*

A. J., June 22.—On Tuesday last between Twelve and One,
the late Bishop of Rochester was brought in a Chair out of his
Apartment in the Tower; and as he pass'd to the Wharf to go
on board the Admiralty Barge, he was allowed to stop and
speak to Dr. Friend at the grating of a Window. His stay was
very short, and then he went directly on board, with Mr.
Morrice and his Lady, &c., Colonel Williamson also, and some
Warders, went down with him, to see him on board the Man
of War. A certain Noble Duke appear'd there, to take leave
of the late Prelate, and went, as we think, down the River
with him, tho' not in the same Barge.† The Wharf Gates were
shut on this Occasion to keep off the Populace.

Against Slander by Insinuation.

A. J., June 29.—Sir, I Remember, in this very Debate about
writing Slander, *in a late Reign,* they came to a greater height
of Plainness than we can pretend to now; for they did not
work by INSINUATION as now, but by downright DEFAMATION,
calling Rogue and Rascal, and the like. The Reason was
plain, the Government let them alone, left them to fight it
out their own way, did little or nothing in it; the Queen was
grieved to be ill-treated, but it seem'd to be an evil without a
Remedy; and her Majesty, secure in her own Virtue and
Innocence, bore with it, and let them not only lampoon her,
but, in a Word, insult her at an inimitable rate; till, as was
very well observed by one Writer *at that Time;* The Tongues
of Slander were really tired in their own Way, and being
as it were weary with trying in vain to provoke the Queen,

---

* The following is the solution of the above cypher:—" When Princes
chuse faithful Ministers and Councellors, these bring Honour unto their
Masters, and themselves, likewise Benefit unto Commonwealths, also they
procure Good-will from their Fellow-subjects towards their Sovereign,
and from their King unto his People. Reason with Experience both shew,
that from contrary Causes different Effects proceed."

† The Duke of Wharton.—*Ed.*

they turned about and tried to provoke Heaven itself; *for Example* :—

They cried the Ballad, called the *Hasty Widow*, under the Queen's very Windows, upon Occasion of the Parliament voting an Address to the Queen to Marry.

. And when this would not do, *I say*, they tried to provoke God Almighty himself, and made a Ballad of *the first Psalm.*

Thus the Government in that Reign was handled by the Three-half-penny Statesmen of the Street, till *at last*, having called one another by all the most exquisite Titles of Honour that *Billingsgate*, the *Bear-garden*, or all the Street Wit between them could supply, they fell out about who had the better of it.

One side called Rogue, Rascal, gave the Lie, and abandoned themselves to all the Indecencies of Railing and Rudeness, and this, it seems, they called WIT; for they Bantered the other Side for want of WIT, though it did not appear they wanted anything but the Talent of Raillery. I shall give a Specimen of the latter.

One of the Papers who opposed the witty People, *as they call themselves*, begins thus :—

" It hath graciously pleas'd *their Wisdoms* The Street Libellers of the Week, to reproach us as not Competent and incapable to Cope with them, for Want of an equal Share of WIT. We joyn Issue upon this weighty Point, they say *Wit* is their Talent; we profess *Truth* to be ours; *let the Fact be Examined.*

" Often have we, in a Dialect suited to our purpose, tho' not in florid studied Speeches, to please *their Wisdoms*, the Party Men, laid them open as Vilifiers of Majesty, Slanderers of Men of Honour, and of Trust in the Government, and Abusers of Crowned Heads, and the like ; we have made them acquainted with their own Pictures, told them the Methods they take to Defame their Superiors ; named the Coffee-Houses they Ply at, where, as in a Market, they Trade in Scandal, and levy Slander against all they please not to like ; and this we have done in such convincing Terms, that it has touched the Tardy among them to the Quick. THIS IS TRUTH.

" In return for this, they fly out, call *Villain,—Pest of Society,—Rogue,—Rascal,—*THIS IS THEIR WIT.

" *Tractent Fabricia Fabri*, every Man to his Trade.ʻ 'Tis
Pity these Gentlemen's good Language should not Boil their
Pots! But so it is, and Characters of the Person speak to the
Case, and the Name of the Man is an Answer to all he
Writes."

I shall carry you no farther on with Quotations *in Nubibus*.
Let us see if the Characters of the Defamers of this Age are
one jot Better, Wiser, or Honester than those of the last;
indeed I must needs say, I think not. If they have any Part
which t'other had not, it is that they are less plain and open,
that is to say, more Cowardly and Base; and, instead of Open
Defamation, they work now by *Insinuation*, and *Suggestion*,
wounding by Mockery, and fixing their Slanders by sham
Praise. But do they think that this is less Criminal? No, *just
the contrary*, neither is it so hard to lay the Hands of the Law
upon them as they Imagine; the most Cautious of those
Libellers, have been dealt with in their own Way; MIST has
been sent to mend his Stockings in the Upper Quarter of
the Province of *Newgate*; *Cato* has been taught Manners
another Way; the *London Journal* keeps himself up by Defending those he raised himself at first by abusing; G——ge has
done, Railing or Flattering, having been lately choked with
the Husks of the stigmatized Cheat, the *Harburg Lottery*.

Let not the new Pretenders to Slander think they are above
the reach of Justice. The Author may write and dwell *in Nubibus*, but he will not get Printers *in Nubibus*, or Publishers
in Nubibus, they must shew themselves, and it will not be easy
to find Printers and Publishers that will stand Gaols, Pillories,
Whipping-Posts and Halters, for so Vile a Cause, as that of
Libelling the Government. If they think they can go on
thus, *let them try their Hands*; we shall soon see the *bold
Briton* turn *Poltroon*, and fly from the Cause, or turn
Renegade, and write against himself, like the *London Journal*.

But if these men think themselves right; if TRUTH is with
them, Why do they hide from the Argument? Why do they
not Impeach the Persons boldly? If Crime be in the Hands
of the Great Ones, the Law is in the Hands of every Man;
every Man, or any Man, may demand Justice. But if they
think this too great a Task, and they shall be Out-Voted by
Numbers, or Oppressed by Money; Let them set by the

Persons, and lash the Crimes; let alone the Ministers, and
attack the Administration. *For Example,* seeing they can
insinuate a Fault in the *Baltick Expeditions,* which I affirm
some of the wisest, and most necessary Steps the Government
has ever taken; let them speak plain *English.* If they can tax
those Steps, with either being guided by wrong Principles,
directed by wrong Views, aim'd at wrong Ends,—either a needless Expense, or not worth the Expense,—I offer to join Issue
with them there; and if they make their Pretence, but so
much as specious, I'll give to them both Government and
Ministry, I'll grant they are no more to be call'd Slanderers,
and say *as they say* in everything, for the future. I think the
Challenge is fair, let them Answer if they can.

Defence of Charity Schools against "The British Journal."

A. J., July 6.—Sir, We have lately taken up a new Method
in *England,* or rather revived an old one in our making a Judgment of Things, and in our Censure of Persons too, namely,
that we argue from the Abuse to the Practice, and if we can
find a Flaw in the Manner, raise our Batteries immediately
against the Principle; as if the bad Effects might not be by
mistaken Conduct produced from good Causes.

If this be at any Time the Case, Justice requires that we
should seek out the Mistake, and Rectify that Abuse; but not
immediately overthrow the Foundation. The *British Journal*
has, according to his Gasconading Manner, taken upon him,—
because he finds room to Complain of the Abuses, which may
perhaps be Committed in some of our Charity Schools,—I say,
he takes upon him to fly in the Face of the whole Body of
Charity Schools now set on Foot in *England.*

As if, because some disaffected Masters, and perhaps Employers of Masters too, may have encouraged the Children
under their Care in wrong Notions of Government,—if any be
so encouraged,—for I do not grant it; therefore Charity Schools
are a Grievance, as if because the Practice may be bad, that
therefore the Institution is so also. This is like the Author's
Reasoning I must confess, which he supports by a bold assert-
ing, (the worst way of begging a Question,) rather than by a
just Arguing.

Some Masters have misguided the Children, instead of

Instructing them, therefore Charity Schools are Pernicious and Destructive: Let us see how it will bear in Parallel Cases.

Some Masters of Colleges, and Tutors in Universities, have been wicked Men, and have set bad Examples to the Youth they are entrusted with; *therefore, no Universities should be suffered.*

Some Children have been Taught by their own Parents as well by Precept, as by Example, to Swear, Blaspheme the Name of God, and talk Lewdly; *Ergo, no Parents should have the Privilege of Teaching or Instructing their Children.*

Some Children, as soon as they could speak have made use of their Voice in taking God's Name in Vain,—Swear and Blaspheme; *Ergo*, no Children should be taught to speak.

If Teaching the Children of the Poor to Read, and to Write,—whose Parents are not able to give them such Learning,—is not a commendable and valuable Act of Charity; then Ignorance is a Blessing, the Word of God no Benefit, or the reading of it no use or Advantage to the Poor.

This assuming Author seems to write, as if he would have us think the Poor have no Souls, or that they were no ways at all concerned in the Affairs of the Christian Religion, turning his Thoughts to the share Politicks have in this Part of the Work; whereas the Charity Schools, in their Institution, and in their Practice too (with very few Exceptions) are pointed at the good of Souls; and, the Encrease of Christian Knowledge, by not only preserving poor Men's Children from being left destitute of Instruction, and exposed to Ignorance, and the worst Sort of Misery, but also to put them into a Way, by the Knowledge of Religion, and the Word of God, to live like Christians, as well as like honest Men.

If he had complained of the abuse of the Institution, he had brought his Charge against the Persons, who endeavour under Colour of instructing the Children, to instil corrupt Principles, either Politick, or Religious, into their Minds, poisoning their Thoughts with Factious Principles as to Government, and Atheistical and Profane Principles as to Religion; and so filling the Nation with a Generation of Enemies, both to God and the King.   I say, if this had been his Complaint, and he could have just Cause for it, I should joyn with him in it with all my Heart, allowing that it ought to be complained of, and to be at once redressed; and those whose Duty it is ought to redress it, yet do not deserve the Censure, nor any Punishment.

But it does not at all follow from hence that the Children of the Poor should not be Taught to Read and Write, or that they should be left in Ignorance and Blindness,—neither to serve God by reading and learning their Duty in the Scriptures,—much less that they should be thought to be made unfit for the Service of God and their Country, by having the Knowledge of the Scriptures, and by having Principles of the Christian Religion infused into them in their earlier Days.

If there are such Abuses crept into the Management of these Schools, as these Men say there are, Where is it? Who are the Schoolmasters? And why are they not marked out by Name, that the Government may be informed of them; and that the Managers of Charities, by which they are supported may be informed of it, and may be led by a Hand to the Redress of it? If any of them are duly informed of it, and do not redress it, why are not the Names of such publickly taken Notice of, that the World may know them, and that the Innocent may not suffer for, or with, the Guilty? For to take up a general Reproach against the whole Body for the ill Conduct of a few, or of any particular Persons; this is highly unjust and unreasonable: If the Masters misbehave, others of better Principles may be found, and the Error rectified before it spread too far; but if, instead of this, the Complainer falls openly and Scandalously upon the Head of Charity Schools in general, Reproaches the Design itself, calls it a whimsical Charity, or worse, and is for the overthrowing all the Schools in Gross, because there are Errors in some particular Persons employed :—this is just as if a Man should inveigh against the Reformation, because there are Sectaries and Enthusiasts, among the Reformed, such as *Quakers, Anabaptists, Independents, Presbyterians,* &c. found among Protestants.

The Scandal of this Method may justly lye at the Doors of such Pretenders to Satyr as this; Satyr rightly placed, is a wholesome Rebuke, but a Sarcasm upon Just and Generous, Pious and Religious Undertakings, because they may be abused, is no more Satyr, but a malicious Charge aimed with Rage against good Men, and supported by Ignorance and Arrogance, unaccountable and unjustifiable.

Subterraneous Fire in Kent.

A. J., July 6.—A subterraneous Fire was lately discover'd to burn in a Wood at North Cray, near Bexley in Kent ; and the Roots of the Trees, supposed to be the chief Pabulum that fed it. However that be, the same was observed to spread so very much, (there being no Moisture in the Ground this Dry Season to give a Check to its Progress,) that the Inhabitants thereabouts were put into a great Consternation thereby ; and for several Days together many Waggons were employed to carry Water from Bexley River to extinguish it.

A Plea for Charity Schools.

A. J., July 13.—Sir, In my last, I hinted to you what a bold Invasion had been made upon the best and most glorious Parts of Christian Charity that had been set on Foot in this Part of the World since the Establishment of *Christ's Hospital,* by King *Edward* VI., I mean of CHARITY SCHOOLS.

Had the insolent Scribbler challenged the Misapplication of Charity Money when collected ; the Misbehaviour of Governors, and Directors, and Schoolmasters that have been entrusted ; had he objected against any Branch of the Management of this important Affair, we should have joined heartily with him in order to Amendment of what had been Amiss, and to obtain any Regulations for the better carrying on those Parts for the future, in a manner most suitable to the good Design of the first Contrivers, and to the true Intent and meaning of those good People, who freely contribute to the Instruction of the poor desolate Orphans that are brought up in these Schools : that Ignorance, and consequently Atheism, and Irreligion may not be entailed on the Posterity of the Poor, and they may be less fitted for Idolatry, than we think they have been before.

But this promoter of Blindness, and ill Principles in the Poor, strikes at the Root, and would destroy the Design, which he cannot deny to be good, in order to cure the pretended Errors in the carrying it on ; nor are the Errors any more than pretended, at least, till they are proved, they are not so in Argument.

But to leave him to the Divine Censure, and to what they may expect who oppose the Work of God, and the good of Souls in the World; let me speak a Word or two to the other Part of his empty Charge against Schools, which he carries up upon the Civil Part, or Political Part, call it which we will: namely, that by this Method, the Poor will be Transposed, as I may call it, out of their Place, and be removed from the Sphere proper to themselves; namely, the Service of the Rich, and be above the Labours necessary to the common good.

This is a strange Principle, I confess; and the most inconsistent with human Policy of any Thing I ever met with. The Danger here suggested, is, in a Word, making the Children of the Poor able to struggle in the World for their Livelihoods, that they may *first* be taught how well they may live by Application to Trades, and Handicrafts, and thereby, *secondly,* have Principles of Diligence and Application infused into them, by which they would certainly grow Rich.

The inconvenience of this, is supposed to be first, that we should want Servants; very well, but then it necessarily implies, that we should be all Masters, *that is to say*, that all the Inhabitants of *Britain* should be brought up to some Trade or Employment, whether of Art and Mystery, as Handicrafts are rightly call'd, or Husbandry and Tillage; and we should want Footmen, Pages, Coachmen, and Grooms; who, in a Word, are at this time the Refuse and Scum of the Nation.

These are they that, generally speaking, being bred up to nothing, are good for nothing; these,—as they are the Offspring of Beggars,—are the Multipliers of Beggars and Thieves throughout the Nation. They spend their Youth at their Master's Heels, or at the Horses Heels; and when they come to Marry the Servant Maids,—who are of like Rank indeed with themselves,—what is their Fate afterwards, but to beg together, to get a Race of Beggars, and fill the Parish with Starving Orphans; the Parents being Hanged or Starved, or Transported, which, in short, are the main Outlets of that Sort?

. But the Charity Schools and Work-Houses will put them out to Trades, both Boys and Girls, teach the Boys to get their Livings, and the Girls to Spin, and to work with their Needles; and in short, to be able to live on their own Labour, keep themselves out of Snares and Idleness, and preserve them from Beggary and Want.

In short, he is afraid the Poor should be made Rich, and the Rich want Beggars at their Doors by Day, and Thieves in their Houses at Night.

But we shall want Servants! I wish for my Country's good, that it might please God that all our People were Masters, and able to keep Servants, tho' they were obliged to buy their Servants, as other Nations do, and as we do in his Majesty's *American* Dominions. Were this our Case, we should be rich enough to furnish ourselves with Servants any where.

But if we were not obliged to buy Slaves of our own, we should have Servants enough from other Countries, all the Nations of the Earth would serve us ; nor would their Numbers be then any Grievance, we could not say they came to starve our Poor, take the Bread out of their Mouths, and the like ; we should want them, and they would add to our Wealth, not diminish it.

But to repine that our Poor should be enabled to make themselves Rich, this is such an unnatural Piece of Policy as I never met with before; and the Author I speak of shews as little understanding in the last Part, as he did Religion in the first Part. I shall in my next, give you a Story apposite to the Case, that may have some Instruction in it to this Author, if he is capable of receiving it. In the meantime

I am, Sir, Your Humble Servant,
M. G.

Defence of Education, and the Universities.

A. J., July 20.—Sir, When I sent you the two last Letters upon the Subject of Charity Schools, and upon the abhorr'd Reproach cast upon the Charitable Designs of well Educating the Children of the Poor, I expected nothing of what I have since seen publish'd, namely, that the Grand Jury had resolv'd to Present the Author, and Publisher of that horrid Libel, at the Court of *King's Bench*, in *Westminster*.

The Presentment of a Grand Jury which some make nothing of, and pretend to talk of with Contempt, I take to be this,—

That the Gentlemen who compose that Body, being justly
aggriev'd at such, or such, a Publication of a Libel; as promoting
Atheism, or Prophaneness, discouraging Virtue, Learning and
Charity,—humbly represent the Grievance, as loudly calling for
Justice ; and, in order to this, lay it at the Feet of the Court,
and of the Judges who preside there, in hopes that some
publick Course should be taken, both to suppress the Crime,
and punish the Offenders.

If the Court find the Complaint just, and that there is
Reason to Prosecute the Offenders; it is in their Power to
Prosecute, and bring to Justice in a manner as Effectual, as if
there were an Information brought by any particular Person.
That the Court does, or does not, always direct a Prosecution
whenever the Grand Juries may present, may be, because all
presented Grievances, or Offences, may not be equally Pungent ;
and it doubtless is, and ought to be, in the Breast of the Court
to Judge of that part of the Matter.

But whenever the Court is satisfy'd of the urgency of the
Occasion, I believe they always direct such Prosecutions as the
Law allows in like Cases; as therefore the Offence presented
by the last Grand Jury about Charity Schools is such, and so
Notorious, as in the Presentment is set forth, I make no doubt
but the Court will act in that Case as Justice requires.

I think it cannot be deny'd that to run with foul and indecent Language upon all the venerable Foundations of Learning at our Universities,—upon the Clergy Educated, and
Educating in those Colleges,—and vilify them as this Author
does, is a Great Nuisance in a Christian, and well govern'd
Nation ; To rail at the Universities, as Promoters of the King-
dom of Antichrist, Debauchers of the Principles of the Nobility
and Gentry, depraving their Understandings, advancing learned
Ignorance, loading the Heads of those they Educate with airy
Chimeras, and Fairy Distinctions, filling States with desperate
Beggars, and Divines of Fortune, who must force a Trade for
Subsistence, and become the Cudgels and Tools of Power and
Faction, What is all this ? Is it Satyr ? No ! no ! true Satyr
Reproves with Justice, in order to Amendment ; whereas this is
Causeless Reproach, with Malice and Rage, in order to over-
throw and destroy.

As I said in the Affair of Charity Schools, so I say of this,

of the Universities, had he censur'd the Misbehaviour of those
that Misbehave, the Crimes and Vices of those who are really
Vicious and Criminal; this had been so far justifiable as the
Fact had been capable of Proof; but this Man flies not at the
People in the Universities, but at the Universities themselves,
not at the Governours, but at the Government itself, not at the
Mistakes and Errors of Christians, but even at the Duties of
Christianity itself. He Reproaches the Founders more than
the Fellows, and the Foundation more than the People Established upon the Foundation; so that according to him, our
Universities should be Purg'd by Fire. They should not be
Reform'd, but Transform'd, not Purified but Pull'd down. The
giving Lands and Revenues for the Educating Youth, and
bringing them up to be Servants at God's Altar; the settling
Estates for the erecting Seminaries of Virtue, and Learning,
that Youth may be instructed in the Knowledge of Religion
and Languages together; this is condemn'd as giving Money
to saucy, lazy, and aspiring Ecclesiasticks; boldly Reproaching
the whole Body of the *English* Clergy, as such, without the
least Reserve for the Pious, Learned, Virtuous and Laborious
among the Clergy, of whom (their Enemies themselves being
Judges,) there are Numbers to be found in every Part of the
Nation.

True Satyr Renounces this Practice as abominable. I say
again, it is not *Satyr*, but *Slander!* And what is Slander?
Slander is made up of two eminent Parts. (1.) Malice.
(2.) Falsehood. To say a Man is a Slanderer, is to charge
him with being neither a Christian, nor a Gentleman; for
Malice is inconsistent with a Christian, as *Lying* is with a
Gentleman. Now to say that the Founders of our Universities
were guilty of giving Lands and Revenues to saucy, lazy,
aspiring Ecclesiasticks, is first Malicious, in aspersing the
whole Body, of the present Members of the Colleges; and
second, False, in saying the Founders gave the Revenues to
such; for the Pious and Charitable Founders certainly gave
their Benefactions for the good and pious Uses of Breeding up
a Learned, Pious, and Laborious Clergy, for the propagating
true Religion and Piety, and Virtue in the Nation; and 'tis a
vile belying of their Memory to say otherwise of them.

To what Purpose else did they appoint Visitors of Colleges

to enquire into the Conduct of the Students and Fellows?
Why make Regulations and Constitutions against all manner
of Irregularities, and Immoralities?   And why exact an Oath
of Subjection upon all that are admitted into their Houses?
Was this done to promote Immorality, or to prevent it?   To
excite, or to discourage Vice?   How then can this impudent
scandalous Writer load the Memory of the Pious Founders,
and Benefactors, as encouragers of the Vices of the Clergy,—
as he does afterwards of the whole Clergy, of being guilty of
those Crimes? But 'tis evident this Man's business is to Rave,
and make a Noise, raising a Dust at the Clergy to make the
Office contemptible,—not the Persons only;—that he aims
not at the Ministers, but at the whole Gospel Ministry; and,
if his Doctrine were adhered to, we should soon have neither
Gospel nor Minister among us.

The first Fire-Engine.

A. J., July 20.—On Tuesday last, Mr. Newsham, in New
Street, Cloth Fair, London, play'd his new-invented Engine at
the Royal Exchange, before several Gentlemen there present.
It play'd several Yards above the Dial, with a constant Stream,
above a hundred Gallons each Minute; which must be allow'd
by all ingenious Men that saw it, to exceed all Sorts of Engines
whatsoever.

On the Insufficient Causes of Great Wars.

A. J., July 27.—Sir, In Reviewing the Histories of Ages
past, it has often been an agreeable, and I think a just Reflection, to look back, and see for what small, and if I may use the
Word, what Sordid Trifles, the Princes and Powers severally
then in being, have disturbed the general Repose; and that,
how, upon the Foundations of such small Matters, they have
involved themselves, and the Nations round them, in War and
Confusion.   And this necessarily brings on another Contemplation, no less worthy our Notice in its kind; namely, how few
of the most Bloody and expensive Wars that have been in the
World, have been raised on just Foundations.   Who must then
answer for the Blood, I might say the Seas of Blood, and all
the other Confusions, which have followed, and been the Con-

sequence of those Wars? That is a Story by itself, and may be spoken of by itself.

What was the Occasion of that bloody War between *Abijah* King of *Judah*, and *Jeroboam* King of *Israel?* The latter it seems was Aggressor, and not content with his Revolt—and carrying off ten Tribes from the House of *Solomon* his Master,—so far God allowed him to go; but,—like as Ambition, where it Reigns, prompts all the Tyrants to do,—would have the two Tribes that were left, and this voracious Thirst after the universal Monarchy cost the Lives of 500,000 Men.

But to leave the many Scripture Examples, which indeed our Bibles are full of, what just Occasion had the *Jews*, seeing they had once submitted to the Roman Government; I say, on what just Occasion did they Rebel and cast off the Yoke? The Romans having neither Oppressed them, or provoked them; and yet, this cost the Blood of above a Million of People, besides the total Destruction of their State and Nation?

On what just Occasion did *Alexander* the Great attack the *Persians*, and conquer *Darius?* The Trifle was no more than a Petulant Letter to the *Athenian* General, of no value, and indeed Offering no Injury; and yet in that War, *Alexander* is said to have killed 300,000 *Persians*.

Upon what just Occasion did the *Carthagenians* break with the *Romans*, when *Hannibal*,—having fallen upon their Confederates in *Spain*,—began his March into *Italy*, and carried the War to the Gates of *Rome*; which War cost the Lives, as History relates, of above 500,000 Men in *Italy* itself, and was after, the ruin of the whole Punick Commonwealth?

On what just Occasion did *Julius Cæsar*, at the Head of the *Roman* Legions, invade *Gaul*, conquer the *Helvetians*, and all the Nations between the *Alps* and the lower *Rhine*, and after, passed over into *Britain*, where the *Romans* carried their Armies even to the *Highlands* of *Scotland*, killing all that resisted them, and destroying Millions of People? Nothing can be, or indeed was pretended for it, but to raise the Glory and Dominion of the *Romans* upon the Bones of Nations, and make Havock of Millions of People, that they might Reign over their Posterity.

But to bring this down to Christian Nations, and to Christian Times, when the Laws not of Reason only, but of Religion too, are, *at least in pretence*, submitted to.   On what just Occasion did the *Spanish* General *Cortez*, and after him the Great *Pizarro*, invade the Continents and Islands of *America*, carrying with them the unknown and amazing Terror of *European* War, fall upon innocent and unoffending Nations, and after robbing them of Immense Treasures, such as the World knew nothing of before ; cut the Throats of Twenty, nay, some say Fifty Millions of People, whose only crime, as to the *Spaniards*, was, that they were Possessed of the unexhaustible Golden Mines of Mexico, and the Silver Mountains of *Potosi ?*

Was this sufficient to justify attacking them, dispossessing them of their Country, and afterwards of their Lives ?   To say nothing of these Things, was the bare possessing that Country a Forfeiture in the *Americans ?*   Or was bare discovering of them in the *Spaniards* a Title ?   Did the Thirst of Gold give a Right to the Gold ?   And did the keeping it by the *Indians* give a claim of War to the Aggressors ?

Come we down to Modern Times, *not to approach too near our own ;* Upon what just Foundations were the several bloody Wars raised and carried on, between *Charles* V. Emperor of *Germany*, and *Francis* I. King of *France ;* when, upon reviling one another with scurrilous Names, they drew out so many Armies, and fought so many Battles, and killed so many Men, only to make it out, which of the two deserved the Name of Liar, Perjured and Dishonourable ; when perhaps 'twas easy for the poor People to make it out, that the Titles belong'd very righteously to both of them ?

To jump a little lower, and within our reach, yet out of Danger.   Upon what just Occasion did the King of *Spain* invade *Sardinia* and *Sicily*, after they had conceded to their Restorative Princes by solemn Treaty,—to which he was a Party ;—and upon what pretence were some other Things done by other People about that Time ?

Upon what Foundation of Right did the King of *Poland* attack *Riga*,—and the *Czar* of *Muscovy*, *Narva*,—and the *Turks* the *Morea*,—in the last Age of the War ?

All these, if I may judge, were trifling, and Unjust ; and yet on these Occasions infinite Ravages were made, Countries and Cities were destroyed, and People Murthered.   It remains to enquire in our next, whether the Quarrels of the present Day are more Righteously begun, than those that are past.

Yours,   D——.

On Defects in the Laws against Murder. Who is Responsible?

A. J., Aug. 3.—Sir, I do not often send Questions to you for your Readers to Resolve, but rather Resolve those Questions that others send to you, yet a Question occurs to me, that I do not care to Resolve any other Way than by Enquiry; and therefore, I shall desire you to propose it to the World in Print, that your Readers may Debate it among themselves, and apply their Solutions, as they think fit, to my Question.

When a Murther is committed, or the Blood of a Man is shed, in a Villainous and Wilful Manner, such as the Laws of the Country call *Murther*, and such as those Laws, in concurrence with the Laws of God, appoint to be punished with Death, and that Murther is not searched into; or, if searched into, the Murtherer, tho' really Guilty, is upon his Tryal acquitted. Upon whom does the Guilt of the Blood lie,—or, to speak in a more solemn Manner,—Of whom will Heaven require it?

I might add, if upon any such Murther, the Murtherer upon Tryal is Condemned, but is respited; or, by what Method you please, is not Executed,—*Upon Whom,* &c.

But the first is the Case I desire at present to insist upon, for the other might be liable to Misconstruction of Enemies, which I shall avoid on many Accounts; I say, suppose a Murtherer really Guilty, is yet upon his Tryal, according to the Forms of the Country he lives in, acquitted.

If any Man suggest there are secret Reflections concealed under this Enquiry, and that particular Persons, or Circumstances of Persons are Pointed at; let such Malicious People know I despise them. I neither Point at any Person, or Case; neither do I know any Person in the whole Nation to whom any such Thing so suggested can be applied, or that are any way concerned in such a Case. If I did, I know no Reason why I should be afraid to reprove that which the Laws of God condemn, or to Censure those who are evidently Censured, and to be Censured by the Sovereign Rule, *He that sheddeth Man's Blood, by Man shall his Blood be shed.*

But what I am upon, is to Enquire, whether, seeing 'tis plain by Scripture that innocent Blood, unrevenged, defiles a Land, and that God says he will require it; the acquitting a Murther,—tho' by due Form of Law,—does not leave the Guilt of that Blood upon the Country where it was shed; or, if not, where else is it to lye; for I suppose it to lye somewhere?

There are many Niceties in Forms, Errors, *or what they ordinarily call Flaws,* in an Indictment; Mistakes in the Processes, and the Like; some committed by Clerks, &c., others by other Means, too many to repeat here. These are by Criminals sometimes taken hold of, and put a Stop to all the Course of Justice; and, because the Jury cannot bring him in Guilty in the Manner and Form, as in the Indictment, he must be brought in *Not Guilty,*—for tho' the Person is Guilty of the Fact, he is Not Guilty in the Words of the Indictment,—and consequently the Jury cannot bring him in Guilty at all; and therefore must bring him in *Not Guilty,* and then, tho' he .was really Guilty, he cannot be punished, because being once acquitted, *he cannot be twice put in Hazard* for the same Fact.

Suppose, *for Example,* that a Man is taken up for Murther, and either for want of Witnesses upon his Tryal, or, that he has bought off, or brought off the Witnesses, so as that tho' they knew of the Guilt, yet they would not swear so positively as to affect the Man, and he is acquitted for want of sufficient Evidence; and suppose then, these Men afterwards confess their having done so, and do affirm that they saw him commit the Fact; or, suppose that more competent Witnesses come in afterward, that saw him do it, and offer to Witness it, who before perhaps had not heard of his Tryal, or of his being taken up; yet the Murtherer having been thus acquitted, and the Law not allowing him to be charged again, Where must the Guilt of the Blood be required?

Take another Example, which if I remember happened many Years ago. A Woman was indicted for Murther, having, as the Charge against her set forth, Murthered her BASTARD CHILD. Now it was said to be Fact, that the Child was Murther'd; that the Woman had Murther'd it, and that it was the Woman's child, born of her Body. But it seems it was not her Bastard Child; for that she was Married to the Man who begot the Child, and the Marriage was proved beyond Contradiction; so the Jury could not find her Guilty of Murthering her Bastard.

By this Mistake in the Process, this Woman, as I understood, came off, yet here was a poor Infant Murthered, in a most inhuman, unnatural Manner; and, if innocent Blood must be punished, or will be required, it comes home to my Question. What can be said, and of whom will that Infant's Blood be required?

It will be said, it cannot lye at the Door, either of Judges or Juries, because they are strictly bound by their Oaths to act According to Law, *and I readily grant all that Part.* Well, the Law cannot be charged neither; *that is, by the Law I mean the Legislature,* who provided Laws for that due avenging Innocent Blood upon the Murtherer. Where must it go then? The Errors of the Clerks drawing such Indictments comes next, and they are Guilty of Neglect, that is certain; but you cannot say they are Guilty of any more,—and can they be put to Death? They cannot be Hanged for a wrong Word put in, or left out; that would be adding more Blood to the Account, unless it could be proved they did it with a Design to save the Murtherer, then indeed something might be required of them; nay even the whole Guilt should devolve upon them, and with the Guilt, the Punishment.

But the Guilt must lie somewhere. That is the Principle which my Question is founded upon;—it must lie somewhere, and where is that? Will it not lie upon the whole Nation, till those Niceties are so removed, or such legal Methods taken, that a Murther may be punished at all Times, and whenever the Murther can be proved; by whatever Flaw, or Mistake, or want of Evidence he might have Escaped before?

If this Question were duly weighed, and fully answered, I perswade myself our Government, or our *Legislature,* would concern themselves to remove all such Niceties, as may open the Door to a Criminal to escape, who ought by the Laws of God and Man to be punished.

Why must not a Man be put in Jeopardy twice? Ay, or ten times for one Fact, if after all, his Guilt may at last be proved? It is not so now indeed, and as 'tis Law, I have no

more to say to it; but if by this Nicety a notorious Murtherer
may escape Punishment, and the Guilt of innocent Blood be
left upon the Nations of whom, for ought we know, God wil'
require it; why, *I say, why* should not the Legislature be
humbly desired to consider of it?

I have only proposed the Question, I may say more to
other Branches of it hereafter.   I am, &c.

Of Public Faith, Theoretical and Practical.

A. J., Aug. 10.—Sir, I have heard the Parsons talk much
of FAITH, as a Religious Act; some say CHRISTIAN FAITH
some CATHOLICK FAITH, some one Thing, some another
Others I have heard swear by their FAITH, and when we come
to talk closely to either of these, 'tis not the easiest Thing for
any of them to make us know what they mean, or what their
Faith is. There is another Kind of *Faith* spoken very much
of too, among the People of these Times; and, for aught I see
some of them, who have it oftenest in their Mouths, are as
much at a loss to explain this, as any other,—and this is the
PUBLICK FAITH. Now I would fain have you tell me what is
this weighty Thing called the *Publick Faith?* For there is
much depends upon it.

In some Countries they understand by it the Honour
of their Princes; their words engaged to their Subjects for
their Liberties, or Religion, or any other Thing; and in
that way *Publick Faith* must be a very sacred Thing to be
sure.

In others they understand by it the Assurances given by the
Government, or one Sovereign to another Government, or
another Sovereign, in Leagues and Treaties of Peace, and
Commerce; and these are always held sacred too, or should
be so.

In *Civil Affairs* they call it CREDIT, when Princes, or
Governments, borrow Money of their Subjects; and engage
their Words, Honour, their Veracity, that they shall be repaid
with Interest.

In *Military Affairs*, 'tis the *Besieger* granting Articles of
Surrender, or Capitulation to the *Besieged*, upon the Faith of
which, they give up the Strengths they were possessed of, give
up their Arms, and Magazines, Cannon and Ammunition, and

put themselves naked into the Hands of their Armed Enemy. Or, 'tis two Generals at the Head of two opposite and powerful Armies, making a Truce, or Cessation of Hostilities, by which they converse freely and friendly with one another, and are good Friends for a Day or two, who were a Day before inveterate Enemies; who when the Truce ends, fall to knocking one another's Brains out as heartily as before.

In immediate Matters of Government, and Transactions between one Sovereign, or one Nation and another; 'tis the said Princes making Leagues, Alliances, and Confederacies one with another, and one against another, to carry on a War, or to prevent a War, and to make Peace after a War, or to guarrantee and preserve any Peace after it has been made; and these Treaties of Peace are always mutually signed by the respective Princes, or their *Plenipo's*, and sometimes are most solemnly sworn to, either side calling God to witness of their sincere Resolution to keep sacred the Articles to which they have agreed.

Now I would fain inquire a little what this *Publick Faith* is? We see above what it means, what it should be, what it ought to be; but let us inquire a little *what it is*, and of what Weight in the Balance of Men's Conduct in the World.

The Question, *I say*, is, of what Weight is this Thing call'd *Publick Faith* in the World? And how far do the GODS *of the Earth* regard it. (I suppose you know who are the Gods of the Earth.)

I observe there is now a general Harmony of Peace in the World. The Temple of *Janus* is shut. There is not the least War, or preparation for *War* among all the Princes of *Europe*. There is not a Regiment of Men anywhere employed, other than in the ordinary Guard of their own Princes,—except some Regiments sent to keep the Peace in the *Dutchy* of *Mecklenburgh;* and they do nothing but negatively withhold the Duke and his Subjects from Violence; and—except what the *Czar* of *Muscovy* is about,—and some say, we have no true Account of that Part neither.

Except those, I say, all the World is at Peace. The Swords are turned into Plowshares, and the Spears into Pruninghooks, *and all the Christian World is at Peace.*

But alas! How long will this Calm last? And whenever

the several Princes fall out again, what shall we say to the *Publick Faith* all the While ?

When the late *Louis*, of glorious Memory, fell into the States' Dominions in *Holland*, because his Majesty had Reason to be *ill satisfied* with the States,—though all his former Leagues and Treaties with them *were subsisting ;*—doubtless that *Male-satisfaction* was a sufficient Ground for him to break the little Trifle call'd *Publick Faith.*

When the same King of *France*, after the most, solemn Ratifications of the *Pyrenean* Treaty, and after having sworn to the Renunciation—upon his Marriage with the *Infanta* of *Spain*,—yet fell into *Flanders*, and seized three whole Provinces, and afterwards great Part of the Rest, on the pretended Right of *Devolution*,—and kept most of them to his Death ; what was this, but from the most profound Regard he had to the *Publick Faith ?*

When the next King of *Spain*, being in profound Peace, fitted out a Fleet, and embarked an Army on Board, and intending a War,—though without any Declaration,—first fell upon the Island of *Sardinia*, (then Imperial,) and then upon Sicily, being under the new King thereof,—whom he had recognized,—and took both these Kings by Surprize ; *what was all this*, but a most exact Regard to the *Publick Faith ?*

What need I go to the *Turks* in *Africa*, or the *Moors* of *Barbary ?* What has the *Czar* of *Muscovy* now in Hand, but to break with the *Danes*, upon the Trifle,—in order, the more effectually, to preserve the *Publick Faith ?*

What did the King of *Poland* intend, when he fell upon the *Swedes*, and particularly upon the City of *Riga*, in a Time of profound Peace,—and at the same Time brought the *Muscovites* and the *Danes* to fall together upon the King of *Sweden*,—then a Youth,—and wholly unprepared for War ; all which Powers were then under sacred Treaties of Peace with *Sweden*, which Treaties then subsisted unbroken, and undisputed ? I say, what did they all intend, but to take the utmost care of, and shew the greatest Regard to—*Publick Faith ?*

How has the *Common Faith* been made a *Common Whore !* And how have these Nations, nay, all the Nations in the World, except *Great Britain*, used her as such ! Nor am I to be reproached for excepting my own Country upon such a momentous Occasion ; I have abundance of good Reasons for it, *and that is enough.*

But to come to another Point. Since then the *Public Faith* is so on all Occasions prostituted to the Lusts and Ambition of Men, how long 'can we expect these Halcyon Days of Peace will continue in *Europe?*

May we not expect, that whenever the *Stronger Party* comes to have an Advantage over the Weaker, that Stronger will find Reason for *Male-satisfaction?* May we not see Reason to expect, that the enterprizing Princes of *Europe,*—when such shall come to reign—will take the like Freedoms with this fair Lady, *Publick Faith,* and make her stoop to their Conveniences? Alas! what is *Publick Faith* to a *Muscovite* Army and Navy, claiming to go Toll-free through the Sound? What is *Publick Faith* to the *Grand Seignior,* if he think fit' to quarrel with the Emperor,—or the *Venetians,*—or the Knights of *Malta?*

I could enter farther into my particular Reasons for this Reflection. But, upon the whole, seeing this is the Case, how can we expect the Continuance of this peaceable Disposition in the World? How can we expect the Harmony should last? I do not expect it indeed, and my Reasons are very good ; and may in Time be said more to, *but not yet.*

I am, &c.

Cautious Reference to the Czar, and his New Fleet.

A. J., Aug. 17.—Sir, As Rumour is no Authority for writing News; so on the other Hand, when News is published with good Authority, I am always for giving Credit to it, at least till some farther Account appears to contradict it. Upon a Supposition, therefore, that such News is true, we that stand without Doors, may I hope be allowed to make some Remarks, especially when at so great a Distance. . . . . I remember a certain known Author was brought into Trouble in former days for putting it into his Paper, that the Duke of *Luxemberg* was hump-shouldered ; and he learned to use foreign Princes and Generals the better for it as long as he lived. I won't, therefore, by any means say that the *Czar* of *Muscovy* is a Mimick,—that he makes a Water Theatre of the *Baltick Sea,*—or that he makes War a Stage Play. Though I can-

not forbear thinking of such Things as these, for my Life.
. . . .

On Cryptography.

M. J., Aug. 17.—Since my first giving the Publick a
Letter in *Cyphers,* which I explain'd, I have receiv'd several
others to the same Effect; and some of my Correspondents are
so fond of the Humour, that they will write to me no other
Way, by which means it takes me up as much Time and Study
to come at the Sense of an Epistle, as it does a School Boy
to construe his Lesson; and, if the Whim continues, I shall be
oblig'd to keep an extraordinary Secretary for decyphering,
which must cause a Deficiency in my private Civil List, and
oblige me to lay a Tax upon the Publick, for the Service of
the Year,—that is, raise the Price of my Paper.

I can assure my Readers, I never had any Notion of
Pleasure in a Fox Chase, where a Man rides till he Fatigues
himself, and then digs to come at the Fox; I say, after he has
taken all these Pains, and has killed his Game, he finds the
Beast is good for nothing.   Thus it has fared with me in some
of these Tryals of Skill; I have pored and studied to unravel
all the Intricacies of one of these Letters, and when I have
discovered all, I have met with nothing to reward my Trouble,
or that could entertain my Readers; so that I have had my
Labour for my Pains.

But perhaps, it may be the Fashion now, to invent new
Alphabets; and the Modes alter in these Things, as much, and
as often as in Dress.   I remember once a Man was reckoned
Ignorant and Ill-bred, who, in writing to a Person of any Condition, did not make at least two-thirds of his Paper to consist
of Margin.   After this Fashion had its Run, it became a Piece
of Rudeness to make any Margin at all, and it was Polite to
begin the Letter very low, leaving a large void *Area* at Top,
so that the first Page of a well-bred Epistle was almost a
carte-blanch.   I expect very soon that some whimsical
Person, who is considerable enough to be followed and flattered; will introduce a new Mode of beginning the Letter at
the bottom of the Page, and writing up to the Top, as the
Hebrews were accustomed to do.   No Time can be more apt
to receive such a Custom than the present, when all Actions

seem to run retrograde, and Men act backwards in all
Things.

But this Maggot of writing in Cyphers and Figures, is not
entirely new, a Whim not unlike it started up some Years
since, when several elaborate Pieces were published for the
Edification of the Youth of this City, under the Title of *Tunbridge Letters ;* in which certain Figures were made use of to
stand for Words and Syllables. It seemed an ingenious Invention of writing Shorthand, after a long laborious Manner ; as
if going round about had been the nearest Way Home.

Yet this was the Summer's Entertainment of our Beaus
and Belles, at which Sport, when a Man had taken as much
Pains as a Dutch Commentator, and was come to the End
of his Labours ; he discovered a miserable Piece of Nonsense,
without Meaning or Design, a Diversion only fit for those
who otherwise would pass their Time at the more ingenious
Amusement of catching Flies.

I find this Folly ridiculed by *Ben Jonson* in his celebrated
Play of the *Alchymist,* where *Abel Drugger* causes his Name
to be writ upon his Sign, with the Letter *A* and a Bell
painted, for Abel, the Letter *D,* with a Rug, and a Dog
grinning, for *Drugger.* So that we find that this is only an
old Folly reviv'd.

This kind of Learning was first borrowed from the
Egyptians, who used it to purposes, very different from what
our Moderns have done ; 'tis said, that under the Figures of
Birds and Beasts, the Mysteries of their Religion were couch'd,
and that the Magicians discovered this Way, in order to conceal
them from the Vulgar.

After this, they used the same figurative Way of expressing
the Qualities of the Body, or Virtues of the Mind, and particularly upon the Tombs of great Men ; as Strength was express'd
by an Elephant, Faithfulness by a Dog, and this was their
manner of writing Epitaphs.

We follow the Example in our Days in Respect to the Living ;
and we find a Way of praising the Qualities of a Man by the
Choice of the Presents we make him,—as a Lion, which is an
Emblem of Courage and Generosity, is commonly presented
to a King ; whereas we give Parrots to Women,—and I have
known a Monkey sometimes presented to a Beau.

And in this Way of communicating one's Thoughts, a Man
may be Satyrical, and give others a Hint of their Vices, as well
as by Writing; for when we find ourselves vex'd and oppressed by Persons too powerful for us to contend with in a
lawful Way, we may ridicule their Vices in a Manner not
cognizable by a Statute.

I have heard a Story of an arbitrary Minister in *France*, who
was a Persecutor of the Wits of that Age in general; but he
pursued one with a more than common hatred. The merry
Sufferer was every now and then sending his Persecutor something to remember him, as an *Ape* or a *Cat*, or other *Animals*,
which are the Images of Malice and Revenge. The ridiculous
Presents were always attended with Crowds of People, to the
Gates of that great Man, for all Men were pleased with anything
that ridiculed him; and he was at length convinced, that he had
better correct those Vices that provoked the general Hatred
against him, than in the Wantonness of his Power, to crush a
poor Man much superior to himself in every Thing that's commendable, only for endeavouring by his Writings to entertain
and instruct the People.

The Turks have a Way of communicating their Thoughts to
each other, different from any before-named. It is a Correspondence invented to carry on the Affairs of Love; and nothing
is more common there, than for a Lady to receive a *Billet doux*
in a Nosegay, which she answers, by sending back another Nosegay, and the Lover knows his Fate, by perusing the Flowers.
Perhaps it may be thought that he who has the finest Garden
may be the most eloquent in this Way of Address; but that
does not always follow, for it is not in the Quantity, but in the
Choice of the Flowers, and the different Manner of ranging
them, by which the Lover signifies the Tenderness of his Passion, and lets his Mistress know his Pain; but be that as it
will, it is certain that an 'Amour is often carried on by an Intercourse of this Kind, and the Lovers, perhaps, never talk to
one another till they meet to have the Ceremony of Marriage
performed.

I could teach my Readers this mystick Art of making up
Love Nosegays, but I forbear it out of a Consideration, that
it may tend to promote Clandestine Marriages, and instruct
young Ladies how to deceive and outwit their Guardians and

Parents; and it is often found that in Love Affairs they are but too witty already.

The Harburg Lottery Bubble. A Word for Lord Barrington.

A. J., Aug. 24.—Sir, Bubbles were grown so Stale a Snare, after the Detecting the Frauds of the late Direction of the South Sea Company, that we thought it was impossible the People of *England* should have been any longer in Danger of being drawn in, or imposed upon, But

> " Of all the flagrant high Extremes of Vice,
> There's none so void of Sense as Avarice."

Had all the Honourable, and the Right Honourable Persons who had raised immense Fortunes by the Shares they had in the cunning Part of the South Sea Affair acted in their Senses at last, and abandoned them in Time, they might not only have saved their Characters, but have been able to have made some Reparation to the Families, whom they had injured; but they went on, and their own Ruin gave the Sufferers some Satisfaction, though not such as in Justice they had Room to demand.

But the Sufferers, not warned sufficiently by their own Harms, permitted two Sets of Bubble Engineers to operate upon them still, and blinded by the general Avarice of the Times, submitted to be cajoled still with hopes of golden Mountains; and so the Crafty found the Way still to dip their Fingers in the Pockets of the Simple, till the Fate of Bubbles in general came upon them.

> " So the unskilful Engineer
> Who fires an ill-charg'd Mine,
> Sinks in the Rubbish of his Works,
> And spoils his own Design."

When I say two Sorts of Bubbles remained, I do not tell you I mean the *Harburgh* Lottery, and the *York Buildings* Company; but this I may say of them both, which I hope can give no Offence; that if any Man of Common Understanding, ever took those two Projects to be anything else but Bubbles, unless it be something much worse; I repeat it again, I may say, *I wonder at them.*

We find in the last of these, a Person of Noble Rank, and unspotted Character, has quitted the Service, or the Command, call it as you please; 'tis not for us to give Reasons for it. The World guesses his Lordship's Reasons to be very good, and indeed so do I, and I believe the World guesses at those Reasons too.

Had the Right Honourable Person concerned in the FIRST of them thought to have quitted, in the same timely manner, I believe he had not given room for Knaves to lay the Scandal of their Designs at his Door; nor for the Public Justice to take cognizance of him to his Disadvantage.

Men of Design love dearly to have high Patrons; not only to Disguise their Frauds, in order to push them with more Success upon the World, but to bear the weight of the popular Clamour, when that Fraud is Detected.

Do Men think there were no Knaves in the South Sea Administration but the Directors, and those few that bore the Weight with them? Was the *Harburgh* Lottery the single Act and Project of only the Person that suffered the Blast of it? No, no! all Projects have a Head, but they have also Members.

Now here is a Bubble made Notorious, and the Right Honourable Person, on whose Reputation perhaps some Men thought they could build a *Babel* of their own Imagination, has quitted; and they are now left to themselves deceived, and are without a Head. Let us see what Measures they will take to lick into Shape again the Creatures they have to nurse.

Will they tell us that a Stock, whose intrinsick was affirmed to be worth between 30 and 40 *per cent.* cannot stand at seven and a half? And that Men could be so blind, as to decline to pay a call upon a Stock intrinsically worth 25 *per cent.* above the Market Price? Can this be, and no Fraud, either in the present Practice, or the past? If the Stock is now worth but seven and a half, How can it be true that it was worth 33 or 40? If it be worth more than seven and a half, Why is it offered so low, and why so few Buyers? If it was affirmed to be worth 33, it was True, or, it was not; if not, then it was a Bubble in those that affirmed it to be worth, really worth it. What's become of the Intrinsick? Who has lessened it? Delude the World no more you Men of Bites and Projects, two Things are before you.

EITHER produce the Money, the Missing of which has made it less; OR, produce the Men that affirmed it to be more.   Your Humble Servant,

                    A SUFFERER.

Protection of Home Manufactures. Arbitrary Proceedings.

A. J., Aug. 24.—They continue to make Seizures of Garments made of India Damask, and Plague innocent People in all Parts of the Town, with searching their Houses, and taking away their Clothes; but 'tis hoped a Stop will soon be put to these Outrages, in regard that last Week they took five Suits of Clothes out of Mr. Pott's Family, an Oil Man in Grace-Church Street, who is resolved to stand Tryal with them the ensuing Term; when 'twill Appear whether these Proceedings are legal or not, and People will know how to act for the future.

A Satire against Dissembling.

A. J., Aug. 31.—Sir, As I was viewing the other Day a new Sign setting up for the Salutation Tavern in —— Street, there comes a Frenchman by, when seeing me stop, he stops too, and looks down upon the two Figures, which were of two Spaniards saluting one another, with Leg and Hand, Grin and Grimace, as is usually the Figure, and the Frenchman falls a laughing, "*Her be de ver prety Show, raree Show, Ma foi !*" says he; "*dis be de Sign of de two Dissemblers.*" I laid up his Words awhile in my Thoughts; but going the next Day into a Friend's Garden, I saw there among other Curiosities, a Glass Bee-hive; a Thing so exquisitely wrought, that it discovered all the Œconomy of that well-governed Society, or Brotherhood of the Bees; and where you might see the Arcana of their Government, with all the Beauties of a regulated Monarchy, that was both Kingdom and Commonwealth. I was musing some while upon this, and it afforded me room for some curious Speculations. But when the two Dissemblers came on a sudden into my Thoughts, all my Reflections wheeled round to this,—how admirable a Light it would afford, and how many useful Discoveries would be made for the inquiring World, could the Heart of Man be formed up into the Similitude of a Glass Beehive; that all the secret Motions, Operations, and

Conclusions formed there, by the Understanding and Will might be looked into; the Passions, the Affections, the Designs, the Resolutions, the Measures taken, and to be taken, be seen and known! What *Terra Incog.* would here be laid open! What Scenes of Treason, Murther, Rebellion, Malice, Rage, Lust, and Love, would here be laid open! How would the real black Ends of the brightest Pretences be laid open; the Aversion concealed under the Veil of Affection; the Secret Frowns of Envy covered under the Pretences of Friendship; the Treachery personated by Sincerity; the Avarice covered with the Smiles of disinterested Love; the Robbery disguised by Services; and the Hate self-mask'd with Charity, be all opened and disclosed!

The fawning Salutations of all the most obedient Humble Servants,—Whores Vows,—Courtiers Promises,—what Inside would they discover! I heard of an Odd Story of a certain Widow, within ten Mile of an Oak, that having a Mind to be undone, sent a Friend to enquire after the Character of her Lover; and that she might be sure to be Cheated, sends him to one of her Lover's near Relations, and the Lover with him.

Now whatever the Widow might learn this Way of her Lover's Inside, she fairly put the Glass Beehive upon herself; that is to say, any Body might see her Inside; that is to say, she wanted to have the Fellow, right or wrong.

There are, Sir, abundance of People whose Conduct is a Glass Beehive to themselves. They betray their own Folly and Madness in the ordinary Conduct of their Lives; we need no other Light into their Meaning than they give us by their Foolish Behaviour. If a Man fawns upon me with an uncommon Meanness; stoops below himself as a Man—as a Gentleman;—laughs always in my Face, and protests his Innocence, when no Body accuses him;—his Friendship, when 'tis good for Nothing, and the like;—why, such a Man, in the Language of common Reasoning, has some secret Design to carry on; something to make of me that I know not yet of. The Glass Beehive is upon him, and I may certainly guess at him, and ought to be shy of, and guard against him.

It is as evident to me, that this Man is a Cheat, and has some Secret Design in his Head; as it is, that the Widow intends to marry the Puppy, that fawns upon, and wags his Tail at her, though she puts on the outward Pretence of enquiring after his Character.

How plainly were the Frauds and Cheats of our late *South-Sea* Bubbles to be seen in the smooth, gilded Wheedles of the late Managers, had not Avarice blinded the Eyes of Mankind just at that Time, and covered them with a general Infatuation to their Ruin!

How easy do the Eyes of the wakened World see now into the like Attempts from our late York Building Bubbles, tho' put upon them with the same Art and more Impudence! Even that Impudence, and those Attempts are like so many Glass Beehives to the Inside of their Practice. Let them refund what's embezzled, let them give a just Account of Calls paid in; and then Something may be thought better about them than we think yet. But, as Things now stand, 'tis the Widow and the Lover; if any Man meddles, it must be, that, like the Widow, he resolves to be bit.

How happy, on the other Hand, is it for the greatest Part of Mankind, that Nature has made no Glass Beehives to the Heart; that it is not in Man to know what is in Man! What a Sink of Wickedness! What a Hell of Treachery and Falshood would be every Day the Subject of our Speculations!

How many blushing Brides would appear to be rejected ——! How many Modest looking Youths would appear distempered, debauched Carcases! How many richly appearing Merchants, to be real Bankrupts! How many, sworn for loyal Subjects, be inveterate Rebels! And abjuring Courtiers appear perjuring Traytors! Blessed Fate of Men! How happy are we, that we see no more than the Outsides of one another! And where is the Man who could bear an Inspection into the Inside of his Soul?   Yours, &c.

On the Oaths of Allegiance and Abjuration.

A. J., Sept. 7.—Sir, I must confess when I read all the witty Works of the Day, and found them all chiming in with one another, upon the Great Subject of taking the Oaths to the Government; I expected some mighty Strength of Argument on both sides of the Question. I thought the *True Briton*, who they say writes fine, would have given us some neat Turns on this side of the Question. And I thought the

Whigs, if they had any fine Things to say, as they boast much they have; would have said something very pungent on the other Side.

But when I came to examine them to the Bottom, I found the first, only Turning the Subject into Banter and Ridicule, obliquely lashing the People he points at, by that odd old Fashioned Thing called *Ironical Praise*. I found that foolishest of all Whiggish Writers, the *Flying Post*, gratifying his Enemies by appearing concern'd for his Friends; and by Consequence, doing them, *as Ever was his Case*, more harm than good.

I am astonished, when, throughout these polite Writers, as we must call them,—and with all the Wit and Satyr, by which the *True Briton*, they say, recommends himself to the World,—there is not yet offered one Substantial Reason, why,—in a Nation, where 'tis apparent, the Government has Friends and Enemies,—some Rule should be Establish'd if possible, to know one from the other. And on the other Hand, the Whigs, so far as I have read them, have not entered into the true Merit of this Part of the Question,—Whether the taking, or not taking the Oaths, as now prescribed by Law, will effectually discover to the Government as above, who are their Friends, and who are their Enemies?

While then they Act thus, (as a poor Fellow said to me the other Day by way of Pun), to what purpose is all this Swearing at one another about Swearing?

If it were as true that Oaths in *England* were binding on all Parties, as it is True, that they ought to be so; I should be most violently for the Government's imposing all the Oaths they thought needful upon the People. Because 'tis certainly true, that all Governments ought not only to bind their Subjects to them in the solemnest Manner possible; but also to know, as above, who are Bound, and who are Free.

But on the other Hand, all the People, who either object against imposing these Oaths, or who talk so wickedly and weakly about them; seem to me not to know well what they are doing.

I. Those who argue for taking them, but give no Reason why we should comply with it, other than Noise and Raillery; write a Satyr upon their Party at least, if not upon their

Masters, for imposing such Things as they (their Champions) can give no Reason for.

II. They who, after all their Banter and Jest at the Oaths, offer no substantial Reasons why we ought not to take them, make a Satyr without a Sting; and if they lash any where, they lash the whole Body of the People of Great Britain in general, as if Oaths were not treated by them with due Solemnity.

What mean the keenest and most Satyrical Turns which we meet with, in either the *Briton*, or any other, about taking the Oaths? They seem indeed to jest at the imposing the Oaths, but then it must be as supposing it to be a needless and use-less Thing; which it is to no Purpose to do, because of no Consequence when done. And this, were it true, would be a bitter Satyr upon all the People of Great Britain, as if they would swear anything, and not value Six-pence what they swore; but as I cannot grant this, so 'tis begging the Question most grossly, for them to advance it without Evidence of Fact.

It may be true, that some do not value all the Oaths you can offer them; but 'tis hard to say so of a Nation, or so much as to think so.

'Tis evident the Parliament were of another Opinion; and we must be so too in Charity, till we have some Evidence of the Contrary.

It may be true, that some Men have taken the Abjuration, and then have Rebelled; but to say therefore, that all that have taken it will Rebel, is saying nothing at all, and can no more be admitted, than it can, that all that take it for the future, will be loyal to King *George*.

Till therefore the *True Briton*, or any of the Writers, assign one good Reason to prove that Oaths are needless and useless, their Jest is lost, and their Satyrs are disarmed; and, till the Scribblers on the other Side can assign some better Reasons for taking them, than I have yet seen among them, they ought to cease Writing; seeing, a good Cause ill Defended, is, in the worst Sense, betrayed.

Upon the whole, I send you here two Questions, One on either Side. If they would enter into the Decision of my Doubts on either of them, I believe they would do a Service to the Government, and to the whole Nation, and perhaps put an end to the Debate.

1. Is it not possible that some Men, who are true and faithful,—constant Friends, and Loyal Subjects, to the present Government, and to the Person of King *George,*—may yet have some Scruples to them; seeming so Justifiable, and to them so Essential, as, that they cannot Satisfy their Consciences in taking the Oaths? And may not such be, some how or other, distinguished from *Jacobites?*

2. Is there any Rule which can, or may be prescribed, by which they may more Effectually discover to the Government, who are, and who are not, Loyal and Sincere in their Fidelity to King *George,* than by this of the Oaths?

On Unnecessary Oaths.

A. J., Sept. 14.—I knew a very good Man, a thorough hearty Whig, a mortal Enemy to the Jacobites, and to all Jacobite Princes, who with the utmost freedom and Sincerity, took the Oaths to King *George.* But coming into some Business which required taking them a second Time, he declined it, and at length positively refused it, whatever Penalty or Danger to himself attended the Refusal; and yet he had not in the least changed his Revolution Principles, or become one jot the greater Favourer of the Chevalier, or his Party; but purely that he thought it Sinful to repeat the taking the Oaths, he having already taken them, and thereby assured the Government of his Loyalty, and giving no Room in any part of his Life afterward to have his Conduct questioned or suspected. By the same Rule, I hope, I may without Offence say, other Men may have other Scruples, perhaps of no more Weight than that above named: But what now must these Men do? Must they be *numbered among Transgressors,* and lose their Estates if they do not? Must they be Stiled Recusants, Convicts, and the like?

Murder of English Gentlemen near Calais.

A. J., Sept. 21.—Colonel Churchill and some other Gentlemen who are arrived in Town, have brought a melancholy Account of the Murder of five English Gentlemen, that were set upon by Highwaymen at a Village about four Leagues

from Calais, in their way to Paris.   Some of the Gentlemen
were in two Post Chaises, and the Villains, as soon as they
had taken from them their Money, shot Mr. Seabright (Brother
to Sir Thomas Seabright) through the Heart, and then made
a Signal for dispatching all the rest; upon which one of the
Gentlemen shot at the Rogues and killed one of their Horses;
but at length they were all Murdered, together with their Servants.   While this was doing, one Mr. Locke, another English
Gentleman, happened to pass by from Paris in his Way to
Calais, and unfortunately met with the same Fate, but his Servants escaped.

On Monday last the Junior, Capt. Adams, did arrive in the
River from Calais, having on board the Bodies of the four un-
fortunate Gentlemen, above mentioned, viz. Mr. Seabright,
Mr. Davis, Mr. Mompesson, and Mr. Locke; the Servants
that were Killed at the same Time being buried in that
Country.

We hear, that the Son of the Woman who furnishes the
Post Chaises at Calais, is violently suspected of being one of
the Murderers; and by the Pains they took to flea and mangle
the Horse which Mr. Davis shot, 'tis supposed that they live
in that Neighbourhood, from whence it is justly hoped that
they will in a little Time be all discovered.   Meantime the
Cause of this Misfortune is ascribed to the English Gentlemen's
exchanging too publickly their Guineas into French Specie; by
which means the Ruffians came to be acquainted with the Sum
of Money they had among them, which was upwards of 300*l.*

On the Same.

A. J., Sept. 21.—Sir, We have a Melancholy Account in
our Newspapers of this last Week, of the Robbing Four
English Gentlemen in *France,* on the Road between *Calais*
and *Bologn,* on their way to *Paris.*   The Robbing them of
their Money had been no Surprize, and would have been no
more than what our *English* Highway Gentry have often done
by the *French* Gentlemen in their Travels over *Gad's Hill,* or
Shooter's Hill, or such convenient Places, in their Way to
London.

But to Murther them all in cold Blood, as we call it, after
they had taken 350 Pistoles from them, and made no Resis-

tance to them ; this is such a Piece of Cruelty and Barbarity that I have not heard of the like, no, not in foreign Parts.

It has been the Custom in *Germany,* and in *Italy,* and other Parts beyond Seas, to attack Travellers upon the Road with their Fusees ; that is, to Shoot them first, and rob them afterwards ; and the Reason of that is something Plain, because Travellers generally riding well-Armed, if they Demanded their Money before they fir'd at them, they might perhaps be Answered *Au coup de Fusil,* from the mouth of their Fusee, and so might be Killed themselves. But to Murther Men after they had quietly delivered their Money, and the Sum so considerable too, as one would think might have Bribed the Rogues to Civility, at least so much, as to spare Men's Lives ;—this I think is unusual, and moves me to make some Remarks for your Observation.

1. The folly of our *English* Gentlemen Travelling in foreign Countries *without Arms,* is not to be excused ; the Way of Robbing in *France,* and other distant Countries, being not such as in *England.* Had these Gentlemen been all well Armed, and their Servants also,—had they carried in their Post Chaises, each Man a good Blunderbuss, or a Carabine, or Pistols ; either the Gang must have been stronger, or they would not so Tamely have been either Plundered, or Murthered. But naked, or at best, having only Pistols ; and, as I am informed, their Servants having none,—they fell a Prey to Villains.

2. The folly of exposing the Charge of Money they carried about them, in a Country where Poverty is at present so much the reigning Distemper, as it is in *France ;* if Occasion makes a Thief, the Occasion of shewing a Sum of 300 Guineas Publickly in *Calais,*—as we are told these Gentlemen did, to get them changed into *Louis d'Ors,*—might very probably be the Occasion of this Robbery.

3. It seems to me out of Question, that some of the Persons concern'd in changing those Guineas, or in procuring them to be changed, must be the Men ; and that this Occasioned the Villains murthering of them, that they might not be afterwards Detected. So Desperate is the Nature of Guilt, that it will stick at no after-Crime to cover the first.

I remember a Highwayman executed at *Tyburn* in King *Charles* II. Reign, lamented the Generosity of his Employment a little before his Execution, on this very Subject; and that, in very extraordinary Terms : " The Gentlemen of the *Highway in England*," says he, " are generally put to Death for their Humanity and generous Usage of those they Rob.   I am not hanged," says he, " for Robbing Mr. ——, but I am hanged for sparing his Life.   If I had bravely Killed him," said he, " as I might easily have done ; if I had Shot him thro' the Head, before I asked him for his Money, I had not now have been in Fetters,—he had not come in against me upon my Tryal,—nor had I been now to dye for it.   But I have spared his Life, and now he requites me by taking away mine."

I make no doubt, but had this Man escaped, he would never have robbed any Man afterwards, but he would have Murthered him at the same Time ; but a just Execution put a Stop to his Resentment, and he was hanged in good Season to prevent the bringing up the Custom among us.

It has been a Dispute among several Men of Judgment in this Affair, whether the general Neglect of our Safety in *England*, as to Highway Robbers, and riding Naked and Unarmed, as almost all our Gentlemen do, be better or worse ; and whether it occasions the more Robberies, or not, encreases the Gangs of Highwaymen, or not.

I shall state it in a few Words, as to the Encrease or Decrease of Robberies. I believe 'tis much the same, and would be the same, did all Men ride Armed, as they do in other Countries ; only, that if Men went Armed, two Evils would follow, which I think would render Travelling much more Dangerous than it is, and so it would be worse rather than better.

1. Highwaymen would rob in greater Gangs than they do now, and would go otherwise Armed than they do now ; they would carry Fusees or Fowling Pieces, and we should have every now and then, not bare Rencounters only, as between Man and Man ; but we should have little pitch'd Battles upon the Highway, between the Travellers and the Robbers ; the first Travelling in good Companies for their Defence, and the other in Troops for securing their Success, and their Retreat after it.

2. Highwaymen would not then bid you deliver your Money, and take what you give them, as they often do now ; but they would Attack you Sword in Hand, and first make the Coun-

quest, killing those that resisted, then leading the Prisoners and Coaches out of the Roads into Woods, and By-places, there Rifle, Strip, Bind, Gag, Ravish, and Murther, and what they pleased, as they do abroad. So that, in a Word, the *English* Gentlemen's riding Unarmed is really their Safety; and 'tis a vulgar Error to think they would be more Secure, if they all rode with Arms. It would only alter the Method of Robbing, and make the Highwaymen Murther first, and Rob afterwards, as is practised in other Countries; and 'tis to give our Gentlemen a due Caution of this kind, that I send you this Letter.   Yours, &c.

On Circumstances affecting Health and Disease.

A. J., Sept. 28.—Sir, Every good Man has an Eye, in all his Actions, to the good of others, as well as to himself, and (in a time of public Calamity especially,) will put to his Hand in every Case where he can be helpful.

We have a very Sickly Time here, and abundance of People die; Nay, if you will believe some People, there are more die than we hear of, and more than is usual on like Occasions. Now, I am no Physician, or Apothecary, neither do I intend to prescribe either Simples, or Compounds; and yet there may be something to be said, for general Admonition on this Occasion.

1. I think we should not alarm People more than need requires, nor give them the Vapours, where the Vapours may be prevented. The famous *French* Comedy, call'd *Malade Imaginaire* might be as suitable to be acted in *London*, as ever it was in *Paris*; and I make no Question but we have a great many People here, every Day, who *Die* for fear *of Death*. I went to visit a Relation the other Day, who they said was at the Point of Death. When I came to her, I ask'd her *how she did*, she answer'd, "O! it is a very sickly Time, Cousin!" " Well, so indeed it is," said I, " But what is your Distemper pray?" " O! Cousin," says she, " I am very Weak, why, there is a Multitude of People die;" *I said Yes again*, but still lay at her to tell me, what ailed her; "O! I am very bad, Cousin, and I was willing to see you before I die. Why, you had a terrible Weekly Bill last Week, Cousin!" And this (over and over again,) was all I could get from her.

At length I heard that the Doctor was come. It seems he

was sent for too, as well as I; and I expected they would send
for the Minister too, after the Physician was gone. The
Doctor after making the usual Compliment of, "*How do you
find yourself, Madam?*" Took hold of her Arm to feel her
Pulse, and found all well there, no Fever upon her; examined
the state of her Intestines, found she had no Dysentery, no
Looseness, neither was she Costive; she had neither Ague nor
Palsy, Gout, Rheumatism, or Dropsy, Stone or Gravel. But
she was very bad, and gave him the same Account of its being
a very Sickly time all over the Town, that abundance of People
died, *and the like*. The Doctor, who saw the Bottom of it, told
her, roundly,—"*Madam, it is a very Sickly time*, that's true,
but you are well enough; I know nothing you ail, unless you
intend to die because other Folks die. *Come, come*," says he,
"*get up, and don't lye Vapouring here; take a Glass of good
Canary and a Toast, and take your Coach, and ride out, and
visit your Friends, and Divert yourself, and you'll be well
enough.*" Upon this, and some cheerful Discourse, my Cousin
mended presently; in a Word, as soon as she knew she *was
not Sick, she was presently well*. One good Glass of Sack did
all the Cure. In short, she was Sick of a *Weekly Bill;* being
frighted, apprehensive, and alarmed at other People's being
Sick, she fancied herself Sick too; and, for ought I know,
would have died in a Day or two more, only because so many
other People died.

I think I see something of this in all the Rumours of Infection, or Unwholesomeness, either in the Season, the Air, the
Fruit, the Oysters, and the like, which People clamour themselves into Mischief with at this Time; and I venture to say
they are generally, if not universally, empty, insignificant,
needless, but not harmless Alarms. 'Tis neither the Fruit, or
the Fish, or the Weather; but 'tis the immoderate Eating of
Fruit, immoderate Drinking of cold Liquors to cool the Blood,
or intemperate inflaming with hot Liquors; these are the
Foundations of our Distempers. Nor is this any more than
is usual, or as I may say, always happens in dry Seasons, and
plentiful Years of Fruit.

He then that would administer good Physick to the Distemper of the present Time, and under the Circumstances we
now speak of, should perswade the good People to abate their

Excesses of all kinds; neither to eat Fruit immoderately, which throws them into Fluxes, and Gripings in the Bowels, Convulsions, and other nervous Diseases, nor drink hot Liquors intemperately, which on the other Side bring Fevers, and Calentures, and destroy them that Way.

For People to live intemperately and immoderately, allow themselves in Excesses either of Eating or Drinking, and then cry out the Town is sickly, the Air is unwholesome, the Season is dry and unhealthy; is as if a Man should cut the Banks of the *Thames*, and then complain that the Marshes were under Water and unwholesome.

We should not say 'tis a Sickly Time, we should say 'tis a luxurious Age; the Town is given up to all Kinds of Excesses, Drunkenness, Epicurism, and Debauchery, and that brings them into Distempers and Diseases. People gorge their Stomachs with Fruit on one Hand, and choke themselves with Coffee, Chocolate, and Tea; and then, they complain of Gripes, Dysenterys, and Nervous Convulsions. Others drink and debauch with Wine and Women, and they cry, " L—d, the Fevers are very rife, and abundance die of Consumptions!"

Let them remove these flagrant Causes, and the Town would be healthy again presently; the Air, blessed be God, is clear and healthful, the Season fruitful and pleasant, no Contagion, no Visitations, the Plague is all in our disorderly Way of Living. Plenty is abused, the Bounty of Heaven applied to gratify a corrupted Palate; Men are gorged with Dainties, they eat to Excess, and drink to Excess, till Nature rejects its due Nourishment, and they grow sick and die. Let them place it to the Account of their Vices, and Exorbitance; and not reproach Heaven with what they ought to give Thanks for.

People are as healthy now as ever they were. All the Distempers which are brought upon Mankind by their own Excesses, and extravagant Living, deducted out of the List of Diseases in the Weekly Bills, 'tis my settled Opinion would be as low as ever they were.

I think it will be a great Act of Charity for you to recommend this to the World, if they will take the kind Hint, and be wary; if they give warning to one another, and live more like Men of Reason, and Men of Religion, the Weekly Bills will abate, Health return, and all frightful Things which

People talk of, would soon vanish; but Luxury will ever bring Diseases, and Intemperance is the Harbinger of Death.

Your Humble Servant,

A. G.

A. J., Sept. 28.—At Maidstone, in Kent, great Numbers of People have been taken ill, and many carried off with violent Vomitings and Loosenesses, which generally hold them three or four Days. The Country People have attributed it to the Eating of Oysters, taken in the Sea by the Copperas Works in Chatham River.

M. J., Oct. 5.—We have heard a Story of two Prisoners that were sentenc'd to throw the Dice for their Lives; and the first Caster threw *Deaux Ace,* which put him into such a Fit of Repentance, Vows, Promises and Resolutions, that there never was so Saint-like a Penitent. While he was in the Middle of his Ejaculations, the other throws *two Aces.* The Dice were no sooner upon the Table, but up starts the *new Convert* from his Prayers, with a bloody Oath in his Mouth, *Ambs Ace,* by ——, says he. This Story hath in it the very Image of human Nature; it lays open our Frailties, the Vanity of our Pretensions, and the Weakness of our Resolutions. How devout we are when we find ourselves upon a Pinch! How ready to promise, and how backward to perform!

M. J., Oct. 5.—We hear from Newgate, that one of the Sheriffs of London and Middlesex, and the Under Sheriff, came thither some Days ago, to inspect the Gaol, and visited the wretched Prisoners in their respective Wards; and, 'tis reported, they signified their Readiness to forgive certain Fines that have been incurr'd during their Sheriffalty, which great Goodness was dutifully acknowledg'd; but, we are told there are several Persons that have been Prisoners for many Years, and not being able to pay the same, are like to continue in that Condition during the Remainder of their Lives. Of this Number the famous William Fuller reckons himself one.* The said Fuller professes that he now humbles himself for the many Crimes committed by him, above 20 Years ago, by the Insti-

---

* A famous Impostor, who pretended to divulge the political intrigues of the exiled Royal Family.—*Ed.*

gation of others ; owns the Justice of God and Man, in his
Punishment ; begs Forgiveness of every one that he hath injured ; intreats them to consider his deplorable Case, and if ever
he is restor'd to his Liberty, he is resolved to bid an eternal
Farewell to all his former Rogueries, &c.

On Temporary Shelters for Unfortunate Debtors.

A. J., Oct. 5.—Sir, It was suggested by some People in
their own Favour, that they did a great Piece of Service to
their Country when, obtaining an Act of Parliament last
Session for the Relief of *Poor Debtors*, they at the same Time
Complimented the *Creditors* with suppressing the Privileges of
Sanctuary, as it was once called, I mean that of the *Mint*:
Whether this has been a Service to the Publick, or no, remains
very doubtful to me. I am not for finding fault with our
Laws ; generally speaking, they are wholesome and good, and
I am willing to grant, in Homage to our Legislators, that the
Good and Welfare of the Publick is really intended in the
Laws that are made in this Nation. But I will never compliment, even the Legislature itself so much, at the Expence of
Truth and History, as to say that all the Laws that are made,
are completely qualified to answer all the good Ends, the Circumstances of the Nation require, no, nor all for which they
are intended. If it were so, why are new Clauses, and Explanations, so often needed in subsequent Parliaments, the
farther to Remedy those Evils which it was thought had been
remedied before ? Why are Acts of Parliament so often Repealed, and New, and sometimes contradictory Laws so often
made on the Neck of one another ?

To bring this down to the Case in Hand ; the Question I
would offer, is this, Has this last Act been for the better, as it
was, no Question, intended to be ; Or, has it not ? Or, to put
it in other Words, Has it fully answered the End and Design
of the Legislature, or has it not ?

That it has been an extraordinary Act of Clemency and
Compassion in the Parliament, to Release out of Prison so
many Miserable Objects, as were at the Time thronged in the
Rules of the *Fleet*, the *King's Bench*, and within the Walls of
Prisons, in several Parts of the Kingdom, I do not at all Dis-
pute ; but whether the Sacrifice on the one Hand made of the

Privileged Places, was not an Extreme the other Way, remains a Doubt with me.

I have heard much said on both Sides, but I could never yet find it proved, that to take away all Security, all possible Retreat from the Miserable and unfortunate Debtor, could be an Advantage to Trade, or a good to the Publick; especially in so great a Trading Nation as this is, at least I never thought it sufficiently proved to me. The abuse of Privileged Places has been great, that's true, and several Parliaments have trenched those Privileges, and laid open the Places to the process of the Law; thus in a former Act of Parliament, the *Fryers*, that is to say, the Place call'd *White Fryers*, in *Fleet Street*, was Dispark'd, laid open, and has ever since been kept so. And it was no doubt very reasonable; the Abuses committed there being then unsufferable by Reason of the height they were grown to.

But my present Inquiry is, Whether no Refuge at all ought to be allowed to the Miserable *Debtor*, no Sanctuary, nothing but a Gaol? No Place of Retreat, where he may treat with his Adversary? I must acknowledge, I think this is driving the Thing too far. Our Saviour says, *Agree with thine Adversary quickly*; the Person there spoken of was a *Debtor*, it was not meant of a Personal Quarrel, but of a Debt, as appears by the next Words, *lest he carry thee to the Judge, and thou be cast into Prison; Verily I say unto thee, thou shalt not come out thence until thou hast paid the uttermost Farthing.*

N.B. *Creditors were always Cruel.*

'Tis plain, I say, the Text speaks there of a Man in debt. *Agree with thine Adversary*; but where shall the poor Man be? Whither shall he fly? Where shall he hide himself till he can agree?

The Thief, the Manslayer; nay, all but the Murtherer, had Places of Shelter in all Ages, and Nations. The Horns of the Altar were a Sanctuary in several Criminal Cases among the Israelites, whence the Church is so to this Day in other Countries. All the foreign Countries that ever I was in, have some Asylum, some Refuge for the Miserable; but here, to be a Debtor, is to be turn'd out of all Sanctuary. Not the Church of God, not the Court of the Prince, not the Army, not the Navy; the poor Debtor is drawn from the Horns of the Altar, and from the very Worship of God, for in some Cases not the Sabbath-Day can protect him from his Adversary.

Then let us Consider the inequality of the Circumstances of one Debtor from another. This Demolishing the Mint leaves still a Place of Safety to a Prisoner, but to none Else; and yet, the Shelterer seems to me to be the greater Object of Charity of the two, for nothing is a more apparent Fraud, for a *Debtor* to turn himself over to the *King's Bench*, or *Fleet Prison*, and the next Day walk about *St. George's Fields*, and all the vastly extended Rules, and bid his Creditor defiance. The Shelterer could do no more in the worst Case, and in many Cases the taking Shelter only serv'd to protect the Person of the *Debtor* till he could accommodate his Business with his Creditor, and then he went abroad by Consent, and this was done without Expense; but the Prisoner comes there at a great Charge,—wastes his Creditor's Effects,—exhausts the miserable Family,—and makes him still more unable than he was before to satisfy his Creditors. So that this Difference seems only to give the Advantage to the Marshal, or Warden of the Prisons; and the Creditor fares still the worse, because there is still less to pay the Creditor with than there was before.

Upon the whole, I must own I think that the poor Shelterer is a much greater Object of the National Charity than the Prisoner; and therefore, a National Refuge I think should be allowed to such, and this I shall farther Explain to you in my next Letter; Meantime,

I am, Sir, your humble Servant,

LIBERTY.

The Same, continued.

A. J., Oct. 12.—Sir, he that pleads for Mercy to his Fellow Creatures in Distress is presently supposed to be in Distress himself; and when we argue for some Clemency to be shewn to the Miserable, we must be presently ranked among them; nay, even with the lowest Class of them. Unhappy People! How are we abused and misrepresented when our Flatterers call us generous, compassionate, kind-hearted, and the like. Where are the like Cruelties exercised upon the like Occasions? Where are Men condemned to Imprisonment for Life upon such mean Accounts, and by such an unauthorised Power as among us?

The Law puts no Man to Death for Debt, that's true,—but the inexorable Creditor making a Tool, or Property of the Law,—how many does he suffer to Languish and Perish ? I might say rather, How many does he Murther in Prisons merely because they are poor, and unable to satisfy his cruel Demand ?

The Cries of these poor perishing Creatures obtained from the Clemency of the Government a late Act of Grace ; that is to say, an Opening of the Doors to many Thousands of them ; but, as if the Creditor was always resolved to poison the Waters, and rob the miserable of the Relief intended them ; they come in, and pray a Clause to take away the Screen which some People,—every jot as Miserable as those in Prison,— enjoy'd from a kind of imaginary Security by the Rules. I say imaginary, for it was no more.

I will not deny but the Security gained by the *Mint* was abused by many, and was not founded upon any legal Privileges, but merely the Usage of the Place ; and the Numbers of those unhappy People, who sorted together in that Place. If a Number of the like People keep together in any Place whatever,—tho' the Practice may be, and is illegal,—yet they will always be formidable to the Bums, or Catchpoles who are their Pursuers ; and a *Mint* may be set up anywhere, as it seems is lately in some degree done in or near *Wapping*. It is necessary that all such Things as these should be subject to the Civil Officer ; but on the other Hand, as the Insolence of those Fellows called Officers,—whom some, and perhaps not unjustly, call Blood-suckers,—is such as the Law no where directs, nor justifies, tho' the Redress is not easy ; I say, as their Insolence to Men in Distress is unsufferable, I must say, I think they, and not the Debtors, are originally the Authors of these Places of Retreat.

In a Word, the Cruelty of the Creditor, and the Violence and Extortion of the Bayliffs, are the Founders, and Patrons of the *Mint ;* and of all the Recourse to the Sanctuary of Privileged Places which poor Debtors are obliged to take. As *Newgate* makes Thieves, and as Poverty makes W—s, so Bayliffs and Creditors make Bankrupts.

Many an honest Tradesman, worried by the impatient Creditor, and hounded out of his Shop, and out of his House, by the voracious Officers, is driven into Ruin before his Time ;

and many Times driven into that Ruin, which he would never otherwise have fallen into.

When shall the Time come, that common Compassion shall prevail between Man and Man; and that no Violencies, more than Justice makes necessary, shall be used? It is true, that the Knavery of Debtors may have been originally the Cause of the Cruelty of Creditors; but all Debtors sure are not Knaves, and Something is due in the Right of Human Nature to the honest Unfortunate.

Upon the whole, it has been a Difficulty long depending in *England*, how to distinguish between the honest Insolvent, whose Unhappiness is his Disaster, but not his Contrivance, and who seeks to pay, not defraud his Creditor; and the knavish, designing, tricking Bankrupt, who devours his Creditors, and advantages himself of his Bankruptcy! Many Proposals have been made in the World to shew a National Pity to the first, and to let loose the National Justice on the last.

But it was ever found, that when any Favour was intended for the honest Debtor, the Knavish, designing, tricking People, come in for the greatest share of it, and in the End the first were defrauded; and the Mercy intended, became thereby, instead of a Clemency to the Debtor, a Cruelty to the Creditor.

The Consequence of this is, that the poor honest Debtor has been left subject to the Rigour and Extremity due to the knavish Bankrupts. I say, rather than let the last Escape by a Clemency which he had no Right to. But as for a Remedy, this may still be thought of. I send you this to prepare the World to receive it, and the miserable to hope for it.

I am, &c.

On Public Spirit.

A. J., Oct. 19.—Sir, I have heard much talk in the World of a Thing call'd *a Publick Spirit*, and of dying to serve our Country. 'Tis a good Thing, without Question, and in former Times, for aught I know, such Things were really to be seen. Great Instances of this Heroick Virtue were found among the Romans; as one who rode a Horseback into the great Chasm, or Gulph in the Earth, to appease the Anger of the Gods against his Citizens. Another, who being a Prisoner of War to the

Carthagenians, was sent back to perswade them to Peace, upon his Parole of Honour to surrender himself if he did not do it; and when he came to the Senate, perswaded them to continue the War, and then went back, and was cruelly put to Death. But those Days are all over, those Fellows they tell us of, were a parcel of Fools, and did not understand the value of Life. It was a Proverb then, *Dulce est pro patria Mori, It is good for their Country that they should die.*

Serving ourselves now, is call'd serving our Country; and this *Self* is so Natural, that 'tis made a Kind of first Principle in all we do. Where's the Patriot now, that serves his Country, but with a good Salary? Where are the Volunteer Gentlemen that serve in the Army, but with a View of Command; or that go into the Field as the Marshal *de Biron* did to *Henry* IV. King of *France*, to have the Honour to die with their King? On the contrary, the greatest Pretenders to serving their Country, — What have they been but the Plunderers of their Country? Witness the *South-Sea* Fraud! Witness the most Brazen of all modern Frauds, the *Harburgh* Lottery Bubble! Witness *York Buildings, Copper* and *Brass*, and innumerable more; some of which have in Part received their just Censure in Parliament, and the Persons been justly expelled, as not thought worthy of being named among the Servants, but rather among the Destroyers of their Country.

The *Publick Spirit* is now become a Strange Medley of Popularity, mingled with Self-Interest. I think much of that which we now call *Publick Spirit* is contained in such Examples as these.

1. The Coffin Maker, near *Fleet Ditch*, who was in hopes of a very good Trade, if the Plague had happened to break out here. He should have put it in better Words, and have said, that if he could have the good Fortune to see a Plague break out here, he should be in hopes of a good Trade.

2. A Fellow going to be hanged; and being desired to pray for the Queen, and for the Prosperity of his Country, as a Testimony, that he died in Charity with all the World, answered—"Yes, I pray for the Queen with all my Heart; but as for my Country, I wish to God the General Conflagration were to come just now, that we might all burn together. For what's

my Country to me," says he, "when I am to be hanged out of it?"

3. But we have a Modern Testimony of a *Publick Spirit* among our Tradesmen very lately, exemplified in a Practice too Notoriously Publick to be denied; namely, that of the late running Goods on Shore out of Ships under Quarantine; that is to say, such Ships as, coming from Places Infected, or near such as were Infected, had been obliged to perform Quarantine to prevent Communicating any Contagion to the Country. If there was no Infection, or Danger of Infection among them, the Parliament then made the Law to no Purpose; and if there was Danger of it, then their Country was exceedingly obliged to those People, who to gain the Profit of a Trifle, would oblige their Country to the venture of it. Nay, I might carry this *Publick Spirit* up to those who Embezzled Goods, ordered to be burnt as really Infected; and ventured to sell those Goods, tho' the whole Kingdom should be Infected by them.

These are Specimens of the Publick Spirit which reigns now among us; and we have just such another Game now upon the Hands of some of our People about the Oysters. A Rumour, if not more than a Rumour, has been raised among the People, intimating that eating Oysters has been the Occasion of the late Distemper among the People. The Oyster Breeders, and Oyster Sellers are affronted at this to the last Degree, and why? Because it Points at their Business, and many Advertisements are published to convince us of the Negative; namely, that the Oysters are not Injurious, not Unwholesome, and the like; all which I must Confess serve to make me believe the first Rumour, which indeed I gave not much heed to before. It is evident however that the *Publick Spirited* Oyster-Catcher, &c. are for having the People eat the Oysters, that they may get the Money; and let the Country run the Risk of their Health and Lives, that's nothing to them.

Upon the whole, that the Oysters may be particularly Unwholesome this year is not impossible; I know some that go farther, and say, 'tis not improbable; others that go farther yet, and say 'tis very probable. I shall not enter into that Part; but this I am sure is right, that upon such a Supposition, it had been no harm for the People to have forborn them for one Season, rather than to satisfy their Palates at the *Expense or even at the Hazard* of their Health.   And the Oyster People had much better have let their *Publick Spirited* Advertisement alone; as I am told,—and own I must believe the Truth of it,—that more People have forborn the Oysters since these partial Advertisements than had forborn them before; and if they go on, perhaps they may move some of the other Opinion to give such Reasons for the Refraining the Oysters as the other Advertisers cannot Answer.

Public Expectation of a Comet.

A. J., Oct. 26.—Sir, I did not think to have meddled with a Matter of this Nature at all, but to have sent you some serious Reflections upon the Times; yet we have all been so set a Stargazing, for these ten or fourteen Days past, that I cannot refrain talking a little somewhat to you out of the upper Regions.

All the Fraternity of you News-Writers have told us,—some from the Authority of one Astronomer, some from another,— That a Comet was seen *Wednesday* seven-night,—somewhere or other, if anywhere,—in, or near the Constellation call'd *Aquila*, or the *Eagle*.

Some said it was to be seen by the help of Telescopes, and Glasses, others that it might be seen by the naked Eye; and, as the Weather has been exceeding Cold and Clear, Thousands of sore Throats, Cricks in the Neck, swell'd Faces, Toothaches, sore Eyes, and the like, are already laid to the Charge of this Comet,—and its Malevolent Influence,—by the Multitudes of People who have star'd and gaz'd at the Stars all Night to find it out, and been disappointed.

In short, nothing has yet been seen, at least not suitable to the Alarm these Men have given to the World, or to the Reputation of the Understanding an Art of those learned Gentlemen, who gave us the first Notice.   Nor can I give any Account of the Reason why they have thus frighted the World; and at the same Time have not been able to make out anything of what they Pretend to.

On *Sunday* Night last, was the first clear Evening we have had since this Alarm was made Publick; it happened that on that very Evening, there was a great Stream of that Vapour,

which our People call the Light in the North. It reach'd across
the Hemisphere from about N.W. by North to N.E. by N., so
that it extended itself in a straight Line, as it were East and
West, from one Horizon to the other.

At first Sight, we ignorant People took this to be the Tail
of the Blazing Star, or Comet, and a terrible long one it was
indeed ; but about Ten o'Clock this Light abated. It cast out
strange Streams of Light as usual, with some moving Gleams
lighter than the other, which went swiftly along, such as in
the North of *Britain,* they call the Dancers ; and by Eleven,
the whole Appearance died away directly North ; ending in a
mere pale thin Light, spreading quite to the Horizon due
North, and went off ; so that all those Observers, who cried
out at first that they had found it, and seen the Star, began
to blush, and sneak off about 11 o'Clock, and Confess they were
all Mistaken. Since that, we have mounted our Telescopes,
rubbed our Glasses, and pored at the Eagle, the Milky Way,
and everywhere else, that we can think of, and no Comet to
be seen. And now they begin to say, it was to be visible not
above ten, or fourteen Days, and then to withdraw ; and that
all that time it was Cloudy, and not to be seen ; and so they
begin to dismiss our Expectations as well as they can.

But, in short, Mr. App, this is a Merry kind of a Story, to
put upon a whole Nation ; and if there is really nothing in it,
I think some Men should be whipped about the Pig-Market,
for amusing the World, and Alarming us all for nothing.
How many Old Women have they frighted to Death, and
Young Women into fits ; and is it all come to this ? Is all the
Comet to end in a Transit of *Mercury* over the Body of the
Sun, which some will see, and be ne'er the wiser ; and Thousands
that look for it, will never see at all ?

After all, if our Astronomers have not found a Comet, why
have they told us so many Fibs ? And if they have, what
is become of their *Solar System,* where they told us there
would be no more of such things seen till 1757, as by Mr.
Whiston's Solar System it is Evident ? When therefore Mr.
Whiston reads his new Lectures upon this Appearance of a
Comet, which he has just now published, pray desire him to
tell us how he came to publish, in his said *System,* that there
would be no Comet, or at least none of those he there describes,
till the year 1757.

And if he did know of this Comet that now appears, (if it does appear, which I must own I do not believe :) How came it to pass that we knew nothing of it when he gave us that Monstrous piece of guess Work, call'd his *Solar System?* And how came he to impose such gross Things upon the World? I think it would be but a piece of Justice to make out this Contradiction to the World before he bestows the Favour of any more Lectures upon us.　　　　I am, &c.

On Comets.

A. J., Nov. 2.—Sir, Since my last we have had more Talk, but not much more certainty about the Comet, that, as it is said, has been seen in the upper World, and we are now bid to believe it as a Thing which admits no Dispute ; and yet they tell us, that as it ascends higher and higher Northward, so it appears smaller and smaller, and will in a few Days be quite out of Sight.

Upon its being thus particularly described, and the Path of its Motions laid out, we must no more dispute the reality of its Appearance, tho' I might have something to say on that Head ; and 'tis easy to foresee something of what this Nation may expect, yet I cannot exert my Gift of Prophecy upon a Phenomenon, which I am no better assured is real ; so I leave that till we hear, or see farther.

But methinks I would have you tell those *Star-Peepers*, who pretend to Calculate the Revolutions of the Comets,—That they should no more impose upon Mankind in their Reckoning, when, and when not, these Things shall return ; seeing 'tis evident this Part of Astronomical Knowledge is above their reach.

It recommends the study of Astronomy very much, and honours that Noble Science extremely, that we can Calculate the Eclipses of the Sun and Moon ; and of the Satellites, or Moons attending other Planets ; can describe the Times to a Minute when those Eclipses shall begin, and go off ; and how much of the Body of the Sun or Moon shall be Eclipsed. Likewise the Conjunctions, and Oppositions, and Aspects of the other Planets ; these are all Testimonies of the verity of Astronomy, and so far 'tis a glorious Study ; nobody can have Room to discourage, or undervalue it.

But when Men affect the Reputation of what the Nature of .

the Thing will not admit; they not only 'Expose themselves, but as I have said, they dishonour the Art itself.   To rescue therefore the Noble Science of Astronomy from the Scandal of Pretenders, let me Observe that 'tis no lessening of the Dignity of the Science to say, that the *System* of the Comets is placed out of their reach and remains, with that great undiscovered Knowledge of the Longitude, as a Mystery reserved for future Ages.

Besides, this may be a Proof, in some Kind, of the suggested Signification of Blazing Stars, or Comets.   For if Heaven has directed these Phenomena to be real forerunners, and Warnings of future Judgment, and approaching Calamities, as after all they have said may be still true, for any thing they know to the contrary; I say, if they are thus directed, it does not consist with the Supposition, that their Revolutions are certain, and may be calculated, as to the Time, and Situation, of their Appearances.

There being therefore no Certainty, *or at least no Discovery of*, the Certainty of the Appearance of Comets, it is highly probable they are reserved for the extraordinary Errands we speak of *viz.*, that they are sent as Signals of the approaching Judgments of God upon Countries where they particularly impend.

N.B. *I say Probable* only.

Another Argument for that Opinion is drawn from History, where 'tis Evident that Comets have often appeared in an extraordinary Manner before; and evidently pointed at some of the most extraordinary Calamities, that ever befel any particular Nations,—so that it would be next to a Defiance of Heaven to deny their Significance.   As particularly, a Comet before the Destruction of *Jerusalem*, which hung for a Year, as it were directly over the City in the Shape of a Flaming Sword.

A terrible Comet before the universal Plague; which, beginning in *Ethiopia*, and then spreading into *Egypt*, visited *Greece*, and afterwards the whole *Roman* Empire.

A Comet before the Death of *Julius Cæsar*, and another just before the Death of *Augustus*.   A Comet before the Sacking of *Rome* and overrunning of the *Roman* Empire by *Totilla* the *Hun*, in which War it was supposed a Million of People lost their Lives.

A Comet before the Massacre of *Paris*, and the Murder of near 100,000 Protestants, in that, and other Cities in *France;*

which was followed by a bloody Civil War, wherein many Thousands of People were also Slaughtered on both Sides.

A Comet here in *England* before the Invasion of *William* the Conqueror in 1066, when 60,000 Men were killed in one Battle.

A Comet in 1664 seen all over Europe, after which a dreadful Plague spread itself over all *England, Holland,* and the greatest Part of the Lower *Germany;* and which was so dreadful in *England,* that it swept away above 200,000 People, whereof near half in *London,* 5000 in *Colchester,* 4000 in *Ipswich,* and parts adjacent, and so in proportion over the whole Nation.

If then it has been certain that Heaven has appointed them, as Foreboders, and Harbingers of the Calamities of Nations,— How should their Periods, and Revolutions be foretold, and regularly Calculated by the help of Art? And if it cannot be, Why do our Astronomers pretend to it?

If they can do it, I should readily grant that the Comets have no Predicting Signification; but then let us see them do it. And why did they not, in all their former *Systems,* foretell the Appearance of this Comet now talked of? And if they cannot do it, what have they Amused the World with so long, but mere Cheat and Delusion?

D. P., Nov. 7.—M. de Beauregard, a reduced Officer in the Regiment of Provence, has obtained a Remission of the five Years' Banishment to which he was condemn'd for striking the Poet Voltaire; but he will be held to pay him 4500 Livres for Damages and Cost of Suit; and the poor Poet is fallen ill of the Small-Pox.

On the New Practice of Concealing Journal Writers.

A. J., Nov. 9.—Sir, Let Peace spread itself with however glorious a Face over the rest of the World, we are always sure to want it here. Nay, *if you will believe some People,* the more Peace we have, the less Peace we have; a Riddle which, to those who know us, is no Riddle, but is understood thus, that the more Peace we have Abroad, the less Peace we have at Home; the more easy some People are, the less easy some People always are, and will be. Unhappy Nation, who so live in Faction that they seem to be nourished by it; and cannot subsist, or at least not with Satisfaction, unless they are always Scolding and falling out with one another!

This WAR is now carried on *chiefly* by the Pen and Ink; (for secret Plots and Cabals, whether Treasonable or otherwise I am not speaking of them now,) but even this *Pen* and *Ink* WAR is now carried on after a new Method too. Our Authors, like the Scotch Highlanders, *fight behind the Door*, whether ashamed of what they Write, or afraid of just Resentment, either Public or Personal; in a Word, whether ashamed of being afraid, or afraid of being ashamed, we are not agreed about it. But they have changed the Scene of Action in a strange Manner, — the Paper Scolds, Raves, and calls Names, while the Men Walk about *Incognito;* and we are neither trusted with knowing *what* they mean, or *who* they are.

All the Wit and Learning, the Spite, the Malice, the Treason, the Heresy, 'tis all delivered like the Heathen Oracles; the God speaks in Nubibus, and Ambiguous Answers are given out by *those Knaves*, the Priests, who, like true Mountebanks, made their Profits of the Game, and cheated the World, *in Nomine Domini.*

The Contests and Quarrels, which in a great Variety are now Carried on in this Part of the World, and which daily disturb us with their Raillery and Wit; are managed in a Way particular to us, and particular to the present Time. In a Word, 'tis all carried on in *News-Papers*, Weekly Journals, and the like.

If Bishops and Learned Doctors fall out about Religion, and think fit to cap Principles,—even till they tell the World they have *no Principles,*—they do it by Advertisements in the Publick Papers; and so it comes into the World recommended by Interest and Party, according to what Paper those Advertisements are published in. How did the Right Reverends and the Reverends, when they lately fell out *about Nothing*, Oppose and Expose one another, with most exquisite Wit and Learning, by way of Advertisement! Some Anger, much Bitterness, little Patience, and less Truth; till they tir'd the World with their Folly, and themselves with the Disappointment of hearing themselves laughed at! How did they Affirm and Deny, Assert and Contradict! Till, in short, the World was Sick of them, and at last the French Hugonot swore them all down; as Conjurors lay the Devil in the Deserts of *Arabia.*

We are now come to a more *covered Way* still; the Publick

Prints go on as usual, Reverend and Right Reverend Bishops occupy Journals, Noble Lords, Dukes, and Persons of Distinction, speak through the Mouths of Scoundrels, and vent their sarcasms upon the Publick behind the coarse Skreen of a Three Halfpenny Scribbler.*

The Liberties they take in this Way of Writing are as scandalous as the Method of doing it; for they *Wound* in the Dark; throw Dirt at Virtue, vent Atheistick Principles, jest at Things Sacred, and advance Things Criminal, reproach Government, slander Governors, expose the Great, impose upon the Mean, and abuse the World.

If Governments resent with the greatest Justice, and proceed even to legal Punishment, poor Wretches may be found to bear the Prosecution for a piece of Money; the real Criminal slips through their Hands, and they laugh at Power that cannot reach them.

He that like the *Scape Goat* can be content to go *into the Wilderness,* may carry with him all the printing Sins of a whole Nation. He that can go to Newgate for his Author, and lie seven Years in Prison for a Skreen, may, without doubt, print and publish what he pleases, and upon whom he pleases. We see this Age has produced a *Shepherd* and a *Matthews,* and 'tis not hard to find Men to load themselves with other Men's Offences, if they are but paid for it.

By this Means *Scandal* walks about the Street in a new Dress, Treason gets vent in Disguise, and all Sorts of Faction and Discontent spread themselves in a new Manner; the publick is arraign'd in Masks; and Kings amd Governors bantered, or rather insulted, by *Ironick Praise.*

The *Coffee House Tables* are now found like *Courts of Justice,* where Monarchs are brought to the Bar, and Subjects judge and pass Sentence; the Journals are the Council which plead the Cause on both Sides, and the Mob are the Jury who bring in the Verdict.

Kings, Parliaments, Ministers of State, Church, Religion, nay, even their Maker, as well as their Sovereign, are judged and condemned here; none can escape these Judicatories; and

---

* Bishops Atterbury and Hoadley, Dr. Young, the Duke of Wharton, Lord Bolingbroke, Sir R. Walpole, &c., are here intended, as among the Journal Writers.—*Ed.*

whether with or without Law, with or without Reason, the
Sentence becomes Popular, and the Nation imbibes it.

Hence Faction and Party Strife grow Popular; then Fer-
ment into Mutiny and Riot, and from thence into Plot and
Rebellion.   Hence what Mischiefs have not proceeded! What
Mischiefs may not yet proceed!   For to what End do Male-
contents appeal in print to the People, but to engage them on
their Sides?   And what is that we call making a Party?   Is
not every Party an Army, *in its Kind,* raised against the Government?   Is not forming Parties a degree of Rebellion?
For what is the Language of any Party but this, in Capital
Letters? *We would be Uppermost!* And what then is wanting
to such, but Power?

Upon the whole then, some Method ought to be found out,
and I doubt not will in Time; for all growing Mischiefs
gradually tend to their own Cure, or to be Incurable.   I say,
some Method should be found out to bring these Combatants
all upon the Stage, that the World may know them; and if
the Bishop will broach his Presbyterian or Independent Principles, let him quit the *London Journal,* 'tis below his Dignity,
and like an honest primitive Bishop let him speak in the first
Person of his Right Reverend Self, and let us know who is a
False Brother, and who not; who confounds the Established
Church, and its Doctrines with *Separatists,* and who, as a
Church of England Bishop, he rejects as *Schismaticks.*   When
his Mask is off, and his Disguise laid aside, he may be fairly
answered; but while he fights in the Dark he evidently defends
the Cause he is ashamed of.

Satire on Journal Writers.

A. J., Nov. 16.—Sir, I had a great Mind, a long while, to
come into the Road of the Times, and Rail at my Superiors;
but it has occurred to me, that there are Abundance of Ways
and Methods to be considered of, for the decent Performance
of such an important Work, particularly that of always preserving the *Main Chance*—which you know Mr. *App,* is a nice
Concern,—*I mean Safety.*   I have seen a great many witty
Fellows have miscarried in this laudable Work, and therefore
I must act with the greater Caution.

Some with greater *Plainness* than *Prudence* have spoken

Bold Truths, which the Governments they live under WOULD not bear; and they have been punished for their FOLLY.

Some with greater *Boldness* than *Truth* have spoken *damn'd Lyes,* which no Government that they lived under OUGHT to bear; and those have been punished for their KNAVERY.

The best Character *the first Sort have* obtained, has been to pass for honest well meaning *Fools;* and even the Party whom they Served, and Suffered for, would at best *only Pity them,* but never Stand by them. Remember that too, Mr. *App!* which is sufficient Warning against ruining one's self for a Party, or a Cause. 'Tis much better to be *Envied,* than *Pitied* in the World.

On the other Hand, the worst Character the Second *Sort* have obtained, has only added that of *Knaves* to the *Fool,* and yet they have perhaps been as much pitied as the former; for the Knaves, *of the two,* have generally the better Luck.

Now all these Ways having been Tried, I see no Encouragement to vent my Gall that Way. But if I fall upon *my Masters,* I think I must begin with *Panegyrick,* for as two Negatives make an Affirmative, why should not two Affirmatives make a very good Negative? The extremes of Panegyrick ought no doubt to be accepted for *Satyr,* and perhaps are the highest accesses of *Satyr,* which an Author, or Poet can arrive to; and if the Persons *so dealt* with cannot see it, they must be blinded with a Folly not many Degrees above *Idiotism.* When *Herod* made a Speech, and was applauded as a God, his Crime was, not the applauding him in that Manner; but his absurd Pride, in accepting the Surfeiting Praise. *Alexander* the Great, 'tis said, had the Folly secretly to wish to be flattered, and yet he with Diligence endeavoured to shun its being known. That was his Prudence. Some of the Roman Emperors, the most Brutal of them, did openly covet it; but *Augustus, Vespatian, Titus,* and all the wisest of them, took the offer of it to be casting the utmost Contempt upon them, and therefore rejected it.

Concluding then, that the extravagant Elevations and Raptures,—in compliment to the personal Virtues of great Men, who understand nothing of Virtue in Practice,—must be allowed to be the keenest *Satyr* that can be written;—why should not I try to abuse some honest great Man or other that Way? Sup-

pose I should write a Panegyrick upon Modesty, and dedicate
it to her Excellency, Madam, the Countess de *Sally Salisbury ?*
Would it not do very well ?   Or another upon Frugality, and
Inscribe it to his Grace of [*Wharton*], and his Grace of [*Ormond*],
or any other Man of Fortune, who may have Glass Windows,
thro' their great Estates almost as soon as they were of Age to
possess them ?   Would not those be taken for Satyr ?

Suppose I was to write a Book in Praise of Honesty, and
Dedicate it to Sir C[*onstantine*] P[*hipps*], or in Praise of Generosity, and Present it to a Lord Mayor ; perhaps these great
Men might be affronted at me, and take it for a *Satyr* upon
them.

If I should write in Recommendation of Voluminous, and
Contentious Writing, and send it in a Penny Post Letter to
a certain dignified C[*lergy*]man, or Praise confounding of
Principles with Contraries in Practice, What would this Dig-
nifiedship say to me ?

In a Word, I am convinced, Mr. *App*, this will do it. *Probatum est.* TRUE BRITON, No. 1629.   From henceforward
then expect—when I write in Praise,—when I swell in Panegyrick,—*it is all Satyr*, and done to abuse my Superior ; according
to the laudable Example of all the Model Journals and publick
Prints, that have gone before me,—Sir *Dick*, as well as the
Duke.

In the first Place then, I think to write a long Encomium
upon the *York Buildings Lottery ;* wherein I shall applaud the
Equity of drawing Lotteries before they are full,—the goodness
of Bubble Security,—the Certainty of having Prizes,—and the
Uncertainty of having them paid ; with a great Variety of
excellent Observations in praise of the excellent Art of
managing Mankind, by Figures and great Numbers.

I thought to have sent you an admirable Poem upon the
late *Harburgh Lottery,* adorned with some Characters of Persons, whereby the Injustice done those honest worthy Gentlemen, might perhaps have appeared to have been greater or
less than themselves imagine ; but in Charity I forbear Treading on the Vanquished.

I have abundance of Panegyrick by me, which would much
exalt the Honour and Glory of our Nation, and shew us what
abundance of Heroes we are like to raise, without a War, more

than ever rose by the Glory of the Field; and how many brave Officers die annually in the Bed of Honour, *Drury Lane*, more than ever did in a Campaign in *Flanders*, or at a *Hochstet*, and a *Ramillies*.

In a Word, Mr. *App*, I can never want Subject of Panegyrick, if Panegyrick may but pass for *Satyr :* So you may expect for the future I shall be very Civil (Saucy) to my Superiors.   Yours, &c.

On the Pleasure of Writing Dismal Stories, Exciting Surprize and Horror.

A. J., Nov. 23.—Sir, I find it very much for my Diversion, and sometimes for my Instruction, to converse with the *Men-Gossips* of the Town. They are very useful People in their Generation I assure you; and, to my particular Satisfaction, we have a tolerable Number, (I was going to say an Intolerable · Number,) of them in our Neighbourhood.

Among the many useful Observations which I have made in my long Conversation among these People, this is one, and none of the least improving; Namely, that tho' they love to have a Story of any Kind to tell, and rather than quite Starve their Friends, or make their Society barren and Empty, they will carefully coin every now and then a Tale for them; or, in good Husbandry, and for the Exercise of their Wit make the same Story serve two or three Times by telling it several Ways. I say, tho' they love to have a Story of any kind to tell, yet their principal Gust is to tell bad News. As many Gentlemen will strain a Tale to its utmost Extent, nay, add a little to it to make People laugh; nay, but to obtain the Favour of a Grin; so these will go five Times as far to make them cry.

If they can but make your Blood run chill, or give suitable Horror to their Friends, then their Taste is gratified to the full; nay, I find, nothing relishes with them like it. They take the most complete Pleasure when their Friends find the greatest Surprize; and therefore you find every Story they tell grows worse and worse every Time they tell it. If they give you an Account of a Robbery anywhere, but especially if it be out of the reach of present Enquiry; they fail not to add some Murther to it, or at least something very barbarous. If a

Fire, they make it burn more Houses than perhaps were in the Town, or Stacks of Corn than were in the Parish; and Ten to one, but they burn some of the poor People alive for you, or at least half roast them, for the particular Diversion, that is to say, Horror of their Readers.

Now the Fact of this is not so strange, (the frequency of it indeed makes it familiar,) but the Fountain of it, the Principle from whence it proceeds is very occult, and hard to be accounted for in Nature; and I send it to you Mr. *App*, that the World may judge of it a little, when perhaps some Friendly Reader skilled in the Sympathetick Powers of Nature, may bestow a Line of good Teaching upon us, and tell us from what strange thwart Lines in Nature, this unnatural Disposition can proceed.

I hope no body that Converses with the polite World will question the Fact; I mean, that the Truth of the Thing is really so. Alas! I can send them to so many of my Neighbours; nay, and perhaps of your Neighbours too, for Examples of the Practice,—nay, to your Brother Journal Men too,—that I can soon give Demonstration of the Thing to general Satisfaction. I'll give you but one Example for the present, and refer you to further Testimonies hereafter; and this is about writing dismal News from Foreign Parts. How diligent were our News-Writers, and indeed, some who carried on the same Thing by the Mouth, to make us believe the Plague in *France* spread this way! How often did they tell us it was come to this Place, and t'other Place, many a Score, nay, Hundred Mile nearer than ever it was found to have been! What Desolation did they tell of! And how many hundred, nay hundred Thousand People did they bury of it, more than ever died! Nay, more sometimes than the Towns mentioned had in them to Bury, tho' they should have buried all the People alive that Inhabited them.

To bring it nearer home, our present Case gives a Taste of the same Temper. With what Diligence do they labour even just now, to have us believe that the Plague is broken out in *Portugal*, and that at *Lisbon* 25,000 People have died in two Months, which, in a Word, were it true, would soon leave *Lisbon* as Desolate of People almost as old *Carthage!*

Nor do these Messengers of evil Tidings consider at all the

mischievous Consequences, which such an Alarm would have
upon us in our foreign Commerce; and the Confusion, which
the fright of it would put us all into at Home. The Consequence, more particularly to us, must be, that Immediately, if
the Fact was true, and the Plague was actually broken out at
Lisbon, we should prohibit Trade with the whole kingdom of
Portugal, and all Intercourse, of Shipping at least; and they
who are ignorant of what would be the Consequence of such a
Prohibition, must be ignorant of this known Truth, (viz.) that
Portugal is next to *Holland*, the Place to which the greatest
Trade—for the Exportation of our Wool Manufactures—is carried on, and perhaps there is not a greater Branch of Trade in
the World,—or where there is a greater return,—than to that
small Kingdom for the Woollen Manufacture. This would immediately stop, the Want of it would be felt by the Poor throughout *England*, and especially by the Drugget and Cloth Trade
of the West, the Shalloon Trade of the North, and above all
by the Bay-Makers of *Colchester*.

But what is all this, to the Pleasure of telling a dismal
Story? What do the People I am speaking of care who they
Injure, or what sudden Damp they bring upon Trade, or what
Disadvantages they put upon our Commerce, if they can gratify
the Itch of a Tale? Were it a true Story indeed, the alarm
would reach other Countries, as well as ours, and we should
injure our Trade less; but to make us believe the Plague has
begun there, when it is not, is but shutting the Door of Trade
against us, and leaving it open to the *French* and *Dutch*, who
being rightly informed, would be under no Alarm.

If it is Criminal to cry Fire in the City, when there is no
Fire, because of the Hurry and Fright it puts the Neighbourhood into; if it be Criminal in the Camp for a Centinel upon
Duty to fire his Musket when he is not Attacked, or sees no
Enemy; what do these Men deserve, who give a false Alarm to
a whole Nation, and for every Fever, or Sickly Season, which
may happen Abroad, cry Fire? That is to say, Plague, which
is worse; when upon a full Enquiry into it, they know nothing
of the Matter.

Revolution in Persia.

A. J., Nov. 30.—We are told that the *Sophi* of *Persia* has sent Ambassadors, and made a Treaty with the *Czar* of *Muscovy;* and the Usurper *Meriwies,* has sent Ambassadors to the *Grand Seignior;* the contents of both which, are, as 'tis said, to demand Aid and Assistance, and offering the Kingdom to Sale to them for that Assistance, that is to say, Dismembering it to both, for help to preserve the whole.

This Treaty of Partition, is no less than a Bargain and Sale, tho' of a different kind; and the Provinces of the Kingdom of *Persia* are fairly offered to the best Bidder. For Example, *Meriwies,* they tell us, offers the *Turks* all *Armenia,* the great City of *Taurus,* all the Frontier Provinces on that side of *Bagdad,* and the *Tigris,* and even to the *Persian* Gulph; which in a Word, is third Part of the whole Kingdom.

The *Sophi,* says the same Intelligence, has actually made a League with the *Czar,* given him up all *Georgia,* the Provinces of *Guilan,* whence our Raw Silk, call'd *Turkey* Silk comes, and all the Coast of the *Caspian* Sea, even to the River *Oxus,* and the Frontiers of *India.*   So that, in short, according to this Bargain, whichsoever of these two most powerful Neighbours can get the better of the other, will Dismember this Kingdom of *Persia,* perhaps a third Part.

But the merriest part of the Jest is still to come, for now the News-Writers tell us, that these two great Neighbours are like to agree together, underhand I suppose; and taking each the third Part allotted to them, perhaps may leave the two contending Parties to fight for the rest, as they did before, or else perhaps turning them both out, may share the *Persian* Monarchy between them.

This is the present Treaty of Partition, and a hopeful one it is indeed, if it be true.   Such is the Ambition of Princes, and thus do they Play at Shuttlecock with Crowns and Empires, when it is for their Purpose to do so.   The poor *Sophi,* or King of *Persia,* has a fine Post of it in the meantime, who between such powerful Neighbours on one Hand, and a Rebel as powerful, in the Heart of his Kingdom, on the other Hand, is like, *at best,* to possess not above one third of his Kingdom, and that Third too, the meanest and the most barren Part of it all.

Here I might give you a very warm and suitable Reflection upon the boundless ambition of Princes, and the Nature of Man; which forbids him being satisfied with anything less *than all he can get*, be his Power and Possessions what they will. One would think the *Czar* of *Muscovy*, and the *Grand Seignior* too, had either of them Kingdoms and Empires enough under their Dominions. When I say *enough*, I mean *enough* to satisfy their Ambition; enough to prevent their coveting any more in this World; but *Reasons of State*, the Ordinary Excuse which the greatest Monarchs make for their Encroachments upon, and Invasions of one another, open the Door for Ambition, and the Ambition is so rooted in the Nature of Mankind, that nothing less than the whole Globe would be a Boundary to it; and perhaps not that, if there were more to be had. But I wave that Part, 'tis this Noble Treaty of Partition that I speak of, I may talk to you more of it another Time.

The Comet again, and on Portents and Signs.

A. J., Dec. 7.—Sir, I am taken off from Moralizing upon the useful subject which I had begun in my last (viz.) the un-satisfied Ambition of Men; to talk a little about a New Enthu-siasm that is gone out among us, which is to Prophesy sad and dreadful Things to us in the Womb of Futurity. This the Prophetic People suggest from the Appearance of the Comet which now impends; which Comet they say has been seen again this last Week more visible than before, and that it ap-pears with a double Tail, or stream of Fire, one pointing South towards *France*, and the other North towards *Britain*. They might as well say towards *Sweden* and Denmark, but it must be as the Star-gazers please to suggest.

The first Thing they hinted was, that the Eclipse of the Sun had Portended the Fall of some great Person in *France*; and now—to their great Disappointment—the Regent of *France* is fallen before the Eclipse has happened. How would these Men have triumphed in their Prophetic Performance, if either the Regent had lived six Months longer, or the Eclipse of the Sun had happened six Months sooner! How would they have boasted that those two famous Eclipses of the Sun should be attended, one with the Death of the King of *France*, (*Lewis* the XIV.) and the other with the Death of the Sub-King, (*the*

P 2

Regent) when it was certain, and perhaps well known, that these Eclipses would happen, and when they would happen, many Years before either the Regent, or his Uncle the King were born or thought of, but this is by the Way.

The main Thing that our whining Astrologers now talk of, is that this Comet with two Tayls shall be not Portending only, but causing great Calamities to these Nations of *Great Britain* and *France;* and that particularly, these Calamities may be, (they are afraid to say will be, for fear of just Resentment of the Government against them for a needless Alarming the People,) I say, they tell us these Calamities may be,—or they may suppose them to be,—Dearth of Provisions, and Contagious Diseases. That is, in a Word, Pestilence and Famine.

I shall not Discourse here of the Improbability of such a *Phenomenon* as a Comet with two Streams, or Tails; that may be reserved for a Subject by itself; but give me leave to set up against these Doctors, who pretend to be *National Fortune Tellers*, and at every Portending Sign in the Event, supposing any to be Portentous, (which however I do not grant,) yet I say, supposing some may be Portentous, I demand whether they always portend Evil, and why not sometimes portend Good?

The Star which appeared at the Birth of our Saviour, is by the Learned *Eckstormius, Riccolus, Rochambuccius,* and other Writers, called a Comet; yet 'tis evident it came with a Message of *glad Tidings,* and ushered in Peace on Earth, and good Will towards Men. Why then may not this Comet usher in good Things to us as well as Evil? And as I have some Room to judge that all these Eclipses, Conjunctions of Planets, and every Comet itself, do, even by the Rules of Astrology, Portend no Evil to this Kingdom; so I think, 'tis very reasonable to say so, when other People are terrifying us with their *Dismals* and *Terribles.*

We read that when *Theodosius* the Great ordered his Governors of Provinces, to Destroy and Overthrow the remains of *Pagan* Superstition in the *Roman* Empire, among the rest of the Temples of the old Heathen Gods which were then Overthrown, the famous Temple of *Serapis* at *Alexandria* in *Egypt,* was Overthrown among the rest. Upon the Destruction of this Heathen Temple *Pagan* Priests obtained of the

Magicians, and Fortune-Tellers (Astrologers) of the Day to spread it about among the People, that the River Nile would not overflow the next Year; for as the God Serapis was the Ruler of the Waters of the *Nile*, he was so Angry with the Insult offered to his Temple, that he would not suffer the Waters to come down out of the Mountains of *Ethiopia*, but had turned another Way all the Fountains and Streams, which usually came down the *Nile* and caused it to overflow; and that now the River not overflowing, a terrible Famine would Ensue, and the People would all perish for want of Food.

This so alarmed the *Egyptians* that it caused a furious Tumult in *Alexandria*, in which the People fell upon the Christians, Murthered a great many, and would have Murthered *Theophilus* the good Bishop of *Alexandria*, if he had not been protected by the *Roman* Garrison. But the Reason of my telling you the Story´is this. It pleased God, (at the Prayers of the Christians, says our Author, and in order to convince the *Pagans* of the weakness of their Idol,) so to order it that the *Nile*, in the next Year overflowed the Country at the usual Season, and that the Waters were five Foot Higher than had been known in many Years before; so that the God *Serapis*, and *Pagan* Superstition with it, lost all its Reputation in *Egypt* for ever after.

I apply the Story to our present case. As these Men have no Commission either to predict the Plagues, or War, or Famine, from those Appearances in the Heavens; so I take the Liberty to say that even by the Rules of their own Art, all the Signs that have yet appeared, or are in our Expectation of Appearing, are against them, and Portend rather Good than Evil. I shall say more of it in my next.

Historical Homily on Proverbs xix. 12.

A. J., Dec. 14.—Sir, *Solomon* tells us, *The Wrath of a King is as the roaring of a Lion.* I want some of your News-Paper Divinities to Paraphrase upon this Text a little, and tell me the Meaning of it; for I must confess, there seems to me to be several Difficulties in it, which I do not well know how to get over.

Indeed, it seems needful to enquire what sort of King *Solomon* means. Whether the wrath of a good King, or of a bad one,

a just Monarch or a Tyrant? And while this Difficulty is
before me, it occurs, that there happened to be but very few
Kings in Solomon's Days, and for many Ages afterwards, but
what were Tyrants. Now if we are to take it as meant of a
Tyrant, the Comparison seems to be very Just, the wrath of a
Tyrant is indeed terrible as the roaring of a Lion.

It is Voracious. The Lion roars for his Prey; and when a
Tyrant shews his Teeth, it is certainly to Devour; when the
Lion roars he is Furious, and when the Tyrant is provoked he
is Outrageous. The Lion is inexorable; the Tyrant knows no
Pity, no Clemency, and shews no Mercy. The Lion is Revengeful; the Tyrant Irreconcileable. When *Justinian* the II.
who was Deposed, and Mutilated by the Popular Fury, had
some prospect of being Restored, by the weakness and incapacity of his Successor; some of the Christian Bishops moved
him to the Heroick Virtue of forgiving his Enemies, (he was, it
seems, in a Boat, passing the *Thracian Bosphorus*, when they
thus exhorted him to Clemency,) he flew out into a Rage,—"*God
drown me this Moment*," says he, "*rather than I shall spare
one of them.*" And he was as good as his Word, for having
been banished into the *Pontick Chersonesus*, and hearing that
the People there had conspired to Kill him; he sent his Army,
after he was restored to the Empire, into the said *Chersonese*,
a large populous Country, and caused them to Massacre the Inhabitants; and—when the Soldiers were glutted with Slaughter,
—the Emperor, not satisfied, but true to his Vow, caused seventy
Thousand survivors of them to be put on Board his Fleet, and
all thrown into the Sea.

This was one of the Kings whose Wrath was really like the
roaring of a Lion; and yet this was a Christian Emperor too,
and one whom the Pope rejoiced over, and Congratulated with
a Letter of Religious Compliments, upon his Restoration;
but of that by the Way.

But to come nearer Home, the Wrath of the Kings of this
Age seems to carry no such Terror in it, as the roaring of a
Lion; not but that Kings are Men in this Age, as well as in
any, and have like Passions with other Men; but the Wrath
of some Kings is now under the Restraint of the Laws, and
the People have learned a Language which Antiquity knew
nothing of; namely, they appeal to the Law, and if the

Monarch pretends not to submit his roaring Anger to the Laws, truly the People appeal to their Arms to support Law. So that it is not now the Wrath of the King, but the Wrath of the Mob, that is as the roaring of a Lion.

Whether this is Right or Wrong,—whether it is as it should be, or as it ought not to be,—is not the Question here, or at least it is a Question by itself. The present Observation leads us to this; namely, what strange Things Kings were in former Days, who had not the Blood of a few, but even the Blood of Nations at their Command, and without Remorse, could shed that Blood like Water spilt upon the Ground! But what strange Things were the People in those Days too, who could tamely submit to such cruel Ravages upon their Properties and Lives!

The World indeed are something Wiser since, and are not quite so passive. Tyrants have been so often sacrificed by the injured People, that the Kings of the Earth grow Wiser, and take Warning; and the Success the People have so often had in their just Resentment of the Tyranny of Princes, has encouraged the People to make use of the helps which the Law of Nature, (now almost become the Laws of Nations,) has put into their Hands; and thus far I must own, I think both Parties are right.

But I have observed, that the Monarchs of the last Ages, having the same gust to Tyrannize, have not the same Power; and seeing the Attempt grow every Day more Dangerous, have found out a Medium how to preserve the Power of Tyrannizing, and yet avoid the Danger of it; and this, by the modern Way of setting up a Prime Minister. 'Tis true they have learned the Method of the *Turks*, for a Prime Minister is nothing more or less than a Grand Vizier; and these are always more cruel and merciless Tyrants than their Masters.

These Christian Grand Viziers have been eminent for Tyranny; nor has their being Churchmen, *as has sometimes been the Case*, mended the Matter at all, as the Cardinals *Richelieu*, and *Mazarine* in *France*, Cardinal *Granville*, in *Flanders*, Cardinal *Alberoni*, in *Spain*, Cardinal *Wolsey*, in *England*, and others; I say, their being Clergymen has not at all lessened the People's suffering, but rather encreased them, Churchmen being not particularly famed for overmuch Mercy.

Under this new Method Nations have often Groaned, and

while the People have been ruined, the Monarch, who was indeed the real Tyrant, has always escaped; and at last, by making a Sacrifice of his Favourite Minister, has pacified the just Rage of his provoked People.

How happy is our Nation, where a mild and clement Prince intrusts the Administration in the Hands of Prudent, Just, and Upright Ministers! The Instruments of Government are not only the Favourites of the Prince, but of the People too; where we hear no Complaints of Injury or Oppression, and have no Petitions in our Hands against the Avarice and Extortion of Favourites and Statesmen!

Long may thy Happiness O! *Great Britain* continue; and may no Evil Ministers be ever Encouraged to make a Prey of the Subject, or abuse the Goodness of the Sovereign, as we have read of in the Records of Foreign Kingdoms, &c., Amen.

On Divers Sorts of Winds.

A. J., Dec. 21.—Sir, I thought to have refined a little upon the Philosophy of the Winds, and the strange Effects which they have upon the Surface of this Globe, as well on the Solid as on the Fluid; and to have taken the rise of my Hypothesis from the late Storms, which have been so Furious and done so much Damage to our Shipping, as well as to our Buildings. But this is so ordinary a Subject, or at least offers itself so frequently to our Observation, that having so much more Material a Subject in my View, I have thought fit to adjourn it till the next great Storm, which upon consulting my private Barometer, I foretell will not happen till the middle of *February;* and that thence, to the vernal Equinox, you will have some Occasion to put me in Mind of it again.

I might also have Dilated my Eloquence here upon the natural Reasons, Why Kings should be Windbound at Sea! And why Monarchs, who can turn the Winds of Faction and Rebellion, this Way or that Way, as they please, should not be able to stem the Torrent of Wind at Sea. (For Air being a convertible Element, may be aptly enough stiled a Torrent, as well as when it is condensed into Water.) But I shall take an Occasion to talk of this another Time.

I desire to speak of Winds now under another kind of Explication, namely, as they are Politically, Nationally, and Ridiculously considered. *For Example ;—*

When a poor Author or Printer comes under the Oppression of a Messenger from his Superiors, and is unhappily sent for to answer, for this or that Boldness of Expression, or for giving Offence to this or that Ambassador, and the like; 'tis an ordinary Thing to say, he has had a STORM upon him.

When a poor Tradesman Fails, turns Insolvent, and Calls his Creditors together, 'tis Ordinary to say he is under a CLOUD; and when the *Cloud* breaks upon him in a Commission of Bankrupt, 'tis fairly represented by a *Thunder-Clap.* Upon the whole we say he is *Blasted,* 'tis a Blast upon his Credit; all which particulars are Stormy Things in the main, and have some Place in the Doctrine of Winds, as now under Consideration.

There are divers Sorts of Winds too that blow among us, besides those at Sea; as particularly, there are sometimes hard Gales, which blow from a Parliamentary Quarter, such was the Blast from a certain Corner, upon the late *South-Sea* Men, the *Harburgh* Lottery Men, and others,—which blew a great many of them quite out of the House, and·well they deserved it indeed, especially the *Latter,*—whom some think should have been blown to the Gallows.

There have been several Times strong Gusts (and Disgusts) about the Courts of our Monarchs. These have overset many a Favourite, before they had been able to set their Sails to it; for (N.B.) *Favourites* GENERALLY *are so Nimble in shifting their Sails, that they can Sail with any Wind; and 'tis not easy for the Storm to blow too hard for them.* Sometimes also there is an ugly Squally Wind, which rises out of the Monarch's reach, and Blows now from this Quarter, now from that, and Oversets, not the Favourite only, but the Favourer too. This Wind is called a *Country Gale;* 'tis worse than the Wind *Euroclydon,* which we read of, that Ship-wrecked St. *Paul;* 'tis generally, I say, a *Country Gale,* and whenever it blows hard, it makes the Court a *Lee-Shore,* that is to say, it makes foul Weather at *Court.*

This *Country Gale* when it over blows, has divers Names too, like the Winds at Sea. When the Wind freshens at Sea, 'tis first called blowing hard; then a Fret of Wind; then a

Storm; then a Tempest; and in some Countries 'tis called a
Hurricane.   So these Country Gales go under divers Denominations. If they blow in the ordinary Manner, 'tis called, as
above, a *Country Gale;* if it increases, 'tis called a *Party Gust,*
then a Faction; then popular Heat, after that, Fury, Rage,
and sometimes at last, it comes up to Insurrection, and Revolution.   We have seen all these Winds blow in *England* some
Years ago.   But of late, blessed be our Fate ! we have had
good calm Weather at Court, and 'tis hoped it may continue
so, whatever some *True Britons* may hope to the Contrary.

But to leave these dangerous Corners, we have other Winds
in *England,* which like Summer are refreshing, comfortable
and cooling; these we call *Court Breezes,* and when they come
kindly, and in the ordinary legal Course, they bring in very
Seasonable Weather with them on that Side.   To some they
Dispense fruitful Pensions, plentiful Crops and large Harvests;
according as they are skilfully improved by the Persons who
receive them from the Sovereign's Favour;—do Good or Evil,
according to the Merit of the Persons, as Corn sowed produces
a good or ill Crop, according to the goodness of the Soil.

Just and wise Governments have always endeavoured to
distinguish Right in the Dispensing their Favours, and cause
this Wind to blow as best serves the Interest of their Kingdoms and Countries.   Tyrants and Designing Princes blow
hot and cold, this Way, and that Way, as their secret Designs
guide them; and that is the Reason we find their Subjects
complaining of Oppression, Injustice, breach of Constitution,
and the like.   These are Storms and Tempests in their kind;
and of these I have much to say in a convenient Season, but
not now.   Thank Heaven we live under a Reign, where there
is a perfect Calm, the *Court Breezes* are all Sanative and
Wholesome; wisely suited to the good of the whole Country;
the Monarch Dispenses his Favours with Justice, and his
Justice with Clemency, Merit commands Respect, and Men
of Worth have always a favourable Gale blowing upon them.

I shall set forth the Advantages of such a fair Wind in its
due Time; in the meantime I must enter in my next upon
the ill consequences of those unhappy Things in a Government,
call'd, contrary Winds.   But I must defer it, I say, till my
next.

On the Keeping of Christmas.

A. J., Dec. 28.—Sir, I know not whether you will have any room for a Story this Week, supposing you will be taken up this Time with wishing your Customers a merry *Christmas*, and the like; but I hope what I shall say may be no interruption to their Mirth.

Our Court is particularly happy this Year, (God sending His Majesty well home in time,) Namely, in having two *Christmasses* fall out in one Year. 'Tis a little odd indeed, but has nothing in it Strange, the difference in our Stile making the *Dutch* Christmas fall out eleven Days sooner than ours, so that the King, if his Majesty had obtained a fair Wind, any time in a Week past, might have kept one *Christmas* in *Holland*, and another *Christmas* in *England*. This difference in the Stile, or Date, occasions the keeping this Festival as we do, all other Christian Holy days falling in a kind of a Confused Manner. The Reason and History of it, that is to say, of the difference between the *Julian* and *Gregorian* Account is obvious to every one that knows but a little of History; namely, that the several Popes *Julian* and *Gregory* rectified, as they said, the Calendar at two several Times, and that several, especially of the Reformed Nations would not agree to the last Rectification, but others did.

When we have said this in brief, we have said all that we can think needful on this Subject; but methinks it cannot be amiss to say something to our Protestant way of observing *Christmas*. Mistake me not, I have no objection against *Christmas*, I am not Puritan enough for the Method. There is no Coherence between the Morning-work, and the Evening-work in the Observation of it; or, if you will, between the Beginning and the End of it.

We begin our *Christmas* with a Religious Observation of the Day, go to Church, receive the Sacrament, and the like, and we do well; and if we concluded the Day with moderate Mirth, Charity, and doing good to the Poor, we likewise should do well. But what to say to all the Debaucheries of *Christmas*, the Drunkenness, the Gaming, the Revelling, Quarrelling, and other Appurtenances of *Christmas*, that is a Case by itself; as I am not Puritan enough for the first, so I am not Heathen

enough for the last; and cannot for my Life find any Coherence between the Feast and the Festival; between Comme-
morating the Birth of our Saviour, and Blaspheming God, and
all Religion, by Revelling and Excess.   This is what is too
openly understood by *Keeping Christmas.*

That there should be a due Expression of Joy and Thankfulness I admit; but what is Joy and Thankfulness to Levity
and Wickedness? And why may we not be Merry without
being quite Mad and Lunatick?   Why not be *Merry and Sin
not*, as well as we are commanded to be *Angry and Sin not?*

As to Drunkenness and *Oaths*, the common Crimes attending all our Mirth in this Nation, and the Essence of very
much of our *Christmas* Revels in particular; who can write
of it but as a Thing which is the Shame of Religion?   But
much more of the Protestant and Reformed Religion; and we
can only recommend it to our Magistrates to restrain it by
the Laws, and to do their Duty both by Punishment and Example, the latter especially.   The Example of Magistrates
'tis acknowledged would go farther than Law among our
People.

I had Occasion to send a Servant some time ago to a
Church Warden's Shop in our Village to buy something necessary on the Sabbath Day; and the good Conscientious Creature asked how she could have the Impudence to come to him
for such Things on the Sabbath Day, did she not know he
was a Magistrate, and could punish her for it?   So the Girl
came home and told me, the Church Magistrate had chid her,
and sent her away without it.   I found I stood in need of the
Thing, and must have it, and bad her go to another Shop; but
the Man that kept the other Shop was a Country Magistrate,
being a Headborough, and he fell upon her, bid G——
D——n her for an impudent Jade to come to buy Things a
Sabbath Days, why could she not have come a *Saturday* Night?
I forgot to tell you the first of these, even that Mr. Church-
Warden himself, is a Notorious Drunkard, and does not scruple it on a Sabbath Day, as well as on any other Day.   This
is a specimen of our Reformation in the Country.   I hope
yours in the City is much better, particularly, I am told you
were very Sober in the City this Year in your Treats for
Common Council-Men; and tho' it is all Bribery and Corrup-

tion, and that of the worst kind, yet being so near *Christmas*, it all goes into the pious Account of keeping the *Good Time*. So that there is Bribery for the good of our Country, and Revelling in Honour of our Saviour; if all this will not atone for, or at least cover a little out of the Way Merriment it will be very hard.

Here's a Justice of the Peace in our Town has lost the good will of all his Neighbours for setting a poor honest Drunken Fellow in the Stocks for being Drunk a *Thursday* last, being the Second Day of *Christmas*; "a cruel unconscionable Dog," say his Neighbours, "to set a poor Fellow in the Stocks for having Drunk a little too much in the *Christmas* Holy-Days! Why if a Man cannot take a Chirruping Cup at *Christmas*, and when he gets it a free Cost too, when can he do it? Why every Body is merry at *Christmas!* What are the *Christmas* Holy-Days made for?" And thus they go Raving about the Justice; but if the Justice himself would be Drunk too, and Drunk with them, not a Dog would wag his Tongue against him.

Thus stands our Case as to the keeping religious Days. For my part, I question whether Drunkenness will not be Counted by some People a Religious Ceremony; they seem already to Mingle it with all Publick Accounts, such as National Thanksgivings, Treats for Elections, *Christmas* Holy-Days, and the like. What Pity 'tis we have no Feast for Godsake such as the *Bacchanalia* were, in Honour of their Gods. I wonder whether the *Jews* are not Drunk sometimes at their Feast of Tabernacles, Feast of Trumpets, and the like; if they are not, I dare say we should, if we had any such appointed Times of Feasting erected by Law, but of that hereafter.

A Piece of Oriental Bombast.

A. J., Jan. 4, 1724.—Sir, The following Letter coming unexpectedly to my Hands upon the Situation of the Affairs in the Eastern Parts of the World, I thought it of Importance to send it to a Man of your Extraordinary Opportunities, I mean in the Way of Publication; that the World may hear some of the Cant of other Countries, for we hear Enough every Day of our Own.

"To the Illustrious Great Renowned Happy Sultan *Ibrahim*

Chan, Great *Vizier Azem*, first Minister, General and General-
lissimo of the Armies of the Invincible Empire of the Grand
Seignior ; *Head* and *Chief Councellor* of the Great Imperial
Divan, and Council of Councellors, who Guide the whole
World under the Light and the Splendour of the Illustrious
PORT.   The Great Right Hand of Empire, and the Director
of happy Measures, whose Days be many, whose Light be
Glorious, and his End Happy.

" I Sultan *Solyman, Eschemai Ismael Schah Miriwies*, Conqueror of the East, whose Court is the Refuge of the Oppressed,
and the dread of Tyrants and Oppressors ; who by the Splendour of my Divine Wisdom, imitating the Sun and Moon, do
good to the Oppressed Nation of *Persia*, and sit on the Throne
of the Immortal *Schah Abbas;* I Protector of the Race of the
Faithful, and Governor of the Governors of the Mighty Provinces of *Persia*, from *India* to *Armenia*, and from the Rivers
Oxus and *Indus* to the *Euphrates* and *Araxis*.

Send Greeting.

" Be it known unto Thee, Prince of the Generals of the Earth,
and Invincible Vizier, That by this Bearer, *Ischan Oglan
Mehemet Ali* my faithful Servant, I have sent my Missive
Letter, address'd to the Footstool of the Illustrious Throne of
the Grand Seignior, thy Lord ; giving his Imperial Greatness
an Account of the Prosperity of my invincible Arms, by the
Assistance of God and under our great Prophet *Mahomet ;* and
how I have Vanquish'd the Power of *Ho Invanoscha Abassi*
General and Vizier to him, who unworthily assumed to wear
the bright Diadem, the Crown of *Persia*, shining with Rubies
and Spotless Emeralds ; and who, flying before my Armies as
Chaff before the Wind, has left me possest of the High, and
Venerable Court and Throne of his glorious Predecessor, *Schah
Abbas*, as also of the Towers, and Immortal Gates of *Ispahan*,
with the Palace of the Kings, and the immense Riches of
Three and Thirty Monarchs of *Persia*.

" Know thou also Illustrious Vizier, That I am possest of
all the Cities of *Persia*, from the ancient *Samarcand*, the Holy
City, to *Erzirum*, and Mighty *Taurus*, and am surrounded with
the Invincible Armies of *Persia ;* so that I am well able to
Support and Maintain my Authority, and even to have

assumed the glorious Title of the *Persian* Throne, whereof I
rather desire to be the Saviour and Protector. Nor do I want
thy Assistance to Chastise the Insolence of the *Unbelievers* and
Rebels of *Georgia*, who have not only presumed to oppose my
Successes, (though without being able to put a Stop to the
Progress of my Power,) but have called in to their assistance
the *Barbarians* under the Dominions of the Unbelievers of
Muscovia, and *Circassia*, the *Tartars of Kalmuck*, and *Cara-
kathay*, and have betrayed to them the Shoars of the Sea of
Baku, whose Pride God will Humble by my Hand; but I seek
the Friendship of the Illustrious Port, and the Favour of the
Grand Seignior, thy Lord, That thou mayest let the World
see the indissolvable Union of all the Faithful *Mussulmans*;
and that the Worshippers of our great Prophet will Assist one
another on all Occasions, to Tread under Foot the Power of
their Enemies. Know therefore Mighty and Illustrious, that
I willingly yield to thy Invincible Lord all the Northern and
Western Border of *Persia*, for which so many Bloody Battles
have been Fought between the immortal Sultan *Selymus*, and
our Ancestors; to the Effusion of much precious Blood of true
Believers; to the End that the Illustrious Port, enjoying a free
Possession of the said Border, from *Erzirum* to *Bagdat*, and
the *Persian* Gulph; a firm and inviolable Peace may remain
between the two Empires for ever.

" Wherefore Illustrious *Ibrahim*, command thy Servant *Chusan
Bassa*, who now leads the Invincible Armies of the *Port* to
take Possession of the said Border, and to sign the said Agreement of ever during Peace. The Bearer also will deliver to
thy Illustrious Hand two Thousand Purses for the Treasures of
thy Lord, as also 500 Purses to thy Slave *Ischaw Ibrahim*,
Master of thy Treasures, for the Service of thy particular
Affairs, which I send, a Part of the Spoil of our Enemies.

" Henceforth Victory attend thy Council, and Prosperity
the bright Throne of the *Sultan's* Glory; may his Name be
Renowned among the Posterity of *Ottoman* and *Orchan*; may
he continue to enlarge his Dominions upon the Ruins of Unbelievers; and, may *Persia* flourish, and be at all Times ready
to aid thee with an Hundred Thousand Horse to carry the
Glorious Half Moon into the Heart of the *Circassian* Kingdoms, and all others the Enemies of thy Lord. *Amen.*"

Here's Language for a Rebel, Mr. *App.* Pray, what a fine Condition do you think the *Czar* is like to be in, between two such Powers as these, if one half of what is here Pretended be True?   But of that hereafter.

On Instinctive Tendencies to take Part in Disputes.

A. J., Jan. 11.— . . . . . . I have observed, that if it be but two little Boys fighting in the Streets; or, if it be anything higher, nay, from the two Boys fighting, to the Gladiators in the Bear Garden; and from thence still higher, to any of the Party Causes so contested among us, either in Parliament, or out of it; still there is some Thing so busy, so meddling, and so very odd in the Nature of Man, that whoever looks on, be he never so Unconcerned; and tho' he never saw, or heard of the Battle before, yet he must take Part, with one Side or other, in his very Thoughts.

If we see the two little Boys fighting, we cannot help it, we must Clap one on the Back, and Discourage the other; even in the common Gossiping of Women in hearing a Story told, where any two Opposites are concerned, we are Byassed from the beginning in Favour of *this*, or *that*, as the Fact is repre-sented.

Man is a busy Creature, and will be meddling with every Thing; and even those that seem to be most Unconcerned,— yet *so it is*, they must be of one Side or the other; they must in their most secret retired Thoughts, wish this Side the better, and that the worse, tho' the Consequence is not one Farthing value to them.

On Impediments to Justice.

A. J., Jan. 18.—Sir, I was accidentally the other Day in Company with two Gentlemen of very different Professions, and having each of them a strong Attachment to the Business he was Bred to; it was not the hardest Thing in the World for a third Man to engage them in a Dispute.

A Friend of mine, who had the art to conceal his Profession, tho' perhaps as liable to Exception as any of the Others; told them that he had a Question to propose to those Gentlemen, which he should be very glad they would decide between them, if they would promise but to keep the Peace, and not fall out.

They gave mutual Assurances of a peaceable Disposition, being indeed both merry Fellows, not at all dangerous to Debate with; and so the Question was stated as follows;— (viz.)—

"Which was likely to be soonest finished, supposing them to begin at the same Time, *a Voyage round the World*, or *a Chancery Suit ?*"

I do not think fit at present to trouble you with the learned Turns, and Returns which pass'd among the Parties concerned in this Dispute; Nor can I resolve you at present, which of the Disputants gained the Victory. 'Tis sufficient to tell you that the Affair, like a long Suit, hangs still upon the Hooks, and your Readers may finish the Argument, if they can.

I have heard that in *France*, Suits at Law have formerly been left from Father to Son, and from Generation to Generation, for near a Hundred Years together, till the Complainants tired with the Scandalous Usage of the Advocates, have been obliged to decide the Controversy, *Au Coup de Fusil*. I am told, indeed, that they have a more Summary Way of late, and that this was a great While ago.

In *Spain*, they tell us, that *Jealousy* and a Game at CHESS, will serve two Neighbours to Struggle with, and Snarl at one another about, from Age to Age; and when, by Assassinating, Killing in the Dark, (and by other Ways and Means,) five or six Heirs, as well of the direct, as collateral Branches, are cut off on a Side, and any one of the said Families comes to be Extinct, then the Quarrel is sure to cease, and have an End, *as you will say*, 'tis Time it should.

Hereditary Malice, I must Confess, is a very pretty Thing, and Family Quarrels are a good Sort of Parish Football, that sets a whole Town a kicking one another most violently, two or three Times a year; while they Drink together very Friendly all the rest of the Time.

It seems to me, upon the whole, that this Thing call'd *Going to Law*, in the usual Form, is a kind of *Civil War* between Plaintiff and Defendant; where, while the *Hannibals* and *Scipios* of the BAR draw up in Array in the Courts of Judicature and Fight with, and Manage that Carnal Weapon the Tongue, with the utmost Fury; Marshalling their Troops

(Arguments) one against another, with such Dexterity and Art
as can never be enough admired; the Judges, like *the* GODS,
sit *spectant Regardant,* disposed to hand Victory down to this
Side, or to that, as the Reward of Merit, and as Right and
Justice require.

All that I can see to complain of is, these Armies, on either
Side, are so long in their Preparation, their *Marches, De-
marches,* and *Countermarches;* and are so Tedious before they
can bring Matters to a decisive Battle, that it makes the War
too chargeable to the Undertakers. The Apparatus of the
Combat costs oftentimes more Money than the Advantage of
the Victory amounts to; so that we often see the Conqueror
a Loser, and he that Triumphs Ruined by the Joy.

Certainly would the Powers of the Earth Study the Peace
of their Subjects, and the Prosperity of Families, there might
be a shorter way to Justice, than is at present to be found in
most Parts of the World; for I am not speaking of the Courts
of Justice in *England.*

The Blessed Apostle St. *Paul* could not get Justice at *Jerusalem;* and was, at his own request carried to *Cæsarea.* Not
able to obtain a fair Hearing at *Cæsarea,* he Appealed to *Rome,*
to be heard before *Cæsar;* a Blessed Course of Law, when an
innocent Man should be forced to fly for Justice to such a
bloody, merciless Tyrant as the Emperor NERO.

We have had several Examples of modern Justice in the
ordinary Process of Law in our Days. Our Merchants have
had Law-Suits in *America,* in the *Spaniards* Dominions; and
from thence have been obliged to Appeal to old *Spain.*

Suits at Law in one kingdom are referred to another, only
for want of Justice. Wherefore do Appeals lie from Inferior
Judicature to Superior, but for want of Justice in the Inferior
Courts? Like as our People in *England,* remove Causes from
the Inferior Courts to the Superior, till they come to the
Supreme; as from lower Courts by *Certiorari* to the Courts of
Westminster-Hall, from the *King's Bench,* or *Common Pleas,* by
Bills of Complaint to the *Chancery,* from *Chancery* to the
House of Peers, and the like.

Some say the tediousness of Suits at Law, has a Tendency
to keep People in Peace,—and perhaps it may be so in many
Cases; but I must acknowledge, if a shorter, and above all, a

cheaper way was found out to determine Controversies between Man and Man, 'twould preserve honesty more, and take away the Occasion of so many legal Battles, as I mention above.

Many knavish Men go to Law in Expectation to Hamper and Perplex, and thereby to tire out the Persons they contend with, and so carry the Point merely by the strength of Money; but if Process at Law was made Easy and Cheap, poor Men would certainly obtain more Justice in the World, and rich Men would not so easily oppress.

A Declaration in favour of Free Trade.

A. J., Jan. 25.—. . . . . These Projectors are the same kind of People, (tho' perhaps not the same Men,) who loaded the Nation with deficient Funds, unperforming Schemes, and preposterous Taxes in King *William's* Time, especially in the beginning of his Reign ; for the King began to be aware of them towards the latter end of it ; These, I say, were the Men who sent the King into the Field without Money, drove his faithful Soldiers to March without Pay, without Shoes, to live without Clothes, nay, almost without Bread, and to fight without Pay;—that oppressed the Nation with Taxes, yet raised little or nothing for the King ; that ate up the Government with Anticipations, high Interests, cursed Discounts, strange Lotteries, and innumerable Cheats, almost as bad as the late *Harburgh Lottery,* and its additional *sham Project,* till in a Word, the King was almost Undone, and the Nation too, and now we are come to say, as in the Text, *These Men who have turned the World upside down, are come hither also.*

I have nothing to say to what the Government are doing, or intend to do ; I am talking of things, and of People without Doors. . . . . I must lay it down as a Maxim in this Case, that Clandestine Trade, however Ruinous, will never cease till we can Abate our Customs. High Duties encourage Smuggling, as rich Travellers tempt Highwaymen.

Defence of Charles I. against Bishop Burnet's Own Times.

A. J., Feb. 1.—Sir, The Day on which we Celebrate the Martyrdom of King *Charles* the First, being but two Days past, I could not pass the Remembrance of it over without

Q 2

giving some few Observations upon the Conduct of a late
Right Reverend Historian, the Bishop of Salisbury on this
Occasion.

That extraordinary Author having thought fit not only to
Rake in the Ashes of the Dead, but in the Sacred Ashes of
the best of Kings, and in particular those of the best King of
that Age, has given me such a Taste of his Sincerity as a
Historian, and especially of his Honesty as a Christian Bishop,
that as well as I love Episcopacy, and as much Veneration as
I have for an *English* Christian Bishop; I think I would
heartily give my Vote for a Law that no more Bishops should
write any more Histories; or at least, that if they did, they
should publish while they were alive. That if they wrote any
false Things, or Scandalous Things, or Things unworthy of the
Christian Name, they might be punished as they deserved.

Whereas, here is an Author, who having complimented an
infamous Usurper, Tyrant and Murtherer, and spent Twenty
Folio sides in a continued Panegyrick upon his Person and
Administration; falls upon the injured Ashes of the Royal
Martyr, with such Fury, such Acrimony, and withal, such notorious Falshood, that it ought to move the Detestation of all
who read it; while the same Author, as if his Malice was carried
to the Grave with him, seems to please himself with Skulking
behind Death, as a Skreen to shelter himself from just Resentment. One would think the Bishop fancied that he should
have the satisfaction after he was Dead, of thinking how he
had incurred the Curses of a just Nation, but was out of the
reach of their Resentment.

Welfare the Bishop, *where he is*; and if we may Judge by
the Falsehood, want of Charity, visible Malice, and other
extraordinary Virtues of his History, no Man will envy him
the present Condition of his Affairs; but as his Memory must
be Infamous, who falsly loads the Memory of just Men with
Infamy, let those that admire the Bishop share with him the
Reward of Infamy, even after they are in their Graves.

It may perhaps seem a little harsh to fall upon any Man's
Character in his Grave; but then the Bishop should not have
begun it, for the History is indeed nothing else. Nay, it
seems to be a general Combustion made among the Graves of
great and good Men. His laborious Work is I think, chiefly

employed in giving his Dogmatick Characters of the Dead.
What Measure he metes, must be measured to him again. How
can he be dealt with otherwise, and good Men be Vindicated?
Yet, after all, when he has, in a most infamous Manner, reproached the suffering King, and used his Memory in the
Worst Manner he can; when he has loaded him with his Dull
and Dirty Sarcasms, and Misrepresented him to the Utmost;
yet speaking of him in his Solitudes and Sufferings, he owns
that his Majesty behaved in such a manner as could not have
been done by Human Nature; that is to say, he bears Witness
to his being Supported by a *Supernatural* Assistance, (Folio 47)
and that he behaved with a composed Firmness, which amazed
all People.

What greater Testimony of a glorious Patience than this!
And that from an Enemy too! I must call him so; for what
greater Enemy could there be to such an unblemish'd Character, than he that can preserve the Rancour of his mind for
above Seventy Years? And after that length of Time, as the
Scripture calls it in another Case, *Murther him afresh and put
him to an Open Shame.* 'Tis spoken by the Apostle,—Author
of the Epistle to the *Hebrews*,—of such hardened ones, who
sinned Knowingly against the Mercy of the Redeemer, of
whom he says, *They Crucify the Son of God afresh, and put
him to an open Shame.* (HEB. 6 v. 6.) I hope 'tis not an
unjust, or indecent Allusion here. The Bishop has not only
exposed the Character of the Royal Sufferer; but has Dis-
honoured his Memory by loading him unjustly, and giving a
false Account of him.

It is the Satisfaction of all to whom the Memory of King
Charles is dear, that he suffers here only under the Weight of
a Collection of Calumny. The Characters in this History are
so universally Scandalous, 'tis not strange that so shining a
Part as this of the Murthered King should suffer among the
rest. 'Tis an additional Satisfaction, as I hear from such
Hands, as I believe are not uninformed; that there is not one
just Character in the Book except his own, whose just Character is drawn from this, that all the rest are unjust.

Another Knowing Person bids me tell you, that if you find
Occasion to draw a Bill upon him for a Hundred Falsities, he
will undertake to pay your Bill, at Sight, out of this History.

If this be true, the Bishop's Character will indeed make some Shew in the Histories of our own Times, that may appear hereafter.

My Friend also bids me Promise you, that if you have a Mind to a Specimen of the History of the Bishop's Life and Manners; he may, in a few Days, furnish you with one as Black and Horrid as any to be found in all his own History.

Your Humble Servant,

♈︎   ♉︎   ♊︎   ♋︎

Aries, Taurus, Gemini, Cancer, &c.

A Merry Astrological Story.

A. J., Feb. 8.—Sir, Being the other Day at a Friend's House where the Family was disposed to be very innocently Merry, our Mirth was all on a Sudden Checked, and the whole Family put into a Hurry, I won't say fright, upon the following Occasion. The Lady of the House, the Mother of the young Family, sent a Summons down Stairs, in more haste than Ordinary, for her Husband; he had not been gone three Minutes, but he came again, runs out in a Hurry, bid his Coach follow him to such a Place, and in short, we were soon told his Business was to fetch the Midwife. Notwithstanding all the haste he could make, (and he was gone but a little while neither,) the Lady was so nimble, that by that Time the good Wife of Business had been with her a Quarter of an Hour, she was delivered of a Son.

Our Joy had so little Interruption, that we began to be Merrier than we were before; but finding our Friend the Husband Absent, and enquiring after him, I understood he was in the next Room; when going to him, I found him busy with the Midwife before him, and a Watch in her Hand, and a Nurse with another Watch in her Hand, and he with Pen, Ink and Paper before him. When I examined farther, I perceived what was the Matter; namely, that my Friend was employed in taking a Critical Account of the Hour and Minute, nay, the Moment that his Son was Born. What he meant by it, was not hard to find out; for I knew he was one that thoroughly understood the Influences of the Heavenly Bodies, Motions of the Planets, &c. But I found, that not content with his own Knowledge, and the Observations he

made from his own Calculations, he was resolved to have the
Opinion of other People also; for he sent his Account of the
Nativity of the child to five or six several Persons, whose
Astrological Skill he had some Knowledge of, in order to have
their Judgment in the Case.

This put me in Mind of a good Story, which happened in
the Court of the Duke of *Mantua* some years ago.   The Duke,
who was a great Horse Master, and kept the best Breed of
Horses of any of the Princes in that Part of the World, had
a Mare, (which he had a great value for,) proved to be so ill
Guarded by the Grooms, that she was big with Foal, and to
his Surprize brought forth a Mule.

The Duke, tho' provoked at the Grooms, yet turning his
Anger into Mirth, causes the Minute, or Moment, of the
Heterogenous Birth to be enquired; and Setting it down ex-
actly in Writing, he sent Notice of it to several famous
Students in Astrology, some at *Milan*, some at *Rome*, some at
Venice, and perhaps several others, intimating, that such a
Day, Hour, Minute, and Second of Time, a Female in his
Court was delivered of a Bastard ; desiring to know the result
of their Calculations, and the Effects of such a Birth.

The Astrologers all went to Work immediately, to shew
their Obedience to his Highness's Commands, and Dispatched
their Conclusions with all Speed ; but nothing in the World
could be more contradicting and inconsistent.   One predicted
it should be a General in the Imperial Armies, and should
gain great Honour in the Field of Battle against the *Turks ;*
another said, he would be a Marshal of *France,* and the Third
made him a *Bishop.   I think he did not say he should write a*
HISTORY *of his own Times.*   Others made him Head of a New
order of Priests, some Knighted him, others Sainted him ; and
at last, one Predicted he should be Pope ; and go, in a Solemn
Procession, at such a Time, from the Vatican, to a certain Church.

But when all came to the upshot, the Birth, was a poor
Mule, who had none of all these great Things in his View.   I
need not tell you what Rage it filled the Calculators with,
which was best exprest by one of them, sending the Duke
Word, that he had Calculated his Nativity for him, and his
Fate should be to Live a Tyrant, and Die in Exile ; but the
Astrologers Account did not prove true.

This was, I confess, an admirable Experiment of the Truth which there ordinarily is to be found in the best Astrological Predictions; and I thought it very suitable to be sent you at this Time, when the Pulse of the Times beats so high for Heresy, and Idolatry; for generally those People are great Astrologers. Also this being a Time when People read much in their Almanacks, and pore much upon the Blazing Star that has lately appeared, and upon the Eclipse that is to happen.

I may give you some farther Hints about it, on Account of the present Revolution in *Spain;* but of that hereafter.

On the Abdication of the King of Spain.

A. J., Feb. 15.—Sir, We have had so many Speculations at Work, and so many Calculators of Times and Seasons upon this new Revolution in *Spain;* that I cannot but think the King of Spain has made more Work for the Sooth-sayers, than ever *Pharaoh* King of *Egypt,* or *Nebuchadnezzar* King of *Babylon* did.

I must own, in my Opinion the Reasons, which they say the King of *Spain* has given for his laying down the Royal Dignity, are the Weakest, not to say the Foolishest, that ever I met with in History. When his great Predecessor *Charles* the 5th abdicated, and gave up the Imperial Crown to his second Son *Ferdinand,* and the Crown of *Spain* to his Eldest Son *Philip* II., among other Reasons he gave for it, These were some, (viz.) That he was weakened *by Age,* worn out *with Cares,* and many Fatigues, and reduced to an infirm State *of Body,* by a declining Health, and Distempers growing Daily upon him; so that he was unable to undergo the Burthen of the Government, and the Weight of so many Crowns. These Things had some Consideration due to them. It was Time for him to apply, if ever, with more than ordinary Seriousness to the Thoughts of another Life. He had one Foot in the Grave. He was loaden with Honour and with Years, and indeed lived but a little While after it.

On the other hand, here is a young Monarch, not yet forty Years Old, that has had no Fatigues to go through, never went out of his Kingdom, but once into *Italy,* that has had always the Administration of his Affairs in the Hands of his Ministry, and the Care of Government as much taken off his Hand too as he pleased; and yet he lays down his Government, and obliges a Young and Beautiful Queen to do the like. Divesting themselves of all the Pleasure and Grandeur of a Court, and the Majesty and Glory of a Crown, and turning recluse; contrary to the common Principles of Nature, and to all that we can Account for in Human Reasoning.

The Reasons his Majesty gives for all this,—so far as we have them handed down to us—are, that he may give up himself to *meditate on Death*, and to *seek his Salvation.*

Now if these are really the true Reasons, I must confess, *to me*, they are very weak ones; and this makes me say, the Doubts which some People have of the Sincerity of those Appearances seem also, *to me*, to have better Grounds than ordinary.

Nor let any one suggest that it is *Maltreating* the King of *Spain* to say those Reasons are weak; on the contrary, I think they are a Testimony of an uncommon Respect for the King of *Spain*, and that I have a great Veneration for his Judgment, and for his Experience of human Affairs, and therefore cannot readily come into the Belief of his quitting the Crown, on Account of Two Things, which he might as certainly, and effectually have looked after with the Crown upon his Head, as he can without it; or else, all the Kings in *Europe* are but in a very ordinary Condition, as to the World to come.

If the Weight of the Crown was too heavy for his Head, or there were some ungodly Things necessary to be done by a King of *Spain*, which other Kings are not obliged to; those indeed are Cases by themselves, but we do not see any Ground for either of them. King *Philip* had worn the Crown about Three and Twenty Years; and, in all that Time, History does not charge him with any Thing so much out of the Way, as to make us think he was very unfit to Reign. We do not hear his Majesty charged with Idiotism, or gross Weakness; and, as to the Crown of *Spain*, I will not insinuate that a King cannot wear it with as safe a Conscience, as other Kings wear their Crowns. So that 'tis very odd, the King should not be able to think of Death, and seek his Salvation, without relinquishing his Crown.

Now if the Crown of Spain is no more liable to these Negatives than other Crowns, What must we say of all the Kings of *Europe,* who occupy the State of Glory in their Degrees? Hard is the Fate of Crowned Heads, if they cannot apply themselves to the Things of another World, and that with the greatest Seriousness and Diligence, without giving up their Crowns.

Dedicating to God is another Word used for this Abdication. Now I can by no means believe but that a King Dedicating the Power, which he is invested with by his Administration, effectually to the Service and Glory of God, is able to Honour his Creator much more, and it is a much better Dedication of himself to God than any he could be capable of in a private retired Capacity. If this is not Granted I am ready to support it with good Arguments, drawn from both Reason and Religion.

But on the other Hand, if it is granted, as it must be, then the King of *Spain* laying down his Royal Dignity, and Divesting himself of his Royal Authority, to Dedicate himself to God; is a kind of Religious inconsistency, to say no worse of it. As to there being a Juggle in it at the Bottom, and that the Design looks at another Crown, that I have nothing to say to just now; but in Favour to all the rest of the Monarchs of the Christian World, I must be allowed to say, a King may certainly be a Christian, with the Crown upon his Head, as well as in a Monastery, or other Retreat; and may give himself a due Latitude of Time to Meditate upon Death, and seek his Salvation, notwithstanding the Cares of Government, and the Weight of Administration. Nay, if they would, as above, apply themselves to Administer their Affairs, in the Fear and to the Glory of God, it might be for ought I know the best way of seeking their Salvation that they could possibly fall into. From whence I must infer, that either the King of *Spain* has been very much imposed upon, or there must be more in it, than we yet hear of.

The Journalistic Propriety of Writing Scandal, Faction, and Treason.

A. J., Feb. 22.—Sir, Upon the News which some of your Journals published last Week, it seems to be received, as a Thing which every Body believes, that the Breach between the

Czar of *Muscow* and the *Turks*, is at last like to be made up, and a general Peace on that Side of the World like to be re-newed.

Upon this Occasion I think I ought to Condole with you News-Writers on a dreadful Famine which is likely to come upon you, and which, in a Word, 'tis likely will not only Starve you all, but all your Readers also; for you will now have no fighting Stories to tell, no Battle and Blood to Distribute. In a Word, the Appetite of the Readers of those Things, their very Taste of foreign Intelligence will wear out, they will be-gin to be Sick of their unsatisfied Enquiries, and leave them off. And what will you do then?

It is true, News-Writers can turn their Hand to any Thing, and when Fighting and Wars are at an End, you can look back to the Ages behind us, and tell of Fightings and Wars that are past, and this may serve you for a while; but it will be but a little while neither, before that will wear out too.

But then you have a never failing Shift, and that is to write Scandal, Faction, and Treason. Let me handle the Three Heads apart; for they are very significant Things, and I know not well how to share them equally among you. There is the *True Briton*, and the *London Journal*; for Scandal, Serious, Bishoplike Scandal, I think they grow Eminent. 2. Nobody will dispute but that Friend *Mist* must be chief among Writers of Faction; nay, he has paid for the Place, and should not be Defrauded of the Title.

And I think, since you call yourself Original, Mr. *App*, you may be reserved for the exclusive Privilege of writing Treason. They say your Operator has been acquainted with it, and you have no Reason to be Offended, for I am for giving you a Lati-tude that will secure you;—(viz.) That you shall not need to begin till you please, and till you find Occasion for it.

However, for your Encouragement, let me hint to you, that it will certainly make your Paper sell. If you want to make your Journal popular, 'tis the shortest Step you can take. A publick Paper never goes off so well, as when the Author goes to *Newgate* for it. There is something so wicked in the Gust of Men's reading palates in this Age, that they love what is Malicious; something Wicked, in every Paper. One Dram of Treason pleases better than a pound of Wit. In lower Things, any Thing that is Malicious; any Thing Slanderous, any Thing ill natured, sells better than the brightest Piece of Virtuous Wit that can be Written. What else makes a certain Bishop's History of Hearsay sell as it does? And why do the most Modest Ladies love to read Bawdy,—the sober Clergy love Plays, and Romances? 'Tis all a Testimony of the Corruption of Human Nature, which is so apt to Embrace what is Evil, rather than what is Good.

But in the Meantime Mr. *App*, for you shall not begin to write Treason till we have a Reign that shall make it a Reason, I say, in the Meantime, there being no more Wars in the World to supply your Paper, I would have you Consider, and turn your Pen to something that may Hit the Humours of the Times; and, in the first Place,—what do you think of Rummaging the Ages past, as the Bishop has done? Do you think the Bishop has not left you enough to Glean after him? Yes, yes, Mr. *App*, depend upon it, and a Gleaning, that would be better than his Harvest.

And tho' he should have Gleaned to the utmost, and there were nothing left for those that came after him, Why, then *a History of the Bishop* would do, as well as a Second Part of the Bishop's History. And this is, I can assure you, so far from being impossible to come at, that I am assured it is to be come at; nay, as I am informed by one who I believe is not misinformed,—*to use the Bishop's own Words*,—it is certainly done, and you may, with the help of good Friends, come to have more than a Sight of it. And so much for the Bishop.

This however, you may Teach the World, from the Example of his Lordship; namely, What a Length this new Way of Posthumous Scandal will go. 'Tis an admirable Way indeed! A Man may know how to secure an Estate to his Children after his Death, when perhaps he can leave them little or Nothing, but that and his Blessing; namely, to leave a Heap of Scandal and Faction for them to publish in his Name; and, be it True or False, it runs, 'tis sure to sell, and the Man who is to bear the Blows is gone, so the Proverb is but a little turned, and it may be expressed thus :—

"*Happy the Son whose Father is gone (to the rest of their Authors of Scandal.*")

Pray then, Mr. *App*, be pleas'd to Advertise the *Secret*

History of the late B—— of *S.* faithfully Collected by Hearsay, (at least) at the Third or Fourth Hand, and founded upon Report; being taken from the Mouths of those who believed they were not Misinformed, ready for the Press, and may be published, for ought we know, some Time or other, after the *Ides* of *March* next.

If such an Advertisment were published about a week after he that would write such a Book was buried, I dare say it would be a very acceptable Work. I would therefore wish you to Consider of it; for indeed the Life of Bishop —— would make an admirable History, as you may Understand hereafter.

A *Quaker Letter* on a *False Lover.*

A. J., Feb. 29.—Friend *App*,—There hath happened an Occasion of much Wrath and Displeasure in our Neighbourhood, in that *Aminadab Undercrust*, whose lawful Calling is the Supplying the People with the Staff of Life, *call'd Bread*, having a Design to take unto him a Wife, has given Offence to the Good People of the Land, by speaking to a Female Neighbour concerning Marriage, and desiring to come in unto her into the Inner Chamber, and then wickedly Desisting, and refusing to Join himself unto her, after she had Inclined her Heart to suffer him to come in unto her, as aforesaid.

This Thing hath not been according to Truth, neither has Friend *Dab* done Righteously in the same; forasmuch, as he, having not obtained her Consent without some length of Time, and many Days importunity, hath Endeavoured to make her a Laughing Stock unto the World, intending to have her be Despised in the Day appointed. It is true, that it is turned much to her Favour, because she behaved Wisely and Prudently in Resisting him from the Beginning, when, as it seemeth unto me, he would have come in unto her without her being Betrothed to him, or given to him in Marriage Rites; which thing, if it be of Verity, bringeth Shame unto him, and verily, good Men speak much Evil against him, by reason thereof.

It also seemeth, that the Female spoken of on this Occasion, is a good Woman, and of a good Report, a Mother in *Israel (England)* and also proceeded, by Birth, from some of the Heads of the House of her Fathers. Whereas *Aminadab*, verily is the

Son of a strange Woman, a mere *Undercrust*, whom we know not; and therefore he hath done wickedly to offer to Defile a Daughter of *Israel*, (*England*) and it will be spoken of to his Shame for many Days to come.

It hath indeed been said, that he has some just Impediment, which he knoweth within himself, why they might not be lawfully Joined together; and therefore he withdrew himself from the Marriage Supper, being ashamed upon that Account. But this seemeth to bear the more Reproach, forasmuch as he should not then have spoken to her thereof at the Beginning. Others also have differed in their Accounts of that Matter, and say, that it is not because of any Impediment, which is call'd *Natural*, being a Deficiency causing Impotency, *and the like;* but the having had his Conversation too much with the Daughters of the Land, who are indeed the children of *Belial*, he had obtained a Gift from one of them, which they say, he may indeed give away again, and yet keep Possession thereof also unto himself, which he was unwilling to do. All which is spoken of, I say, in his Favour, forasmuch as he could not be an honest Man to Join together the Sound, and the Unsound. Wherefore they say he is Resolved to be *Baked* in his own *Oven*, Or, as the Profane call it, be *Pickled* in his own *Powdering Tub;* and then he will speak further to her of this Matter.

But now, poor *Dab* has another Evil Thing happened unto him; namely, that the Female hath resolv'd, with Speed, to join herself unto another, to take away her Reproach from among Women; and, that if Friend *Aminadab* offers to ask her in Marriage again, she will answer him, that verily she is given unto one more worthy. It is farther known, that this Female is a Woman of great Substance, which would have accrued unto him; and the loss of which, we hear is already a great Subject of *Down Casting* to our Friend *Dab*.

All these I signify unto thee Friend *App*, that thou mayest put him to Shame, for his Unrighteous Doings; and moreover, for his Folly. For verily he deserveth Rebuke from thee. Let him then be made a Scorn of to the Daughters of the Land, and let him be scoffed at in the Streets; nay, let Songs of him be made, and let the Vile Ones sing them in the publick Places of the City. When the Woman that he has thus Misused rides by him in her Leather Tenement, (*the Convenience of the Vain,*) let him be Laughed at to Scorn, and let him behold it with Sorrow and Shame; let him even swell with Envy, and let him be Despised of all that know it; let him Eat what he Bakes, and no Body come to Buy; let him be rejected of Women, and let even the Ugly say him nay; let him be ever asking, and ever denied; let the young Women mock him, the Middle-aged Spit upon him, and the Ancient speak evil of him.   Forasmuch as he intended to cast Blame upon the Innocent; but that his Folly is fallen back upon himself, and has loaded him with Infamy.

Farewell, Thy Friend,

OBADIAH BLUE HAT.

Character of a Wicked Landlord.

A. J., Mar. 7.—Mr. *App,*—Exposing Scandalous Crimes is a Debt due to Virtue, that if the Criminal be out of the reach of Justice, or find means to Evade it, the Country may not bear the Scandal of the Crimes they Abhor; and also, that the Person may have some of the Shame due to his Wickedness, tho' he Escapes the Punishment of it.

It is true, that no Subject, I mean in our well ordered Government, is out of the reach of Justice, in a legal Sense; but yet, some Men, by their Situation among the People, whom they have a particular Influence over, and also, by the particular Nature of their Crimes, have greater Opportunities to be scandalously Wicked, than others; and this favourable, or rather partial Distribution of Justice, is one of the present Grievances of this Nation.   Let me suppose a Case to you for the exemplifying the Thing, and shewing what I mean in this Introduction.

Supposing there is a Man, *I don't say a Christian Man, much less a Protestant Man, but a Person,* dwelling in a civilized Christian Nation; where they pretend at least to an excellent Governing Magistracy, and to wholesome Laws, for the regulating both Property and good Manners, and for Preserving them.

Suppose then a Thing called a Gentleman, vested with a particular Influence among the common People, by the happy Incident of about 3000*l. per annum* Estate.   Supposing this

Estate so conveniently situated for the Purpose I mention, (viz.) of giving him an Influence over the People, that he has no Superior near him. That it lies contiguous with itself, almost all in one uninterrupted Line or Space, so that he has several Villages, and some considerable Towns, all, or almost all, his own; by which means he has a universal Homage within his Bounds,—as being Lord of the Manor, or rather many Manors together,—all the Inhabitants being Tenants, and consequently his Dependents, and almost all the Women among them in his power.

Suppose even the Peace Officers, and even some Justices of the Peace, so far his Tenants, or under his Influence, as they either Care not, or dare not Disoblige him; and which is worse than all, suppose him entrusted with a Commission of the Peace himself.

Suppose then this Man acting with so much Rigour, not to call it Tyranny, among his Tenants, as to have them at his Command; even beyond the lowest degree of Submission, almost to that of *Vassal* and *Slave.*

If in pursuit of his Game, he breaks down their Fences, leaves open their Gates, rides over their Corn, or does them any other kind of damage, they dare not complain; much less dare they demand Reparation of Damage, or a Stop to the Depredations of their Tyrannical Landlord.

But to crown all, or rather, to make him a finished Tyrant, and shew his Tenants completely subjected Animals and Slaves, suppose him not riding over their Fences only, and over their Corn, but over their *Wives* and *Daughters;* openly Debauching them, and committing all manner of Rudeness with an unresisted Authority; as if his Right to their Farm, gave him a Right to their Properties, their Virtue, their whole Persons, Consciences, Souls and Bodies; his own virtuous Lady, at the same Time, obliged to turn out of Doors, and live-from him.

Suppose again, too many consenting to his Wickedness by a Depravity of WILL, owing to the general Decay of Virtue, and the badness of the Times; but many others by a kind of Fear, lest their Husbands should be deprived of their Livelihoods, and turned out of their Farms. Suppose him, however, to Let good Pennyworths, and his Tenants get good Advantages under him, in order to make room for this Exorbitant Behaviour.

Suppose now one of his Tenants marrying a young hand-some Wife in a Country distant, and bringing her home to his House, the Landlord comes to him with a *D—— ye* Goodman *L——, you pitiful Dog, do you intend to keep that pretty Woman there all to yourself? No, no, I must talk to you about that!*

Suppose a few Days after, he sends to the Man to send his Wife to him, on such and such pretended Business; but the Tenant tells him he understands him, and his Wife is not for his Worship's turn. Suppose then he is in a Rage, and the next time attacks the Wife, but she repulses him; and the next Thing you hear of, the Tenant is turned out of a good Farm; but is so just to his Country, and to his Landlord, as to defy the last, and proclaim his Conduct to the first.

Now Mr. *App*, as we may for Argument's sake, suppose all this *really to be*, tho' indeed it were really not so; what must we suppose if such a Case should be True? What must we say of the Execution of Justice in the Country, where such an Example should be found? How does the Parson do, if such a one there be, to manage the *Ecclesiasticks* in his Neighbour-hood, that they do not proclaim his Shame from the Pulpit? And the Ecclesiastick Courts that they do not take him into their Hands *Notor Adultery?* Or the *Civil Justice*, that he is not Indicted for Rapes, or Trespass? What can be said, why such a flaming Example of Vice should not be made a flaming Example of Justice, and why the World should not know the Man, that he may be stigmatized as he really Merits, that all honest Men may publish their Detestation of his Crimes, and he may be the Shame of the Gentry, as he is the Plague of the poor People about him?

Hitherto I have suggested such a Thing to you for your Censure, on the Supposition that such a Person may be in the World; but what if I should also tell you, that within a few Miles of the famous River *Trent*, something of this kind may perhaps upon good Enquiry be heard of; and, that if any En-quires of you Mr. *App*, you may, if you desire it, hear farther.

Your Humble Servant,
N—— Upon Trent.

Death of the Sheriff of London, and its Consequences.

A. J., May 14.—Sir, I am a Friend to all the just Proceedings of the Law, and acknowledge that Corrections themselves are absolutely Necessary; but what then? Tho' we are all willing a Murderer should be hang'd, yet all men hate the very looks of the *Hangman*.

Hence there is some little particular Satisfaction, even in People that are quite unconcerned in the Case itself, to see the general Mortifications of the whole Families of the *Catchpoles* at this Time; whose surly Looks, and Hawks-Eyes are so abated for some Days past, that they carry no Terror with them, as they used to do.

The Skulker and Shelterer who kept within Bounds, and appeared but in the Dark, go now boldly by Daylight abroad from *Old Gravel Lane,* and from the *Mint,* and fear no Colours. Even *Guildhall,* where a Thousand good Livery Men durst not come, has been Witness to Numbers who have strenuously Poll'd for some new Sheriffs, that when they have chosen them, will (that's ungrateful you'll say,) Seal the Warrant to Apprehend the very Men who so kindly Poll'd for them.

How many hidden *Courtiers* have these few Days of *Interregnum,* sent out of *the Verge* to visit their Friends, and Solicit their Enemies! A Clap on the Shoulder is now no Surprize, and the Question *at whose Suit,* is not the Language of the Day.

As I was coming thro' the Back Street behind St. *Clements,* I happened to look into a House, where I lately went to visit a Friend in his Affliction, and found a Bill upon the Door, HELLS *to be Let;* and coming the same Afternoon by the *Compter Gate,* in the *Poultry,* behold! there were the two Posts hung in Mourning, and all the Sergeants that used to Sit there, look'd like a Parcel of Hunger-starved Slaves, that had fed upon Bread and Water of Affliction.

From thence to satisfy my Curiosity, I took a Walk down *Wood Street.* There all was Shut up, and in great *Chalk*-Letters was written on the Bench, *These are Fasting Days;* and without the Gate, thus, *Chambers to be let unfurnished.*

All this, it seems, has been the Consequence of the Mortality of Sir —— *F—st,* our late Taskmaster, for whom the

Bums, the *Followers,* the *Bites,* and all the several Families of the Takers, are it seems made *to Mourn,* tho' not all *to go into Mourning.*

But to pass by all these, *Newgate* itself, it seems, is in great Tribulation, for by this *Interregnum* of the Magistrate, The Turnkey has no Hands, his great Keys have no Wards, and the Bolts will not stir; in short, the Gaol has been in Travail for *a Delivery,* but no Midwife can do it, but a Sheriff. Poor *W*——, and Vile ——, can't get at the Gallows on any Account whatsoever, till a new Sheriff is chosen; and all the Merry Race of the Common Side of the College are adjourned for almost a Month.

This stagnation of Business is mortifying indeed to the numerous Army of Bailiffs, and Sergeants, and their Attendants, which are subsisted in this Trading City, and its adjacent Parts; and they seem to walk about very Melancholy. But we must remember too, that in a very little while the Vacation will be over, and then they will be expected with double Wrath; so they that are in Apprehension, may take the Hint, for the Swarm of Locusts will Issue forth, and spread the Face of the Earth, as their elder Family did the Land of Egypt.

Some have enquired how many of the Generation of People call'd officers are employ'd in this Wicked tho' necessary Work, within the Bills of Mortality; or, if you will, within Ten Mile round *London.* When I proposed it to a Friend of Mine, he told me he believed they were in all about Twenty Thousand. One that stood by, answered that they were double the number, including all the Kinds.*

And in a Word, all that are any Way concerned in Restraining the Liberty of Mankind, whether of Criminal, or Trespassers and Debtors. A black Army indeed they are, and tho' 'tis true, that as the Law employs them, they are a kind of needful Rogues; yet I am of Opinion that some wise Measures might be taken, and Matters might be directed, that Nine Parts in Ten of them might be Disbanded, and voted Useless, and the whole Business of the Law be as effectually done without them, and this is the Reason of this Paper, of which more in my next.

---

* Here follows an Enumeration specifically of 25 different kinds of Officers.

On the Death of Pope Innocent XIII.

A. J., Mar. 21.—Sir, Upon the Death of his Holiness the Pope, I find our People are acting in very indecent Manner, instead of Condoling with the Church, they really Triumph. And tho' I am no Roman Catholick, Mr. *App*, I cannot agree to that neither; and therefore desire to explain a little upon those Things with you, that you may come off of the Scandal of it. Many Things make People Merry upon this Occasion.

" O !" says one of my Neighbours, just now, in a Jeering way, " do you hear the News ?"   " No," says I.   " What News ?"   " *Why the Whore of Babylon is dead ! the great Scarlet Whore !   The Red Dragon !*" &c., according to the Language of *us Hereticks*.   I said nothing to it a good while, till he came upon me again with it, by the way of Question. Thus, " The Pope is dead," said he, " and is not the Pope the Whore of Babylon ?"   " Nay," says I, " that is another Question, and an old one too ; and the Learned are not fully agreed about it to this Day."   Well, we fell at last to Dispute it, and I must Confess, tho' the Argument did not amount to Evidence, yet the Similitudes came up so near to it, that we agreed that the learned Author was in the right, who had the Merry Expression about it ; " That's, I will not say," says he, " that the Pope is Antichrist, as some pretend to declare positively ; but I must Confess, if there was a *Hue and Cry* after Antichrist made Publick, and I should meet the Pope in my Way, I should go near to Stop him upon Suspicion, and so leave Authority to determine his Quality."

In the mean time the Clamour of the World is very wrongly pointed at the Pope ; for as Matters now stand with the Princes and States of *Europe*, the Death of the Pope seems to me to be of no more Consequence than that of any other old Woman, in that, or any other part of the World. For, as for the Whore of Babylon, if any Thing about the Pope is concerned in making such a Pageant as that, 'tis the Roman Hierarchy in the Gross ; 'tis the Romish Constitution, the Pontificate itself. There lies the Ecclesiastick Pride, the Tyranny ; there lies the Usurpation upon Religion, and Christ's Church.   The Pope himself is nothing but the Statue upon the Triumphal Arch,— the Image upon the Pageant ; or like the Picture before a Booth in *Bartholomew* Fair. When he is taken down, the Shop shuts for a while; but the Actors carry on the Grimace of the Matter, set up the Picture again, and the Whore of Babylon (*that is to say, the Actions of the Stage,*) is just where she was.   So the Death of the Pope is no more than chusing a new *Harlequin* to every Opera; the Place and the Manner of Acting is the Same to a Tittle.   Let therefore none of our old Women, however zealous for the good Protestant Cause, flatter themselves about the Death of the Pope; for the State of Popery is but just the same.   If one Pope goes, another Pope comes.

And this brings me to observe, that the Kings and Princes of Europe have really very much changed their Measures, with respect to the Homage and Veneration which they formerly paid to the Chair of St. Peter; and they can now, at all Times, Crush, Slight, and Evade the Power of the Pope, and laugh at the Anathemas of the *Vatican*, making the Pope and his Interest subservient to their Power, and scruple it no more than they do turning a single State Minister out of his Post, or deposing an ordinary Bishop.

On the other Hand, the Pope's power for Excommunicating Sovereign Princes, Deposing them, and giving their Crowns to others, are Things the Popes of these latter Ages have not thought fit to venture upon; and if they should, the Princes concerned would sufficiently have been laughed at.

Now for choosing a New Pope, it seems to me, to be of as little Weight as the other. 'Ti snot two Farthings Matter to us who they Choose, or when they Choose; but let them have a Care they do not Choose a Protestant Pope, as they said of Innocent XI., for should such a one Reign, the Protestant Interest would perhaps obtain a Sanction from their own Hands, which they never had yet. 'Tis said of the Pope, that he admonished King *James* II. not to take the Rash Measures which he afterward run into, and which were the Cause of his Ruin. If that was true, he shewed himself the more Politick Person of the two. Whether it was a Mark of his Infallibility, or no, I will not say; but indeed any Persons whose Eyes were in their Heads might have seen, that the Measures King *James* took, would End in his Destruction, tho' he could not see it himself.

If any Body has a Loss in the Death of the Present, or rather of the *late* Pope, it is the Chevalier, to whom the Pope was, as they say, wondrous Kind and Beneficent. The Chevalier seems to be left Fatherless in a double Sense; but he may perhaps find his Way into the Cabinet of the next, so the Matter will not suffer much.

Cardinal *Alberoni* has lost a great Friend too, but as the Cardinal had but a few Days before received his Hat, and had his long Affair brought to a Period; he is happy in being out of the reach of his Enemies.

These are the only Cases of any Moment that I remember in the Affair of the Pope; so that his Death seems not two Farthings value to us, one Way or other.

Sir, Yours, &c.

The Elevator.*

A. J., Mar. 28.—Sir, I am a great Lover of Projects, and of Ingenious Men, as well as of the Instances of their Ingenuity. I write this to you on Account of an Advertisement which I saw from a certain Society of Ingenious Men, called *Water-Work People ;* whether of *York Buildings,* or otherwise, it matters not either to you or to me.

These Gentlemen, they tell me, have given Publick Notice, that they will give great Encouragement to any that will furnish any *New* or *Extraordinary* Engine or Machine, for raising the largest Quantities of Waters, and that certain Persons at their certain Water House in —— are Employed to treat for the same ; and, as above, will give all fitting Encouragement, as by their publick Advertisement may farther and more at large appear.

Now I have been inclined to make some Proposals to those Gentlemen for the Information of their Society,—*or for Information of the World concerning them,*—take that as you will ; in which I may perhaps tell them how to raise the Water, (or raise the Wind ; which, of the two, 'tis said, is the main Thing they want,) in greater Quantities in certain Places, than ever yet was done, or will be done, or can be done, by any other Art, or Artist whatever.

My Proposals consist of several Parts, and I have various Engines to present them with, which may deserve their Consideration ; as first, I have an Excellent Wheel call'd an ELEVA-

---

* The York Buildings Company, with their Water-Works and other Projects, survived, for some time, the general bursting of Bubbles.—*Ed.*

TOR, which is particularly qualified to raise Water in a Manner invisible to the Eye, and in some Measure inscrutable by Mortal search. This Elevator I recommend to their Use, because, in a particular Manner, it will raise *Water in the Brain;* and that, the Learned say, is highly necessary, in Chymerical Elevations; in order, especially, to condense the fluids in the airy Part of the Understanding, which inclines Men to build Castles in the higher Regions.

Now a due Quantity of Water being raised up to a proper height by this Engine of mine, so Tempers the Volatiles in the Head, as completely qualifies Men for a particular kind of Management call'd *Knavery;* and in especial Manner to act with some less Art, and a needful Quantity of *the down Right,* as 'tis called in some Countries; and therefore, may be very useful to those particular Gentlemen who publish this Advertisement.

Where this Engine is not used, the volatile Salts of the Brain, are so carried away by the Indraft of Hell, and a Flux of Subtil Matter from the Abyss, and are often so managed by the Prince of the Air; that they often lead Men into the Secret untrodden Paths of Villany, and so they become Knaves of a more Subtil kind, supported by Craft and Art, so as rarely to be discovered, and Scarce ever fully found out, which, by the way, are the most dangerous of Knaves.

But the Humid, being condensed by the Water of my Engine, the Brain becomes more Solid, and the Conceptions more Gross; and consequently more Intelligible; and then they begin to discover a new Way of Acting. For Example, Things formerly concealed become clear and exposed. Men lay Snares that every common Sight can Detect. Tell LYES that may be felt with the Foot. Draw Schemes that may lose, but cannot gain. Draw Lotteries with Prizes ever to be paid. Buy Estates without Money, and draw in Fools without Craft. Now these, being less dangerous Knaveries than the other, my Engine must be very valuable to the Publick.

Also, as all these barefaced Things were in themselves more wonderful than ordinary, wise Men had been long musing by what extraordinary Operation they have been made Successful; but all that Difficulty would be solved at once, if the secret Power of this Water Engine of my Invention, comes to be more effectually understood in the World.

It would contribute also to their Success in these Things, if they would make use of my *Elevator*, or *Water Engine*, to throw up some due Quantity of Phlegm into the Heads of their Adventurers against the next Eruption of Project from the Prolifick Brain of *Don Ferdinando Bellisandro*, Engineer General, for the Present, of the said Society; that so, he may meet with no Opposition in the eminent Things he has to offer at the next Meeting, &c., and which, he doubts not, the Adventurers will come into.

This Water Engine of mine also would be particularly useful, if rightly employed, in order to quench some dismal Fires which have been formerly kindled in the Society, and may be still of dangerous consequence, upon that Occasion of converting Prizes and Blanks into Annuities, Demandable *Sine Diu*, and Payable when we can Catch, and the like. And as these frequent Fires are in themselves formidable, and threaten the Company with a general Conflagration, there may indeed be the more need of so extraordinary an Engine; and therefore, please to tell them, that, according to their Advertisement, I expect all due Encouragements to

Your Humble Servant,
ELEVATOR.

On the Government of the City.

A. J., April 4.—Sir, This has been a Time of Hurry in the City, and your struggling Parties have made the utmost Efforts that they were able, as must need appear by the equality of the Division on both Sides; since, upon the whole, there is a majority but of Eighteen of one Side against another, upon the nicest *Scrutiny* in so large a City.

That there have been false Votes, and foul Practices on both Sides, has not, *as I understand it*, been the Question at all. No Side denies it, as I hear of, but which Side has been dipp'd the deepest in Knavery; so that, *as it was said formerly*, in a like Case, the Scrutiny has not decided which Side were *honest Men*, and which *Knaves*; but having detected *Knavish* doings on both sides, has determined which were *deepest in the Dirt*.

This gives me but a dull Idea of the Times, and a mean Opinion of Party Men of all Sides; and, in short, I much doubt, that when we talk of them, *especially of the Hot ones on both Sides,* the old Song may come up, and may not be thought unreasonable,—*Tantara, rara, Rogues all, Rogues all !*

I happened to be in Company of some honest Gentlemen of the City t'other Day, and they were mighty wavering in their Discourse upon these late Elections; and after some Time, in order to strengthen their Party, a Proposal was made; *I don't enter here into the Merits of the Case, and therefore I do not say on which Side they were;* but the Proposal was, that a great Number of Gentlemen of the first Rank, or at least of *high Rank* and Quality, should come in and take up their Freedom of the City, in order to support the Cause of an Election. Upon which a Friend of mine stept in, and told me a Story, which as near as I can remember, I shall relate to you, as follows, (*viz.*)

In the Days of King *Charles* II., *said he,* his Majesty was pleased to Honour the City of *London,* with accepting of his Freedom.   I think, *says he,* it was the *Grocers'* Company his Majesty was made Free of at first, and afterward of the City. Upon this Precedent, it began to be a fashionable Compliment to Favourites and great Men at Court; and after that, it became a Party Bite too, (*viz.*) to make Freemen, &c.   The King, who, as he was the best Humoured Man in the World, was also the most ready at a smart Repartee; talking one Day upon that Subject with the Duke of *Buckingham,* Complimented his Grace upon his Freedom, which it seems he had accepted too, among the rest, and called him *Alderman Buckingham.*

Some body it seems took the Hint, and whether with, or without his Grace's good liking, set about the Thing in good earnest, and it was the current News of the Day, that the Duke of *Buckingham,* being a Freeman, should be put up for Alderman; I think, *says the Gentleman,* it was *Vintry* Ward, or *Queen Hithe,* or thereabouts, for there the Duke had a House of his own, and was an Inhabitant.

But it happened at that Time, that between the occasion of chusing an Alderman, and the time of the Election itself, the usual time of chusing Parish and Ward-offices intervened, *namely, the latter end of December;* and some unlucky Ill-natured Fellow of a Citizen, put up his Grace to be chosen Scavenger.   This Scandalous Motion, *says he,* you may be sure was very surprising.   But this was not all; for when he had done, he voted against him too, and so his Grace was not chosen.

It was wondered much, upon this Affront to his Grace, not that the Duke was put up, but that the Man that did it should vote against him too; but he gave for Answer, that he had no Mind the Duke should be an Alderman, and as he was sure he could not be chosen Common-Council Man, till he had been Scavenger, so neither could he be chosen Alderman. *Thus far the Story.*

Now as I have only told the Tale, but have nothing to do with the Application, I would know of you, Mr. *App*, if any Man, whether a Lord, or a private Person, can be chosen into the Office, or Place of an Alderman of *London* that has not served the City in that needful Office of Scavenger; and if you answer Negatively, *that they cannot*, as I believe, then I think the Gentlemen above, will the better know what they have to do in Time to come.

There was another Motion, to this Purpose, some Time after, tho' perhaps somewhat more in Jest (*viz.*) that all the Noblemen of a certain Party, then in Opposition to the Court, should bind their eldest Sons Apprentices to Tradesmen in the City, in order to make them Freemen, and Qualify them to be Aldermen; but the Duke above named, who was as ready at a Jest as the King was at a Repartee, was mightily for it, and told the King his Reason for it; namely, that then they might have a Court of Aldermen full of Peers, and a House of Peers full of Aldermen.

There was abundance of Mirth passed at Court in those Days upon that Subject; till at last these popular Steps of *Anti-Courtiers* grew into Fashion, and to Male-content Principles; and then it became a Tragedy, instead of being the Subject of Raillery and Jest.

However let me put in a Caution to you, about these Honourable Freemen.   Let as many of them come and be made Freemen, and put on Leather Aprons as please; but I would have the city take Care that they take no Apprentices.   I say no more at present, I may explain myself hereafter.

Your Humble Servant, &c.

On Variety of Tastes.   A Story.

A. J., April 11.—Sir, We that every now and then write Letters to the World by your Hands, to supply your Readers with Speculatives for their Daily Diversion, cannot but observe with what different Taste the World read your Papers; some bring their Party Passions to the Paper, and if you have nothing of Politicks, nothing of Court Alterations, City Struggles for Sheriffs, Pulpit Battery for and against Heresy, nor Town Rattle for and against Whig and Tory, cry, D—n this Fellow, he's dull, empty, insipid, not worth reading, and the like.

Others, happening to come in a merry Humour to read, why, they look for Wit and Gallantry, Mirth and Humour, from us; and if they don't find some suitable Stories to the Pin they are just raised up to, they d—n us as fast for want of Mirth and Humour, tell you there's nothing in us capable to make the merriest Fellow in the World laugh, or the wantonest Girl in the Parish smile.

A Third come with their Martial Spirits about them, perhaps from a City Muster, or a *High Park* View, and they d———n us again for want of Fighting Stories; and thus, in a Word, we run the Gauntlet, not for real Barrenness, but as the different Tastes of the People that read, happen to be disposed at the Time. And what must we do to reconcile those Differences, and bring your Readers all to relish us at the same Time, whatever Temper they are in? To this I shall answer by telling you a short Story; the Conclusion of which, I hope your Readers will take for a Solution of the Difficulties.

Four several Persons were met together one Evening at a Tavern, to drink a Glass of Wine, and Converse agreeably together. But when they were set down and proposed what to Talk, one of the gravest began, and said, there was a particular Misfortune in their Society, which, tho' they were Neighbours, and very well pleased with one another's Company, would, he doubted, soon put a Check to their design'd Conversation; and that was, that they were of such different Professions, that none of them,—being to talk in their own Way,—would be able to talk either to the Understandings of the other; or, at least not to their Taste and Satisfaction; so that he thought they could never Converse agreeably. Now the several Professions were these.

1. One was a *Physician* and *Surgeon,* and he said, that if he talk'd in his Profession; if as a Surgeon, he should enter into a System of Anatomy, the Contexture of the Microcosm, the Nerves, capillary Veins and Arteries, the Seminary and Blood Vessels, the Ureters, the Ventricles, the Bowels, the Coats, the Glands, &c., 'twould be both unintelligible, and unprofitable. Or if, as a Physician, he should run into the *Materia Medica,* read a Lecture upon Simple and Compound, of Volatiles and Humids, of Acids and Alkalies, and the like; it would be equally tedious and impertinent, and therefore he could not talk to their understanding in his Way.

2. The Second was a *Lawyer,* and he said he was a useless Fellow in Conversation, to any but his particular Clients or Company, as they were in at that Time. For what Edification can it be *to you,* Doctor; says he, turning to the Physician, to hear me talk of the Civil and Statute Law, the *Justinian* Codes, or the *Magna Charta,* the Constitution Rights, and the Statute Rights, the Courts of Equity, the Common Law, and Ecclesiastick Jurisdiction, their Independencies one upon another, and their Subordination one upon another, and the like,—it would be all Heathen Greek and Enigma to the Company; and therefore, 'twill be very unprofitable for me to Talk.

3. I am in the same Case, says the Third, who was a *Divine,* for Doctrine and Practice is Work for the Pulpit; and for me to enter into Modern and Ancient Disputes,—Examining who are Orthodox, and who are Heterodox; enquiring into the Doctrines of the Trinity, and of Infallibility, Tradition and Revelation, Reprobation and Predestination, Rewards and Punishments, Heaven and Futurity, you would both, Gentlemen, turning to the Doctor and the Lawyer, tell me I might hold my Tongue; that I did not talk to the Understanding, and that you desired I would talk of Things capable of Demonstration, and not of Clouds and Darkness. So that really, Gentlemen, I have nothing to offer that I can talk to the Purpose.

4. It came then to the fourth Man to speak, who was a Rustick, and yet who at last solved the whole Difficulty. Why really, Gentlemen, I am in the same Case, for as you say well,

in all your Respective Professions, that you could not Talk to
the Understanding of one another ; and indeed, in any of your
Professions I should understand little of the Matter ; so I also,
tho' I am but a mere Farmer, or Grazier, could talk out of
your Way too, as much as you could talk out of mine, for if I
talked of Breeding and Feeding, of the Weight of a Bullock,
the Suckling of Calves, the Method for early Lambs, the Improving of Lands for Pastures, and the' Culture of Arables, by
different Mendment, *and the like*, you would any of you tell me
you Understand nothing of the Matter.   But I have one Proposal to make, says he, to make us all Talk intelligibly, and
put an End to the Difficulty.

Come, says he, let us talk Bawdy, and that we All understand.   Whether the Company agreed to the Proposal, or no,
tho' they all agreed they understood it, that Part of History is
silent.   So I can give you no Account at Present.

I am, &c.

Choice of a Subject on which to Write.

A. J., April 18.—Sir, I have for a long Time had very low
and humble Thoughts of myself, when I looked upon myself as
Stooping to this Mean, Mortifying Business of Writing Letters
to you Journal Men. The Dignity of which seemed to be much
lower than that of *Servus Servorum ;* and this Thought has made
me many Times think of laying down my Pen, and to see if I
could not employ myself to better Purpose.

But all those low-priced Imaginations are vanished on a
sudden, I am quite another Man than I thought myself to be ;
For, said I, am I not Ranked with the Highest ?   Is not the
Business of writing Journals justly esteemed Honourable ?   Do
we not see the greatest Pens think it an Honour to be seen in
the first and second Folios of a Weekly Journal ?   And have
not Men of Rank thought it no Disgrace to be Author of News
Papers ?   So that I find myself agreeably Rank'd with L——ds,
D——kes, B——ps, D——ns, D——rs, and what not.   This,
I thought, made me look a little like myself ; and, that I might
not act below my Quality, namely, of *an Author*, I enquired
how I might find out some Subject worthy of so eminent a
Person.

I considered Faction, but found it a poor and little Thing,

far below me, and too dirty for my Pen; and besides, Brother
Mist has some capable Hands, ready whenever he thinks fit,
and I would not Invade another Man's Property.

I was tempted to think of Lampoon, and Satyr upon the
Government, but being under some Elevation at this Time, I
answered, no, *hang it*, I am above that too; if the Tempter had
mov'd for Rebellion and Treason, something might have been,
but as he did not go so high, I scorn to be hanged for Trifles,
so I declined that too.

Religion came next into my Thoughts; but I, that always
had a Veneration for sacred Things, could not reconcile it to
my Principles to PREACH in a Journal.   In short, I do not
think People come to read. News-Papers with their Polemics
about them; nor is the Coffee-House the most agreeable Place
to brighten an Argument about Religion.

Let the B——p if he pleases, bring the Doctrine of *the
Trinity*, down to a level with a *News Journal;* and argue against
Clark and *Emlin*, by way of Libel and Ballad.   Perhaps his
L——p's Works may be more suitable there, than *Viva Voce;*
and he may do more good in the Coffee-House, than in the
Pulpit.   Or, perhaps his way of Talking here, may be more
suitable to the Price; and he may deal in Three Half-Penny
Divinity with more Success than he has done while, *as the
World thought*, he rated himself above the Market.

Let the Bish——p, I say, do thus if he pleases, for my Part I
cannot avoid thinking, that the sublime Subject of our Blessed
Redeemer's Divinity, is too solemn to be made the Point of
our Buffoonery, and be mingled with the Trash, the Falsehood,
the Fiction, the Slander, the wicked Things, and the mean
Things, which are generally in the other Part of a Weekly
Journal.

How decently are these Papers put together! While the first
Part is taken up with the most solemn and serious Arguments,
from the Right Reverend Pen of a Christian B——, in Defence
of the Orthodox Faith, and in Honour of God, and his Gospel;
in the very next columns, perhaps a Story of the *Czar* of
Muscovy, and his Preparations for his Coronation Feast at
Moscow; the next perhaps shall be a Story of a Justice of the
Peace and a W——; and after that a Bawdy Song, and the
like; and to close the elaborate Work, a Column or two of

filthy Advertisements, not fit to be read. So that we dare not, in short, bring the B——p's labours home to our Wives and our Daughters to read, because of the Advertisements at the End of them.

In a Word, the Journal is like a Witch's Prayer; you read backward all the way; you begin at Heaven, come on into the World, then in the World, you go down from the Actions of Kings and Princes, publick Affairs, and Politicks abroad and at Home, to little sorry Paragraphs of home Forgeries, called News; thence to Slander and Malicious Advertisements, and so on to Lewdness; and, in short, Hell! You begin with God, and end with the Devil.

Is this a Stage for a B—— to act upon? Is this Piece of low Life suitable to the Dignity of the Mitre, and the Reverence it calls for from the World? One would think, if his Lordship had thought fit to Preach once a Week in the Kennel, yet still he should not let his Divinity be the Handmaid and Harbinger of Rubbish, Lies and Slander, and Lewdness.

He might have the Paper at least so far as to be separated from the Filth of the Town Laystall. People will say his Divinity stinks of the Anti-venerals, &c., and that 'tis Blended with the Nastiness of the Town; it will corrupt more than it will Correct, and do as much Harm as Good.

At least the B—— is made Accessory, by this, to the spreading of those vile Things over the Nation; for if the Sale of the Paper is advanced by the most admirable, and indeed the most wonderful works of his Lordship; that very Advance of the Paper spreads with it all the wicked Part, as a flourishing Title spreads a Book. And thus, the B——, in a Word, may be said to cry the Paper about the Country, and fill the Ears and Heads of the People with Filthiness and Debauchery.

I am, &c.

On Cruelty and Inhumanity.

A. J., April 25.—Sir, They that would please the World, as it seems the World now goes, must be sure, they say, to make them *Laugh*. But how shall we do to be always sure what will make the World Laugh? Some Laugh when they should Cry, and some Cry when they should Laugh; and particularly, some people always Laugh at *Mischief*.

In *Yorkshire,* they tell us, 'tis the Custom of the Country to Laugh when they are Angry, and look Sour when they are pleased ; because they say, a Man of Sense ought never to be thoroughly discovered, but when he pleases.

It was said of *Charles* the IX of *France,* that he always bestowed his Favours with evident Tokens of Disgust and Displeasure ; and, when he had taken up Resolutions fatal to the Life, or Fortunes of any particular Person, or Persons, he would treat them with Smiles, and Caresses, and all the Tokens of Endearment in the World. Nay, it was said that two or three Days before the bloody Massacre of *Paris,* he caressed the Admiral *Coligni,* the Head of the Protestants, whom he had doomed to Destruction, and one of the first that was Murthered ; I say, he caressed him with the utmost Testimonies of Affection and Tenderness, embraced him at his coming into the Court, made solemn Protestations of a sincere Reconciliation to him, and the like ; yet the very next Morning beheld, with Pleasure, his dead Body dragged about the Streets of *Paris,* by the enraged Mob, after it had been Murthered by his express Command.

The best Way that I see to make the World Laugh, at this Time, is not to talk to them of any thing *very Merry,* but of something, very, VERY WICKED. There is something of NERO left still in the Nature of Men, that would shew itself, and exert its Power perhaps in more than Ordinary manner, if *Nero's* Power and unlimited Opportunity were put into their Hands.

It is said *Nero* played upon his Fiddle while *Rome* was on Fire ; and that he pleased himself with the Terrors and Cries of the frighted and impoverished Citizens, as with an harmonious Sound, bearing Concert with the nicest Strokes and Touches of his Instrument.

We have some secret degrees of Cruelty and Inhumanity break out, every now and then, among us in this Nation, which were hardly ever seen or heard of. In *Rome,* it was an Observation of a Learned Antiquary, that tho' there were more Suicides, or Self-Murthers in *Rome,* or under the *Roman* Government, than there are now in our Christian Times, yet there are infinitely more Homicides now, than there were then.

Here we have Killing of Fathers and Mothers; murthering of Bastard Infants; and, in a Word, innumerable Slaughters of all Kinds that were then abhorred. And, which is still more wonderful, we love to hear such Stories; and your News is hardly agreeable, if there is not some strange Story of a Murther or Robbery, and even a Robbery does not please, if there is not some Blood in it.

Now what shall we do to make the People laugh? To talk of Murther, and Robbery, is none of our Business, 'tis out of our Way; the News Jobbers deal in that by themselves. But to make the People grin, and look pleased, and that not the *Yorkshire* Way neither, give me leave to tell you a wicked Story.

An honest poor Man, in our Country, had a very handsome Wife, and a certain rich Gentleman had cast an ill Look or two at her for some Time; that is, in short, had a Mind to be wicked with her, and used all the Applications to her for such Purpose that he could invent, but without Effect, the Woman preserving her Virtue with an Obstinacy, as the Gentleman called it, beyond common Civility.

However, the Person being one that had more than common Influence upon the Family,—and could go a great Way towards ruining them all, if made an Enemy,—really was, or at least pretended to be, so angry at the Repulses that he received, that he fell upon the Woman's Husband in a Cruel Prosecution, and threw him into Gaol.

The Case was altered,—the Tables were turn'd,—for as, before this, he Courted the Woman, and used all his Rhetorick to prevail on her Virtue, so she was made Suppliant now, and oblig'd to use all the soft Entreaties and Perswasions, mingled with Tears, to move him to be merciful to her Husband. By the Way, you are to understand, that the Husband was really in Debt to the Gentleman; and he Prosecuted him on a just Demand, tho' with an unjust Design.

But the Gentleman was now inexorable, and no Prayers, no Tears would prevail, unless she would consent to him; which she had still an utter Aversion to. At length the Gentleman went to the Prison to the Debtor, and Frankly told him the Case, that he had long solicited his Wife, but she would not comply; that it was no such great Matter for him, the Husband, to give his Consent to that; and, that if he would

yield to it, and perswade his Wife to Consent, he would withdraw his Action, and give him longer Time.

The Man told him it was an unreasonable Request to
Demand; and that, only to give him longer Respite upon his
complying, would be a selling his Wife to him for Nothing;
that whenever his Worship had a Mind to repeat the Sin, he
would Caress him again, and so on; but if he would forgive
him the whole Debt, which was 300*l.*, he would give his Consent, and endeavour to persuade his Wife to Comply.

The Esquire capitulated that 300*l.* was too much; but that,
if she complied, he would strike him 100*l.* off the Bond, only
that the Husband should allow him a Week.

In short, the Husband agreed, but there was a great deal of
difficulty still to gain the Wife, who had always been a modest,
virtuous Woman; however, at length, the Distress of her Family
prevailed upon her. The Squire brought the Bond, put it into
her Hand, and bid her tear it; only made her promise that her
Husband should give another Bond for 200*l.* in the room
of it. And upon the Appointment being made, the Action was
withdrawn, and the Man was let out.

The Woman took the Bond,—tore it as she was bid, and
when she had done, she leads the Gentleman into a Chamber,
and pretended to withdraw; in a Word, she made her Escape,
and bilked her Gentleman.

The Cause I hear is to be tried in Course of Law. Pray
let's have your Opinion, how will it go? The Husband, it
seems, protests his Innocence, declares his Wife is run away
against his consent; and, that the Cancelling the Bond was done
by the Squire's own Consent and Order. Whether will he
recover the Debt? For 'tis plain he can't recover the Condition.

Your Humble Servant, &c.

Character of a " Dundreary" in 1724.

M. J., April 25.—Dear *Nath,* Take Pity upon one of thy
constant Readers, and give me a Word of Advice; my case is
this. I am just turn'd of 30, have a good Estate, a Genius for
Books, and live in a sociable Part of the World. I am neither
the Jest of Men, nor the Aversion of Women. Every
Thing seems to conspire my Happiness, which notwithstanding
is still wanting. I cannot, for my Soul, of late, stick to any

one particular Business; I can neither tarry Abroad, nor
abide at Home.   When I retire to my Books, I do nothing
but tumble them over; running from Page to Page, and
from Author to Author, without any Application or Improvement.   When I retire to my Garden, the Scene of Pleasure
and Contemplation; instead of walking, I rather traverse the
Alleys; am possessed with ten thousand fluctuating Whims,
and tire myself, before I know what I am doing.   When I
recover a little, and begin to reflect,—which, by the by, is very
short, and seldom,—I fancy all this proceeds from Melancholy;
to shun which, I immediately repair to Company, where I
never answer one Question directly, never say one Word to
the Purpose, and am always either breaking of Pipes, humming
to myself, or drumming with my Fingers on the Table.   I
know all this too; and yet 'tis impossible for me to help it.   I
sometimes resolve to apply myself to my Studies very earnestly,
but, instead of confining myself as I had determined, my
Horse is call'd for, and up I get, without ever knowing whither
I am Bound, or with what Intent.

   Now prithee tell me, *Mist*, if this ben't Madness, or rather
worse, because I know it? I am lothe to call it voluntary
Madness, because I cannot help it; but sure 'tis the most extravagant kind of Frenzy in the World, and such as I believe
Bedlam can't produce an Instance of.   I am sure it does not
proceed from any innate Principles of Inconstancy, because I
have been able, some Years since, to stick to my Study with
the greatest Severity and Intenseness of Thought.   I am con-
fident it cannot arise from any affectation of Wit, or Humour;
for I know there is neither Wit nor Humour in it, and I despise all others that are guilty of it.   Neither will I allow it to
proceed from any Levity of Mind; because I am sensible of it
myself, and despise myself for it too.   In the Name of common Sense, Friend *Mist*, what is it then?   Some of my
Friends tell me I must marry; and tho' I have no Inclinations
that Way, yet I would do any Thing that may conduce to my
Recovery.   When I say I have no Inclinations to Matrimony, I
would not have you think, that I have any Aversion to it neither;
for, as in all other Things, so in this, I am perfectly indifferent.

   They tell me of many strange Cures effected by Love.   But
certainly if Love would do it, I need not have recourse to

Hymen for a Remedy, for I love every Soul upon the Face of the Earth. But my Notions of Love, they tell me, are too general and unconfin'd, which Marriage will collect and reduce to one particular Object; and, that then, I shall find the Advantage of it. If it be so, with all my Heart; I will do any Thing to change a Course of Life, which I can neither cease to disallow, or to practice. So I have given them my Word and Promise to marry. But when, or how, I shall be as good as my Word, hang me if I can think, or imagine! I cannot bear the Thoughts of running thro' the many tedious Addresses of a Courtship. When I should be talking to my Mistress, I shall be whistling, picking my Teeth, or playing a Minuet on my Fingers : And if I should happen to deliver myself of a premeditated Sentence or two; as soon as ever I had spoken it, I should be for marching off, without expecting any Reply. This Humour must need ruin me for an humble Servant with the Ladies; so that I can think of no other Expedient, but of recommending my self to the Ladies through your Means, as an unaccountable sort of a Fellow, that is willing to marry, if he could get an agreeable Woman, who would consent without Ceremony.

I am too much a Philosopher to stand upon the Pence. Symetry, or a Fine Face or Shape, will not break Squares with me; every Figure being alike useful to a Mathematician. Neither shall I insist upon Complexion; Mr. Locke having long since convinc'd me, that there is no such Thing as Colour. Let me have a little Sense, a great deal of good Nature, and I desire no more. I have therefore drawn up a general Address to all our British Females, which I desire you to publish in your next; hoping that it may hit the Humour of some or other, amongst so many, and you will oblige your constant Reader, and very humble Servant,   H. S.

To all unmarried Ladies, Gentlewomen, and Spinsters, whether Maids or Widows, old or young, rich or poor, tall or short, crooked or straight, wise or otherwise, black, white, red, yellow, or blue, to whom these Presents shall come, greeting. Whereas, a good condition'd Bachelor, at present under a Necessity of marrying, having no other Incapacities, as he knows of, but only that of making his Addresses; He hereby humbly begs the Favour of any good natur'd Female, who is willing to take Pity upon him, that she would direct to him, with some short Account of herself. He is five Foot high, aged 30, has a good Estate, of a sanguine Complexion, strong Supporters, loves roast Beef, and can procure a Certificate, under the Minister and Churchwardens of his Parish, for his good Behaviour.

London Catchpoles.

A. J., May 2.—How great the Crowd of those Fellows are ! How unsufferable their Violence and Rapine ! How many poor Debtors perish under their Hands, and are ruin'd by their Extortions, is too long, and too black a Story to enter upon here ! But let the oppressed Debtors be comforted, the Grievance is so flagrant, so crying, that it hastens its own Remedy; it cannot be long before the Complaints of the Miserable will reach the Ears of the Merciful.

How often, by the horrible Violence of those People called the *Marshalsea* officers, I say, How often is a poor Man arrested for a Trifle, perhaps a Shilling, and put to fourteen or fifteen Shillings charge before he can get clear, tho' he pays the Debt too ! How many Thousand Pounds do poor Debtors pay to One Hundred Pounds that the Creditors recover ?

Whenever the Parliament of *Great Britain* shall think it proper to take such a Matter into their Consideration, I will not fail to give you a Scheme for the Disbanding of *eight* out of *ten* of all the Catchpoles in the Nation; which, if we may believe some Men's Calculation, are in this Time, no less than forty Thousand.*

Satire on the Impending Election of a Pope.

A. J., May 9.—Sir, We have a Witticism published in one of our last Week's Papers, upon the Proceedings of the Conclave and the probability or improbability of *who*, or *who*, shall be POPE, (*viz.*) That Heaven is for *Orsini*, the People for *Corsini*, the Ladies for *Ottoboni*, and the Devil for *Alberoni*.

I do not say that I believe this mean Jest has yet reached *Rome*, or that *Pasquin* has really any Hand in it; but I must needs say, I should be very sorry to hear it should prove True, for then I should conclude that Cardinal *Alberoni* would certainly be chosen Pope.

---

* Parliament, shortly afterward, suppressed many monstrous evils of the Marshalsea, and other Debtors' Prisons.—*Ed.*

As to poor Cardinal *Orsini*, who they say Heaven is for, I cannot think there is any Hope for him, unless Heaven has more friends in the Conclave than I believe is the Case; and let Heaven be for whom it will, (unless by some Influence or other, Secret or Open, Natural or Supernatural, it procures a Majority of Voices for the Cardinal whom it befriends,) he can never be chosen.

As for Cardinal *Corsini*, the People it seems are for him; but as they do not choose Popes by the Freeholders, as in *England*,—nor by the Liverymen of the City, as in *London*,—or by the Inhabitants paying Scot and Lot, as in *Southwark*, &c.,—nor by the *Pot Wallopers*, as at *Taunton*, in *Somersetshire*, and other Places;—that is, *in short*, that it is not to be a popular Election,—it matters not who the People are for, but who the Cardinals are for.

Then, as to Cardinal *Ottoboni*, it seems he has gotten into the good Graces of the Ladies; one might make some Mirth upon that Head, if we were Sure of the Truth of the Fact. Whether Cardinal *Ottoboni* has recommended himself to the Ladies in the manner usual for the merry Priests of the *Roman* Church to do, I cannot say; therefore I would not wrong his Eminence neither, so I let that Part alone. But let it be which Way it will, that he has obtained a Majority at the Tea Table, and in the Circles of the *Roman* Beauties; yet, as it happens, the Ladies have no Votes in the Conclave, and so, the Cardinal may go near to lose it.

But now to come to the other Party, Cardinal *Alberoni*; on my Word, I know not what to say, or what to think of it. For if the Old Gentleman be really in his Interest, I shall be very much afraid he will carry it,—for I doubt not but the Devil has a great many Friends in the Conclave; nay,—which is still worse,—I will not say but he has Admission into the very Cells of the Cardinals at the Conclave itself. No Wonder, then, if whatever Cardinal the old Gentleman is pleased to Favour, he should have the Majority.

How, and by what Means this politick Cardinal has made so powerful Interest, and when he contracted his Friendship with the Prince of Darkness, that I do not undertake to say, or upon what politick Principle Satan acts, in promoting the Cardinal *Alberoni's* Interest; doubtless he has some Game to carry on, of a Secret nature, for the Devil is a Devilish cunning Fellow, and never meddles in such Affairs without some visible Design.

Perhaps he expects to embroil *Europe* a second Time, by setting such a violent Spirit at the Head of the Church, and who went so far towards enflaming all *Europe* before!

Perhaps he is in hopes to bring the *Spaniards* into *Italy* again by this Means, and, by Consequence, the *French;* and to drive the Imperialists once more out of *Sicily*, and the Kingdom of *Naples*. Who knows what the Devil may be able to do, when a Tool of his own is gotten into the Infallible Chair?

But how come we to forget the Chevalier? May not the Devil have some Views in his Favour too? We have been told that the Chevalier and Cardinal *Alberoni* have been strictly allied together a great While; and if the Devil comes into the Confederacy, and makes it a triple League, what may not be the Consequence?

To this, I must needs say, that I differ exceedingly from those who talk of the Chevalier and his Interest, with Apprehensions. And were Cardinal *Alberoni* chosen Pope, and the Devil and he in as close a Confederacy with the Chevalier as could be possible; they would be yet as ill able as ever to do us any hurt in this Nation. The Government here is too solidly established; the Constitution of this Protestant Kingdom too well settled, and King *George* too well guarded to give us the least Chagrin on that Account. So that let the Devil and the Pope, (be it *Alberoni* or any other Person), do their Worst, they can do nothing this Way, and I believe the Devil himself to have more Wit than to attempt it.

Sir, your Humble Servant, &c.

An Eclipse.

A. J., May 16.—Sir, The Eclipse, being eclipsed on *Monday* last, and the Expectations of most People very much disappointed, by the Dulness of the Day; but especially upon the finding, that if it had been a clear Day it would not have been Total, as it was Nine Years ago; allow me to make some brief Observations to you on the Temper and Disposition of our People in *England,* not on this Occasion only, but on all Occasions, in which anything of Novelty appears.

Unless the worst of every Thing happens, we are never pleased; like the People that go to see our modern Gladiators, at his Majesty's Bear-Garden. If the Fencers do not cut one another, and the People do not see the Blood fly about the Stage; they are quite disappointed, grow uneasy and dissatisfied, and cry out, "A Cheat, a Cheat!" Whereas, to those who understand the Art, or, as the *Back-sword Men* call it, the Noble Science of Defence; the best Sight is, to see two bold Fellows lay heartily at one another, but be so dexterous, and such exquisite Masters of their Weapons, as to ward off every Blow, parry every Thrust, and after many nice Closes, and fair Attempts, not be able to come in with one another, or so much as to draw Blood. This shews them to be both good Swordsmen, and perfectly skilled at their Weapons; whereas, if either of them was to Fight with a Person less expert, he would cut him down presently.

It was the same Thing in the Eclipse on *Monday* last. Because the Sun was not entirely shut in, and the Darkness, Cold, and Damp, which was so Remarkable, and so Surprizing in 1715, was not to be found now; our *would-be Artists*, and almost all our Common People, made a Jest of it, mocked the Astronomers, and think there was Nothing in it.

"D—— these *Clipse-Mongers* and *Stronomer Men*," says a learned Cit, that gave a Guinea to come into Mr. *Whiston's* Great Room; "they picked my Pocket," *says he*, "of a Guinea, and when it come to, there was nothing to be seen. Why it was not an Eclipse worth a Farthing! I expected it would be quite Dark, that the Birds would fall down dead; that it would be Cold, Damp, and Dismal, as it was nine Year ago; that the old Women would fall down to their Prayers, the young Women be frighted into Fits, that the breeding Ladies would Miscarry, the Children would be born with the Eclipse marked in their Faces; that the Catholick Women would run to Confession, and all the Maids that had been Lewd would Cry, and tell their Mistresses of it, for fear the Day of Judgment was come. But instead of this, there was a great piece of the Sun left uncovered, and Light enough to harden all the Pretty Sinners; so that none of those little useful Secrets came out, which would otherwise have been told."

A certain grave Matron in our Parish, resolving she would

not die in her Shoes, and believing that she should hear the
last Trumpet very soon, put herself in a good Christian Way
of Dying; and so, having said her Prayers for three or four
Days before hand, went to Bed, had the Curtains all drawn
close about her, a Watch-light set in her Chimney, ordering
her Maid to sit up with her, to jog her if she was called for;
and so, in a most Christian Way, lay and quak'd and trembled
by herself till it was all over. And now she has the Vapours as
much for being Laugh'd at, as she had before; has been sending about for Cunning Men, and Almanack Makers, to tell her
when another shall happen; and being told it will happen
again in two and forty Year, she is much concerned how she
shall fare when it comes, being at present only nine and fifty
Year old.

In a word, Mr. *App*, these two Eclipses of the Sun, (*viz.*)
That in 1715, and this on *Monday* last, have made Sooth-
sayers and Magicians of half the old Women in the Country.
One came to me to Day, and bid me tell the World, that as
the King of *France* died in the same Year as the last Eclipse
of the Sun, so another King of *France* will certainly go this
Year; and then she read me a long Gipsy Lecture of what
Revolutions should follow, not only in that Kingdom, but in
many other Places in *Europe*, where the Eclipse has been
Total. I do not tell you that I believe her; but if any of her
Predictions should come to pass, I should go near to call her a
hard Name for her News.

For my Part, I lay no stress upon it that Way at all. The
two particular Planets, the Sun and the Moon, know nothing
at all of the Matter; and I believe, can as little Predict what
shall befal us, and have as little Hand in it, as we can have
Knowledge of, or, have any Hand in the directing their
Substance and Conjunction. All the rest I take to be Foolish
and Enthusiastick.   VALE.

On Death and a Future State.

A. J., May 23.—Sir, This is a merry World, that's certain;
and, if we can but arrive to the Perfection of ONE THING, which
we heartily push at too, and which I must confess we bid
fairer for than any Age that ever went before us; I say, if we
can but arrive to this ONE THING, we shall be the Merriest

Generation that ever lived, and you shall hear what it is presently.

First, The sting of all the bright, fine, polite, pleasant Things of Life, is this ugly Thing, call'd DEATH. "O Madam,"—said a Lady of Quality the other Day, to another Lady, that admired the Felicity of her way of Living, her Plenty, her Equipage, Attendance, Furniture, Jewels, and fine Clothes,— "O! *Madam*," said the Lady, "*it is true, I live very agreeably, and if it was not for this Dying it would be all very pretty ; but that cursed Article takes away `all the Comfort of my Life.*"

Secondly, the being called to an Account *afterward*. This is another Sting of all the bright, fine, polite, pleasant Things of Life : "*Who dare call me to an Account for anything ?*" said a harden'd Creature that I knew ; and yet, when a grave Person that stood by, told him, that *He that made him* could call him to Account, *he turned Pale*, in spite of all his Insolence.

Now, I understand, Mr. *App*, that there is a new Way found out, to take off all the Chagrin of the Mind from these two Things : And if this Project, (for I hope I may be allowed to call it a Project), succeeds, I say, it will make us all merry Fellows indeed. This new Project is to scratch out all the Ideas of Futurity, and that unknown Thing call'd GOD. I say, scratch them out of the Book of the Mind, and this, they say, is now very easy to be done.

Deism and Scepticism, with wonderful Application, and no small Success, have reduced our ideas of a Deity, to be less frightful, by much, than they used to be, and we have brought Him to be just such a *Gentlemanly Being* as will suit with our Occasions ; namely, that he is so Merciful that he cannot be Just ; so Good, that he cannot Punish ; so Forbearing, that he cannot be provoked. That we ought not to think he can entertain Thoughts of inflicting Pains intolerable, and eternal, upon his own Creatures ; pass a Sentence so infinitely disproportioned to the Offence ; that he regards not the trifling incidents of Man's Life ; that having created the World, he has left all the rest to Cause and Consequence ; that 'tis below him to meddle with what happens in the ordinary Course of Life ; that he is so infinitely happy in himself, that 'tis his Nature, and Delight to make all his Creatures happy also ;

and that any Peccadilloes of theirs cannot be capable of hin-
dering it. So far the Deists; and a very merry Story they
make of Religion indeed!

But we have a new *Apostle of the Devil*, set up among us now;
who tho' he be but a Quack, or *Hell-Fire Mountebank* at best,
has lately started a new Point in the World, which out does
them all. He seems to tell us we are not capable of some of
those Things, which among Christians pass for the greatest
Offences; for Example, we are told in the first Place, that there
is no such Crime as *Blasphemy* in the World.

This merry Fellow, I must confess, seems not to be a Papist
in disguise, no, nor can I call him a concealed Atheist; but,
in Short, he must *be a Devil in Masquerade*, or to give him a
Name less dignified, he must be a *Devil in a Hop!* One that
begins a Dance *a la Infernal*, as the Rat Catcher in *Germany*,
who piped till he made all the Town Rats, and after that, all
the Town's Children, Dance into the River, and be drowned.
So this merry Fellow sets up a Tune, that must make all his
followers Dance away to the Devil directly.

This is that Perfection of Devilism, which, as I said above,
if we can but attain, we shall be the merriest Generation that
ever lived.

Would it not be a merry World, if we could Sing my Lord
Rochester's Atheistical Song :—

> "After Death nothing is,
> And nothing Death."

Wou'd any of us value what we did in this World, if no
body was to call us to Account in the next? Certainly these
Men are in the right, if they are but sure of the Thing, and
that they can but find out this Philosopher's Stone; for let
them depend upon it, if there *is no God*, they need be afraid
of *no Devil!* And if there be *no Devil*, the D———l a bit will
they care what comes in the next World; and so I say, they
may live very merrily in this.

Thus the World goes merrily on Mr. *App*, for if, according
to our Friend *the British Journal*, there is no such Crime as
Blasphemy; which is much the same as to say, there is no
Deity to Blaspheme; then, whatever that Thing called *a God*,
is, and whatever *his Being* be, it seems we may say all the

wicked injurious Things of him we will, without Offence, or
without being Blasphemers. And so I come back to my Text,
'Tis a Merry World, for by the same Rule, all Men may be as
wicked as they will !

Sir, Yours, &c.

South Sea Company's Trade.   On Voting.

A. J., May 30.—Sir, We are now under a kind of Interval
in an affair of Moment in Trade; namely, the *South Sea*
Company setting up the Greenland Fishery. The Debate, they
say is adjourned for a Fortnight, and then the Proprietors are
to Ballot for the Question; the Substance of which I doubt,
very few of them understand. But 'tis no Matter for that, this
is not the first Question that has been put, in a Society much
greater than these, which those were to Vote for who did not
understand it; nor as things go in the World at this Time, is
it necessary that every Man that is to Vote in an Affair of
Moment, should thereby understand the Question ! 'Tis enough
they give their Vote; and as Numbers, not the Merit of the
Question decides it, the great Work generally is, to get those
Numbers to give their Votes, whether they understand what
they Vote for, or no.

Suppose an *Old Woman in Trade* comes to give a Vote, or
give in the Ballot for, or against, the *Greenland* Trade; and
suppose this HE *old Woman*, upon Examination, does not know
whether they go to *Greenland* to catch *Crabs*, or to catch
Whales; or, as one learned *South Sea* Man, *the other Day,*
said very wisely, that they were to go to *Greenland* to Fish for
Bears; which by the way may be true, both literally and
figuratively, yet I say, What is all this to the purpose ? If
these People give their Vote, as one or other, who does
understand it directs, 'tis as effectual to a Deciding the
Question, as if all who Voted understood what they voted about.

Thus, upon the whole, we see it is generally acted, in several,
if not most of the great Societies of People where things are
carried by Numbers, (viz.) that a few Men lead the whole
Society,—whether by the Nose, or not,—I will not determine;
but they lead them, that is, Sway and Bias them, by the Credit
of their greater knowledge, and so the greater Number follows
the less; which, in short, is contrary to the ordinary Course,

and the Nature of Things, where 'tis usual for the greater Number to lead the less.

I would fain perswade People, in an Age so clear-sighted as this is, or at least pretends to be, that they would learn for once to see with their own Eyes; especially in Things of Moment, in which they are concerned so much, and may Lose or Gain considerably. That they would learn for once, to let their Votes follow their Understandings, not go before them; and instead of Sacrificing their Reason, and their Interest, to the Opinion of others, learn to Judge, not only what they are Voting for, but why they give their Vote this Way, or that Way, in a Case of such Moment; lest they give away their own Money, as it may appear in the Event, and know nothing of the Matter.

Let them ask themselves the *previous Question* first, which I think is of Moment to every Member of the Company. The *previous Question*, as I put it, is this:—

Ought I, who am a Proprietor in the *South Sea* Stock, to give my Vote for, or against, the Company's entering into the *Greenland* Trade, before I know something of the Trade, and whether it is like to be profitable to the Stock, or hurtful? In short, ought I to Vote on it before I understand it?

Suppose the Answer should be, *as every wise Man's Answer ought to be,* in the NEGATIVE, then the next Question we think should be:—

How shall we get a right Understanding in this Matter, and of whom must we Enquire? To this last Question something should be said here, that Men who desire to be informed, may take right Measures for their Information.

And first then, Negatively, when you seek for Information, you should not go to those who are already known to have determined their Votes for it; have embarked themselves, and are making Interest for the Affirmative; this is asking my Fellow if I am a Thief. This may be going to Enquire of the enemy; at best it is going to ask Advice of him, who before you go has told you what Advice he will give you. In a Word, it is just like going formally to the Directors of the said Company to ask their Advice, whether you should sell or keep your Stock; and methinks there is something Ominous, if not Fatal, in going to the same Oracle for Direction,—tho' 'tis true, the same Devil does not give Answers,—yet we do not know how far the Action may be the same in its Degree. The same Rock may be split upon, tho' the same Pilots do not Steer.

But why ask Advice of any body? Let us Enquire into the Business of every Body, and then we need ask Advice of no body. Get a right understanding of the thing itself, and then you may be your own Advisers.

Enquire then, how it comes to pass, that having been so often attempted by the *English* Merchants, they have so always Miscarried? Has it been all Ignorance, or Negligence, or Misfortune; or have they been outdone by their Neighbours, or No?

Enquire again, whether the Trade itself is not nice in its Nature, and extremely Hazardous, so that it very often Miscarries in General; and consequently, may be too difficult to be Undertaken by a Company. And then, enquire whether it is carried on by a Company in *Holland*, which we believe it is not.

Enquire whether even the *Dutch* themselves, with all advantages they have for carrying on this trade, do not Miscarry; and whether, for Example, they did not universally Miscarry the very last Year in Particular.

Enquire then, whether such a Miscarriage of a whole Year's Equipment, when all falling upon one Stock, might not be fatal to a Stock, which subsists so much upon its Credit, and upon the popular Opinion.

Enquire then, what would have been the Case; supposing the Company had begun, and fitted out Twenty Ships last year as was proposed, and they had come all Empty Home,—as would have been the Case,—to the Loss of ten or twenty Thousand Pounds. What a Clamour would it have raised, and how ill-satisfied would the People have been with their Conduct!

I may send you some more Enquiries in my next; in the meantime these may be worth considering.

From your Humble Servant, &c.

The South Sea Company.

A. J., June 6.— . . . .
. . . . Now, When one of these Negative Gentlemen comes to Ballot, he first swears thus, " I *A. B.* do swear that I am a Proprietor, &c., in the Corporation appointed by the

Authority of Parliament to carry on a Trade to the *South Seas*, &c., and for encouraging the FISHERY." Well, and what then? ·

"*I therefore Vote against the Fishery!*"

"How Sir! Do you swear that you are a Member of a Company for encouraging the FISHERY, and then Vote against the Company encouraging the FISHERY? It is a little *Merry!* Pray how is this to consist?"

This is a kind of Trade Blunder, and wants a little of Mr. *Law's* over-the-Water-wit, to explain it.

I don't say it is a Perjury, because the Oath does not particularly oblige every Man to go a Fishing. But is there not a Breach in the Consistency of the Thing? . . . . . . *A Friend of mine*, talking a little merrily upon the Subject, said, he likened the New Act to an Act formerly proposed in the House of Commons, in the time of the late Duke of *Buckingham*, and upon that he desired leave to tell a Story.

"A Bill," says he, "was brought in, or proposed to be brought into the Parliament, to punish *Adultery* with *Death*; and the Title was, an Act for the better preventing the Sins of *Fornication* and *Adultery*. The Duke," says my Friend, "stood up against it, and said he disliked the Title,—a Bill for preventing, &c.—No", says he, "I move it may be entitled a Bill for the better concealing the Sins of Fornication and Adultery." "Well," says I to him, "but how do you form a Parallel between that Jest, and this New Act for removing the Duties upon Coffee and Tea from the Custom House to the Excise?"

"Why," says he, "I think I would not remove the smuggling Trade from one Set of Knaves to another;" and upon this Subject we joined Issue, and had a very warm Debate. He would insinuate that there is much room for Concealment now, as there was for Frauds before. I alledged that there was not, and have undertaken to prove it, but this is too long a Discourse to begin at the End of a Paper. I shall give you the Trouble of it perhaps for your next.

I am, Sir, Yours, &c.

A. J., June 6.—On Tuesday last, Mr. Jonathan Wild petitioned the Court of Aldermen for a Gratuity, for Detecting

Persons returning from Transportation before their Time. And they were pleased to order him a very handsome Sum for that Service. And 'tis hoped Mr. Wild will double his Diligence for the future.

On Wednesday last there was brought in a Sedan to the Royal Palace at St. James's, one Mrs. Eleanor Stewart, an Inhabitant of St. Giles's in the Fields, aged 122 Years and upwards; being born at Kendall in the County of Westmoreland, in the Year 1602. She has had one Husband, and by him 20 Children; 9 of whom were born, and she big of the 10th, at the Time of (the Death of) King Charles I. She is in perfect Health and Strength of Mind; and was brought to Court by his Majesty's Order, with proper Certificates of her Age, &c. And his Majesty was pleased to order her a handsome Donation.

Village Love—Scandal, and the Ducking Stool.

A. J., June 13.—Sir, We have a great Parish Controversy in our Country, which, having something very new in it, I thought might divert your Readers very much. A venerable Matron in our Town, being of an Age sufficient to bear the Scandal that followed, was sentenced to a certain Punishment, which is not usual in any Country that I read of, but in *England*; I shall let you into Part of it presently, but must in the first Place tell you something of the History of it.

The grave Person above mentioned, had very unhappily discovered a Love Intrigue, concerning a young Lady, (I mean a Lady of the lower-sized Gentry). She was something of the Degree of a Shopkeeper, call'd a Milliner, or Haberdasher; which in our Village contains many other Callings.

The love of Virtue was at first, without doubt, the Reason why this ancient Lady disliked the Levity and Vanity, as she call'd it, of the young Body her neighbour; and she took frequent Occasions to reprehend her, on which Occasions they often fell out, and that so publickly, that some of the Neighbourhood were disturbed at it, and gave it the Nickname of Scolding. Nay, sometimes they would come to them, when they were thus hotly engaged, and bid them, for Shame, leave Scolding, and say, they were two common Disturbers, and the like; which the ancient Lady, especially, took very heinously.

She took it the worse also, because, as she said, she did only seriously reprove a young Hussy for her wicked Life, and that she had a right to do it, being so much her Senior in Years,—and withal her betters too, for she was a Gentlewoman, she said, and came of a good Family, her Father having been Clerk of the Parish,—and therefore some Regard ought to be had to her, whose Ancestor was an Officer in the Church.

Well, but Neighbour, says a sober, honest Man, that lived near her; methinks you might let your Reproofs be with a little more Calmness, and you need not be so loud, for as it is, really you disturb your Neighbours.

It happened that the next Time this grave Matron had Occasion to Reprove her Neighbour was upon a very extraordinary Occasion; namely, that discovering some of her Haunts, she not only found that she (the young Trader) was pleased to play the ———, but that she took Occasion to make her Assignations in a little empty House, that stood in a bye Place, which the ancient Lady had but too much Opportunity to watch the Entrance to, from a back Window in her own House.

Here she frequently saw the young Woman go in, and come out, and a Man to be always with her; but as their Meetings were generally in the Dusk of the Evening, she could not very plainly discern who the Man was.

Fate is not always propitious to Love! The old Woman having thus discover'd the Place, resolved to discover the Person too, with whom this Love Affair was carried on; and to this purpose she, examining the empty House, finds there were two Doors to it, as is not unusual. She managed Things so dexterously that she got a Key made to the back Door, so that she could let herself in, as well as the Lovers had done, and in order to detect the guilty Persons, she places herself in the Garret of the House where they used to meet, a little before the ordinary time of their coming. Here she had the Opportunity to see them both come in, and when they were in, she found they went into a Chamber, which she thought had been empty, but it seems they had conveyed some convenient Furniture into it, for their Purpose.

When they were in the Chamber, the grave Matron came softly down, and by some unhappy Opening, had the Opportu-

nity to see all that passed on that Occasion; but to her great
Surprise, found the Man to be a Neighbour of hers, with whom
it seems she had formerly used the same Familiarity; but who
had left her on Account of her Age, and had found the Way
to accommodate himself with a younger Mistress.

Rage and Jealousy fired her Spirits on this Discovery, you
may be sure, but Guilt and 'Discretion bridled her Passion, so
that she did not discover herself; but having seen sufficient
to give her great Vexation, she withdrew to the Garret again
without being heard, and waited till they both went away.

The next Day, she falls foul of her young Neighbour, and
with a Volley of her usual Thunder, alarms the whole Neighbourhood; insomuch that the Neighbours, believing the young
Woman innocent, take the old Lady up, and carrying her
before the Justice, his Worship, at the common Request of
the good Women around, sentences the poor old Lady to the
Ducking Stool.

How the Sentence was in vain attempted to be executed
upon her,—how she swam upon the Water like a Cork,—how
they carried her back, upon that Emergency, to the Justice, and
accused her of being a Witch; and, what was the Issue of the
whole Prosecution,—being too long for this Letter, remains to
give you an Account of in my next.

I am, Sir, Yours, &c.

The Same, Continued.

A. J., June 20.—Sir, In my last I gave you a History of
a most eminent Transaction between two of our Country
Neighbours, Females of right worthy Fame, which issued in
the publick Application of a Parish Remedy for the cure of a
Scold, namely, the DUCKING STOOL; of which Engine of Justice I have had some Thoughts of giving a more particular
Account,—as it is Historically, Mathematically, and Enigma-
tically to be considered,—but of that more hereafter; and in
the meantime, I must return to the Tragical Part of my
Story.

The good old Lady mentioned in my last, being piously
inclined to detect the Vices of the young Gossip her neighbour, and having in particular been immeasureably provoked
to find, that she not only intrigued in the empty House hard

by; but, that it should be with Mr. *Such-a-One*, a Person, that the good Wife had formerly engrossed, and perhaps had the folly to believe she had still kept wholly to herself; being, I say, immeasurably provoked at these Things, she had given her Tongue a Liberty very offensive, and destructive to the Peace of her Neighbours.

But this not being satisfactory, she carried it on too far, (for who can set Bounds to their own Passions in such dismal Cases,) in a Word, she was daily, and every Day, so Loud, so Termagant, so Abusive; and the young Hussy had so much the art of governing her Passions, beyond the old one,—insinuating into the Opinion of her Neighbours so much, by her seeming Mildness, that they believed her to be innocent. At length the good Wives of the whole Street came in a Body to the old Lady, and told her, in a few Words, that if she would not let the young Woman alone, and if she would not cease her daily Clamour, they would present her, as they called it, as a common Disturber.

It was in vain for her to tell them the young Creature was so and so; they answered that she was a very modest young Woman; and, in a Word, that every Body said so, and no Body would believe her.

In fine, the old Lady, insisting upon the Fact, and continuing her Clamour, they proceeded in a Way of *Parish Justice*, as I said above, and got an Order of the Bench of Justices to have the poor old Lady dous'd for a common Disturber, that is to say, have the Exercise of the Ducking Stool.

Against the Time of Execution, the poor Sufferer having some reasonable Time allowed to prepare herself, had among other Necessaries provided herself, by the Advice of some People; (I suppose who had passed the Trial, and made the Experiment before,) I say, she had provided herself with a large under Petticoat of Oilcloth, such as the Market-Women usually cover their Hats with; the use of which was, innocently to keep the Water from her Body, the Weather being some Thing cool.

When she came to the Place of Execution, she found it was on the Side of a River, at a Mill-Tail, but some Space below the Mill; the Water was indeed very deep and broad, but in the middle was a small Island.

The Officers being ready to fit her into the Seat, a Woman

T 2

or two, who came to her Assistance, tied her Coats close about
her Feet, alleging that if they did not, the Water would at first
throw them up, and she might be a little exposed.

While they were tying her in the Chair, and perhaps not
very expert at their Work, and the unwilling Sufferer struggling
hard with them,—it happened they had not put in a Piece of
Wood, which fastens the Body down ; and, making an Essay to
turn the Chair off,—only to see how it would perform,—the old
Woman, having her Hands at Liberty, suddenly—with a Pair
of Scissors, which she had concealed about her,—cut the Ropes,
and giving a Spring out of the Chair, threw herself desperately
into the Water.

At the first plunge she seemed to dip a little under the
Water, but suddenly she appeared again, and her Coats being
tied close about her, and the Oil-Cloth keeping out the Water,
behold she swam above the Water ; and the Wind blowing that
way, she drove towards the little Island.

As soon as the People saw her, they cried out, " A WITCH,
a WITCH ! " and, " The DEVIL, the DEVIL ! *look yonder*," say
they, " *Why she swims like a Cork !* "

The old Woman, tho' frighted to the last degree, and crying
out for fear of being drowned, yet could not be heard for the
Noise ; but after some Time finding herself driving towards the
Island, she paddled with her Hands, and so, helping herself
forward, at last she arrived at the Port, and got safe on shore,
where she sat down, untied her Coats, and then held her
Hands up to the People, to beg they would have Mercy on her,
and help her from being drowned.

But the Mob, seeing her hold up her Hands, cried out the
louder, " O! Look how the old Wretch raves, and now she
curses us," say they ; at which the Boys threw Stones at her,
the Women ran away, and hailed their Children away, for fear
of being bewitched ; and, in short, the whole Crowd, for fear
of Witchcraft and the Devil, dropped away, by little and little,
leaving the old Witch all alone ; and there she was fain to stay,
wet enough, and cold enough, all Night. At last the Miller
took Compassion of her, in the Night ; and making a little
Float of Wood,—for he had no Boat,—he fetch'd her off in
the Night, and bid her begone, and no Body see her any
more.

In the Morning, the People came to the Water side to see for the old Witch, and the Constables were ordered to fetch her away, that she might be tried for a Witch; but she was gone, and nothing found, but one of her Petticoats, which being too wet, it seems, she had put it off, because it was too Cold for her. In the Pocket of the Coat was found a Paper of Brimstone and some Matches; with some writing on a Paper, which the Water had spoiled, so that it could not be read, and about Nine pence of Money, in Halfpence.

Upon this they cry'd out more Witchcraft; and that the Devil helped her to that Sulphur to carry on her Witchcraft, and the like. They examined the Miller, and he, a Cunning Rogue, confirmed them in it; telling them, that in the Night he saw a great Fire in the Island, heard a horrible Noise, shrieking, and the like, and on a sudden, there rose a great Gust of Wind, and then, he heard a Voice say, "Miller THOMAS, Miller THOMAS, *tell them I am gone!*" and so, says the Miller, " I suppose she flew away :" Upon which, our Folks made no Doubt, that the Witch rode away upon a Devil, and has got out of their Hands; but a little after, all the Murther came out, and the old Woman is no Witch, Mr. *App*, any more than you or I; No, nor a Devil either,—only a Devil of a Scold.   Sir, I am, Yours &c.

Against Fears of Popery.

A. J., June 27.—Sir, The Scribblers of the Town tell us. every Day, by the dullness of their Papers, what a scarcity of Intelligence they are under ; and what I foretold you long ago, of a Famine of News, seems to be come upon you, and what you will do in this Case is hard to tell.

Here's one of your Brethren Journal-Mongers is turned Divine, and he Harangues once a Week upon the Errors of Popery; I would advise the Man to transpose his Work from *Saturday* to *Sunday*, and from the Press to the Pulpit, and so, borrowing a black Cloak and a Band, to Hold it forth Decently where such Things should be held forth : I mean in a Sermon, to a full Congregation.

But why must we fall upon Popery at this time a Day? Is not Popery all dead and buried ever since King *George* came to the Crown ? Nay, I might have said, is it not dead and

rotten? Sure Popery is out of the Question now, or it never
will be!   Besides have not half the Nation sufficiently testified
they have no Inclination to Popery; that it does not Relish
with them, and will not go down upon any Terms?   Did we
not take an *Emetick* of Popery *Anno Dom.*, 1688?   Did
we not Vomit it all up at the Revolution, and do they talk to
us of Popery again?   Alas! 'tis such a dismal Farce, 'tis
enough to make us Sick at the very mention of it.   The very
Name is Nauseous, and there is no Need of troubling us
about it any more these Hundred Years.

I might · enlarge here upon the establish'd Securities, by
which our Religion is sufficiently fortified against Popery : so
that according to King *William's* Declaration, we need never
be in a fear of a Return upon us.   Our Securities, I say, are
many; we are surrounded with Strengths, Bulwarks and
Bastions, Ditches, Forts, Mud-Walls, and Wooden-Walls;
Armies, Acts of Parliament, a Protestant King, and a Succession of Protestant Princes, all adding to our other Assurances;
so that as to Popery, 'tis quite distanced; quite left behind
us, and that so, that it can never recover itself in this Nation.

To talk then of Popery at this time of Day, and raise a Hue
and Cry after the Whore of *Babylon;* is a Work as much to
the Purpose as a large Comment upon the Witch of *Endor*, or
a Dissertation upon Witchcraft.

'Tis a sad Sign indeed, that we have little to say when we
come just to tell our Beads over again, and say what our
Grandfathers had said over and over, so often, and so long ago,
that 'tis grown Thread-bare, and time it should be forgotten.
I wonder these Men do not write us a History of the Revolution, and print the *P.* of *O*——*s* Declaration again, for fear we
should forget it.   That would have some Sense in it; but a
long serious Preachment against Popery at this time of Day,
who can bear the Thoughts of it?

If the learned Casuist had set up a substantial Argument
against Arianism and Socinianism; if he had summoned
Whiston and *Emlin* to appear at his Bar, and employed his
mighty Talents in Defence of the Orthodox Faith, against
our Modern Hereticks we should all have joined with him,—
cried, O Yes! and beat a Call to bring a good Audience to
him, to hear what News he could tell us upon that Subject;

but to bring a Tale of a Cock and a Bull about Popery, and to spend his Breath to inform us against Popery, is as much to the Purpose as if he should beat an Alarm of the Emperor of *China* coming, with a vast Force, and an Army to Invade us, and bring in Father *Confucius* among us, or set up the great Idol *Szan Chi* to be worshipped in *Guild Hall*, in the room of the old Giant *Hogmagog*, and his Son.

In Charity therefore to your zealous Brother of the *Saturday* Morning Tribe, I desire you would acquaint him as a piece of News,—That poor, decayed Popery is dead, and has been interred some Years ago ; and therefore, instead of Disputing against it, I would advise him to preach its Funeral Sermon, and print it in his Journal ; and, to help it off, we will give him a short Epitaph, to add at the bottom, alluding to Old *Shakespear :*

> " *Here lyes old Popery in the Ground fast ramm'd,*
> *And let him that goes to raise it again be Da——d.*"

Sir, Yours, &c.

On a Trade Strike at Colchester.

A. J., July 4.— . . . .
. . . . . . The Masters, or the Bay Makers, are Hurtful and Injurious to us poor Weavers, and therefore we poor Weavers will go, and do Mischief to *ourselves.* For, in short, it is so, and no otherwise ; all such Things, without fail, ending in Mischief to the poor Rioters *themselves. Item,* We cannot get enough to feed us, not enough to *support our Families,* and therefore we will take care to get ourselves into a Jail *for the better support of our Families. Item,* Our Masters the Bay-makers say, they cannot afford to give us more Wages for our Weaving, therefore we will pull down their Houses to make them be more able to keep up their Payments.

Then as to the reasonable Part of this particular Sort of Justice. A Bay-maker will not give us a due Price for our Weaving. And what then? Why to punish him we will go and pull down his Landlord's House, who knows nothing of the Matter.

It was a memorable piece of Justice, that a certain Mob of this kind did, in King *Charles* II.'s Time, in *Spittle Fields ;*

when the Weavers rioted about Engine Looms. A certain
Master had discharged three Journeymen, and the Mob came
and demolish'd a good Part of his House; but while they
were at Work at it, in comes a poor ancient Woman, with her
Eyes full of Tears, and her Hands lifted up, and she begs the
Mob to spare her House, for it was all she and her three
Children had to live upon, and she was a poor Journeyman
Weaver's Widow. This so damp'd the Mob, that unreasonable
as they were, they left the House, and dropped away by little
and little and fell to Work some where else. Now, after all,
when the Matter came to be examined, the Man that lived in
that poor Woman's house had no *Engine-Looms*; but only dis-
missed three Journeymen because the Trade fell off, and he
had no Business for them.

(In his reflections upon this he justly remarks :—)

In a Word, this Mob Justice is a strange Thing; and, as a
Flood spreads over the lowest Grounds it can find, and without
distinction, over those first that lie next to it, so 'tis here; the
Bay-maker that comes first in their Way meets the first of
their Fury, not because he is the most concerned in the
Oppression, if it be such, but because he stood next them,
and then down goes his House; not that they know whether
'tis his own House, or whether it may not belong to some
Weaver's poor Widow, or other. So that 'tis all one to them
who they hurt, or whom they wrong, no more than the Flood in
the River considers whose Ground it overflows, and whose not.

(He recommends mutual forbearance of Masters and Journeymen both in bad and good trade.) As Seamen that embark in a Ship must take their Lot, for Calms and Storms,
good Weather and Bad, fair or foul. But if they will indeed
Mob the People that are Guilty, they must go over to *Portugal*
and *Spain*, and tear the Clergy to Pieces for not wearing more
Gowns, and the Gentry for not wearing out their Bays Cloaks.

Against a Bishop Writing on Armies and War.

A. J., July 11.—Sir, I have been long solicited to Write to
you in a different Stile from what I think most of your Correspondents have yet talked in, and to treat of Things Solid;
and truly, if I thought your Readers would bear with Things
of that Nature, I should take the Liberty sometimes to be

very Grave. But I know the Town at present seems to relish
nothing but Trifles, and it is discouraging to enter upon
Matters of Moment, when People are not disposed to hear
them.

Again 'tis discouraging to see how unacceptable what others
have written upon these weighty Subjects has been, even the
Bish— himself has had but poor Success in it. It is indeed,
they say, something out of his Way ; and therefore he may not
discharge in it, with the same Vivacity, or Write with the
same Spirit as he himself might do in Matters of another
Nature. To hear a Divine comment upon Trade, and tell us,
that all Trade is carried on to the Gain of one Side, and the
Loss of Another, which is as contrary to the nature of Commerce, as the *Poles* are opposite to one another :—To hear
again, the Men of God, and of the Gown, talk of Standing
Armies, and Reason upon the Convenience of entertaining a
Body of Soldiers; why, either we ought to believe them in a
Plot, or expect they will talk of those Matters very Oddly.

It is true, that the Clergy, in all Ages, have been said to be
too forward to promote War and Bloodshed. Not that I pretend to say they ever cared for Fighting themselves ; except
it be here and there that such a Son of Thunder is found
among them. I say, tho' they seldom care for a Share of the
Blows, yet they have not a little assisted in blowing the Coals,
as well as in blowing the Trumpet.

But for this very Reason, I think, when I hear the Parsons
talk of Armies, and maintaining Soldiers, in time of Peace,
and the like; I always fear there's some Crusado in Hand,
and that the World may expect Mischief in a very little Time.

And yet when I read the Learned Labours of the Right
Reverend *Britannicus*, in Defence of a Standing Force, and
also the Arguments used by his worthy Pen, to convince the
Nation that we are in no Danger from such an Army ; I must
confess, I thought it very wonderful; and had I not had a
great Veneration for my Lord *Britannicus*, I should have
thought he had been in the Interest of the *Chevalier*, and that
the *Chevalier* had employed him, *and that under a good Pension
too*, in order to expose the Thing he seems to Defend, and to
magnify the Danger of the return of *Popery*, and of the
Chevalier, as a Thing so certainly approaching, that nothing

but a very considerable and Newly Augmented Army could prevent it, and indeed, hardly that.

This Step is so preposterous, and so unaccountable, especially to come from the Pen of One, that seems to speak as the Scripture says, *As one having Authority, and not as the Scribes;* That I think 'tis enough to give all the Women the Vapours, and all the quiet and wealthy Citizens the Spleen, to think how dreadful our Danger is, and how the *Chevalier* is, as it were, at the Door, with the Lord knows how many Thousand of *Jacks* and *Papists* ready to cut our Throats, overturn our Government, subvert our Religion, and do everything that is Terrible and Frightful to, and with us.

Now with his Lordship's Pardon, and with the Pardon of all that write in this Manner, I must say, this is very Scandalous; and I think they are not writing for the Government, but for the *Chevalier de St. George.* Is not magnifying the Number, and the Interest, and the Danger of our Enemies, encouraging our Enemies? Is it not doing them a Service in their Negociations and Solicitations Abroad? Is it not telling their *Popish* Allies how formidable their Party is at Home? And that they only want a little Assistance from Abroad to Make a Stand, and that then, they are able to do, God Knows what, for themselves; the contrary to all which is indeed True?

What do these People mean thus to dress up the *Jacobite* Interest *a la Diable?* Is it to Terrify us into the Consenting to, or bearing with, a Standing Army for our Defence? Sure, on the other Hand, they intimate, that there is very little to be said in Defence of the Parliament's Voting a Standing Force needful; that they should resolve it all into the Danger of Rebellion, and the Chevalier.

I am clear in my Opinion, that a Standing Army is necessary in this Kingdom, and at this Time, and that even the Number is also needful; and that we are in no Danger of losing our Liberties by such an Army, as some would Suggest. But I think 'tis doing more Reverence to the Popish Party, than I think we owe them, or than is any Way their due, to say that we stand in need of a considerable Force to keep their formidable Figure at a Distance; or to prevent their Rebellions and Insurrections, to oppose the many Thousands of their Friends at Home, and to keep off the Invasion of their great Allies from Abroad.

Nothing like it! I look upon them as a Routed, Contemptible, and Despicable People, not worth one Hour's Anxiety about them, or worth the least Shadow of our Apprehensions. Routed in their Strength, Contemptible in their Numbers, and Despicable in their Circumstances. That they are Down, Down; and not only will never, but can never, no never, rise any more; and so I think they need not be named any more, in all the Debates about keeping up a Standing Army in this Nation. Nay, I believe the wisest, and most thinking Gentlemen in *England* are of my Mind.

Now having laid down this Fundamental, Let no Man ask us, *What then do we keep up an Army for?* Seeing I think 'tis easy to make it appear, that a Standing Body of Troops is needful at this Time, tho' there were not a *Papist* left in the Nation, and this I dare undertake to make Good.

Sir, I am Yours, &c.

A Standing Army, with Consent of Parliament, not Dangerous to Liberty.

A. J., July 25.—Sir, I wrote to you, some Time agon, my Opinion concerning Liberty, Standing Armies, and the Reason and Danger of them both; and tho' in that, my Opinion perhaps may differ from the general Notions of the World, yet as I think I am able to Defend my Opinion, without any Room for Objection, I make no Apology at all for it, but send it you Naked as it is.

I then told you that *I believe* there is, at this Time, a justifiable Necessity for a Standing Force to be kept up in this Kingdom, leaving the Number to be judged of and determined by King and Parliament; and this, tho' there were no Chevalier, and no Jacobites in the World, they being all out of the Question.

I now take the Liberty to add, that *I believe* our Liberties are not in any Danger from a Standing Army, that is to say from such an Army, and so stated, as is, at this Time, the Case in *Great Britain*.

'Tis something Merry, that such great Fears, and such mighty Arguments, should be raised upon so small a Part of

the point in Hand.   The Gentleman that wrote lately upon
this Subject, and expects our due Regard, says the Army kept
up before, *upon the ordinary Establishment*, was sufficient *to
Enslave us*, and yet argues against nothing but the last Augmentation.   If we were in Danger before, and that the Ten
Thousand Men in *Great Britain*, and Twelve Thousand in *Ireland* were *sufficient ;* then why so much Noise about the Augmentation ?   For we can but be *Enslaved*, and if the 22,000
mentioned in *Britain* and *Ireland* are enough to do it; then 'tis
likely, that Augmentation *is not made to Enslave us*, for there
was it seems no need for it, the Forces being sufficient before.

But I say, and undertake to shew, that neither the *Ordinary Establishment* of 22,000 Men, as before, nor the Augmentation made since, are either sufficient to enslave this Nation,
or that there is any Danger to our Liberties on that Account.

And here it would be necessary, if there were Room for it
in this Paper, *to cull Witnesses* as in Cases of other Tryals.
Let us look back, and enquire whenever this Nation has been
so overpowered by a Standing Army, kept up in Time of
Peace.

The Instance given is *but One*, and that is the Army in the
Time of the late Rebellion, which indeed is no Instance at all ;
As I undertake to prove in a few Words.   (1.) It was not a
Time of Peace, but a Time of War and Confusion.   (2.) It
was a Time of Conquest and Tyranny ; the King was Subdued
and a Prisoner, all the Loyal Nobility and Gentry, the Staff
and Defence of *English* Liberty were cut off and destroyed in
a long, furious, and bloody War.   (3.) The Parliament were
grown Contemptible, even to their own Armies, as well as to
the whole body of the People ; were odious •to the Nation,
divided among themselves, and as it were by Providence itself,
lay an open Prey to the Army.   Nay, if the Accounts of those
Times are true, the People themselves concurred with the Army
in pulling down the Power that had Tyrannized over, both
their Sovereign, their Liberties, and Destroyed the very Face
of Government in the whole Island.   So that, it was really the
Parliament, not the Army that Enslaved Us ; and the Army
only Usurped upon Usurpation.   No wonder, if in Times of
such Confusion, Liberty fell a Prey to every Power that proved
Strongest.   So I think, as I said above, this is no Instance at

all.   If this then be laid aside, I do not see one more in the whole *English* History, for as to *William* the Conqueror, his Title tells you what he did ; namely, he came in by Force, and he Reigned by Force, and is no more an Instance of a standing Army in Time of Peace, than the Landing of *Julius Cæsar*, and the Government of the *Romans*, or any other of the Invaders of those Times.

Take then the other Side of the Question, and how many Times have Standing Armies attempted it and have Miscarry'd ? Nay, I pretend to say, that no Standing Army was ever able to Enslave us, nor did they ever Attempt it, but they miscarried in that Attempt ; even tho' much stronger than the present Army, and when they openly and avowedly Resolved upon it.

In my next I shall go through it Historically, 'tis too long to come in at the end of a Letter, and therefore I only at present Advance it, as a General ; and repeat it thus, that no standing Army, in Time of Peace, was ever able to subdue our Liberties, and all that ever did, either Design or Attempt it, have miscarried.

If this can be proved, as is Evident it may, then the Fright and Alarm which some People would fain bring us into, on Account of the Troops at present kept up in this Nation, will all Vanish, and die of themselves ; as shall be farther Evident in its Place.

I am, &c.

A. J., July 25.—The Library of Samuel Pepys Esq., Secretary of the Navy in the Time of James II., late in the Hands of — Jackson, Esq., of Clapham, deceased, is now placed at Magdalen College in Cambridge, in a handsome Gallery fitted up by the College to receive it.   It is a very choice and numerous Collection, consisting of three thousand Volumes, in most Sciences and Languages, containing several curious Books and Papers relating to Navigation, &c.   Secretary Pepys desired in his Will that his Library might be disposed of to some College in one of our Universities, that it might be serviceable in the Advancement of Learning in general ; and rather to Magdalen in Cambridge than any other, as a grateful Acknowledgement for his Education in that Society.

*Lewdness not to be Defended.**

A J., Aug. 1.—Sir, I am diverted from my last Subject, however useful, and indeed at this Time necessary, by a demand which Justice makes upon me, and upon all honest Men in whose Station it is to do it Publickly; namely, to shew their just Abhorrence of Flagrant Vice, and to set it forth in its proper Colours, that the World may both see and know the Degree of its Guilt, and testify their Detestation, both of the Offence and the Offenders.

We see in some of our late Advertisements, a new Book to be published, and as I am assured, it is since Published; Entitled, an Apology for the Stews, or a Defence of them. In short, 'tis an Apology for those Sinks of Hell, which this Town is but too full of, call'd, Bawdy-Houses.

Nor is the Title of this infamous Work so plainly offensive, but the Work itself, as I am informed, is every way as Wicked as the Title can suggest it to be; and not so only, but is performed in a Manner, which makes it rather an Incentive to the grossest Lewdness, than exposing it, as every modest Writer would have done.

How, and with what Face such a Writer could expect Connivance in the common Justice of the Nation I cannot imagine. What every sober Magistrate must necessarily Detest and Abhor, sure some will be found to Censure and Punish. It cannot be but that a Work thus Qualified for Justice to take hold of, would receive its due Discouragement some way or other; and tho'. there are indeed too many Advocates for Wickedness among the dissolute Part of Mankind, there are yet none so audacious as to dare to plead for such an open avowed Defiance of it as this is.

It is true that there are said to be Allowances given to publick Stews or Houses of Sin in *Italy,* and that Bordelloes are said to pay an annual Tribute to the State; but shall we argue for being Wicked, because others are so? We are told strange Stories of the Lewdness of *Friars* and *Monks* in Religious Houses, and how they have justified those Things from the Necessities of Nature, and from its being Medicinally good for the Body; but let me add a Word even to the Papists

---

* Against Dr. Mandeville's notorious Pamphlet.—*Ed.*

themselves,—namely, let them shew me any of the Precepts
left behind them by the Institutors, or Founders of those
Orders, and let me see there the Latitude left them for such
Wickedness.

If then it was not permitted by the Founders of those
Orders, from what Dispensation do they who wear the Habit
of those Orders allow themselves in such Liberties? But
suggesting that it was so; how does that Militate in defence
of us? And which is it that we call ourselves? Are we not
called the reformed Countries, the reformed Churches? And
what are we reformed in; are we reformed in Doctrine only,
and not in Life? Do we resent the Principles of Popery only,
and not the Practice? Are we more Holy in Doctrine, and as
wicked in Conversation? This will by no means do, when we
come on the other side the Stars.

But suppose we are not yet so thoroughly reformed, as it is
to be wished we were; are we pleading for them? We ought
to repent of defending that which Scripture and all the Rules
of Morality, as well as Christianity Condemn. To Offend, is
the Weakness of Nature, but to justify and defend our Offences, is an Impudence born from Hell, and ought to be
punish'd by the Magistrates.

We have often Proclamations for Fasts and Days of Humi-
liation appointed; the Reason given is to confess our National
Sins, and implore the Mercy of Heaven, and to avert impending Judgments. These are some of the Reasons given in the
late appointed Fast, when we were all in dreadful Apprehensions of the Plague. But did ever any Christian reformed
Nation but this, publish a Defence of those very Sins, which
on these Occasions they are to confess. This is setting God
and Religion at Defiance; and, by the way, is a gross Scandal
upon our Magistrates, thinking them to be just such as we are
ourselves,—suggesting that they will approve, or at least connive—at such a Wickedness, as all good Men must abhor.

It is true there is an unbounded Liberty taken, I will not
say given, in this great and populous City, to open Lewdness,
and the wicked Houses where such Deeds of Darkness are
carried on, are too many, and too Publick. But then we
must acknowledge, to the Honour of our Constitution, that
they are unlawful Houses; and were the Magistrates just to

their Offices, and to the Trust reposed in them by the Government, they would soon Root them out, for there are very wholesome good Laws to suppress them. But to set up now to support them by Arguments, and write Books in their Defence, this is such a Liberty, as I never knew suffered in this Nation before; and if it pass unpunished now, it must be because the Power of Crime Encreases, and the Power of the Government Decays.

The very Rabble, as wicked as they have been, and are in other Cases, always testified their abhorrence of the Liberty such People as these took; and the open Bawdy-Houses in Moorfields, Whetstone's Park, (as it was called,) and such like Places were frequently Demolished by the 'Prentices and Mob, in Testimony of their abhorrence of the Liberty they took, till those Places are, as we may say, Rooted out, and Vice has been obliged to affect a little Decency, and Walk in Disguise.

But to publish Books for Restoring the Audacious Trade,—to lay down Arguments to prove the Necessity of Whoring, and the many Conveniences of it,—to encourage the abusing other Men's Wives, and Debauching the Youth of both Sexes,—and to Argue for it; What is this but Mobbing God Almighty himself, and playing Liberty against Religion, and the Laws of Men against the Laws of God?

I shall take some Time with the Language and Manners of it, and see how Ruinous both are to the Morals of the Nation, and how directly tending to Destroy all Sense of Virtue and Religion from the Minds of Men among us; and in Conclusion shall, with all Decent Earnestness, call upon the Magistrates to do Justice to their Maker, and to do their utmost to suppress the bold Attempt, before it spread too far among us to the Ruin of our People.

Your Humble Servant, &c.

Attempt of John Sheppard to Escape from Newgate.

A. J., Aug. 1.—Sheppard, the notorious House-breaker, who lately escaped from New Prison, and was retaken by Jonathan Wilde and committed to Newgate, attempted to escape also from that Gaol a Day or two ago, several Saws and Instruments proper for such a Design being found about his Bed. He is since confined in an Apartment called the Stone Room,

The manner of
John Shepherd's Escape
out of the Condemn'd Hole in Newgate.

kept close, and sufficiently Loaded with Irons to prevent his Designs for the future.

A Defence of the Female Sex.

A. J., Aug. 8.—Sir, I make no Question, but upon a profligate Paper appearing last week in a kind of Triumph, with an Insult upon the Women, Reproaching the Sex with being worthyless, useless, and only fit for breeding-Nurses, and Servants; and reproaching ENGLAND with over-valuing them, &c., I say, I make no Question but the Ladies of *England*, whose superior Merit needs no Advocate, would easily be able to List Armies in their Service, on this Occasion, if it was worth their while

But I shall take up this Quarrel for them, if they please, and shew the World, by a different Way of Discourse, that this Enemy is *not Competent*,—that he is not qualified for the Undertaking; namely, of Attacking the fair Sex in *England*, till he first clears up an Objection, or *Demurrer* against his Plea, which I shall bring *in Form*, after laying open the Case a little beforehand.

The Case is this, it has been thought by our Ancestors, Time out of Mind, (and that in *England* we call a Title by Prescription,) to give all the due and just Privileges to the Ladies which they now enjoy.   *There's their first Title.*

We are not to Question; and if we did, could not maintain it, whether the Ladies, when first they obtained these Advantages, merited them from the Men, or not, either by their extraordinary Gallantry, their Assistance, as well in the *Field of Battle*, as in the Toils of the *Field of Labour*.   For we find they had their Share of both, and can, if Occasion require it, go far to make Proof of their Service in both, and consequently of their Merit; but that, I say, is not the Question now.

As our first Ancestors bestowed all those Favours, so their Successors, in all Ages, thought fit to continue them, and rather to Encrease than Diminish them; from whence, in Justice to the Senses as well as Honesty of our illustrious Grandfathers, we are bound to conclude, that they found the same Merit which moved their Ancestors to bestow such Honours on the Women, moved them to Confirm and Continue them.

Now, unless this wiser Gentleman can shew that the Ladies
of this Age are unworthy of their Grandmothers' Honours,
which the Ladies of former Ages enjoy'd, he cannot expect to
perswade us to Repeal, or *Re-assume* the Grants which our
Ancestors made them; and as he will find this a very hard
and difficult Task,—so, if he attempts it, he will *no doubt* be
fully answered from every Quarter. For there are such Potent
Batteries ready in Defence of the Virtue, the Beauty, the
Sense, the Wit, &c. of the *English* Ladies, that I may say to
him, as my Lord *Rochester* said to another Writer, upon a
different Occasion :—

> " Fellows that ne'er were heard or read of,
> If thou writ'st on, will write thy Head off."

But to waive this Part, I come to my Demurrer; which I
venture to say, *with Submission to the Learned of the Long
Robe,* will stand good in Law. I humbly move the Author
may produce his Pedigree, *if he has any;* and prove the Legi-
timacy of his Pen; for if he is not an *Englishman,* but should
appear to be a Native of a Country where the poor Women
are the Slaves, and the Husbands the *Corregidores;* where
the Husbands Dine, and the Wives wait at table; where the
Salique Law is universal,—and reaches to private Families, as
well as Crowns; namely, that the Women never Reign; where
the Women carry the Burthens, and the Men receive the
Wages :—Then, I say, he is not Competent to this Question;
for being bred a Tyrant, he neither Knows how to use, or
bestow Liberty.

Nay, if this Author be a *North Briton,* tho' they may in
some Sense be of ourselves, yet I think he could not claim
even the *Post Nati* on this Occasion; unless the *Scots* will
first loose the Rigorous Bands from the Women in their
Country, and set them upon an equal Foot with the Women
of *England.* And that, he will not pretend is yet done.

What then does the Judgment of a Foreigner weigh in this
Case? Is he angry that the Ladies in *England* enjoy some
Privileges, which the Ladies in his Country do not? Reason
dictates then that 'tis because they deserve it better; Or, that
the Men in *England* are Honester than the Men in his
Country; let him take it which Way he will.

I might enlarge upon the usage of Women in many Nations

in *Europe*, even the most civilized; and Argue the inhumanity of setting up to Tyrannize over the Sex. Also the Cruelty of denying them that early Erudition, which would make them Equal, if not Superior in all manner of Science, and even more capable of all possible Improvement than the Men.

But I cleave to my Demurrer : Let me first see that I am Arguing with an Adversary, who has not Principles of Domestick Tyranny mingled with his Mother's Milk ; and who, *as I may say*, is born a Tyrant, then I shall say more. But if the Opposer be Partial, and that Partiality be an Error of his Nature; his Pen is *an Alien*, he knows nothing of the Matter, he is prepossessed, and the Ladies have nothing to say to him.

Your Humble Servant, &c.

On Defects in the English Law of Divorcement.

A. J., Aug. 15.—Sir, You have been pleased to be Merry, with the poor Wheeler's Wife of El—m, but you do not consider the Latitude the Women take on that Side the Water ; and I doubt you do not Compassionate your own Sex as you ought to do, but Compliment the Ladies at our Expence, as if unfaithfulness to us their Husbands, were a light Matter in your Eyes.

But to take you short, give me leave to tell you, tho' I am not for Encouraging any Man to Abuse, Impose upon, or Oppress his Wife, yet I think there is one Thing in which we (the Men) have not Justice done us ; nay, the very Laws themselves are Deficient, and there are some Inconveniences attending it, I assure you ; and that is, in short, the Difficulty a Man has in proving his Wife to be false to him, (so as to take the Legal Benefit the Law allows,) tho' he really knows it to be so.

My Case is very Particular. It was my Misfortune to go a Journey, in which I intended to have stayed out a Fortnight, but business not succeeding as I expected, I came Home in about Five Days. Coming pretty late in, yet my Family were not all in Bed, and I found my Man, and my Maid, grinning and whispering, and shuffling about strangely, but neither of them would say anything to me. However, supposing all well, I asked for my Wife; one said she was above ; the other said she was a Bed, but still, like a Fool, I suspected

U 2

nothing, but ran up Stairs to go to my Chamber: when on a
sudden, the Chambermaid met me on the Stairs; " Sir," says
she, " my Lady is gone out, they are at Cards at Madame
L——'s, and they sent for her."

She made no doubt but I would go to her, but I was
weary and willing to go to Bed; so I said, " Well, *Betty*, go
tell her that I am come Home, and am so Weary that I can't
come out to-Night," so I goes on, to go to Bed. The Jade of
a Chambermaid, not in the least seeming Surprized, Returns,
" Lord, Sir, my Lady has the Key of the Chamber in her
Pocket, and you can't get in. Be pleased," says she, " to go
into the Parlour till I go fetch the Key."

To that Minute I suspected nothing, but I innocently answered, " You need not fetch the Key, I can open the Door
without it." With this, the Girl, having no other Shift, falls
down on the Stairs in a Swoon,—that is to say, a Counterfeit
Swoon; and I was so innocently Foolish still as to think
nothing of the Matter. But in short, the Noise the Wench
made, discovered the whole Story, for up jumps my Wife,
opens her Chamber Door, and asks, what is the Matter? And
I presently answered, and told her how *Betty* was fallen down
in a Swoon. I had little thought that my Wife would be in
such a Fright at hearing my Voice;—but she was struck
Speechless in a Moment, and indeed, then, so was I.

Now, tho' late, I began to see. I immediately put my
Hand up to my Forehead, astounded at my Disgrace; in a
Word, I took them both together, both Undressed,—the Lover
and the Lady,—for they had no possible Way to avoid me;
and this I think now, is as good a *Rem in re* to my Satisfaction, that is to say, that I am cornuted. Neighbour *App*,
Mark that!

And yet, after all, they tell me this is not enough; that
upon this Evidence, I cannot convict my Wife, nor obtain a
Divorce, which is what I would have in this Case.

If this be so, then I say the Men have hard measure; for
now my Wife may go and be unfaithful to me every Night,
and I must not only continue bound to own myself to be her
Husband, but must keep the Children too that she shall have,
and let them call me Father, and come in for a Share of my
Estate. What think you of it, Mr. *App?* Is not this a very

dull Story for a Poor *Englishman?* Do you think 'tis thus in *France*, or anywhere else in the World?

Now, Mr. *App*, if you can redress this Grievance you may defend the Women as you please; but till this is done, it must be acknowledged it is a great Hardship upon the Men; and what no Men suffer but us *Englishmen*; I say, 'tis a Hardship, for to be so disgraced and wronged may be a common Fate, but to see it, and not be able to do one's self Right is unbearable.

I am answered by our Beaus with a Question. Why did I not do myself Justice, and send the Fellow of an Errand into the other World? A pretty Story indeed; a Man Robs my House, and I must turn Hangman, and Execute him, because the Law will not; nay, the Law will not bear me out in it neither, but I must be brought into Trouble, tried for my Life, and think it a favour to be brought in Guilty of Man-Slaughter, and come off with the Mark of a Rogue in my Hand. This is very hard Mr. *App*. Indeed, very hard!

Or suppose the Adulterer wore a Sword; what then? Why I must fight him, must I? And that's another good Tale; that because he has debauched my Wife, I must lay an Even Wager who shall Die for it, he or I? For fighting is but laying an Even Wager, who shall Live, and who shall Die. I will State that Case upon a better Foot, for you, in my next.

Your Humble Servant,
Thomas Horncastle.

The Same Continued. Faults on both Sides.

A. J., Aug. 22.—Sir, In my last, I hope I satisfied you about what I am (I assure you) very sorry for; namely, that I am (and shall please your Worship,) a ———, that my Wife is a lewd woman, and all that; and I have given you a sufficient Testimony of it, so that it cannot reasonably be suggested that I am mistaken. The young Fellows, my old Companions, Laugh at me, and make Tricks at me, and say I ought to have Fought the Rogue that has thus Abused me, and Killed him. Now tho' I must take upon me to tell you that the World does not take me for a Coward; yet in this Case, as I said before, the Hazard is not equal at all.

First, I am the Person injured; he is the Person that has

abused or injured me, Must I then stake my Life against his upon an equal Hazard? No, No! That is a new Bargain, let me debauch his Wife first, and then I am upon an equal Lay with him; then I will fight him with all my Heart, that is to say, let him make me first an open Reparation for the Injury he has done me, and then I'll fight him; but to fight him because my Wife is unchaste, there is in my Opinion no Sense in that.

But what then must I do in the Reparation of Honour? Why the truth is, I cannot tell, and this is the Hardship I complained of to you in my last; and 'tis such a Hardship that I do not see how I can come off of it.

I may, you will say, turn my Wife away; yes, I may put her out of Doors, but she shall go and take a House at next Door to me, and make me pay the Rent; nay, tho' she become even more wicked there, as it were before my Face, 'tis all one; the very Rogues that associate with her shall lend her Money, and Arrest me for it; and, in a Word, she may Ruin me, as well as abuse me, if she thinks fit.

Nay to go further, as I mentioned in my last, if she have children not mine, the children being born in Wedlock, shall be called by my Name; and I am obliged to own them, or at least provide for them, so great are the Privileges of married Ladies in *England*.

Now what must I do? If I use any open Violence to my Wife, then I am called Cruel and Barbarous, a Tyrant, and I know not what. I am advised to put her into a Mad House, and indeed considering all, she is worse than a Mad Woman; but she is too cunning for me in that Case, and being aware of such a Thing, she tells me she won't be Tricked, or Kidd-napped; and, in short, she won't go, so I see no Remedy, but to be quiet, and put my Disgrace in my Pocket.

Now if the Ladies of *England* have not Liberty enough, Judge yourself, and send me Word, and tell me what Course I shall take with my *Gillian*. But now, let me tell you, after all, Mr. *App*, I cannot tell how to be cruel to this Lady of mine, or how to move one Step in any thing Severe against her; all I have yet to reproach her with, is to Upbraid her, and tell her I will be Divorced from her. As to the first, it seems to make some Impression upon her, and not being able to deny the

Guilt, she falls into Tears; but when I talk of Suing for a Divorce, she Laughs at me, and tells me I cannot do it, and that she knows what the Law says in that Case, as well as I do.

Now, Mr. *App*, I have a Neighbour of mine is much in the same Case with me, but his Wife has not been so wary as mine, and he has gotten good Witnesses against her; so he resolved, they say, to Sue out a Divorce against her. And he employed a Proctor to that Purpose; but when it came to the Upshot the Man cannot do it, the Law of the Land hinders me, and the Law of the Land hinders him.

In short, Mr. *App*, the Woman is a ———— that is certain, and the Man has Proof enough of it too, as I have said; but he loves the Woman, and notwithstanding all her ill Conduct, he Doats so much upon her, that, in a Word, he says, he cannot think of putting her away. And thus it is with some more that I know, that, in short,—what with Law, and Love,—the *English* Women may do what they will with us, and what would you Advise me to do in this Case? For my Part, I see no Remedy, but to be Contented with our Fate, and try by Kindness, and good Usage to win our Wives.

I acknowledge, I believe, if I had not been a loose, cross, reprobate Fellow to my Wife, I believe she had never been drawn away to be so Wicked, and she makes me a fair Proposal, that if I will abate my Scandalous Living, she will convince me of her Fidelity for the Future; and indeed, the Proposal is so reasonable, that I am a little inclined to make a new Bargain with her, for I am still of Opinion that the best way to reclaim a Wife, is to reform the Husband, and that in particular, as to her, I am fully perswaded, that had I been Sober, she would never have been Wicked.

As to my Neighbour, I believe 'tis much the same, for he Loves his Wife to a kind of Distraction; yet, he has played her the same Trick some time ago, and has no Body to blame more than himself. Not that I think the Wickedness of a Husband justifies that Wickedness of the Wife; but I must own, it stops his Mouth very much, when he Challenges her with it; and that's my Case. Yet I find it very hard to pass over this cursed Slip in my Wife; and thus I come to you in a double Difficulty, for I know not how to keep her, nor to put her away.

Your Humble Servant, &c.

What is Courage.

A. J., Aug. 29.—Sir, We have had some wise Church Dissertations of late upon Courage.   I must Confess, the learned Author has in my Opinion taken as much Pains to say something that is nothing to the Purpose, as most Men that I have lately heard of; for we still remain at some Loss to know whether it be a Habit, or a Quality.

I have something of an Aversion indeed, to hearing Churchmen talk of Courage; it looks as if they were telling us what Occasions they would bring us to have for our Courage, and that they would find the World Business for their Arms.

Methinks when, in a profound Peace, they enter into an Enquiry after that Thing, which is so useful in the Field; they are at least willing to take Care of us, that we should not forget how to appear in the Face of an Enemy again.   *'Tis very kind indeed,* but they may for the present set their Hearts at rest; for PEACE, blessed be God, however ill. pleased some People *delighting in War* were willing to be, or rather seemed to be, at the making it, is now so much the Nation's Blessing,—and his Majesty has so apparently, and so vigorously appeared in preserving it, not to us only, but to all the World,—that we are out of Fear of any Body, no, not the Ecclesiasticks themselves, breaking in upon it.

Not but that turbulent Spirits may, at any Time, embroil the World, in some degree or another; but let them remember too, that 'tis generally at their own Expense, and they pay dearest for it at last; and so I doubt not, it will be here, if they attempt our Peace.

I have observed of late, and have been often thinking to write to you about it, how quiet our Clergy are as to Popery; as if they thought the Church, when once powerfully protected by the Civil Power, was in no danger from Error and Heresy. Now, if they would but shew their Courage in pushing against the Devil's Kingdom, in matters of Principle; I think they might leave the Civil Power to struggle with all our temporal Enemies; and they would do it well enough, and find Men of Courage equal to any of their Opposers.

But in the needful Opposition to Popish and Arian Errors, which plainly and daily get ground upon us in this Nation, I think there is a Call upon the Clergy to shew their Courage, and to blow a Trumpet, and lift up the Voice,—so the Scripture calls it,—against those Invaders of the Church; and had they sufficient Courage for this Work, it would be much better employed, than in Debating, whether other Men have Courage or no, or what true Courage is.

What the Reason is, that the Protestant World is thus asleep, while the Agents of Popery gain Ground upon us, by their Diligence and Application; is a Thing worth our Discoursing of by itself, and I shall take up some of your Time upon that Subject, as much to the Profit of your Readers as I can.

In the meantime to return to the Subject,—What is, or is not, Courage? The Question is not difficult, tho' many have given differing Accounts of it. Setting aside then the Physical and Philosophical Accounts given of it, my Opinion is, with my Lord *Rochester*, that Fear is the original Cause of all Courage. A Musketeer is Bold in his Ranks, and Fires in the Face of his Enemy, even when he is ready to foul himself for fear of being killed. He pushes on, even to Desperation, for fear of the Blows of his Officer, or for fear of being Hanged for quitting his Post. One Fear overcomes another, and the greatest Fear gives the Man Courage, makes him Desperate, so that he rushes upon his Enemies like a Madman; whereas could he avoid it, he would never Fight at all! For says the same Lord *Rochester* :—

" *All Men would be Cowards if they Durst.*"

Thus *Cato's* Courage, so much talked of, was a base Cowardice; finding himself Conquered by *Cæsar's* good Fortune, he run desperately on his own Sword, for fear of being taken alive by his Enemy, and suffering the Shame of being carried in Triumph through the Streets of the City. Had *Cato* acted the Hero, he ought to have Encouraged his Train of Officers, for he had a Gallant Body of Gentlemen left about him, and with them he might have retreated into *Spain;* and there he should have fought against *Cæsar* to the last Drop, as the two Sons of *Pompey* did, who was then there, and had two Gallant Armies; and who, if they had been assisted by *Cato* and his Followers, might perhaps have gained the Victory, and they were near gaining it as it was.

I shall give you a Specimen of this Thing called Courage, very much to this purpose, in my next.   I am, &c.

Opening Bartholomew Fair.

A. J., Aug. 29.—On Saturday last (22nd) in the Afternoon, the Lord Mayor came with great State and Solemnity to Smithfield, and proclaimed Bartholomew Fair. His Lordship's Coach stopp'd at the Lodge Door of Newgate, where Mr. Reuse, the chief Turnkey appeared, in the absence of Mr. Pitt, the Keeper, (who is indisposed,) and treated his Lordship, the Sheriffs and Aldermen with a Lemonade, after a very handsome and pleasing Manner; which Custom is observed to all the Mayors, at the Proclaiming of Bartholomew Fair.

To Dare to be Good; or, To Dare to be Wicked, as Tests of Courage.

A. J., Sept. 5.—Sir, I promised you, in my Last, a little farther Discourse upon that nice Thing called Courage. A thing so many talk of, and so few understand. We have a modern Attempt made to Philosophize upon this Article of Courage, and that by the Reverend Bishop, lately turned *Speculation Man.* But in my Opinion his Lordship has neither Philosophized, nor Christianized upon it, or at least not to any Purpose; nay, if I may be so free with his Lordship, he has talked of Courage,—as if he neither knew the Thing he wrote of, or himself, who wrote of it,—as if he was neither Philosopher, or Christian.

To call Acts of Desperation by the Illustrious name of Courage, to call Madness, and the Height of Lunacy, a Species of Gallantry, and Recommend a Demented Rage to us as an Act of Bravery; this is such a Way of talking, as is fitter for the *Circus,* and the *Amphitheatre,* than the *Rostrum* of the Divine, or the School of a Philosopher.

A wise Man, and a Truly brave Man, writes *Nil desperandum* upon everything that is before him; he gives up no Cause that ought to be Defended, while there is the least Room to defend it. To abandon his Cause and his Country is the worst of Despair; and Despair is the Extreme of Cowardice and Fear.

But to leave this Part of the Discourse, as what I find his Lordship does not understand much of, for he allows the *Roman*

Custom of Killing themselves to be a Species of Bravery, which, on the Contrary, I think is the worst Part of Desperation, as Desperation is the worst Part of Cowardice; let us look into times more Ancient than of the *Romans*. *Saul* is an eminent Instance, who seeing the Battle went sore against him, fell upon his own sword. Why? Not as an Act of Courage, but for shame of falling into the hands of the *Uncircumcised*. As to Courage, that was apparent in *Jonathan*, and *Abinadab*, and *Malchishua*, *Saul's* Sons. There true Valour shewed itself. *They died fighting*. See 1 *Sam.* xxxi. 2, 3, &c.

The like was the Case of *Abimelech*, *Judges* ix. 54. When he found himself Wounded by the fall of a Stone upon his Head, he caused his Armour Bearer to Kill him. Why? Not from a Principle of Gallantry and Courage, but *fear*, fear of Infamy, " *that Men may not say of me, a Woman slew him.*"

Thus Cato died, not by a superior Act of Gallantry, but a mere dread of being taken alive by *Cæsar*; and Gracing his Triumph with Cato *Captivated*. To say this is to be judged of by the Customs of the Times in which they lived, is to say nothing to the Purpose; for tho' indeed Times may alter the Circumstances of Things, yet they do not alter the Nature of them, that is, and will be the same for ever; and Desperation will for ever stand in direct opposition to true Magnanimity.

But to come to the Matter of True Courage. I would ask these nice Discussers of the difficulty one nicer Question than any they have yet spoken to, and I would be glad to see it soberly and gravely answered, so as becomes a Philosopher and a Christian, whether taking Courage to be a *Quality* or a *Habit*, (for that part I will not dispute,) I say, taking it which Way they will, whether is the greater Testimony of Courage—

To *Dare* to be *Good*, or to *Dare* to be *Wicked*?

Both of these, as the Circumstances may happen which they are attended with, may require a vast Share of daring Boldness; and that, according to the Moderns, is called Courage.

I shall venture my own Opinion in few Words, and leave it to be further resolved by those who differ from me.

1. *To Dare to be Good*, in some Cases, and in some particular Times, is to bid defiance to all Power, of Men, and Devils; 'tis to sacrifice Life, and as certainly to spend the Blood of

the Person, as it would be to leap down a Precipice.   Thus
in the early Times of Christianity, for a Man to say *Christianus
Sum*, was as certain Death as shooting himself through the
Head would have been, and only differed in the Morality of
the Fact!   It would be the same Thing now in *France* for a
French Man to go up to the Duke of *Bourbon*, the Prime Minister, and say, " *Sir, I am a Protestant.*"   And we have seen
that Death has been the Consequence, and Death with the addition of complicated Cruelties and Tortures in those Cases, I
mean, of the primitive Times of the Church.   So that here is
a most sublime Courage exercised in Daring to be *Good*. But,—

2. On the other Hand, to *Dare to be Wicked*.   Here is another kind of Courage exerted, which, though in the particular
Circumstances of it, is detestable, yet, in its Nature, is a wonderful Thing ; and how human Nature can be brought up to
such a height of Courage is hard to describe.   In the first
there is the Terrors of Men, and the Terrors of Death to
struggle with.   But in this, there are the *Terrors of the Almighty*
to struggle with ; those Arrows which *Job* says *Drink up the
Spirits, Job* vi. 4.   There is another most emphatick Expression on this very Subject, and I think 'tis the most elegant in
the whole Bible, I mean of this kind, *Job* xv. 25, 26. Speaking
of the wicked Man : *He stretcheth out his Hand against* GOD,
and strengtheneth himself against the ALMIGHTY.   *He runneth
upon* HIM, *even upon his Neck.   Upon the thick Bosses of his
Bucklers.*

Here's the Man of Courage indeed ; he must be a bold
daring Fellow.   Let the judicious Reader apply the Case, and
let us judge of Courage by the just Inferences.

It is true, this is a Subject too Grave for a Paper of so
narrow a Compass as this; but as 'tis an important Question,
and since a Wise Man has entered upon it, every Man is call'd
upon to give his Opinion.   I shall treat it in a less serious
Way in my Next.   I am, Sir, yours with Respect, A. G.

Sheppard Escapes from the Condemned Hold.

A. J., Sept. 5.—The Escape of John Sheppard from the
Condemn'd Hold in Newgate, on Monday last, was contrived as
follows, viz. His Wife having furnished him with a Saw, File,
&c., he proceeded to cut off one of the large Iron Barrels from

his Links; and then, to prevent their Shackling, made them fast to one Leg, at the same time setting the other at perfect Liberty. He next cut an Iron Spike over the Door of about six Inches in Length, and one and a half square, his Tools being dipt in Oil; and his Wife with another Woman, pretending to be in close Conversation with him, he soon sawed it asunder, without being heard or suspected. The Interval thus made, being capable of admitting his slender Body to pass thro', and assisted by the Women, he instantly perfected his Liberty, and went out at the Lodge Door, together with them, in a Night-Gown, which concealed his Irons, at between Seven and Eight in the Evening; the Turnkeys being at the other end of the Lodge at that Instant, concerting Measures for his farther Security, as well on Account of his notable Escape not many Weeks before from New Prison, as his present Circumstances, being ordered for Death with them who were executed Yesterday. The other Prisoners, having no Friends at Hand, and being withal too Corpulent to pass thro' the Breach; then called to the Turnkeys, and told them Sheppard was gone. He is about 22 Years of Age, by Trade a Joiner, and is suspected of having committed many more Burglaries, besides that of which he was convicted. He has a Brother named Thomas Sheppard, convicted in last July Sessions for Felony, and lies in Newgate for Transportation. It has since been known, that a Waterman's Boy plied him at Black Friers Stairs the same Night, and landed him at the Horse Ferry at Westminster, the Boy observing his Irons under his Gown.

On Tuesday Night his Wife was Committed to the Compter for assisting him in his Escape; having been apprehended and taken that Day by Mr. Jonathan Wild.

Obedience to Law, the People's Happiness.

A. J., Sept. 12.—Sir, It is a Question not easily determined in the World, which are the happiest Part among Mankind, the *Governing* or the *Governed;* much has been said on both Sides, and much more might be said, but want of a Temper in Mankind to be easy in the Circumstances which Heaven has made their Lot, is certainly the Reason, why 'tis so hard to bring it to a Conclusion.

I am far from thinking Happiness tied down to Grandeur
and Magnificence.   Crowns are fine gay Things, and Dominion is Glorious; but who can weigh the Weights of Government, and how few understand the Secret of Governing?
Every Crown does not sit easy upon the Head that wears it;
and when it sits uneasy, that Uneasiness is of a Nature very
much differing from the common Uneasiness of lower Life, and
not so easy to be supported.

Tamerlain the *Scythian* Emperor, is said to have reflected
with great Seriousness on his own Unhappiness, when he heard
a poor Shepherd upon the *Caucasus* piping to his Flock, on a
little Pipe made of a Reed, for want of a higher priced one;
and told his great General that Shepherd was happier than he,
or any King in the World,—(perhaps had he asked the Shepherd, he had his little Uneasiness too,) but of that by itself.

King *Charles* II., a Prince who had a true Taste in the
many Species of Pleasure, was never so sensibly touched with
this just Reflection, as he was by one Line in the Play, call'd
The Jovial Beggars, which Line had really more in it, than even
the Poet who composed it had in his View when he wrote it.
The Words are thus :—

> " *Then who would be a King, when a Beggar lives so well?*
> *And a begging we will go, will go, &c.*"

Upon the whole, I cannot but, in my Opinion, give the Prize
of Happiness to Persons *Governed*, rather than to the Persons
Governing; provided the first live under a well ordered regular
Constitution, and the King, or Person Governing is content to
Govern by the Rules of that Constitution, and the People willingly submit to it. But where is that happy Spot to be found,
and where is it placed?

I came thro' a certain town in *England* but a few Days ago,
where the Magistrates had, as they assured me, studied always
to administer the Civil Government of the Place with all possible Mildness and Moderation,—endeavouring on all Occasions
to make the People easy, and to keep them so; but I found
the People there, notwithstanding this gentle and easy Usage,
all up in Arms; and the whole Town possest with the Fury of
Tumult and Rabble.

One of their Manufacturers, or labouring Poor, had been
Arrested by his Employer, on a matter of Debt, or a Question

of Right and Wrong; and the Fellow who was Arrested, not being able to find Bail, was carried to the Town Prison. Immediately the Mob rises, some bring Hatchets, and other Iron Instruments, proper for the Work, and others Clubs and Staves; and away they go to the Prison, to the Number of a Thousand, or upwards. Then, in Defiance of the Magistrates, who could do no more than look on, they fall foul of the Prison, break the Windows first, then the Walls; and at last find Means to get open the Door, or have it opened to them, and let out their Man, who they afterwards bring along the Streets in Triumph, threatening the Mayor and Aldermen with their further Resentment, if they offered to disturb them any more in that Manner. And who pray is King where these People live?

If now, there could be any such Thing as Felicity to a People in, and under a mild, just, and a gentle Government, these poor People might be said to Enjoy it, and that in a most distinguished Manner; and yet they had so little a Share of that Felicity, or so little a Sense of it, that they could by no means submit to their own Felicity. And what must be said then to the Happiness of the *Governed?*

As to the Felicity of the Persons *Governing;* how little a Sense of their own Happiness have most of the Monarchs of the World ever had! How soon has Ambition, Avarice, Pride, or Envy, disturb'd their Tranquillity! and how Unhappy are they often made! This is indeed a long Subject, and may be spoken of again hereafter; but my present Enquiry is, What must a good and just Prince do, when his Subjects, whom he endeavours sincerely to make perfectly Easy, and Happy; understand it so little as to disturb his *Peace and Tranquillity?*

What must he do, when they defy Magistrates, break open Gaols, release Prisoners, and insult Government? Must he to obtain, or preserve the Name of a Merciful and Clement Prince; I say, must he suffer Authority itself to be contemn'd and despis'd? The Subordinate Servants, I might say Representatives, (I mean the Civil Magistrates) oppress'd by Dirt and Disorder? What must the mild, merciful Prince do in such a Case? If he punishes, he is immediately thought Cruel and Severe, and if he does not, the Rabble Insults him, and he sees his Authority trampled under Foot. And where then is the Felicity of being a Governor, unless the Persons Governed please to make him Happy, by cheerful Submission to him?

Hence then, to be Tumultuous, to be Riotous, to insult Magistrates, and break the Publick Peace, is not only an Act of Rebellion against the Government we live under; but it is an Act of the greatest unkindness and disregard to the Prince also, depriving him of that which is the only true Felicity of a Sovereign; I mean the willing Submission of his Subjects.

Never let such People drink their King's Health, or publish their Party Loyalty. As Christ said to his Disciples, *If ye Love me, keep my Commandments,*—I say, they that Love their Sovereign, must shew it by obeying the Laws, for no Man can Love the King, and at the same time disturb the Peace of his Government.

Your Humble Servant, &c.

Capture of Sheppard at Finchley.

A. J., Sept. 12.—On Thursday last, about Noon, John Sheppard, the Malefactor, who made his Escape from the Condemned Hold of Newgate, on Monday the 31st August; was apprehended and taken, by the Officers and Turnkeys of that Prison, at the Town of Finchley, near Highgate, in Company with one William Page, an Apprentice to a Butcher in Clare Market. The last, patiently surrendered, and Sheppard took to the Hedges, where being closely pursued and discovered, and Pistols presented to his Head; he begged them, for God's sake, not to Shoot him on the Spot, trembled, was in great Agony, and submitted. There were found upon him two Silver Watches, a large Knife, and a Chisel, and a Knife only upon his Companion; they were both disguised in Butcher's Blue Frocks, and Woollen Aprons. Being brought to Town, Sheppard was immediately carried to Newgate, loaded with heavy Irons, put into the Condemned Hold, and Chained. William Page was carried before Sir Francis Forbes, examined, and committed to Newgate; with Orders to be double Ironed, and to be kept from Sheppard. He was accordingly put into the Castle, and his Friends are not permitted to see him.

· In the evening a Divine and several Gentlemen went into

the Condemned Hold to Sheppard, who seemed composed and cheerful, and acknowledged the manner of his Escape, viz. That having got out of the Condemned Hold, he took Coach at the corner of the Old Bailey, (along with a Person whom he refused to Name,) went to Black Friers Stairs, and from thence to the Horse Ferry, at Westminster, and came in the middle of the Night to Clare-Market, where he met his Companion, and they disguised themselves in the Manner above mentioned.   From thence they rambled to a Relation of Page's, within seven Miles of Northampton, where they were entertained a few Days, but growing uneasy at their not being able to make Satisfaction for their Bread, returned towards London.   He has hinted in dark Terms, that he hath Committed Robberies · since his Escape; he denies that he ever was Married to the Woman who assisted him therein, and who is now in the Compter for the same; declaring that he found her a common Strumpet in Drury Lane, and that she hath been the Cause of all his Misfortunes and Misery.   He takes great Pains to excuse his Companion Page of being any Ways privy to his Crimes; who, he says, only generously accompanied him after his Escape.

On Tyrannic Power.   A Pleasant Story.

A. J., Sept. 19.—Sir, In my last, I gave you a Sort of Specimen of Riot and Tumult, where the Magistrates were all Subjects and Vassals, and the People all Kings and Monarchs. Certainly they were glorious Days, when there was no King in *Israel*, but every Man did that which was right in his own Eyes.   But 'tis Observable, that whenever that Circumstance happens to be spoken of, some Extravagant publick Mischief or other attended it.   *For Example*, 'tis first mentioned, *Judg.* 17. 6.   Immediately comes the Story of *Micah*, and his setting up a House of Gods in the Land; that is, an open bare faced Idolatry, in defiance of God, and his Tabernacle Worship. The next is *Judges* 18. 1. and immediately follows the Story of the *Danites* taking Arms, on pretence of seeking more Room for their People, then plundering their own Tribes, then setting up the same Idol, and forsaking the Worship of the true God; which Idolatry continued among them, even to the Time of the Captivity, *Judges* 18. 30.   The third Time this Expression is used, is *Judges* 19. 1. And immediately follows the black Story of the Outrage committed on the *Levite's* Wife by the Men of *Gibea*, and the almost total Extirpation of the Tribe of *Benjamin.*

Well, those were brave Times for all that; and such Days, we see, have been bid fair for among us, several Times. But Heaven has mercifully interposed, and several of the Attempts to have us brought into those democratick Extravagancies, have ended at the Gallows. Let our Friends at *Colchester*, at *Taunton*, and at *Collumpton*, consider of it. But that by the bye; my View at present lies another Way.

Being lately at a *Tea Table* Conversation, where some Female Elevations were carried on to an immoderate height; we had a very learned Discourse concerning the deposing of Tyrants; and a particular Lady, famous for a due Quantity of Fire in her Temper, as well as Acrimony in her Blood, argued very warmly for the Liberty of the Subject, and pulling down Governors. She pleaded natural Right, and ancient Usage, like a Civilian. She talk'd of the *Roman* and the *Grecian* Governments, as if she had been born there, and lived in the Time of the Consular Government at *Rome*; and she held her Discourse a full quarter of an Hour, which was a great while *you will say*, to obtain the Attention of a Tea-Table.

But before she had well done, she was violently Interrupted by a Lady, for the glorious Principles of High-Church Obedience; and this Lady was Seconded, and Thirded by other Ladies, who all imagined the Doctrine of the Divine Right of Monarchy was struck at. So the first Lady was in great Danger of being censured for a Republican; or at least one tainted with republican Principles.

In this Discourse, I must acknowledge there was some Heat; and afterwards some Indecencies. Nay it wanted but a little of breaking out into a Civil War; and I began to think of reading the Proclamation to them, for I verily thought that *Jacobite*, and *King George for ever*, had been the Game, and Arbitrary Government and Revolution had been the Substance of the Argument, as indeed so it was, in the first meaning of the Parties. But O! the *Power of Eloquence!* The first Lady, who found she was got into bad Company which she did not approve of, and that the whole Circle was

against her; that her Doctrine would not do at that Time, and
that she might be perhaps expelled the House, made earnest
Motions to be heard; and after much Difficulty, raising her
Voice to a violent height, she told the Ladies they were all
out of the Question, that she had nothing of those Things in
her view; but that if they would give her leave but to explain
herself, she would in three Words satisfy them all.

This gaining her a little Attention, she told them that they
quite Mistook or Misunderstood her Meaning; and were bringing a Subject of Politicks upon the Stage, which she had not
in her Thoughts.   And then running on with an inimitable
fluency of Tongue, and a Flux of Wit and Eloquence, she told
them they were talking wide of her Design; that she was for
deposing Tyrants indeed, but not for destroying the Tyranny,
not for pulling down the Government, but putting it into
better Hands.   Then with an incomparable Turn of Wit, she
applied her Discourse to the Usurpation of Men over the Sex,
and that it was their Tyranny which she said, she was for
Deposing; that yet, she was not for destroying Family Government, but for restoring the Ladies to their Right, and to that
Dominion that Beauty and their own Merit naturally gave
them over the Men; and that, as they were found Kneeling
and Adoring, Whining and Sighing, Hanging and Dying, before Matrimony, they ought to be kept so; that all their After-
Game, and the Tyranny they practised after they were got
into Possession, was an unjust Usurpation, and the Ladies
ought to Claim that of Right they should Resign; which, if
they refused, she was of Opinion they ought to be Deposed as
Tyrants and Invaders.

This Surprizing turn of the Discourse gave an immediate
check to all the Resentment which was breaking out against
the Lady; she gained a sudden Applause, and the whole Circle
of Ladies joined in the Proposal.   What dreadful Effects we
are to expect from such a Unanimous Resolution of so powerful a Party in the Nation, I may acquaint you of hereafter.

I am, &c.

John Sheppard's Recent Proceedings.

A. J., *Sept.* 19.—The Recorder, as well as his Deputy, being
at the Bath, the Execution of John Sheppard will not be so

expeditious as expected.   He has confessed that on Tuesday
the 8th instant, two Days before he was taken, he came from
Finchley into Bishopsgate Street, and drank at several Publick
Houses; and in the Evening came into Smithfield, went
thro' Christ's Hospital, pick'd two People's Pockets in the
Cloisters, and from thence passed under Newgate, down the
Old Bailey, and into Fleet Street; where taking Notice of
Mr. Martin's, a Watchmaker's Shop, against St. Bride's Church,
and only a little Boy to look after it, he meditated to rob the
same, and perfected his villainous Design in the Manner
following, viz., He first fixed a Nail Piercer into the Post of
the Door, next fastened the Knocker thereto with a Packthread,
and then Cut out a Pane of Glass, and took three Silver
Watches out of the Shop Window; — the Boy seeing him
take them, but could not get out to pursue him, by reason of
his subtle Contrivance.   One Watch he pawned for a Guinea
and a half, and the two others were taken upon him at Finchley.   He denies that his Fellow Traveller Page was privy to
this Robbery; but, if we are rightly instructed, Mr. Page was
accompanying him all that Night, and was aiding and Assisting him in this Fact; and, just before it was executed, came
into the Shop, and asked the Boy some trifling Questions, the
better to observe the Inside, &c.   This with some other Circumstances, will, as we are told, be proved against Page.   If
so, in all probability he may accompany his Friend Sheppard
in his Cart and Two.

On Saturday Night the Rev. Mr. Wagstaff, being attending
John Sheppard in order to prepare him for his approaching
Dissolution, discovered a small File concealed in his Bible;
which is supposed to have been conveyed to him by his Brother, (who is a Prisoner on the Common Side Felons over his
Head, in order to Transportation,) and between whom there is
a sort of Communication through a little Hole.

And on Wednesday Morning the Keepers, going into the
Condemned Hold to Sheppard, found two Files, a Chisel, and
a Hammer, hid in the bottom of a matted Chair, with which
he had begun to file his Irons.   Now, when he perceived his
last Effort to Escape thus discovered and frustrated, his wicked
and obdurate Heart began to relent, and he shed abundance
of Tears.   He was Carried up to an Apartment called the

Castle, in the Body of the Gaol; a Place of equal, if not superior Strength to the Condemned Hold, and there Chained to
the Floor.

A Satire on City Politics.

A. J., Sept. 26.—Sir, I have been mighty busy among our
Friends in the City for some Time past, to get Hands to an
humble Petition of the Citizens, against all the late loose doings in the Choice; and seeing the Election of a Lord Mayor
is so near at Hand, we are very sorry the Parliament is not
sitting, otherwise we should have been in Hopes that we might
have obtained such an Answer to our Petition, as might have
secured the Election of Such a Person as WE, (I say, WE in
general, for you may easily know who I mean,) should desire
to have.

Previous to this famous Petition, we have had divers Meetings of worthy Citizens, to consider what it is we were to
Petition for,—and how we should word our Petition; and, as
our Debates were very Wise and Weighty, and the Subject of
them may be of Moment for future Ages, in their Reflections
on Times past; it may not be improper to give you some
Account of them.

First, Then, it was moved to consider the State of the City;
in which several Things offered themselves to be spoken to.
(1.) As particularly, That the *Tory* Interest in the City was
grown formidable.   (2.) How it came to be so.   (3.) How to
pull it down again.   And (4.) How to preserve the superiority
of the *Whigs*, when they had it.

The first of these was granted.   *Hinc illæ Lachrymæ!*   The
second was warmly disputed.   Some laying it upon one, and
some upon another.   At last a grave Citizen told us very
plainly in a handsome calm Speech, that we had lost our
Friends by our Roaring and Ranting, Rabbling and Fighting
in the Streets; by our Mug-house Riots, and raising Mobs
and Rabbles, and by our high flaming Bonfires; breaking the
Peace, and encouraging those very Tumults we pretended to
suppress.   That if the *Jacobites* and *Tories* were Riotous and
Tumultuous, we should have quelled them, and by the Magistracy, or the Civil Power; and if that failed, by the Military,
as the Law directs.   But that setting up to Mob, and Fight

with *High-Church* in the Streets; beating them, as it was called in their own Way, was practising the very Thing we condemned. *He added*, That Capt. *T——*, though Right Noble, and his Deputy Capt. *B——*, the ignoble, *he thought*, deserved as much, for Rabbling, as the poor Fellows, who were (*tho' justly too,*) hang'd in *Fleet Street*. That, as these Things were carried, many wise and sober People, who had the Peace of the City, and of the whole Kingdom at Heart, show'd their dislike of them, and withdrew from the Party; and, finding that Way of Mobbing encrease, that it broke into the general Conduct of Things, and that in Time the Mayor, Sheriffs, Common-Council Men, &c. might come to be Nominated, nay Chosen, at Mug-houses, or by the Votes at Bonfires, or Assemblies, not at *Guild-Hall*; I say, this brought them to Vote for Men of a more peaceable Disposition, in mere Regard to their Liberties; and thus, and by such other degrees, *says he*, as, if there is Occasion, may be enumerated; we lost our Interest, and the *Tories* got a Superiority. As to the Means how to recover this Loss, that *he said*, was to be now considered; and as for preserving it, that was time enough to Consider, when it was first obtained.

Secondly, It was moved, that according to the said grave Citizen's Motion, it should now be considered how to Recover the Superiority they had Lost; and this brought on the Proposal for a Petition to the approaching Parliament.

What the Petition now imports, is not my present Business; doubtless they will ask nothing but what they think the Parliament may grant; but my Business is, to tell you what was Proposed in that worthy Assembly of Citizens, that I have mentioned above.

1. One wisely moved, that they should Petition for a qualifying Test; that none should have the Liberty to Vote that would not comply with it, and that a Mark of Distinction should be set upon who should Choose, and who should be Chosen. But this ran them into innumerable Divisions, for as in the famous Triumvirate of *Augustus, Anthony*, and *Lepidus* in *Rome*, every one proscribed those they had a Quarrel at, till almost all the Men of Note in the City were proscribed and Murthered; so here, every one was for incapacitating his opposite Faction, till in short, the whole Livery would have

been in a fair Way of being excluded.   At last this Dispute
ended by one Man's starting an ill-Natured suggestion;
namely, that they had best consider, when they Petitioned,
that they did not Petition to exclude themselves.   So the
Project for a Test for Qualification of Votes dropt at once.

In the next Place, it was proposed that they should be sure
to petition against Nothing that they had thought fit to allow
by their own Practice.

This Motion was received with a kind of silent Murmur.
" Hum !" said an ancient, considering, Christian Citizen,—" this
is an ensnaring Proposal, for lo ! have we not practised most
of these Things ourselves, when we have found it to our
Purposes ?"

At this, one started up in a kind of Rage,—" Thou hast
spoken rashly, Neighbour Livery Man," says he, " I do not
allow that we have ; and I was going to move that *Ex Post
Facto,* a Law might be petitioned for to hang all those who had
polled twice at one Election,—had personated any Man that was
absent or dead,—or, that had given any Man Money or Rewards
to do so.   Thus also, that a Law might be made to fine every
Man to half the Value of his Estate, who had Treated, or
Feasted, Bribed for, or bought Votes for Aldermen, Sheriffs,
or Common Council Men ; as being a just Punishment for Corruption, in Breach of our Liberties."

" Hold !" said another.—" Pray, Brother Common Council-
Man, stop your Motion, and let us hear no more of it ; lest,
when we hang a great many of our Enemies, and fine a great
many of our High Neighbours, we may be obliged to hang
and fine some of our own People too ; and that the Livery of
the City of *London* may chance to be too much diminished
upon such an Occasion."   ˌ

Upon these Debates our little Assembly broke up at that
Time, without coming to any Resolution ; but at the next
Meeting the Sense of their own Merit made them a little more
moderate, and tho' they resolved to Petition, yet it was also
Resolved only to ask a Redress of Things for the Time to come,
without any Retrospects, or Resentments for Things past.
And did they not do wisely, Mr. *App ?*   Very wisely !

Your Servant,

LIVERY MAN.

Sheppard to be Legally Identified.

A. J., Sept. 26.—John Sheppard, the Malefactor, having escaped from Justice after his Conviction and Sentence, we are now assured that it must be proved in a regular and judicial Way, that he is the same Person who was so convicted and escaped, before a fresh Order can be made for his Execution; and that this Matter will come before the Court at the Old Bailey the next Sessions.

Pleasures in the City and the Country Contrasted.

A. J., Oct. 3.—Sir, I know 'tis *Michaelmas* Time, and you are very Busy at *Guild Hall*,—*Voting, Mobbing, Caballing,* &c., and the like noisy Work, which generally takes up much of your City People; and we find it here in *Hampstead,* for almost all our best and gravest Inhabitants are gone to *London* for the whole Week, to look after the Publick, cultivate their Interests, keep up their Factions, and nourish Parties, according to their annual Duty, and the ancient Practice in the City.

But what is all this to those more important Affairs which are successfully carried on here among the *Beau Monde* of our Town? We are above all your little Quarrels and Wrangles; as we breathe a freer and purer Air, and live half a mile nearer Heaven than you do at *London,* so our Thoughts soar in Proportion, and our Spirits are sublimated in a Measure proportioned to our Situation.

Hence by the just Rules of Natural Philosophy, we move in a different Manner from the grovelling World; and have Views and Ends superior to the Common Ultimates of your CITS. *Love,* and *Honour,* engage our Passions, and divide our Time. The Hours, winged with Joy, fly over our Heads, with an imperceptible Swiftness; and we measure Time not by Pendulums, and Pulsations, but by the noble Rotation of our inexpressible Pleasures.

We laugh, sing, drink, play, and enjoy, while Day and Night are not felt; and the Remembrance of the passing Hour is lost. Clocks, Dials, Watches, Light, Dark, Sun, or Moon; they are indeed known here, and seen in their ordinary Places and Courses; but are of very little Use to us, whose Moments are felt to pass, only by the Succession of our

Pleasures, and measured by the constant Revolutions of our Enjoyments.

If we do sometimes doze, 'tis always in the Arms of Beauty, and we ought not to call it Sleep; but only, that, *we lost ourselves a little while* in the Excesses of our Love.

Thus we live. This is living, my Friend; you can't be said to live. You struggle a little indeed in the horrid Shades of Smoke and Death. You breathe Hell, in the Noise, Dirt, and Darkness of your Streets; and in the Scandal, Fury, and Hypocrisy of a clamouring Crowd; but 'tis we only that may be said to live, who enjoy Mirth and good Company, in the Perfection of a calm Soul, or a serene Air.

I told you, how all our grave ones, our City Politicians, and *Guild-Hall* Statesmen, are gone to *London*, to make Aldermen and Lord Mayors, and 'tis often so, sometimes on one Occasion, sometimes on another; but you cannot imagine what a Turn it gives to Affairs here. How are the Visiting Days of the Ladies at those particular Houses crowded with an Unusual Circle of Company! And how do the pretty Recluses, that were visible but on High Days, and Apostles' Eves before, move about, see Company, and take a Ring to the Walks, &c.!

Nor is it a fruitless Time; the Hours are not misimproved; for as 'tis the Perfection of the Place to abuse a Citizen, so no Season so proper as when Politicks possess the Brain of the Husband. Alas! his Head's turn'd, his Soul is possess'd, he has no Room for Jealousy, or any of his usual Tyranny; the Lady, or the Daughters, may take the Coach, Range the Heath, troll to *Belsize*, raffle at the Walks, and, in a Word, *as they will, and at their Will*; 'tis our Jubilee, and we make Use of it, I assure you, to our Satisfaction.

While then this is the Case at our Town, and at the neighbouring Villages, we give you Joy, in the City, of your Huzzas, and holding up your Hands in the Hall, your Clubbing, and Caballing at the Coffee Houses, and your whole Mass of City Clamour on the present, and other publick Occasions; and to add to your Felicity, we shall endeavour that your Families may be no losers by your Absence.

Your Humble Servant,

HAMPSTEAD, HIGHGATE, ENFIELD, SOUTHGATE, &c.

The Story of an Injured Wife.

A. J., Oct. 10.—Sir, Love and Courtship has, I find, been much the Subject of your Introductory Letters of late, and you seem much to desire that your Paper should be the Centre of the Injured Ladies' Complaint ; which if you obtain, you need not fear but you shall be quickly thronged with Clients of this Nature. Pray let me be one to make a beginning?

I am the unhappy Woman lately exposed in a certain Publick Paper, call'd the ———, for having, as the Advertiser insolently says, elop'd from him, my Husband; to which is added, that no Body should trust me, for that he will pay none of the Debts that I shall contract. Now pray, Mr. *App*, let the World hear the Probability of a Wife's Story being just, as well as that of a Husband !

Suppose a Man, having little of his own, marries a Woman with a tolerable good Fortune. I will not say he ought to use her the better for her Money ; she should have considered that Part before she bestowed her Money and herself upon a Scoundrel that had neither good Humours or good Manners. Suppose him then, having gotten Possession both of the Money and the Wife, to waste the first, and abuse the last.

Suppose then, Mr. *App*, that after having played the Extravagant without Doors, and the Tyrant within, till he made himself not only Odious to his Wife, but Intolerable ; and that, at last, he has added that Wickedness which is above all other most abominable to a Wife, namely, the Entertaining other Women, and this not privately even, but as may justly be said, under his Wife's Nose. Supposing that to prove this upon him, most undeniably, he may have been taken with two such at a Time ; and suppose upon all this, his Wife did indeed leave him and go away from him, ought such a Rogue as this to publish his Wife's parting from him as an Elopement?

Now, Mr. *App*, I desire to know of your Wisdomship, what must an Honest Woman do to have full Revenge of such an inimitable Villain? Shall I publish his Name and Place of Abode, Mr. *App*? That he may be known to be what he is, where he goes for a Saint? Or shall I publish the Names of his two Strumpets, and invite all my Friends to go in a Body

and pull them out by the Ears, and have them to the Horse
Pond; for this, I believe, I am able to bring to pass?

Or shall I raise the *Posse* of my Neighbours, the good
Wives of the Parish where I live; for I believe I am well
enough beloved to do that too, and shall we go and pull the
Tyrant Husband out, and set him up for a Shew, upon his own
Sign Post, as he deserves, that all the Town may see him?
Tell me, Mr. *App*, whether this shall be done, or any Thing
else which the just Rage of a Provoked, but Potent Wife can
dictate? And assure yourself that any Thing but Murthering
the Rogue shall be immediately put in Practice, and even that
of Killing, only excepted for my own Sake, not for his; because
it would be hard to have an Honest Woman hanged, for
ridding the World of a Monster.

You are to know also, Mr. *App*, that among our Sister-
hood, we have concluded to Solicit the Further Punishment
of all such Fellows who thus abuse their Wives; and that
a Law may, if possible on the first Occasion be past to
bring such Criminals to Female Justice, in which Case, it
should be out of their Power to Cry us down, and Post us up
as they do. But instead of that, every Man guilty of Lewdness, his lawful Wife being at Home, and in good order, as a
Wife may be supposed to be, should be posted at every Corner,
be pelted by every Rabble, and the Woman being discharged
from her Bonds of Wedlock, be at Liberty to Marry again
who she thinks fit.

Also, we think, the Ways and Methods of proving that
Incontinency of the Man, ought to be made more Direct and
Easy; and the Proceedings to be Summary and Short. For
Example. To prove that her Husband was found in Circumstances from which his Guilt might be fairly and reasonably
concluded should be Evidence Sufficient; and the Man thus
detected should for ever after be obliged to wear, above all his
other Cloathes, a Green Coat with a yellow Shoulder Knot,
and such other Brand or Mark of Infamy, that he should be
always known by it.

That at the same Time he would be obliged to give
Security for his good Behaviour; and that he would never
take any Revenge, or any way Injure or Affright, or
threaten the Person of his Wife who had thus done herself

Justice upon him.   All this we think but reasonable Mr. *App*,
and we hope you do so too.   Your Servant,

PENELOPE FIREBRAND.

Sheppard again Attempts to Escape.

A. J., *Oct.* 10.—On Wednesday John Sheppard, the
Malefactor, found means to release himself from the Staples
fixed in the Floor of the Apartment, called the Castle, in
Newgate,—where he was confined alone,—by taking off a
great Padlock from his Legs.   He attempted to pass up the
Chimney, but by reason of Strong Iron Bars in his Way was
prevented.   In the midst of his Endeavours the Keepers came
up, as usual, with his Necessaries; when, to their very great
Surprize, they found him at Liberty in the Room.   They
searched him from Head to Foot, and found not so much as a
Pin; but when they had Chained him down again, the Head-
Keeper and others came, and intreated him to discover by what
Magick Art he had thus got himself from the Staples.   He
reached forth his Hand, and took a Nail, and with that, and
no other Instrument, unlocked himself again before their Faces.
Nothing so astonishing ever known! He is now Hand-cuffed,
and more effectually chained.

On Saturday last Joseph Blake, alias Blueskin, was, by three
of his Majesty's Justices of the Peace, committed to Newgate;
being Charged, upon the Oath of William Field, a noted
Evidence, for that he, the said Blueskin, together with John
Sheppard, and himself, did break and enter the House of Mr.
Kneebone, a Woollen Draper in the Strand, in the Night of
Sunday, the 12th of July last, and steal Goods to the value of
45*l.*, for which Fact Sheppard received Sentence of Death, and
was to have suffered on the 4th September, but escaped.
This Blueskin was himself formerly an Evidence, against
Junks, alias Levee, Flood, and Oakey, who were Executed at
Tyburn for robbing the Honourable William Yonge, Esq. and
Colonel Cope, near Hampstead.   His companions Charles
Vendersman, commonly called, the Long Drover of Newport
Market, and Charles Roley, a Wheelbarrow Fellow, taken
with him at his Lodgings in St. Giles's, and who are suspected
of having together with him, committed many Robberies, are
continued in the Gate House, for farther Examination.

Story of a Captain in Unfortunate Circumstances.

A. J., Oct. 17.—Sir, I am a Half-Pay Officer, and indeed 'tis very Low with me, for I have always lived like a Gentleman, but could not subsist, after my Way, upon about 50*l.* a Year, and having outrun the Constable, I am surrounded with Enemies; for I am in Debt.

I would not have exposed myself to you, as I do at this Time, if I could have got my Living in an honest Way as a Gentleman; but, alas! I am in a Gaol too. That is the worst of the whole Story, or else I could have made a Campaign or two upon the Highway; and perhaps have made a good honest Livelihood that Way.

But this is it. I was drawn into an Ambuscade, being out upon a Party at a Tavern; and being surrounded, and overpowered, was obliged to call for Quarter, and Surrender upon Articles. One of which was to this —— Hole, and here I am, a Prisoner of War.

Now I really know not what Course to take; the Jade of a Landlady that put me in, has received several Favours from me, which deserved better Usage, for I have served at Bed and Board, when no Man that had not a Horse's Stomach would have touch'd her at all, that is forgot; now she will hear of nothing but her Money. I call her foul names, but 'tis all one to her; she Locks me up here, and tells me, let me but pay her her Money, and I shall call her what I will. I reckon up a Thousand merry Things to her, that have passed between us; but all I can get of her is again,—" Captain, that's very true, but that won't pay my Brewer."

In short, I am d——ably put to it; pay her I cannot, and yet she is so barbarous that till I do pay her, she will never let me out. She is so lewd, that she will let me do as I please even when she comes hither to Dun and Teaze me for her Money, and yet she will not abate me an Inch of the Law without her Money.

Now what must a poor Soldier do? I could cut her Throat for her a little, if that would do any good; but I don't see my way out of Prison by that at all, so I have given over the Thoughts of that some Time. I have Thoughts of removing myself, by a gentle Brace of Bullets through the Head,

and so go off like a Soldier.   But, upon Second Thoughts, I
found that kind of *Habeas Corpus* might be only going from
one Gaol to another, with the addition of a worse *Jailor* too,
tho' the latter is hardly possible neither.

Being thus hardly put to it for Ways and Means to dispose
of myself, I met with an Offer yesterday, which at first I
thought would have been in my Favour; and that was a proposal of Marriage, and by a Person able enough to pay all my
Debts; and more than that, she promises to do it too.   But
here Mr. —— is my great Difficulty; the Woman, as I have
said, has Money, but she ·is Old, Ugly, and has, in short, a
Character for every thing that is Horrid and Terrible.   In
Short, I hate her, I loath her, I am sick of her, I had rather
Storm a Counterscarp, than come near her; and what can I
do. To take her, as we do a Town, by Storm, and so Plunder
Madam and leave her,—that I could do as a Soldier very well;
but as she is a Woman, tho' bad as the Devil, I can't do that
neither.   So that, in short, I am at a *Non plus* there too.

On the other hand, I am in Love with a dear Angel, a
Picture of Perfection, a charming, young, sprightly Gay and
Fair,—that has Wit, Virtue, and Beauty to an Extreme; but,
she has not Money, that is, not enough for my Purpose.   To
marry that Rich Wretch, the Object of my Aversion and
Abhorrence; and break all my Vows to that beautiful Creature
I love! Can I do this? No, No! Not to gain all the
Heavens and Earth can bestow.   What then must I do,
pray tell me? For I see no Remedy, but that cursed Vomit
called PATIENCE.

I read your Papers sometimes, and other News-Writers,
and they talk of New WARS at Hand.   O! that you could
bring them on with your Pen! Pray try Mr. ——, and
see if you News-Paper Men, Masters of Politicks, cannot
inflame the World a little, and bring us another War.   Then
we Men of the Sword should get some Business.   Then the
Prison Doors would be set open; at least to Men, Gentlemen,
and we should not Lie and Starve upon Half Pay, as we do.
Pray try your Hand a little, that a poor demolished *Aid de
Camp* may get out of LOBBS POUND.

I am Yours, Dear Sir,

Yours for Ever,   A. A. A.

Satire on the Dutch.

M. J., Oct. 17.— . . . .
. . . But let their (the Dutch) Sentiments upon that Head be
what they will, the Portuguese have lost all the *Molucca*
Islands by them. They have taken from them *Macassar* on the
Island *Borneo* and *Solor*, and another Island; and many other
Settlements whose Names do not at present occur to me. They
are charged with spiriting up the Massacre by the Natives or
Japan, committed upon the *Spaniards* and *Portuguese* settled
there some years since; but whether the Accusation be just, I
cannot determine. Immediately after which Massacre, a Law
was pass'd in that Country, which made it Death for any
Christian to land there, or to attempt to settle any Trade
or Commerce with them; but soon afterward, it was
observ'd, the *Dutch* settled a Factory at *Magasaqui*, the
Capital of *Japan*;—and, it is said, being questioned at their
first coming, what Religion they were of, they answered that
they were Dutchmen! And, it seems, that to this Day the
Japaneez observe the Formality of searching every *Dutch*
Ship which comes in, for Christians, according to the Law
before mentioned, but I cannot learn that they ever found
any.

Sheppard Escapes from the Castle in Newgate.

A. J., Oct. 17.—On Thursday Night, John Sheppard found
means to Unchain himself from the Staples fixed in the Strong
Room, called the Castle in Newgate, twisting and breaking
some of the small Irons, and unlocking a great Horse Padlock.
He got off his Hand Cuffs, and then, with the help only of an
Iron Bar, which he found in the Chimney, broke through a
Nine Foot Wall into a strong Room, the Locks whereof
(having not been opened in ten years before,) he broke and got
farther to another Door belonging to the Chapel, then forced
the Locks and Bolts of that also. In all, he broke through Six
Strong Rooms, where People had formerly been confined, but
had not of late been in Use, and got up to the top of the Gaol,
then descended from thence by two Blankets tied together,
on the Top of a Turner's House next to Newgate, broke
through,—without being heard by any therein,—let himself

out at the Street Door, at about One Yesterday Morning, and so made an entire Escape.

Threatened Insurrection of the Ladies.

A. J., Oct. 24.—Sir, I hope you, who pretend so much to the publick Good, will not fail to promote the humble Application of your own Sex; especially in such a Time of imminent Danger as this is, wherein the ancient Constitution, Established from the Creation, is in a Manner subverted, and overturned; or at least, is in danger of being so reduced as to bring us all into Misery, *nay, worse than Egyptian* BONDAGE.

In this exigence, I apply myself to you in order to raise the *Posse* in behalf of the Freeborn People of *England;* at least, that part of them who come under the denomination of *Lovers* or *Husbands*, and those you know make the most considerable Body of the Nation. The Case is this; the Women, who you know have for a long Time been very uneasy under the Yoke of Subjection,—which the Laws of God and Man have put upon them,—seem now to be in a dangerous Plot; and, as I do not pretend we are well and sufficiently prepared for our Defence,—so, I could not but give you this notice of our Danger, that you may give the Alarm to all the well meaning Part of Mankind, that they may not be surprized, and reduced to Captivity unawares.

I have indeed often thought the Sex would, one Time or other, take up Arms; that they would not be content to be unfaithful to us, Elope from, and Beggar us, but that they would indeed furnish themselves with offensive Weapons, and in short, would wage War against us. But little did I think that they were so far advanced in the wicked Design, as to furnish themselves with Arms and Ammunition so Secretly, and in so surprizing a Manner, as they have done. *For Example* :—

I happened lately to come into a certain Family in our Country, to make an innocent mannerly Visit, when I was surprized with a sudden Breach between the Master of the House, and his Lady. The beginning of the Quarrel was too long, and too trifling, to trouble you with now; but the Man, it seems, had let fall some Words which seemed a little Menacing, when on a sudden the Lady starts up, and marching up to his Teeth :—"*How Sir !*" says she, "*What, do you pretend to use your Authority ? What, do you threaten me ? Be it known to you I scorn to be threatened. Come hither niece Alicey,* (says she) *and Sister Tammy. Look you,* SIR, *I would have you to know, we are prepared for you, the Women have known and felt so much of your ill Usage, and so long, that we are resolved to bear it no longer, and are now sufficiently prepared to use the Remedy Nature has put into our Hands, and to resist Violence with Force ; and so begin when you please.*" With that she held up, and shook at him, the most formidable FAN that has been seen ; nay the ancientest Record, I believe, does not mention the like. The *Niece* and *Sister* drew up to her, and shew'd him, (FAN *advanced,*) that they were armed after the same Manner, and that they were ready to fall on, if she gave the Word of Command.

The good Gentleman, surprized, you may be sure, to see himself thus, on a sudden, surrounded with an armed Force ; and having good Reason to believe that his Wife, who had Threatened with an Oath to *split his Skull,* with her most terrible FAN, would be as good as her Word. I say, the Gentleman, having no Reinforcements at hand, thought fit to give way to his Circumstances, and began to Capitulate ; told her he hoped she would not Murther him for *a rash Word,* that he intended not to have provoked her to such Extremities ; *in a Word,* he begged a Truce, and that she would be Quiet and Easy, and he would say no more. This did not fully satisfy, till she had brought him to accept of very hard Conditions. After which, she yielded to a Truce for some Time, and so the Broil was ended, and they came to some tolerable Composure again; after which we went to Supper.

I, who had been witness of this Insurrection of the Women, was *you may be sure,* mighty willing to see the Weapons, which the Ladies were thus armed with, and, in Confidence of which, they had thus fallen upon the Husband ; so with a great deal of Caution and Ceremony in my Application, I at length obtained the Favour of the Ladies, to let me see their FANS. It seems they had been at a Neighbouring Fair, where they had furnished themselves, and they assured me that all the Ladies in *England* were furnishing themselves with the like ; so that, they said, they did not Question raising a prodigious

Army of Women, well Armed, with FANS of a mighty Size,
Strength and Weight, so that the Men might probably soon
feel their Indignation, in a different Manner from what had
formerly been known.

These Fans are first, unusually heavy; the Sticks large, and
generally made of the Teeth of Wild Beasts, in order to make
them the more really Terrible. The *Butt-end*, where there is a
Conjunction of all the rest, is more than ordinarily thick, and
at the Extremities there is a strong Piece of Iron running
thro' the *massy Teeth* above mentioned, which is Keyed at
both Ends, to band the said Teeth together; all which put
together, are unmercifully thick, and more than sufficient for
the wicked Design of Splitting the thickest *Skull* that any
reasonable Husband can be supposed to wear.

Upon the whole, you are desired to publish to the World
the imminent Danger that the Men are in; and to move all
those whom it may concern, to take timely Care, that the
Women may not go Armed in this terrible Manner, but that
they may be obliged to wear FANS of an ordinary size, such as
the good Matrons their Ancestors have been contented with.

Your Servant, good Mr. APP.

Sheppard and his Prototype.

M. J., Oct. 24.—The great Talk which the strange Escape
of John Sheppard has occasion'd, has reviv'd an old Story
which happen'd in the Reign of Queen Elizabeth, when Wal-
singham was Secretary of State. This Minister, suspecting
that Spain was carrying on some Designs against the Queen's
Government, suppos'd that he cou'd discover the bottom of
the whole Affair, if he could have a Sight of the Spanish
Ambassador's Papers. He might have seized him, but that
was look'd upon as a Violation of the Laws of Nations; he
therefore compass'd his End by a Stratagem. He sent for the
then Keeper of Newgate, and ask'd him, if he had a Thief in
his Custody who was very expert at opening of Locks? The
Keeper told him of one who was wonderful that Way, a
Fellow that lay in for several Robberies, and who would
certainly be convicted. The Secretary order'd the Fellow to be
brought to him, and gave him Instructions to convey himself
into the Ambassador's House, and open such a Cabinet; but to

take nothing but Papers from thence, promising him not only a Pardon, but also a Reward. The Fellow executed his Orders without being discovered, only that he could not forbear the Temptation of taking a Parcel of Gold which lay in the Cabinet with the Papers. Upon his delivering the Papers, the Secretary ask'd him, if he had taken nothing else? He frankly own'd he had; at which the Secretary seeming very angry,—the Thief gave him to understand that he was out in his Politicks; for if he had left the Gold, the Ambassador would have known it could be no common Thief who had broken open his Cabinet, but now he would never suspect from what Quarter the Robbery came. It is said farther, that the Name of this famous Thief was Sheppard, and they carry it so far as to say, our Sheppard is lineally descended from him.

Since I'm in the Way of telling Stories, I shall give my Readers one more, (but a short one,) concerning our Sheppard lately escaped. The Keeper, upon a certain Day, going in to examine his Irons, found that he had been tampering with them; and said to him, "Young Man, I see what you have been doing, but the Affair betwixt us stands thus: It is your business to make your Escape, if possible, and mine to take Care you shall not." Sheppard answer'd coolly, *Then let's both mind our Business.*

The first Account of this Fellow's Escape appear'd so extraordinary, that many were tempted to believe he had some Assistance, or at least there was some Connivance in it; but since several Persons have seen the Places thro' which he escaped, and the Manner of it, they are convinced it is all fair. Though when we consider what Work he went through in the Space of four or five Hours, we may almost compare his Escape to one of Hercules's Labours.

Complaint of One Graduating an Old Maid.

A. J., Oct. 31.—Mr. App,—I am obliged to give you this Trouble, my Case being very Deplorable, and in hopes of some Relief from your making it thus Publick.

I have for some Years past made some Ladies in my neighbourhood the Subject of my Drollery, on Account of the Danger they were in, of falling into that worst of all Conditions, (viz.) OLD MAIDS.

I was Young, Handsome, Gay, Rich, and out of all Manner of Apprehensions of falling into that miserable State of Contempt myself. I had Flatterers, Admirers, and pretended Lovers innumerable; and thought myself the Queen of the Company, wherever I came. But guided by what Fate, or under the malevolent Influence of what Witchcraft I know not, all the Applications that were ever made to me, were such, that I, who of all the Women alive, had the greatest Aversion to the Negative Particle, and thought that those two Ugly Letters N and O ought never to be joined in one Word, without other Letters to alter their retrograde Signification; yet was obliged to say No to every one that came near me. Either they made Love of a wrong Nature, and aimed at the Crime, not the Virtue of Love; or they were such Fools and Idiots, as no Woman of Sense could bear the Thoughts of; or else Poor and had nothing, *and I was too proud for that too;* that in short, tho' I have had a thousand Bees and Butterflies, buzzing and fluttering always about me, yet I never could find anything, but what I was obliged to Fly-flap away, with the same Indignation that we do those troublesome Insects in an Evening, when they swarm about a Candle.

And now, in spite of Wit, Beauty, and Money, I am Night and Day under a continual Alarm at the dreadful Apprehensions of being an OLD MAID! Horrible! Frightful! Unsufferable! An OLD MAID! I had rather be metamorphosed into an *Humble Bee,* or a *Screech Owl;* the first, all the Boys run after to Buffet it with their Hats, and then pull it a Pieces for a poor dram of Honey in its Tail; and the last, the Terror and Aversion of all Mankind, the forerunner of Ill-luck, the foreboder of Diseases and Death. Should I be an OLD MAID, I shall certainly run distracted, and make the World a *Bedlam* all about me. Nay, I am Distracted, at the very Terror of it, and the Notion of its Approach; for I am already Three and Forty, and they say at Four and Forty, that Title begins to be our due. Wherefore I see no Remedy but to take the first Fop that comes, be he of what degenerate Race, or of what contemptible Character soever; for if I live to be an OLD MAID, I am Undone, Ruined, the May Game of *Islington,* the Jest of every Tea-Table, the Pointing Post and Scoff of every saucy Wench that has but a round-eared Cap upon her Head;

in a Word, there is no enduring it.   Therefore some Remedy must be found out.   Pray Mr. APP, do your Endeavour for us OLD MAIDS, that are drawing on to this Misery; for I must own there are a vast many of us.

And after all, Mr. APP, I beg your Wisdom to have the goodness to tell us if you can, under what Malignity of Planets, under what old, envious, second-sighted, malicious, old Witch's Evil Tongue I must have been brought forth.   That I, with all the Perquisites of Nature which are usually thought Requisite to dispose of a young Lady to Advantage, should thus lie on Hand.   What have I done?   That neither Youth, Beauty, Wit, or Money, would put me off?   That I alone, of all my Companions, School Fellows, and Neighbours, should have none but Fops, Fools, or Beggars lay Claim to me?

Teach me how to remove the spiteful Charm that has thus Bewildered my good Fortune; and, in a Word, what shall I do?   For to be an OLD MAID is the Devil.

I live nigh ISLINGTON *Church.*   *Octob.* 24, 1724.

Your Humble Servant,
ANNE.

Sheppard Still at Large.

A. J., Oct. 31.—The Keepers of Newgate have received certain Information, that the famous *John Sheppard* came a few Nights ago to the Brewhouse of Messieurs Nichols and Tate, in Thames Street, and begged some Wort of the Stoker, which was given him; and, that before the proper Officer could be got to secure him, he went off.

On Wednesday the Mother of the famous John Sheppard was at St. James's, to wait on his Majesty, and to beg a Pardon for her unfortunate Son.

A Heroine in Love Escapes à la Sheppard.

A. J., Nov. 7.—Mr. APP,—As the Taking and Retaking of *John Sheppard*, the Housebreaker, is the Subject of all Conversation, pray let me entertain you with a Parallel *Story*, of a less criminal Nature; indeed, my Case will let you see, that all the Art of *breaking Prison* is not contained in SHEPPARD's supposed Ingenuity.

You must understand, then, that I am a young Body, such

as in common Speech you call a young *Lady*, and having a good Fortune left me by a distant Relation, I am much in the same case with *John Sheppard*; for I am condemned, and imprisoned, having twice made my Escape, and being unhappily taken the third Time, believe the Sentence will now be executed upon me without Mercy. My Story, in short, is much like that of *John Sheppard*, as follows :

First I was desperately in Love; that you must know, is called a most wicked, abominable Thing in our House, worse than *Sheppard's* Crime abundantly. My Father is of an austere, rigid Disposition, full of invincible Aversions against my being married. He says, his Daughters are his proper Goods; every one of us, he says, is a *Chattel*. I suppose, if he should die, he would have us appraised, and put into the Inventory of his Household Goods. I had Application made to me by a young Gentleman of a good Estate, and in the most honourable Way possible; only indeed, that he made Love to me before he spoke to my Father of it. This my Father took Occasion to resent, and that to such a Height, that it threw him into Indecencies, and he charged him with a Design to rob his House; that is, by the Way, to rob him of one of his Daughters. But I put an End to that; for I told my Father, in so many Words, that I was willing to have him. My Father told me, and him too, that *it was all one for that*; that I had no right to dispose of myself without his Consent; that I was his Property, as much as his Horses, or his Cows; and, that if I would stray from the Pastures, I ought to be pounded. Accordingly that very Night he caused the Stair-Head Door to be locked at the Top of the Stair-Case, after I was gone to Bed, and setting an OLD MAID,—which by the way, is the worst Jaylor in the World, for they have a natural Aversion to any Body's being married;—I say, he set this withered Thing to be a Centinel over me, made me a close Prisoner up two Pair of Stairs, and sent my Lover an insulting Message; namely, that he had secured me, and he might take me if he thought he could come at me.

This at first put me into such a Rage, that I could hardly forbear laying Violent Hands upon myself. However, in a few Days I composed myself, and from that Time applied myself wholly to make my Escape; and first I found Means to let my

Lover know my Condition, by calling out at the Window to a
Neighbour's Maid, who faithfully conveyed the News of my
Circumstances to him : and he and I conversed freely together
afterwards through a back Window over an Alley, where we,
by her help, contrived all that followed.

This indefatigable Girl making her Way over two or three
Houses, came round the End of the Alley, and with infinite
Hazard got into the Chamber to me about Midnight, I opening
the Garret door, on the Top of the House; here we decently
tied the OLD MAID, my Jaylor, fast down in her Bed, bringing
the Rope about her Neck, so that if she stirred or struggled
she would be Hanged, and Gagged her to Boot.

Having done this, we went both out at the Top of the House,
and got over the Houses the same Way she came in, shutting
the Door so after us, that they never imagined we went out
that Way ; but thought I had let myself down by a Rope from
the Window, which we left open with a Rope hanging to it on
purpose ; and thus with most desperate Hazard I escaped the
first Time.

My Lover had been contriving my Escape all the while
another Way, but waiting an Answer from me, could not proceed, and heard nothing of my Escape, till afterwards, when
it was too late.   When I was at Liberty, the first thing I did
was to give notice to the Family to go up, and to Relieve the
old Jaylor, who I was lothe should be strangled, as indeed she
was in danger of being ; and this brought it to my Father's
Ears that I was gone.

Mr. *Wild* never made more diligent Search after SHEPPARD,
or his Brother BLUESKIN, than my Father did after me ; had I
been half as sharp in securing myself, he had never found me
at all.   But to my no small Surprize, some Days after, my
Father having by his indefatigable Diligence found me out;
comes furiously into the House where I was—with a Lord
Chief Justice's Warrant—seized me, as if I had been a Thief, or
a Murtherer, and carried me away almost frightened to Death.

Being thus brought back to my Prison, my Father, after a
great many Outrageous Words, and fierce Looks, carried me
up Stairs to the same Apartment ; and, to my no small Mortification had Iron Bars made to the Window, where he thought
I had Escaped.   And though he did not suspect that little Door

thro' which I had really Escaped, yet he had it Nailed up fast, so that there was no getting out that way neither; and to make the securing me his own Care, caused my Mother, who if possible, was more Severe than himself, to lie with me every Night.

He endeavoured, by all the threatening Words imaginable to make me confess, who it was that got into the Room to me, and which Way; but I would never confess any Thing, but denied there was any Body there. The OLD MAID affirmed that she saw her; at last I carried it so cunningly, that in short, my Mother concluded it was the Devil, and it began to work upon her old Heart so far, that she was afraid to lie in the Room with me alone, so got the OLD MAID to bring a Bed into my Room, and they both lay there to guard me.

In the meantime, my trusty Friend, the Maid Servant, who had let me out before, finding how it was, found Means to throw a Letter in at the Top of the Chimney for me, in which she proposed a Way to get the little Door open a second Time; and, in a Word, I, by Signs to her out of the Window, desired she would help me to something to open it with by Force. Accordingly, she tied a strong Claw-Hammer, and a File, to a String,—gave me Notice of it by Signal at the Window, and let it down the same Chimney; and so I got it safe, without Discovery.

Having gotten this Implement, I filed the Hinges off the little Door, and with the Hammer I wrenched open the Door gently, and got out in the Day Time, when my two Keepers were gone down Stairs; and now I thought I had been safe enough.

But this being in the Day Time, some unlucky People of the Neighbours, seeing me clambering over the Houses, gave the Alarm, and behold! when I was got down Stairs at the House where the good honest Girl, my Assistant, had secured my Passage, and I was just going out at the Door, behold! I say, there stood my cruel, hard-hearted Father, ready to receive me, and carry me back to my old Prison again; and thus far you see I am in a kind of a Case much like JOHN SHEPPARD's, though a thousand Times more disconsolate about it.

My Crime, it seems, according to my Father, is Robbery, which by the Law is punish'd with *Death*, and my Sentence is, that I shall live to be an OLD MAID; than *which, you know,* to be hanged in one's Youth is much more Bearable. Now, as some of my Neighbours (I hear) pity SHEPPARD, and say, 'tis pity he should die, but that he should be let go for his Ingenuity; then why should not I escape for my Ingenuity too? But I hear my Father is inexorable, so that I know no Remedy, but I must *lead Apes,* unless I can escape a third Time, which I am resolved to try, come of it what will; and if I do get off you shall hear further.

Yours, &c.

Sheppard's final Apprehension.

A. J., Nov. 7.—On Saturday Night last, the famous John Sheppard was apprehended and taken, in the Manner following, (viz.) between Eleven and Twelve of the Clock, he came to the Shop of one Nicks, a Butcher, in Drury Lane; and having agreed for three Ribs of Beef, he desired Nicks to go with him to Mrs. Campbell's,—a Chandler's Shop, a Door or two farther,—intending to treat him with a Dram of Brandy, and to pay him for the same. Nicks went accordingly, and while they were drinking, an Ale-House Boy,—belonging to Mr. Bradford, who keeps the Rose and Crown against the House,—came in to ask for Pots, and seeing Sheppard, went and acquainted his Master, who being a Headborough, took to his Assistance the Watch, and seized Sheppard in the Brandy Shop. He was dressed in a handsome Suit of Clothes, a Diamond Ring, and a Cornelian Ring on his Finger, and a light Tye Perriwig of about Seven Pounds Value, three other plain Gold Rings in his Pocket, two Tortoise-Shell Snuff Boxes, a Tortoise-Shell Watch, and Five Guineas and two half Guineas, besides two loaded Pistols, in his Pockets. Mr. Eyles, a Constable, was sent for, who, with the Headborough aforesaid, Watch, &c., put him in a Hackney Coach, and conveyed him to Newgate, several thousand People being assembled in Holborn; as he was in the Coach, he called out, "Murther! for God's sake; I am murthered, and am in the Hands of Blood Hounds; help, for Christ's sake," &c. Being brought to Newgate, he owned, that on Friday Morning last, he did break open the Shop of Mr. Rawlins, a Pawn-Broker, at the Four Balls in Drury Lane; and took from thence a Suit of

Black Cloth Clothes, a Light Tye Perriwig, a Bob Perriwig, a Gold Watch, and a Tortoiseshell Watch, two Tortoiseshell Snuff Boxes, a Silver-Hilted Sword, a Night Gown, and other Goods, to the Value of about 60*l.* He is now put into an Apartment, called the Middle Stone Room, adjoining to the Castle, and is loaded with 300 Pounds Weight of Iron.

On Monday last several Noblemen and Persons of Distinction went to Newgate to see the famous John Sheppard.

We hear, that his Majesty has been pleased to send for the two Prints of Sheppard, shewing the Manner of his being chained to the Floor in the Castle of Newgate, and describing the Manner in which he made his Escape from thence on the 15th of October.

Marriage Proposal to the Old Maid, and her Reply.

Kensington, Nov. 2.

A. J., Nov. 14.—Friend APP, Yours of *Saturday* last, I read, and do much commiserate the unlucky Fate of the unmarried Lady. Her dread of being an OLD MAID may be laid aside, if willing to enter into a Matrimonial Way with a brisk young Fellow. I have but one Misfortune that attends me, and that is *Inopia Pecuniæ,* a Matter of great Importance, especially in this Affair ; for according to the Modern Way of Love, the principal Thing consulted is·MONEY, which too often makes Marriage Bonds set so uneasy ; for were pure Love and real Esteem, the Things aimed at in this solemn Union, very few would deny listing themselves under *Cupid's* Banner. But as to this, there is no Reason to expatiate farther at this Time ; but return to the Point, and let the Lady know, if she will accept of one under the above Misfortune,

I am Your Ladyship's most devoted

Humble Servant,

TRUE LOVE.

Mr. APP, I have received your Letter you sent me from the kind Gentleman who is so willing to take me, and rid me of the dreadful Apprehensions I am under of being an OLD MAID ; and I here send you back the Gentleman's Letter, that you may let the World see how I am used, and whether I had not just Reason to make my Complaint to you as I did.

Sure this Gentleman did not read the Letter I sent you, where I honestly owned to you that I had had many Lovers, (as they call them) but they were such, as (1.) made Love of a wrong Nature, or were (2.) Fools and Idiots, or else (3.) were Poor, and had Nothing; and, that I was forced to say No to them all, on these several justifiable Accounts. That *in short*, I had a thousand *Bees*, and *Butterflies* buzzing and fluttering about me; but I could never find anything, but what I was obliged to drive away, as we fly-flap the Insects from us in a Summer Evening.

Now, to help me out of this Distress, here comes one of the same Sort, which I told you I had been troubled with before, that is, one that has nothing. No Money! Why *Friend?* I told you *I was too proud for that too.* No, no! Mr. *App*, pray tell the poor Gentleman I should have been very glad of his offer; only the *Money, the Money*, I say, is such a Top Article, that Love is all *Wishy-Washy* without it. I would fain be Married; that I told you, but not to go a begging neither. No, No! That is a kind of Love I am not for being acquainted with, I told you that before. Therefore, good Sir, if he is *without Money*, let him know that I must be *without the Man*; for as to Marrying to be Starved, that won't do indeed, to be an *Old Maid* is bad enough, but to be an old Beggar is still, much worse. So that, Mr. *App*, I am just where I was (viz.) in great danger of being an OLD MAID still. But again, Mr. *App*, I am not so far gone neither, as to be quite given over, for it was your Mistake, Mr. *App*, to print that I was three and Forty, for which I think to have you Indicted for Slander, as really, I am but three and Twenty; and a great deal too, for as I said in my Letter, *four* and *Twenty* commences *Old Maid*. I did not tell you I was an *Old Maid* already, but only that I was dreadfully frightened at the Apprehensions of it, and going distracted with the Fright; for, that I was within a Year of twenty-four, which is the first scandalous Year of Virginity. However, to give some Comfort to this new Lover, who takes me to be three and Forty, I allow you to tell him that I accept his Proposal; and, if I do not Marry till I am an *Old Maid* of three and Forty,—such as he already takes me to be,—I'll take him, with, or without

Money, for if it should come to that frightful extremity, I must be contented with anything.   Your Humble Servant,

NANCY.

Sheppard before the Judges.   Ordered for Execution.

A. J., Nov. 14.—The Constables and Headboroughs of the Liberty of Westminster, &c., have Orders to be out to preserve the Peace on Monday next, when Sheppard is to be executed; and the Sheriffs have also ordered an extraordinary Number of their Officers to guard him to Tyburn.   He is to be carried thither in his Handcuffs and Fetters.

Sir James Thornhill, the King's History Painter, has taken a Draught of Sheppard's Face in Newgate.*

On Tuesday last *John Sheppard* was conveyed in a Hackney Coach from Newgate to Westminster, being Handcuff'd and Fetter'd; and guarded by a great Number of Constables, &c. from Temple Bar.   In Westminster Hall his Handcuffs were taken off; and being brought before the Court of King's Bench, the Record of his Conviction for Burglary and Felony at the Sessions in the Old Bailey, was read; and he, making no Objection, Mr. Attorney General moved that his Execution might be speedy, and· a Rule of Court made for Friday next. Sheppard addressed himself to the Bench, earnestly beseeching the Judges to intercede with his Majesty for Mercy, and desired a Copy of a Petition he had sent to the King might be read, which was complied with; but being asked how he came to repeat his Crimes after his Escapes, he pleaded Youth and Ignorance, and withal his Necessities, saying he was afraid of every Child and Dog that looked at him, as being closely pursued; and had no opportunity to obtain his Bread in an honest Way, and had fully determined to have left the Kingdom the Monday after he was retaken in Drury Lane.   He was told the only Thing to entitle him to his Majesty's Clemency would be his making an ingenuous Discovery of those who abetted and assisted him in his last Escape.   He averred, that he had not the least Assistance from any Person, but God Almighty; and that he had already named all his Accomplices in Robberies, who were either in Custody or beyond

---

* Hogarth also visited him, and painted his portrait.—*Ed.*

Sea, whither he would be glad to be sent himself. He was reprimanded for profaning the Name of God. Mr. Justice Powis,—after taking Notice of the Number and Heinousness of his Crimes, and giving him Admonitions suitable to his sad Circumstances,—awarded Sentence of Death against him, and a Rule of Court was ordered against him for Monday next. He told the Court, that if they would let his Handcuffs be put on, he, by his Art, would take them off, before their Faces. He was remanded back to Newgate, thro' the most numerous Crowds of People that ever were seen in London; and Westminster Hall has not been so Crowded in the Memory of Man. A Constable who attended, had his Leg broke; and many other Persons were hurt and wounded at Westminster Hall Gate.

On Wednesday John Sheppard was brought down from the Middle Stone Room, and put into the Condemned Hold,—along with Houssare, the French Barber,—stapled down to the Floor, and a Watch of two Men set upon him.

We hear that upon searching the Lodgings of John Sheppard, near Newport Market, the Handcuffs and Irons have been found there, which he had on when he made his last Escape from Newgate; as also several Instruments which he made use of in breaking open Houses.

Moll Flanders' Niece an Admirer of Sheppard.

A. J., Nov. 21.—Mr. APP, I am a poor unfortunate Creature, as my Story will tell you at large. I was born in *Newgate*, the famous *Moll Flanders* was my Aunt; but she met with good Fortune to set her above her poor Relations, and I am left under infinite Disappointments.

I have been Transported twice, and have both Times found Ways and Means, not only to come back again, but to avoid being taken again, till Acts of Indemnity, and length of Time, gave me leave to appear Abroad.

I have followed the Trade of Pilfering and Stealing some Years, and was got to a tolerable State of Life, that I could now have lived without it; but the habit has so become a Nature to me, that I believe I should have walked in my Sleep to pick Pockets, if I had denied myself the Liberty of doing it waking. So I have continued the Trade a great many Years with uninterrupted Success; and now, what strange

Thing do you think has befallen me? Would you think it
Mr. *App*, that I should have fallen in Love, after so much good
Education as I have been Mistress of?

But so it is,—I have been so deeply in Love with your late
Friend *John Sheppard*, that I have been quite distracted.   His
Escaping with such Dexterity as you have heard out of
Newgate, charmed me; and if I could have found him, during
the little Time of Liberty he enjoyed, I had certainly had him.

What tho' I am 20 year older than he, we should have
made a suitable Match in all other Things; For as he was the
most dexterous Housebreaker in *England*; so I pretend to be
the cleanest-handed Shop-lift, and the nicest Pick-Pocket in
Europe.   I offer, Mr. *App*, to go into a Mercer's Shop, and
tell him I come to take such a Piece of Silk, by sleight of
Hand, and he shall neither miss the Piece, or perceive me
touch it; but shall think he sees the piece of Silk lie upon the
Counter all the while.

I never went to *Salter's Lecture*, or St. *Lawrence's* Church,
and came away without a Gold Watch, or a Tweeser, or some
other valuable Prize, in my Life.   I rarely come empty-
handed from the *Theatre*, especially if the Play was anything
Popular.   I assure you *Cato* was worth above 100 Guineas to
me, and yet I reckon the Things taken, as we generally sell
such Things; namely at half Value.

The last Opera of *Tamerlane* has done pretty well, and as
'tis likely to take, and to be acted pretty often this Winter, I
won't take a 100 Guineas for my Marketing; especially if the
Quality come pretty much to it.

Harlequin has been tolerably beneficial to me; but the Au-
ditories were a little too much *French*.   There were not so many
Gold Watches there, as on other Occasions; however, I don't
Complain.

Now the Parliament is met, and the Term in being, I am
pretty much at *Westminster;* nor is my Success there so mean,
but I may get a fair livelihood.   And all this while, Mr. *App*,
if you will believe it, I not only have never been taken, but
I have brought the Art of Picking a Pocket to such Perfection, and have such Exquisite Skill at it, that I not only
have not, but I will not be taken, no never; I say, if you will
believe this of me, you must believe also, that I am an extra-

ordinary Person, and that I have an Art something beyond
the D——l.

Perhaps you have never heard of me, nor does the Fame
of our Profession ever, spread to any extraordinary Degree,
till they come to *Newgate ;* but I have been so long forgotten
there, that the present Incumbents, not Mr. ————— himself
knows anything of me.

Now had *John Sheppard* and I made a Match, what a clever
Couple should we have been, and what Pockets, what fastened
Watches, what Purses of Money could have escaped us by
Daylight, and what Bolted Shops, or Barricaded Houses have
kept us out by Night! In a Word, Mr. *App,* we would have
visited *Lombard* Street itself; no Iron Bars could have kept us
out, no Iron Chest have withstood us within. But all is over,
poor SHEPPARD is gone, and in him the expertest House Breaker
in *England* is gone.

And am I not under a vast Disappointment now, when
poor dexterous *Jack* is thus snatch'd from us by his evil
Fate; after two of the inimitable Escapes, and after having
twice had his Liberty, but not been able to preserve himself?

Alas poor SHEPPARD ! I have lost my Love, and all the
hopes I had cherished of a universal Plunder, are gone so far,
that I am left under an inexpressible Grief!

Your Humble Servant,

BETTY BLUESKIN. (Catch me if you can.)

Nov. 16, 1724.

Execution of Sheppard.

A. J., Nov. 21.—John Sheppard, the famous Housebreaker,
was on Monday last executed at Tyburn, pursuant to the Rule
of Court of the King's Bench, Westminster. He being an
enterprizing Fellow, it was thought necessary to put Handcuffs on him in carrying him to the Gallows; which could not
be done but by Main Force, he struggling against it with all
his Might. And being searched, before being put in the Cart,
they found concealed about him a Clasp Knife; with which,
'tis thought, he intended to cut the Cord wherewith he was
tied, and then to leap among the Mob, as his last Refuge.
The Crowd of Spectators all the Way was prodigiously great.
An Undertaker with a Hearse followed him to Tyburn, in order,

as we were told, to bring back the Corpse to be interred in St. Sepulchre's Church Yard ; but the Populace, having a Notion that it was designed to convey him to the Surgeons, carried off the Body upon their Shoulders to an Ale House in Long Acre ; and the Undertaker and his Men got off with great Difficulty.

Madam Blueskin proposes to Publicly Exhibit her Art.

A. J., Nov. 28.—Mr. APP,—I wrote you something last Week of the great Disappointment I was under for the Loss of my new Acquaintance, and particular Favourite, Mr. *Sheppard;* and how all my Measures were broken by that sudden Disaster. That I had laid a Design so good in its Nature, and so certainly advantageous to him, as well as to me ; that had he but kept out of the Hands of Justice for this last Time, we should have done Wonders.

But now, Mr. *App*, since this great Artist at Housebreaking is disposed of, I desire you will find me out a Help-meet, a suitable Rogue, whose Dexterity, bearing some Proportion to mine, we might still be able to carry on the Trade of Housebreaking with as much Success, as I have hitherto carried on that of Shop-lifting and Diving.

I gave you, in my last, some Account of the Perfection I was arrived to in general. I have had some Thoughts of leaving off that Criminal Part of my Trade, having made a pretty good Hand at it, and being now pretty well to pass; and to set up with my Friend, Mr. *V——s*, to shew it as a new-fashioned, and true Sleight of Hand ; in which I make no doubt to give full Satisfaction to all the Gentlemen and Ladies that shall come to see me, and they shall acknowledge that Nothing of the like was ever shewn in this Age.

In this Case, I make no Question to let the Ladies see, that let them fix their Gold Watches and Tweezer Cases ever so fast to their Sides, at their coming, they shall not be able to carry one of them off again, without their falling into my Hands, and without I please to restore them ; which I shall very generously do.

A Gentleman, coming into the Room as well guarded as he pleases, only his Hands not being in his Pocket ; shall see me present him with his Gold Snuff-Box, which he had placed in the securest Fob he had about him, before he can think any One but the Devil knew where he had put it.

No kind of Trinkets shall hang to the Ladies' Watches, or Tweezer Cases, longer than I please, after due Notice taken of the Position they are at first placed in.

These, and many other most wonderful Performances, may be seen upon my Stage, if you think fit to encourage me so much as to make due Publication of my extraordinary Design, and bring me Customers to supply my Undertaking.

I have also many other ingenious Pieces of Art, that I may make Experiments of before your Faces, for the disposing of Silver-Hilted Swords, Gold-Headed Canes; and such Trifles as the Gentlemen, being vain of, upon all Occasions, twirl about in their Fingers as they go along, or as they sit in Coffee-Houses, Chocolate Houses, &c.

Also, for the coming at Pocket-Books, and Letter Cases, in *Exchange-Alley*, where the Men of Business are pleased, for Dispatch, to deposit them in their Coat, or Waistcoat Pocket ;— and, for the nimble running to the *Bank* to receive the Bills, if any are found, or purchasing Plate with them, before publick Notice can be given of them in the Prints.

Also, for Slight of Hand, in getting Accompting Books, Cash Books, and Day Books, out of the Tradesmen's Shops, and Merchants' Compting Houses; which always fetch a good Premio upon being honestly returned,—with no Questions asked.

Upon examining all these dexterous Performances, the Spectators may receive infinite Satisfaction, *as well* to see to what extraordinary Proficiency our Trade, or Science is arrived, as to see what Measures they ought to take ; and, in short, the only Way to be sure not to lose a Gold Watch, or Gold Snuff-Box, upon going into any publick Company, Crowd, or Show, is to carry none about you ; for that, as long as the Ladies will shew their Vanity, and the Gentlemen will shew their Pride, in carrying such Things about them, they will certainly fall into such Hands as mine some Time or other.

I have been for some Time studying the Art of unlocking Fetters, and Irons ; breaking through Locks, Bars, and Stone Walls, getting up Chimnies, and over Spikes, scaling Walls of 20 Foot high, &c. But as I am a Woman, I find it will not be to my Purpose, so I have only looked into the Theory

as yet; but I am told there is a young Fellow in the World,
that as much out-does *Sheppard*, as *Sheppard* did *Tom Crabb*
of *Spittle-Fields*, and that pretends, if ever he gets into Lob's
Pound, nothing shall stand before him. I shall tell you
more of him, if I find it is Matter of Fact; but at present I
can say no more than that I expect Wonderful Discoveries to
be made in the Art of *Free-Masonry*, or Gaol-breaking, in a
few Years more. And that they must find out other Sorts of
Castles than that of *Newgate* to confine the Gentry of our
Occupation in; or they may have them to look for, when they
want them, as they had *Sheppard*.

Your Servant, Mr. APP.

Description of an Unmanageable Wife.

A. J., Dec. 5.—Mr. APP,—I have for a long time expected,
and hoped, to have found some Parallel case to mine sent to
you, or some other of your Fraternity; that so, seeing some of
your wise Answers, I might have been instructed what to do
in the most difficult Case that perhaps ever happened in all
the Matrimonial State.

My Wife, and please your Worship, is endowed with two
d——ish Qualifications, which I can by no means Manage her
in; and yet I once thought myself able to have managed any
Woman, that ever was of Hea——n's making. She is, in
short, a Scold, a ——; and yet, as I tell you, I can deal with
her in neither of them.

That she is a Scold, a Teazing, Tormenting, unsufferable
Scold; and yet she Scolds with such polite Language, and
such admirable Turns of Wit, such Dexterity, such Slight of
Tongue, and such Sense; that, in short, I cannot Answer. If
she has a Mind to provoke, she has such bitter Expressions,
such Sarcasms, such pointed Reproaches, such devilish, fierce,
and furious Vollies, and yet wrapped up in such Words, that
they at once raise a Storm in my Soul, and yet lock down the
Passions, and suppress the Rage, which are ready at first to
make me lay violent Hands on myself, and her too; that I
am no more able to lift up my Hand, than to open my
Mouth. I can neither be in Jest nor in Earnest with her; if
I would Laugh, she makes me Furious, and if I would Rage,
she enervates all my Gall; so many Devils sit upon her

envenomed Tongue, that she is enough to Embroil a Man with himself, and with all about him; and yet, with such Magick she dozes the Understanding, that I am not able to make my Passions appear Rational, or to Reconcile my Resentments to my Senses. If I enter into Arguments with her, tho' I have the most evident Claim of Reason on my Side, she baffles me in a Moment, and I am as stupid as a Brute in a few Minutes; in a Word, I am talked out of my Reason, my Understanding, and my Argument all at once, and in a few Moments I have nothing to say. All my Rage intended to be shewn, and with greatest Cause, as well as Occasion, is turn'd into a kind of Calm; found, not so much by Conviction as by Wonder and Amazement. In a Word, I am perfectly reduced, she remains Victor to all Intents and Purposes; and then, Womanlike, she Tyrannizes in her Conquests, her Triumph is attended, not with a Moderation becoming the greatness of Soul she pretends to, but with the height of unsufferable Insolence, and she uses her Victory with the utmost Cruelty. But if I offer to take her at that Advantage, and Reproach her with Haughtiness and want of Temper, she takes up the Cudgels again,—Rallies me upon the Measures of human Prudence, and the Rules of Generosity and Justice, as they regard one another; and again she talks me down with a Torrent of Words irresistible, and yet inimitably fine. To conclude; she is the D——l of a Wife, and yet has the Tongue of an Angel.

But 2ndly, *which is a Blank Article upon me*, I assure you, Besides all this, *she is Lewd*, that is to say, I am fully satisfied of it; but I and all the Art of Man, can never find her out. She reads Lectures upon Jealousy to me till I am ashamed of it, and have not a Word to say; and if she does wickedly, *as*, I tell her, *I am sure she does*, I think verily she flies up in the Air to do it, and associates with her Lovers in the Middle Region, for no one can trace her. I have laid a Thousand Snares and Traps to catch her in, but she Defeats them with such Dexterity, and throws back the Crime on my Uneasiness, in so dexterous and extraordinary a Manner; that I am as ashamed as *Saul* was, when *David* shewed him the Spear and the Pitcher.

Now, Mr. *App*, if ever you had such a Case before in your

Life, let know what Remedy you directed the Parties to, and
if all the State Physicians you are acquainted with, can prescribe a Dose of Pills for a She-Devil, let me have them I beg
of you; for there's no Living thus in an everlasting State
of Bewitchedness as I do.

Your Humble Distressed Servant,

ANDRONICUS.

*Inhumanity of a Female Mob.   Andronicus becomes
Abel Peaceable.*

A. J., Dec. 12.—Mr. APP,—I had the Curiosity on *Monday*
last, to go to *Shoreditch*, to see Monsieur, the *French Barber*,
that is to say Executed, and tho' I was not able for the prodigious crowd to come near the Place, and withal came too
late,—yet the Example has done me some Service I believe;
for I cannot but say that the Temptation might some Time or
other have prevailed with me in my Case of a Wife, of which I
sent you some Account in my last. For who do you think can
be able to live with such a Wife as I described to you, and not
sometimes give way to the Secret Desire of being entirely rid
of her one Way or other?

But of all the Terrors that have been upon my Mind in this
Case, that of going out of the World with such universal
Torrent of Curses upon me, as the poor Barber had, has not
been the least horrible in my Thoughts. The Women, who
in my Conscience made up the two-thirds of the Throng, How
they did Rail! "*A Barbarous Dog!*" says one, "to Kill his poor
Wife!" "Ay, a *French Dog!*" says another. "A bloody *French*
Cut-throat Rogue," says a third. "It's Pity he should be only
Hanged," *says another.* "They should have pull'd him piece-
meal with burning Pincers," *says another.* "They should have
torn him in Pieces with Mad Horses," says yet another, and
thus the poor Barber was handled everywhere among them.*

As he was carried along to the Gibbet, there was no Room
to pity him; a poor Man did but sigh, as he saw him carried
along, and cried, "*Poor Soul!*" but a whole Gang of Wives
surrounded the Man. "Poor Soul! poor Dog, poor French

---

* Mons. Houssare, a French Barber in London, hung for murdering his
wife.—*Ed.*

Devil! Ay, 'tis no Matter and half the Men in *England* were
so served, for ye are all Tyrants to your poor Wives." This
they run upon so eagerly, and Hemmed the poor Man in,
that he began to see his Danger, and gave them a Thousand
good Words to be rid of them; and indeed I thought at first
he would not have got away so quietly as he did, for the good
Women were indeed desperately enraged.

In a Word, a general Spirit of Railing and Clamour was
among them everywhere, and if a Man had appeared but to say
a Word in favour of the poor Wretch that was hanged, he was
in danger of being *Woman-Mobbed*, and pulled to Pieces. For
you know how that Sex is famous for being empty of Mercy;
Cruel and Revengeful to the last degree, and grossly Partial in
their own Case.

I took care therefore to preserve a decent Silence in the
Crowd; made my Observations, as above, walked off for my own
Safety, and came home very Chagrin and Disturbed I assure you.

And now, Mr. *App*, I am in a very Sad Condition, by Reason
of my *Wit* of a *Wife* (as I have described her to you in my
last), for I see, if I rid my Hands of her, tho' it be done with
ever so much Decency and Slight of Hand, yet, I shall fall
into one Gulph or other; either be hanged, or tortured in
pieces by the Women, there's no avoiding it. Therefore she
must live and she will, for I won't be hanged for her. .But let
us consider the Reason of this Case. If a Woman is condemned for Killing her Husband, she is hurried to a Stake; if
a Man kills his Wife, he is hurried to the Gallows. But which
of the Sexes suffer the most on this Account, is a disputed
Point too. I appeal to the general, whether there are not
more Women executed that have Murthered their Husbands,
than there are Husbands that have Murthered their Wives?
The Matter seems to be pretty equal, and yet I believe the
Causes of the several Furies are very different, the Men commit
the horrid Crime, generally in the Excess of Drink, which
Dementing the Creature, Carries him out of himself; and the
Devil prompting his Rage, puts as it were the Weapons into
his Hands, and urges the very Fact; or, the provoking Tongue
of the woman, *set on Fire* as the Text says, *by. Hell*, pushes the
Man on beyond the power of bearing, and so she becomes the
Agent to her own Destruction.

This last Part deserves a Dissertation by itself. Who knows the Power of a Provoking Tongue? I have felt its Fury, as I told you in my last, till I have been at the Point of Murthering, not my wife only, but myself; and I cannot therefore but Pity all those poor Creatures, who provoked by the ungoverned Insolence of a Scold, beyond their Restraining Power, let loose their Passions to do Mischief.

Wherefore, Mr. *App*, tho' I do not justify the abusing of Wives, much less the Murthering them; yet I wish all honest Men would join with me, in a modest, but serious Application to the Legislature, to obtain a Law :—

1. To make the Proofs of Adultery in Man, or Woman more certain and possible.

2. And secondly, to restrain the unsufferable Insolence of the Tongue, and to punish what we call *Scolding*, more especially between Man and Wife; and that should make it Criminal for a Man or Woman to give each other any Abusive Names, or provoking Language; and Capital to give Blows, or to throw anything at one another, capable to Hurt or Injure, upon any Account whatever.

Such a Law as this would go a great way to preserve Family Peace, and you would soon see that, as I say, foul, urging, provoking Language is the great Occasion of the Family Murthers, which so often happen among us; so that it would be proved by this, that when those hateful Causes were thoroughly removed, we should have less of that Mischief happen, and we should have no more Stakes set up for Murthering Husbands, or Men hanged in Chains for killing Wives.

You see I make no difference here between the Men and the Women, so the good Wives will have no Charge to lay at my door of Partiality. I abhor a Man-Scold as much as a Woman, and I am no more for allowing Teazing and provoking Language in the Man than in the Woman. Let it be equally forbidden in both, and equally punishable in both; and as for Blows, *ill Names*, giving the *Lye*, and the like Rudenesses,—I mean between Man and Wife,—they ought to be so effectually Suppressed, that they should be heard no more among us.

Your Servant,

ABEL PEACEABLE.

On the Decay of true Friendship.

A. J., Dec. 12.—The following Letter seems to be written, tho' not with the greatest Eloquence, or in the politest Stile, yet with so feeling a Sense of the Calamity, which the World at present so much groans under,—we mean the Decay of true, sincere, disinterested Friendship, and the Treachery of false and ungrateful Friends, that we could not do the Author more Justice than to put it in his own Words, and shall endeavour to give a fuller Answer to it in the next Journal.

Nov. 25, 1724.

Mr. *App,*—Having had some Occasion to try the Fidelity of Man, and the true Value of a Friend, in which I have been disappointed, gave Ground for the ensuing Lines ; which, if worthy to be communicated, insert when Opportunity offers. If not, the Paper may serve for some other Use. The Theme is beyond my Ability indeed, but however, take my present occurring Thoughts, which run on FRIENDSHIP,—a Noble, an Excellent Endowment ; a Thing much talk'd of among us, but very seldom on any Emergent Occasion found by those that unhappily want the Experience of it. Tho' many Promises, and seemingly real Kindnesses have been shewn in a prosperous State, yet when Adversity frowns on Man, when *Tempora sunt nubila*, how seldom they have been performed, daily Experience, and a Thousand recent Examples too unhappily demonstrate. How many Families now are, and have been, who have laid a Foundation for others to build a Superstructure, by which they have been raised, who have denied a grateful Assistance to their kind Benefactors ! How many, I say, who fatally know the lack of a FRIEND ; and verify the Truth of what I am upon ! So long as Man enjoys the Smiles of Fortune, what Crowds of Acquaintance, what an innumerable Correspondence, shall such an one have ! An Acquaintance, who by their hypocritical Fawns, ensnaring Speeches, and betraying Behaviour, can't easily be discerned from real and sincere Friends ! Yet let the Table be turned, and Prosperity obliged to give Place to Adversity, what a surprizing and unexpected Change for the most part, doth such a one meet with ! They that before, even with a thousand Oaths, expressed and promised an inviolable Friendship, begin, so soon as they perceive Calamity approaching, to grow cool, and gradually relinquish their too kind Friend. Those very base Persons, that before received their Subsistence from such an unfortunate calamitous Man; now, instead of relieving their quondam Associate, often endeavour to lay more heavy Oppressions on him. They that were chiefly instrumental to his Ruin, now scorn and deride him. The best a man gets is a helpless Pity, a poor Relief, a sorry Recompence for past Favours. FRIENDSHIP! The Name indeed continues, but the Substance hath been long extinct! A Man may at Noon Day, with as little Success as the Philosopher of old searched with a Light for an honest Man, seek now to find a faithful, uninteresting Friend; *Rara avis in Terris.* Friendship! Sure from the length of Time she has been absent from us, she left this Sublunary Part to take a Tour with the Goddess *Astrea* to visit the upper Regions, where she hath made her Residence ever since. Certainly, a true Friend was never more difficult to be found than in this Iron Age; and happy is that Man, that hath the Enjoyment of one. But more happy the Person that hath no Occasion to make the Experiment of trying the reality of one. I would have every one beware, and keep in Mind, *Felix quem faciunt aliena Pericula Cautum.*

Yours,
T. EXPERIENCE.

On the Baseness of Ingratitude.

A. J., Dec. 19.—Mr. *Applebee,*—In your last you published a very feeling Complaint in a Letter signed Mr. *T. Experience,* on the excellent Subject of the Decay of Friendship, which Letter I suppose you sent me to answer. 'Tis a Complaint so general, and yet so just, that few will doubt the Truth of what that Gentleman has found, and perhaps by dear Experience knows so much of; and therefore what Answer to make to it I really cannot tell.

Friendship is so nice a Part of Life, and so few know how to act it, that indeed 'tis no Wonder to see it broken and betrayed. Most of the World mistake it for Interest; and such People therefore, whenever their Interest and their Friendship come to test, stick to the first, and throw up the last. The first they allow to be Material and Essential; the last they Esteem as a Circumstance only and of no great Value, and therefore always to be dropt when the former comes in question.

A wise and learned Man, tho' not over engaged in the Thing called Honesty, used always to say that Friendship depended upon Property; that if ever Property clashed with Friendship, the latter was destroy'd of course. And therefore, he usually said, with more plainness than discretion, if any Man claimed Friendship or Kindness with him, that he would serve them with all his Heart, and do them all the Acts of Friendship in the World, provided they would not touch his Pocket; but farther than that he would not go with any Man.

It is true, it would be very fair if Men would all do thus, I mean, that all those who practice it would also profess plainly that they would do so; but the Offence is that they practice it indeed, but profess just the Contrary.

Nothing is more common now than the highest Expressions of an elevated Friendship, without any Reserve either to Property or any other exception; and yet, as *Sathan* said of *Job*, do but put forth your Hand and touch them in their Property, and they will curse you to your Face.

Hence Ingratitude, which in its Nature is the worst of Crimes, is the most practised in this Age; and with the more shameless, open, avowed Profession of it, than ever it was in any of the more ancient Ages of the World. Formerly, to say a Man was Ingrateful was to sum up all the Vices which the Nature of Man was capable of in one Superlative; but now, to call a Man Ingrate, is laught at as an ordinary Thing, worthy of no Notice, meriting no Censure, and, in short, a Thing of nothing.

I know some have said this last is a Crime peculiar to *England*, and owing to the Climate; but I have more respect for my Countrymen than to grant it. I remember two Highwaymen brought to the *Old Bailey* to be tried. The first was condemned, at which the second was so concerned that he embraced him in the most passionate Manner imaginable; and when he came to his own Defence answered, he could say many Things, but as his Friend was Cast, and the World without him was of no Value; they might do as they pleased, he would die with his Friend; and so, they were both condemned.

Whether they were executed or not I do not remember, but the first Part I saw and heard myself.

My best Advice to the Gentleman who sent you the Letter, and to all People who are in the same danger, is, that since Friendship is a Thing so universally decayed, and the rever e is so generally the Practice, take care no more to depend upon it; have good Testimony of it before you trust to it. No, not on any Account whatever, depend on an Obligation. I know a Person at this Time, abused and insulted by one who, without the least Obligation, he had fetched three Times out of Prison. Nothing can oblige an ungrateful Mind. It will bully Parents; trample upon Relations; ruin those it ought to uphold, and starve those that have fed it. I have heard a Person of very great Experience say, he had been five Times ill treated, and in a Manner ruined, by the very particular People that he had kept from Starving.

I would not perswade any Man against Acts of Beneficence and Charity, tho' the present Usage of Benefactors is enough to harden any Man's Heart against the most moving Objects; but let every broad hearted Christian act like himself, only expect no Returns, expect nothing on the Account of Friendship, for as the World goes now, 'tis Odds but he will be disappointed. We must therefore now act upon a higher Principle; namely, to do good without hopes of receiving, and to be a true Friend, but expect no Returns; for if we do 'tis Ten to One but we come to our Penitentials, like the Gentleman who wrote his Letter.

Friendship is indeed too refined a Specie to suit with the gross selfish Ideas which the Men of this Age entertain. We are come to my Lord *Rochester's* state of Soul, which however he recommended by the strongest Irony:—

> " *In my dear Self I centre every Thing,*
> *My God, my Soul, my Country, and my King.*"

Self, in a Word, governs the whole World; the present Race of Men all come into it. 'Tis the foundation of every prospect in Life, the beginning and end of our Actions; and where those Actions, at any Time, do not answer this End, they are so far eccentrick and out of square. 'Tis to move retrograde to the general System of Life; and to stand as it were by ourselves. Therefore 'tis not at all to be wondered at that Men trample on their Friendship, break Vows, Oaths, Asseverations, and forfeit all that Thing they call Honour and Gratitude in the World. And this I hope may be a full Answer to Mr. *Experience's* Letter.

Your Humble Servant,
GRATEFUL.

That True Friendship is founded on Virtue.

A. J., Dec. 26.—Mr. *Applebee,*—Among all the good Things you have lately said of Friendship, in a Letter or two you published in your last Papers; methinks he that wrote to you seemed himself to be a little Ignorant of the greatest and best Part of Friendship, I mean Virtue. And when he recommends Friendship by the Example of a couple of Highwaymen, who, having. joined in the Devil's Work together, had such a true Taste of Friendship as to take their Wages and hang together; I say, in this, he testifies that he is not thorough Master of the best and most refined Principles of true Friendship; in a Word, I must tell your Letter-Writer, that he has not a right Notion of true Friendship, nor does he understand it at all. The only true Friendship is founded on Virtue. Honest Friendship must act upon honest Principles. To tell me of Friendship where there is no Virtue, is to talk of a Chain without the Links being locked together. Virtue is the bond of Friendship: all Friendship that is not thus cemented is a Confederacy, but not an Amity.

Hence it is, you so rarely meet with any Villainous Action done in the World; but, on the publication of a Reward to the Discoverer, or of a Pardon, you seldom fail of their betraying one another. The Reason is plain, the Thing is a Crime, there is no Foundation for true Friendship to act upon; and therefore no Mutual Confidence, which is the basis of true Friendship, can be established between them.

I remember at the conclusion of the late *Preston* Rebellion, there were two intimate Friends, who had professed entire Friendship to one another; they were also of the same Profession, and that no mean One indeed. I need name no Names. These two Brethren in Rebellion, and Friends, happened to act a very different and opposite Part; for being both made Prisoners at the defeat of their Party, one of them was tried at the *Old Bailey*, condemned, and afterwards hanged; and the other, his most intimate sincere Friend, was Witness against him, by which he was convicted, and by which the latter saved his own Life.

After the Tryal was over, they had a short Interview, in which he that was the Evidence salutes him.—"My dear Friend," says he, "I am very sorry I am obliged to go this length, but I hope you will forgive me; you know I could not help it, unless I would have died too, which would have done you no good." "Indeed, my Friend," replied the other, "I have nothing to blame you for; I must only tell you, I am unhappy in your being too nimble for me, for if you had stay'd but one Day longer, I had done the same for you."

This, I say is the Fate of Friendship which is not founded on Virtue; but honest Friendship is quite another Thing. And that brings me to the other Part of Friendship, which your Letter Writer mentions, namely, Gratitude. Where Friendship is founded on just Principles, there can never be any Ingratitude; and therefore when Friends break off, and turn Enemies, it will generally appear there is some Breach in the Morality of their Friendship, and if there is, their Gratitude ceases; for if I do dishonestly by my Friend, I am no longer a Friend, nor can his breaking with me be called ungrateful.

When, therefore, I hear of true Friendship broken off between any particular Persons, I am always for inquiring into the Foundation on which it was begun and carried on; if the End and Design of it was corrupt and dishonest, no wonder it broke off, for it was built on no Foundation. But if the Design and Beginning of that Friendship was open, a disinterested View of doing Good and receiving the mutual Returns of a virtuous Friendship; such Friends seldom break off, and are seldom ungrateful. Now, I would refer it to the Gentleman who signed his Letter *Experience*,—who complains so much of broken Friendship,—to bring his own Part to this Test, and try whether the Reason of the Breach he complains of, is not in himself as well as in others; and whether the Friendship was founded in Virtue or no. And let him judge impartially as he finds it; perhaps he may not find the World so bad as he talks of.   Your Servant, &c.

Mr. T. Experience, on a Case of Ingratitude.

A. J., Jan. 2, 1725.—Mr. *Applebee,*—Your several Answers to
my Letter about Friendship and Ingratitude are very good in
Speculation, and your Writer I acknowledge has spoke very
well, perhaps as Things have occurr'd to him, and within his
own Knowledge ; but my first Complaint to you reaches the
general Practice of Mankind, which my Experience tells me is
now more than ever tainted with this Crime.   And tho' it is a
Thing of so odious a Nature, as a learned Author says, that to
say a Man can be Ingrateful, is to say he can be everything
that is wicked ; and everything that qualifies him for a Companion of the Devil !

Wherefore seeing your Writers are not pleased to reach the
particular Case which I complain'd of, and which I cannot
well enter into any Explanations of, for some particular
Reasons : Seeing, I say, I cannot enter into the Particulars of
my own Case, I'll carry it back to its Original, and my next
Question is,—Whether Ingratitude was the Sin which turn'd
the Angels in Heaven into Devils ?

But let me explain myself a little in this Part.   I know that
the Divines tell us Pride was the great Sin which first communicated Crime to the Seraphick Nature ; that this Pride
swell'd up to Ambition, and rais'd the Grand Rebellion against
God, for which the Angels were expell'd the heavenly Mansion.
But after this Revolt, and their Defeat, all the succeeding
Wickedness, which was the Consequence of their Rebellion, is
to be resolv'd into Ingratitude to their Great Maker ; this has
blacken'd their other Crimes, and rendered both them and their
Conduct monstrous.   In a Word, while they were only Rebels
they continued Angels ; but when Ingratitude came into it,
then they commenc'd Devils.

Hence I infer that Ingratitude has an assimilating Poison
in it, and it comes from Satan, and made a Devil of him ; so
where e'er it breaks in upon Mankind, and breaks out in
Practice, it makes Devils of Men, it makes Men act like Devils
to one another.

In a Word, when Men have arriv'd to a capacity of acting
Ungratefully to those who have serv'd and oblig'd them ; so far
they deviate into Devils, and will afterwards act like Devils

when Opportunity presents. Whence, by my own Experience, I must say that the Apostle's Advice, given in another Case, is good, *with such a one no not to Eat.* Nothing is so vile, so horrid, so base, but such a Man can be guilty of it if the Occasion present; and this is so much within the reach of my own Experience, that I therefore sign'd my Name *Experience* to my Letter.

My particular Case, as I have said above, I cannot yet publish; but that you may judge a little of the Nature of it, and whether I give a right Judgment or no, let me tell you, your Friend's Answer does not in the least come near it. My Case concerns Blood and Life; and abundantly makes good that proverbial Saying, *Save a Thief from the Gallows and he will cut your Throat.* Take it at a distance thus: Suppose a Man has an Opportunity to save a Gentleman from the utmost Distress, and the immediate Danger of Life, say it were from Thieves or Enemies, or what you will; and suppose that very Person, (I may not call him Gentleman any more,) basely using, insulting, and provoking him, and at last drawing his Sword upon his said Benefactor, and using his utmost Endeavour to destroy him. But his Efforts failing, and being disarm'd fairly at his Weapon; you are to suppose then that his Friend, however provok'd, gave him his Life, embrac'd him, sent for a Surgeon to dress a Wound he had, in his own Defence, been oblig'd to give him; and after this shewing him several acts of Friendship and Kindness: Suppose this Man thus a second Time oblig'd in a degree so Extraordinary, yet on all Occasions returning Abuses of the worst and grossest Nature; I say suppose all this, and you reach a part of my Case, tho' but a Part.

Now is all this enough to denominate a Man a Devil, or is it not? Mr. *Applebee,* pray let me have your Opinion in this Case, and if you can give me anything like it in the History of low Life, let me hear it; for I cannot deny, that it is my Opinion, no Man in the World has been used like me, in this great point call'd Friendship.

If then you would have me believe that there is any such thing as true Friendship left in the World, pray give me some Instances of where, and when, and in what it has been shew'd; for if hazarding my Life for my Friend, to save his, nay, if giving him his Life, after all his Endeavours to take away my own, will not tye a Man to be a Friend, what is it that will or can oblige?

In a Word, Interest prevails. The World is govern'd by Self. No Man values the Hazard, the Loss, the Pains that another takes to serve or save him; but the Service is the Thing. Whatever is wanted is expected; and till it is done the Suitor fawns, and stoops, and is as humble as a Spaniel; but when the Service is done, the Obligation has no Effect, but on the least Occasion is return'd with Insolence and Affront.

Your Humble Servant,
EXPERIENCE.

Against Unlawful Proceedings of Insolvent Debtors.

A. J., Jan. 9.—Mr. *Applebee,*—I have nothing to do with the Dying Speeches on one side or other, of the late Capt. *Towers,* executed at the New Mint, as 'tis call'd; but now the Man is gone,—for I would not meddle in it before, because I would not anticipate or hasten his Execution on one Hand, or prevent any Mercy that might be shewn him, if it had been intended, on the other Hand. But, I say, now the Man is gone, give me leave to say a Word or two to the Sanctuary of Knaves, to say no worse of them, who have taken Post in that Part of the Town call'd *Wapping,* and pretend to make it really be as they had called it, a NEW MINT.

The Parliament of Britain may see, in this piece of Roguery in Miniature, what good the sort of People call'd poor Insolvents had reap'd; and how much the better they are by all those acts of Mercy shewn them for these few Years last past. It is remarkable, and worth our Observation, that the frequency of Acts of Grace to those petty Debtors seems to have rather increas'd their Number.

In former Times, the Parliament have shewn their Compassion to the Miserable, and pass'd several Acts for the Relief of Debtors and Creditors also; but then, those Acts of Grace were at longer Distances of Time, and the Number of Insolvents did not seem to be so many, especially of those who lay by for small Sums, as they are now.

It is sad we should think that they should be so hardened by Mercy, that they should run into Debt on purpose to be delivered by the publick Mercy; nor will I carry it so far as to say it is so, tho' I must confess it looks very like it. But this I doubt may be said, viz. That it would be well worth the Consideration of the Legislature whether the little-thinking part of Mankind are not made less Considering; and whether they do not more freely embarrass themselves, not caring whose Debt they run into,—depending upon the Clemency of the Legislature, that they shall beg themselves out again,—pay their Creditors with an Oath, and a Summons, and come off by the Grace of an Act of Parliament.

If this be so, as I fear there is too much of fact in it; then I would query whether these frequent Acts of Compassion, as they are now ordered, do not really tend more to the multiplying Knaves and Thieves, (for they are no better,) than to the delivering honest Unfortunate Insolvents who merit our Compassion?

How else comes it to pass, that notwithstanding such frequent Acts of Grace, and such unusual Clemency of the British Parliament; the enlarged Mint and Rules, the Verges, and Privileg'd Places, and even the Prisons themselves, are scarce able to receive the Prisoners and Shelterers that fly to them, and thrust themselves in there, in hopes of new Relief, but that they stand in need of harbour in new Retreats; as if driven to the extreamest Necessity, run desperately together, Consecrating Sanctuaries by their Numbers, and forming Priviledges to themselves, upon the dangerous Foundation of Tumult and Rebellion?

This unsufferable Violence offered to the British Constitution, Reason would tell them could not serve them long; and that every Step they took to defend it would entitle them to the Gallows; which now, by one Example, being successfully made for them, they may be convinc'd of. For I must insist, that the Justice executed upon this One, is a most merciful Step taken to warn the rest; and, that they ought to look upon it as the greatest act of Clemency the Government could exert. Had they lived under a *French* Government, what might have been the Fate of their new Adventure? In all probability two or three Regiments of Soldiers had been sent among them, have taken every man of them out of their lurking Holes, and after Hanging, or breaking on the Wheel forty or fifty of them, have sent all the rest away to *Mississippi*; that is to say, to *Virginia*, or as it is, to a Place five hundred Times worse.

But now, Mr. *Applebee*, to leave those desperate Creatures at Wapping to go on their own Way, and bring themselves to the Gallows gradually, and in order; or, if it may be hoped, to grow Wise, and abandon the State of their Lives which at present exposes them so much; let us consider a little what Course can be taken, if possible, that the Madness of these People,—for it is no less,—or the Knavery of real, but willing, Insolvents,—who run into Prisons and Shelters on purpose to be delivered, and whose Cases call rather for Justice and Punishment, than Compassion from the Parliament;—I say, let us think if some Course may not be taken to prevent the Knavery and Wickedness of these from giving a check or Interruption to the clemency, the Christian Compassion, which the Parliament of Great Britain are always willing to shew to the Misery of those, who, appearing Honest in Principle, tho' Unhappy in their Circumstances, have become Insolvents, neither by Vicious or Criminal Practices, and that are willing to pay as far as they are able, but made unable and destitute by their Disasters in the World.

Such, every Christian will plead for, every Merciful Man wish may be delivered; and, as above, 'tis hard that such should be shut out from Mercy by the outrageous Behaviour of the wicked, outlaw'd Rabble of New Minters, or by the thronging of the Knavish Debtors to Jayls and Privileg'd Places, on purpose to be delivered.

Now it has always been a Difficulty upon the Legislature how to distinguish between these two; and how to make a Law that should punish none but Knaves, and deliver none but honest Men. If this happy Medium can be now found out, Sir, I hope we may do an acceptable Service to our Country, and of this I shall furnish you to say more hereafter.

I am, &c.

Against Pandering to Vice.

A. J., Jan. 16.—Mr. *Applebee*,—You have been talking pretty much lately of Friendship, Virtue, Gratitude, Honesty, and such Things as those, most of them out of the reach of the Men

of this Age, or at least much out of their Practice; and as you
do not pretend, I hope, to stem the Tide and Current of the
General Inclination, I wonder you trouble us with those dull,
phlegmatick, unwelcome Discourses. I dare assure you, tho'
they may Instruct, they will never Please the World, as the
Genius of the World now governs; for this Age, tir'd with
Wit, Mirth, Gallantry and Gaiety, will not relish things so
Grave, and therefore unsuitable a Gust.

But if you will please the World, if you will suit their Inclination, you must change your Subject; in a Word, if you
will write to be read, you must write what People love to read,
teach the pleasant Age how to taste their Pleasures, shew
wicked Mankind how they may be as wicked as they are able,
and if possible, how to be wickeder than they are.

Several of the Roman Emperors kept Persons employ'd, and
I suppose allow'd them Pensions, to turn their Thoughts wholly
to gratifie the Pleasures of the Emperor, that is to say, to study
new Ways of Pleasing their insatiate Lusts.   And this in particular as they found the Gust of the Emperor's Vices lay this
Way or that.   If it was a libidinous *Caligula*, they sought out
the most beauteous Women, whether Married or Virgin, to
oblige his Taste; if it was a luxurious *Heliogabalus*, they sought
out the most delicious Sauces, and the greatest Dainties, to
gratify his vitiated Palate, and the like.   Thus, if you will
please a corrupted Age, you must study the particular Corruption of their Taste, and furnish such Things as you may be sure
will please, not judging by what will yield them Profit; but
what will give them Pleasure.

I might run out here in telling you what it is will, in a particular Manner, please the Taste of the Town at this time.   I
might tell you, that to teach them to be superlatively Wicked
is one of the first Steps towards pleasing them. But then I must
enter into the *Modus* for you, and shew you how to set up a
school of *Venus* and of *Bacchus*, and teach the Sciences of
Hell; and, as I am not fully qualified for a pedagogue in *Satan's*
Systems, I cannot be supposed to be fit for that Work, or to
instruct you in it.   I am not *Posture-Master* enough for that
yet,—so I lay that Part by; but, I must confess 'tis hard, that
the less this is done, the less you will attain to the power of
Pleasing among them in any thing you write.

However, I am prompted to talk a little in the Dialect of the Devil too; and to begin, I shall touch upon a new Topick, which some say is much wanted in the Town. We have a flaming Instance here, of late Days, of a certain Lady, who having thought fit not only to dishonour the Station of a Wife, but to do it so openly and notoriously as to put it into the Power of her Husband to divorce her, and put her away, has sued for a Maintenance too, and this has been attended with two Circumstances much in her Favour, and which, as I say, shews much of the Taste of our Times.

> 1st. That they perswade us she is now in a state of simple Independence, and that she is made capable to marry again; and

> 2nd. That notwithstanding *Notor* (or Notorious) *Adultery*, as is already prov'd, yet that the Husband is obliged by our Law to give her a large Allowance out of her Fortune, nay almost equal to it, for her Subsistence.

This I think is so absurd, and were it really so in Fact, would be such an Error in our Constitution, that I cannot but refer it to the Consideration of the judicious World; what ought rather to be done in the like Case?

First, I can assure you that in other Nations, and no farther off than a part of our own, I mean *Scotland*, the Fact itself being punish'd with Death; there would be no need, ever since the Offence, to do any thing for the Offender, but assist to bring her to the Scaffold, that is to say to the Gallows, the Offence being in the highest degree Capital, and seldom failing to meet with its desert.

But, Secondly, tho' our Law does not punish Adultery with Death, yet our Law is far from suggesting that Adultery is not a Capital Crime, and deserves severe Punishment; but to talk of allowing a divorced Adultress to marry again, methinks that is such a Piece of Front that it speaks out the Character of our Times in a very particular Manner.

Not that our Law says any such Thing, let no man mistake me, I am not going to bring such a Scandal upon our Laws as to suggest such a Thing; but I say, we have some among us who would set up for such a Law and openly plead for it.

I know they plead a learned and valuable Man as their Authority for dissolving the matrimonial Covenant, and for parting effectually, both sides giving Consent; but neither will the Laws of God or Man come into his Scheme, and all that can be said for so great a Man coming into it, and arguing for it, is, that he shew'd he had his Foibles, in the midst of all his forcible Reasonings, and that his Case was, in short, that he had a bad Wife; nor had his Wife the most agreeable Husband.*

But what is all this to giving an Adultress leave to marry again? The very proposal smells of a debauch'd Age. I shall say more to it hereafter.   I am, &c.

Confession of a Termagant Wife.

A. J., Jan. 23.—Mr. *Applebee,*—I am a married Woman— help me! and have been so some Years, to my Sorrow and Woe. I liv'd a Dog's Life with him a long Time, and had scarce a quiet Hour; for among all his good Qualities he had a devilish provoking Tongue, and gave me a great deal of bitter∙ Language on every Occasion, or indeed without any Occasion; and though I was always a Woman of Spirit, yet I saw no Way to deliver myself, for I had this Tyrant always at my Elbow, and there was no resisting him.

He did not indeed beat me, at least not for some Time, but he often threatened me, shook his Cane at me, and doubled his Fist at me, and swore he would be the Death of me; so that I trembled under him like an Innocent just going to be murther'd.

The grossness of his Language, and his Outrageous Usage of me, sometimes put me into a Passion indeed, and I could have kill'd him a Thousand Times if I durst; but then the apprehensions of his being too strong for me, and that he would do me some Mischief or other, cow'd and daunted me, so that my Passions generally turn'd upon myself, and I was more likely to Mischief myself than him. Nay two or three Times my making him believe I would lay violent Hands upon myself, made him relent and grow cool; and for a Week or two he would be better, but it lasted but a very little while at a Time.

You may easily judge my Life has been very uncomfortable, and that I have been several Times made desperate, nor has

---

* John Milton is undoubtedly intended. See p. 379.—*Ed.*

the old Gentleman been wanting to prompt me, in those Fits, to many Hellish Things,—the utmost and most Devilish that Rage and the Devil could devise; sometimes against myself and sometimes against my Husband.

Hence, Mr. *Applebee,* I desire you would take Notice, that Women, in my Opinion, ought never to be put to Death for Murthering their Husbands, unless it be where the peaceable Disposition of the Man, and the violent and unquiet Temper of the Wife, be first duly attested; and that, not from one single Action, but from the whole Tenour and Course of their living together. For else, I cannot think a Woman provok'd even to Distraction and Madness, ought to be deem'd any more *Compos Mentis;* or to be punish'd for any Violence she may be unhappily guilty of afterwards, especially in the heighth of the Provocation.

For Example,—This Fool of mine,—for such he was to the highest degree,—pretended at last to be jealous of me, would come home and upbraid me with this Man, and t'other Man, who perhaps I had never seen in my Life, or at least had never spoken to, call me —— and ——, and such Names as those; Things which I never had been us'd to, nor had my whole Conversation given the World or him any ground for. Nay, the Wretch would confess it to others behind my Back, and that he did it only to vex me, for that he lov'd to see me in a Passion; which when I heard, I thought was the most barbarous thing in the World.

It happen'd some Time after this, that one of his own Friends, with whom I had Intimacy enough to communicate my Sorrows, gave me a hint of her own, perhaps from her Experience of his Temper, for she was nearly related to him before I was. "My dear," *says she,* "tho' he is my Relation and you are not, yet as you are a Woman, and I see how you are wrong'd, I'll tell you how you shall deal with this mad Creature, and perhaps, if you have Courage to try it, you may reap the Benefit of it as long as you live. My —— is a great Coward, and if a Man does but give him a threatening Word, he trembles and is frighted out of his Wits; I am perswaded if you stand up to him and talk boldly to him, and do but take anything in your Hand as if you would strike him— tho'," added she, "I would not have you touch him for the World, yet I believe you would have the better of him, and perhaps he might be the better for it a great while." Then she gave me some Examples of his base cowardly Spirit.

I took the hint, and, in short, was soon of her Opinion, for I had observ'd something in his Conduct that look'd like it, on several Occasions; so I resolv'd the next Time he gave me a Provocation,—which I knew would not be long,—to let him know my Mind.

It was but the very Evening of the same Day that he fell upon me with his usual Language, calling me Names; and upbraiding me, as usual, almost with every Body that came near me.

After I had borne some Time, I flew out in a most furious Passion, indeed, I was provok'd to the utmost, but I made myself seem to be more enrag'd than I was; and, in a few, but very bitter Words, I told him how villainous a Manner he had used me with, and if he continued to use me so I would not take it of him, in short, that he should either kill me, which was not so bad as the Treatment he gave me, or I would be the Death of him.

He grin'd and sneer'd at me, and made a jest of my threatning him;—"No, no! Madam," says he, "I won't kill you, I don't desire to be hang'd for you, but I'll correct you, Madam, I'll correct you for your sawcy Tongue." This he said with an insolence unsufferable in itself, but not stopping there, he shook his little Cane at me, and at last strook me with it, tho' not very hard, upon my Shoulders.

"You Dog you!" says I, "do you strike your Wife!" and with that I snatch'd up the Fire Fork, for it was in the Kitchen; and at one blow I lay'd him at my Foot as dead as a Stone. I began to be frighted when I thought I had Kill'd him, but I soon found he came to himself. I expected the utmost of his Fury; and therefore held the Fire Fork ready in my Hand to defend myself, and told him, if he offer'd to come near me I would stick it in him.

But contrary to my fears he sits him down in a Chair, falls a crying like a Child, gave me all the submissive Words imaginable, and has been so good ever since that you can't imagine how the Case is altered with me. Pray, Mr. *Applebee*, what think you of publishing the Experiment?

Your Servant,   TERMAGANT.

P. S.—Pray give me your Opinion, whether you think, or
do not think, that most Women that Kill their Husbands, do it,
as this might have been, in the height of their Provocation.
And why should not the Law be favourable to us in such Cases,
as well as to Men who are not *Compos Mentis?*

An Old Maid's Views of Polish Courtships.

A. J., Jun. 30.—Mr. *Applebee,* I have several Times troubled
you in behalf of those most deplorable Circumstances which,
as I told you, I was afraid I should fall into, and which I
truly represented to you as the most frightful and formidable
Thing in the World; I mean that of being an OLD MAID.

I told you that I was already 23, and that I was told at a
certain Circle of Ladies at Madam ———'s Tea Table in
Hatton-Garden, that 24 begins the fatal Denomination, so that
I am just entering upon the last Year that can be call'd Youth,
in a Person of my Character; and that it is the most egregious
Nonsense to call any one a young Lady, after she is 24.

But you are a *cruel Dog!* so you are! To take no notice of
a poor Lady's Complaint, tho' made to you in the most moving
Terms imaginable, and I am very glad of the Opportunity to
insult you upon it; for be it known to you I shall never
trouble you any more upon the Occasion of not being marry'd,
a new and effectual Remedy being provided, which has been
already practis'd and approv'd of in Foreign Countries, and I
doubt not to bring it in vogue here in *England.* If not, we
Maiden Ladies that are in danger will soon have a Remedy
for it, and go over to the Place where we are told the Gentlemen are as handsome, as brisk, and as well behav'd as they
are anywhere; and so, Mr. *Applebee,* if we are not ask'd in
Time, we can say Good bye to ye, and be gone. But I will
hold you no longer in suspense,—the Story is this.

Hearing a great deal of Discourse the other Day of the City
of *Thorn,*—for we talk of News pretty much at our Tea-Table,
—after something about a Rabble there, and of several bloody
Executions afterwards,—Things which perhaps you may know
something of, tho' I have other Business to mind,—some of the
Ladies began to sigh and pity the poor Protestants, and how
hard a Fate it was to live in such a terrible bloody Country as
Poland, where the Men were so cruel; and the like. " I

wonder much at it," says a Lady in the Company who was just past the critical Number, " for I heard Sir *William C——* but last Week, giving the most agreeable Account of *Poland* that is enough to make us all in love with it, and for my part," says she, " I have wish'd a Thousand times since, that it had been my good Luck to have been born in that Country."

We were mighty earnest with her to tell us what Sir *William* had said, for we knew he was well acquainted with the Customs and People of the Country, having liv'd some Years at the City of *Warsaw*, so we all had a very good Opinion of his Judgment, and we prest her earnestly to tell us what it was.

" Why first of all," says she, " there are no *Old Maids* there' nor has any young Lady that has the least share of Address any need to fear coming into that scandalous state of Life.' This heighten'd our Curiosity still farther, and we call'd out for an Explanation, and that with an impatience which she might see was not to be resisted, so she went on.

" Why," says she, " the Ladies are in general allow'd the Liberty to fix upon the Gentleman they have a Mind to, and then 'tis not counted any Disgrace to take a Friend or Relation with them, and go to the Gentleman and let him know it that is, in so many Words," says she, " the Ladies go a Courting there just as the Men do here."

We all look'd a little surpriz'd that she should recommend this for a Practice, and began to talk very contemptibly of it " But," says she,—" hold Ladies ! Do not take it in bulk too hastily, there are a great many Circumstances in it which alter the Case, and give the Ladies less Disadvantage than you may imagine,—for this is so far from being look'd on as forward and indecent, that the Gentlemen think it a great Honour to be thus singled out; and the Clergy have work'd it up so far that a Woman is never us'd ill upon it; for when she goes to the House she is, first of all, sure to be receiv'd well by the Lady of the House,—suppose the Gentleman's Mother,—and lodg'd in her own Apartment; and, whether they agree or not she never goes from them again till it is settled, and quite broke off, and she consents to quit her Design.

" If she should be in any way affronted, the Clergy on one Hand would censure the whole House, and perhaps Excommunicate the Gentleman, and then he is undone, for no Body will ever have him after it; besides, all the young Woman's Relations are sure to resent it, and draw their Sabres at the Man wherever they meet him.

"As soon therefore as the Lady comes to the House the Thing is immediately discours'd of between them, she is far from being asham'd to say she has pitch'd upon the young Gentleman to make her happy; and the other receives it as an Honour, and then they fall to work upon the Conditions, which are not so difficult as here, because they do not make Smithfield Bargains, as we do here, for Portion and Joynture, but the Lady's Family is known, and the Custom of the Country is known; 'tis debated what Equipage she shall have, and what Servants, what Castle, for every House is call'd so there, and the like; and the Matter is not long making up unless she happens to be an Heiress, and to bring some Titles with her;—then indeed she Capitulates for Honours, and for the Titles being preserved to her eldest Son, and the like; but still she chooses for herself."

"Now Madam," said the first Lady, "I take the benefit of this Custom to be infinitely to the Advantage of the Women many Ways, but especially thus: 1st, that they have by this means an Opportunity to choose the Man they like, and, 2ndly, may always be sure to be marry'd if they please." If this is not enough to make us all run away to *Poland*, judge you.   Yours, &c.

Description of a Jealous Husband.

A. J., Mar. 6.—Mr. *Applebee*,—I have often found that distressed Ladies have recourse to your Paper, to make their Grievances publick, and I doubt not they have found Redress, or else they would have ceas'd their Application. Whether you are one of those we call Cunning Men, or whether you deal with Cunning Men, or no, that's a Question by itself; but my Case being very Particular I must lay it before you, and that you may shew your Skill, I shall give you some Light into the State of it.

I am a young married Woman; whether I am Handsome or Virtuous, Wise or Rich, is not much to the purpose with him I am to talk about, for my Husband is as jealous of me as

if I was the worst Woman alive. If a Gentleman does but
look up towards the House, as he goes by, he takes it for
granted I am at the Window, and have given him some Signa
for an Assignation; then out he runs into the Street and looks
up too. If I am at the Door, or in the Street, and any
Gentleman happens to pull off his Hat to me, he marks the
Man, runs after him and dogs him to his House, if it be possible to know who he is, and to see if he can make anything
out of it, tho' it be but in his own Fancy; and did he live in
Italy, as he does in *England*, he would have hired Ruffians and
Banditti before now, to have stabb'd forty or fifty honest
Housekeepers for only looking at his Wife, when he did not
think it proper.

The other Day a powdered Spark came by the Door, as I
was standing with my Husband, just in the Entry, and my
Gentleman looking in, pulls off his Hat and made an extra
ordinary Bow; being, it seems, over full of Manners that Day
upon a particular Occasion.

My Husband, with an air of great Surprize, cry'd, "Who is
that?" I took the hint, and told him with a kind of haughti
ness,—a little more than usual,—a Gentleman of my Acquain
tance. This heighten'd his Curiosity, and he asks again, in a
kind of Passion, "I ask you who he is?" "A very honest
Gentleman," says I, "I assure you." "Very well," says he
"I will know who he is," and out he runs after him; he had
not follow'd him far but he found he went into a Shoemaker'
Shop in St. *Martin's le Grand*.

In goes my Gentleman, for (seeing the Person he follow'd
went into the Shop, and thro' it into the House), he did no
doubt but he was a Lodger in the House; and that he had
pitch'd upon the Mark he aim'd at. When he went into the
Shop he knew not what to say, or who to ask for, but sits him
down, and calls for a pair of Shoes; but was sadly baulk'd when
he found the Fellow in the Shop rung a Bell for his Master
and saw his Gentleman whom he had pursu'd, having laid aside
his powder'd Wig, and edg'd Hat, come running down Stairs
and making him a low Bow, call'd him by his Name, and ask'd
him what Shoes he would please to have.

"Why, are you Master of the Shop?" says my Spouse. "Yes
Sir, at your Service," says Crispin. "Why you was a Beau just

now," says he. " A little Cap-fine, Sir," says he, "just upon this Occasion;" in short, my Spouse understood by his Discourse that he was just married, but that he did not use to go always so gay. This baulk'd my Master, and away he came without any Shoes. When he came back I jested with him, and ask'd him if he had found out my Spark, for which he gave me two or three hearty Curses, and so that went off again. A few Days after, I call'd my Maid,—having a mind to vex him,—and gave her my Message before his Face, bidding her take one of my Shoes in her Hand, and go to such a Place, being the same Shop, and fit a pair of Clogs to it. I saw it provok'd him, but he kept his Temper a while, at last turning it into an angry jest, said to me, " *You need not send for your Scoundrel, Madam, if you please I'll take a Coach and fetch him to you, and cut your Throats together,*" and out he went, in a Passion.

I have been ill us'd since upon several Occasions, on account of this Shoemaker, which provok'd me to the last degree, that he should think me so low priz'd too as to take up with such a Fellow as that; however, in a little Time that wore off, for some few Weeks after a Clergyman came to our House with a Relation of his, to make us both a Visit.

The Devil could not have contrived a worse Thing to set my Brute on Fire; for tho' the Person who brought him was his own Cousin, and tho', upon Enquiry, the Clergyman is a grave, reverend, and sober Person, and of an unspotted Character,—and tho' I never saw him before or since,—'tis all one, I have him thrown in my Teeth every Day; and am used by my Brute like indeed what he is, and as Brutes will use their Wives.

Now, at the same Time, I am to tell you that I am as jealous of my Brute as he is of me, only with this difference :—

I. That I am pretty sure I have Reason, and Know very well the Person; and would I take half the pains to expose him that he would take to expose me, I believe I could fix it even to Evidence of Fact.

II. That I am more indifferent about it, and do not care one Farthing whether he is Lewd or no, or whether he leaves it off or no; because I am resolv'd upon my Measures, for which Reason I send this difficulty to you.

My Question is this,—

Whether, seeing I am satisfy'd of the Truth of it, and that he is really guilty; I may not as justly separate myself from him as I might, on a publick Evidence, do it by Tryal and Process? For though perhaps I might compass him that way, yet a Woman runs thro' so many Difficulties in such an Attempt; is at such an Expence, and runs so many hazards of a Miscarriage, that I do not think 'tis prudent to venture it. But as I am a Judge for myself, and have Proof enough to put it out of doubt with me, I think I may declare him divorced so as is sufficient to myself, go from him, and let him clear himself if he can. And this Question I ask you for the Use of the whole Sex, as well as for myself. Pray Mr. *Applebee*, give me your speedy Answer. Your humble Servant,

ABIGAIL.

A Story of Matrimonial Stratagems.

A. J., Mar. 13.—Mr. *Applebee*,—I am a distress'd Female, tho' I confess I am partly the Cause of my own Distresses too; but that cannot be help'd now. I was put to my shifts a little too young, and falling into Cunning Hands, I was advis'd to set up in the World for a Fortune; and that nothing could get me a good Settlement like it.

The Person who put this hint into my Thoughts wanted no Art either to prevail upon me to comply with it, or to direct me in the Management of myself in order to carry it on, and undertook upon certain Conditions, scandalous enough too in the End, to be at a considerable part of the Expence; for, indeed, tho' I had something of my own too, yet it was not considerable enough to support an Equipage and Figure, which, it seems, she said I was to make.

Upon the whole, I consented, and was accordingly dress'd up for a fine Lady, and one of a great Fortune; and, after a great many Intrigues and subtle Management, in which I play'd my Part always as I was directed, I was at last pitch'd upon by a young Gentleman, who not only pretended, but really was, Son to a Father vastly rich; who was able to do wonders for him, but that he was not of Age, and his Father, having been a little disgusted at his Conduct in some small Matters discourag'd him much, and would not do for him yet, but that, as he was the Heir, he must have a great Estate at last, and the like.

This Gentleman was represented to me with infinite Advantage, and indeed, if he had been in worse Circumstances than he really was, if he had courted me fairly, I should not have been very shy of him, nor should I have had any Reason.

But now, as I was to act the part of a Person infinitely above what I really was, I appear'd to be shy of him, to the last degree, and when I did admit him it was with Reserves, and with Arguments rais'd upon mighty good Grounds, namely, that I could not think of it except his Father and my own Relations had a meeting; and, that Things of that Consequence might be settled, for that I could not be satisfy'd to throw away what little I had, without such Settlement as it was reasonable to expect.

This look'd so like a Lady of Fortune that he knew not what Answer to make, but pretended to act upon another Foot, (viz.) that he was deeply in Love, that he would do anything that lay in his Power to secure my Fortune all for myself, or in my own Hands, and the like; and so lay'd close Siege to me, in a Manner that look'd like one very sincere, and I believe was so.

But all this while I was instructed to hold off, and to appear the more obstinate the more eager he appeared; and I did so, till my Gentleman began to despair, when on a sudden the cunning Manager takes him into her Apartment, and talking very seriously to him, told him she, had us'd all the Means possible to perswade me, but that nothing would prevail but to have the Consent of Friends, and so asked him if he could not find some Friend to move it to his Father; but he shook his Head, told her she did not know his Father's Temper so well as he did, and that he knew it was not to be done. "Why then," says she, "there is but one Way left, and that I am sure will do." "What's that?" says he. "Why to come one Evening and take us out in a Coach to take the Air, and drive away with her."

He smil'd at the Offer, and tho' he said it was dangerous, yet said he would venture ten Times as much to obtain the Lady, and so began to court the Assistance of the cunning Lady, who pretending a vast Kindness to him, told him she would venture her Life to serve him; and so, in short, they concerted their Measures to take me out to the Play at such a Time. I was directed to make a Scruple of going unless she, my Friend went with us, which he readily consented to, knowing she was in the Design.

Accordingly, at the Time, he brought a Coach, and we went into it, but when we were in, he starts it as a new Thought, *"What if we should take a Turn into the Country a little to take the Air?"* My Companion immediately answered, "Ay, Ay!" So away we drove to the Spring Garden at *Kensington*, where we stay'd till it was dark, and when we came away I was insensibly put into another Coach with four Horses, tho' I did not see the Horses, and Hurry'd away to *Brentford*, where being carry'd into a House, he came to me and told me in a very obliging Manner, that he had laid his Life at my Mercy, and there was no Remedy, but I must either hang him or Marry him, and used abundance of earnest Importunities.

I desired he would let me consider a little of it, and shew'd myself very uneasy and surpriz'd. He said, to give me Time would be to put himself into immediate Ruin, that he would not stir out of the Room, but that if we two had a Mind to consult anything he would retire as far as the Door, upon my Word of Honour that I would not go to the Window and cry out.

After some importunities I promis'd, so we consulted together, and she made herself two or three times an Ambassador to go between us; however, by her Conduct he was made believe I was obstinate, which also I pretended, and seem'd to be in a great Passion, so that he might see it.

When this was carry'd on as far as was requisite, she told him I was come to crying, and was at a stand, that she believed I would comply, and so bid him get a Minister, but there was no need, for he had brought a shabby Fellow in a Gown, who came behind the Coach.

In a Word, I was at last huff'd and threaten'd, and seemingly frighted into it, had the Office of Matrimony read, and whether I said yes or no, was afterwards put to bed, and lay with him there three Nights together, tho' pretendedly ill pleas'd.

Now since all this, it appears too plainly that I am no

Fortune, tho' I am not a Beggar neither, but my Lover and Husband is ruin'd by it. He does not know to this Day but that he forced me to it; and may be hang'd if I please, but he dares not speak to his Father, nor differ with me, so that he is desperate and miserable on both Sides; and as for me I know not what Course to take. Pray Mr. *Applebee* give me your Advice.

I am, your Humble Servant,

Nelly.

On Matrimony, and the most Suitable Age for the Ladies.

A. J., Mar. 20.—Mr. *Applebee*,—I have sent several Letters to you in consequence of my most earnest Desire to avoid the most scandalous Circumstances of Women, call'd an *Old Maid*, but last Week I happen'd to meet with some very agreeable Conversation among Persons of both Sexes, where this great Question was propounded,—Which was the best and most likely Age of our Sex, for a Woman to expect to be well Married in? Three stages of Life were proposed:—

I. Young Maids from fifteen to five and twenty.

II. Young Widows from eighteen to thirty.

Or,

III. Old Maids from five and twenty to forty.

IV. Middle aged Widows from thirty to forty five.

And

V. Old Maids from forty to five and fifty.

VI. Antient Widows from five and forty to sixty.

It would be very diverting to give you an Account of the wise Debates which happen'd upon this Occasion, and very long they entertain'd the Company; but not to detain you too long with the Particulars, 'tis sufficient that the Company almost unanimously gave it for the middle Class, namely, for the old Maids and the middle aged Widows; and affirm'd, that one Time with another, the old Maids, tho' they had staid long, and suffered some Reproach upon that Account, were yet, generally speaking, better Married, had better Success, and made better Wives, than the younger Ladies, who went off between fifteen and five and twenty.

First. It was suggested they had more Experience in the difficult Part of a Lady's Life, call'd the Negative Voice, and

had more Courage at saying No; whereas, what between the
Motions of Friends, and the pressing persuasive of Inclination,
they could not easily be prevail'd upon to say No in their
younger Years, by which Means they were often betray'd,
abus'd, ruin'd, and undone.

Secondly. It was added in their Favour, that all the middle
aged Widowers look'd into their Class for Wives, not caring
either to look back too far, or forward too far, for divers good
and weighty Reasons, and especially Reputation for the first, and
Inclination for the last; and that therefore the middle Class
of Ladies had abundantly the more Choice, and stood a better
Chance to be taken off, than either the very young, or the
very old.

Encourag'd by the cogent Reasons which were used on both
Sides, and which at length prevail'd in favour of the last Opi-
nion, I recal all my Solicitations to you to furnish me with
Argument to support my self under the fear of being an *old
Maid;* that I must tell you I am resolv'd to run the risk of
staying, and being taken off to my Advantage, than of being
Boy-match'd in my Youth, and tied down too early to a Fool
or a Fop, the two hateful Denominations which the smart
Youths of the Town are generally sorted into.

But then, take it also as you go, that it is not at all to be
suppos'd that I act in a state of Indifference as to being Married at all. No, No, Heaven forbid! But a pure Piece of
Discretion, in order to be well Married. Of which hereafter.

It is true, there was a long Debate upon this main Point,—
Whether there were not more Men than Women also ruin'd by
the disasters of Matrimony, than by all the other Kinds of
Human Casualty in the World; and it was at length carried in
the Affirmative, tho' much against my Opinion, I confess. I
say it was carried in the Affirmative, and concluded, that really
Matrimony was a most fatal Circumstance of Life; nay, one
Man advanc'd that it kill'd more than the Plague,—beggar'd
more than the War, and ruin'd more than Vice. Upon which
it was inquir'd, whether there might not some other Way be
found out for the propagation of Mankind, with less risk both
to the Male and to the Female; an important Question, I assure you, had the Fact been prov'd.

Many learned Debates took up our Time upon this Head,

but they were all so much to the Advantage of the Men, and to the Disadvantage of us Women, that we were forced at last to grant, that tho' it was true we ran great risk in Marrying, and the Men were, in short, Brutes to us on many Occasions, yet upon the whole, we had better trust them, under the bounds of Law, than trust them without Law, and take them *for better*, *for worse*, than be their humble Slaves, to be toss'd about the World like Tennis Balls, and make nothing of it. And so we all voted for Matrimony, as much the least Evil of the two. But being not fully resolv'd in this Case, I desire your Opinion, and am   Your Humble Servant,

LADY MARJORY.

Conjugal Forbearance Inculcated by a Story.

A. J., Mar. 27.—Mr. *Applebee*,—I am a Married Wight, so the Fates decreed, and so my Unhappiness is fix'd, for, may it please your Worship, the Devil and I entered into Wedlock now almost forty Years ago; nor let this surprise you. For as the Devil,—by the concurring Testimony of the Learned,—is incarnated in divers and sundry Shapes, Places, and individual Persons, and appears in almost every relative Station of Life; so there is no doubt remaining with me, but that I have met with him in human Shape, and entered into a formal Contract with him,—tho' not really as a Devil, but at all hazards,—for I took him for Better for Worse, Devil or no Devil, Wife or no Wife, *hab nab at a venture*, as the Boy says, and with him, in Female Shape, I committed Matrimony, as I told you before.

From this horrid Conjunction, for my *Sybil* was but touch and go, a fruitful numerous Offspring has proceeded, of both Sexes; some are as dull and stupid as *me*, their wretched Father, some as arrant Imps as *that Devil* their Mother, and we have thirteen of them Alive.

We liv'd together, that is, we carried on the Civil War against one another almost 20 Years, till,—as in human Affairs it often happens,—being tyr'd with Strife and continual Battle and Bloodshed, we at last came to a Treaty; in order as you will suppose to Peace, and a reconciliating the Matter.

Plenipotentiaries were appointed, and Preliminaries settled, and the Treaty began as formally as that at *Cambray*, the weighty Matters of the Treaty were debated; and, upon the whole, Things tending all that Way, we very soon came to this Agreement,—namely, to Disagree as long as we liv'd. In order to which, we met one Morning, Friends and Relations being present, and turning Back to Back, she walk'd out at one Door South, and I walk'd out at the other Door North, and Cursed one another very heartily, if ever we came into a House together again as long as we liv'd; and thus our matrimonial Relation ended.

In this separate Capacity we have liv'd now almost twenty Years longer. I very well satisfied at being parted from a Monster, and she as well pleas'd, *so she always profess'd*, at being at liberty from a Tyrant; and yet we have not liv'd very remote from one another neither.

And now, after such a length of distant Reflection, Reason and Nature beginning to take Place again with both of us, and being somewhat worn off of former Heats and Exasperations, we have either of us strong Inclinations to come together again, and be Friends with one another; but having had some Meetings about it, the Notion of having forsworn one another, and cursed ourselves if we joyn together again, is so frightful, that really we are afraid of it, and keep asunder now upon that Account only. Nor do I see who can absolve us of this Oath, or how we can come off of it, without incurring the Penalty which we wish'd upon ourselves.

This horrid Case keeps us now asunder, and we dare not meet but in the open Air, for fear the House should fall upon our Heads; which is one part of the Imprecation mention'd, and so of another part not fit to name. Now we have been with the Minister of our Parish, and he makes light of it, and says it was an unlawful Thing for us to separate, that we are oblig'd to come together; and that, for the Curse or Imprecation, we must repent of it as a Sin, and not commit another Sin in keeping asunder for fear of the Punishment. But that does not satisfy our Scruples, and so we are at present where we were, and are likely to continue so for ought I see.

Nor do I give you my Story for your Advice in it, for I question whether we should be able to comply with it, tho' it were ever so good; but to let you give the married Quarrellers a Specimen of the ill Condition such wrangling Families necessarily bring themselves into, by their rash, violent Doings;

which,—tho' they may afterwards sorely repent,—yet leaves a
Sting in their Minds, which does not fail to torment them like
a lingering Disease. And it may be very useful on many
Occasions, to the forward Ladies of the Day, and to the hasty
Lovers also; for indeed I like turning Back to Back before
Marriage, much better than twenty Years afterwards. Besides,
as to the cursing Part, there seems to be no great matter in it,
for if two Lovers part with a Curse if ever they come together
again, they have no more to do but to keep to it, and stay
asunder; and if they never see one another again they may be
never the worse.

Upon the Whole, I believe my she D—l and I shall go near
to set our Horses together, and perhaps be wiser than we have
been, to the Instruction of all our Neighbours; and if we have
the good Fortune to act a different Part from what we have
formerly done,—as I believe we shall,—we may not have spent
the last twenty Years much amiss, whatever we did the twenty
Years before it.

I am your Humble Servant,

FURIOSO.

Story of an Unfortunate Matrimonial Adventurer.

A. J., April 3.—Mr. *Applebee*,—Having seen some merry
Cases sent you by your Friends concerning the great Advantage of cross-Questions in Matrimony, and the Blessings of
bad Husbands and bad Wives; I have thought very often to
send you my Case, which is very particular, but have been
hindered by my Apprehensions of being discover'd; however, at
last I have ventur'd to let you know what a Condition I have
been reduc'd to for want of a good Wife.

It is now above 20 years ago that I began to think I should
be very happy if I could get a good Wife, and I assure you I
resolv'd, with the utmost Sincerity, to make a very good Husband; and had I been well us'd, I believe I should have done
so; but my Fate directed Things quite contrary to my Expectations.

To come to the Fact,—I chose, woo'd, obtained, and married
a young, handsome, merry, good humour'd, clever Girl, and
very happy I thought myself indeed; and we liv'd together near
two years, had one Child, and expected another, when on a

sudden, one of your Half-pay Frenchmen came and took a
Lodging in our House. I was pleas'd well enough with the
Man, being a civil, mannerly Person, and who gave me a good
Rate for his Lodging, and Dyet, little thinking of what follow'd. But my Gentleman had not been long with me but I
found him very sweet upon my Wife. At first I took it for
good Manners only, and what they call a French Freedom ;
but, in short, to my great Uneasiness, in a little Time more, I
found my Wife as fond of him as he was of her, and in a little
more Time,—to cut the Story short, for what signifies telling a
long Story,—being grown, not only jealous of ill Usage, but
convinc'd it was so, and resolv'd to find it out, I laid a Snare
for them, and that, so as they were not wary enough to foresee,
or not cunning enough to prevent ; and, in a Word, catch'd
them in the very Fact.

The Frenchman, being made desperate by the plainness of
the Discovery, was too much a Soldier for me to venture upon
him in my first Fury ; and having his Sword and Pistol within
reach, stood a Parley with me, so that I only d——d him a
little and withdrew ; and my Wife, afraid of my Resentment,
sheltered herself under his Protection, and the same Evening
pack'd up and fled, her Gallant bringing up the rear made his
Retreat also.

It was not long after this Disaster, when making my Complaint to a Learned Friend, he undertook the Question, and
with a great many cogent Arguments, too many to report
here, urg'd me to marry again, argu'd the Lawfulness of it,
made a trifle of the Forms of Divorce, and insisting that it
was Lawful in itself, and that the rest was but Ceremony, told
me I ought to make myself amends upon the Woman for
abusing me, that I ought not to sacrifice the whole felicity of
my Life upon the Accident of a Wife, and live single because
she was debauch'd ; upon being easily perswaded to what
Nature prompted me to, I resolv'd upon it, and having good
Intelligence that my Wife and her Spark were separated, and
that she was gone away with another to Jamaica, I concluded
I should hear no more of her, so I gave out she was dead,
call'd myself a Widower, and soon pick'd up another Wife.

You must Note here, that being in pretty good Circumstances at this first part of my Life, I took more care to please

my Fancy than my Judgment, and chose much by my Eye,
for I resolv'd always that I would have a handsome Wife; my
first was handsome indeed, but my second was a Beauty, and
I was mightily pleas'd in the Match.   But I, that was to be
the Subject of the Story, was as much disappointed here as
before; for in short, in about four Months, I found that my
Wife not only was with Child, but that she increas'd so fast,
and grew so near her Time, that it was impossible it should be
mine; so, taking the Occasion one Day to Question her plainly
upon it, and she seeing it was in vain to deceive me, fell into
Tears and confess'd it; giving me a full Account how she was
drawn in by a Sea Captain, upon solemn Engagements of
Marriage, and how he afterwards basely abandoned her.   And
indeed, her Story was so moving, that I could have forgiven her,
but the grand Article of not staying, but venturing to marry
me before she either had been delivered, or was sure she had
not been with Child, stuck so close to me that I would not be
reconciled to her; so she walk'd off, and now I was single the
second time.

I have not room here to give you the Detail of my sundry
Adventures after this, but you may take it in the gross
thus :—

I married a third, and she prov'd a common D——, gave me
a Disease, and used me like a Dog into the Bargain; had two
Husbands alive at the same Time, and then ran away from
me.

I ventured a fourth Time, the former three living, and she
prov'd such a Termagant that she fought me fairly, once or
twice, and indeed box'd me to such a Degree, that at last I
was forced,—not to drive her away, for she would not go,—but
to pack up my All, and run away from her, or I believe she
would have murdered me.

Away I went into the North of England, in order to live
cheap and retir'd, for I had a little Estate, just a sufficiency
to maintain me; there I married a fifth Wife, thinking to live
quietly, and out of sight, having chang'd my Name.   But it
was all one here; for she Yorkshir'd me, after her own
Country Fashion, cheated me, and at last robb'd me, and ran
away from me.

From hence I went to Liverpool, and shipp'd over to Ireland.

I married two Wives there, and both of them prov'd unchaste;
so I ran away from them, and took Shipping for New York, in
America. I had the misfortune to Marry three more Wives in
several Plantations abroad, but never got one that I could stay
with, or that would stay with me; and now, I am come back,
and am going to venture again. Pray give me your Opinion,
not as to the lawfulness of Marrying now the eleventh Wife,
the former ten, *for ought I know* being all alive; but whether
you think there is *an honest Woman* left in the World, that a
poor Wretch may think it safe to venture on, *or no?*

Your Humble Servant,
Tom Manywife.

On Polygamy : a Satire.

A. J., April 10.—Mr. *Applebee*,—I told you in my last Letter
to you how I marry'd eleven Wives, who for ought I know
are all alive, as I am, at this present Writing, praised be God
therefore. And now, after having told you this Story, I hope
you know better than to ask me my Name; especially because,
being newly arrived in Town, I hear some of the worthy
Ladies have been inquiring after my Health, whether for good-
will or ill-will, whether to have me, or to have me hang'd,
that indeed I do not know, neither do I lay much stress upon
the Question.

But I write to you now to tell you that you need not make
a strange Thing of it, for coming lately into some good Company, where I told my own Story publickly,—only as in the
person of an absent Man,—I found the Ladies mightily pleas'd
with it; and one Lady said openly, she believed it would be
much better if it were allowed to be so every where. For, says
she, this unhappy confining One to One, Leaves the World
unmatch'd and unprovided for; and is in a great measure the
Reason why Women go off so ill, and such a vast many are
fain to live and die Maids, or do worse, from the Power of
meer natural Necessities. .

Then she run on to tell us, it was her Opinion that there
were abundance more Women in the World than Men, nay,
she said it was her Opinion it was always so from the Beginning; why else, said she, were Men allow'd plurality of Wives,
some to have Two or Three, some Ten or Twenty, as King

David, some a Thousand, as King *Solomon*, and the like? For, added she, if the Number of the Sex had been equal, then the rest of the Men would have wanted Wives, and a Thousand poor Jews must have died Batchelors, to have help'd King *Solomon* fill his Seraglio.

Then she descended to the Times, and she gave it as her Opinion, that in the present State of Things there were in this Nation abundance more Women than Men; and that, she said, made the Market go so hard against her Sex, and that it was impossible all the Women could be married, because there was not Men enough in the Nation for them.

I objected the Wars which had carried off so many thousands of the Men. She said that was no Reason at all, and that, if I would give myself the Trouble to inquire, I should find there were so many Women more than Men that sold themselves to go over to Virginia, and our other Plantations in America, that I should find it was equal to all the great numbers of Men who went away in the time of War; nay, she alledged that there was above 30,000 Wenches in a year carried away, by their own voluntary Consent, and that the most of them went away for want of Husbands.

After a long Discourse of this kind, I ask'd her what Remedy she could propose for this Mischief; she answer'd very readily, she knew a Remedy well enough, or else it would be imprudent to complain of the Mischief; that this was not incurable, if the Parliament would but take it into Consideration. And presently, as if she had taken me for a Member of Parliament, she explained herself, and told me, if the Parliament would but make a Law by which all the Men should be obliged to marry two Wives, that would effectually cure it.

I laugh'd at the Proposal you may suppose, but she went on with her Explanation for all that, and held me in a long Discourse about it, proving the Lawfulness of it,—but especially the Convenience of it; and in short, that there was no other Way to put a stop to the wickedness of the Age, and to prevent Lewdness, which was grown up to such an extravagant Height, as that there were few honest Women, she said, to be found.

I heard her out, but answer'd her coldly,—told her it was against the Protestant Principles, nay, against the Christian

Religion; and that, in short, she could never think such a Thing could be allow'd in such a Nation as this, where all our Laws were squar'd by the great Rules of Religion.

"Don't tell me of Religion," says she, "if some such Remedy be not applied, I do not see how the Reputation of our Sex can ever be preserv'd, or that much above half the Number of Women that are in this Kingdom will ever be married;" and with that she told me she was resolv'd, and knew of above 20 more Women of good Fashion that were resolv'd with her, they would go to the East Indies, and seek their Fortune. So she ended her Discourse in a kind of a Female Fury. Pray let us have your Opinion of her fine Proposal.   Yours, &c.

Description of a Quarrelsome Wife.

A. J., April 17.—Mr. *Applebee*,—I find you are applied to by the Ladies of late, upon the most material Subject which is at present the great Grievance of the Sex, I mean *a bad husband.* What good you do them, or how you come to be so much in their Favour I know not. I hope you will make a good Use of it.

But pray, as the Counsel say, when they are pleading Causes, pray your Worship to favour me a Word on the other Side. There may, indeed, be a great many bad Husbands, and I doubt there are so; but, pray Sir, are there none of those Creatures in the World call'd bad Wives? What, are the Men all Devils, and the Women all Angels? Pray leave Room for a few of our Stories too, for I have something to say as well as other People, and perhaps as much to the purpose too.

I am a marry'd Man, and 't please you; and if my Neighbours say true, none of the worst Husbands neither. I have done my endeavour to keep a quiet House; and, had it been possible, to have pleased my wife too. I have labour'd with the utmost diligence to provide for my Wife, and all about her, every Thing necessary and convenient, and have had so much Success too, that my Wife cannot say she has wanted anything, that she either would have, or should have; and yet after all I have done, or have been able to do, I cannot say that ever I yet had one quiet or one pleasant Hour with her for the last twenty Years, and we have been married now about two-and-twenty Years in all. But all her ways have been continual Discontent, Passion, Noise, and Uneasiness, and that for the most senseless Trifles imaginable, such as it would be ridiculous to mention.

Nor is this continual Unquietness such as a Man ought to slight and contemn, and so make himself easy let 'em say what they will; but the Devil has furnish'd her with such a hellish Art, that she will not go unanswer'd or unquarrell'd with. 'Tis as impossible to sit still and say nothing, as it is to say anything that can silence or satisfy her.

In a Word, Strife is her Element, and she cannot breathe out of it, or subsist without it; 'tis her daily Business to argue, contend, be spiteful, insolent, and abusive. The calmest Words beget contention, Words cannot be so put together as to please her, or when stirr'd to appease her; to slight and say nothing is not to be done, unless I could fly the House and be absent. If I am from her, she grows so uneasy that it's terrible to think of coming to her again; if I am with her, I am like a baited Bull, kept always in a Sweat; always upon my Defence, always fighting for my Life.

All this while she pretends to be a very good Wife, is mighty Religious, constant at her Prayers, very devout, very honest in her Person, modest in her Behaviour; in a Word, every Thing but quiet and peaceable. And what must a Man do; for, in short, she is an eternal Scold, and 'tis impossible to be quiet a Moment in her Company.

At length, I was so tir'd with her perpetual Unquietness, that I fell sick with mere vexation and uneasiness, entirely disappointed in the general felicity of human Nature,—I mean, my Peace and my very Blood being inflamed with being in a continual agitation; it threw me into a Fever, upon which, opening my Mind to some of my Friends, and to my Physician among the rest, they have unanimously given it as their Opinion that I ought not to live with her, and in Truth it admits but of very little debate, for to live with her would not be to live, but to die, and indeed would be a Kind of *Felo de se*, or Self Murther.

But to make out the point of Conscience, 'twas thought but just, that I should tell her the true Reason of it, and expostulate the Case with her, letting her Know, that if she did not think fit to alter her Conduct I must remove; but here re-

maiued a Difficulty (viz.) who should break it to her; as for
doing it myself I declared against that, for I knew that to
attempt it would throw me into a Fever again, and endanger
my Health, nay, I declared l dare not do it.   It went round
all my Friends, but none would adventure; at length by
unanimous Consent, it was resolved· that the Physician should
do it, or the Parson of the Parish, for both were present; they
contended long about it, so dreadful a Thing is a contentious
and angry Woman.   At last, importunity prevailed with the
Doctor to undertake it, and he performed it with a great deal
of Temper and Prudence.

But to hear what a Rage she flew out into, and how she
abused the poor Gentleman for being a Messenger of such
News, and, as she call'd it, my Counsellor in it; she denied the
Fact, declared that she was not sensible of the least Unquietness
or Unkindness in all her Life to me, that it was only an Abuse
upon her, and an Excuse in me to go away, leave my honest
Wife, and live with some other Woman, and that he, the
Doctor, was Confederate; and then she abused him again most
plentifully.

The Doctor,—a Gentleman that had abundance of good
Humour, and abundance of good Temper naturally, besides
being a Gentleman of Education and Manners,—gave the
hearing of all her passionate Eruption without any Manner of
Motion, only told her he was sorry he could not prevail upon
her to consider a little better of the Matter, and that he would
leave it to some Person that had more interest in her Respect;
and so, making his Leg, came away infinitely satisfied that he
was delivered. And coming back to me, said no more but this,
shaking his Head, " Alas! she is fit for nothing so well as
Mr. *Guy's* New Hospital; for she is certainly one of the *In-
curables.*" Upon this Attempt, and all Men agreeing that I had
no other Way, I am at last resolved to leave her, for the mere
preservation of my own Life, and have let her know it; but
that I might try all Means possible before I come to Extremities, I have publickly sent this to you, and if you know any
other Method, you may give your Opinion before 'tis too late.

Yours, &c.

On Divorce, and Mr. Milton's Arguments.

A. J., April 24.—Mr. Applebee,—I came lately out of *France*, where riding from *Blois* to *Orleans*, I had the pleasure of meeting the little Queen of *France*, that was to have been, going back to *Spain* again, to make room for the new Queen of France, that is to be, and I fancied there was a melancholy Air upon the Countenances of the whole Retinue that attended her, and that they were going on an Errand they were a little ashamed of; but the little Infanta, for so she is now to be called, was as bright and as cheerful as it is possible to suppose anything could be, that was not either perfectly pleased with, or perfectly ignorant of the Occasion of her Journey.

The last, we were told, was her Case; and that she neither did know anything, or was to know anything of what was her Condition, till she had been at Madrid some Months.

This way of Marrying and Unmarrying put me upon Reflecting on us poor *British* Mortals, who being once wed, are wed for Life; and can have no relief, against all inequalities either of Age, Temper, or Circumstances, let them be never so disagreeable to one another.

The famous Mr. *Milton* insisted upon it, that Disagreeableness of Tempers, when it once appeared to be irrecoverable, was sufficient to justify a Separation; and to leave either Party, or both Parties, at Liberty to try their Fortunes in another Venture. He gives strong arguments to prove the Justice and Reasonableness of his Opinion; I cannot say he brings any Scripture Arguments, or at least that he does them Justice.

But when we come to examine the Matter with more exactness, it seems, the Case was, that Mr. *Milton* had a cross Wife, or was himself a very cross Husband; and, in short, that he would very willingly have made a Separation, and have married another Wife. This indeed takes off a great deal from the Weight of his Reasonings; and he was so jested with, and bantered, and written against, that he, who was himself not the most patient Man alive, was put out of all Temper, and at last laid down the Dispute.

Well, be it as it will, Mr. *Milton's* Arguments go a great way with me; for, in short, if my Wife and I,—by mere agreeing upon Terms,—came together and married,—why may not my wife and I,—by the like mere agreeing upon Terms,—separate again ? For if mutual Consent be the Essence of the Contract of Matrimony, why should not the dissolving that mutual Consent dissolve likewise the Marriage, and disengage the Parties from one another again ?

But let this be my Opinion as much as it will, we find ourselves deceived in the Thing itself, for I fear we cannot alter a Case within itself; the Laws of our Country compel every Man to live with his own Wife, and what then must we do that have bad Wives?   *Miserere !*

But I have another Grievance, which afflicts me as much as all the rest.   We have here a constant Clamour against the ill Consequences of Matrimony, and the bad Husbands which make the Women all Miserable; but not a Word of the bad Wives, and the Misery of the Men who are plagued with them. Now, it is true, my Wife has a bad Husband,—a very bad one indeed,—there is no denying of it, nay (which is worse) there is no help for it, nor any likelihood of its ever being otherwise.

But then, Mr. *Applebee*, take it with you as you go,—my Wife too is a very bad Wife; pray tell me, how shall we do in this Case ?

A Story of an Exorbitant Lawyer.

A. J., May 1.—Mr. *Applebee*,—I think I have a Story to hansel your new Model'd Paper, which may be worth the Price that any Body shall give for the Journal.* A Friend of mine obliges me in giving the following Account of a Passage, which, as he assures me, happened very lately; and which I think well worth being made publick, for Caution to such as are in danger of falling into the Hands of the merciless Attorneys of the Age.

A certain Lady, (says my Friend,) being left a Widow, tho' with a good Estate, found it absolutely necessary, in order to get in the Arrears of Debts due to her Husband's Estate, to employ an Attorney to sue some of the Debtors, and to threaten others with Prosecution, in order to quicken the Payment; and she pitch'd upon a Man who had been long acquainted with the Family, and had been often employed also by her deceased Husband, and whom she, and her Husband also, thought, *as Lawyers go*, had been a very tolerable honest Man.

---

* *May* 1, 1725. Additional Stamps were imposed on all Journals.   Many were suppressed, and the survivors, including *Applebee's*, remodelled.—*Ed.*

He did her Business for her to her Satisfaction, only she thought his Bills were something Extravagant; however she always paid them without abatement, and gave him what he ask'd, till at length, hardened by her Easiness in paying former Bills, and having two or three Suits depending for her Ladyship, he staid a little longer than usual for the bringing in his Bill, till the Lady pressing him to give it to her, he at last, to her very great Surprize, gave her a Bill amounting to 317*l. Sterling.*

The Lady was exceedingly surprized at such a Sum, knowing very well he could have done nothing to make such a Demand reasonable, and spoke to him about it. The Attorney told her he had served her Ladyship a long Time, and she always found his Bills so reasonable, as to pay them without any Difficulty, and he wondered she could find so much fault in it now; insisting still upon his Demand of 317*l.*

The Lady, being yet dissatisfied, and considering well the Exorbitance, yet being willing to make an Amicable End, she came to this Resolution; she sent for the Lawyer, told him she thought his Bill very unreasonable, and that she would be willing to refer it to any indifferent Person he· could name; the Attorney affirmed his Bill was reasonable, and refused to refer it. Upon this the Lady told him that tho' she thought it was more than his due; yet for old Friendship, and on her late Husband's Account, who had a Respect for him, and withal for Quietness sake, she would pay him 200 Guineas if that would content him.

The Attorney at this flew out in a violent Passion,—told her he did not make Taylor's Bills, to have them cut off with a pair of Shears,—that he expected his Money, and did not think she would have used him so; that, in short, he would be paid, and if she did not think his Bill a fair and lawful Demand, she might go for her Remedy where she could find it, and the like; beseeching her not to give him the Trouble of her Objections, for that if she would not pay him he knew how to get his Money, and he would pay himself; and with this, flew out of her House in a Rage.

The Lady however, having gotten into better Hands, did not yield to his Motion, but making the best of her way towards *London,* came up to Town ; where her Case, being so very evident, she having got other Lawyers to advise her, her first Step

was to summon her old Friend the Attorney before a Judge;
after which,—whether it was that she followed her Cause so
well, or whether, really, the Merit of her Cause made her obtain Relief, in the ordinary Course, sooner than other People,—
she obtained an Order to have her Lawyer's Bill tax'd; which,—
though much against his Will, he was obliged to submit to,—
the Issue of which was, that, after having everything allowed
him that he had any just Pretence for, his Bill was reduced
from 317*l.*, or thereabouts, to 35*l.* 13*s.* 4*d.*

I would have concluded my Story with giving you an
Account how ashamed the Gentleman Attorney was, and how
he blushed, when he received a Reprimand in Court for abusing
his Client, and offering to impose, at such a Rate, upon a Lady
to whom he had been so much obliged; but I was mistaken in
the Man, and I find, that whether it belongs to the Profession,
or no, not to blush at any Thing, it certainly was a Part of his
best Qualification; for all the regret I hear he shewed, was,
that he had not taken her 200 Guineas, which the Lady offered
him, as you have heard.

I think you would do well to bless the World with this
Story, that it may direct some abused Clients in the Managing
their Country Attorneys, and bringing their Bills to a little
Moderation; a Thing they are at present not much acquainted
with.   **Your Humble Servant,**

HEN. ANTIFOGGER, Junior.

Against a Prevalent Factious Spirit.

A. J., May 8.—Mr. *Applebee,*—I have of late observ'd your
Paper taken up with the Miserable Complaints of the direful
Effects of Matrimony, and that alternately on both Sides; the
good Husbands complain of bad Wives; and the good Wives
complain of bad Husbands, and I have some Times thought, at
reading them over, that really it was ten to one whether the
Complainer was not the Agressor, and that the worse did not
complain of the better.

Indeed, sometimes the Stories were Tragical; and if true,
summon'd our Compassion. But then, after we had parted with
a sympathetick Sigh or two, in Commiseration of the Suffering
Lady, or oppressed Husband, we were shock'd presently with
a Suggestion, that perhaps there might be nothing in the

Story; like the old Woman that was set a Crying with hearing a Sermon on the Passion of our Saviour, but comforted
herself afterward, upon asking the Minister how long ago it
was, and how far off it was, that, *Grace a God*, she hop'd then
it might not be true, seeing it was so long ago, and such a
long Way off.

Upon the whole, Mr. *Applebee*, unless any of the like Things,
of very pressing Necessity to be published, intervene, I beg of
you to give Way to some more Important Affairs, of a different
Nature; and let you and I look a little into the Times, as
other People tell us they do. Tho', I confess, if we do it to no
better Purpose, I think we had as good let it alone, and sing
Ballads; and not do as *Job* says,—and as the Right Reverend
London Journal seems to have been doing a long Time,—I
mean, *Darkening Council by Words without Knowledge.*

Here's your Brother, *Mist*, he, at a Distance, flatters one
Party, with Hopes of now and then speaking a good Word for
them; tho' hitherto, *Sysiphus* like, they only roll up the Stone
to have it fall back upon them with a double Weight.

There the *Right Reverend*, being come from the Pulpit to
the Primer, like the Child at School, reads what Lesson the
old Woman points out with her Fescue, and calls everything
by what Name she bids him.   And so of the rest.

Here they tell us long Stories of the New Establishment of
City Privileges, *there* they make as loud Complaints of Corporation Tyranny, which by the way, *for ought I know*, is one
of our present National Sins, I mean in Politicks; and what
are they both doing? *The last*, to be sure, are talking nothing
to the Purpose, *for the Act is passed*, and *the First*, in my
Opinion, seems to be writing a Satyr upon the Parliament
that passed it, as not being Intelligible, not being Explicit, or
as if it had a *double Entendre*, and wanted the wiser Head of
the Learned B——p to tell the People the Meaning of it.

Now if the Law be passed on one Hand, what need anything to be said to perswade us not to like it? And if it be
wisely made, and intelligibly Worded on the other Hand, what
need of long Harangues to make us understand it? Either
those Harangues are a Satyr upon the Legislators, for not
making it Intelligible, or a Satyr upon the general Understanding of the Nation, that we cannot read plain Laws when

they are made, and intelligible English when it is printed.
Neither of which, (with submission to his Instructions, and to
the old Woman's Fescue,) are our Case.

We are now come to an Age very different from what our
Fathers lived in, if their Histories do not deceive us; when
they were oppressed by Factions and Parties; when they went
to Loggerheads, and hard Knocks, the Wits of the Day
employed their Pens not so much to justify the Honesty of
the Quarrel, as to encourage and hearten up their Champions,
whet the Swords, and furnish the Weapons.

But in our Day, if we have a Burthen tied fast upon our
Shoulders, supposing it to be really Just or Unjust, our Pen
and Ink Labourers are Employed, to shew us the Reasonableness of our bearing it; and submitting to lie down, *Issachar*
like, with the Pack upon our Back. Now certainly our present Teachers are Wiser and Honester than those of the last
Age; for whether are wiser, they that submit, or they who,
(when 'tis to no purpose especially) resist?

For my Part, if I may turn my Speech to my Fellow-
Citizens, I would have them to do as a certain Member of
Parliament in *Scotland* did, after the Union was past there,
much against his Will; a Noble Person, who was then and is
still a Malcontent, ask'd him, what he would do now the Act
was passed? "Do, my Lord," says he, "look on, and see
what will come on it." "Why," says the Nobleman, "will
you submit to it, sure you'll not do that?" "My Lord," says
the Gentleman, "I opposed it to my utmost in a legal Way,
but now 'tis made a Law, 'twould be illegal to oppose it; let
us see if they do not make an illegal Use of it; if they do, the
same Law that is now for them will be against them, and
what is Law now, being made a Grievance, we shall get it
repealed in the same legal Manner as they got it passed."

On Peace between Germany and Spain.

A. J., May 15.—Sir, Since my last to you another Incident
has happened to amuse the World, which gives our Speculators
some Business, and in which nevertheless their eminent Pene-
tration is greatly deficient; and this is, the sudden clapping up
a Peace between Spain and the Emperor. . . . .
. . . .

Every one that looks into Foreign Affairs with any Observation must know, that the French King, or to speak in the more polite modern Stile, the Court of France, have acted in a very particular Manner with the Court of Spain, in the late sending back the Infanta of Spain; who was, as the Spaniards say, fairly and honourably married to his most Christian Majesty, and, as I believe, had the Honours and Title of Queen paid her in France; how young soever, and unfit to understand those Things, her Majesty might be.

(He then goes on to say that this was a great Offence if not an Affront to the Spanish Nation. This in his opinion is the reason why the hasty Peace between Spain and Germany has been made, at the instance of Spain.)

Without the Ceremony of sending or returning one Courier, the whole Matter has been concluded at once, without the least Communication of it or of the Design of it, to the Court of France, at least that we know of; a Contempt which the French have no Room to resent.

Let me conclude this Letter with this Remark only; namely, How effectually does Time wear off the Strongest Resentments. Even National Animosities, the strongest of all other, yield at length to Time, and popular Reconciliations succeed, by the very Consequence of forgetting Quarrels. No two Nations have been at greater variance, for some Years, than the Imperialists and the Spaniards. Nor has any War been carried on with more personal Heat and Resentment than the late War between those Nations, as well in Spain as in Sicily; and yet, Time and some little Incidents concurring, has brought them not only to a Cessation of Hostilities, but even to a perpetual Amity. All the Rebels and Deserters are to be pardoned, the Exiles and Refugees return, Forfeited Estates restored, and Offenders received not to Mercy only, but to Favour. May the Example spread into all Christian Nations, and may it descend to all pardonable Offences; that all the jarring Interests may be reconciled, Justice mixt with Mercy take place, and Peace, with Truth, o'erspread the World!

On the Same.

A. J., May 22.— .... Now to look back a little; if a Man should have ventured to have

told the People at that Time, that within five or six Years of
the Peace then making, France and Spain should declare War
against one another; fight, kill, burn and destroy, as, in all
Wars, is the Case; and, that this Repulse should be made in
favour of the Emperor, and under an Alliance with England,
pray what do you think such a Man would have been thought
of? Would he not have been call'd Tory, and Jacobite, a
Friend to France, and an Enemy to King George?

(After similarly adverting to other unexpected changes between the three Nations referred to, and the failure of all the
prognostications of past speculation in our own Country, he
concludes :—)

Let such dogmatick Speculators then see, and be humble
under the view of their weak Politicks; and learn to know,
that those very Events which they then thought so improbable
are all come to pass, and others more unlikely may,—as we
may tell you in our next.

Trial of Jonathan Wild.

A. J., May 22.—On *Saturday* last *Jonathan Wild* was
try'd at the *Old Bailey,* upon the new Act for more effectual
Transportation of Felons, which makes it Felony without
Benefit of Clergy, to Receive and Return Stolen Goods, knowing them to be so, and not apprehending and prosecuting the
Felon, in which Case such Person shall be deemed to stand in
the Felon's place; and he was found Guilty. It was also
sworn that he set the Robbery; it being of a Box of 50*l.*
worth of Lace, from a *Lace-Woman* near *Holborn Bridge;* for
returning which, he received a Reward; but of that he was
acquitted. The Counsel for the King were Mr. Attorney
General, and Mr. *Whitaker;* and for the Prisoner, upon a
point of Law arising, Mr. Serjeant *Baines* and Mr. *Kettleby.*
We hear he was to have been try'd upon more Indictments;
but this being Capital, it was judged needless.

The Sessions concluded that Evening, and there received
Sentence of Death five Persons, viz. *Jonathan Wild, Robert
Harpham, John Plant, William Sterry, and Robert Sandford;*
the two last for Robberies on the Highway, and *Plant* for a
Street Robbery.

On the Great Influence of Public Journals.

A. J., May 29.—Sir, I have been often contemplating with a particular Satisfaction, the eminent Station we Journal Writers, and the Printers of Journals stand in, and what high Characters we bear in the World.

Our younger Brother *Mist* lately took Notice, very well too, how Posterity would observe the Usefulness of such eminent Men as we are; how we were made use of to raise the Publick Funds, and how even the Publick were assisted by us in their laudable endeavours for lessening the heavy Debts of the Nation.

But I think this is the least Part of our Fame, and we have a more just and lasting Character from the extraordinary Usefulness in our Generation, and the Opportunity we have of doing Good to our Fellow Creatures, and that, even to the greatest and most distinguished Persons, as well as to the Miserable and Distressed; and what can speak more in our Praise than to be thus Useful to Mankind. But let it be duly observed then, how Persons of all Ranks acknowledge our Beneficence, by many undoubted Testimonies, as well of their Want of us upon many Occasions, as of the Services we do them when we please to enter into their particular Cases, and set them forth with our particular Artifice to the World. How, by the irresistible Power of good Language the prejudices of the worst Enemies are removed, and the affections of Friends roused in favour of the Causes which we plead; for who can resist the force of sound, harmonious, well-placed Words?

"Song charms the Sense, but Eloquence the Soul."

Upon this Occasion likewise, the rate of our Reputation rises every Day; for this is an Age of Clamour, in which it is become fashionable for Men to vent their private Passions in Rage and Slander upon one another, without regard to Innocence, Honour, Virtue, or (that least of all human Considerations,) Religion; and, in a Word, to heap up, and publish, Scandal and Personal Reproach, is become a kind of Custom, and allowed upon a general sufferance in the World. The injured Complainer finds us, Mr. *Applebee*, I say us, to be the Refuge of his Innocence; hither he flies to do himself Justice upon the World, and we, like Men of true Honour, with Cheerfulness, (a light Fee concurring,) accept the Office of vindicating the Character of the oppress'd Sufferer; and we do it so effectually, that he who yesterday was dejected and oppressed by ill Language, and even run down by the Persecution of the Tongue, in one Week turns the Tables upon his Opposer, and washes himself, by our Art, as clean as with Salt and Nitre.

Even the great Actions of Heroes and Generals, who Serve for Fame, and Traverse the World for Glory, receive a double Lustre by the assistance of our Labour, which spreads their Characters, and expatiates upon their Exploits,—carrying the news of their Victories into every Corner, and enlarging on the Particulars—builds a Fame for them in the Minds of Thousands, who, but for us, would scarce hear of their Names; and records their great Undertakings in our more lasting Works, where they are read by those who could no other Way arrive at the knowledge of them.

How do the Statesmen secretly court our Favour! How many times have the Senators, in former Days I mean, (I will not venture to say it is now so,) sent us Copies of their fine Speeches, that the World may hear of them abroad, and some times hear more without Doors than was really said! Nay, how often have some, who would be thought Eloquent, talk'd in our Language, have come to us for fine Speeches, and then had them published again for their Own!

Nay, that we are very Considerable; and, that what we say makes deep Impressions on the present reading World, and is esteemed to be of weight with Posterity, is abundantly acknowledged by the furious Resentment which Men of Power, nay of the greatest Rank, are apt to shew, if they but feel themselves touch'd in any tender part of their Characters by our more eminent Hands. Even Kings have thought it not below them to shew their Displeasure, if but in any Manner attack'd in our Papers; and how severely some of our unhappy Fraternity have suffered on that Account, let Brother Mist tell you, who groans under the Hand of Justice to this Day.

On the other Hand,—How grateful has it been to the greatest Men, in all the latter Ages of our flourishing Circumstances, to have their Actions handsomely spoken of by us, and the Fame of their Conduct well set forth; or, to put it in

a modern Stile, to have us, the mighty, important Authors of
the Journals, do them Justice!

Some great Ones I have heard of, in former Times,—for as
for the present Age and Government they are above all such
Measures,—I say, I have heard of some who have given great
Rewards, nay, even Pensions and Stipends, to the Writers of
Journals, to set forth their Actions with the flourishes of Wit
and Eloquence; and to publish their otherwise languishing
Fame to the World.

So capable are we to Save or to Destroy a sinking Reputation, or a tottering Fame, and so considerable are we in our
Station in the World.

And since it is so, Mr. *Applebee*, and no Man can deny it,
I desire that for the future you will take due Care to maintain
the Dignity of our Office; and the Value the World will put
upon us by the same.

Execution of Jonathan Wild.

A. J., May 29.—On *Monday*, (24th) about the usual Time,
Jonathan Wild was executed at *Tyburn*.   Never was there
seen so prodigious a Concourse of People before, not even
upon the most popular Occasion of that Nature.   The famous
Jack Sheppard had a tolerable Number to attend his *Exit;* but
no more to be Compared to the present, than a Regiment to
an Army.   And, which is very remarkable, in all that innumerable Crowd, there was not one Pitying Eye to be seen, nor one
Compassionate Word to be heard; but, on the contrary, where-
ever he came, there was nothing but Hollooing and Huzzas, as
if it had been upon a Triumph.   Nay, so far had he incurred
the Resentment of the Populace, that they pelted him with
Stones, &c, in several Places, one of which, in *Holborn*, broke
his Head to that Degree that the Blood ran down plentifully;
which Barbarity, tho' as unjustifiable as unusual, yet may serve
to deter others from treading in his Steps, when they find the
Consequence so universally odious.   At the Place of Execution, the People continued very outrageous, so that it was impossible either for *Jonathan*, or any of the rest to be very
composed; however he behaved himself better than could be
well expected, considering the perpetual Insults, Peltings, &c.
that he suffered.   All the Indulgence he received was, his not

having his Hands tied all the Way; and at the Place of Exxcution he was admitted to sit in the Cart, till the Minister came, the others having been tied up a Considerable· Time. When he was turned off, there was a Universal Shout among the Spectators. As the Cart drew away, his Arms being loose, he happened to catch hold of the Coiner, but was immediately parted from him. His Body was carried off in a Coach and four to the Sign of the *Adam and Eve*, near *Pancras* Church, in order to be interred in the Church yard there; where one of his former Wives lies buried, which was done on Tuesday Night last. About two of the Clock in the Morning he had taken a Dose of Liquid *Laudanum*, in order to have dispatched himself; but swallowing too much, it proved too strong for his Stomach and came up again; however it seemed to have a stupifying Effect upon him. So desirous he was to avoid the Execution of one Sentence, tho' with the utmost Hazard of suffering another unspeakably more dreadful. At the same Time and Place were executed *Robert Harpham*, for High Treason, in Counterfeiting the current Coin of this Kingdom; and *William Sterry* and *Robert Sandford* for the Highway.

Against the Reproach of MERCENARY *applied to Public Writers.*

A. J., June 5.—Sir, Detraction is one of the missive Weapons which Envy throws at the most consummate Virtue in the World; and they who, envying the Reputation and Honour of the truly Great, would do anything to blacken their Character, while at the same Time they confess their Merit, generally do it by this particular Method; namely, to lessen the Value of their great Actions, and thereby to lessen their Fame.—" *Ay, ay," said the Pharisees, " 'tis true he does do such Things as those, but how? He casts out Devils, 'tis true, but he deals with the Devil to do it, he casts out Devils by Beelzebub the Prince of Devils;"* and the like; and thus they would, by Detraction, have lessened the Value of the great Works which our Saviour did to the astonishment of the Jews.

Thus, to illustrate small Things by great, they who envy the just Fame, of our Brethren the Journal Writers, and the Printers of Fame, who are concerned with them, attempt us by Detraction; tell us we Write, and we Serve, and we plead the Causes that are brought to us, for Money, that we are Mercenary, that we do all for Bread.

Now as our Blessed Saviour asked the Jews,—" *If I by Beelzebub do cast out Devils, by whom do your Sons cast them out?*" So we, with all humble deference to the Comparison, say, if we for Money, and for Bread, plead the Causes that come before us, and give Characters of great Men, applaud their Actions, erect Monuments for the Dead, and give Compliments to the Living; pray, by what Spirit, and for what Consideration, do all your great Men Act?

The Jews could make little or no Answer to the close Question our Lord asked them, and as little to the purpose can those Men of Envy say to us, when we ask them, thus,—If we for Bread, that is to say, for Money, write Journals, and print and publish them, in order to possess the World with the Knowledge and Fame of great Actions and great Men; for what, and why, and upon what Foundations do you all Act in the World? And, what other Principle is at this Time to be found among Men?

For what do your Ministers preach, your Lawyers plead? On what Account do your Physicians heal,—your Surgeons restore dislocated and mangled Nature,—your rich Men trade,— your poor Men labour,—and the meaner Sort beg? What fills the Royal Exchange with Merchants,—the Sea with Ships,— Streets with Throngs,—and those Throngs with Thieves? To carry it yet higher,—For what do the Soldiers fight,—the Generals lead,—the Ministers of State manage,—and even their Masters govern?

Does not the whole World swim down the same Stream? Are they not all employed the same Way, and all act from the same End, or Worse? Where is the Man does Good for the mere sake of doing Good? And, not to slander the Devil, he does not do Mischief for the mere sake of the Mischief! If we then, Mr. Applebee, who are capable of both doing good and hurt, by the extensive Power of our present Office as Journal-Writers, act from the common ordinary Principles of Mankind, viz. for Money; how much more do we Merit of the World than the rest of our Fellow-creatures can do, in that we do honourable and just Things for Money, whereas the other People I have mentioned corrupting both their Labours, and the End and Design of those who pay them, receive the Pay, and deceive their Masters?

How do the Clergy,—who are paid for performing Acts of Religion and Devotion, and for instructing us in the Way to Heaven,—sometimes take our Money, and cursedly inverting the End for which they receive it, broach Error, wrest Scripture, set up Factions, and form Schisms in the Church, confounding Doctrine and Ceremony, Morality and Discipline, and dividing, instead of preserving the Unity of the Faith, carrying up Religious Breaches, under pretence of a warmth for Truth, to a Religious Frenzy?

> " And make Men fight like mad or drunk,
> For Dame Religion as for Punk."   Hudib. lib. i.

How do the Judges pervert Justice, the Masters of Consciences take Bribes, Courtiers sell Places, and Governors of Garrisons sell Towns? Nay, in a Word, have we not heard of Kings that have sold their People, and People that have sold their Kings; and to sum up all, we have heard of some that have sold their Selves, and others that have bought the Devil.

But we do Justice for Money, that is, we do Right, and take our Fees,—our poor Three Halfpence,—and if it shall be called Bribery, we know who gets a Halfpenny, so that we are in good Company there too.

No, no! Mr. Applebee, if we do well and are paid for it, we Act the honest Part, and do our Duty; the Service for the Wages, and who acts better in the World? We have no corrupt Views, no bad Cause to wash Clean, no Harburgh Lottery Cheat to vindicate, or Charitable Corporation Fraud to recommend. We have no South Sea Company upon our Hands, of which 'tis hard to say, whether the lifting it up, or the pulling it down was the greater fraud; no Directors to Examine, of whom 'tis hard to say, whether the Things they did, or the Things they suffered, were the more Unjust. But our Reputation is Established upon doing much Good for little Reward. Let the best of you all shew us a better Character if you can.

Your Servant,   Epidemicus.

A. J., June 5.—Yesterday was 7 Night the Body of *Jonathan Wild*, that was buried in *Pancras Church Yard*, was dug up from the grave and carried off, three or four Days after Interment. The

Coffin was afterwards found near *Kentish* Town. Enquiry is made for the Persons concerned in that inhuman Action, which is Felony by the Law.

An Essay on Fools.

A. J., June 12.—Sir, There is a strange, pressing, importuning Something in the Nature of Man, which ever pushes him on, in the Search after something Strange and Surprizing; if he can but find out something New, and which the World has not heard of before, that he may say he is at the first of it, he is pleased, were the Discovery no more than a new Snailshell, a new Butterfly, a new Species of Frogs or Toads, or of any Thing, however mean and contemptible.

But I wonder much, that notwithstanding this Curiosity, we do not find them equally diverted with the various new Species and Kinds of Fools which the Age supplies us with; and yet, we find the Times are very fruitful in that kind of Production too. Wherefore I think we cannot do Mankind a greater Piece of Service, than now and then to enlarge upon the wonderful Productions of this kind which have assisted to make the present Age particularly Remarkable, more than all that went before it; and which might, in the due Improvement of New Discoveries, serve to Instruct us, as much as any New Butterfly, or new Insect, which had never been seen before.

We have had Fools of various and sundry Sorts in this Nation, who have made their Appearance at various and sundry Times, and in various and sundry Places; some remarkable for one Thing, and some for another, some shewing in one Shape, some in another, and from all of them something might be learned by those who would not be Fools themselves. But of all the Sorts of Fools the World has been troubled with of late, I think the Wise Fools have disturbed the World most; and more than ever, within the compass of a few Years past. It would have been no small Undertaking, had some learned Author, or Society of Authors, taken up some of their spare Hours, in letting us see farther into the wonderful Follies of the Wise Men, the Wits and Sages of the Age.

Certainly a Satyr upon the Universal Folly of the Wise, would have been much more Entertaining than that weak Thing, lately talked of, upon the " Universal Passion,"—but every Fool will be meddling.

I have been thinking sometimes to propose an Order of Knighthood among such People, in order to preserve the Honour of the Fraternity; and were it not that a revived Knighthood is just now upon the Stage, against which I have not a Word to say, I should perhaps enlarge upon my Proposal.

But I had a Difficulty too about the Titles I should bestow in Case of a Knighthood of Fools, and which I cannot well get over, namely, what Appendice of Honour to give to such a Degree, for the addition of Sir is so stale, and so, in common, annexed to the most ordinary Knights. Nay, and so many Fools are already Sirs, and so many Sirs already Fools, that I gave over that Thought.

To talk of the Fools of this Age would be a tedious tho' indeed a useful Undertaking, and I may hereafter lead you farther into it than you can expect me now; but as it is, let me tell you for the present, we have a great shew of such People about us at this Time, particularly methinks the Humour of the People seems to be running much into this Part of wise Folly, viz. Condemning a thing by Law, and then running into the Practice of it again, in a kind of condemning the Law by which it was forbidden, and we see Examples of this in the publick Practice, every Day.

How have we run up in our aversion to Bubbling, to an Extravagance equally mischievous to the Bubbles themselves! Run upon, and ruined abundance of Gentlemen only because they stood unhappily in the way of the Torrent, and at the same Time, or within a little, tolerated some of the most tricking and bare-faced, raise-Water, kill-Fire Bubbles, that ever were talk'd of.

And even to this Time Bubbles go in Masquerade, and the still, noiseless Way of Tricking and Bubbling, goes on as much as ever.

The Exchange seems to be made thus, that the Method being damned by Law, makes the Practice full of Fineness and *Leger-de-Main*; but the Game, and the Humour of Gaming, runs as high as ever, and Men are raised and ruined, made hastily rich, and hastily beggared, as much as before, only the Fools are Wiser Fools than ever.

I think the Knavery of this Age lies as much in concealing

their Honesty, as in betraying their Craft; and though we make more Noise now in sometimes discovering a particular Man to be Tardy, yet there is so much Cheat covered in discovering Cheats, that I know not which is worse, the Knave exposed, or the Knaves exposing.

What a Stir has been made here, when one great Man has been found guilty of Bribery, as if there was not ten Thousand great Men, who own themselves corrupt in the very Noise they make against Corruption! For my Part I hate all discovered Roguery; but if I can cheat you, and rob you, and take Bribes of you, and deceive you in a thousand Ways, without your Believing I do so, and then bring you not to believe it, tho' you see it, I think I am as Honest as any of you, and something Wiser into the Bargain.

So your Servant, Mr. Applebee,
Antho' Hubble Bubble.

On Fools, Continued.   Criticism on Dr. Young.

A. J., June 19.—Sir, I hinted something in my last to you of the solid Usefulness of Fools in general; I hope you will not take Notice how near that Subject came, after my having treated so solemnly of the great Value of Us,—Writers of Journals, in the present Age, lest they should Rate us with the Fraternity.

However, should our over-witty Gentlemen take us at such an Advantage, I hope they will consider that an ill-natured Question might follow; namely, If we that write are ranked among the Fools, of what Class must our Readers be denominated, who borrow from our Wit, and pay their Money into the Bargain?

The Truth is, the reading Vice of this Age seems to be rated among the Incorrigible; how would it be possible else, that so many Scribbling Doctors should not have cured them of that Itch before now? How many memorable Histories of John Sheppard, and of Jonathan Wild, have we extant at this Time, laid up in the Archives of every Corporation, and bound up in the Learned Collections and Libraries of the Reading Gentry? While such valuable Things as these are treasured up, sure the Wisdom of the Day can never be called in Question, or Fools of any kind be complained of!

Who then need be afraid to write, while every Thing that can be written will be read? In short, writing Nonsense, dull Satyr, low-prized Praise, and the like, is now so common, that 'tis the UNIVERSAL PASSION, and makes the Subject, which has so lately been so dully handled, be the very figure of its Author. Strange, that a Man that writes once tolerable, a second Time scarce tolerable, should not be able to see, that a third would be intolerable; and yet, be so blind as to harras the World with a fourth, more Monstrous than all the rest.

Let us then write without Fear, for as the Age goes, the worse the Subject, the more the Admirers, like Things made rare by their Deformity; the worse the Performance, the more the Readers, and the Rate of the Work rises, as the Merit of it decays. Hence, some valuable Things have not met with Success after the Rate of others of a meaner kind; as Mr. Milton said, when they told him his Poem of Paradise Regained did not please the People so well as that of Paradise Lost. " No," says he, " that is because they have not so strong a Sense of the Joys of Heaven, as they have of the Torments of Hell; so they taste nothing of the Pleasure on one Side, like what they do of the Fright on the Other."

I remember, in the hurry of our late South Sea Stock, the Loss made infinitely more Clamour than the Gain. Men stood silently admiring at the last, treasured up what they got and said no more; but they made a horrid Noise when the Tide turned, and they lost their Money. While they got Money in an extraordinary Manner, they smiled upon every Body, and the Directors were the most wonderful People on Earth; but when they came to fall, and the Loss fell heavy, then they vented their Spleen at the very Men they admired before.

Thus, when the Bells ring in a Town, Men look pleased, and say to one another, " You are mighty merry here, who is Married pray ?" and the like; but let the same Bells but ring backwards, fright and horror sits upon every Face; " Lord," says one, " there's a Fire somewhere! Where is it? Where is it? Oh! there 'tis, Fire! Fire!" and out they run into the Street like Men frighted out of their Wits.

Upon the whole, the Taste of the Age being thus degenerated, we that write must turn our Pen, and write to please the Times; that is, in short, we must endeavour to please Fools,

as well as Wits, and I must tell you, the former are sometimes
the more difficult of the two.

In order however to make the Attempt, let me observe, that
the first way to please Fools is to perswade them that they are
very Wise.   Immediately you set them to admire themselves,
and after that the grossest Things in the World will go down
with them; for what may not such a Wretch admire, after
once he is thoroughly possessed you believe him Wise?

We have an eminent Instance of this lately near the Town,
of a Gentleman of Figure, whom his Neighbours would perswade
to believe that he understood Physick; and, that he was a Man
of such good Judgment, that they needed no other Doctor in
the Town, but that all the poor People should come to ask his
Advice when they were ill. This being carried up to a suitable
Height operated immediately upon his Fancy; for the Gentleman himself falling very ill, ordered himself to have a Vein
opened, and would be let Blood to the tune of 120 Ounces, by
which he opened a Door for himself into the next World; but
his better Fate interposing in the very Moment, clapt it to
again for a little while, so that the new Doctor is not dead
yet.   Whether, if he lives, he will be a little wiser, Time only
must discover.

Thus, if my Lady is but once perswaded she is handsome
enough to be admired, why should we call it absurd in her to
think that every Body was in Love with her? And why
should we question whether she will run mad or not upon the
Occasion?   Do but then perswade the World that they are
good Judges of Sense and Wit; and you need not fear pleasing them, write or print what you please.   And upon this
Foot I shall make an Essay at a General Benediction in my
next.

Your Humble Servant,
MODERN.

On the Fallibility of Human Judgment.

A. J., June 26.—Sir, It was a saying of a truly great and
eminent Philosopher,—That a Wise Man never does anything
to repent of.   It is true, that the Thing called Repentance was
not understood as it is now among Christians, that is to say,
that the best Man in the World, and the Wisest Man in the

World, stands in need of Repentance; but they spoke of it then, as Actions among Men respected one another, and I speak of it now under the same Consideration; and so I may truly say still, a Wise Man does nothing to repent of.

But where then, and among what Societies must we look for this wise Man? And what will become of an old English Proverb which is too Significant to be lost,—"That the Fool peeps out of every Body sometimes?" The Practice of the wisest Men I meet with, (our Governors excepted, for we must take the City Proverb along with us too, and always add, except my Lord Mayor,) I say, except as before excepted, the Practice of the wisest Men that I have met with, consents to and confirms it; that there is a Mixture of the Fool among the best concerted Part of their Conduct; and scarce a Man lives, without doing or saying something, every Day, that the next Day he wishes he had not done or said.

Whether this Difference, between our Wise Men and those who were called so in former Times, happens from the Overplus of our Sense of Things, or the want of it, I think is easy to determine; and judge which you will, it will at least Appear, that the Sages of our Times act with the least Deliberation of the two.

How many Sentences and Censures even of the greatest Bodies have we seen revoked? Laws repealed, others amended; Clauses explained, even by Bodies of Men who would have taken it as a high Affront, and perhaps have Resented it powerfully, to have been told, while they were passing those Censures, that they would themselves revoke them in time to come! Have we not seen one Sanhedrim repeal what another has decreed; one Age condemn what the past Age, every Jot as wise as themselves, transacted? One Council order directly contrary to what another, nay, sometimes to what themselves had ordered before?

Nay, to look abroad, do we not see even the Roman Councils, who demand to be reverenced as Inspired, and who say they are led by the Holy Ghost; I say, do we not see them, at every Meeting, repairing the defects and decays of the Infallible Decrees of those that went before them? And notwithstanding all their Pretensions to the guidance of an unerring Spirit, the wisest and most learned of their Doctors frequently dispute the Usefulness and Necessity, nay, and even the Justice of their Canons; and if they do not carry on those Disputes to a Negative, 'tis owing merely to a blind Subjection to the Power and Authority of the said Councils, rather than a Conviction of the Truth and Soundness of their Canons and Decrees. Hence we see, in the famous Council of Trent, some of the Bishops, nay even of the Cardinals, who sat there arguing strenuously for some Things which Nature and Religion demanded, and which several of the most Powerful Princes of Europe desired at that Time; as particularly that of admitting the Cup to the Laity, the allowing the Priests to Marry, and crushing Pluralities, and enjoining Residence to the Bishops; but being over-ruled, they submitted their Consciences to the Number of Voices, and joined with the Multitude to do Evil.

Even in Judicial Affairs,—where Men are supposed to act with the greatest Deliberation, and with the utmost power of Human Prudence,—how are Sentences passed, and even Punishment inflicted upon Innocent Persons, and Men frail and subject to Mistakes themselves, suffer themselves to be influenced, or awed, by the powerful Motions of other Men's Passions, and sometimes of their Own; and how have the future Judicatures recognized the Innocence of the Persons so Condemned.

Nay, we have seen the same Actions of Men adjudged to be Treason in one Age, which have been called Patriotism in the next; and the Sufferers be esteemed Criminals to-Day, and Martyrs for their Country's Liberties to-Morrow. The Heads and Quarters of Men executed as Traytors in one Reign, and exposed on the Principal Gates of the Cities and Towns, for the Terror of others, have in the next, been taken down and buried with Veneration, and Magnificent Monuments been raised over them, to preserve their Memory to Posterity.

We see Men dignified with New Honours in one Reign, and the very same Men,—nay, those pretended Honours themselves,—trampled under Foot and made Contemptible in another; so that, in short, instead of being Infallible, in Council or in Action, we see all the Actions of Men exposed, every Day, to their own better Judgment, to be altered, corrected, rescinded, and sometimes Condemned.

Where then shall we fix the Standard of human Wisdom?

And where is the Wise Man who, (even with respect to Man,) does nothing to repent of, or to be ashamed of? We shall search for him further in our Next.

A Plea for Charity to Destitute Labourers.

A. J., July 3.—Sir, Without all Question, Charity is not only one of the principal Graces, but the Glory of a Christian Life, and it extends to abundance of generous Things, perhaps more than we imagine it does; and, to come directly to the Point, the Relief of the Poor is one of the main Branches of a Christian's Charity. 'Tis also an Act of Beneficence, which human Nature dictates to Men of Fortune, as the Consequence of their own happy Circumstances; and therefore, as no Man can be more willing than I am to prompt this noble Principle in the Minds of all the Readers of this Paper, so I will not fail on due Occasions, to excite you to Acts of Charity by all the proper Motives, as well of Religion as of Humanity. And this, I say, lest any carping, narrow-minded Animals should take Occasion from those due Cautions, which I shall mention for regulating of Charity; to suppose it needless, and that they may withold their Hands from the Poor.

And first, I must tell my Charitable Friends, that the Poverty of this Nation does not lie chiefly among the noisy, clamouring Poor; such as knock at your Doors, run after you in the Streets, and follow you with their never-to-be-answered Importunities, not only to your Houses, but even into your Houses. These call equally for your Correction, as well as your Relief; and indeed, stand in need more of the first than the last.

The present time of Distress, by the long continued Rains, and the threatening Clouds which still hang about us, gives us a very clear Instance of this. The poor Labouring People who come up yearly to the Southern Parts of England for the Haymaking, that is to say, for Harvest Work of all kinds; I say, they come up hither in great Numbers. If you will believe common Fame, there are not less than thirty Thousand, who every Spring remove from their Huts and Cottages in the Northern and Western Parts of England, and come this Way to seek Work; and let them be as poor and despicable as you please in your Eyes, they are as Necessary to us, as any People can be; nor could these Southern Counties of Hertford, Cambridge, Essex, Middlesex, Bucks, Surrey, Sussex and Kent, be able to get in their Hay, Corn, Hops, Cherries, &c., without their Help, except they gave exorbitant Wages, such as they are not able to afford.

These People come up to Labour, and often Times get and Save little Sums of Money sufficient to carry them Home, and help them to live Comfortably in their little Cottages thro' the Winter, and many of them get good Settlements and Services here, and never go Home at all.

But this Year has distressed them to a very great Degree, and they have, in some Places, suffered the very Extremity of Hunger and Want; as well as Sickness and other Distresses, from the want of Lodging and Shifting, being continually in their wet Clothes, lying on the Ground, and the like.

This has brought them to beg, and to be really Objects of uncommon Charity; and some of them that cannot beg and cry at your Doors, have perished, and do daily; and Others in desperation destroy themselves, as some sad Examples have shewn us.

What can I say more to excite the Charity of Christians? And to move you to be kind and open-hearted to them at such a Time, when it is evident that Misery is fallen upon them merely by the visible Hand of Providence, the inclemency of the Season, and the exceeding Rains; when their Work in the Field is taken from them, which indeed cuts off the Bread from their Mouths.

At the same Time, I ought also to acknowledge,—to the Honour of the Gentlemen of the Out Parts and Villages, where those People are more particularly found,—that they have and do generously, and in an extraordinary Manner, relieve the Haymakers; giving them Bread, and Meat, and Broth, and Money, and in a constant kind of a Stream of Charity daily, some one Day, some another. And this, not in one Place only, but many, and by Gentlemen whom I could name; but they neither seek the Occasion, nor Court the Praise.

But at the End of all this, it were to be wished some few Regulations might reach your Charity, and that Things might be brought to some such Order, as that this Charity might not be made a Grievance; and that Care be taken by relieving them now,—in this extraordinary Exigence,—you do not Incorporate them into the Trade of begging for good and all. And this obliges me to observe,—

I. That the fame of the Bounty,—as well of the Gentlemen above, as the Citizens at the Exchange, and in the Streets,—has listed all your common Beggars, Mumpers, and Street Runners, into the Army of Haymakers; and, armed with Fork and Rake, away they March every Day to the Exchange, and to the Churches, and to all Public Places. And, as they devour your Charity, so they rob the real Haymakers, in such a Manner, that few, compared to them, of the true Haymakers, will in a little Time be to be found among them; nay already you find it hard to distinguish or know them from one another.

II. The Haymakers themselves, Encouraged by the extraordinary Bounty of the People in the City, run all away thither to beg; so that, if a little Interval of fair Weather shines out between the Showers, and there happens to be a fair Day, the poor Farmers, who have entertained and relieved them too, as far as their Ability will allow, cannot get a Hand to help them, whatever Advantage it might be to them, but they are all run away a Begging.

This is indeed so much a Grievance, that if not Rectified will make your Charity hurtful rather than helpful, and yet I would be very lothe to be an Instrument to lessen the Charitable Disposition of the Citizens to the Poor; but for the present, one single direction may be of Value, namely, never to Relieve a Haymaker on a fair Sunshining, or Windy, dry Day, for then 'tis certain they may have Work, and that Farmers want them. Then, if they beg, they both injure their Employers and abuse your Charity.

Besides, by this Method the Citizens will distinguish between the common Mumpers and the true Haymakers; for the first will beg as much in fair Weather as in foul, pretending they are Sick, or Lame, or some such like, whereas the true Haymaker will be gone earnestly to his Work, as an honest Man ought to do.

This one Caution will go a great Way to direct your Charity. I shall say some other Things when the present Exigence is over, which may serve against another Occasion; and which I am lothe to enter upon now, lest I should damp the general

Charity to the truly indigent Haymakers, which I would not do by any Means.   Your Humble Servant,

                                                    THE FARMER.

Against Astrological Predictions of Famine and Pestilence.

A. J., July 10.—Sir, You are not ignorant that the present Year, so far as it has now run, has been divided, so the Great Director of Nature saw.fit, into two almost equal Parts, I mean as to the Seasons, (viz.) three Months severe and constant Drought, and the other three months almost continued, and in some Places extreme Rains.

I make no Question that our Barometer Men have valued themselves upon their frequent Predictions of these unseasonable Extremes, from the conjunction of Planets, and the Aspects of the Heavens; and 'tis fit they should have, now and then, a seeming concurrence of the Effects,—whether at all owing to those Causes or no,—that the gainful Science of Scoth-saying and Gipsy-making, may not be lost in the World, in which direful Case, our Chimney Corners would be quite barren, Mother Shipton be worn threadbare, and the old Women be quite exhausted of their important Stock of Tales, to initiate the young, and to support the gossiping Manufacture in the Kingdom.

But, as we have a great Veneration for the Ass-trologers of the Age, and would by no Means have their Ware sink in its Price, or in the Market; so we cannot but, on the other Hand, oppose that ill Natured Spirit of false Prophecy, which runs thro' the Veins of the whole phlegmatick Part of the Nation, and which, upon every such little intemperance of the Seasons, is always filling our Heads with terrible affrighting Notions and Predictions, of Famine and Want on the one Hand, and Plague and Pestilence on the other; which, at the same Time they have neither Warrant for from Heaven, nor probability of from the Earth, and I cannot think one of your Papers will be misspent in laying open their Criminal Delusion, and making the World easy upon this Account.

In order to do this, I desire you a little to expose these chimerical Terrors which such People spread among us, by Stating the Case in a few plain Words; letting the World know how far we are from such real Dangers, and how far we ought to be from the Apprehensions and Frights which those People would have us entertain about them.

The Truth is, the greatest Plague we have in view is that of Luxury; and the greatest Famine that of Honesty. We have a Scarcity of Morals, and a Fever of Pride, raging among us with great Violence; and what Extremes they may run us into I know not. But as to Famine and Pestilence, Heaven has so far Confounded those Rumours already that we have;—

I. The most hopeful prospect of a prodigious Plenty, both of Corn for our Bread, and of Grass for our Cattle, that has been known in the Memory of Man; and the small damage suffered by the late Rains is not worth naming in proportion to the rest.

II. The Bills of Mortality were never lower, or the People healthier, at this time of the Year, in the Memory of the oldest Man living.

What then is it that our vapourish People would have? And why must the whole Nation be frighted, because they see double, and are over-run with the Hippo?

It is true, that by the late Rains, a great deal of Grass and Hay has been damnified, and in low Grounds some Corn; but it has pleased God to send fair Weather so timely and so seasonably, that the Damage is abundantly repaired in the goodness of the rest. And let our Melancholy People take their Horses, or their Coaches if they please, for I hear some, that are not without these Equipages, are foolish enough to talk thus; and let them go a Day's Journey into the Country, no matter which Way, East, West, North, or South, for they will find it much the same every Way,—and I can assure them they will see the greatest prospect of Plenty, and of the finest Harvest both of Grass and Corn that has been seen upon the Ground these half hundred Years; and, that the Damage pretended to be done by the Rain is hardly to be discerned. Nay, even where the early Hay, near London, did receive some Damage, even there, the Farmers are abundantly recompensed in their after Pastures; so that every where, unless Heaven still punish us for our Murmuring and Unthankfulness, we have the greatest view imaginable of Plenty, and a good Season.

Nor is this all, but I desire the unthankful Generation I am speaking of, to look abroad, and there they will see that England is like to have all this Plenty at the same Time that our

Neighbours, especially in France and Spain, are under the greatest Consternation imaginable from the evident Destruction of their Harvest, and of the Hopes of it, by much greater Rains and Floods than have been here; and, which is still worse, by violent Storms and Tempests of Hail, Lightning, and Rain, which have laid the Corn flat on the Ground, destroyed the Vines, and almost all the Fruits of the Earth. So that our Plenty being like to be their Supply, will necessarily transpose their Money into our Country, to our great Encrease and Advantage.

I shall in my next tell you, that our pretended Fears, and Prophecies of Famine and Scarcity, are so groundless, that had we not such a view of a plentiful Harvest as we have, and were there no Seas open, to bring Supplies from Abroad; nay, were there not to be a grain of Corn of any kind grow in the Nation, or be brought into it, for two Years to come, yet we could not have a Famine in this Kingdom, except it be a Famine of Unnecessaries and Superfluities; and this I shall demonstrate beyond any possibility of a just Objection.

On the Fears of a Famine.

A. J., July 17.—Sir, The unseasonable Weather seeming to return, and more Rains and Cold to come on, I find our phlegmaticks too return pretty much upon us, and our propheciers of evil Tidings threaten us again with Famine and Pestilence, and I know not what dreadful Things; the most of which that they can have reason yet to say is, that it is true God can send it, and it is possible such a Thing may happen, and that therefore it will happen, which I think is no Consequence at all.

It is but a few Days ago that one of these foreboding Prophets was at it, thus :—

1. Says he,—for the old Woman, you must know, was a Male, and yet an old Woman too ;—" first," says he, " God can send a Famine, that I hope you will grant." " Yes, yes, Sir," says I, " God can do many Things which we hope and have good reason to believe he won't do. So pray go on !"

2. Adds he, " If those terrible Rains continue we shall have no Harvest.

3. " To make it out completely, if no Harvest, no Corn ; if

no Corn, the Poor must be starved; and that's a Famine, is it not?" and so he thought he had cleuch'd it.

"Well, but," says he, "to make it completely out, you will say we may make Shift in England to live without Bread for a while; but if the wet Weather holds, all the Hay will be spoiled, and the Sheep will rot, so that we shall have neither Mutton nor Beef, then we shall be in a terrible Condition I am sure, won't that be a Famine pray?"

Now, tho' blessed be God, neither of these Cases is likely to happen, and that the Hay in many Counties is secured already, and in others is not in danger of being spoil'd; nor is the Harvest yet lost, or, we hope, in Danger of it.

Yet, because these old Women-Men come with their Supposes, if the Rain holds, and if we have no Harvest, and the like, that then we shall have a Famine, I desire to take them at the utmost extent of their unreasonable Suppositions; and I affirm still, that first as to Bread; If the worst Weather they can imagine should happen; if we have no Corn, which God forbid, I say, no Corn, no, not at all, for the next whole Year; nay, I believe I might say for two Year, yet we have such Stores of all kinds in hand, and such Means to lengthen those Stores out, that we could have no Famine.

(He then proceeds to explain how Famine may be avoided, and the Plan would doubtless surprise and amuse the Economists of the present Age, but would not be otherwise interesting. He concludes that this would not be an absolute Famine, and adds, for the comparative comfort of his readers :—)

Even let us but look, at this very Time, over into France; if I am not misinformed, and I believe I am not, Bread is at this Time in Paris, and other Places in France, at sixpence per Pound, and flesh Meat at ten Pence per Pound. I dare say the People there are well content to eat brown Bread, and so should we too, if it were at such a Price here. But at present I see nothing like it, for our Beggars eat as white Bread as the best of us, and the coarsest Bread, which is ordinarily sold at our Bakers' Shops, is what we call Household Bread; and at this Time is, with all our Fear of Want, not yet sold at above five Farthings a Pound, nor if the Government please to order Things, as may be done, need the Price be much higher, let the Harvest be how God pleases to order it. For it is not

Scarcity here that makes Corn dear, but the Knavery and Folly of our People, raising the Price of Corn by the mere Clamour and Noise of Scarcity, a great while before it comes.

Essay on Suicide.

A. J., July 24.—Sir, I have observed, and not without some horror I assure you, in the Weekly Bills, for some Months past, two very melancholy Articles of Self Murther; a Thing which tho' we have always had some of, and that more than any Nation in the World, yet never I think so many in so little Time as just now.

If I do not reckon amiss, I can give you an Account of no less than six and twenty, poor, unhappy, demented Creatures, who have been their own Executioners in London, and within fifty Miles of it, within the space of seven Weeks past.

Of those, six or seven have destroyed themselves, for I call it no less, by excessive Drinking of Geneva; or, if you please to take it in the Drunkard's Cant, Royal Gin.

I shall not take up your Paper, or your Readers' Time, with enquiring into the Manner how, or the Causes why, those poor Creatures thus laid violent Hands upon themselves; the Histories of the Facts, and of the Occasion, are too solemn, and too phlegmatic for a Journal. Our Readers do not care to be made too serious.

Nor shall I enquire, at this Time, what has Occasioned the dark Cloud to spread itself over so many Minds just now, when no publick Calamity is upon us, at least as I see. We have no South-Sea Stock falling upon our Hands; the current of Distractions and Self-Murthers which happened upon that Occasion was very great, and who are to answer for it? Those who made our Hearts too glad, by raising a Hundred to a Thousand? Or those who sunk our Spirits with our Stocks, from a Thousand to a Hundred? I say, who are to answer for it remains to be revealed. We have no War, no Famine, no Plague, except that of Pride and Party-making; what then it can be I know not, nor, I say, will I enquire at this Time: But two difficult Questions lie before me.

1. What can be the Reason why, not only now, but at other Times, nay, I might say at all Times, there are more Self-Murtherers in England than in any, nay perhaps, than in all

the other Nations of Europe? That it is so, in Fact, I believe will be granted me, for 'tis very rarely heard of in other countries in Christendom; and I am told, 'tis never heard of among the Heathen, Pagan, and Infidel World.

What then is there, in the Christian Nations to be the Occasion of it? Has the Christian Religion any Hand in it? No, certainly, it is destructive of all Religious Principles, at least of all Christian Doctrines. Nay, so opposite is the Christian Profession to it, that we do not allow, arguing as Christians, that such as die thus, are so much as in a possibility of Salvation; so that Self-Destruction, by all the Principles of Christianity is, in a Word, a Self-Damning Action, and the unhappy Wretch that lays Violent Hands upon himself, is supposed to Kill both Soul and Body at the same Blow. The Knife that cuts its Throat, cuts the Soul's Refuge off, and sends it directly, without Hope, into the eternal Gulph, wherever it is; for it commits a Crime in the very opening of the Door, and so near to the shutting of it, that not a repenting Thought can be said to go through, along with it.

This, I say, clears the Christian Religion entirely of it, and consequently, no Christian Church, either Catholick or Reform'd, Roman or Lutheran, Episcopal or Presbyterian, Socinian or Anabaptist, will admit such as thus go out of the World, to be named among them, or to be so much as buried with them; but, as if they were to be punished after Death, they are buried in the Highway, with a Stake driven through them.

Since then the Christian Religion abhors the Principle, and rejects the Practice, what is the Reason that this, so dreadful a Practice, is found more frequent among Christians, than among Turks or Pagans; and still more frequent among English Christians, than in any other Nation whatsoever?

I have often proposed this Question in Society, as well to the Learned as to the Religious, and have received abundance of differing answers, and indeed, seldom do two of their Opinions agree; however, I shall name some of them, and leave it to the Readers to judge of them, only, previous to the particulars, I must add,—that the several Answers which I received, differed according to the Professions of the Persons to whom I proposed the Question.

The Physician placed it to the Account of Distemper in the

Blood; scorbutick Inflammations, and tormenting Pains in the Nerves, which they tell us, English Bodies, by their gross Feeding, are more subjected to than any other People, and have not Temper to support.

The Philosophers placed it to Natural Causes, and those rising from the Climate, and the inclemency of the Season, stagnating Vapours from the Earth, and fumes from the Quantity of Minerals in the Soil, and the Nitrous and Sulphurous Particles in the Air, which the Isle of Great Britain is fuller of than any other Nation.

The Divines gave Religious Reasons for it, and told us, that the English, being left to wander in the untrod mazes of mysterious Principles in Religion, were unguided and mistaken; they often lost their Way, those Dilemmas run them oftener than other People into Darkness and Despair.

The Politicians placed it to the innumerable variety of Men's Circumstances in the World; and that, as more Families were raised, from mean Circumstances to great, in this Nation; so, many more fell from Wealth and Plenty, to Misery and Want, which sudden Alteration, of Circumstances were so shocking to Nature, and the Spirits of Englishmen were naturally so great, that the Soul could not support the Change, and the Chagrin turned into Fury and Melancholy.

I allow that all these were Reasons, in their Places, and each of them were supported by Experience, that is to say, by frequent Experience. But I must add another Reason, and that is, that there are in England more Lunaticks than in any other Country, and when the Physicians can give us a Reason for that, I believe we may give the same for the other; for we may in Charity believe that most of those People who destroy themselves are first Lunatick, and they that can give a Reason for the last, may give the same for the first; but that Part I believe will be very hard to do.

On Pope's Translation of Homer.

A. J., July 31.—Sir, I suppose, among the rest of your Friends, you have not been ignorant of the Clamour which has been made upon a certain Author, for publishing his Translation, or Version, of your old Friend *Homer*, under his own Name, when it seems he has not been, nay, some have had the hardiness to say, *could not have been*, the real Operator.

I must confess, I cannot come into all the Resentments of the learned World upon that Subject ; and I am not without my Reasons for my Opinion, as I suppose they have shewn their Reasons for theirs.

Writing, you know, Mr. *Applebee*, is become a very considerable Branch of the English Commerce ; Composing, Inventing, Translating, Versifying, &c., are the several Manufactures which supply this Commerce. The Booksellers are the Master Manufacturers or Employers. The several Writers, Authors, Copyers, Sub-Writers, and all other Operators with Pen and Ink, are the Workmen employed by the said Master Manufacturers, in the forming, dressing, and finishing the said Manufactures ; as the Combers, Spinners, Weavers, Fullers, Dressers, &c., are, in our Clothing Manufactures, by the Master Clothiers, &c.

If a Clothier employs a Master Workman to weave him so many Pieces of Cloth, and agrees with him for so much Money, the Weaver brings them home finished, and puts his own Mark on them ; and this Weaver, being known to be a good Workman, the Master Clothier recommends the Cloths to his Customers, as the Work and Weaving of such a known and eminent Weaver. At the same Time, this Clothier knows very well that the said Weaver could not be able to weave them all himself ; perhaps also he knows that some of them are of a much meaner Workmanship than that Weaver used to Work, yet the Weaver and the Clothier conniving together, they all carry the same Mark. Nay, sometimes the Weaver brings a better Workman than himself into the Loom ; but having an Opportunity to get his Work cheaper, he takes him in. And thus, a Medley of Goods are put off together, all under the Mark, and in the Name of the Master Weaver.

Now upon the whole, pray, Mr. *Applebee*, who is the greatest Cheat in this Affair, the Clothier or the Manufacturer, the Master Employer, or the Weaver ? Not but that they may be both Rogues, Mr. *Applebee*, but who is most concerned in the Fraud, seeing it is the Master Clothier who puts the Goods off in the Weaver's Name, tho' he knows there are 'Prentices, and Scoundrels, for the sake of a low Price, employed in the making them.

As to Writing, Mr. *Applebee*, Do we expect that every Man that publishes a Book, and sets his Name to it, should *Bona fide*, be the Author *of it all* himself? Do we not know how several Booksellers of Note at this Time, keep Authors of different Fame employed, some at one Price, some at another, to form the same Pieces of Work? And have not several Authors, who are particular for being voluminous, their several Journeymen that work for them, some in one Jail, some in another, some in one fluxing House, some in another? Nay, has not the Right Reverend Author himself, who made this very complaint, his Deputy Journalist, and his supply of Operators, as Occasion requires, tho' the Labourers receive their Esteem from his own illustrious Character, and are all called his Own?

Did not the late celebrated *Tatlers* pass, even to the end of the Work, for the Labours of the worthy Editor Sir *Dick Steele?* And did it not come out at last, *when he could conceal it no longer*, that he had abundance of *Aid de plumes* under him? And might we not give the same Account of several laborious Tracts, which the World to this Day honours the Names of Authors for, who had the least share in the Labour?

But to carry this Complaint higher, a Merry Fellow of my Acquaintance assures me, that our Cousin *Homer* himself was guilty of the same *Plagiarism.* Cousin *Homer* you must note was an old blind Ballad Singer at *Athens,* and went about the Country there, and at other Places in *Greece,* singing his Ballads from Door to Door; only with this Difference, that the Ballads he sung were generally of his own making. Hence I suppose it was, that one of the same Profession here in *London,*— who, tho' blind too, made his own Ballads,—was so universally called *Old Homer.* But, says my Friend, this *Homer*, in process of Time, when he had gotten some Fame,—and perhaps more Money than Poets ought to be trusted with,—grew Lazy and Knavish, and got one *Andronicus* a Spartan, and one Dr. S———l, a Philosopher of *Athens*, both pretty good Poets, but less eminent than himself, to make his Songs for him; which, they being poor and starving, did for him for a small Matter. And so, the Poet never did much himself, only published and sold his Ballads still, in his own Name, as if they had been his own; and by that, got great Subscriptions, and a high Price for them.

Now, Mr. *Applebee*, if my Friend be in the right, was not Cousin *Homer* a Knave, for imposing thus upon the *Grecian World*? *In a Word*, it seems to me that Old *Homer*, was a mere Mr. P(ope), and Mr. P(ope), in that Particular, a mere *Homer ;* so that there's ne'er a Barrel the better Herring, except the *Master Manufacturer ;* who, like a Bawd to a ———, knew the Fraud, and imposed it upon his Customers, and so has been worse than both of them.

Your Servant,

ANTI-POPE.

The Same, and on Literary Frauds.

A. J., Aug. 7.—Sir, I wonder much your Friend who wrote you a Letter, published in your last Journal, should make such a serious piece of Work of a little Plagiarism, and one Author borrowing the Labours and Fame of another, as if Mr. *Pope* had been the first of that kind, or the World had never been imposed upon before; whereas I make no difficulty of telling you there are abundant Instances of the like or worse Doings than that; and in Books celebrated for their Wit, Learning and Usefulness.

What Long disputes have we had about the famous Εἰκων Βασιλικὴ of King *Charles* the First, the *Basilicon Doron* of King *James* the First ; nay King *Henry* the Eighth's Book against *Martin Luther*, was said to be the Labour of a certain Archbishop, who sacrificed his labours to his Majesty's Fame. And if we recur to a late celebrated Piece, in vindication of the Orthodox Faith, against Mr. *Whiston*, we find it suggested, that instead of the eminent Person who enjoys the Fame of it, his Lordship's Chaplain had a Share in the Labour.

Nor does it diminish the Fame of a Learned Poet, contemporary with Mr. *Pope*, who has received many Honours besides that of Knighthood for his most sublime Performance, that his Yoke-fellow is said to have a just Claim to, at least a Moiety of the Honour due to his latest Labours.

But to descend to the Times, and to Persons nearer home. Alas! How many of our Reverend Fathers are at this Time made florid by delivering, with a good Grace, the borrowed Labours of their Ancestors, and speaking like an Oracle, Words not at all of their own Composing; and even sometimes above their Understanding, tho' not above their Expressing!

Why should we put such Hardships upon the Clergy, as to oblige them to be the Authors of all the fine Things they inform us of in the Pulpit? Nay, why should we be so unjust and injurious to ourselves as to tie ourselves to hear their own Compositions, when they may so easily oblige us with better Things of a prior Decoction, and formed perhaps by a superior Genius, and for some extraordinary Occasions?

I remember a Reverend Clergyman being called to preach on the Anniversary of the Revolution, before a great Assembly, and in which were some Persons of Rank, as also Magistrates; and he made, or rather delivered an excellent Sermon, which was mightily Applauded, gave very great Satisfaction, and the Minister gained much Reputation by it. After Sermon, the Minister had the Honour to dine with the Corporation, and most of the principal Gentlemen of the Audience. After Dinner, one of the Gentlemen, discoursing with the Minister, complimented him much upon the extraordinary Discourse he had made them from the Pulpit; a second Gentleman that heard it, joins in applauding the Discourse, " but Doctor," says he to the Clergyman, " how come you to take no Notice of the Day? You had not one Word of the Revolution in all your Discourse, tho' that was the Occasion of your Sermon."

The Doctor, not answering so readily as was expected, a third Gentleman excused it, and said he supposed the Doctor forgot it; but a fourth unluckily put in, " I believe," says he, " I can give a better Reason for the Omission, viz., That the Sermon was made before the Revolution;" which it was indeed, about five and twenty Years before.

The Taste of Mankind in these Cases being therefore so dull as not to distinguish without a verbal Discovery; why should they expect they should not some Times be a little imposed upon? And, where is the Damage, that we should resent so much the Thing? Why must the Name sell the Work? If the Performance be equal to the Man, why not approved as well?

Suppose the Work better done than the Person pretending could do it, which is often the Case; if we reject it then, 'tis plain we bought the Name before, not the Work. I would therefore advise all the cheated World to keep their own Councils; and as Cuckolds, they say, when they cannot help it, should put their Horns in their Pocket, so let them take the Book, say nothing, make no Satyr upon themselves, but go Home, and take care they be not cheated a second Time.

Yours, &c.

Of Bankruptcy in Manners, Morals, and Religion.

A. J., Aug. 14.—Sir, I observe abundance of Noise and Clamour raised in the World about People's being in Debt, and not paying our Debts; and nothing is thought more Scandalous, than that Men should not pay their Debts. Nay, so Criminal is it taken to be, not to pay what we owe, that several Laws are made to oblige Men to pay their Debts; that is to say, to force them to do it where their own Principles of Justice and Honesty are not sufficient to move them. And particularly, Commissions of Bankrupt, as they are called, are appointed to take the Effects of the Insolvent into Possession, to appoint Trustees or Assignees to manage them, and to see Justice done to the Creditors whether the Debtor pleases or no; and, where the Debtor cannot satisfy, there are merciful Laws too to consider him.

But notwithstanding all that natural Justice, or religious Obligation can do, I find an infinite Number of Bankrupts and Insolvents in every Place where I come; nay, they are the worst sort of Insolvents too, for they are generally knavish Debtors that can pay and won't; that are able, and more than able abundantly, but have no Principle; in a Word, these are such as in Trade we call *Knavish Bankrupts*, that make no Conscience of running into Debt, and then make no Conscience of Payment; *for Example* :—

There's Friend *Zachary*, the Quaker, runs in *Debt to all his Neighbours, for good Manners. The Man had Respect shewn him by every body in our Street; and when we met him walking along, or standing at his Door, we all pull'd off our Hats. *Zachary* in return, standing bolt upright, paid nothing, but went upon Tick unconscionably. The most that could be got of him was, now and then, a Nod of his Head, or a, " *How dost do?*" softly expressed, as if he was afraid you should hear him; all which, placed honestly to Account, would not amount to Sixpence in the Pound; a Composition so low that 'tis not worth namiug. Yet, when he is spoken to about it, he answers coldly, that he can make no other payment, and if his Creditors won't accept of it, they must take their course,—upon which we resolve to take out a Statute against him.

There's *Formal Stiff*, Esq., Justice of Peace in our Division; he's worse than Friend *Zach*, for he runs in Debt with an Air of Insolence to every Body. His broad Hat cock'd up on three Sides, sits fast on his Head, and when he meets any of his Parishioners,—tho' of as good Figure as his Worship,—when they pull their Hats off, he pulls his Hat on; so running in Debt most abominably to all Mankind; and that, in a Manner that he will never be able to pay if he should live a hundred Years.

On the other Hand, there's my Lord *Plausible*, a Man of Quality, and he is in the other Extreme. For tho' he is run behind hand extremely in *Sincerity*, and 'tis feared, will in a little while, be quite Bankrupt in that Way; yet he brings every Body into Debt to him for *Ceremony*, and I am told, he makes no question to quit Scores with most of his Creditors that Way, and balance their Accounts, which if he does, it must be confess'd 'tis an easy way of paying Debts. Perhaps it may come in fashion towards the year 1800; for as we have much encouraged the Lying Manufacture in the last Century, another Posterity perhaps may bring it to Perfection by the end of this.

In the next Place, what an infinite Mass of perjured Oaths, broken Vows, and unperformed Promises are Mankind in Debt for, one to another? An eminent Magistrate in the Town where I live, having, for some Years past, made it his Practice, tho' on the wrong side of Seventy, to lie with all his Maids, upon a solemn Promise, that as they doubled their Work he would double their Wages, has not yet, as we are told, performed it to any of them, but the poor Girls have been turned off without the Additional Article; and have been told it was payment enough that they had the Honour to be with Child by their Master.

Nay, to such a Length are we arrived, that we endeavour to bring God Almighty himself in Debt too, if possible, to his Creatures; having so often endeavoured to engage him to Damn us all, according to his Word; which, not being yet brought to pass, the Age seems to be Creditor of Heaven for the Performance.

How many of us are in Debt to King George, receiving the Protection of his Government, and not paying the Debt of Gratitude and Obedience, which Loyalty and just Principles demand of every Body; but insult him in opprobrious Language, and dedicate our simple, worthless Homage to his impotent Enemy, and a routed Party. And yet, even Thousands of those good People too are in Debt to their own Party, for whom 'tis said they promised to fight; whereas, when it came, we find they could do nothing but run away *for him*, which in short, was but cheating him at best.

Nay, we have some among us who seem to be in Debt to the Devil, for boasting of more Wickedness than ever they have been able to commit, they thereby promised the Devil to be as bad as they said they were; and, no doubt, Satan expects prompt payment of them, unless he should be so kind as to take the Will for the Deed, and make good Dr. *Fuller's* old Maxim in Divinity :—

 " That he that would be wickeder than he is, is certainly as wicked as he would be."

I could descend to Matters of human Conversation, Love, Virtue, and Vice; we run in Debt every where, and in so shameless a Manner, that we act in everything as if, like true Bankrupts, we not only did not pay our Debts, but never intended it.

I may in a little Time give you a List of Bankrupts of this Kind, to be published in your Journal Weekly, as you do the Bankrupts in Trade; for why should one Sort be less exposed and less Publick than the other. And if I should do so, you will find abundance of Bankrupts among some Men who perhaps the World thinks at this Time are very well able to pay their Debts, and make a fine show, as if they really did so.

I doubt too, we should find Bankrupts among People who seem to be exempted from the Word, and against whom no Commission would lie according to our Law; *for Example :* How many of our Clergy are in Debt to their People, while they promise them Heaven upon those moral Principles that will never carry them thither; while they recommend to them the Virtue that they will not be at the Expense of Practising, and while they promise to preach Orthodox Doctrine to them, and then, paying a false and Counterfeit Coin, put them off with Arianism and Heresy.

But as I must do Justice too on every Side, in our Parish we are even with the Parson; for, as he puts us off with counterfeit Doctrine, we pay him in a worse Coin; for while we pretend to go to Church to receive his Ghostly Instructions, we talk to one another all the while in the Language of the Eyes, and mind not a Word of what he says.

Your Servant,
Tom Bankrupt.

On the Tricks and Contrivances Incidental to Journalism.

A. J., Aug. 21.—Sir, I must confess it is a most lamentable Thing to see the Condition of this poor City of London, at this Time labouring under a severe, cruel Scarcity of Intelligence. The great Rains which have fallen so unseasonably of late, and which are now returned, just at the entrance into Harvest, have, together with some insalubrity of the Air, occasioned, that the Councils of Europe, as well as the Fruits of the Earth, have not come on kindly, or ripened up into Occurrences of Moment, as they usually do at this Time of the Year; so that, in short, we have great Reason to fear a Famine of News.

The King is indeed Abroad, and the King of Prussia and his Majesty have had an Interview, and are separated again. But whether it be that the Councils of Princes are better kept than usual, or that Princes do not care to expose their Measures to be handed about among the lower Gentry, as in former Times has been the Custom, we cannot tell; but we do not find Things come abroad as they used to do in Days of Yore. So that, in a Word, our News-Mongers have not wherewith to sustain themselves, nor can their Readers subsist upon what few Morsels are allow'd them. It will not maintain the Speculators in the due Exercise of their ordinary Talents, nor bring the Coffee-Houses a sufficient Number of Politicians to read the ordinary Lectures to their Pupils; all which are Grievances requiring an immediate Redress.

Nay, I must observe also, that the Calamity is so great that it will be felt by the Publick; for the Duties upon Coffee, Tea, and Chocolate, and the Excises upon Beer, Ale, and other Liquors, are in danger of not being paid, or at least may be very much lessened, for want of suitable Amusements at the Time of drinking them.

Besides,—those Liquors were found very necessary to wash down the crude, and gross, unconcocted Stuff which Men were sometimes obliged to swallow on those Occasions, and which required proper Vehicles to take them in; and for that Purpose the Journals and Newspapers were not only properly placed in Coffee-houses, Inns, Ale-Houses, and such like Places, but they had of late been taken in much by the Women, especially the Politick Ladies, to assist at the Tea-Table, and at the Chocolate in the Morning repast, and so, One might help to digest the Other.

But all this seems under an extreme Disappointment, and NEWS, the very Nourishment and Support of human Society, is cut off from us. Our foreign Prints are barren of Intelligence, and are only filled up with hard Names, of great Courtiers and Ambassadors of Princes, running to and again of their Masters' Errands to no purpose; and if they get a State Marriage, or a State Prostitute to talk of, they tell it so often over, and cook it up so often for want of a Supply, that it grows tedious to the very Relator, and nauseous to us who relate it again after them.

If they are so empty, from whom, and from whence, our Papers drew their Nourishment, what must become of our Papers? See, alas! how they look, one foreign Paragraph serves a whole *Post-Boy*; two supplies a Journal; all the rest we owe to Invention; and how barren! Or, to Domestick wit; and that, how dull! Or, to Quack Doctors; and they, how fulsome! Or to Home News; and that, how fabulous, how monstrous, and, in itself too, how mean!

This Article called Home News is a new Common Hunt, tho' upon a Cold Scent, after Casualties. The Miseries of Mankind are the Chief Materials, such as Death and Marriage in the First Class; the Disasters of Families, such as Robberies and Bankrupts, that's the Second Class; the Jail Deliveries, either to or from the Gallows, that's a Third Class.

If indeed a flaming Rogue comes upon the Stage, such as a *Sheppard*, a *Gow*, a *Jonathan Wild*, or a *Blueskin*, they are great Helps to us; and we work them, and work them, till we make Skeletons of the very Story, and the Names grow as rusty as the Chains they are hanged in.

Nay, to tell you the Truth, we marry Couples that never woo'd, bury those that never die, bankrupt those that never break, and rob those that never met a Thief,—but this goes but a little Way. I have thought now of a new Method to restore Plenty to our hungry Palates, and supply the World with News; and that is, to raise a War in the World, that we may have those dear Things called Battle and Blood to talk of again, and that we may not be all undone by Peace and Quietness.

How this may be done is the Question, and the Question we are prepared for answering, for having made a Confederacy of our Own, in which, if we design War, you may depend the Clergy are not excluded ; I say, having made a Confederacy in the World for the inflaming Mankind, we doubt not to work Wonders in a little while, for a War we must have, of one kind or another, whether of the Pen or the Sword, it matters not much. Your Humble Servant,

CombustIon.

Proposed Remedies for a Dearth of News.

A. J., Aug. 28.—Sir, Your Complaint in your last, is indeed very moving, about a famine of Intelligence, which you intimate as coming upon *you Journalists*, and upon all the Speculators of this lower World, who we call your Readers.

The Distresses you are put to for *Home-News*, are indeed very lamentable, and I most heartily pity your Condition ; and the more, considering the great Hardships you are all driven to for the present Subsistence of the People, to keep your Readers from Starving, and your Papers from coming to the Parish. How, as you say, you are forced to marry Couples that never woo'd, bury those that never die, bankrupt those that never broke ; and, you might have added, commit Murthers, Ravishments and Robberies, *in Nubibus.* Those are sad Things indeed, and I must confess the Publick ought to take some Care that such useful Fellows as you are, should not be driven

to such Exigencies; lest Necessity, (for what will not Necessity
drive Men to?) should, one Time or other, put you upon seeking
to get your Livelihood by some honest Employment; and so
bring you and your Journal, and all the many Thousands that
are employed your Way, to utter Ruin and Distress.

In order, therefore, to save you and your Dependents from
Destruction, and prevent, if possible, the imminent Dangers
that threaten you, I have spent some serious Moments in trying to beat out some new untrodden Path for you, in which
you might, *if it be not too late*, retrieve your Fortunes, and
bring the People about you again; for, *Mountebank like*, you
only want a Crowd about your Stage, that your Ware, being
useful, or at least thought to be so, they may throw away a
little Money upon you, and if we can but make a Noise among
them for you the Business is done.

In order to this, I was first proposing to you to talk mys-
teriously and unintelligibly, and sometimes to discuss Religious
Difficulties, and leave them more entangled than you found
them; but I was informed this had been so admirably well performed, and yet with such dismal Discouragement, so Unsuc-
cessfully, and so to the Ruin of a well-disposed Paper, by our
Right Reverend Friend and Favourite, the *London Journal*,
that it quite discouraged me, and I concluded that 'twas Nonsense to talk Sense to the present impenetrable World.

Hereupon, I considered, whether I should put you upon the
Reverse of that Conduct, raise Batteries against not the Church
only, but against all Churches; banter Religion in general,
insult the Minister to make the Parish merry, and insult the
Doctrine to make them mad; make a Jest of Things Sacred,
and ridicule Things Civil; and so, if possible, to bring the
World to be wiser and wickeder than they are. This I
thought would be a very laudable Undertaking, and especially
that it would be profitable to you, as I knew it was agreeable
to the Times; but I was told it had been tried already by our
other *British* Brother, and without Success, tho' after infinite
Expense of Wit and good Reading, so I despaired on that
Side too.

It then occurred to me to propose *writing Truth*, and thereby
distinguish your Paper from all the Fraternity. I had no
sooner mentioned the Word, but all that heard me began to

make Mouths at me, and wry Faces, and at last they broke
out into a loud Laughter.   " *Why, the Fellow is crazed !*" says
one; " *write Truth !*   Why, who does he think will buy the
Paper ?   Who will meddle with such out o' th' fashion Ware
as that ?"   " He may pretend to it indeed, if he will," *says a
Second,* " but it will never do."   " Nay," *says a Third,* " but
to pretend to it is foolish ; the very naming it would damn his
Paper at once ; 'tis such a dry, barren, stale, worn-out Thing ;
there's no Taste of it left among us."   " *Truth* in a News
Paper !" *says a Fourth,* " why, 'tis a Contradiction, 'twould be
no News if it had any Truth in it."   Truth, like South Sea
Stock, was run down under PAR ; and tho' sometimes it may be
jobb'd up again by Art, I assure you it was indeed ART, not
TRUTH that did it.   For how can Truth run up the Rate of any
Thing above the Value ?

Like the late Cry of a mighty Whale-Fishing, *at first* it was
magnified to a great Gain, and up went the Stock, which was
the best Whale in all the Fishery ; but when the Whale was
caught, then the Account came out as it really was (*viz.*) Good
compared to Bad, and Bad compared to Good.

Upon the whole, it is concluded that *Truth* would never
make the *Journal Stock* rise ; and, that if you expect to supply
the World with News, you must start some new Hare,—you
must see if you can, *Phaeton-like,* set the World a-fire in some
Place or other, that we at Home may listen daily for an
Account how it burns.

Nor is this so remote from our Business, as we are *Journal-
Writers,* as some may imagine ; for have not our Ancestors in
Pen and Ink Manufacture been all Incendiaries, even from the
Beginning ?   Has not the Press thrown more Bombs than the
Mortar piece, and the Pen done more Mischief than the Hand
Grenadoe ?   Certainly as the Brain of Mankind has hatched
more Mischief than the Hand could execute, and his Will has
done less harm than his Wit ; so, there is no doubt, but that if
the Writers of the World would join heartily together, they
may soon set the Readers together by the Ears, and so, in Time,
the Pen may perform more Wonders than the Sword.

The grand Question is, How shall we do to bring this Pacifick
Generation to a Temper suitable to our Design ?

Answer, *First,*—In order to a Religious War, preach up

ZEAL. Cold Christianity is no Religion at all; 'tis red-hot
Piety and scalding Zeal must do the Work —

> " *Zeal makes Men fight like Mad or Drunk,*
> *For Dame Religion as for Punk.*"—HUDIB.

How brave an Example did our Brethren the *Jesuits* shew
us lately at *Thorn*, not only in the bloody Affair itself, but in
the several Speeches and Pamphlets, Papers and Prints, published and dispersed over the whole Kingdom of *Poland*, ani-
mating the Nobility and Gentry to stand by what they the
Reverend Firebrands had done !

And how comes it that We, (who hope we are equally qualified for Mischief with the best of them,) have not used the
like warm Endeavours to animate the Protestants to *run before
they are sent*, and in spite of wiser Measures, to fall on before
our Masters think fit ; and in defiance of all Satisfaction to
be had by Treaty ? And so, make a War of it, right or
wrong ?

Secondly, For the propagating our laudable Design of kind-
ling *a new War*, why do we not second the grave Efforts of
those who move the Dutch East-India Company to attack the
new Ostend Traders in the Indies ? Whether their Masters the
States will or no ? The Treaties of Peace made in *Europe*
having, as we say, no force beyond the Line.

Thirdly Why do we not inflame the Reckoning a little between *Spain* and *France*, for sending home the *Infanta ;* and
between the *Turk* and *Venetians* for the Affair of *Spalatro ;*
between the *Czarina* and the King of *Denmark*, on Account
of the Duke of *Holstein ;* and between *France* and the *Poles*
on account of King *Stanislaus ?* These, and many others, are
Fields of Action proper for your grand Design ; for certainly
they that are willing to do Mischief can never want a
Handle.

Evils of the King's long Absence.   Perambulation of Westminster.

A. J., Sept. 4.—Sir, In this State of Emptiness which, as
by your last Papers, all our Journals suffer the Affliction of, I
took a walk the other Day out of the City to the Court ; or,
as the Citizens vulgarly call it, *the 'tother End of the Town.* I

did it indeed in Charity to your Paper, thinking to pick up something at that Part of the Town for your Service; that being the usual Place for Intelligence, where the greatest People and the greatest Number of People resort.

But 'tis impossible to express my Surprize to you, when I came thither and found that Part of the World all as it were in Desolation; indeed I may liken it to Hell in one respect, for I think there was *Weeping and Wailing and Gnashing of Teeth*. In one Thing indeed it was unlike, and that was in the fewness of the Inhabitants.

The *Weeping* in the first Place I found among the Principal House-Keepers, most of whose Houses had Bills upon the Doors, of Rooms to be Let, and they made a great Moan that they could not let their Lodgings; that the usual Income, or Rent of Apartments let out for Lodgings, was the Means by which, at least, they paid their Rent, and sometimes maintained their Families; and that this Year they saw nothing before them but Ruin, for that they not only had no Lodgers now, but were like to have none a great while; and as for the return of the Court, they had no Account when that would be, and if it was late in the Winter, or towards Spring, as some People made them Fear, they should be undone.

Sick with these Complaints, and being able to give the poor People no Comfort, I left them, and went away towards *Hyde Park*; being told of a fine new Avenue made to the East Side of the Park, fine Gates, and a large *Visa*, or Opening, from the new Squares called *Hanover Square*, &c.

In this Tour I passed an amazing Scene of new Foundations, not of Houses only, but as I might say of new Cities. New Towns, new Squares, and fine Buildings, the like of which no City, no Town, nay, no Place in the World can shew; nor is it possible to judge where or when, they will make an end or stop of Building.

Before I came into this new World of Brick and Tile, I saw abundance of empty Houses, as well as empty Lodgings, and Bills upon the Doors, even in some of the principal Squares and Streets of that Part of the Town, such as the Streets about *Covent-Garden, St. Martin's*, nay even in *Leicester-Fields* itself.

This was the most incongruous thing of its Kind imaginable to me, when I considered the Addition of Houses and Streets

in one Part, and the spare Houses in the other; especially
when I reflected that many of those Houses with Bills upon
the Doors, wanting Tenants, were some of the most considerable Houses in the Place. Certainly then, said I, the City does
not encrease, but only the Situation of it is a going to be removed, and the Inhabitants are quitting the old Noble Streets
and Squares where they used to live, and are removing into the
Fields for fear of Infection; so that, as the People are run away
into the Country, the Houses seem to be running away too.

All the Way through this new Scene I saw the World full
of Bricklayers and Labourers; who seem to have little else to
do, but like Gardeners, to dig a Hole, put in a few Bricks,
and presently there grows up a House. The Streets are at
present Peopled only with such as these; and with Carpenters,
Joiners, and other Workmen, and Alehouse Keepers to receive
the Money they spend. When, and from whence Inhabitants
are to come to fill up the void Spaces, is as mysterious as a
double Tongued Oracle; for while they build Streets, as if
they intended to make the Town, *Nineveh like, be Three Days
Journey long,* we see the rest of the Town empty and abandoned,
weeping for want of Inhabitants, and looking like the Picture
of Desolation.

Coming back from this Prospect, I went to *Charing Cross,*
among some Shop-keepers who owed me some Money, thinking
to receive a good Sum to pay Bills of Exchange with; but if
they were *Weeping* before, they were *Wailing* here. Money
they gave me none, they rather upbraided my Unreasonable-
ness for expecting it when every Body was out of Town;
Court, Term, Parliament, all in Recess. "Money," said one
of my Customers, "How should Shop-Keepers have Money
without Trade? How Trade, without People? Why," says
he, "Don't you see every Body is gone? We'll pay you some
Money when his Majesty, &c. comes home again, but you
must stay till then." However, they said nothing undutiful
of his Majesty, only lamented the Case of poor Tradesmen,
with an absent Court, and an empty Town.

*Meditations in Palace Yard, Westminster Hall, the Abbey,
and the Park.*

A. J., Sept. 11.—Sir, History has recorded, and it is still more authentically attested, by the living Testimony of many good People of venerable Antiquity,—especially of the Female Sex,—that in the time of the late Visitation, (so we, of the precise Speakers, politely express the Plague Year 1665,) the Town was so empty of People, and those that were left went so little Abroad, that the Grass grew in the Streets; nay, I won't be positive that they did not say the *Royal Exchange* wanted Mowing, only that no Body could be found to make the Hay.

Be that as it will, I could not forbear calling the Memoirs of those evil Days to mind,—when the other Day I had Occasion to cross over the Street from *Channel Row* to *Westminster Hall*,—all that unfrequented Vacancy called *Palace Yard*, once so thronged with Coaches, seem'd to me to be a Void in Creation; a useless Spot of Ground, like a barren Common in the Country, laying open to the Road, neglected and Waste, as neither fit for the Plough nor the Hoof, neither for Corn nor Cattle.

While I stood staring about me, and wondering a little,—at least diverting my Thoughts with the Difference of the Face of Things,—I saw a Man walking across the Yard, out of the ordinary Path, in a direct Line, and taking large Strides, as if he was measuring the Ground by Paces. As I found by his stepping he would come near the Place where I stood, I waited till he came close up to me, when, on a sudden, he stopped;— " *a Hundred !*" says he aloud, and then cut a Notch in a Stick, with his Knife, which he held ready for that purpose.

" What are you doing Sir," *said I to him*, " are you measuring the Ground ?" " Yes Sir," *says he very courteously*, and seeming, as I thought, a very civil Fellow, and willing enough to talk, I ask'd him if I might be so free with him as to enquire into the meaning of it. " Yes Sir," *says he*, " with all my Heart. I had heard, the other Day," *says he*, " that this Piece of Vacant Ground was to be let to build on, and as I am a Projector," *says he*, " I have been measuring it out, and I think it will make a very handsome Square this Way ;" and with that he points it out with his Finger ; " or that Way, Sir," *says he*, " it will make two very fine Streets."

I smiled, but perceived he was not pleas'd at it. " I find Sir," *says he*, " you seem to laugh at my Design, I presume you do not understand those Things so well as I. 'Tis my

Business, Sir, I laid out the Plan of all the ancient fine Buildings in the Town, I built *Dunkirk House*, and St. *James's Square;* I laid out all the fine Streets in *Hatton Garden,* and the Noble Pile of Buildings call'd *Portugal Row* in *Lincoln's-Inn Fields;* all your new contracted Squares of *Soho, Golden Square, Red Lion Square,* ay, and your *Hanover Square* too, are Fools to them."

" Pray Sir," *said I, and made him a Leg,*—" do not mistake me; I did not laugh at you, but smiled to see how our Thoughts agreed, for I was just musing upon the same Thing, namely, the Uselessness of this Piece of Ground, only that I was laying it out for other Business, for I am no *Builder.* But Sir," *said I,* " in your Design, what Care have you taken to keep a Way open to the Great Hall there, for that you know is a place of Business?" " O dear !" *says he,* " that's true, indeed I had forgot that. Why, will the Lawyers come to it again ?" " Yes, Yes," *says I,* " 'tis very likely they may." " Well, Well," *says he,* " 'tis but giving a new Turn to my Design, and I shall make a Passage, broad enough for all honest Men I warrant you." " HUM !" *Says I,* " for honest Men ? But you must allow Room for the rest too," *says I,* " or it won't do." That troubled him a little, but I perceived he went to take a new Survey of the Ground, and so I left him, after we had, upon this short Acquaintance, appointed where to meet in the Evening to finish our Conference.

I went on then to the Hall, where I found the Doors open indeed, and the Spider-left Ceiling preserved the ancient dull Lustre of *Irish Oak.* The Trophies of *Blenheim* seemed to be following the Memory of the Great Duke of *Marlborough,* and indeed of Mankind, for they hung in Rags, and began to rot; so certain is it, that Fame, like the Bones of Men, must return to its first Nothing; and, that *Immortal Memory, is Nonsense, in terminis.* Neither Marble nor Brass, no, nor Tombs of Adamant, can prevent the sinking of every Thing into Nothing; but that by the Way. In a Word,—there was the venerable Old Pile, the vacant Throne of Justice stood at the upper End, and the Ruins of the most eminent Shops for Trade remained; but for all other Things, all was silent, empty, and void, and put me in mind of the Ruins of the old World after the Deluge. So I resolved to do as the rest of Mankind seem'd to have done, (viz.) abandon it; as they tell us the Inhabitants of *Arch-Angel* do, who leave the Country during the vacancy of Commerce, and return again at the proper Season.

From Hence, I went into the *Abbey*, and there, indeed, I found the Royal Tombs, and the Monuments of the Dead, remaining and encreased; but the Gazers, the Readers of Epitaphs, and the Country Ladies to see the Tombs, were strangely decreased in Number. Nay, the Appearance of the Choir was diminished; for setting aside the Families of the Clergy resident, and a very few more, the Place was forsaken.

" Well," *said I*, " then a Man may be Devout with the less Disturbance ;" so I went in, said my Prayers, and then took a Walk in the *Park*.

Both sides of the *Park* look'd Gay and Green, but *alas !* all the fine Company was gone, the Benches were vacant, the Beauties were absent, I miss'd the noble Train of Ladies, the Glory of *Britain*, that used to shine there; all the Gentry I could find were some few Officers of the Guards, whose Companies I suppose were upon Duty,—now and then a Barber, going with his Instruments to Shave,—some Footmen going of Errands, and here and there a fallen Woman ; for the rest, the Parade was quite empty, the Mall wanted weeding, the very Ducks in the Canal miss'd their ancient Benefactors the Nurses, and Nursery Maids with the Children, to give their Breakfast to the Wild Fowl. The Houses round, whose Windows enjoy'd the pleasant Prospect of the *Park*, look'd all heavy, the Window-Shutters fast closed, and not a Face to be seen. Upon this melancholy Day I took up a sudden Resolution, that since all the World was gone Abroad, I would go and look for them ; for why should I live alone when the Company was perhaps as Merry as ever, if I could but find them out? Accordingly I took my Horse for *Tunbridge*, and there I found them, to my inexpressible Satisfaction, as you shall hear in its Place.

Your Humble Servant.

Lament on the Loss of the " Charming Fanny," laden with Brimstone.

A. J., Sept. 18.—Sir, In one of our last Week's News-

Papers we found a very unhappy Piece of News.   Unhappy!
not only to the Persons concerned, but many Ways so to that
laudable Design, which I had the Honour to propose to you
in my last; namely, of embroiling Mankind, and setting the
World in a Flame.

This unhappy News was, that the Ship called the *Charming
Fanny* was cast away in her Voyage, bound home, from *Italy*,
laden with *Brimstone*.   Unfortunate Vessel!   How cam'st
thou to miscarry, fraught with so necessary a Merchandize,
and at a Time too,—for Disasters are doubled by their Circumstances,—I say, at so critical a Time, when Combustibles
are so much wanted?

What a noble Foundation for inflaming the World might
this charming Lady *Fanny* have laid among us, had she
brought her Loading safe home!   Bless me!   What could not
about two hundred Ton of Sulphur, had it been rightly applied, have contributed to so glorious a Work as that of inflaming Mankind, and setting Fire to the already prepared
Heads of us Scribblers!

The learned Mr. *Burnet*, in his *Theory of the Earth*, boldly
intimates, that the Whore of *Babylon* shall burn with the
First, and that the General Conflagration shall begin at *Rome*;
because the natural Soil of *Italy* being supposed to be all Com-
bustible, the grand Store is laid up there for the Work, and
Heaven has no more to do than to touch it with a Match,
that is to say, an Eruption a little deeper than ordinary from
Mount Vesuvius, and the whole Magazine would blow up at
once.

In like manner, give us but one *Charming Fanny*, loaded
with *Brimstone*, and let us Writers touch it with an inflamed
Pen, a Pen rightly dipped in *Styx* and *Phlegethon*; and if we
don't set all *Europe* on Fire, we must have less Skill than we
think we have, and less Power of doing Mischief than we hope
we have.

Do but take our late *London Journal* for a Leader, who with
but one Touch of his Pen, destroy'd a Lover, and two beautiful
Ladies at a Blow, in his very last Paper, and all in Shadow;
but the Merriest Thing of all was, that he had, but the Week
before, given poor *Robinson Crusoe* the LYE, most courteously,
and genteelly, for writing an Allegorick History of his own

Life, and yet could, the very next Paper, work out a most tragical Story, I do not say (LYE) of his own Brain, merely to fill up his Paper with, and Murther three innocent Creatures that were never alive. All done most accurately to convince the Reader, that his former Censure was just, according to the Honour of a Journalizing Critick.

Is it not apparent by this, what noble Achievements we Writers of Journals are capable of; and what wonderful Efforts we might have made by this Time, had not the *Charming Fanny* been lost,—the Brimstone Lady, that was charged with such a Quantity of Combustibles, such a Bulk of Sulphur, that the *Hell-Fire Club*, if ever there was such a Race of Devils, could never boast; in short, Dear *Fanny*, if she had but arrived, might have been able to have made a *Hell-Fire Club* of our Journals all at once. But alas! the poor Girl has miscarried, and has quenched her Flame in Salt Water, and so our Rockets cannot go off, nor are we half so well qualified for an universal Conflagration as we should have been.

But, Courage, Bullies! There's more *Brimstone* in *Italy;* and tho' *Fanny* has miscarried, there's the *Lovely Betty*, the *Charming Nelly*, and the *Charming Molly*, all Ships of as good Fame as their Owners. They may all take Freight for Mount *Strombolo*, and load Home with *Brimstone;* and let us alone to blow our Match. I warrant you we'll illuminate the World upon their Arrival.

Nor is the World so barren of Combustibles as we imagine. Come, come, Neighbours! A Religious War, or an Irreligious? For 'tis all one to us, so that it be but a War, and may not be so far off as some think, the *Polanders* having scorned the Offers of Accommodation.

I could tell you where, for your Encouragement, some other Things don't look so peaceable as some People pretend. I wonder whether the Drum does not beat in the Well at *Oundle?* If it does, depend upon it there will be War somewhere or other, some Time or other; and then, we shall have Business to do again.

Your Humble Servant,
GUNPOWDER.

Reflections on Death.

A. J., Sept. 25.—Sir, Such are the Vicissitudes of Human Life,—such the Chequer-Work of its Outside, or Surface ; the Light, the Dark, the Rough, the Smooth,—so many various Stages do we make, and so many Strange Ways pass through the World, that I think it is not capable of a Delineation or Description. Some have compared it to one Thing, some to another ; but, in short, no Simile, no Allusion, no Comparison will reach it. 'Tis even the whole Work of Life to describe Life.

Every single Man's History, were it to be written down, would be a History of odd Incidents, new, surprizing, and particular to itself ; as there are not two Faces, nor two Voices alike, so not two Men go through the World in the same Track, or out of it by the same Door. One goes away by a Halter, and he is said to die an infamous, ignominious Death ; and another by a Mortification, another a Canker, some terrible Thing, and he dies in Torture, and as miserable as the other. Here's a Man cut for the Stone, and perishes in the Operation, torn and mangled by the merciless Surgeons, cut open alive, and bound Hand and Foot to force him to bear it ; the very Apparatus is enough to chill the Blood, and sink a Man's Soul within him. What does he suffer less than he that is broken alive upon the Wheel ? Another is burn'd in his Bed by Accident,—goes to Sleep in Security, and wakes in the Flames,—as was the Case but a few Days ago near *Fleet Street*. Death is a Calamity wherever it comes ! How few bear it with Patience, or think of it without Horror !

It was my Lot, Mr. *Applebee*, to be at *Jamaica*, in the late terrible Hurricane and Earthquake ; *that is to say*, we thought there was an Earthquake too, but were not certain of that Part. Could I give you a Description of that terrible Day ! Could I represent, in lively Colours, the Calamity and Horror of it, you would say there never was a more affecting Sight seen in the World ! But I reflected on it only as a Picture of Nature's Disorder ; and that the rest was Nothing but a greater Number of People dying together than usual. I found the Thing had nothing more in it than this, that Death came with more funeral Attendants than he ordinarily does, and that this was nothing to the Horror of a Plague, or the Carnage of a general Battle; and so my Surprize at it wore off, even at the very Place. I had also another View of Death lately, that shewed it in a different Aspect from that. The other Day, I chanced to cast my Eyes from my Chamber, where I lodged, towards the Street, where I saw a great Hurry among the People, running and crowding after a Couple of Carts; upon this I ran to the Window, and, behold! four Condemned Criminals were carrying to the place of Execution to be hanged.

"Poor miserable Creatures!" *said I*, and so said some Ladies that were with me. "No, no," *said I*, "not those in the Carts; I do not mean them, but those that run after them. The first indeed are miserable, as they are in the Hands of Justice, and going to receive immediate Punishment, the Reward of a Wicked Life. But what are all the rest?" *said I*,— "only Criminals reprieved. Are they not all under an absolute indefeasible Sentence? Execution is only respited, for awhile, by the Favour of the Judge; but that will as certainly be executed, in a little Time more, as those Four now are to be; and with this Difference too, that many of the rest shall die in Torture and Terror, ten thousand Times more grievous than those Four. Nay, perhaps few of the Thousands who go to see these four People die, shall get so easy a Passage out of Life. And how many would not choose to go out of the World at the Gallows, *setting the Ignominy of it aside*, rather than by the Tortures of the Stone, the Strangury, the Cholick, and the like terrible Distempers?"

The Manner of Dying has certainly a great Influence upon Mankind; but 'tis all founded upon a wrong Principle. 'Tis not the Manner of dying, but the Reason of Death that ought to influence us. The Guilt makes a Publick Execution infamous; but where there is no Guilt there will be no Shame. Innocence knows no Infamy. A publick Punishment upon an innocent Man stigmatizes the Judge, not the sufferer. Guilt or Innocence only distinguishes between the Criminal and the Martyr.

I have seen Death in many of its most frightful Shapes; and I must acknowledge, that the cold-blood Way of dying in the Arms of our Friends, the Chamber crowded with Relations,— one crying here, and another there,—Children coming for their

Blessing,—the Parson, like a Ghost, appearing with his Book, to prepare the dying Man,—and all the ordinary Apparatus of Death,—waiting, till the two Friends, Soul and Body, part, leisurely, and by Torment ;—I say, these seem to me much more frightful than an Executioner, with an Axe or a Halter ; who gives the Soul an easy, and sudden Passage,—lifts up the Sluices,—and lets Life out, at one Gulph.

How often do the most exalted Mortals die more miserable than a mean ordinary Person! How died the great *Herod*, the famed *Antiochus*, the late *Louis* the XIV., and, to go no farther, the Czar of *Muscovy* ? The printed Account had an Article in it, enough to make the Blood of the Reader run chill in his Veins ; his Surgeons having, I suppose, done him some Hurt in searching or probing the *Urethra*, a Mortification ensued, which tortured his Majesty for several Days till he expired.

We cannot, I say, know anything of the Truth of the Particulars ; but supposing the Relation good, how much happier would one of the meanest of Subjects be, than Majesty itself, in such a Passage out of Life !

In a Word, Life may be a Scene of Pleasure, but Death is a Scene of Horror ; and nothing but Virtue, and a Mind fixed upon a State of Blessedness beyond Life, can support it.

Public Rejoicings.   Instability of Mobs.

A. J., *Oct.* 23.—Sir, You have been mighty merry this last week, and I rejoiced with you most heartily ; the Truth is, I love to have an Occasion, now and then, for National Mirth, for it seems *to be,* or at least to *begin to be,* less familiar to us than formerly.

We used to rejoice most famously in ancient Days, with Processions to St. *Paul's,* and giving Thanks with the *Te Deums* of the roaring Cannon, praising God in the Morning with Drums and Trumpets, and at Night with Squibs and Crackers. I want some Fighting Stories, and some Bonfire Nights again, for Victories and Conquests ; nor is it material if they did sometimes pay more for them than they were worth, as some maliciously said. But what was that to us ; 'tis enough 'twas Victory ; and who can buy Joy too dear ?

Besides, we, without Doors, do not always trouble ourselves

with the Causes of Publick Rejoicing; but when they bid us
rejoice, we toss up our Caps immediately, and shout and
holloo,—as Dogs wag their Tails, and skip about, when their
Masters bid them,—not knowing what 'tis for, and whether it
is for anything or nothing.   Nay, and for ought I know, 'tis
our Felicity, in such Cases, that we do not always enquire into
the Causes and Reasons of Publick Joy, but that when our
Masters laugh we can laugh too ; as Papists, in their Idolatry,
know when to bow, this Way or that Way, when to kneel, when
to stand, when to adore, when to say *Amen*, by the Motions
of their Leaders and Priests, not understanding any Thing of
what they say, or whether they bless them or curse them, buy
them or sell them.

Nor, to give our Masters their Due, do they, if they are in
their Senses,—*I mean their Politick Senses*,—lay much Stress,
or value themselves much upon the *highty-tighty* of the Street
Salutations, or the Excesses of Bonfire Joy ; for we of the Street
Gentry bestow our Acclamations sometimes with as little Judgment as Sincerity, and there is very little but the Noise to be
found in it.

It is most certain that we know what our Rejoicings have
been for *this past Week*, and have as real and just Causes for
it, on several Accounts, as we have had for any publick Joy in
our Age, or on any Occasion since the Revolution, exclusive
of the Revolution only ; namely, the Coronation of the King
on the Throne, the Advancement of a Protestant Prince, and
a Protestant Family, and I as heartily join in it as any Body
does, or reasonably can do.

But what is the Case, and always has been the Case of
Mobs ? Do not the same Mob holloo out, and holloo in ? Did
we not see them one Day holloo, and set one another on, to tear
Popery to pieces, make Bonfires of all the Mass Houses, or at
least of their inside Furniture, and, run to meet the Prince of
Orange by Hundreds and by Thousands ; and, within but three
Days after, when King *James* came back from *Faversham*,
halloo him back again, and toss up their caps as high as
before ? And if this was not an Instance, can we not find one
Seventeen Hundred Years ago, and farther back, when the
Rabble of *Jerusalem* cry'd *Hosanna*, and strewed the very
Ground he trod on with Flowers, at their Saviour's entry into

Jerusalem; and, within a few Days, raise those impious Clamours to Crucify him; and reclaimed a Murtherer instead of him?

Reading the Foreign Prints, the other Day, I saw a living Example of this, in a Prince now in being; the variety of whose Fortunes has given him a Taste of both these Extremes, and who now seems rising again to at least a distant View of a New Turn in his Affairs, I mean King *Stanislaus*.

How often have the *Poles*, and in how many Places of that Kingdom, shouted at receiving him, and shouted at rejecting him; just as he was, or was not, backed with sufficient Power to maintain himself in Possession? And how contented do they, *since that*, sit still, in the view of his lowest and most dejected Circumstances? And, no doubt, if a Time should come that he should be able to take Possession of the Throne there again, and be able to keep it; the Shouts of the People would be as much his again as ever. Nor would I answer for the Rabble, if King *Beelzebub* were to be exalted in Royal Robes, but he would have a Rabble to huzza for him, and throw Squibs at his Bonfires, as well as in other Cases.

The Sum of all my Discourse is this; I would fain have the People of this Nation rejoice with their Understandings, and distinguish themselves in their Joy, as the Occasions justly and rationally ought to be Distinguished, shewing something of Judgment in their extasies, that they might not be taxed with the levities of other Rabbles; and, that consequently, some weight may be put upon their Appearances, more than has ordinarily been due to Rabbles in other Times.

The present Occasion gives them also ground, and an Opportunity, for this alteration of their Conduct. It cannot be doubted but that they have as much just Reason for the Commemoration of the Coronation of his present Majesty, as of any Prince that ever sat on the *British* Throne; and that, (to omit the great variety of other Reasons, for I am not going to write a Panegyrick on the King,) if it were nothing but the settling the Minds of the People of this Nation in their dependence upon the Protection of a powerful Prince,—and a race of Princes of a Protestant Line,—and, that we have no Room to stand wavering between right and wrong, Possession and Claim. The only just Claimer being the strong Possessor, and the Protestant Interest secured, in a Protestant King.

As better Reasons then for our Joy can never be given, let us Keep to the Substance in our Joy; and never rejoice but upon some such like substantial Foundation. As Children they say cry for Nothing, so Fools laugh for Nothing. We have now a solid Cause for Publick Rejoicings; let us hold there, and never more Keep Holiday for Trifles, or for Contraries. Could we Keep to this, the Mob in *England* would attain the Reputation which they formerly said the *Dutch* Rabble had, namely, *that they never were in the wrong.*

On Learning; illustrated by his own Attainments.*

A. J., *Oct.* 30.—Sir, I observe with some Concern, a great Stir made among Mankind about the word *Learning*, and many Disputes, of very little Consequence, are raised upon the very Word itself; nor is it yet determined among the Learned World, what we are to understand by Learning. Nay, to tell the Truth, there is some difficulty to find out who they are we ought to call the Learned World. I must own to you, I do not judge of it as some, that would have themselves a part of the Learned World do.

I remember an Author in the World, some Years ago, who was generally upbraided with Ignorance, and called an "Illiterate Fellow" by some of the *Beau-Monde* of the last Age. He was run down in this Manner by some, that upon enquiry, had a much clearer Title to the Character of a Blockhead, by a great deal, than himself; but his Enemies were Noisy, and the Man was negligent in his own Defence. Nay he would frequently own he was no Scholar, and be perfectly unconcerned at the Calumny of being thought to be Illiterate.

I happened to come into this Person's Study once, and I found him busy translating a Description of the Course of the River *Boristhenes* out of *Bleau's* Geography, written in *Spanish*. Another Time I found him translating some Latin Paragraphs out of *Leubinitz Theatri Cometici*, being a learned Discourse upon Comets; and that I might see whether it was genuine, I looked on some part of it that he had finished, and found by it, that he understood the Latin very well, and had perfectly taken the Sense of that difficult Author. In short, I found he

---

* Although in the third person, Defoe undoubtedly speaks here of his own learning. *Vide* Vol. i., pp. 12-13.—*Ed.*

understood the *Latin*, the *Spanish*, the *Italian*, and could read the *Greek*, and I knew before that he spoke *French* fluently,—*yet this man was no Scholar.*

As to Science, on another Occasion, I heard him dispute, (in such a Manner as surpriz'd me,) upon the Motions of the Heavenly Bodies, the Distance, Magnitude, Revolutions, and especially the Influences of the Planets, the Nature and probable Revolutions of Comets, the excellency of the New Philosophy, and the like; *but this Man was no Scholar.*

In Geography and History, he had all the World at his Fingers' ends. He talked of the most distant Countries with an inimitable Exactness; and, changing from one Place to another, the Company thought, of every Place or Country he named, that certainly he must have been born there. He knew not only where every Thing was, but what every Body did in every Part of the World; I mean what Business, what Trade, what Manufacture was carrying on in every Part of the World; and had the History of almost all the Nations of the World in his Head,—*yet this Man was no Scholar.*

This put me upon wondering, even so long ago, what this *strange Thing* called a Man of Learning *was*, and what is it that constitutes a *Scholar?* For, *said I*, here's a Man speaks five Languages, and reads the Sixth, is a Master of Astronomy, Geography, History, and abundance of other useful Knowledge, (which I do not mention, that you may not guess at the Man, who is too Modest to desire it,) and yet, they say, *this Man is no Scholar.* What then will become of me, *said I*, who know nothing but a little mere Greek and Latin? What must I do to preserve the Name of a *Scholar*, for such I pass for now; but certainly must quickly forget and disown it, nay the very Name of it, if such as these pass for Men of no Learning?

But meeting with a brisk, pretty Fellow, at *White's* Chocolate House, the other Day, whom I took to be a little in my Class, for we had studied, that is, *fooled a little Time away together*, at the University formerly, and as I thought were Classic Dunces together; I say, meeting with him one Day, I made my Grievance known to him, and ask'd him what I must do.

"Phoo!" *says he*, "you are all wrong, and the thing is right; the Fellow you speak of was a meer Blockhead, for as the World has a different Taste of Learning now from what it had in former Days, so if you will pass for a *Scholar* you must take up a new Method." I was mightly pleased to find that I had met with a Director, for I knew he was conversant with the Modern World; and so I pressed him to adjourn to a Bottle, and let him and I talk it over a little. We did so, and I am perfectly reconciled to things now; and dare undertake to shew you,—Time and Place convenient, and in a few Words,—*what Learning* is, and what it is not,—and to let you see how mistaken you all are about it. But I must not begin the Relation at the heel of my Paper, you shall have it at large next Time you and the World meet together.

I am, &c.

On Learning; illustrated by the Character of a Pedant.

A. J., Nov. 6.—Sir, In my last, I made Room for an Inquiry into the modern acceptation of the Word *Learning;* and who it is we are to understand by a Man of *Learning.* I gave you an Example of a Person, within the Compass of my own Knowledge, who could speak five Languages, and could read Six, who was a Master of Science, who discoursed of the Stars and the Regions above, as if he had been born there, who had the History of the World all in his Head, the Geography of it at his Fingers' Ends, and understood the Interests of all Nations, as if he had lived among them; but all this would not reach it, this Man would by no Means pass for a Scholar.

I went some Years under the Amusement of this cramp Question, who was a Scholar? When, after some Time, I had occasion to put my Son to a Grammar School, and enquiring after a proper Person, I had a Friend, who hearing of it recommended a Man to me; and among all the rest of his Qualifications, he told me he was a great Man, a profound Scholar, that he had been eight Years Fellow of a College in *Cambridge*, that he had written a Book upon the Pointings of the Hebrew, and had made some Learned Amendments to the Greek Grammar; that he spoke the Latin better than the English; and, in short, he was known and valued for a Man of extraordinary Learning. Upon which you may be sure I put my Son to School to him most readily.

Having committed my Son to his Care for Erudition, I

had frequent Occasions to converse with this great Scholar; and, as near as I can, you shall have his just Character.

He was, in the first Place, of a sour, cynical, surly, retired Temper; this I suppose, though some of it came from mere Nature, yet had grown upon him by Time, being the consequence of poring upon his Book.

In the next Place, if he performed anything as a Scholar, it came from him by the violent Labour of his Head, violent mortifying Application, and with not only twice the Labour, but twice the Time that other Men ordinarily took for such Things.

At the same Time that he was a Critick in the Greek and Hebrew, he hardly could, or at least did not, spell his Mother Tongue, English.

·His Stile was all rough Laconicks, thronged with Colons and Full-Points; and he seldom made his Paragraphs above a Line and a half.

He was in Orders, and sometimes read a Sermon or two; but preached away all his Hearers, not being able to suit his Discourse to his Auditory. He made his ordinary Sermons the same as if he had been to preach *ad Clerum*, or to the Heads of the University.

Writing a Letter to me once, upon a Disaster which had befallen one of his Scholars, he wrote that there was a sad Accidence fallen out in his School; and, when I shewed it him, and would have mentioned it as a mistake of his Pen, he began to be Warm, would needs justify the Orthography of it, and began to talk of the Etymology and Derivation of the Words.

He knew no more of the World abroad than if he had never seen a Map, or read the least Description of Things. He could give no more Account of Africa or America than if they had never been discovered; only, that he knew St. *Cyprian* and St. *Augustine*, but not whereabouts they lived, or whether Africa was divided from America by Water, or by Land.

He understood not a Word of French, Dutch, Spanish, or Italian. He had read the Roman Histories, and the Church Histories, and had the Names of all the great Cities and Kingdoms in the Grecian, Persian, and Assyrian Monarchies by heart; but knew nothing of what Part of the Globe they were to be found in.

He had Horace and Virgil in his Head, and was as good as an Index Verborum to Juvenal and Persius. As for the Bible, *give him his Due*, he was a walking Concordance, and had a local Memory for Chapter and Verse; but when he preached, he was all Exposition, without either Inference or Application.

Take him among his Books, everything that was ancient, crabbed, and critical, suited; everything modern, smooth, eloquent, and polite, provoked him to Wrath. He had Learning enough to find fault, but not good humour enough to mend; he liked nothing, and nothing he performed could be liked. His mere Learning must be buried with him, for 'tis like a · great Crowd pressing out at a little Door, for Want of Room to come out all at once, it cannot come at all.

In a Word, he knows Letters, and perhaps could read half the Polyglot Bible, but knows nothing of the World,—has neither read Men nor Things; and this, they say, is a Scholar. Why then that SCHOLAR is a LEARNED FOOL.

Your Servant, Mr. APPLEBEE.

Fashion, a Cause of National Degeneracy.

A. J., Nov. 13.—Sir, We live in wicked Times, that's true, but I always find a Contest between the Ancients and the Moderns, about the Wickedness of the Times; and how we shall do to reconcile them I want very much to know.

I remember an old Saint of my Acquaintance, who departed in Peace about Number 80, six and thirty Year ago, used to tell me often, that he had heard his Grandmother say, there were mighty happy Times in her Uncle's Time. It seems, she being an Orphan, lived with her Uncle when she was a Child, and he had let her know, that he had seen good Times. "O Child!" says he, "the World was not so wicked, as it is now, when I was a young Man." Now my Saint, as I call him, dying thirty-six Years ago, at the Age of 80, and having heard his Grandmother, when he was 16 or 17, tell him, (perhaps she might be 90,) what her Uncle told her at the Age of 15, he had seen 60 Years before that; I say, upon all these Evidences, we may believe the People were mighty good at that Time. You may cast up the Distances, Mr. *Applebee;* or your Readers may do it at their Leisure.

Now if the World has been, ever since that Time, growing downwards and degenerating, and yet are no worse than we find them, I think 'tis pretty well. What they may come to, two or three hundred Years hence, *indeed*, I cannot say; let the *Democritans* weep about that, if they think fit; for my Part, I think 'tis none of our Business. The best Use we, of this Age, can make of the present Degeneracy of the Times, would be, to see into our particular Part, and every Man to undertake that the Age should not be the worse *by him;* and that no Part of the declining Virtue be laid at his Door.

It is certain that no more is required of Individuals than relates to Individuals, and if every Man that complains thus,—for I find the Complaint of the Badness of the Times mighty flush, in almost every Body's Mouth; I say, if every one of the Complainers would but reform one, the Case would quickly alter. Example would cease. Crime would blush, and walk alone, and in the Dark; be ashamed to come abroad by Daylight,—and at last, for, Want of Encouragement,—would die away, and grow out of Fashion.

And this brings me to the main Thing, upon which I lay the general debauchery of the Age, namely *Fashion.* It is a strange Influence, that the gust for the Fashion, or Mode, has upon the People; and it unhappily runs at this Time into even our Morals, Religion, nay even our Passions and Temper.

By Fashion (for 'tis only a fashionable Word,) I mean a Pride of imitating those who are above us, or whom we think so. I must acknowledge, if we were fond of mimicking those who were wiser than ourselves, there would be less Danger in it; but such is the gust of Imitation, that we will affect the most ridiculous Things, if it be but to follow others who are above us.

I remember, that in King *Charles* the Second's Time, the Court thronged with French of all kinds; nothing could go down with the People but what was French. French Claret, French Cooks, French Sauces, French Silks, French Taylors, French Fashions, to say nothing of French W——s, though there it all began. At length a French Ribbon Weaver in *Spittle Fields,*—finding a decay of the Trade of Narrow Ribbons, and not knowing what to do,—hires a French Taylor, to go over to France, and bring back some new Fashion that should bring the Men all to wear Ribbons.

The Frenchman went to Paris, but could find nothing worn there but what we had gotten here already; and, after racking his Invention a great while, began to be in despair of Success, and afraid he should be obliged to come back (*as we say*) without his Errand. At last, passing the *Pont Neuf* at *Paris*, he happens to see a parcel of Swiss Strollers who had gotten a Puppet-Show; and among the rest of their Puppets, their *Harlequin*, or Merry Andrew, was dressed up in a very antic Manner, and particularly with open kneed Breeches,—hung all round at the bottom with narrow Ribbons about six Inches deep,—so that it took up seven or eight hundred Yards of Ribbon to train them about.

Immediately the Taylor, (for it hit his Fancy to a Tittle,) falls to Work, got a Suit of Clothes made in *France*, with some Addenda suitable to the purpose, and a pair of Breeches exactly like the Jack Pudding he had seen.

As soon as he comes over hither, the Weaver, ravish'd with Joy at the Discovery, falls to Work, five or six Suits were made very fine and gay, and Frenchmen found to appear at Court with them, as a new French Mode; and immediately it took, the Taylor had more business than he could do, the Weavers were all employed of a sudden, nay Friends being perhaps made to a certain French Lady, but to say it was a fine Dress, and in a little Time, the King and all the Court appeared in *Pantaloons*, that was the Name they obtained, so great was the Pride of Imitation.

The Degeneracy of the Times Denied and Confuted.

A. J., Nov. 20.—Sir, I gave you a hint in my last, of the Wickedness of the Times, and how it proceeded from the mischief of Imitation, or following the Fashions. I could carry that Part on a great Way, but it would necessarily bring me to a kind of serious Reproof, and sober Satyres; and I know that will not please your Folks at this time of Day, so I drop that Part, be it ever so Useful and Profitable.

But I can not but tell you, I think we are mixing the very Reproof with the Crime, for when our People cry out of the Badness of the Times, as above, even this is but an *Imitation;*

and because 'tis the Fashion to do so, therefore they do it. The same, the very same Humour by which the Badness of the Times is grown to the Height it is now at.

Hence it comes, that those very People who complain of the Times, not only have a great share in the Degeneracy, but practice the Things which are the Cause of it, while the very Complaint is in their Mouth. " L——d," says a Woman of the Street, " how wicked this d———d Town is grown !" when a certain Gentleman picked her up in the dusk of the Evening, but did not like her, and moved off. *" You should say so at Home, Madam, not at the Corner of Salisbury Court,"* said a virtuous Lady that happened to be just behind her.

So the *London Journal,* the other Day, gave poor *Rob. Crusoe* a taste of his Breeding, and told the World it was a Lie ; and at the same Time the very *London Journal,* bless me ! how many Fables and forged Stories, not to say *Lies,* is it full of ! How many borrowed Tales, imaginary Heroes, invented Names, has he given us, as well before as after that Reproach, almost in every Paper, so Shameless is the World grown, and so wicked are the Times !

But why are our Times worse than those that went before them ? I affirm, and dare enter upon the proof of it, with any impartial Historian, that the Times past were much worse than they are now ; aye, and that the farther you go back, the worse the Times have been, even as far back as you can read anything of them, making only allowances for Circumstances, and particular Obstructions of Things. And if you will but capitulate with the World for me, that they do not from hence infer that I am justifying the wickedness of the present Age, I will come to Particulars when you please. For Example,—

Take the World in the three crying Crimes that now rage among the People, and in which the Common People especially are (that's certain) grown very wicked, and growing worse and worse every Day ;—I mean Whoring, Swearing, and Drunkenness.

For Whoring, let us look back to Popish Times, and the Days when, before the Reformation, the Monasteries, the Religious Houses, reigned in their Ecclesiastical Rogueries in England, and lived on the Fat of the Land. What voluptuous, luxurious Living ! What debaucheries with Women ! What

Murthers of innocent new born Infants, aye, and of Mothers too, for Concealing Crime and avoiding Shame, does History record of them! Nay, is it not made the very Reason of their Houses being demolished, and the Societies being Dissolved? And to add to the Scene of wickedness, and that the Clergy might not be alone in Crime, how were the same and other Crimes Winked at, nay allowed to the Laity by the Priests? Sending them away from Confessions with a *go in Peace*, and a free Absolution from all manner of Debaucheries, on the highest Penance, or perhaps, instead of it, a Payment of Money; so commuting with Heaven for what is past, and running on Tick for more.

Can any one think this was not a proclaiming Liberty for Crime, and an Encouraging all kinds of Wickedness; in a Manner which, blessed be God and the Reformation, we see nothing of now.

To say People are debauched still, and there is a great deal of Whoring and Lewdness among us still, is to say nothing to the Purpose; for so there is a great deal of Atheism and Irreligion still, but Atheism and Irreligion is not allowed by the Church for Money, nor is it the Practice of the Time, Nationally Speaking, to encourage it. Vice, however prevailing, is yet a Crime, and is concealed as such; and sometimes, tho' indeed but seldom, punished as such. The Clergy do not preach upon it as a venial Sin, or give tacit Licenses for it, as formerly.

In the next Place Whoring is not allowed by Law; we have no Bourdelloes, as at Venice and Naples. No Stews allowed at the Bankside, as was formerly the Case, and no longer ago than even at the Heels of the Reformation, I mean in Henry VIIth's time; we have no Statutes made for Limiting the number of Bawdy Houses, and setting up a Sign at their Doors to have them known by, or for restraining them to who, and who not, when and when not, how long and how long not, any they should receive and entertain, as Lodgers in their Houses. So that, even in this very Part, which is so notorious, and so much and so justly complain'd of; I say, even in this Article, we are not yet so bad as the Ages that have gone before us.

Nor, if I should instance in the upper Ranges of Mankind, and should rummage the lewdest Part of the Town; could we

find such flaming Instances of Wickedness as in the Times of
King *Charles* IInd, of Pious Memory? We have no Roches-
ters, no Sedleys to be found, who gloried in Crime, and by
their Wit and Examples, gave a Sanction to all Manner of
Lewdness, in defiance of Justice, and above the reach of Law.
Nor were there a Set of Men who were able to act equal to
them; (for it was his boast that meaner Men did not know
how to Sin like a Lord,) I say, were there any flagitious Branch
of degenerated Quality inclined to be thus wicked, and able
to be so, yet they have not the same Example, nor have they
the same Encouragement from those above them.

I go no further, 'tis enough to say there is no Comparison;
the Times are bad enough, God mend 'em! But not quite so
bad yet, as those that went before us. The Complaint then of
the Degeneracy of the Times is all Grimace. All a whining
modish Way that Men have got, to make us believe they are
better than other People, when the very Complaint is a Falsehood in Fact, and is an Addition to the Wickedness they complain of, by adding their Hypocrisy to the barefaced Debaucheries of the Times. If they would have the Times better,
let them leave whining over the Crimes of other Men, and
diligently reform their own.

Journalists, like Mountebanks, profess to Benefit the Public.

A. J., Nov. 27.—Sir, We that print Publick Papers, ought,
like Quack-Doctors, always to act, or at least pretend to do it,
for Publick Good. It was but the other Day I had the
Curiosity to stand gaping among a Crowd of People, not much
wiser than myself, about a Mountebank Stage; where, after
Monsieur Jack Pudding, (that's English for a Harlequin,)
had played his Game very well, gathered a large Assembly,
and entertained them to their full Satisfaction, forth stalks
Mr. *Doctor*, Grave as a Senator, *Tout Brilliant*, (as the French
call it,) with Gold and Silver Embroidery, a fine full-bottom
Wig, a gold snuff-box in his Hand, and all his *et cetera* of
suitable Accoutrements. And after jesting a little with his
Merry Andrew, he turns to his Gentleman, who attended, and
beckoning him to come forward to his Assistance, he addresses
himself to harangue the Mob.

His first Topick, after a few introductory Words, was to tell them what admirable Cures he had wrought among them; how a Fortnight before he had cut off a poor Man's Leg, and pointing to a poor Fellow, who was brought up on purpose, told 'em, there he stood, in so fair a way of Recovery, that no Hospital Surgeon could shew a Man better in two Months; that the week before that, he had cut off two Women's Breasts; and that, by and by, they should see them both come upon the Stage.

N.B. That was prolong'd, you may be sure, to keep the Crowd together, for the Women were both behind the Curtain at the other end of the Stage, at the same Time; and it did effectually keep them.

After this, he told them, these were Operations that other Surgeons had great Sums of Money for doing, but the Poor might perish for any Thing they cared, unless they could be paid, or have good Security before hand, they would do nothing; and besides, says he, they will have Security beforehand, because, it being as likely they will kill the Patient as cure him, they need not then care one Farthing whether he lives or dies.

" But I, Gentlemen," says he, " act upon another Principle. These poor People, 'tis well known, were able to pay nothing for their Cure; they are your Neighbours, and you know their Circumstances. I have performed the Operation, and finished the Cure for Nothing. I act upon a higher Motive. I thank God I have a plentiful Fortune, and I don't keep a Stage here for what is to be got. I don't suppose you can believe, that what I get by coming once a Week here among you, can maintain me, or support the Figure I live in. No, no, Gentlemen! I come abroad and expose myself thus, to do good; the very Physick I dispense among you, is rated so low, and given out so cheap, I may say, 'tis rather given you, than sold to you. The Price I take, all my Servants can testify, is but just sufficient to pay the Charge of the Ingredients. As for my part, 'tis a full Satisfaction to me to be able to do good to the Publick. I had rather have the Blessing and Prayers of the Poor, than the Money of the Rich."

By this Time, the two Women were brought out upon the Stage and shewn, and he opened their Breasts, and dress'd them both before the People; and indeed the Women were strangely well, considering the dreadful Operation they had gone through.

But now, what was the End of all this? Why, 'tis true the Doctor had made the Amputations dexterous enough, and the People recovered apace, and he had done it all for nothing; and yet the Doctor was paid for it too, for what was the Consequence? Why, the People, astonished at the Wonder, and elevated in their Opinion of the Doctor, bought his Medicines and Packets, at such a Rate, that he took 15*l.* in less than two Hours time, in Sixpences, Twopences, and Groats; and in the Evening had his Chamber thronged with Patients for sundry Ailments and Grievances, to all of whom he gave Advice and Physick, taking nothing for his Advice, only that his Gentleman, who stood at a Scrutoire in a Corner of the Room, took of some 1*s.*, of others 1*s.* 6*d.*, and the like, as the Doctor directed; and here he took six or seven pounds more the same Night, and in the Morning while he is Dressing. Then, away he goes to the next Market Town, where he does the same, and thus the whole Week round; with this Addition, that where he stays a Sunday, he has as good a Chamber Practice all Day, as before in the Evening.

Now all this is for the Publick Good; and have not you and I, Mr. *Applebee*, as much right to doctor up a Journal, and take three halfpence, for the rectifying the Brains of Mankind, as this dressed-up Gew-Gaw of a Mountebank has to give his Packets out, with his good-for-nothing Plaisters, and his *Pillæ Rud*, and *Pillæ Roff*, and the like, and take Sixpence? Sure we may have as much Room to pretend to Publick Good for curing the Head, as he has for healing a Cut Finger? For rectifying the Passions of Men, as he for checking the Vapours? For curing the Scurvy Humours of the People, as he for purging the Scorbutick Humours out of the Blood? Therefore, upon the whole, I think we act more upon the Publick Good, than e'er a Mountebank of them all.

I might go from these Quacking Mountebanks to another Sort, I mean your Politick Quacks, your State Mountebanks, who make long harangues too, and boast of their Zeal for the Publick Good—their Patriotism, and such as that; but at bottom we all know what they aim at, and what Measures

they take.   But hold! Mr. *Applebee!* what are we doing?
Tace they say, is Latin for a *Candle!*

> " *To hold our Hands I hold it good,*
> *Whether we are, or are not, understood.*"

VALE.

Merry Days and Doings.   A Satire on the Times.

A. J., Dec. 4.—Sir, Whoever complains of the Badness of
the Times, (as it seems he that wrote you the last you printed
insinuates,) I assure you I don't; I dare say there never were
merrier Days, nor merrier Doings, in this part of the World,
than we have, even just now, upon the Stage. To talk of bad
Times, in such a gay, rich, thriving, topping Day as this, must
be very strange; let them tell me the Time, if they can, when
ever People lived so merrily as they do now? As to Whoring
and Lewdness, your last Author tells us of the *Stews* on the
Bankside, near Southwark, which were allowed by the Government, limited by Act of Parliament, and the like, and calls
that an Instance of the Badness of the Times. Pray let him
take a Walk into the Hamlet of Drury Lane, or ask him if he
remembers *Whetston's Park?* Let him then ambulate from
Ludgate to Temple Bar in an Evening, or (if you do not think
the Journey too long for him,) let him begin in that modest
Part call'd the City, and extend his walk to Charing Cross,
and thro' the Park at Eleven at Night, and let him tell me if
Wickedness is not as merrily carried on our Modern Way, and
without the help of a *Bourdelloe*, as ever it was then? And
much more to the Scandal of Magistracy? *But that by the
bye.*

As to the Laws conniving, *as it seems your Friend supposes
they did formerly*, I do not say our Laws Connive at Fornication and Adultery; but this I say, the Trouble, the Difficulty,
the Expense of Suits, the Nicety required in Proofs, and the
many Ways the Devil finds to creep out, are such that I know
not which I would choose, either to wear the Horns quietly,
or make the Knave that bestows them on me pay for their
Ornaments; witness the Quaker at Chelmsford, mentioned in
our late Newspapers. Why, *Friends*, in good Truth, Why
should a Man sue another for an unnatural Crime when the
Owner was gone to the East Indies? Would any Man expect,

or should he expect any other, in such merry Days of Cock
Fighting as those? For my Part, if I go to the East-Indies,
and leave a Wife unprovided for behind, Would I sue any
Man for Damages that should take care of her in my long,
long Abdication? No, No, Friends, Thrones are never to be
Vacant, All breaches in Fences must be repaired, and Justice
done. Let us never enter too far into such nice Matters, in our
Times, lest we find worse doings at Home, that should be
looked after as much, and want it more.

For what is it we make so many Laws against Bankrupts,
and fill our Jails with poor Debtors, when we all run on Score
with the Devil for our Morals, and turn Bankrupts in point of
Faith and Honour every Day? Heavens! What drunken
Doings is there among us, and how merrily do we reel about
Streets every Night! But that which is the merriest Part of
all, is to see the Vice creep into the Kitchen so fast, and go
round the Tea-Table; for Female Drunkenness was never so
much in Fashion in this World as now, nor were the Merry
Consequences ever so visible. But of that I think to write you
a brief Diary in a few Days, that may perhaps give some Satisfaction to the Ladies for the Scandal thrown upon them on
this Occasion. Also, I may give you a new Scheme for the
Quality, instructing the Sex how they may be merry according
to Law, and drink in due Proportion to the Dignity of their
Families; for, in short, 'tis a Scandal never to be retrieved,
that Ladies of Distinction should be drunk in the ordinary
Way, and Dutchesses drink *Gin* like the Fish Wives.

But to return to the merry Times I was speaking of, we
lately heard tell of a JEW, who bilk'd the Bank of a few Guineas,
18 or 20 Thousand, I think they call'd 'em,—and as this could
not be done but by dint of down right Forgery,—for the Bank
they say, are as cunning Fellows as a Man need ever employ
or trust one's Money with; I say, as it could be done no other
way, so here, they tell us, was no want of Forgery upon Forgery. Well, and what then? The Money they say is paid,
and so the Man may go hang himself, or Pillory himself, if he
will, for no Body as I hear troubles themselves about the Crime.
Now, Mr. *Applebee*, I have been told, when I was a little Boy,
that no Man can, or at least ought, to Commute a Crime, or
acquit a Criminal, but by Law; and, that he that compounded

a Felony, was next a kin to him that committed it; but perhaps that may not hold in these Days.

What merry Doings should we have here, Mr. *Applebee*, if Forgery and Adultery were Felony, as they say is the Case with our Neighbours on the other side of the Tweed! No wonder the Gentlemen on that Side the Country, when they take Occasion to divert themselves in that uncouth Way, come into a milder Climate, where, tho' the Sun may shine warmer, and Blood boil hotter, yet the Laws are a little cooler in those particular Cases. Bless us! To hang Folks for lying close to one's Neighbour! Well hast thou scaped, honest Friend ———— of Chelmsford! Hadst thou been in Scotland I doubt thy outward Man had been suspended. But not to run too hard upon Neighbour ———, What merry Work, as I said above, would it make among us if all our seducing, debauching Nobles and Gentlemen should be deemed worthy of Death! Among the rest, what would become of the worthy Nottinghamshire Magistrate, who, if you believe Fame, suffers not a Tenant of his to go free, unless protected by some particular in the Wife more than ordinary disagreeable.

We have many Occasions of this kind present to our Thoughts within the Compass of our Climate, which give me Occasion to say, it would seem to be a merry Turn of Affairs if all those that have been over Civil to their Neighbours should be brought into Jeopardy; and I fear we should have some People's ——— make Buttons, who at present we look upon as too demure so much as to think of, and who it would be thought next to uncharitable but to suspect.

As to some other light Offences of the Times, such as Irreligion, Anti-religion, no Religion, and false Religion, Heresy and Hereticks, I think we have Room to be very merry upon that Head, for I must own they seem to make all Religion a kind of Mirth now, and to find something in every part of it to be very merry with. Whether they may not at last jest themselves out of all Religion, that is for themselves to consider, not me.   Your Humble Servant,

                                        DEMOCRITUS.

Self Murder.   Royal Gin Recommended.   A Satire.

A. J., Dec. 18.—Sir, I once took the Pains to write to you
upon a very solemn Affair (but I find the Times do not much
relish anything serious,) I mean the Subject of Self Murther;
as whence it proceeds, and why so many Self Murthers happen
in this Country more than in any other, and why more, even
in this Country, at this Time, than ever before; for both these
Particulars are apparently true.

But seeing, whatever is the Occasion, and from what Principle soever it is practised, *so it is,* and *so it is like to be,* and
there is no putting an Englishman out of his Way; I am thinking that it is to no Purpose to talk to them upon that Point
any longer, but to put them in a Way, for the future, *how to
do it* with more Ease, and less violence to Nature. So that there
need not require so much screwing the Spirits up to a Pitch,
and raising a Storm in Nature for it; till which, many People
have wanted Resolution to go through the Operation, and
dally'd and *dally'd* a great while with Death, before they durst
venture. Nay, at last, they have been forced to be beholden to
the Devil, or to (that worse than Devil) an *ill Wife,* to put
them into a Rage; and then they do it off hand, *Sans Ceremony,* Monsieur.

Now, my Way is certainly *a Nostrum* to this Age. 'Tis the
softest, easiest Way! A Man slides out of Life with the utmost
quiet; so calm, 'tis like an Opiate. He neither feels himself,
no nor hears himself die; in a Word, he is dead and gone with
Decency, and knows nothing of the Matter till he comes into
t'other Country, *Lord knows where!*

I know by this Time, many a melancholy poor Wretch that
has Occasion for it, is uneasy to know my new Method; for
there are many poor uneasy Creatures in Life who long to be
out of it, (they know not why,) and would *do it,* but they can't
bear the Thoughts of a Knife in the *Wind-pipe,* or a hard Knot
under the *Ear,* or an Ounce of Lead in the inside of the *Skull.*
These Things sound too harsh to 'em; and they can't get up
Resolution enough *to die, for fear of Death.* There's an Old
Gentleman, of my Acquaintance, is so hasty to die, for fear of
Poverty, with about 10,000*l.* in his Pocket; that I doubt not

he would give me 500*l.* beforehand to teach him my Method, that he might be sure he should not be starved.

But hold, Mr. *Applebee*, I don't love harsh Measures, they never do well in any Thing. I have been considering, whether you and I might not make a good Bubble of the Project, and if we can't get a Patent for it, we may find some Way or other to keep the Property of the Undertaking to our own Use and Benefit; and to bring it to this, that no Body shall have the Privilege of Killing themselves without our Consent, and without paying us such and such Fees for Direction. As the King of *Denmark* lets no Body in or out of the Baltick Sea-Door (*the Sound*) but at such a Price.

Well, however, Mr. *Applebee*, upon second Thoughts, and being myself of a publick Spirit,—and willing to do all the good I can to my Fellow Creatures—which you must own is a very honourable Account of myself; I say, being of this Publick Spirit, I have thought fit to make this valuable Secret known to the World, by which any of our frantick Folks that are resolved to be gone *(the shortest Way,)* may do it with less Pain, less Terror upon the Mind, and without any of the Devil's assistance at all; for, *by the Way*, what has he to do with it? And this easy Way, Mr. *Applebee*, is, in short, nothing but——

DRINKING OF GIN.

Royal Gin! Exalted Gin! Mr. *Applebee!* You can hardly conceive how never-failing, clever, and easy a Way it is. We have had about 13 or 14, that I can call over by Name that have tried the happy Experiment, within this Month past, in the narrow Compass of my Acquaintance, and not one of them has miscarried. In a Word, 'tis as sure *as a Gun*, nay as sure as *Inoculation*,—if the Body be but rightly prepared,—as the Doctors call it; nor did I ever know it fail since made use of regularly, according to the modern Way. As to the Manner of applying this infallible Remedy, that, Mr. *Applebee*, I think I may very lawfully keep as a Secret, till farther Enquiry is made, being a Matter of some Nicety; at present there are so many *Gin Doctors* lately set up in England, that I think no Body can be at a loss for Direction. The main Business is, frequent Application and a suitable Quantity, both which the said *Gin Doctors* will at any Time, *(so generous is the Age at this Time*,) be readily assisting, without Fee or Reward, other than simply paying for the Ingredients. And of these Physicians, I am told there are above 5000 new set up, in and about this sober City, within a few Years past ; and, that all or most of them have very good Practice.

How happy are we beyond our Ancestors, and beyond even the Ages within our own remembrance! We, who have discovered to us, by the Wisdom of our Sages, so wonderful a Specifick to cure all the Maladies of Life ; and so easily to open the Door, at any Time, out of this dark State, into the general *Ecclaircissiment* of Nature. Our Ancestors were forced to do this by outrageous Methods, *Swords, Pistols, Garters, Tape, Packthread*, anything that came next to Hand ; putting Nature into such Convulsions, that our Coroners' Juries generally brought them in *Non Compos*, as if it was not to be done till Men were besides themselves. But now, it appears practicable, without the least Disturbance or Discomposure ; and you have nothing to do but DRINK and DIE.

PROBATUM EST, Mr. *Applebee*, farewell.

Wanted, an Honest Man.

A. J., Dec. 18. — Mr. Applebee,—I have a Proposal of Weight to make to you. I do not know what great Interest you may have in the World among Persons of Business ; but 'tis my fate to converse among Men who it seems have received some very bad Usage, somewhere or other, and are always complaining. I never meet with anything from them of the Management of Mankind, (I mean in Trading Affairs, Mr. *Applebee*, not Governments. Pray don't bring me into a Scrape !) I see nothing, I say, but continual Complaints, Rogues, Knaves, Cheats, d——d Rogues, Bubbles, and the like good Words. Now pray, Mr. *Applebee*, inform me, for sure such a Thing is somewhere to be had, I say, pray inform me, if you can, where I may find an HONEST MAN? I doubt not but such Things there are, but where? Where does he dwell? And who, and what is his Name? I beg of you to enlighten me a little in this Matter ; for, at present, I am much in the dark upon the Subject. I am loth to send into foreign Countries, Mr. Applebee, for after all, I am in hopes he may be found here as soon as abroad ; nay, Charity tells me here or nowhere. But O that I knew but where he lived! And how I might direct a Letter to him, for indeed I have at present great Occasion for him.

> " Diogenes, the Ancients say,
> Walked with his Lanthorn duly
> At noon among
> The mortal Throng
> To find a Man speak Truly."

Your Servant, URGENTISSIMUS.

Murmuring at the King's long Stay in Hanover.

A. J., Jan. 1., 1726.— . . . . Come we next to a modern Head of Complaint from the Inhabitants of the Western Part of this great City, for the absence of their Parliament, their Court, and their Sovereign. While they complain'd only, and with decency wished his Majesty would come home, and the like; I pitied the poor Sufferers with all my Heart, and wish'd and complain'd with them, and for them. But, Mr. *Applebee*, when Wishing and Complaining exceeds its due Bounds, and comes to Clamour and Disaffection, and People write Pamphlets, next Door to Treason and Mutiny, or to excite them against the Government, and against the Sovereign; *hold then*, Mr. *Applebee*, I know you are too honest, as well as too much your own Friend, and your Country's Friend, to expect or assent to that.

Kings would have but a very mean share of Trust reposed in them, if it was not left to them to judge, while they were Abroad, when it was proper for them to return. And suppose the Sovereign to be Abroad, engaged on important Occasions, for the Publick Good of his Kingdoms; or if it were of the Protestant Interest, *as we have Reason to believe is the present Case*, is it not highly reasonable to think, that if his Majesty is able to direct those Negociations, as we see he is, and is the centre of their Motions, he is a proper Judge of when they are, or are not sufficiently settled, and may be left.

We have formerly had glorious Kings, who having been possessed of large Dominions Abroad have, some for one Occasion, some for another, thought fit to go abroad, for the managing their Affairs beyond the Seas; and did not they always go and come when they pleased?

King Edward III., a King whose Wars Abroad were not for the Defence of Liberty, not for Establishing Religion, or Preservation of Commerce, but merely for *Conquest* and *Glory;* yet King Edward went into Flanders, and to Cologne, to form secret Alliances against France, and that King staid at Antwerp, and other Places above a Year (mark that) at one Time, viz., from July 1338, and he staid Abroad till September, *Ann.* 1339. Yet we have nothing said of the People's murmuring for want of Trade, or the Westminster good Wives for want of letting their Lodgings, nor do we hear that there were any Pamphlets written, to excite ill-Blood ; especially, we did not hear the preposterous Part, namely, that those People should exclaim loudly at his Absence, who had least Desire he should ever return at all.

I could give you an Account, if I had Room too, how great expense that King was at abroad, and how he contracted heavy Debts there, which is not our Case at all ; and yet the People gave him half their Wool the next Year to pay his Debts, so far were they from crying out of spending their Money abroad, *even when it was so.* But see how Englishmen may alter ! Mr. *Applebee.*

Yours, &c.

The Duty of Journalists towards the Government.

A. J., Jan. 9.—Sir, By a Letter lately sent you, and which you published in your Journal some Time ago, you are pressed, as I understand it, to write upon publick and politick Subjects, as a Thing which would be useful and agreeable to your Readers. I remember once, in a Reign when there was much more *Malecontentism* than I hope there is now, and I am sure much more Reason for it, a Person *Incog.* pressed the Printer of a Paper to let him Write for him, and he would write his Paper gratis, which the Printer readily accepted, (as who would not, Mr. *Applebee ?)* and so they set out.

As it happened, he advanced the Paper presently, for he wrote bold Things, and such as surprized the World; he attacked Great Men, because they were Great, and satirized the best Actions, as if done with the worst Designs. And the World were mightily pleased, for Scandal is the universal Passion of the People.

Encouraged by the Shouts and Huzzas of the Mob, the Man,—knowing no Bounds of either Reason or good Manners, Duty or Law,—ran his Head at last against the Stone Walls of the Government; and the publick Justice alarmed and roused at the Insolence, call'd for an Account of it. The Sequel was, the poor Printer was taken up, and, not being able to produce his Author, took a Walk to Newgate; what followed was Merciful indeed in the Government, but without Merit in the Man.

Now, Mr. *Applebee*, I would have those who prompt the Publishers of such Papers as yours, first assure the Printer they will go to Newgate for him, and then let them send what Sort of Papers they please.

But this is not all, in the next place a Publisher of a Paper should Judge a little, whether the Government he lives under is just, and the Administration right, or no, before spreading Reproach and Complaints of either. They should consider if we complain with Reason, or without Reason, and Square their Writings accordingly. If the Government merits Praise, let Panegyrick be without Flattery; if Censure, let the Remark be with Modesty. Just Governments, and Righteous Administrations will equally bear with, nay accept these; and no Honest Man will offer them any other.

If then, upon this Foot, you are willing to have, now and then, a Letter, upon the publick Affairs of Great Britain, or any other Nation, I shall bestow my best Labours to oblige you; but if you expect Panegyrick with fulsome and nauseous Palaver, or censure of Superiors,—with rancour and indecency, virulence and disaffection,—tell 'em, Mr. *Applebee*, you are their humble Servant, and they may be pleased to Note you understand yourself better than to merit Newgate on that Account. Besides, where is the Occasion for it? And to complain and Insult without Occasion, is to be (as well as to suffer as) an evil doer, which we are equally forbid.

Take then a Specimen of the Manner in which I will, to serve you, talk of publick Affairs, and see how you and the World may like it.

The Pulse of the Times, they say, runs high for——what? I suppose it would be expected I should say, for *a War*. If I should say so, I should say what I neither see nor believe; and

unless I should speak to favour Parties, I would not be willing
to Slander the Nation, and say they desire they know not
what.   Have not we, and the World, had War enough?   Are
the Wounds of the late War fully healed?   Is War a Pleasure
to the World, or is it a Judgment, and is the Sword sent as a
Punishment to the Nations?   To say the Pulse of the Nation
beats high for a War, and not give the Reason of it, would be
to write a Satyr upon the Nation.   I would speak of a War
as the late Duke of Marlborough (when he was Lord Churchill,
and as young and full of Fire as any Man) said in a Speech to
the House of Commons, on the Motion of a War with France;
If a War be unnecessary, let us not be fond of it, if necessary,
let us not be afraid of it.

The Enemy we have in view is not so inconsiderable that
we should Court a Quarrel with them, and yet I hope not so
formidable that we should abandon the Nation's Interest, or
the Protestant for fear of them; as then we are in a state of
uncertainty in the Measures taking, or taken, about War or
Peace, so let us be in a state of Neutrality in our desires between War and Peace.

I make no doubt but his Majesty brings over with him, not
only the Reason, but the Resolution for War or Peace, and
that you will know them in due Time; in the meantime I
shall observe a little upon the Subject, as things seem to look
Abroad and at Home.

At Home I observe People speak of War and Peace, not as
the publick Good is concerned, but as their own Affairs call
up their Politicks into the Discourse.

Talking with a Stock-Jobber the other Day, I found him
mighty anxious about the Public Affairs, and whether we should
have War or Peace.   "Why," says I to him, "do you seem
so concern'd about it?   What is War or Peace to you?"
"Nay," says he, "I don't care one Farthing, only that if I
could know a little before my Neighbours, I should know
how Stocks would go, and so might know whether to Buy or
Sell."

Just thus, talking with a Half Pay Officer in the Country,
and he was in great hope of a War; I entered a little into the
Causes upon which a War was to be hoped for, or shunned.
"Ay, ay," says he, "that is for you to talk of; but we Gen-

tlemen who have been in the Army, we may hope to raise our Fortunes by a War; we can get nothing by Peace."

Talking with a Merchant, he said, " A War! God forbid! That's a sinking Fund, I am sure," says he, "to Trade. We Merchants shall get nothing by that." " But, Sir," says I, " the Protestant Religion is concerned." " Prithee," says he, " don't tell me of Religion, Protestant or Popish; we are a trading Nation, let us look to our Trade."

Thus, Mr. *Applebee*, in short, the Pulse of the Nation just seems stated, and every Man wishes as his Interest guides him to wish; few understand the true Interest of their Country, or a true State of Things in the World.

Our Business therefore, I think, about a War, is as a good Christian's should be about Death,—neither to wish for it, nor fear it; but let us leave 'em both where they should be left; Death, to God and his Providence; War to the King and his Parliament; and resolve to be satisfied with what shall be determined there. In my next I'll speak something of the Parties abroad.

On the Spread of Unfounded Public Rumours.

A. J., Jan. 22.—Sir, This has been a Stormy Winter, can you tell if it will be a Calm Summer? Many wise and skilful Navigators have been Shipwrecked in the late tempestuous Weather; many Politicians are like to be run aground in the Councils and Consultations for the next Summer.

" Why," says a grave Gentleman to me, upon talking thus, " are you of Opinion then that there will be a War next Summer?" And he listened earnestly for my Answer. After but a Moment's pause I readily answered; " Yes, I make no doubt there will, it is impossible it should be otherwise."

I then went on, musing and uttering strange Things, till another, as grave as the former, asked me another Question as full of Wisdom as the first, namely, How the War would be maintained? " For," said he, " the making a new War here, would make Mad Work." I answered, " That was a Question by itself. That the World generally went to War first, and then found out Ways and Means to carry it on; that a small deal of Money may be sufficient to make men Quarrel, and sometimes Men and Nations too quarrell'd for want of Money. At

length, one graver than the rest, and who began to see a little
farther into the Millstone than the rest, came with a serious
Air, and a low Voice: "Sir," says he, "You seem to have a
little of the Waterman in your Discourse, it looks another Way
than it aims; you say there will certainly be a War, but where,
pray? And who is it will make War?"

I told him I spoke directly. If their Question looked
another Way they should have explained themselves, I answered it plainly, and that I was satisfied there would be a
War. "Ay, Sir," says he again, "but where?" "Why, in
Persia," said I, "where could you think I meant?" "Why,
Sir, we meant quite another Thing, we meant a War here at
Home." "At Home?" said I, "why now you must explain
yourself again." Then one run on with a War in Poland for
the Protestants; "Well," says I, "If that should happen, how
do you call that a War here at Home? And what are we
concerned in it? Only as Protestant Allies we may lend them
a little Help." "But," says he, again, "a War with the Emperor." "For what?" says I. "If you let three or four of
his Ships alone at Ostend, the Emperor has nothing to say to
you, or you to him."

In short, the Notions we have of an approaching War seem
to be built upon the weakest and most incongruous Foundations imaginable. : . . . . .

Incapacity of Spain and Poland for War.

A. J., Feb. 5.—In a Word, for these two Nations to pretend
to bully the World, and talk of making War, deserves no better
Answer, in my Opinion, than a certain Grand Vizier of the
Turks gave once to the Muscovite Ambassador at the Porte,
who talk'd big, and threatened the Turks with his Master's
Arms. "Go home," said the Turk to him, "and tell your
Master that I say, *he understands neither how to make War or
Peace.*" . . . . . .

On the Folly of Hazardous Pleasures.

A. J., Feb. 19.—Sir, I have heard some of our *hot-blood
Philosophers* say, there is no true Pleasure like that of having
some little Difficulties mixed with their Delight, and meeting
with some Fatigue; and in consequence of this Notion, these

People generally choose the most robust, and sometimes hazardous Exercises, and this they call taking of Pleasure. I happen to have met with the excess of these Experiences in this Case in my Time.

I would fain know, if any of these wise Gentlemen come in your Way, how, and which Way, the Pleasure is conveyed to the Mind, that arises from needless Hazards and Dangers, which we expose ourselves to without a justifiable Reason for them; and on what Reputation with others, or Satisfaction to ourselves, the Mischiefs which befal us on those Occasions, are to be supported.

In the late *French* War, a young Gentleman in *Sussex*, to compliment his Mistress, a young Lady of a pretty Good Fortune, would needs take her out in a Boat, to toss her a little, as he call'd it; (he had better have been tossed in a Blanket than have taken his Recreation with her in that Way.) " O," says she, " *I shall be sick;*" " Why *that's the pleasure of it,*" says he; " *O but,*" says she, " *I shall be wetted and frighted;*" " Why ay," says he, " *that will make it still the pleasanter when we come back.*" In short he prevailed, and they rowed off a Mile or two, the Weather warm and calm, in a Boat with two Seamen.

When they were off, the Wind began to blow, and blew fresher and fresher, and harder and harder, from the Shore; till in Short, they could not get back again, but lay upon the open Sea all that Night. There was a little fatigue for them to make it pleasant.

In the Morning, being half over to *France*, and the Sea going very high, they were in great Distress; but at length they saw a Vessel under Sail coming towards them, and glad they were to be taken up, and saved from drowning. But, to the encrease of their pleasing Difficulties, when they were taken on Board, they were surprized to find they were gotten into a French Privateer, and the Seamen fell to pulling and hauling them; and, in a Word, almost tore all their Clothes off their Backs, and glad the Gentleman was, by promising the Captain a good Ransom, to get him to protect his Mistress from the worst of Violence. *All this was to heighten their Pleasure.*

In a Word, they carry'd him into *France,* and it cost him enough (before they got home again,) to allow him to call it his Dear Pleasure, as long as he lived.

Again, we find Gentlemen in *England*, mighty fond of sliding with Skates, upon the Ice, when we have a hard Frost; and this violent Exercise they gratify their Fancy with, and 'tis very well if it ends so. It is true in *Holland* and *Germany*, where the Ice is often strong enough to bear a piece of Cannon upon it, there is some Sense in it; and, which adds still to the Reasonableness of the Risk, the *Skate-Riders* use it to go upon their ordinary Business, to Markets and Fairs, and on Journies, and the like. But how strange is it here, to see Men skating in *England* upon thin Ice, and deep Water, and without Consideration, hazard themselves, for the pride of being look'd at by the People; and, if they can but hear a looker on say, *that Gentleman does it cleverly*, why then that Fool (Gentleman) exerts himself to the utmost, and at the utmost Hazard; and at length, not foreseeing the weakness of the Ice, he feels it give Way, plunges in, and is drown'd; and, could he hear it then, he would find all the World blaming him for a Fool.

The *Spanish Bull Feasts* seem to have been much of a kind with this, where the Noblemen and Gentlemen to gain the esteem of a Mistress, or the Reputation of being Brave, encounter with the strongest and most furious Creature in the Universe; and that, with all possible inequality of Weapons and Strength, and oftentimes, 15 or 16 are wounded, to one that comes off with Applause.

Now I would fain know, Mr. *Applebee*, upon what Point of human Reasoning these Men act; and how such irrational Hazards as those can be answered by a Man of common Sense to himself.

It is commendable in a Soldier to be Brave; but this Bravery does not consist in Madness and Desperation. He is truly brave who coolly stands his Ground when he is attacked, and repulses the Enemy; who, when he is commanded, falls on with Fury, but can receive the Enemy's fire with Flegm till he is. As a Man can never keep his Credit, that cannot keep his Post, so he never gains any Credit who falls on without Order. No man runs needless Hazards in War; it is enough to be bold and daring when he is drawn out to the Action. Not the utmost Bravery in Action will bear him out when he is not; nay, he is blamed tho' he succeeds, but if he is wounded or killed it is presently laid at his Door, and they say, who bid him go?   What Business had he there?

Three Gentlemen, in the late deep Snow, about three Weeks past, took a Boat, to go a shooting, upon the River *Trent*, in *Nottinghamshire*.   By eagerness after their Game, or want of Skill, or Accident, they lost one of their Oars; having no Rudder, and but one Oar, and the Current exceeding Swift, they were driven down the Stream.   At length the Boat lodged them among some Osiers in the Stream of the River, where they could neither launch her off, nor had Land to get out upon; so for their particular Satisfaction, they had the pleasure of lying in the Boat all Night; while, for their particular Comfort too, a deep Snow fell upon them to warm 'em.   In the Morning they strove, but in vain, to get the Boat off, none of 'em could swim; and if they could, it was but very indifferent Weather for a Cold Bath.   So they breakfasted upon Snow-Balls, and dined upon the Same, their *Sauce* being continual screaming and hallooing for Help.

At length, kind Providence, who was pleased to correct their Folly, rather than fatally to punish it, directed a Countryman so as to hear, and follow the Noise they made, and come to the opposite Bank; when he had seen their Distress, and heard all they had to say, he told them he would go and get some Help, if he could.   After about an Hour's more Exercise for their Pleasure, the Man returns with a long rope in his Hand; this put them almost to Despair, for how should they get the Rope? It was too far to cast it to them, and they had nothing to reach it with.   "Well, well!" says the Countryman, "be easy, I'll send it to you presently;" and with that he calls a Dog to him, and taking the End of the Rope, and giving it the Dog in his Mouth, "Here," says he, "carry it over to that Boat."   Away goes the Dog, and takes the Water at once, and swims over to them with the Rope; and then the Countryman pull'd over their Boat.

I leave the just Reflections upon the Folly of the Men, and Sagacity of the Dog, to your judicious Readers; especially those that love to have their Pleasure attended with some Difficulties and Fatigues.   As for the Story, you may depend upon the Truth of it.

A Pie worth Stealing.

A. J., Feb. 19.—Mr. Barry, the Exeter Carrier, who was sued by Mr. Kennedy, Collector of Customs at that Port, for losing a Pye, in which was said to be 1500 Guineas belonging to the Government, which he was bringing in his Waggon to London, hath obtained a *Noli Prosequi*.

The Jesuits in Poland Outwitted.

A. J., Feb. 26.— . . . .
. . . . . . But the Jesuits reckoned without their Host.   One private pique, which they, as cunning as they are, could not foresee, or foreseeing, could not prevent, lost France entirely as to their Cause; for King Philip, making a Secret Treaty with the Emperor, without the Participation of France; and that Treaty, as it were, pointed with resentment at France; Interests of State roused up the French Court to counteract this Piece of Spanish Policy, and threw France as it were into the Arms of the Protestants; and so the Jesuits are defeated in their great politic Gunpowder Plot against the Protestant Powers.   Nor can all their Interest and Cunning, or all their Influence, as Confessors to Princes, bring them to bank their Civil Interests in favour of the Church.   And what is the Consequence of all this? Popish Measures seem to be broken, and the lofty Powerful Princes whom they depended upon, see themselves over-matched. The Balance of Europe turns against them, and now they change their Note; the Bishops in Poland talk of giving the Protestants Liberty, and the Affair of Thorn to be left to the King. . . . .

On the Increase of Robberies and Murders; and the Character of the Army affected thereby.

A. J., Mar. 5.—Sir, I have often been Considering, in our late Discourses of Peace and War, of what I find in the Mouths of abundance of People, in their Ordinary Discourses. — " O !" say they, " we want a War ! The Nation is in Distress for a War, to rid them of the horrid Crews of Rogues, Thieves, and Murtherers, that overspread the Country everywhere to such a degree, that they know not what Course to take. People cannot be safe in their Beds; no, nor in going about, from Place to Place, upon the most necessary Occasions." Among which they reckon up abundance of Particulars; and especially, robbing Gentlemen coming in Chairs from the Ball, a most needful Avocation indeed.

Then, they give us an Account of this wretched Gang of Murtherers lately spread among us; such as *Blewit* and his Gang, who are now taken in Holland, upon his Majesty's Proclamation, for a barbarous Murther of Thomas Ball, and several other Murthers and Robberies, some of their Accomplices being apprehended in England, before they went over.

The like Account they give us of a frightful Gang of Robbers on the Frontiers of Gelderland and Germany; no less than 18 of whom have been already executed at Gueldre, the Grove, and some other of the Towns of that Government. And more it seems were in Custody, and not like to escape.

Then, they go over into France, and the Frontiers of Picardy; where, they say, they have had the Impudence to lay the Country under Contributions, give People safe-guard for their Houses and Habitations, and while they have paid them, have tolerably well performed the Conditions with them.

As to the City of Paris, notwithstanding the Troops of Cartouchcans, who have already passed the Operation of the Wheel,—and it must be acknowledged France has made no Truce with those bloody Creatures,—yet we have scarce any Advices from Paris without giving an Account of some barbarous Street Robberies and Murthers, which are committed there every Day; such the last French Mail was full of, as particularly the murthering of a Goldsmith in his Shop. The disguised Thief entering a Lady's House, with a Footman at his heels, and robbing her of 60 Pistoles, while his Footman stole her Plate; and many more such, too many to enumerate here.

As to what we meet with in our own Streets, they are indeed such as are without Example, and it is a new Thing in England; a kind of bloody Humour is spirited up among us, which Englishmen, however wicked and desperate, have generally been Strangers to. Our People have generally been more humane, in their worst Villainies; but the Spirit of the Devil is, I think, got uppermost. Blood and Murther seems the Companion of even the least Robbery; and some Remedy must, and I believe will, speedily be applied to it.

But that this should call for a War, is a most scandalous Reproach to the Gentlemen call'd Soldiers. His Majesty's Officers, who bear his Commission, and fight for their King and Country, I dare say, desire no Murtherers to be listed in their Companies. Though there is a kind of Poverty and Distress necessary to bring a poor Man to take Arms, and list in the Army, and run the risk of Life and Limb, for so mean a Consideration as a red Coat, and 3s. a Week. Yet those poorest of Men may have Principles of Honour and Justice in them, at least it should be supposed they have, till something appears to the Contrary; and therefore, to suppose all that List in the Troops are Rogues, and that the King's Armies rid the Land of Thieves and Murtherers, is to lay the Service too low; and, no honest Man would care, for ever after, to be a Soldier, if he could avoid it. In a Word, this, instead of proving that the Army was made up of such, is to make it so; and to bring the Captain under a necessity of rummaging the Gaols, and the Houses of Correction, for Soldiers, and no others to make up their Companies.

Whereas, on the Contrary, our Armies have been often raised by Gentlemen of Figure and Estate, among their Tenants, among the Husbandmen, and the Farmers Sons, the Cottagers, and the poor Plebeii of the Country; and a Captain, to my knowledge, has been able to call every Soldier of his Company by his Name, and to give an Account of his Father, or Mother, or Original; true these Men have been poor, but brave and honest. Nay, that it should be supposed that all the Soldiery are Rogues and Thieves, all Murtherers, *Blewits* and *Dickinsons*, is a most scandalous Reproach to the Character of a Soldier, and very unjust to the poor Men themselves.

It is the same Thing with the Gentlemen of the Fleet, who seem to be more degenerated into Brutes, and to have less of Humanity among them,—I mean when they turn Pirates, run away with Merchant Ships, murther the Captain they go to Sea to serve, and commit such villainous Things which nothing but the worst of Villains can be guilty of; such as Gow and his Crew were executed for. It would however be hard to suggest that all Seamen would be Pirates if they had Opportunity. But I shall speak more upon that Point hereafter, and some thing perhaps of the Reasons which have made so many poor Seamen turn Reprobates, but enough of that here.

War with Spain.

A. J., Mar. 12.—. . . . .
. . . But not to lessen the weight of this Argument,—which is very good on our Side,—I believe we may find another good Reason for this turn of the Affair in Spain, (if it be so turned) and that is, the preparing a strong Squadron of English Men-of-War to go to the Spanish West Indies, or to the West Indies, take it in General, for that includes the whole. . . . . .

Were a strong Squadron of British Men of War kept constantly in the West Indies, cruizing thro' the great Gulph of Mexico, and insulting their two principal Ports of La Vera Cruze, and Cartagena, I would ask the Spaniards what would become of their Commerce in those Seas? And how would the Galleons find their way out or home? It is said by the boasting Spaniards, that the Havanna is the Key of America; but I must add to them also, that a Fleet of English Ships would be a Key of the Havanna. . . . .

Character of a Good Writer.

INTRODUCTION.

U. S., Oct. 12, 1728.—If this Paper was not intended to be what no Paper at present is, we should never attempt to Crowd in among such a Throng of Publick Writers as at this Time Oppress the Town. But we have other Views, and shall give you an Account of them in very few Words.

The Main Design of this Work is, to turn your Thoughts a little off from the Clamour of contending Parties, which has so long surfeited you with their ill-timed Politicks, and restore your Taste to Things truly superior and sublime.

In order to this, we shall endeavour to present you with such Subjects as are Capable, if well handled, both to divert, and to instruct you; such as shall render Conversation pleasant, and help to make Mankind agreeable to one another.

As for our Management of them, not to promise too much for ourselves, we shall only say, we hope, at least, to make our Work acceptable to every Body; because we resolve, if possible, to displease no Body.

We assure the World, by way of Negative, that we shall engage in no Quarrels, meddle with no Parties, deal in no Scandal, nor endeavour to make any Men merry at the Expense of their Neighbours. In a Word, we shall set no Body together by the Ears. And tho' we have encouraged the ingenious World to correspond with us by Letters, we hope they will not take it ill, that we say before-hand, no Letters will be taken notice of by us, which contain any personal Reproaches, intermeddle with Family Breaches, or tend to Scandal or Indecency of any kind.

The current Papers are more than sufficient to carry on all the dirty Work the Town can have for them to do; and what with Party Strife, Politicks, Poetick Quarrels, and all the other Consequences of a Wrangling Age; they are in no Danger of wanting Employment; and those Readers who delight in such Things, may divert themselves there. But our Views, as is said above, lie another Way.

Let no Man envy us the celebrated Title we have assumed, or charge us with Arrogance, as if we bid the World expect great Things from us. Must we have no Power to please, unless we come up to the full Height of those Inimitable Performances? Is there no Wit or Humour left, because they are gone? Is the Spirit of the SPECTATORS all lost, and their Mantle fallen upon no Body? Have they said all that can be said? Has the World offered no Variety, and presented no new Scenes, since they retired from us? Or did they leave off, because they were quite exhausted, and had no more to say? We think quite otherwise.

However, you may pardon a just and modest Ambition, and allow us to say, we desire to please you; and, if you are not too difficult, hope we may. At least, we resolve to try. This is the grand Design of our Undertaking; we leave the Success to Time; and that's all we shall trouble you with about it.

Universal Spectator.

No. I.   Saturday, October 12, 1728.

I have heard with some Impatience, the wise, but weak Speculations of the Journal-Makers, and other Publick Intel-

ligencers of the Town, concerning the mighty Value they think
the World ought to put upon what they call *a good Writer*.
How certainly, and yet modestly, they all suggest themselves
to be of the Number, though it is too evident, yet as the
Remark would have some Satyr in it, 'tis out of our Way !

I most readily agree, that *a good Writer*, or Author, is a
useful and valuable Man to the Commonwealth, and for that
Reason, ought to have a due Regard paid to him ; but I do
not find it so easy to settle some other Points about it ; such
as :—

    1. What particular Qualifications go to the Composition ;
       or, in a Word, what is required to denominate a
       Man *a good Writer ?*

    2. Who, and where, is the Man ?

One says, this is a polite Author ; another says, that is an
excellent *good Writer ;* and generally, we find some oblique
Strokes pointed sideways at themselves ; intimating, that
whether we think fit to allow it, or not, they take themselves
to be very *good Writers*. And indeed, I must excuse them
that Vanity ; for if a poor Author had not some good Opinion
of himself, especially when under the Discouragement of
having no Body else to be of his mind, he would never write
at all ; nay, he could not ; it would take off all the little dull
Edge that his Pen might have on it before, and he would not
be able to say one Word to the Purpose.

Now whatever may be the Lot of this Paper, *be that as
common Fame shall direct*, yet without entering into the Enquiry who writes *Better*, or who writes *Worse*, I shall lay down
one Specifick, by which you that read shall impartially determine who are, or are not, to be called *good Writers*. In
a Word, the Character of a *good Writer*, wherever he is to be
found, is this, *viz.*, that he writes so as to PLEASE and SERVE
at the same Time.

If he writes to *please*, and not to *serve*, he is a Flatterer,
and a Hypocrite ; if to *serve* and not to *please*, he turns Cynic
and Satyrist. The first deals in Smooth Falshood, the last in
Rough-Scandal ; the *last* may do some Good, *though little ;* the
first does no Good, and may do Mischief, *not a little ;* the *last*
provokes your Rage, the *first* provokes your Pride ; and, in a
Word, either of them is *hurtful*, rather than *useful*. But the

Writer that strives to be useful, writes to *serve* you, and at the same Time, by an imperceptible Art, draws you on *to be pleased* also. He represents Truth with *Plainness*, Virtue with *Praise*; he even reprehends with a Softness that carries the Force of a Satyr, without the Salt of it; and he insensibly screws himself so far into your good Opinion, that as his Writings merit your Regard, so they fail not to obtain it.

This is Part of the Character by which I define. *a good Writer*; I say, 'tis but Part of it, for it is not a Half Sheet that would contain the full Description; a large Volume would hardly suffice it. His Fame requires, indeed, a very good Writer, to give it due Praise; and for that Reason, (and a good Reason too,) I go no farther with it.

But the main Question is still behind, (*viz.*) WHO, and WHERE, is the Man? As the wise Man says, in another and superior Case, I doubt we must all acknowledge, every one for himself, *it is not in me*. The City! The Court! The Country! Will they not all say, *it is not in me?*

> " *If such a Man on Earth*, ye Gods! *there be,*
> *Let Thunders speak aloud his lofty Eulogy.*"

Having thus touched this tender String, and hinted to you how difficult a Thing it would be, after the strictest Search, to find out such a Man, I cannot quit the Subject, without observing how weak a Thing it is in you that read, to expect the shining Quality of *a good Writer* among the empty Lucubrations of our voluminous News Papers; and how arrogant it is in any of us to reproach one another for the Want of it. Alas! it is not yet heard of, among the whole Clan! What may be, in Time to come, who knows?

But I meet with an Objection of some Weight here; and I would fain remove all Difficulties, from what Quarter soever they may come. A timorous Friend of mine, as if he was frighted at the Boldness of the Attempt, at first Sight, cry'd, " HOLD! Stir not a Step farther," *says he*; "you are lost if you go on; you will fall by your own Sentence. A good Writer must please and serve! Why, do you know the World no better? Pray, what if they won't be pleas'd, though they are serv'd; where's your good Writer then?"

It shocked me a little at first, and I began to grow fainthearted, and doubtful about my new Undertaking; but my Discourager being gone, I soon recovered myself, assisted by the exceeding breadth of my own Charity, and I answered the ill-natured Suggestion to myself thus;—Not be pleased, when they are served? It cannot be! 'Tis against Nature. Common Reasoning will prevent it; nay, common Sense will be on my Side. Then the Story of *Andronicus* and the Lion with the Thorn in his Foot, came into my View; and it argued in my Favour, thus,—The very Brutes are grateful; they will lay aside their Terrors, hold in their Claws, and be pleased, if they are served. Upon this I concluded, that in common Civility to the World, I should not give Place to such a base Suggestion, but steadily believe my Fellow Creatures all too good to be so rigid.

However, lest some such unnatural Thing should appear in the World, and I should meet with a *Monster*, (for, I dare say, there will be very few such,) I have this Remedy, viz., To leave him where I find him, and let him be neither served nor pleased. In which Case, I ask Leave to conclude with a short Story.

A certain Countryman travelling on the Road, his Horse got a Stone in his Foot, and went very Lame. The Clown got off, and went very kindly to Work to ease the poor Horse, and get the Stone out of his Foot. But it seems, it stuck so fast in his Shoe, that he could not get it out, or, at least, not so soon as the Creature desired; and the Horse, perhaps a little pained, with his knocking upon the Stone, snatch'd away his Foot, and kick'd at his Benefactor. The Countryman, provoked to be so used for his good Will, gives the Horse a kick with his own Foot,—" *Say you so, Sir,*" says he to his Horse, " *There's kick for kick, and the Stone in your Foot still.*"

On the Complete Tradesman.

F. J., Jan. 11, 1729.—Sir, I have upon many Occasions shewn the World that I am a constant Friend to TRADE, and Commerce, which I take to be the third general Head in the Essentials of a Nation's Good. For,——

1. To be Uniform in orthodox Principles of Religion, adhering strictly to the common Faith. 2. To be established

on one and the same Foundation of Right and Property, Loyalty and Subjection; and 3. To be flourishing and prosperous, in just Measures, for Encouragement of Commerce, &c. These three, in my Opinion, constitute a happy People.

The *Romans* indeed pursued the two first, but not the last. *Numa* the great Giver of their Law, and Founder of their religious Rites, made the Worship of the Gods the first Principle in the good Government of their Commonwealth, and the Subordination of the People the Second; but as they lived by the Sword, and not by Trade, so *Numa* himself knew nothing of it.

Hence, as the late Author of the *Compleat Tradesman* well observes, the *Romans* were no Encouragers of Trade, but on the contrary, where other Nations had laid the Foundations of Colonies and Manufactures, they destroy'd all again by their Conquests, as was particularly observ'd in the Ruin of *Carthage* and *Corinth*, both famous and flourishing in Wealth and Trade.*

Trade is a Circulation of Wealth, which never fails its Course, if encourag'd; and if, at any Time, by the *Ignorance* or *Oppression* of our *Rulers*, it receives a Wound, and has a Check given to its Vigour, so that it suffers from any *Convulsions*, how soon is the *Stagnation* felt to the very Vitals of a Government!

How miserable, how dejected, do a People look, (however prosperous before,) if by any Accident of an unprosperous *War*, or an *ill manag'd Peace*, Trade receives a Blow! And how cheerfully do men Fight in a War, and Work in a Peace, if the Channels of Trade are but kept open, and a free Circulation of Business is preserved!

All this, I bring down to a mean and trifling Thing in Appearance, but which I take to be so essential to Trade in general, that the highest Thoughts are not too great to illustrate it; and therefore I bring the Excellency of Commerce, in general, to enforce the Argument made Use of, for the propagating it in all its Particulars.

---

* In recommending, even anonymously, a work written by himself, although the copyright of the Complete Tradesman belonged to the publisher, yet Defoe delicately speaks of the Author as if deceased.—*Ed.*

If Trade is the Life and Prosperity of a Nation in general, and the next valuable Thing to Religion and Civil Government in a Commonwealth, then the Tradesman is a most useful and valuable Creature to his Country; and it is of Importance to the Publick, that he should thrive in his private Capacity, as well as it is that Trade, in General, should prosper as a publick Good; and this, (with the present Time of Year concurring,) brings me down to the Case in Hand.

We are just now arrived at one of the grand Periods of Trade. The Close of the Old Year, and the Beginning of the New, makes the annual Revolution of a Tradesman's Business, when careful and judicious Tradesmen generally make up their Books, and, as the lower sort of Dealers call it, *Case up Shop*, and inspect, whether they go backward or forward in their Business; and this the *said Author* justly lays so much Stress upon in general, that he demonstrates,—That the Tradesman who is afraid to inquire on what Bottom he Stands, must know in the Main, that he Stands upon no Bottom at all; and that he must needs Stand ticklish, and unsafe, who is afraid to look into, and see his Condition.

From this Foundation, I cannot but join with that Author, and Press all our good Citizens and Wholesale Men, (to whom that useful Book is directed,) that they would, at this solemn Period, spare a few Hours from their daily Diversions, to look into their Warehouses and Accounts, that they may know how it Stands with them, and how they go on.

Then they may return cheerfully to the Diversions of the Season, dance, play, eat, drink, feast their Friends, and feed the Poor; and, in a Word, live cheerfully and happily, which they cannot *justly* do, either with regard to *Themselves* or *Creditors*, while they are ignorant of their own Circumstances to afford it.

'Twould fill a Book to treat at large upon this Topick; but that is already extremely well done to my Hand, by the Author above mentioned, call'd *The Compleat Tradesman*, to which I refer the Reader.   I am, &c.

FINIS.